FALLING POMEGRANATE SEEDS DUOLOGY

WENDY J. DUNN

Poesy Quill Publishing
www.poesyquill.com
Copyright © 2022 by Wendy J. Dunn

Contents:

The Duty of Daughters

Wendy J. Dunn

THE FIRST PART OF THE KATHERINE OF ARAGON STORY

I dedicate this novel to my first born, my beloved son, James. I am so proud and happy you now walk the same road I started walking so many years ago. May you discover what I have learnt – that teaching is a true privilege and calling, where our students teach us more than we can ever teach them.

Those who know, do.
Those that understand, teach.
~ Aristotle

SCHOLAR

I cradle the books
that found me.
Tonight, I prop them
on my knees
one by one; each
offering up
a lesson I must timely absorb.

The rain speaks of days like these,
in dim light, with
only my wit as guide.
No feat of voluptuousness;
of womanhood, shall aid me here.

I tiptoe down these halls,
a quiet predator in the shadows,
light feet, steel-trap cunning,
and wily defiance; I shall show them
what a woman of iron mind can do

~ ELOISE FAICHNEY, 2016

(Once my student and now a dear friend, Eloise, with great joy, I
watch you fly high.)

"That's where the truth of history comes in," said Sancho.

"They could as well have passed over such matters in silence out of fairness," said Don Quixote, "for there's no need to write down actions that neither change nor alter the truth of history if they must result in disesteem for the hero. In truth, Aeneas was not so merciful as Virgil paints him, nor Ulysses so prudent as Homer describes him."

"That's so," replied Sancho, "but it is one thing to write as a poet and another as an historian: the poet can relate or sing things, not as they were, but as they ought to have been, and the historian has to write them, not as they ought to have been, but as they were, without adding or taking anything at all from the truth."

Miguel de Cervantes
Don Quixote de la Mancha

HISTORICAL CHARACTERS

LIST OF MAIN HISTORICAL CHARACTERS USED FICTITIOUSLY IN THIS WORK, BUT INSPIRED BY HISTORY

Beatriz Galindo (b? – 1534)

Years ago I discovered a footnote about this fascinating woman, known as La Latina (Lady of Latin), in an essay about Isabel of Castile. A Latin expert, poet, so knowledgeable about medicine, rhetoric and the philosophy of Aristotle, she tutored on the subjects at the University of Salamanca. Beatriz was also a friend and advisor to Queen Isabel, as well as being a wife and mother. She is yet another woman forgotten by history – and a woman who deserves notice. I hope she forgives my imagination for the liberties I have taken with her story in these pages, but if it makes people interested in finding out more about her, then I am happy. Beatriz was a student of Antonio Elio de Nebrija, a

Renaissance scholar and a man known in history for writing one of the first books of grammar for a romance language.

Francisco Ramirez (b? – 1501)

Known as "the Artilleryman" during the war of Granada. Husband of Beatriz Galindo, Francisco Ramirez died in the taking of the Villa of Lanjaron in Granada, Spain.

Cristóbal Colón (c. 1451 – 20 May 1506)

Christopher Columbus, as he is known in English speaking countries, was born in the Republic of Genoa which is now part of modern Italy. He is well known for his exploration of the Americas.

Isabel I of Castile (1451 – 1504)

Isabel ruled Castile from 1474 to 1504. My imagined construction of Isabel is drawn from these following works: Isabel the Queen: Life and Times (Peggy K. Liss); and Isabel of Spain: The Catholic Queen (Warren H. Carrol).

Ferdinand II of Aragon (1452 – 1516)

Ferdinand, Catalina's father, was one of the rulers Niccoló Machiavelli used in The Prince as a benchmark for other rulers to follow. A wily fox and able politician, he made use of whatever he could, including members of his own family, to achieve his own ends. This influenced my imagination in the creation of his character. Machiavelli wrote: "...always using religion as a plea, so as to undertake greater schemes, he devoted himself with pious cruelty to driving out and clearing his kingdom of the

Moors; nor could there be a more admirable example, nor one more rare" (Machiavelli 1532).

THEIR CHILDREN

Isabel (1470 – 1498)

Prince Juan (1478 – 1497)

Juana (1479 – 1555)

María (1482 – 1517)

Catalina, later Katherine, Queen of England (1485 – 1536)

María de Salinas, kinswoman of Catherine of Aragon (? – 1539)

Her parents Doña Josefa Gonzales de Salinas Don Martin de Salinas

Ahmed, son of Boabdil, King of Granada

Doña Elvia Manuel

Francisco Jiménez de Cisneros

Fray Hernando de Talavera (1428 – 1507) confessor to the Queen

Alfonso, Prince of Portugal

Margaret of Austria

Manuel, King of Portugal

GLOSSARY

Spanish words used in this story and glossary
Alcázar: palace
Amigo: friend
Andas: litter
Cadis: judges
Chopines: platform shoes
Converto: a Jew who becomes Christian
Doña: Lady
Don: Lord
Hidalgo: Spanish noble
Habito: a loose day-gown
Hija: daughter
La Latina: The Lady of Latin
Prima hermana: first cousin
Si: yes
Toca: head covering
Mi chiquitina: little one

1

"Follow your star and you will never fail to find your glorious port," he said to me.
~ Dante Alighieri

Burgos, 1490

Doña Beatriz Galindo caught her breath and tidied her habito. She shook her head a little when she noticed ink-stained fingers and several spots of black ink on the front of her green gown. She sighed. *Too late now to check my face.* "The queen has sent for me," she told the lone guard at the door of the chambers provided for Queen Isabel's short stay at Burgos. The young hidalgo straightened his stance, then knocked once with the back of his halberd on the door, his eyes fixed on the white, bare wall across from him. The door opened and a female servant peeked out at Beatriz, gesturing to her to come in.

In spite of the hours since dawn, the queen sat in bed, her back against oversized cushions. She still wore her white night rail, a red shawl slung around her shoulders, edged with embroidery of gold thread depicting her device of arrows. A sheer, white toca covered her bent head, a thick, auburn plait falling over her shoulder.

Princess Isabel, a title she bore alone as the queen's eldest daughter, and named for both her mother and grandmother, sat on a chair beside her mother, twirling a spindle. Her golden red hair was rolled and wrapped in a cream scarf criss-crossed with black lines, a wry grin of frustration formed dimples in her cheeks before she discarded the spindle in the basket at her feet with the others. She nodded to Beatriz with a slight smile. "Good morning, Latina," she murmured, using the nickname bestowed on Beatriz by the queen. Beatriz hid her stained fingers behind her back and curtseyed her acknowledgement.

Straightening up, Beatriz gazed at the bed-hangings, unfurled behind Queen Isabel. A naked Hercules wrestled with a golden, giant lion, his club on the ground beside him. Turning to her queen, she fought back a smile and lowered her eyes, pretending little interest in Hercules, especially one depicted in his fullest virility.

Queen Isabel balanced her writing desk across her lap, scratching her quill against the parchment, writing with speed and ease. A pile of documents lay beside her. An open one, bearing the seal of the king, topped all the rest. Beatriz's stomach knotted, and not just through worry. She closed her eyes and breathed deeply. *I am free; I am always free while the king is elsewhere. Pray, it is not bad news about the queen's Holy War.* The knot in her stomach became a roaring fire. *Holy War? Jesu' – how I hate calling any war that. Pray God, just keep my beloved safe.*

She almost laughed out loud then; as one of the king's most important artillery officers, Francisco Ramirez, the man Beatriz loved and had promised to marry, did not live to be safe but lived to live. It was one of the things that made her fall in love with him. Waiting to hear the reason for her summons, she gazed around the spacious bedchamber, composing in her mind the letter she would write to him tonight:

My love, my days are long without you...

No – she couldn't write that. If she did, it would be a lie. Her days were full – most mornings she spent tutoring the girls before relishing in the long afternoons free for her own studies. She missed Francisco, but still lived a rich life without him, a richer one when he was at court.

What to write to him then? She could not tell him of her hatred of the Holy War. She could never name as holy a war stamping out any hope of another golden age, when Jews, Moors and Christians lived and worked together in peace. Francisco was a learned man, but a man who used his learning to win this war. Her learning taught her otherwise. It taught her to keep silent about what she really felt to protect the freedoms of her life. Could she tell him then of her joy of teaching the infanta Catalina and her companion María de Salinas? For six months now she had been given full responsibility for their learning. She looked at the queen. Surely the queen was happy with the infanta's progress?

As if Beatriz had spoken out her thought aloud the queen

said, "I want to speak to you about my youngest daughter." She waved a hand to a nearby stool. "Please sit."

The queen put aside her quill and pushed away her paperwork. She lifted bloodshot, sore-looking eyes. A yellow crust coated her long, thick lashes.

Seated on the stool, Beatriz gazed at the queen in concern. If there was no improvement by tomorrow, she would prepare a treatment of warm milk and honey for her eyes, even at the risk of once again upsetting those fools calling themselves the queen's physicians.

"Si, my queen?" she murmured.

"Tell me, how do you find my Catalina and our little cousin María?"

Beatriz began breathing easier. Just another summons to do with the infanta's learning. "Both girls are good students, my queen," Beatriz smiled. "The infanta Catalina is a natural scholar. She relishes learning – even when the subject is difficult, but that does not surprise me. Your daughter is very intelligent, just like her royal mother. María, too, is a bright child. Slower than the infanta, but already the child reads simple books written in our native tongue, as well as some Latin. The method of having books written in Latin and Castilian placed side-by-side is working well." Beatriz straightened and lifted her head. "It was the method used to teach me when I was the same age as the infanta."

The queen exchanged a look with her listening daughter.

"I have been pleased to see how much my Catalina, my sweet chiquitina, enjoys her mornings with you." Queen Isabel brought her hands together, drumming her fingertips together for a moment. "Latina, I believe the infantas Juana and María can be given over to other tutors now that you have provided them with an excellent grounding in Latin and philosophy, but I desire you to be Catalina's main tutor, of course that includes María, her companion." Queen Isabel twisted the ring on her swollen finger. "One day, my Catalina will be England's queen. It will be not an easy task – not in a country that has known such unrest for many, many years. I want to make certain my daughter is as prepared as I can make her, but I need your help. Can I rely on you to stay with us, and teach Catalina what she needs to know of England's history, its customs, its laws?"

"My queen, of course..." Beatriz halted her acceptance when the queen raised her hand.

"Think before you commit yourself. You are betrothed. What will happen when you are wed and, God willing, have the blessing of children? We talk of an obligation of perhaps ten years, and for you to be not only my daughter's tutor, but act also as her duena."

Beatriz smiled at Queen Isabel. "Francisco and I are both your loyal servants. When the time comes, we will do what needs to done for our marriage and children, but I will confess to you that my real life is here, and as a teacher at the University of Salamanca. I am honoured that you wish me to continue in that role for the infanta. And to be entrusted with teaching your daughter, now and in the future... my queen, words can not describe what that means to me."

Light. So much light. Beatriz Galindo walked back to the library in light, and not just the light from the high archways of the royal alcázar. It was the light of life. Her life. Before the shadows engulfed her again, one archway opened to a garden where running water from a fountain sparkled like diamonds, light and water flashing rainbows onto the high, white stone walls. Beatriz halted by the arch, holding her habito away from her feet, and gazed out before treading into the garden. She sat on a stone bench and looked around her.

At summer's end beauty and ugliness competed for dominance. Most of the flowers were now gone to seed, even the well-tended roses drooped their heads, crimson petals and desiccated leaves of

every shade of brown scattering upon an earth sucked dry and cracked by days of relentless heat. Life passed so quickly, one season dying, re-birthing into another.

Beatriz closed her eyes for a moment, raising her face to the sunlight. *Dear God, I have much to give thanks for – I will always be grateful for what I've been given.* Then she thought how complicated was this gratitude. It was a gratitude birthed from sorrow, and from loss.

A shadow fell upon her. She opened her eyes, relieved to see her dearest friend, Josefa de Salinas, smiling down at her. "You are fortunate, Beatriz, to have time to enjoy the day. I am on my way to the queen." Josefa laughed a little. "My royal cousin has summoned me to embroider the hems and collars of her new shifts. Sometimes I wish my mother had not taught me so well my skills with the needle. I may then be like you, amigo, more at liberty to spend my mornings in the garden."

The sheer, white fabric of Josefa's toca wafted in a breeze against the sides of her face. Apprehension stabbed Beatriz. Her friend's face was too pale, too thin. The deep hollows under her high cheekbones were as if strong thumbs had bruised her wan skin. A flowing black habito revealed the swell of her belly, a jewelled scallop, made of gold, gathering together the points of the toca at the breast of her gown. Beatriz did not need her knowledge of medicine or midwifery to know that Josefa's pregnancy was proving difficult. Beatriz swallowed, thinking of what she could make to help her friend. Hiding her anxiety, she smiled at Josefa. "I was thinking of my own mother."

Josefa sat beside her. "Did she not die when you were but a child?"

"Si – I was three when the black death took her. My father never forgave himself that he could not save her from suffering a terrible death. I think I have told you that my father was a famous scholar of medicine, highly regarded in all Castilla – yet all his knowledge proved useless at that time. I was just wondering how different my life would have been if my mother had lived. My father's grief was such he never married again. It no longer mattered that I was but a daughter. He consoled himself by teaching me."

Josefa laughed. "And found himself with a prodigy."

"Prodigy?" Beatriz shrugged. "I'm not certain I was ever that. Rather a child with a great passion for books and learning. I was twelve when my father's great friend Antonio de Nebrija took me under his tutorage. It changed my destiny from that of a religious order to a respected teacher of Latin at the university itself. So respected Queen Isabel sought me out when I was twenty to teach her to read and speak Latin. I have found complete fulfilment these past five years and more – not only as a teacher at Salamanca, but in my work as tutor to the queen's children." Beatriz lifted her gaze to a rose dropping its petals. *Si.*

Death not only destroyed the life I had then, but also planted the seeds for the life I have now. The life I was meant to live. She refused to ponder about the dues she sometimes paid.

"You have told me the story before. But what makes you think of this now?" Josefa asked.

"I am happy today – the queen wants me to continue as tutor to her youngest child, and your daughter."

Josefa lifted her dark eyebrows, and grinned wryly. "So – I hear it first from you."

Beatriz eyed her friend. "Do you mind?"

"Does it matter if I mind, or not? Martin or I could not say no to the queen when she asked for María to grow alongside her daughter as her companion. It was a great honour for our family –and all of us saw how much the young infanta loved María. We are close kin, after all, with the queen. I must accept with good grace my daughter shares the same education as the infanta." Josefa glanced towards the archway leading back into the building. "While I would like to sit and talk with you in the sunshine, I must be away if I have any hope of finishing even one of the queen's chemises before the day grows too hot."

Josefa stood up, shook out the folds of her habito and headed towards the sunlit corridor. "No doubt I will see you soon enough," she called over her shoulder.

Beatriz watched her friend go. For a time she sat there, content to be alone with only her thoughts as company, content this sunlit garden held no dark memories for her. At last, she sighed and rose from the bench, heading towards the library. Almost at its door, she heard voices of children. She slipped into the alcove that hid her from view but also allowed her to look into the room.

Catalina and María bent their heads over a book, opened wide upon María's lap. The girls sat in a pool of light from the window behind them. It burnished their hair with gold – lighting Catalina's to a fiery red and covering María's black hair with a veil-like sheen. Even at only five, both girls took great care of precious books. *But where is Doña Teresa Manrigue? She should be here.* A tender-hearted woman, Doña Teresa carried in her pocket a seemingly endless supply of rose sugar as rewards for the children. The last time Doña Teresa left the girls alone in the library she had told Beatriz the infanta had commanded her to go. No wonder the queen desired a new duena for her daughter.

"My turn to be Arthur!" María said, placing her finger on the page closest to Catalina. Her face a picture of concentration, María licked her top lip. "And as they rode, Arthur said, I have no sword." María's sigh was one of clear relief.

Catalina pulled the book closer to her. "No matter, said Merlin, hereby is a sword that shall be yours."

Beatriz restrained a laugh, hearing the infanta deepen her already low voice. But while one child loved learning, the same couldn't be said about the other. When Catalina pointed to the next passage there was no mistaking María's discomfort as she shook her head. "You do it. You read better."

Catalina's grin revealed missing milk teeth, giving her round face an endearing look. "I only try harder."

"You forget," María said quietly, glancing towards a hoop with an uncompleted embroidery some distance away, "Mamá doesn't care whether I read or not."

Catalina turned to María a look of determination, it was one that mirrored the queen's. Just like her mother, altering the girl's chosen course was nigh on impossible. "I do," Catalina said. "I want you to be as good as me at this. Think, when we learn about herbs from Latina and the good sisters, you can go to my mother's library to know more. Latina says knowing Latin is like having a key that will open many doors. You read now."

Beatriz grinned. Her lessons were not falling on deaf ears.

María read in a halting, uncertain voice: "So they rode till they came to a lake, which was a fair water and broad, and in the midst of the lake Arthur was aware of an arm clothed in white samite, that held a fair sword in that hand..."

"Catalina!"

Beatriz almost jumped out of her skin when the young, grating voice called. Stepping out of the alcove, she saw the infanta Juana rushing down the corridor, followed by her duena and two female slaves. A child of ten, Juana's slight form was outlined in sun-edged shadow.

"Latina! I did not think to find you here too." Juana looked into the library. "Sister, our lady mother desires our presence in her chamber."

Catalina gazed at her older sister and then back at the book. "Come, my sister. Latina, you come too."

The infanta Juana disappeared from view, her women picking up their skirts and rushing after her. Beatriz smiled, reminded of the goose girl she had seen only this morning, searching for herbs not grown in the royal gardens. The swish of long dresses and under-breath protestations hissed after the infanta like a gaggle of annoyed geese.

Her face pensive and full of regret, Catalina shut the book, caressing its engraved leather cover before passing it to María. The two girls got to their feet, María cradling the book in her arms. Catalina ran after her sister. Silken slippers padded against the tiled floor until fading to a whisper. Now all alone in the library, María stood on her tiptoes, returning the book to its rightful place. Beatriz hurried back to the queen's chambers with the others.

The guard blinked in surprise, seeing her yet again, when Juana knocked and Catalina beckoned to Beatriz to follow. One by one they entered the queen's bedchamber, Juana's duena and slaves stepping aside to wait outside the door.

The queen was still abed, still writing, appearing disturbed, even downhearted. Wondering what could have changed the queen's mood so quickly, Beatriz noticed the queen was writing a letter to the king. Looking around the room, she thought of her unwritten letter to Francisco. Should she write to him of Prince Juan, now perched on the edge of the bed, his head bent, silver-blond hair half covering his face? The prince strummed his small harp, one long, slender leg folded under the other. Or should she write of his sisters – Isabel, the eldest child of the queen, Juana, María, and small Catalina? Beatriz lowered her face to hide her smile. Perhaps her letter would turn out like her last – one where she wrote to Francisco about the Aristotle tract she was translating from the Latin to Castilian, and yet more suggestions about what he should do to protect his hearing. She had even quoted to him from her lecture about Bartholomew the Englishman to underscore her seriousness. But then too Francisco's love letters did not fit the usual pattern of a lover. So many times his letters were full of his experiments with gunpowder, even sharing different recipes he'd tried in his efforts to discover a trustworthy composition, and the success, or lack of it, he had in weakening the fortifications of the Moors. Sometimes he even asked her to seek out in the queen's library for books that would help him in his task to blow up walls that had stood for centuries. She only agreed to his proposal of marriage when he promised her their mutual quest for knowledge would never change. She had no reason to doubt him. They had been good friends since she first took up her position at court. A widower ten years older than she, with two grown sons and one married daughter, Francisco was a man who understood the passions of minds.

Beatriz returned to the present moment. Prince Juan blinked as if waking from a dream, his handsome, sensitive face that of a poet. Humming in accompaniment to her brother's song, Infanta María, three years older than Catalina, twirled her spindle, sitting next to her adult sister, Isabel. Not one to love learning for the sake of learning like her three sisters and brother, the infanta María was a kind child who never seemed to share the melancholic natures of her more sensitive siblings. Sometimes Beatriz wondered if she was born under a kinder, happier star.

Princess Isabel reached for *Livy's Decades* on the table beside her and opened it to a page deep within the book. Her index finger pulled at her bottom lip, eyes scanning the page, turning it quickly to the next. Catalina and her small companion watched on in fascination. Beatriz smiled. She could guess the girls desired to read just as fast.

Suitably serious as the eldest child of her mother, Princess Isabel rarely wasted her time with books of courtly romance. Her mother sometimes teased her, as she also did her second daughter, Juana, by calling the princess 'my mother-in-law'. But while the queen called the infanta Juana thus because she inherited the dark bold beauty of her father's mother, Isabel gained the name because she shared her grandmother's solemn outlook on the world and desire for study and prayer. The queen held up the king's mother as yet another example for her daughters to mirror.

Small Catalina, fifteen years the younger, wanted to be just like her eldest sister, Isabel. As the companion of the infanta, María had little choice but to follow after. Both girls still preferred tales of King Arthur or El Cid, favouring the chivalry intertwined with magic and love and longing of King Arthur's court. It was a good thing the queen had a well-stocked library with a full collection of the Arthur legends, from French poems to their favourite Latin text written by an English knight. The girls were always asking Beatriz for new stories.

The queen lifted her gaze from the half-finished letter. Her worn face softened into a welcoming smile as she looked over to her youngest daughter. Letting go of the parchment, she pushed her desk aside and held out her arms. "Mi chiquitina, come! Come and embrace your mother."

Josefa, putting aside her sewing, grinned at Beatriz, placing a hand on her daughter María's shoulder. The child flung her arms around her mother, cushioning her face against her breasts. Josefa bent her head, kissing the top of María's head. She looked up at Beatriz and smiled again. "I said I'd see you soon enough." Without waiting for an answer, Josefa took her daughter's hand and led her from the royal family to the far end of the room where there were, prepared already for the night, two bed-pallets.

With not enough rooms in this beautiful but small alcázar for the queen and her court, her four daughters and their most trusted attendants slept on pallets in the large chamber near the queen's private rooms. The queen never slept alone. She shared her chambers with her daughters because King Ferdinand stayed too long away from her side. No one could doubt the queen's honour or wifely virtue while she slept with her own daughters and favoured women. Now the time approached for the court to leave Burgos to join the king at Sevilla.

A finger to her lips, gesturing to her daughter for silence, Josefa sat on a chair, picked up a border of black material, and returned to her needle. She stitched the gold, even loops of punto real, a favoured stitch of the queen. On the nearby stool was a neatly folded chemise waiting to be joined to the finished embroidery.

Firelight flickered, glinting upon the gold, silver and jewel-decorated vessels set upon a nearby table. Beatriz stepped into deeper shadows, where no candle or firelight reached, seeking not to be noticed. Her eyes rested on the royal family. The queen's blessing done, Catalina clambered onto her mother's bed and kissed her cheek. The queen wound her arms around her youngest child. She laughed softly, caressing Catalina's hair.

Prince Juan, Catalina's twelve-year-old brother, dropped his harp on the bed. His blue eyes glowing with mischief, he tickled his sister's underarm. She giggled, nestling into him. The prince stood on the threshold between pretty boy and beautiful youth. Blond down intermixed with a darker, thicker colour upon his cheeks. He tickled Catalina again.

The child giggled. "Stop it, Juan!"

Juan laughed. He flicked back the straight fringe from his eyes before reclaiming his harp and plucking a short tune. The black velvet of his doublet increased the bright blond lustre of his hair, candlelight creating an aureole around his head. Angel, his mother called him. Prince Juan well deserved his nickname. All loved him. "Your command is mine! What song shall I play you, sister?" asked the prince.

The queen's smile embraced them both. She rested her fingers on her son's arm. He returned a gaze full of love.

"Son, not yet. I want to first speak to Catalina." She encircled her daughter with her arms, drawing her closer. "Mi chiquitina, can you remember what happened two years ago?"

Catalina looked up, bewildered. "Mamá?"

The queen sighed. Her jaw slackening, she no longer smiled. A candle gusted out, casting her face into deep shadow. Communing as if with the unseen, she tightened her hold on her daughter.

"I forget – 'tis long for a small child to remember... In truth, you were little more than an infant when the English came and I, holding you on my lap, showed you the bulls." The queen smiled slightly. "You wore your first gown of black velvet that day, one rich with jewels. The next day we promised you to their prince." She looked again at Catalina and stroked her hair. Wrapping a lock around her finger, she studied it and let it go, her face becoming strong again. "I have just received word from your father. We have promised another of our hijas to another king's son. My Isabel?"

Princess Isabel playfully peered over the book. "Mamá?"

"Come, and tell your sister your news."

Isabel strode over to the bed with all the grace and confidence of a young woman of twenty. She sat on the other side of her mother's wide bed and took Catalina's hand. "I'm to be wed."

Catalina cried out and threw herself into her sister's arms, pulling at the long chain of Isabel's heavy, gold crucifix. Princess Isabel's laugh overlaid the silence of the other occupants in the queen's chamber. Disentangling herself from her sister, she said, "Be careful, Mi chiquitina."

"Married! But to whom?"

"Can't you guess?" Isabel laughed, but didn't wait for Catalina to answer. "I'm marrying Prince Alfonso of Portugal. One day he'll be Portugal's king, and I its queen."

Queen Isabel gazed at her eldest and youngest daughters with cheerless eyes. "Isabel, I hoped that service for your sister, María, many years hence. Whilst your father, before he owned to the French king's treacherous heart, wished you wed to the French prince, I wanted so much to find you a husband of suitable birth to keep you with us in Castilla. You are my first born, after all. But Alfonso remembers you too well from the time when you both were hostages together. He wants you, and only you."

Princess Isabel smiled, stretching out her hand to her mother. The queen clasped it and held it against her cheek. Catalina's wide eyes travelled from her mother to her sister. "You're leaving us?"

Isabel's eyes shone with sudden tears. "I must, Mi chiquitina."

Catalina wrapped her arms around her sister. "Don't go, I beg you!"

Over her head, Isabel the mother and Isabel the daughter gazed at one another. Lines of pain scored deep in the queen's white face, rending her almost ugly. She shut her bloodshot eyes, biting her bottom lip. In the heavy silence, Beatriz could hear the drum of her own heart in her ears.

The prince swung from the bed with nimble grace. Standing between María and Juana he clasped their hands. All three of them gazed at the bed.

With a short laugh, Isabel's arms tightened around her youngest sister. "Catalina, listen. Portugal is not so far away that I cannot ever come home. In any case, I know my duty and do it willingly."

Catalina grabbed her sister's habito, as if she wouldn't let her go. Isabel frowned and shook her head, not one strand of hair daring to shift from its rightful place. "When you're older, you too will do your duty and marry your English prince. You will not fail God or your country then. I will not fail it now."

Gently Isabel extricated Catalina from her arms and dried her sister's tears. A finger under Catalina's chin, she forced her small sister to look at her.

"Child, needless weeping is not for Castilian princesses." Isabel looked at the queen with pride. "Especially hijas of our mother, the greatest queen ever known to Christendom. And what reason for tears? I am happy to wed Alfonso. I learnt to love him long ago and go to him with joy in my heart."

2

Mujer que sabe latin rara vez tiene buen fin.
Hija hilandera, hija casadera.

The woman who knows Latin seldom ends up well. The daughter who spins is a daughter who is marriageable.

Night fell. Cold, Beatriz curled up in her narrow trundle bed, trying to get comfortable, trying to sleep. The infantas talked softly to one another in the shared chamber, the older ones engrossed in the plans to celebrate Isabel's wedding in Sevilla. At last the excited infantas settled down, their discussions dissipating to a lulling word here and there until the breathing of Juana and María became that of the sleeping. Beatriz closed her heavy eyes and began to drift towards dream, only to be startled back into wide-eyed wakefulness by Catalina's excited voice. Very young, the child's tone punctuated the growing silence. "You never spoke of him."

Covered with white furs, Princess Isabel twisted on her couch, grey shadow falling like a blanket on her slender form. Near night candles lit up her teeth and eyes.

"Alfonso? How could I? The match wasn't set in stone. Indeed, our father fought for years to dissolve the contract of my betrothal. And for good reason. I am the heir to our mother's throne after Juan, God protect him." Isabel crossed herself. "That might prove true for our father's kingdom, too. Mother wants Father to force Aragon to stop insisting on male succession." She glanced at Catalina. "Also, the King of Portugal may have agreed to settle for our sister María, once she reached marriageable age."

Catalina rolled on the narrow pallet to face her sister. "You did not want that?"

Isabel shifted like one discomforted. "You're no longer an infant. You should know by now that what we want for ourselves matters very little. We serve, and obey."

"But, sister, your heart?" When Catalina gestured with palm upraised, it seemed to Beatriz she held to her sister the heart she spoke of.

"Heart?" Isabel's muted, grim laugh resonated in the high ceiling chamber. She glanced over to Beatriz. "Our La Latina likes to sprinkle too well her lessons with tales of romance. I beg you, don't believe them."

She lounged back, letting out a deep breath. "But you are right. For my own sake, I did not want our sister María matched to Portugal's prince. Alfonso and I became good friends during the time we were held hostage together." Isabel shrugged. "He is three years younger than me. I cared for him as I do for Juan, like I do for you all.

"But we also shared that we're both eldest children of ruling monarchs. Such children do not stay children for long." Isabel's teeth shone with an unexpected smile. "He kissed my lips when we said farewell." A dreamlike shaft of light showed her straightening her form on the couch, hands locking behind her head. When Isabel spoke again, it seemed she spoke to herself rather than her little sister. "My first kiss from a noble-born youth, not a brother or close male kin. An innocent boy's kiss, si. But even then, a kiss that promised much." Isabel turned again to her sister. "Mi chiquitina, no more questions. Time for you to sleep. Would you like for me to provide a lullaby by reciting your favourite part of *El Cid*?"

With a squeal of delight, Catalina nodded. Yawning, Beatriz rubbed her eyes. Rolling on her side, she listened to Isabel's melodious voice:

> *"Ah Cid I kiss thine hands again,*
> *but make a gift to me*
> *Bring me a Moorish mantle*
> *splendidly wrought and red."*
> *"So be it. It is granted,"*
> *the Cid in answer said,*
> *"If from abroad I bring it,*
> *well doth the matter stand...*

That same night Beatriz awoke to the sound of Catalina weeping. She sighed and slipped from her bed to go to sit by the child. Catalina looked up at Beatriz. The girl took a shuddering breath, bit her bottom lip, her tears stopping. Beatriz touched the child's wet cheek, smiling at her in reassurance. Too many nights Catalina awoke like this. It was one of the reasons why María de Salinas had come to companion the young infanta. She was one who knew how best to comfort her in her night terrors. Before María, Catalina had wept until the break of dawn, or when the queen sent a priest to pray over her. Beatriz believed the child was unsettled by the long, arduous journeys from one part of her mother's huge kingdom to another. She was also a girl blessed with a deep awareness of good and evil, attuned to the world of the spirit.

Catalina sniffed and rubbed her eyes. She inhaled another shuddering breath. "Forgive me," she whispered. "I'm all right now. Teacher," she pointed, "I beg you to re-light that candle."

The oscillating saffron light of the near fire revealed the dim tower of the blown-out candle, placed near Catalina's bed. Beatriz lumbered sleepily to relight it. The candle burning bright, she returned to Catalina and sat by her side. "Why are you so afraid of the dark, child?" she asked quietly, aware of their sleeping companions.

Catalina shook her head. "Not the dark... only what it brings." "Bad dreams come to all, my infanta." A slant of blue moonlight slipped through the window and showed Catalina lowering her gaze, as if ashamed.

"Si. But this bad dream won't leave me alone." "Would you like to tell me about it?"

Catalina stared up at her. "An eagle sits on my chest." She brushed away fresh tears. "It pulls out my heart."

Taken aback, Beatriz rubbed the side of her face. Why would a child have such a dream? What could she say to her? She weighed up her words slowly and with care. "Believe me, night-mares don't hurt us. Even in dreams we can call for God's help, and protection. He turns nightmare back into dream. When you dream this dream, pray to God to make the eagle fly away."

Catalina looked at her in bewilderment. She seemed struggling with knowledge far beyond that of a child's. "You don't understand. 'Tis when the eagle flies away I wake up weeping."

A few days later, Beatriz sat by the window, reading, near to where Queen Isabel and her four daughters twirled their spindles from their distaffs. Lifting her eyes from her book, she saw Catalina's companion stick out her tongue and Catalina's answering grin. The two five-year-olds reddened when Princess Isabel glared at them. Scowling, she gestured to them to return to their task. Beatriz closed her book, listening to the queen.

"One must first give battle before claiming victory. If you do nothing, you end with nothing. Remember well my words – those who do not recognise opportunity when it comes, find misfortune in its place. My hijas, you go to rule alongside your husbands..."

The queen placed a finished spindle in the basket beside her feet before picking up an empty one. Holding it in one hand, she sat up, the fingers of the other hand slipping under her white toca. She combed her fingers through her hair not once or twice, but three times, each time her fingers slower than the last, as if measuring out her words. "Si, you will rule too, but never let them know that. Men believe they possess the upper hand. The wise woman never lets her menfolk know otherwise."

Twisting her spindle back and forth, Princess Isabel stroked back a few loose strands of fine red/gold hair escaping from her silver hair net, seemingly far-away in her own deep thoughts. Shimmering with rainbows, tiny pearls glistened like tear drops throughout the weave of silver. On her stool, Juana swivelled from watching her older sister, her deep blue eyes now turned to the queen.

"Mother... may I ask who has the greater power – you or our lord father?"

The queen's face spoke her surprise with a lift of her thin eyebrows. Taking in her daughter's seriousness, she smiled. "Your question gives me pleasure, my Juana. You should think about such matters. As for the answer – your father and I work in partnership and I share my rule with him. He is my king, and my beloved lord."

Twirling her spindle with confidence, María piped in, her usual reticence seemingly all forgotten. "I don't understand, Mother. I hear the priests say husbands are always the heads of their wives. But you and Father –" the infanta shifted upon the stool, clearly ill at ease, "'tis not like that at all."

The queen dropped her spindle onto her lap, now swinging her approval to her third daughter. "My Joy," she said, using María's nickname. Queen Isabel used it so often her siblings had taken to using it, too. "You're right to remember well the teach-ings of the church. But God places us in a peculiar position – a position where we serve Him by offering up ourselves. That is the duty of our royal blood."

"But will not our husbands be our heads, Mother?" Infanta María darted a look at Beatriz. "Yesterday, Latina discussed with us the words of Aristotle." The young infanta's face frowned in concentration. "Juana – do you remember?"

"'Men's courage is shown in commanding and women's in obeying,'" Juana answered.

Thoughtfully, the queen picked up the spindle again, her long fingers pulling at the woollen thread from the distaff, keeping the thread taut and even. She glanced aside at Juana. "And the male is naturally more fit to command than the female, excepting where there is a miscarriage of nature.'" The queen laughed with grimness. "I have heard it all before, and too many times. Aristotle also said, 'The male is by nature superior and the female inferior; one rules and the other is ruled.' I confess something to you, my hijas. I think often of the words of our ancestor, Alfonso the Wise. He said, 'Had I been present at the creation, I would have given some useful hints for the better ordering of the universe.'" Her spindle stopped twirling and she yanked at the thread. "This world is a hard one for women, but we make the best of our lot. Since time began, men and women suffer and learn... women most of all."

The queen straightened. "Learn from me here, my hijas. Let your husbands think they are the head, let them be the head when times allow, but always be ready to do what God tells you is right. Listen to your hearts and souls, as well as to your minds." She drummed the spindle against the black velvet of her habito, pulled taut over her thigh. "You four are hijas of two proud royal houses. Your marriages will work towards giving our land stronger ties and power throughout Christendom, all for the glory of God. Think too what it means for your brother if we place his sisters in positions to help him as king of two kingdoms.

"My hijas, work towards forging strong friendships and alliances with people who will best aid and shield you in the future when you no longer have my protection. Whatever befalls you, be watchful. Keep your people close. Never forget to reward those who deserve it, those close to you, and those you want closer. Punish those who betray you and never, ever show yourself weak.

"Hijas, remember this, too – keep your hearts and minds chaste and your bodies from ill and wanton company. Your grandmother raised me in honesty and with much care for my purity, and I have done the same for you girls. 'Tis not just your bodies I speak about here. I tell you in truth, we gain nothing if we lose our souls. Rulers, too, must remember this." The queen grinned, a smile embracing all her daughters in its warmth. "We are the blood of the Trastámara. Strong, God-fearing women make up the fabric of our royal house, women you can be proud of – think you of your ancestress, Saint Isabel. My four girls will be worthy of them, for already you make me proud. Enough said." She glanced at Catalina. "Child, do you wish to begin us in Latin conversation?"

Dropping her spindle upon her lap, Catalina sat straighter, her hands holding the sides of her square stool. She nodded, her eyes alert, shining, eager.

The queen laughed, a gentle laugh she saved for private moments with her children. "Mi chiquitina, your poor mother became a student far later than you. Pray, give me at least a few minutes before you outpace me. Indeed, if all you girls could remember who is queen here?"

Seeing the queen's proud gaze, Beatriz joined in with her daughters' laughter before re-opening her book and resuming her reading.

3

If you can't bite, don't show your teeth
~ Castilian proverb

"Could we not go and see my brother?" Catalina asked. Beatriz sighed. Their imminent departure had disturbed today's lesson, again and again. All morning, servants came and went, emptying the library of the queen's most precious books. Bad weather slammed the door shut on any hope of being allowed outside this morning. The girls had struggled for the last hour to complete their reading in the midst of what seemed the confusion of an overturned beehive. No wonder Catalina wished to escape from the hectic bustle of a court making ready to move once again.

Putting down her quill, Beatriz gestured her defeat. Without any more discussion, Catalina pulled María in the direction of a far more secret door, hidden underneath a huge wall tapestry at

43

the side of the room's fireplace, with Beatriz following close behind. The secret door opened to a secret passage going from one wing of royal apartments to the other – not only to ease the way for the king to come to his wife, but also to aid a safe and quick escape for the royal family. For years now the prince had possessed his own establishment, practising the art of ruling within the security of his mother's court. While the king was with the army, the prince occupied his father's apartments.

One guttering torch, set high in a blackened sconce, lit dimly the short passageway to the spiral staircase at the end of the corridor. First to bound over the last, shortened step upon the staircase, designed to trip and announce an unknowing assassin, Catalina pushed open the hidden door to the prince's bedchamber. A sudden burst of light from a nearby window illuminated Princes Juan and Ahmed playing chess together. Ahmed, the nine-year-old son of Boabdil, Moor king of Granada, had been held as a hostage for his father's freedom and good behaviour since the age of two. Lovingly called Infantico by Queen Isabel, he was treated like a member of the royal family and raised as a Christian, and a loyal Castillan.

Catalina called out her greeting and the two princes turned. Ahmed's dark, huge eyes flashed in welcome, his smile stretching across his plump face. Only his thickly lashed, dark brown eyes showed his Moorish ancestry, for his skin was as pale as all of Queen Isabel's family. Blond-haired like Prince Juan, the boys could have been mistaken for brothers. Prince Juan frowned. "Sister, pray tell me that you asked permission of our mother to visit me?" The prince coughed.

Catalina coloured, biting her bottom lip. Her brother sighed. Rising from his stool, he paced over to his chamber's door and opened it. He stuck his head into the next room. "Miguel," he called. "Tell the queen the infanta Catalina is here with me." Shutting the door he turned back to his sister. "Thank God, I hadn't sent Miguel on another errand, and he was alone. He is one of the few who knows of the secret way between these chambers and our mother's. Anyone else would have wondered how the three of you slipped by the guard."

Ahmed chuckled. "'Twas the way I used today, too."

Prince Juan returned to the stool and grinned. "With my royal mother's permission – something my small sister often forgets to seek in her eagerness to visit me." Crossing long leg over long leg, his tapered fingers tugged at the sag of his red hose. Juan lifted his gaze to his sister. "Or have you come for another reason?"

Beatriz curtseyed. "I beg your forgiveness, my prince. It was my place, not your sister's, to ask the queen's permission. I'm afraid all the disruptions today caused me to forget."

Catalina glanced around the room and almost skipped towards an unused stool. Sitting on it, she placed her hands before her, fingertips touching fingertips, studying her brother. She smiled her most enchanting smile. "We could not study, could we Latina? Even in the library we were made to feel in the way. Is it then wrong to want to see my brother?"

Prince Juan laughed. "Moving court does not trouble me. My men refuse to let such trivial matters concern me." He studied the unfinished chess game. "All I need to do is sit and play with Ahmed until I'm wanted again."

Ahmed pushed forward one of his pieces and picked up one of the prince's pawns. "I'm winning this game."

Prince Juan screwed up his face and rolled his eyes. "Not for the first time. My father is right. I dream too much."

Catalina bounded off her stool. "Can I play against Ahmed next?"

Rising from the chess table, Prince Juan gazed towards his harp. He coughed again – and took a deep breath, as if fighting it. The prince was unwell so often Beatriz kept a well-stocked supply of soothing mixtures of horehound, honey and lemon for his coughs. But hating his times of weakness, Prince Juan worked hard at hiding any sign of illness from everyone, especially his parents.

The prince wiped his mouth. "Take over the game, Mi chiquitina. I have a tune in my head I cannot silence." He dipped his head to Prince Ahmed. "Do you mind? Catalina will give you a better game than me, especially today."

Prince Ahmed gestured to the empty seat across from him. "Come, Mi chiquitina. Let's see if you can gain victory."

Watching Catalina consider her move, Beatriz put her hands in the deep pockets of her gown and drew them out again in disappointment. Staring down at empty hands, she sighed. Usually, she had small books in her pockets to read at times like these. Now she prepared for boredom. María too shifted from foot to foot, but then Prince Juan turned and spoke. "María. My vihuela is still unpacked. Take it up, cousin, and sit by me. I need your help with my song."

Happiness lighting up her face, María grabbed the vihuela next to Juan. She gazed at him with joy, with worship, as if unable to believe he trusted her with one of his most loved musical instruments, let alone believe he asked her aid to make music. The prince had played vihuela for years and María only for the last nine months since companioning Catalina.

Knowing the gentle prince would not expect her to ask permission in his private rooms, Beatriz settled on a stool, words of Aristotle coming to mind:

> *... shall we rather suppose that music tends to be productive of virtue, having a power, as the gymnastic exercises have to form the body in a certain way, to influence the manners so as to accustom its professors to rejoice rightly? Or shall we say, that it is of any service in the conduct of life, and an assistant to prudence? for this also is a third property which has been attributed to it.*

Beatriz turned to the window, and began planning her next lesson for the girls.

Later that day Prince Ahmed plopped down next to Beatriz on the stone seat built as part of the protruding oriel window. The boy gazed down at the steep, rocky cliff-face that defended one side of the queen's alcázar just as surely as did her soldiers, maybe more so, as it was difficult to imagine any – friend or foe – surmounting the sheer, inhospitable cliffs. Turning to her, Ahmed commanded. "Tell me of my mother."

Her mind distracted by wondering how long it would take the royal court to reach their next palace, Beatriz laughed, shut the book she was reading and placed it on her lap. "Again, my prince?" "Pray, one more time," Ahmed flashed a wide smile of perfect white teeth. "Until I ask the next time."

Beatriz settled against the cushions, preparing to tell the oft-told story. "She was a daughter of a famous general who spent his fortune in defence of your father's kingdom. In gratitude, your father, my prince, showered a constant stream of titles upon him: Alcaide of Loja, Lord of Xagra, Mayor of the Alhambra and Sheriff of the Kingdom of Granada. With such a renowned father, it is not then not too surprising your mother became the wife of the king." She smiled a little, knowing she had reached Ahmed's favourite part. "I saw her once with you... Your mother held you in her arms before surrendering you for your father's freedom. The veil on her face did not hide her unforgettable eyes. How piteous they looked when she passed you, her infant son, to the queen's chamberlain."

Ahmed yanked the sleeve of his white shirt. Edged with lace and bordered with embroidery, every stitch of it came from the queen's own hands. "Would she remember me, do you think?"

Beatriz stared at him. She hooded her eyes, compassion flooding her heart. "A good mother never forgets the child she bore into the world. My prince, never doubt that your mother is a good mother. She did not need to come and hand you over at the queen's court. Only when Queen Isabel promised she would care for you like her own children did she let you go. One day, you'll know from your mother's own lips how little she forgot you."

Furious, Ahmed bounded up from the cushions and stood over her. "Why doesn't she write and tell me that now? My father writes to me but my mother, never."

Beatriz bent towards him. "My prince, your father always writes a message from your mother."

Sitting again beside her, Ahmed's lower lip trembled. "A few words – that the king, my father, includes for her."

Gathering her thoughts, Beatriz gazed at the book on her lap before eyeing Ahmed again. "Your mother would write if she was able. Do not fall into the mistake of believing what you see at Queen Isabel's court is the same elsewhere. Dear prince, not all women know how to write."

Ahmed's thick brows puckered in confusion. "Time after time you've told me my mother is intelligent. And my grandmother too. I can easily read, why not them?"

"Many know how to read without knowing how to write. 'Tis a far harder skill to learn, my prince. Do not think harshly of your mother when countless men have also not learnt to wield a pen." Beatriz opened the book. "Do you know what I have here?"

Ahmed peered at the cover page. "*Garden of Noble Maidens*," he read without hesitation.

Beatriz grinned. "Well done, my prince, and from the Latin too. I would not expect you to know the story behind this book, but the queen received the first copy as a gift for her seventeenth birthday. By then, she had lost her younger brother and it seemed more likely that our queen might succeed her brother, the king. An Augustinian friar wrote this book for her, to guide her, so he said. It speaks of all the attributes expected of a maiden – chastity, modesty, watching her tongue and humility. The friar also writes that women descend from Eve, the original sinner. He wrote this book as a reminder to Queen Isabel, a reminder of women's inferiority. My prince, our queen is perceived by many men as the best of the worst, a woman who must also strive to be an example to other women. And so she has done – from the time she first became queen. So many women at court – and I count myself amongst their number – reap the benefit of being ruled by one of our sex.

"Many men of your father's faith also do not question women's inferiority. One day, Prince Ahmed, you might fully understand why your mother never writes."

4

An ounce of mother is worth a ton of priest
~ Castilian proverb

The huge andas shook, shuddered, and jerked. Pitched almost off her seat, Beatriz bit her tongue, swallowing back the metallic wash of blood. Outside, the oxen master yelled and cracked his whip. Pity filled her heart for the poor beasts pulling the heavy andas along this ill-made road that jarred her very bones, the scream of protesting oxen cutting into her as if she was whipped, too. But she already felt whipped. The queen's court at Sevilla would include the presence of the king. Listening to the loud voice of Josefa's husband commanding the queen's escort today, she squirmed again, unable to find any comfort from the hard seats or the beautiful brocaded cushions, made mostly for display.

Queen Isabel sat across from her, little disturbed by the constant jar and rock of the journey, hand overtop the other in her lap. Josefa de Salinas and the infanta Catalina dozed close on her left and right. Just like Beatriz, little María, seated next to Catalina, shifted her position yet again, unable to find the same escape.

Heads close together, Queen Isabel and her eldest daughter murmured with Doña Beatriz Bobadilla, one of the queen's dearest friends, speaking too softly for Beatriz to make out any more than a few disconnected words. Juana twisted beside them, her heart-shaped face dark and scowling. She peeked through the thick curtains, allowing in a sliver of piercing light. Juana's eyes glowed catlike. Her jaw jutted out and another furrow appeared between her dark brows. When her mouth twisted like her body, Beatriz dropped her gaze and clasped her hands tight together. She well knew the signs. Very soon Juana's hot-blooded temper would break, unable to withstand the long hours of both heat and confinement.

Strong wind slapped the untied leather on the outer walls of the andas, while the shell breathed in and out as if alive, buckling and expanding with every hot gust of wind. The air stifled rather than offered any relief. Juana leaned across her sister. "Please, Mother, can we not open them further?"

The queen turned to Juana with a frown. Her eyes stern, she shook her head. "There is a time and place to show ourselves, but not while we dress to avoid the heat of the day. And hija, do not interrupt while I am speaking to others."

Tears of frustration fired Juana's eyes. She slumped back in her seat, wringing her hands. Her eyes raked the back of the andas. The strong wind pulled at the unsecured opening, revealing a momentary glance of the outside world. The hot sun already seared the earth and the very air itself, assaulting the winding road and the long cavalcade before them in a dazzle of blinding light. Juana's voice almost whined when she spoke again. "Mother, please, I beg you, I cannot bear to be thus enclosed. Please, when we next stop, can I not ride a mule?"

Jutting out her own chin, Queen Isabel stared at her daughter. Seemingly defeated, Juana cowered in her seat.

"Learn to bear, hija, learn to bear." The queen clamped her lips shut as if biting back harsher words.

Juana grabbed her mother's arm, in one last desperate attempt. "But Mother –"

Queen Isabel shook her off. "Must I always repeat myself with you? Don't be foolish, girl! I have already told you that when we near Sevilla all of us will make ready to change into one of our new gowns for Isabel's wedding celebrations and ride together into the city." The queen's face softened. "My Juana, can you not be patient until then?"

In answer, Juana shifted in frustration and swung out a leg that connected with María's knee. The child yelped, her gaze crossing swords with Juana. But Juana already seethed with repressed fury. María dropped her eyes, wisely choosing a hasty retreat, and made herself smaller against the wall of the andas.

Offering her little cousin a glance of sympathy, the queen turned a face to Juana as hard and unyielding as their wooden seats. Paling, Juana muttered a quick, under-breath apology to María.

Queen Isabel drew a cushion behind her and settled back against the thick padding of the andas. She inhaled and let out a deep breath. "Shall I tell a story to pass the time?"

Excepting for those still dozing, everyone seemed to sit straighter, the groans of creaking timber, the snap and whip of untied leather, the continual crazed rocking of the andas, the early afternoon heat that caused them to drip with sweat, all forgotten. Juana and Isabel turned to their mother, identical eyes wide, delighted and full of yearning.

"Oh, Mother, please," murmured Isabel.

Catalina stirred in her seat, sleepy and annoyed, half-opening her eyes. "Are we stopping again?"

"The queen is going to tell us a story," her small companion answered. All the girls wide-awake now, the sisters riveted their gaze on their mother, reminding Beatriz of the long-necked swans swimming last summer in the river near the royal residence.

The queen laughed, teasing humour returned a vivid beauty to her eyes. "Has it been that long, my hijas?" Her mouth thinned into a straight line. "Organising your sister's wedding has taken much of my time." She straightened her shoulders. "But you must realise an event like this takes days and days of careful preparation to ensure all is done properly, and as it should be. Your father and I both want Isabel's day to be glorious. We've engaged the services of the finest musicians in the land and commanded the making of many fine jewelled gowns for our beautiful girls to wear." She smiled for Isabel alone. "This is the wedding of our first born. We will show the Portuguese how much we treasure you."

Isabel kissed the queen's hand. "As I treasure you, Mother."

Juana leaned across Isabel. When Juana's older sister frowned in response, Beatriz found herself thinking, not for the first time, how much Princess Isabel resembled her mother. Not only in appearance but in spirit.

"What of the story?" whined Juana. "Please don't forget the story."

The queen considered Juana, her face becoming more lined and full of worry. "And what story shall it be? A true one or a fable? Perchance a story from the good bible?"

"A true one." Juana glanced aside at Isabel. "Our sister is leaving us. Mother, could you not tell us again the story about how you rescued Isabel when she was a child?"

Princess Isabel beamed, and Catalina stirred in excitement. "Mother, yes, that one! Please!" the child said.

The queen patted Juana's hand. "Good. You make my heart happy that you ask for this story, my Juana. It shows you've put aside your jealousy of your sister." She glanced at her eldest daughter. "Very soon, Isabel will be counting on you to take her place."

Imparting a gentle smile to her sister, Isabel nodded. "Juana will do this well. Father will see my sister better when I am no longer here. She only needs this chance to come into her own and show him how truly able she is."

Queen Isabel pursed her lips, the lines of age deepening around them. Her eyes fixed on the tapestry that backed the wall of the andras before her. As if caught up in the scene showing Saint Michael fighting the dragon, she seemed oblivious to her waiting daughters. At last, she gave a short laugh. "Your father may not be so observant, but I know well the abilities of my hijas." She reached across Isabel and clasped Juana's hand. "My passionate, beautiful Juana, in a family of great hearts, you truly have the greatest heart of all. I know it has been hard for you to grow up in Isabel's shadow. I do not wish to ever speak against your father, but he has had little time to know you as I do. He lives a hard and dangerous life as a soldier. That must remain his focus while we fight our Holy War.

"With Isabel gone, he will see you more clearly and look more to you with approval. Try to keep your emotions under control, my Juana. Nothing annoys your father more than to see his hijas forgetful of who they are. Never forget you're a royal daughter twice over."

Intertwining her hands tight in her lap, Juana blinked away tears. She grimaced in pain – or perchance for other causes. She spoke in a barely heard whisper. "My mother, I pray every day for my lord father to look more kindly upon me."

The queen's eyes darkened. Before she shut them, for several heartbeats, Beatriz saw a door opening to deep wells of pain and grief.

"I know you do, child." She sighed. "Isabel's marriage gives our hearts reason for joy. As for your father, he is only harsh because he wants what is best for our kingdoms, and the best for all our children. Let's begin this story."

Queen Isabel smiled at Catalina. "Isabel was then little older than our chiquitina," the queen laughed grimly. "If you think today is hot, my children, it compares little to the heat we endured then. None escaped it. It scorched the land in the hottest summer in living memory. In the middle of that awful summer, word came to me that Isabel was imprisoned at Segovia –"

Princess Isabel laughed. "Not right, Mother?"

The queen glanced at Isabel with a merry glint. "Pray, mine own young Mother-in-Law, are all my girls interrupting me today?"

Beatriz turned away a smile, hearing the queen use her often used nickname for her eldest daughter.

Her laughter ringing out like bells, Isabel lounged against the andas and waved her hand. "My esteemed and most prudent queen, forgive me. Pray, lady mother, go on."

Her gaze again on Saint Michael and his uplifted sword, Queen Isabel's eyes darkened as if with memories. "Even at six, my Isabel acted older than her years – much like chiquitina." She shrugged. "Isabel was yet my only living child. For seven years, before the birth of Juan, she wore the mantle of my successor. She needed to grow up fast. Your father and I made certain of that. Your sister did not panic at the sound of near battle. Despite her young years, her quick thinking ensured she and her attendants escaped to the inner tower of the alcázar, fleeing from the clutches of men who soon captured Don Pedro de Bobadilla. He was left in charge of Segovia whilst my dear amiga and her husband Cabrera spent time at my court." The queen smiled aside at Doña Beatriz Bobadilla.

"'Twas one of the few times I ever saw you weep, hearing of the imprisonment of your good father."

Glancing aside at Queen Isabel, Doña Beatriz shrugged. "My queen, I foolishly allowed myself to become distressed. You soon had the situation in hand."

The queen nodded and returned to her story. "The messenger told us Isabel and her people were in safe-keeping. But for how long? It was only a matter of time before these disgruntled rebels realised that they could gain a greater hostage for their bargaining if they turned their attention to Isabel.

"Thank the good God, I was then a young and hardy woman, used to spending days in the saddle. Without wasting any more precious time, I mounted my best horse, leaving orders for Cabrera and Doña Beatriz to follow with a troop of cavalry. Only two companions did I take, two men I judged could aid me best – the Count of Benavente, a man well-proven in battle and wisdom, and Cardinal Mendoza, whose advice had rarely led me astray. We left Tordesillas as the sun reached its zenith and rode and rode. The only time we stopped was to give ourselves a chance to speak of the best course of action once we arrived at Segovia.

"At night we journeyed without torch-bearers, but a full moon helped us find our way through mountain passes. Refusing to give way to sleep, we rode until the break of dawn and well into the next morning.

"My heart lifted at the first sight of the Roman aqueducts, and then I saw the alcázar, shadowing its beauty high over the city. I spurred my horse to greater speed, leaving both the count and the cardinal in the wake of my dust. The poor cardinal," Queen Isabel gave a short laugh. "I yelled at him, 'Dig your heels in! Use your whip, make the horse gallop!' A ghost of a man by this time, the cardinal struggled to keep himself upon his mount. But this mission was far too urgent to stop or give him any pity. That could wait. The sun attained its zenith again by the time I reached the city gates. I held my head high, drawing to myself every iota of my being when I said to the rebels: 'Tell those cavaliers and citizens that I am Queen of Castilla, and this city is mine.' Without showing fear, I rode through the gates. None dared shut me out. None dared doubt I came to take back what rightly belonged to me. Si, what was mine. I spurred my poor, exhausted horse one more time, galloping straight to the tower where my Isabel took refuge.

"As good fortune had it, a large number of loyal citizens had added their numbers to her bodyguard. They opened the gates with joy. When I took Isabel into my arms, I praised God for keeping her safe and vowed out loud, whenever possible, Isabel and all my children, yet unborn, would stay protected by my side. But our tears of relief needed to wait for another time. Events in this rebellious city had not come to an end.

"Outside, the people bayed for blood, howling their hatred and demands. Fearing the fury of the mob, the good cardinal and Count Benavente wished for me to bar myself safe within the tower. "But they spoke to a queen hearing well the voice of her unhappy people. My heart told me they wouldn't hurt me, that their hatred wasn't for me. I showed no fear standing at the tower window, my little Isabel holding my hand." The queen's eyes met her daughter's. "How proud I felt of my girl. Without showing any trepidation, I asked my people what they wanted. Voices called as one: 'Remove Cabrera!'" At the name of Doña Beatriz Bobadilla's husband, Queen Isabel smiled reassuringly at her friend. "I told the crowd I'd give the city into the keeping of a servant, loyal to me, but who would also honour them. I wanted no further dealings with those involved in leading the insurrection, only those faithful to my rule.

"'Long live the queen!' echoed between the towers, and I knew victory was mine. The rebel leaders escaped with their lives and peace was restored without further bloodshed.

"For a time, I relieved Cabrera from his post and stayed in Segovia for two months, attending to the complaints of the city. Most of the problems stemmed from a long list of misunder-standings." Queen Isabel shrugged. "Perchance a little over-eagerness to be firm with the city on the part of my loyal Cabrera —"

Men shouted in sudden warning. Whips cracked, oxen bellowed in pain. The andas pitched forward and then violently to the left. The queen grabbed onto the stiff tapestry behind her, sewn securely into the wall. Her head whipping around, she looked at her daughters, as they fell hard against one another, crying out in pain and fear.

Flung one way and then another, Beatriz snatched at the stiff tapestry, grasping for a handhold. Loud cracks, snapping leather, bellowing oxen muffled the incoherent cries of her companions.

The andas jerked again, jarring to one side. Josefa, seeing her daughter perched perilously on her seat, reached out to little María. One more time the andas tottered, tilting over to one side. Josefa lost her balance and toppled between the facing seats. Her body thudded loudly on the floor, her cut-off cry smiting all to a terrible stillness. Josefa remained there, unmoving, silent. "Mamá! Mamá!" her daughter cried, her eyes entreating the queen for help. A babble of voices rose to a crescendo outside. The andas now steady, Beatriz, with caution, followed the queen, moving from her place on the upward slope. Crouching over Josefa, they gently rolled her over to her back. She lifted her eyes to meet the queen's eyes. Queen Isabel waved Josefa's daughter back without even glancing her way. She gently shook Josefa's shoulder. "Cousin?"

Fanning out her hands either side of Josefa's belly. Beatriz let out a breath of relief. "I felt a kick. The babe lives!" she said.

Josefa moaned. Beatriz gazed at her friend's white face and now opened eyes, and her heart skipped a beat. Her pupils enlarged and skin as white as pure alabaster, Josefa looked terrified, and in great pain.

Beatriz helped the queen seat the dazed Josefa between them. Outside, men's voices boomed, shouting over one another until the sound became a cacophony of confusion. Horses squealed and snorted, their hooves thundering around the andas like a violent storm.

One side of the andas opened up with a loud slap of leather. Beatriz blinked her eyes at the sudden rush of light. Josefa's husband appeared, the strong angles of one side of his face all harsh shadows, the other bathed in light. After an anxious glance at his drooping wife, he vanished from sight. Beatriz heard him take charge. "Heave! Heave! Heave! Come on, men, work together. Get your backs into it, keep it steady. Right that wheel on its axle! You – over there. Check the ropes of the oxen. Remember, the queen is inside!"

With another violent jerk and shake, the andas became level again. Emitting a soft whimper, Josefa's head fell against the queen's shoulder. Queen Isabel bit her bottom lip and glanced aside at Beatriz. "How far to Sevilla, my friend?"

Trying to hide her growing fear and alarm, Beatriz lowered her head. "Hours away, my queen."

"Shall I call a physician?" asked Queen Isabel.

Placing her palm on Josefa's chest, Beatriz concentrated on counting the beats of her friend's heart. She rubbed her face. *Mother of God, help me. Josefa's heart beats too fast.* She gazed at the four infantas. Even Juana stayed still and quiet. It seemed a door had opened to a part of life none of them wanted to see. Even Isabel, a woman full-grown and old enough to be mother of both Catalina and María, kept her eyes fixed upon her lap.

Beatriz turned to Queen Isabel, keeping her voice down. "My queen, you know I speak the truth when I humbly say I am as learned as them." She smiled grimly. "Remember, the two physicians accompanying us today were both once my students at Salamanca." She put her hands upon Josefa's belly. "I can care for her. I do not think her labour has started, but she's hurt. I cannot easily judge how badly this might be while we remain cramped up here. The sooner we reach Sevilla the better."

"I can care for her." The enormity of her words echoed in her ears. She looked at the child María wiping away her tears. Comforted, the small girl gazed at her as if she seized onto her words with hope. The child believed in her. Beatriz found herself praying that the child would still believe in her in the coming days.

5

If you have the moon, ignore the stars
~ Castilian proverb

Beatriz cursed the hours it took them to reach Sevilla, more aware than ever of every rattle, every sway, every bump in that teeth-chattering andas. Those terrible, drawn-out hours seemed as slow as a dreadful winter changing into spring. The infanta María whispered in her mother's ear. Nodding in reply, Queen Isabel popped her head out of one of the openings. She uttered a brisk command, and the cavalcade came to a stop.

"Children, not much longer now. Go and stretch your legs for a few minutes."

The crest of a high hill overlooked the outskirts of Sevilla. The infanta Catalina and her small companion wandered a little distance away, gazing at the winding track leading to the city. The panorama of unyielding, sun-scorched landscape, hills and valleys went on forever. Catalina twirled around as if in dance, her arms outstretched as if claiming freedom. Her older sister hurried over to her. "Stop it, Catalina," said Isabel. "You're showing the men you do not know how to behave."

An agonised scream cut through the andras. Beatriz spun around to Josefa like a spinning-top.

"Mamá!" María yelled. Her skirts bunched up in her hands, exposing naked legs, the child ran back toward the andras.

Beatriz gazed down on Josefa. Lines fanned out like fine webs around her tightly closed eyes. Other lines deepened from nose to outer lips. She looked grey, older than her years and almost unrecognisable. Opening her eyes, Josefa snatched at Beatriz's hand in desperation and screamed again. Beatriz's fear rose, real, solid, and impregnable.

Josefa moaned, more softly this time. She turned to Queen Isabel, voicing a few words of a strained apology before a louder cry strangled her words. Pain darkened her unfocused eyes to almost black. Shifting side-to-side, her agony was plain and horrible to see. Rubbing Josefa's belly, Beatriz whispered to the queen, "I fear her travail has begun." Little María clambered inside the andas.

Beatriz glanced her way, unable to speak one word of reassurance to the child.

Queen Isabel took something out of her pocket and placed a small, golden rectangular box into Josefa's limp hand. She closed her hand over it. "Hold this to you, cousin. 'Tis my fragment from the robe of the Virgin I carry always. I had it with me for all my childbirths. The good Mother of God will keep you safe."

Josefa didn't seem to hear, or see. She gave another moan and shifted again. "Pray, forgive my weakness." Removing her hand from the queen's, Josefa stared at the tiny gold reliquary with distaste. "The fall hurt my back. 'Tis not my babe, 'tis not that!" Her eyelids fluttered closed. "'Tis not that..."

Beatriz rubbed at her wet eyes.

Josefa came to childbed before her time, giving birth to a dead boy the very same night they reached Sevilla. For days Beatriz and the queen's physicians feared her lost too, a knowledge sweeping Beatriz to the brink of a deep, bottomless void. For Josefa's little daughter it was more than the brink. For three days María haunted the doors outside her mother's chambers, knowing her mother fought a battle for life. Within, her father refused to budge from his wife's side. Forgotten by her parents, shut out from their lives, María barely registered when, sooner or later, Beatriz led her back to the royal chambers.

On the third day the chamber's heavy door swung open. Fray Hernando de Talavera, the queen's elderly Hieronymite confessor, came through its narrow opening. The dark brown scapula covering the priest's white habit served only to make the harsh angles of his fleshless face more severe and deepened his dark, cavernous eyes. Beatriz strode over to him, María closely following. Like so many times in the past, the priest gazed kindly at María, but this time a kindness overlaid with pity. Despite his unhidden disapproval of her, Beatriz held Fray Hernando in great regard. Like her, he was a respected professor of the university at Salamanca. He always spoke to children just as he would speak to adults – and always what he believed the truth.

María ran to him, clutching at Fray Hernando's scapula and then Beatriz's habito before falling to her knees. Her efforts to question them became lost and muffled in tears. Beatriz raised María up, keeping her arm wound around her.

"My mamá..." she sobbed.

With a helpless gesture, Beatriz turned to the priest. Fray Hernando paid her no mind, his eyes were only for the child. Never before had Beatriz seen him so gentle.

"Come here, child," he said, taking María from Beatriz. Bending down, his aged bones cracked as he gripped María's thin, frail shoulders. "The crisis is coming, child. Perchance in the next hour we'll know... Pray, child, as we all are. María, if death does take your mother..." His grip tightened on her shoulders. "Little one, she goes to God's care. Go with your teacher, child, and wait for us to send word to you." The priest shuffled away in the direction of the chapel.

Beatriz clasped María's hand and led her to the library. María stopped her. Her eyes were wide, her mouth opening and shutting.

"What is it, child?" Beatriz asked.

"I don't want Mamá with God. I want her here, with me."

Tired, miserable, Beatriz hugged María. "I know. I want that, too, as do all the people who love her. I promise you, we never give up while there's life. My heart tells me that God will hear our prayers and let paradise wait for your mother a while longer."

María wept. It took all of Beatriz's control not to weep, too.

Early morning of the next day, María stood again outside her mother's door. One hour passed and then another until

Beatriz sent a hesitating Doña Teresa Manrigue to approach her.

"María, come with me," she coaxed, her voice sugar sweet, just like the rose-sugars she kept in her pocket. "Our queen does not want you here, little one. Becoming so upset does not help your mother. You're upsetting the infanta too. She refuses to do her lessons unless you are with her. Look, your teacher is waiting to take you back to her."

Doña Teresa took the child's arm, but she shook her head and refused to budge, rooting herself to the ground. María stared at the door of her mother's chamber. Doña Teresa pleaded with her, bribing to give María her own bag of rose-sugar if she returned with Beatriz to the library. Tut-tutting and muttering her frustration, Doña Teresa scurried down the corridor. She came back with a tall and broad manservant. Without a word, he picked the child up as if she weighed nothing at all.

"The infanta commands your presence," he said. María sobbed her helplessness as he carried her back to the royal apartments, with Beatriz close behind. Letting the child down outside the library, he strode away to other concerns.

María entered the large library like a sleepwalker. Catalina gave a cry, bounded up from the table and ran to embrace her friend. For the remainder of that day, María sat next to Catalina. Catalina held her friend's hand as if that alone would prevent María from being pulled down into the depths of terrible currents of grief and despair. Carefully choosing a book to read to the girls, Beatriz once more attempted the motions of everyday life. It was impossible.

The dark tide drew back the morning of the next day. A few words of hope travelled down to them that the queen's physicians believed the battle won and María's mother's life saved at last. Unable to say no to María, Beatriz took her to her mother's chamber. As if the child conjured him out of thin air and unvoiced yearning, her father flung open the door. Almost a stranger to them, he stood against the light, hollowed cheeks, face unshaven, curded from his usual tan to an unhealthy paleness, dark rings under red-rimmed eyes. María ran into his outstretched arms.

"Mamá, Mamá," the child said through her tears, as if she could speak no other words. He hugged his small daughter tighter to him, before gesturing to Beatriz to approach them. "Come. Come and see her."

Whiter than the white chemise she wore, Josefa outstretched her arms to her daughter. María became an arrow shooting to its target.

"My María." Stroking María's hair, Josefa said her daughter's name like a caress.

Sobs racking her, María nestled her face into her mother's breast, tightening her grip on her shoulders. Her father gently pulled María from her mother. "Careful. She's still not well."

Josefa gazed at him, her dark eyes wells of grief and loss, wells with depths that Beatriz could only imagine. "I am better today." Chalk-white, Josefa's hand curled in a tight fist upon the bedclothes.

Martin squared his chin, his usually generous mouth a hard gash in his wan face. He clasped the limp hand at her side. "Si. Better today." He shut his eyes, the skin around them wrinkling into fine lines. Tears beaded his thick, long eyelashes and fell down his bristly skin. María edged closer to her mother's side, her frightened eyes going from one parent to the other.

Believed blithe by many, these days changed María's father forever.

Josefa's hand tightened on her husband's. "I am here, and I will bear you more children."

Her husband opened anguished, tortured eyes. Raising his chin, he tightened his mouth, and shook his head. "This is not the first time I've sat by you, wondering if you'd die. No more. I've spoken to the queen this morning. When you are better, you will go home to our other children and no longer stay here at court."

María let out a cry. Her mother's arm wound around her daughter, pulling her closer. "Hush, I go nowhere."

Martin grasped his wife's shoulder. "Josefa, what of our other three? Don't they also need their mother?"

Turning her head, Josefa wiped her wet face with the puffed sleeve of her chemise, staring at the white pillow next to her. "My mother cares well for them, you know that. 'Tis far better that they stay safe at home." Her distressed eyes veered back to her husband. She took a deep breath. "I wish María had remained there too. I have told you, she who goes with wolves learns to howl."

Beatriz stared at Josefa. Did she mean the royal family? She knew Josefa loved the queen, her cousin. Catalina? Catalina a wolf? Never. The king, though... he was a wolf like none other.

Martin shrugged, and then spoke out loud the very thoughts pounding in Beatriz's mind. "Those prowling too near our wily king may turn wolf." He smiled at his wife. "'Tis your good sense that has always guided me best about him. But the queen, your cousin, keeps our daughter safe with her children. There's no danger for our child."

Josefa acted as if she didn't hear him. "I tell you again, husband, I like it not she and the infanta remain so close. We but lose another child."

He stroked a falling tear from her cheek, rubbing it between index finger and thumb as if he caught something precious. His grim face softened. "My love, were you not also close to your cousin, the queen, from childhood? You, Latina and Beatriz de Bobadilla are trusted as none other." Martin reclaimed his wife's hand. Shaking it gently, he brought her eyes back to him. "Beloved, we cannot change the fact the little infanta befriended our María so the child asked her mother for her as a companion. Our family serves the royal family with their lives. But our noble queen is your good amiga too. She has listened to me and agrees you must go home."

"Martin, I –"

"No more arguments, sweetheart. This is the third child lost to us while journeying with the court, and every time the physicians battle for your life. They tell me you will die if something like this happens again. Josefa, enough is enough!"

Josefa's far-too-wan face pinched more around eyes and mouth.

"You want me gone from you? Our youngest child left alone at court?"

Martin nuzzled into her neck, his cries tearing out of him.

Beatriz led María away to the nearby embrasure. How she feared for the child. The last few days had seen the threads of María's childhood snap, one by one. Soon, it may be too late to prevent the snapping of the final threads.

Josefa wrapped her arms around her husband. "Beloved, don't. I cannot bear it."

Martin gazed at her with bloodshot eyes. "And I cannot bear to lose you. I beg you, please listen and go home. Please, Josefa."

In answer, Josefa moaned softly, as if fighting a different type of pain to what she experienced in the andas. She shifted her head one way and then the other on the pillow, before wiping her face and kissing Martin.

"I'll bear you more children. Going from court won't change that, or the fact that childbirth is always a woman's war."

Their black hair intermingling on the pillow, Martin rested his head next to hers. He brought her hand to his mouth, kissing its inner palm. "You speak of war, beloved. Hear me... given the opportunity, leaders worth their salt map out their battle engagements. In my own soldiering, what aids me to victory is the study of war and my own experience. For my own safety and that of my men, I remember well the lessons taught to me by both history and life."

He kissed her cheek. "I learned this here. Three times you've journeyed far with the queen while with child, only for you and the unborn babe to suffer for it. Three sons have been lost to us, in almost as many years. When you stayed at home, you did not lose our babes. Thanks to the care of your good mother, you bore our children safely there, and every child lives and thrives.

"Coming to attend the queen has worn you out, and put your life in unnecessary danger. Not once, or twice but three times now have I seen the priest make ready with the last sacrament. You hold my heart, Josefa. Take you from me, and I am little more than dead too. Beloved, I beg you, please go."

Josefa held his face between her hands. "I want to stay at court." She took a deep breath. "What if you need me? I would never forgive myself if you're hurt soldiering with the king, and I discover it too late… far from you at home…"

Martin drew her closer to him. He kissed her, first a rain of kisses along her brow and then her cheeks, before taking his mouth to hers. Still holding María's hand, Beatriz blushed, stepped away and stared at her feet for a moment. Martin traced down from Josefa's temple to the corner of her kissed red mouth. Her lips opened to the gleam of white teeth.

"Believe me, love. I could not forgive myself if I caused your death by giving you a child when you are too unwell to bear it. I love you, body and soul, Josefa. The doctors tell me it will be long before we can bed together again. Having you here, close to me, is too much temptation. You must go, beloved!"

Josefa wept and wept. Beatriz stood in the shadows, forgotten, with their daughter, swirling in her private ocean of desolation.

6

Walk until the blood appears on the cheek,
but not the sweat on the brow
~ Castilian proverb

Dear Francisco,

Soon I will be very lonely at court. Not only have you been gone for months, but the queen's cousin and my good friend Josefa returns to her home in Vitoria. Poor Josefa is unhappy about leaving, but her fragile health has forced the queen to command it. The queen well knows what it is to lack the strength of body to bring forth a living child. In the early years of her reign, she lost baby after baby due to waging battle for her crown.

At the moment, Josefa waits for the queen's physicians to give permission for her departure. I –and the queen, too – visit her every day. I take her daughter, my little student María. The poor child cannot hide from me how she dreads the day when her mother leaves. Whilst five is very young to lose a beloved mother, we can only thank God the loss is not permanent.

We are in the midst of celebrations for Princess Isabel's wedding...

"Come home with me," Josefa pleaded.

Alarmed, Catalina looked aside at María. She shook her head so fast it could have been a spinning top.

The queen laughed. "Look at María. And my Catalina, too. We'd need horses to drag these two apart, just like when our girls first met over a year ago. I remember well that day. The storm that drove us to your home to take up the hospitality of my aunt, your good mother. Come the morning of the next day, few could separate Catalina from María." Queen Isabel studied the two girls. "Do you wish me to make the command?"

Josefa frowned and lifted her gaze from her sewing, dropping her embroidery onto her lap. Her skin remained as white as the sheets of her bed, but the aging shadows around eyes and mouth lessened with every new day. Her natural vitality slowly returned the youthfulness of a woman who, like Beatriz, had seen no more than twenty-five summers.

Josefa considered her daughter and then Catalina, shrugging her slight shoulders. "I kiss your hands in gratitude, my queen, but I think not. Our two remind me of two girls I once knew – two cousins, one older, the other younger – who called themselves sisters. Every time life separated them, the younger one's heart broke. God willing, I would rather not give our girls reason for the same grief."

Queen Isabel picked up Josefa's still hand. "Si – love binds us to those we love. I would want it no other way." She lifted her chin. "I make this vow to you, I will be as a mother to María. Even without kinship, our long, loving friendship means I could do no other."

Josefa gave a wry smile. "I am grateful, Isabel. I cannot lie to you, my prima hermana, I'd prefer María to grow up with my other children. But like the sun rises in the morning and sets at night, María already knows her place is to serve your hija. My heart tells me this is what God wants. And why should my daughter not love your daughter? All my life I have loved her mother." Tears welled in Josefa's eyes. She spoke in a voice both trembling and plaintive. "Who will care for you, Isabel, as I do when you cannot sleep, and work throughout the night? None attend to your needs as well as I." She glanced over at Beatriz. "Latina forgets the whole world when she loses herself in her study. I always make certain you at least have a drink by your side during the long hours to Matins, or ensuring there is enough candlelight for you to work by."

Queen Isabel shook Josefa's clenched hand. The smile she bestowed upon Josefa was one Beatriz had never witnessed from her before – young and tender, speaking of a lifetime of loving memories. "Don't cry. Don't dare think you've failed me. You have not, my Josefa. You have exhausted yourself in my service and suffered because of it.

"Now it is time for me to take care of you. I will look forward to your letters. Si, María and I will write to you. Let you revel in your hija's improving hand and sharpening wit. My Catalina will make certain of that.

"Next summer I will journey through Andalucia. I give you

notice today I will visit you at Vitoria and see you as I pray to see you – healthy and more than ready for argument once again."

Brushing away tears, Josefa laughed. She gazed up at the queen as if she was the only person in the world. Her mouth trembled. "How I shall miss that. These years spent in your service have meant much to me. How I wish I could stay. My greatest regret is my body proved too weak to both serve you and give my husband more living sons. My body betrayed me." Josefa wiped her face with the sleeve of her chemise. "My Latin will grow rusty while I care for my children and my apricot trees."

Queen Isabel bent to kiss her cousin's pale cheek. She framed Josefa's face with her long, gout-swollen fingers. Their gazes met again.

"Your apricots and horses will make you strong and well again," the queen laughed. "Not forgetting your older children. They have been too long without you." She rested her hands on Josefa's shoulders. "I'll send you books. Many books – books for my good aunt to enjoy too. As long as I know you remain safe and well at Vitoria with your orchards, riding your horses, and improving your Latin, my heart stays light." She kissed her cousin again. "Let's us enjoy these final days together while you regain your strength, and remain content our separation will only be through distance and not yet death."

Alone, Beatriz leaned against the garden's high wall in the royal alcázar at Sevilla. Her black cloak and sheer toca lying at her feet, she held her arms tight across her chest, trying to control her breathing. A shaft of sunlight struck and hurt her eyes. She rubbed them, her fingers coming away with her tears. She crossed her arms over her swollen, painful breasts, swallowing the blood in her mouth from when she had bit her tongue. The tears started again – she let them fall, unchecked.

Gathering an assortment of herbs growing in abundance in this private royal garden, she had not expected to be disturbed, disturbed by the loud snapping of dry twigs that had announced the arrival of the king.

Don't think of it. Forget it. She yanked up the neck of her gown, covering and hiding from view the bruises left by his fingers on her breasts. She rubbed her neck and tried to swallow, her throat hurt. She didn't need a mirror to tell her she would need to find a dress with a high collar to hide what the king had done to her.

She tried to repair her dishevelment, and began to walk slowly towards her rooms. Beatriz cocked her head, stepping into a part of the garden awash with green light. She felt unreal, as if she had fallen in another world of nightmare. Without thinking, she crossed herself, resettling on her head the toca. She wished it could make her disappear.

Beatriz stepped into the garden's deeper shadows and saw María coming through the gate. The child looked at her with surprise. "Latina," she blurted out.

"Have you come to enjoy the sun's warmth, too?" Beatriz said quickly. As if in denial of her words, she shivered, averted her face and swallowed, her hand going to her throat again. It hurt. Really hurt. This time she feared the king had meant to strangle her.

María, disturbed and frightened, stepped towards her. "Mamá –is all well with her?"

"Your mother?" Beatriz narrowed her eyes against the bright light streaming on her face. She untied and retied the loose ends of her girdle, as if letting loose the beads of a rosary in prayer. "When I saw her this morning she gave me no cause for concern. Has something happened since then?"

María looked even more bewildered. She gazed down at the toes of her black leather slippers, peeping out from beneath her skirts, and then back at Beatriz. "Something is wrong, my teacher…"

María glanced at the path leading to the royal chambers. The doorway was open in the high stonewall. A climbing rose spread its certain claim over the grey stone. Butterflies flittered a graceful dance around the yellow roses creeping above the door. Only the royal family ever used that door, for its path led straight across a courtyard to the chambers of the king and queen. Go too far and guards barred the way with pike and sword.

María turned and faced her. "Why is the door open, Latina? The queen commands it locked."

Beatriz shifted uneasily. "Why should I know, María? You ask questions for no good reason." Her words broke and snapped, like the very twigs under their feet. She gazed at the sky. Not one cloud – so beautifully blue, it seemed to mock her.

María blinked. Distressed, her eyes filled with tears, she repeated, "Something's wrong…"

Beatriz bowed her head, straightening the folds of her gown, refusing to meet María's eyes. She shrugged. "Si, something's wrong, but 'tis not for a young child's ears. Go from here, María.

Go and enjoy these days too soon ended, when childhood gives you freedom denied to us who are no longer children."

Her eyes shining with tears, María gave Beatriz a deep reverence. Her head pounding, Beatriz felt like she had lost her footing. Again the abyss opened up before her. She raised her hand to her aching temple. *I should not have taken it out on her. Next lesson, I'll beg her forgiveness.*

Before she left the garden for her own chambers, Beatriz shut the door, watching María head in the direction of the library. The wind brought to her ears the gay long notes of the hunting horn threaded with the muted rumble of galloping horses leaving the grounds of the alcázar. In the distance, she saw the billowing dust of the party accompanying the king on his morning hunt. Soon, the sounds of men and horse became but a whisper of rumour upon wind.

Despite the warmth of the day, Beatriz gathered her cloak around her body, and tossed her hood over her head. She cloaked herself in another sense than the physical. Following the path that would take her back to her rooms, her eyes no longer saw the world around her, but looked blindly around, overcome by despair and defeat. Beatriz stumbled. Wanting to vomit, she sat on a nearby stone bench and bowed her head. *I am trapped. Trapped, with no way to escape.*

***

Catalina and María stared at her when they came to the schoolroom for their morning lesson the next day. "You're wearing a nun's habit," stated the infanta.

Beatriz glanced down at her shabby grey gown of the Franciscan order. The girls had been little more than babies when she had stopped wearing it every day. "I am still a lay member of my order in Salamanca. I almost took my final vows, but realised my problem with obedience is one I never want to solve." The girls looked disconcerted. "I am allowed to wear the habit if I wish. I'm a member of the third order of Franciscans." Catalina and María continued to gaze at her in bewilderment. Beatriz took a deep breath. "I'm wearing it today because I needed a reminder of humility. Yesterday I was unnecessarily harsh to María. I hope you can forgive me, child?"

María beamed. "Si. But you don't need to wear your habit, Latina."

Beatriz eyed the child almost skipping and dancing with Catalina to the table where their books were waiting. The coarse fabric of the habit chafed her skin, as if reminding her of her lie.

She swallowed, touching the wimple of her habit. She had pulled its cords a little too tightly this morning, but at least it covered her bruised neck and chest. She prayed to God the habit would give the king reason to think again before coming her way. He respected the church. Surely if he remembered how close she had been to taking her vows he would leave her alone.

***

Sweet heart,

I miss you sorely. I do not often say that, do I, love? But my dear friend is gone. Last week, Josefa left with her husband for Vitoria. The queen's physicians deemed her well enough for travel, but, love, how bitter sweet that day was.

Her daughter María is bereft. Court life never disturbed the child overlong with Josefa also here. Josefa offered a buffer, a semblance of normality for the child. I pray to God I can do the same. The queen promised her cousin she will be a second mother to the little one. As yet, María can not hide she aches for her own.

Once a year, before the onset of Lent, María will go home with her father to spend Easter with Josefa. No doubt the passing of time will teach the child to adapt with ease from one place to another without Josefa's help.

Si, María's home is no longer with her family. Catalina is the child's true home, her place of belonging. As I, too, belong – to you. Today I find myself yearning to be your wife. Is that strange for me to say? I – who always tell you, 'There is no hurry. Let's be patient, and marry when you can leave the king's army.' Farewelling my friend leaves me melancholy... These last days, only teaching gives me any joy...

7

Every man is a fool in some man's opinion
~ Castilian proverb

Beatriz saw him again and again during the weeks leading up to Princess Isabel's wedding. He stood alone in shadows, away from sunlight, away from the hum and bustle of court, his eyes full of dreams. *Just like a mystic,* she thought. A mystic burning bright with the fire of a zealot.

Noticing Beatriz's curious eyes on him again, Catalina whispered. "'Tis the Italian, Cristóbal Colón. Father calls him the Jew." Beatriz looked aside at Catalina and lifted an eyebrow. Catalina answered with an embarrassed shrug. King Ferdinand made no effort to hide his dislike of Jews.

With so many Jews in powerful positions in his wife's court, Beatriz knew Catalina often felt confused about the different standpoints taken by her parents. Beatriz hoped to guide the girl —hoped to help open her eyes so she appreciated people for their hearts and souls, rather than view the world through unnecessary prejudice. God knew she received enough of that herself as a woman scholar navigating a world mapped out by men. "He wants my parents to pay for ships and men. The king, my lord father, says the man is a charlatan and wastes my mother's precious time with some foolhardy plan to discover a sea way to India and the land of the grand khan."

María gazed blankly at Catalina.

"Do you know what grand khan means?" Beatriz asked. Frowning, María gave it quick thought and offered an answer.

"King of kings?"

Beatriz smiled. The children were listening to her lessons.

"Si," Catalina said. "Mother told me that the khan sent word to the pope for men of God to come to him. None have because the journey is too full of danger. Cristóbal Colón believes he can discover a way to make it not so."

"I think the king is right. Seafaring ships disappear over the ends of the world," María said earnestly.

Catalina laughed. "That's only a fable. Don't you remember Latina telling us otherwise?" she reminded her friend, with another glance in Cristóbal Colón's direction. "Geraldini and Santángel both have my lady mother's ear. My mother likes the Italian. She believes God has sent him to her. He will get his ships." Catalina pulled María back into movement. One more time, Beatriz gazed over her shoulder. Seemingly a true Italian – even if a Jew – with heavy, hooded eyes, large, hooked nose, sensual lips, and strong chin, the man reminded her of a bust found in their present alcázar, a bust of a long ago Roman Caesar. Cristóbal Colón took no notice of two small girls and their woman tutor padding softly in the long, narrow corridor, away from the shadows and into the light of a new day. Even Catalina, a daughter of the royal house, aroused none of his attention.

Behind the infanta Juana, a frowning Doña Teresa Manrigue gestured to them to quicken their pace. Beatriz ceased wondering about this stranger, forced to face the moment at hand. With her trailing skirts slung over an arm, she rushed with the small girls to join the queen and her other children to attend yet another festivity celebrating Isabel's proxy marriage to the Prince of Portugal. Two more of the queen's women followed a few steps behind.

Beatriz hurried faster than usual, but for far different reasons. If she didn't hurry, concentrating on walking in her long gown with grace, she might succumb to her desire to run in the opposite direction. She had no wish to watch another bullfight.

Beatriz hated bulls. She had always hated them. An immense, overpowering primeval fear made it so, a fear surging up within her whenever the inescapable smell of a bull came near. Seeing them, smelling them, even from a safe distance, swamped her in a violent tide of terror. Her heart beating hard and furious against her chest, Beatriz felt sick and dizzy. It took the clasp of and Catalina's hands to stop her from dashing away from the entrance of the arena. Already, the heady, ripe smell of beast walled her in its imprisonment.

Looking down at their white, pinched faces, it seemed the girls also shared her fear. And not only the girls. The queen also hated bullfights. Time after time she sat there with a white, drained face, empty of expression. Her head set against the high back of her chair, she kept her eyes fixed, watching the bull rage and fight for its life against the matador.

Just days ago María had experienced her first bullfight. The child wept – and the queen had noticed. Later, when Beatriz accompanied Catalina and María to the queen's private chambers, Queen Isabel took María aside, crouching down to speak to her in the embrasure of her huge window.

"I detest bullfights." She lifted María's chin, making the child look straight into her eyes. "Can I trust you with my secret of how I pretend otherwise?"

María nodded and attempted a smile.

Queen Isabel rested her hand on María's shoulder. "You are your mother's good hija, si?"

María nodded again and the queen laughed. Cocking her head to one side, she peered out the window before turning back to María. "I must appear brave before my people, small cousin, but –I tell you in truth – only the stupid and those lacking any foresight do not fear. Little cousin, you too descended from kings, please believe the truth of my words. When we pretend bravery the pretence often becomes real. Very real. If we face fear we often find we turn a lion into a cat. A cat is easily dealt with, si?" Queen Isabel smiled when María nodded. "My small kinchild, promise me you'll pretend to be brave until mantled by true bravery."

Remembering now María making that promise, Beatriz steadied her gaze upon the queen's thickened fingers, drumming on the arm of her seat. The jewels in her rings winked in the sunlight. Overheated in her gown, Beatriz attempted to push down the fear and horror swirling in her stomach, making her feel ill again.

Loud laughter erupted from the king's stall. His vulpine face full of eagerness for the kill, King Ferdinand leaned forward in his chair and joked with the grandees standing near him. Beatriz lowered her head, praying he would not notice her. The king always took great delight in the battle of life and death waged before their eyes. A vivid, magnetic and pragmatic man amongst men, he seemed to live for such moments.

Beatriz hooded her eyes against witnessing the men's enjoyment, but she lifted her head when she heard the excited laughter of Prince Ahmed and Prince Juan. Watching Prince Juan copy his father depressed her. A poet and scholar, Juan was a youth who never revelled in bloodshed. His behaviour today disturbed her. Why, she asked herself, must he assume the mask that belonged to men like his father? Could he not show the public the sensitive, gentle boy he really was?

Still and silent, the queen and her daughters sat with rod-straight backs against their chairs. Placed behind Catalina, Beatriz kept her hands locked together in her lap and steadied her breathing. She thought of the morning song of birds, new books she wanted to read, tomorrow's lessons – anything and everything rather than to return her eyes to a bleeding animal full of justified fury, no longer seduced by the matador's dance, but fighting for its life. Hearing the king laugh again, Beatriz recalled the words of Aristotle: *Man, when perfected, is the best of animals, but when separated from law and justice, he is the worst of all.*

The bull gave a tortured bellow. Beatriz looked down to see the matador pull his short spear out of the bull's back. She hated bulls? Watching the animal's pain-glazed eyes roll back in its distress it was no longer hate she felt but great pity.

Side-stepping with a dancer's grace, the matador again speared the bull deep into its shoulder. The open wound gushed an outpouring of blood, a red rivulet against the bull's black skin. The crowd roared its approval and so did the king. In answer, the matador flourished a half-turn to the royal stand. A foolish, costly mistake. The bull lowered its head and charged.

Beatriz closed her eyes. She heard Catalina gasp and Juana scream, a scream penetrating the silence in the royal stands.

Below them the bull gored the matador to death. Sickened, faint, Beatriz swallowed back vomit. Hot urine splashed down her thighs. Her heart in her throat, the matador's terrible screams cut through her. Twisting, she looked behind her, seeking an easy way of escape through the queen's crowd of women. She just wanted to grab Catalina and María, and run away from this living nightmare, but obedience to the queen forbade it.

Holding long spears, twelve men or more rushed into the arena. From a safe distance, they aimed and threw their spears. The bull, focused on its revenge, stayed oblivious to the arching spears until too late. One last furious bellow sounded below. The beast buckled, collapsing on the dying matador.

Catalina turned and looked at Beatriz with terrified eyes. The child had grabbed the back of her seat, holding it so tight her knuckles became white. Hysterical, Juana sobbed and sobbed. Beside her, a very pale Isabel took her arm, and shook. She whispered, "Quieten yourself, I beg you. Father watches."

Juana hiccupped, her tears stopping, as if knifed at their very source. Ducking her head, Beatriz looked aside at the king. Black fury darkened his already dark skin to a frightening guise. Reminding Beatriz of the bull just minutes before its death, his gaze snapped upon the queen's as if a bolt of lightning. Without warning he stood, his anger making him seem tall. His men followed suit. The king turned his back on his daughters and the queen, striding fast from the stands. Queen Isabel sighed, stirring in her seat, her face stern and pale. "Let's follow."

Stiff brocade gowns rustled in a chorus, skirts swept the ground. With their women helping to hold up their trailing gowns, the queen and infantas carefully manoeuvred through the stands. High and low, the multitude watched the royal family's every move as they left the arena.

After entering her chambers, the queen commanded the majority of her attendants to stay in the outer chamber. Only those closest to the royal family were admitted to her private bedchamber.

Turning on her heel, the queen faced her second daughter with worry and frustration.

Juana fell to her knees. In a hoarse voice, she pleaded, "Mamá, I beg you, forgive me."

Wordlessly, the queen shook her head. Her eyes huge, Juana visibly shuddered. Isabel rested a hand on her sister's shoulder and stood protectively beside her. Swallowing hard, Isabel's gaze veered to her mother. Her eyes pleaded, begged.

Looking at her two daughters, the queen's shoulders slumped, her face softening. "Hija, be warned. Your lord father will surely take you to task about your behaviour today."

Juana's mouth trembled. Tears ran down her cheeks. "I didn't mean to do it," she said.

Shaking her head again, the queen sighed. "I hate the blood of the bullfights too, Juana, but they belong to our land just as surely as we do. Even Catalina did not cry out like you, and you are five years the older. You must never show fear, not now, not ever, my daughter. Showing fear renders you powerless." Queen Isabel swallowed. "You gave your lord father and I much reason for shame today, my Juana."

Juana crumpled against her sister. Isabel, putting her arm around her, looked at her mother and spoke. "Mamá, can you not please talk to Father and crave his forgiveness for my sister. It was a terrible thing that happened today. Surely he can understand the reason for my sister's great distress."

Queen Isabel's eyes narrowed. Lifting her chin, she gazed at Juana, but spoke as if she wasn't there. "Your sister shamed us. Shamed our family in front of the whole court and our people." Rubbing the side of her face, she took a deep breath. "Si, I will speak to him, but if he calls for Juana to come to him, she must go."

"Oh, please, no." Juana sobbed. Anguished, she gazed beseechingly at her mother.

Her arm still around her ten-year-old sister, Isabel tried again. "Mother, we celebrate my coming wedding..." Isabel's eyes filled with tears. "I cannot be happy if my sister is punished. Pray, Mamá, could you not tell Father that?"

Queen Isabel ran her thumb's knuckle across her forehead and between her eyebrows, her teeth worrying at her upper lip. Forgotten, the trail of her gown dragged on the floor as she paced to the window. Flinging open the shutters she leaned on the stone windowsill. The harsh sunlight fell on her face, aging her.

"Dear God, dear God, give me strength," she muttered, turning back to her daughters. "What if I ask your father to let me punish you instead, Juana?"

Juana dropped to her knees again. She knotted her hands before her, looking up like a reprieved criminal. "Oh, thank you, Mamá." She grabbed her mother's dress, kissing its dusty hem.

Her eyes narrowing with sudden pain, the queen pursed her lips. "My hija, I cannot promise this will suffice with your father." She reached down, then drew back her hand to clench it for a moment. With a deep breath, she touched Juana's bent head. "Child, get up now. I will do my best."

———

Juana's great fear did not surprise Beatriz. When the King of Aragon deemed his children guilty of wrongdoing, he punished them sorely. If he witnessed it, that alone ensured his quick anger and chastisement. But for Juana, the king always reserved a crueller punishment. Many times in childhood he whipped her bare buttocks with a rope and ordered her locked alone in a chamber, often for a day and night. She saw no one but a silent servant who brought her food. Sometimes a whole week passed before Juana was allowed to resume her place with her sisters. Beatriz heard Juana often crying in the night when her father was at court. The king seemed to possess little love for Juana. He gave more kindness and love to his bastards – even to hunting dogs he sometimes kicked in passing – than to his second eldest daughter. He suffered the infanta's presence with barely hidden contempt.

Many of the court paid Juana little attention because of this. None desired or wished to bring the king's disfavour upon themselves. Each time he resumed his place by his wife's side, the king eroded Juana's confidence, making her fear him more with every new and greater punishment.

Time after time he dismantled the queen's careful care of their most sensitive daughter. The king made the intelligent Juana feel stupid, worthless, defenceless – a shame to the royal houses of Aragon and Castilla.

When he returned to the battle-front or vanished to his kingdom of Aragon or to the distraction of a new mistress – Beatriz thanking God for it, even knowing it caused the queen great pain – it took weeks of the queen's tender nurturing to stop Juana from jumping at shadows, biting her nails to the quick, screaming in the black of night. Beatriz pitied the girl. The infanta craved her father's love, his approval, but all he gave her was pain.

Despite the closeness of Princess Isabel's wedding, this time was no different. The king refused to allow the queen to buffer Juana from his anger. First whipping Juana, he then locked her in her chamber for two days. When the infanta returned to her sisters' side, she was a frightened waif who recoiled at her father's every glance.

8

A strong attack is half the battle won
~ Castilian proverb

Two weeks before Isabel's marriage, Beatriz brought Catalina and María to watch another tournament and noticed the queen fixing her attention on a tall man standing amongst the group of men gathered behind the king. The queen beckoned to Catalina. Approaching her mother, she dipped a curtsey, her eyes alight with curiosity.

Queen Isabel took her daughter's arm. "There's an English lord you should meet." The queen turned again to her husband and his companions, catching the gaze of the more plainly garbed man with the king's grandees. She gestured to him. "Pray, come, my good Lord Darcy."

The Englishman, squinting against the bright sunlight, walked towards Queen Isabel. His hood slipped back. To her surprise, Beatriz saw a handsome youth rather than a mature man. His sky blue eyes shone brightly, perchance brighter because the sun had tanned his skin to a dark golden honey. Streaked almost white by the sun, his blunt mane of silver-blonde hair, cut far shorter than the long French style favoured by the grandees, framed an oval face. He bowed low. "Your Highness, gracious and noble queen, you greatly honour me by your notice."

Queen Isabel proffered her be-ringed hand for his kiss, a slight smile teasing at her lips. She held out her free hand to Catalina. "My good lord, pray indulge me in the pleasure of introducing my hija, one day your future queen, if it so pleases God, many long years hence." The queen smiled broadly. "My youngest and beloved hija, the infanta, Doña Catalina and, with great pride, also known here as the Princess of Wales."

The young lord bowed. His bright eyes blinking against the glaring sun, he bowed once again to Catalina. "The queen honours me by this greatly desired introduction. Elizabeth, by the grace of God, Queen of England, consort of our gracious King Henry VII, spoke of you to me, as also did Arthur, our well-beloved Prince of Wales. We look with pleasure to the day when you come to our fair land, Your Highness."

Catalina blushed. "Thank you, my lord." She licked her dry lips, then spoke to the English lord in slow but perfect Latin. "I am eager to see England."

Lifting an eyebrow, the queen gave a short, gruff laugh of pride. She glanced at her husband. "That day will come soon enough. But I think Lord Darcy can see for himself the reason England must wait. Perchance he could write now the truth of it to King Henry, our good brother. My small hija needs time to grow to maturity. What better place to do this than by her mother's side?"

The English lord dipped his head. "I cannot argue against your wisdom, noble queen. Perchance I can beg a boon and talk to the princess. I am told I am a good teller of tales. I am certain she would enjoy hearing about the English court, and Prince Arthur."

Queen Isabel smiled. "Lord Darcy, come you to my chambers tomorrow. I want to know everything of England." Her eyes lost their light as she gazed down at her small daughter.

Before noon the next day, Queen Isabel summoned Beatriz to bring the infanta and her companion María to her chambers to meet again with Lord Darcy. Greeting her mother and the English Lord, Catalina sat on a large cushion by her mother's side. María quickly sat on the floor next to her. The infanta's eyes glowed with interest as the young man began to speak of England and its royal family. Darcy spoke long about Prince Arthur. The small infanta bent forward when he mentioned how the heir to the English throne loved his lessons and playing his harp. He told Catalina of the prince's new puppy, a recent gift from his mother. Beatriz could see the English royal family come alive for Catalina. The bright, blond, blue-eyed Arthur teaching his little dog tricks, reading books, playing with his little sister, Margaret, learning music from his own mother and sometimes King Henry himself. Darcy also told them his queen hoped for another child to add to her nursery soon.

"Her last letter told me the same," Queen Isabel said, sewing at the altar cloth she worked on for the Church of the Holy Sepulchre. "Very soon her children will out-number mine. She is a good mother, I hear." She smiled down at Catalina. "Already she acts as mother to my daughter, troubled she will find English water unfit to drink." Queen Isabel laughed. "There's no need for her concern. One day, your queen will discover that her son's bride is no weakling."

Time passed and the stories of the royal family changed its direction to other members of the English court. "I believe you knew Lord Rivers, my lord, a man I was proud to own as kin?" the queen asked, handing to Doña Beatriz Bobadilla the still unfinished altar cloth before taking up her spindle. Amused, Beatriz noticed Doña Beatriz folding the altar cloth into a perfect square. Bending down to María, the older woman whispered, "María, show me your hands." The child held out her hands, while Beatriz turned back to listen to Darcy's reply.

"Yea, Your Majesty, I knew him." Lord Darcy crossed himself. "May his soul be at rest with God. It was because of his tales about this most glorious Holy War that I decided to earn my spurs here when the time came. My father was not pleased to let me go, but I am near to nineteen." He lifted his chin. "Old enough to act the man's part."

"Both sides, child," Beatriz heard Doña Beatriz murmur nearby. María looked bewildered, turning her hands backwards and forth. She paled when Doña Beatriz placed the altar cloth into her hands. "Put it back in the queen's sewing chest."

María's face lit up. Straightening her shoulders, she almost skipped by the time she reached the open, nearby chest. Turning with empty hands, she gazed towards Doña Beatriz, and then, at a loss of what to do next, to her tutor. Beatriz smiled, beckoning María to come to her side.

Queen Isabel frowned and put aside her spindle, and began to twist her rings on her swollen fingers with difficulty. *Dandelion tea. When I return to my rooms I will brew dandelion tea and make certain the queen drinks it tonight.* "Rivers was a brave and handsome man, despite losing his front teeth fighting for us."

"My husband and I liked him well." Her eyes became thoughtful. "He lost his teeth fighting in the manner of your countrymen. While I did not witness the engagement, the king told me of it. Rivers dismounted from his steed at the head of his three hundred men and, armed with sword and axe, amazed all with his battle frenzy. He scaled the walls of Loja as if he wished to take the conquest single-handedly. But a stone hit him in the face and shattered his teeth, and knocked him unconscious. His injuries kept him abed for some time.

"The king and I visited him once he began to recover. I told him of my sadness that such a handsome man could be left with such inconvenient an injury. My lord husband has lost teeth in battle, so he also commiserated with him. Rivers replied, ''Tis little to lose a few teeth in the service of He, who has given me all. Who reared this fabric has only opened a window, in order to discern the more readily what passes within my soul.'"

Women's laughter rippled through the chamber like the chiming of bells, and Lord Darcy grinned. "Rivers was a good commander. He fought for King Henry at Bosworth, the battle that vanquished that evil York tyrant-usurper, and child-killer.

"Queen Elizabeth had no desire to see her uncle to leave their court, but 'tis hard for men to be younger sons, as I am, and be always in the shadow of the older. Poor Rivers was shadowed by four brothers. For certes, he died doing what he wanted and shining none but his own light."

Queen Isabel took hold of her spindle and twirled it. She sighed. "I wish he had remained with us. He was an amusing man, proud of his race and his relationship with my family, as well as your noble queen. Rivers was forefront at our pageants and festivals. His magnificence feasted our eyes. I miss him greatly. Perchance, he might be now still living if he had stayed here. Even if he had lost his life here, dying fighting a crusade is a far more glorious death than dying as a mercenary against the too often faithless and Godless French."

The queen's eyes hardened when she mentioned the French. Leaning back in her chair, she screwed up her lips as if tasting something unappetising that she wished to spit out.

Lord Darcy sipped from his goblet, and then placed it back on the table. "I agree, Your Grace. I can only applaud your great dedication and sacrifice to this holy enterprise."

Queen Isabel smiled at him. "My lord, I am queen for God's purpose, and what better one than this?"

"May I have permission to speak, Your Grace?" Doña Beatriz Bobadilla stepped from the embrasure to the queen's side.

Queen Isabel turned to her, and then back to the English Lord. "Of course. Lord Darcy, Doña Beatriz Bobadilla is like a beloved sister to me, and has been so since we were children. She has aided me many times in my life." She clasped Doña Beatriz's closest hand. "Once she even took an assassin's dagger meant for me. Praise the good lord, the dagger simply glanced off her padded gown and gave enough time for my soldiers to seize the would-be murderer." Queen Isabel laughed with grimness.

"Men might wear armour, but Doña Beatriz proved that day we women sometimes embroider our gowns so densely they may serve the same purpose. I will never forget, but for the grace of God, I could have lost one of my dearest amigas that day. I trust her with my life, and the lives of my children. Pray speak, Beatriz."

Beatriz Bobadilla dropped a curtsey. "Beloved queen, I thank you." Her face grave, she turned to Lord Darcy. "I desire for you to know more about Queen Isabel, so you can tell my words to your king and queen. Our beloved and illustrious queen is achieving what no other Castilian monarch has done before, ridding Castilla of the blight of the Moors. You are right to mention her sacrifice, for Her Highness works tirelessly and sacrifices much to gain this victory."

Darcy bowed once to Doña Beatriz and then swept a deeper one to Queen Isabel. "Good queen, you but need to talk to the soldiers to know the great love and esteem they possess for you. Your men call you a saint and gladly lay down their lives in your service. Madam, I am honoured to count myself one of your knights."

Smiling with all her charm, Queen Isabel outstretched her hand. "It has been a very pleasing visit, my lord. I look forward to watching you in our tournaments and speaking again with you at the nightly revels. These weeks are joyful times for myself and my family. I am most glad you are here to share them. Until we meet again, God go with you and keep you safe from harm."

Darcy bowed and backed towards the door. One last bow and the room again became the queen's chamber, empty of men.

Queen Isabel sniffed and lay a hand on Catalina's shoulder.

"Hija, listen now to your mother... I see you like Lord Darcy, he seems a good man. But, child, the English vice is treachery, more so than our countrymen's. They keep their kings looking over their shoulders and worrying every shadow hides an assassin or traitors of their own blood plotting their overthrow. Trust is a gift that must be earned. Catalina, do not trust any of them until given sure proof of their mettle..."

Her heart sad, Beatriz stared at the small infanta. *Assassins. Traitors. Treachery.* The five-year-old looked wide-eyed, anxious and uncertain. Since Catalina was three years old, the child had learnt lessons of queenship whether she wanted them or not.

***

Merry music swelled and throbbed in the huge, candlelit chamber where another night of festivities hailed Isabel's approaching wedding. The king's return to court brought many of his closest men from the most recent battlefield. One man was Beatriz's betrothed, Francisco.

Standing next to him, she gazed over to the half cycle of courtiers. "Our first meeting in months, and we are surrounded by the court," she said.

Francisco smiled wryly at her. "While you keep delaying our marriage, sweetheart, it is probably best we meet not alone. I might be tempted to persuade you otherwise."

"Do I need to crave your forgiveness, Francisco?"

He laughed. "Now I am with you, perhaps. But I'm not a youth. I am willing to be patient for what I want. Just as long as I have your promise you will not make me wait too much longer to call you my wife."

Beatriz eyed him. "Did you not tell me you desired no marriage until your skills are no longer so needed by the Queen?"

"I'm beginning to think that day will never come. I only wait now for you to say it is time."

She reached for his hand. "Soon, I promise we'll call the banns soon. Just be patient a while longer, please."

Francisco enclosed her hand in both of his. "I am a man of my word. I promised to give you all the time you need. As long as I have your promise to be my wife, I'm content."

Beatriz smiled at him. Francisco had asked her to marry him not long after the king had first assaulted her. Still coming to grips with that, his declaration of love and proposal of marriage had left her sobbing in his arms, the arms of her good friend. She confessed to him her lack of virginity, telling him of her rape, but not of her rapist. She feared what would happen if he knew. She had expected her confession would douse cold water on his desire, but discovered anew Francisco was a man of compassion, and still determined to offer her his love. Eventually, it seemed right to agree to be his wife.

A flash of bright colour caught Beatriz's eye. Close to the wall, near the door, the infanta Catalina and her companion María giggled together, imitating the dance moves of their elders. Both girls wore what looked like their best gowns.

Still holding Francisco's hand, Beatriz pushed her way through the seemingly endless crowd, ducking her head when she noticed the king, hand-in-hand with the queen, measuring out another dancing step, suddenly swing his eyes towards her. She shivered. He seemed an unhooded, hungry falcon catching sight of its prey. How she despised the man. She glanced at Francisco. She could never tell him her rapist was the king. In the work he did on the battlefield, he needed his wits about him. Giving him cause to hate the king could place him in greater danger. At least she was safe from the king's unwanted attentions while Francisco was at court. Beatriz reached the girls. "Infanta! María! What do you do here? Doña Teresa will be beside herself if she discovers you not in your chambers."

Appearing suddenly guilt-stricken, the little girls stepped closer to one another.

Amused, Francisco, winked and grinned at her. Beatriz couldn't stop herself grinning back. "Forgive me, Francisco, I must take these two back to their chambers before the queen discovers their disobedience."

Francisco nodded, adoration shining from his dark brown eyes. "I look forward to continuing our conversation and the pleasure of your company on your return."

Beatriz smiled at him, her dear friend, the man who wanted her as his wife, and turned her attention back to the two small girls. "No argument from either of you. Come now."

Taking their hands she hurried to the door that would take them back to the royal chambers. "Night is no time for two small girls to take it into their minds to leave the safety of their bedchamber. I should by rights tell the queen," she scolded.

She almost laughed when she saw Catalina and María share a smile. She shook her head. They knew her far too well; she would never tell on them. Tomorrow, translating Aristotle or some other dead philosopher would seem far more important to her than their small transgressions.

Catalina stopped her at the door. Some distance away but in view, the king, queen and Princess Isabel sat on the dais.

Cardinal Mendoza, a man both respected and feared throughout the queen's kingdom and beyond, occupied the chair beside the princess. A duke sat next to the cardinal, and next to the duke another noble, the Portuguese lord, an elderly cousin of Alfonso and his proxy at the coming wedding, two bishops, and finally Ahmed. The only child at the table and white-faced with exhaustion, he looked uncomfortable and unhappy

"Why is Ahmed there?" Catalina whispered to Beatriz.

She shrugged. "He is the first born son of the Moor king. The queen believed it right that he should be here, for the Portuguese to see him."

Garbed in regal gowns, twenty women danced with cavaliers before the king and queen. Applause and murmurs of appreciation rippled around the chamber as the dance ended. Again the music rose and fell, the women returned alone to the floor, with girdles tied around their waists. The royals on the dais clapped, and Princess Isabel bent towards her mother and whispered. Queen Isabel smiled and nodded. Glittering with jewels and in a golden gown almost exactly like the queen's, the princess stepped out to the floor with a lady from Portugal. Servants handed them girdles, and they joined the jubilant dance.

The women left the floor and the musicians struck up a solemn tune. This time the king and queen, hand-in-hand, stepped from the dais to dance a measure both grave and graceful. Jewels emblazed their royal garb, glittering and flashing with every movement in the light of countless candles and high torches.

"I love it when they dance." Catalina drooped, her face pale and miserable. Breaking free of Beatriz and María, she stepped towards the dim corridor. "I want to leave. I want to go back to my chamber."

"Why?" María asked, gazing back at the slow dance of the king and queen and around the chamber blazing with candle-light. Music throbbed and soared, and then plummeted to speak to all hearts.

"I hate it..."

Bewildered, María looked at Catalina, and then up at Beatriz.

"Hate?"

"What do you hate, child?" Beatriz asked the infanta. Catalina knotted her hands together. "My sister is leaving."

Gazing back at Princess Isabel now talking animatedly to Cardinal Mendoza, Beatriz tried to think of words of comfort. Nothing came to mind.

***

Beatriz stood a short distance behind Catalina on the royal dais near the high altar. In the cathedral of Sevilla, a thousand and more lit-candles, reflected by mirror, gold and silver, mimicked the brightness of day. The smell of incense was heady and sickly sweet, making her head spin and ache, adding to her depression. Called back to battle, Francisco had left that very morning. Beatriz hoped it would not be long before the king followed after, or that it was true that the king had found himself a new leman. She had never been that. She was but the bitch he kicked in passing.

Below, her hand atop the king's, Princess Isabel walked down the aisle of the cathedral to Alfonso's proxy. Isabel, pale and petite like her three sisters, was so beautiful she could have been a figure painted in an illuminated book. Beatriz had never known her other than as an adult, but today, on her wedding day, the stillness of Isabel's face made her appear utterly young, and vulnerable. *Thank God she possesses her mother's strong mettle. The girl will need it.*

With her head held high and eyes fixed straight ahead, Isabel displayed every iota of her usual pride as she paced towards the taking of her vows. The measured steps of Isabel and her father seemed a strange dance timed to the slow chanting of monks.

Isabel's slender form gave her the illusion of height, an illusion aided by high chopines. With every step she took, gold-patterned heels peeped out from under her gold-cloth gown. Each short, determined, cautious step bespoke constraints, constraints her position placed upon her. Even if she wanted to run away, her chopines forbade it as surely as if she wore fetters, fetters no one saw, but securely locked upon all the daughters of the queen. Beatriz sighed. Fetters placed too well on all women. But for the daughters of the queen the fetters were merciless.

Isabel stepped closer to Alfonso's proxy, and closer to her heart's desire. This marriage was one she never dared to voice and hope for. Taking her place next to the prince's proxy, Isabel, her face solemn, knelt for the cardinal's blessing.

The Princess Isabel now utterly and indissolubly joined to Alfonso in marriage, the weeks of celebrations arrived at an end. Another week passed and the queen and king and their two courts accompanied their eldest daughter to the border of Portugal and Castilla. Following closely behind Catalina and the rest of the royal family, Beatriz rode her mule to crest the last hill of their journey. Spread out far and wide on the green, lush valley below shimmered the colourful pageant of the richly dressed courtiers of Portugal. Mounted on horses, the king and prince were far more richly dressed than the superbly garbed men and women of their court.

Prince Alfonso leaned forward, eyes scanning the approaching company. The wind blew his long blond hair around his tanned face. He smiled – a smile of joy blazing out across the distance. The seventeen-year-old prince forgot royal protocol. With a loud cry he heeled his horse into a gallop, heading towards the mantle-covered, slender girl riding down the hill.

Reaching level ground, Isabel halted her mount. She bent low, patted the mule's neck and murmured soft words, all the time watching her prince ride to her. Coming close, he vaulted from his horse and ran the short distance separating them. A gentle wind lifted Isabel's thin veil and brushed its caress against her pale cheeks. The gossamer veil could not hide her smile. From the way her shoulders shook, Beatriz suspected she laughed, or perhaps wept – tears of happiness. She had hoped for this day for so long.

Now at her side Prince Alfonso held out his hand to Isabel, with palm upraised. Beatriz grinned at Catalina, trying to lift the child's spirits. Not too difficult to discern the desire of the prince – he wanted Isabel's hand in his.

Caught up in the moment, Beatriz heeled her mount closer to the royal family, wanting not to miss a moment. Isabel clasped Alfonso's hand, her eyes glittering with unshed tears. Beatriz had never seen her so elated. Isabel leaned towards Alfonso, whispering something to him, her face hidden from all but the prince by the falling mantle hood. Seized by a sudden gust of strong wind, Isabel's hood fell back as she lifted her head. Silken red tresses, aflame in the sunlight, escaped her veil to intertwine with his golden hair. The prince laughed, kissing the inner wrist of Isabel's thin hand. It seemed to Beatriz that an illuminated page came to life.

Sharing their joy, smiles of two courts encircled the young couple. Despite years of reservations about this match, especially from the still disgruntled King Ferdinand, their union symbolised and strengthened the new peace between Castilla, Aragon and Portugal.

Queen Isabel and King Ferdinand gazed at one another. The king shrugged and, in the full view of everyone, he exchanged a rare, tender smile with his wife. They bowed in their saddles to King João, King Ferdinand lifting his black velvet bonnet to him. Returning the courtesy, King João's countenance spoke to all of his great pride and delight. There could be no doubt of his love for his treasured and only legitimate son.

Taking the bridle of Isabel's mule, the prince led his bride across the border. King João and his Portuguese subjects followed close after them. Cries of jubilation and the beat of many drums and trumpeting of horns marked the crossing from one country to another.

Princess Isabel turned in her saddle, gazed at her parents and waved. Almost in unison, they dipped their heads to her and raised their bonnets. A final wave and then Isabel faced Portugal. She did not turn again.

In Portugal, Isabel wedded once more the heir of its throne, but this time without proxy. For months Beatriz heard news of Isabel's happiness with Alfonso. The queen reassured those closest to her, and so herself, that Isabel dwelt in peace and joy with her husband. Deciding upon this marriage had been the right and only decision for her eldest daughter.

Isabel's wedding signalled the new era of concord between Castilla, Aragon and Portugal. Queen Isabel trusted her oldest daughter to do everything necessary to assure peace remained in that quarter, because a far more important war demanded her attention – a war moving closer to victory.

Her daughter's departure aged the queen. For twenty years she had doted on her eldest daughter. In recent times, Isabel was one of the few to whom the queen opened up her true and secret heart. With the king now returned to the battle-front, Catalina seemed the only daughter able to raise her mother's smile.

9

War at the outset is like a beautiful maid
With whom every one wishes to flirt.
At the end it is like a despised hag
Bringing tears and sadness to whomever she meets.
~ Samuel Ibn Nagrela

From a distance, flower puffs of white and myriad vibrant colours seemed to embroider the brown, summer-seared hill. Closer still, Beatriz picked out the magnificent silk and brocade tents of the king and his grandees, surrounded by simpler soldier tents. Banners fluttered in the air everywhere. The tent city competed in colour and beauty with the looming Moorish city of high, reddish stone towers.

It was not simply the rich hues of the royal camp bespeaking the glory many found in the queen's Holy War. Gazing at men in battle gear, hoping to find Francisco at the camp, Beatriz remembered María recounting her father's conversation with her mother Josefa on their last visit home: "Castilla belongs only to those of the true faith. Soon our land will be cleansed of those heathen unbelievers."

"Mamá was sitting by the fire, sewing a new shirt for Father. Flames reflected in her eyes, and she looked at my father with fear. I could see my father's eagerness to share the thrill of battle did not enthral her. When she returned to sewing, her needle flew in and out of my father's shirt in unspoken anxiety.

"She hates this war, Teacher. But she is a soldier's wife. Her duty binds her to silence just as Father's duty means for him to go back to war.

"My mamá does not like women who farewell their men with whining and beating their breasts for what none can change. She told us she will not be like Andromache, the wife of Hector of Troy, and plead with our father not to fight. She always bids my father, 'Godspeed' when he rides away from our home.

"As soon as we see him no more, Mother goes to her chamber. I believe she weeps there."

Beatriz stopped the pull of memory. Up ahead, Queen Isabel, mounted on a chestnut mule covered by trappings of crimson edged with gold embroidery, gently rocked within her stately saddle-chair. Catalina's proud gaze was all on her mother.

A beat of drums, a swelling of trumpet notes and a roar of thousands rose to the heavens at the queen's approach. Many soldiers broke rank, rushing towards her, kneeling, uncaring of the dirt, along the road bringing her to them. Beatriz caught the answering cries of dismay from the defended citadel of the Moors in the wind.

His dark eyes alight with grim merriment, and garbed in a crimson doublet with breeches of yellow satin, the king rode his favourite black stallion towards his wife. A group of proud grandees closely shadowed the king. The men galloped their mounts as if invincible.

Queen Isabel tossed aside her deep scarlet mantle, freeing one arm to rein in her mule. Her agitated movements opened up her black velvet brial to its skirt of scarlet brocade underneath. Her three daughters wore gowns similar to the queen, even down to wide black hats with thick gold thread worked around top and edge.

The queen straightened her shoulders. Beatriz noticed pain flickering across her face. Travelling about Castilla caused the queen immense discomfort, swelling her legs to almost twice their normal size. Days of journey forced her to stay abed for as many days. She became sicker and sicker with every new year.

Coming within speaking distance and pulling hard at the reins of his horse, the king saluted her. King Ferdinand's huge black beast pranced beside the queen's mule as if eager to return to battle. "Did I not vow to you I'd pick out the seeds of this pomegranate? One by one, I have done so until there remains only one seed left."

Angry shouting came from the walls of the fortress. On the battlement flashed the glint of armour and scimitar. Clusters of men waved lances, threatening to throw them on the queen's soldiers below. Tossing his brocade mantle over his shoulder and displaying his sword with its eagle-winged hilt, the king grinned. His missing front tooth caused a slight whistle when he spoke.

"Hear the Moors, wife! They rent their clothes and tear out their hair at seeing you come hither. They know time runs out for them. By sword or gunpowder, be assured, lady wife, conquest will soon be thine."

Studying the citadel of their enemy, she offered a smile half-shadowed by her sunhat. Her bow almost touched her mule's neck. She gazed back at the king. "Yours and mine together, husband, as it has been for every day since we first joined hands and our two kingdoms."

The nearby stallions disturbed Beatriz's nervous mule. Calming her mount before it decided to break away, she wondered yet again about the king and queen. She long knew the queen's devotion to her husband surpassed his shallower affections. Almost every year she bought off another mistress whilst publicly and affectionately caring for the resulting bastards. It seemed to Beatriz the king loved his wife as the queen, and all the power her queenship brought him, rather than the ailing, fast-aging woman too often following him with doting, increasingly anguished eyes. Suddenly ill, Beatriz trembled, hunching under her cloak. *Dear God, please make the king leave me alone. Make him forget me, please.*

Removing his bonnet, the king dipped his head and smiled. "My queen and lady wife, there is a loyal subject you must congratulate." Catalina reined in her mule, restless like Beatriz's, and watched her parents. She beckoned María de Salinas to come closer. The bells on the harness of Queen Isabel's mount rang a discordant sound as her eyes searched the men at her husband's back. She gestured, calling out: "My good Marques of Cadiz and Count of Cabra. Pray ride to me, my lords."

Two men heeled their horses toward the queen. Followed by his banner bearer, one man edged his coal-black horse away from the other, stopping the huge beast before it chanced to overtake the king's.

Forced again to attend to her fidgety mule, Beatriz recognised the banner of the Count of Cabra. Set upon a sanguine field was a crowned Moor, a gold chain around his neck, with twenty-two banners placed around a shield. The queen had told her the tale behind it. Seven years ago, the count had taken into custody the King of Granada after the defeat of his army, which saw the death of many and the taking of twenty-two banners of their enemies. Thus, the king and queen gave to the Cabra family the title of Don and awarded the gift of this banner. That same victory had seen Prince Ahmed handed over as an infant hostage for the release and good conduct of his father.

Before the count rode the Duke of Cadiz, a hot-tempered man who yet possessed a great heart, with the one-eyed ambition that came from proving himself worthy of the titles he inherited despite being his father's bastard. With no other son to inherit, his father had wed his mother when the duke was a youth and already a demonstrated victor of famous battles. Coming from the enemy side in the early and uncertain years of Queen Isabel's reign, now he was Godfather and sponsor to Prince Juan himself, having long proven his loyalty to the queen and her cause.

He squinted against the bright sunlight. Yanking his costly helmet off, his hood slipped back with the shake of his head revealing a mature face, older than the king's or the queen's, but a face so comely it drew Beatriz's attention and made it difficult for her to look away. Long days in the sun had tanned his skin to brown leather. His dark, deep-set eyes glittered like jet. Firm cleft chin, sensual mouth, long, red hair streaked by silver curled around his face. The magnificent lord bowed low in his saddle to the queen. The duke lifted eyes that widened before hooding against the glaring noon sun. A hand shading his face, he bowed once more. "Gracious and most noble queen, pray forgive me for staying on my horse."

Riding closer, Queen Isabel proffered her hand for his kiss. "My good duke." She exchanged an amused look with her husband.

The Count of Cabra, a dark-haired man with a network of lines mapping a story of humour and careful diplomacy on his face, approached to give the queen homage.

The queen gazed at her two leaders. "Now, my congratulations must be to either of you, or maybe both, as has proven the case for many years in the past. Tell me, which is it now? Cadiz or Cabra?"

With a gruff, deep laugh, the count came closer. "The duke this time, Your Highness!"

The duke smiled. "A small thing, my queen."

Horse hooves shuffled and shifted in the dirt. A protesting neigh pierced the air, as the king half-wheeled his horse to face the queen. "A small thing, Rodrigo? I do not think it a small thing when you saved so many from a grim fate. When bad weather caused soldiers to lose themselves in the mountain passes, the duke here lit beacons around his tent to guide the stragglers back to the campsite. Without that action, I would hate to think how many good men we would have lost on our journey here."

"I was but in the right place at the right time," the duke shrugged. "Any man with common sense would have done the same."

The queen patted her restive mule. "You have a gift to be always there at the right time and the right place, my lord duke. I count myself fortunate to have you in my service. Your good sense and great prowess has brought great glory and victory to our Holy War."

The duke bowed. "My queen, I am proud and honoured to serve you."

"And I am proud and honoured to number such men as yourself and the good count as my leaders." Queen Isabel grinned. "Now this tent my husband mentioned, 'tis the same magnificent tent I have seen on other occasions? If my eyes do not mistake me, I see it yonder?"

Beatriz followed the direction of the queen's pointing finger. The duke's pavilion travelled with him to every new battlefield. Decorated in Moorish taste, with inner compartments divided by walls of painted silk and curtains, the tent's splendour left the tents of all the other nobility pale and lacklustre beside it. It dominated the city of tents as if an alcázar itself, even daring to compete with the tent of the king.

The duke bowed in the saddle. "Gracious queen, allow me the pleasure of surrendering it to you."

Her objective achieved, Queen Isabel's eyes glinted with humour. "I thank you, my lord duke. You are as generous as always."

Before settling her court into the camp of her army, Queen Isabel kept her eyes on the king and his men as they returned to the battlefield. She became so still, her face acquiring a strange look —as if her apparent calmness hid a thousand thoughts, a thousand heartaches. For the rest of the day, not even her daughters dared speak to her.

10

Habits are first cobwebs, then cables
~ Castilian proverb

Sweet Francisco,

I thank you for your letter explaining your absence from the camp. How like you to not send another to search for gunpowder supplies – and how wise are you to not trust this task to another. Your work is dangerous enough without you chancing your life on ingredients of inferior quality.

Here at the camp we grow more impatient day-by-day for the king's summons telling us that Granada is at last conquered. While the days are slow, their pattern remain the same: Matins, morning meditation, state business. The queen often attends to this abed – her strength diminishes daily and is not what I desire to see...

"Who will care for you as I do when you cannot sleep and work throughout the night?" Josefa had asked the queen before leaving her service. The queen's sleepless, too often pain-fraught, nights distressed Beatriz, her children and all those loving her, and for good cause. Most days Queen Isabel ruled her kingdom with no more than four hours sleep, sometimes less. But an arduous day ruling rarely caused her to neglect her other roles. By late afternoon, when the worst of the heat had passed, she allowed time to attend to her duties as wife and mother. She wove fine linen to make her husband's shirts, setting her daughters and her women also to this task. While they wove and sewed, she instructed her daughters on the word of God and lessons in statecraft. Listening to her lessons on ruling, Beatriz's pity grew for the queen's daughters. *Thank God I am a teacher and not born into royalty. Life is hard enough without that.*

Catalina listened to her mother with great devotion. Day-by-day she learnt from her an example of patience and hard work, an example that never wavered despite her mother's increasing ill-health. Every evening night fell to the ringing of bells that called to Angelus when the queen chanted the much-loved prayer, "The Angel of the Lord declared to Mary: And she conceived of the Holy Spirit."

Her three young daughters responded in unison with the next part of the prayer, leading in the other women. Beatriz saw Catalina drinking in her mother's closing words: "Behold the handmaid of the lord: Be it done unto me according to Thy word. Hail Mary..."

These daily rituals of the church seemed to serve yet another purpose. The queen stamped upon herself and her daughters the conviction that, through their royal birth, they were God's handmaidens, committed to serve God through the ruling of Earthly kingdoms. That God placed them thus allowed them no other choice.

***

June brought with it not only the hottest days of an unrelenting summer, but also their long-awaited summons. The queen and her court re-joined the king at Gozco, camping closer but still at a safe distance from the battlefield. There, the court watched victory ripen like the pomegranate itself in summer, and see it fall – fall, luscious and red, bursting with its jewelled seeds ready to eat, seeds of death and life, into Queen Isabel's waiting palm.

While soldiers readied the queen's encampment again, Beatriz looked over at the near hill, blinking against a noon sun, inhaling and exhaling air so hot it seemed to scorch her lungs. On the apex of the hill, King Ferdinand's splendid tent commanded the highest view, overlooking the combined armies of Aragon and Castilla and the red walls of their ancient enemies.

Beatriz turned her head, rooted to where she stood, hearing the loud flap of canvas. Strong winds billowed out the huge banners of Santiago, Castilla, and Aragon into confusion. Set before them, shards of cutting sunlight broke against the ornate, silver standard of a fourth banner. The holy banner of the crusader's cross flapped and whipped uncontrolled against the banners of the two kingdoms. All the banners seemed engaging in battle for supremacy when Hernando de Talavera, the queen's confessor, emerged from the king's tent into the strong wind. Windblown, his body bowed before the wind, his face ageless in its austerity, his long, white robes joined the flap and billow of the banners.

Another dawn broke, awaking Beatriz to the hand-bells of priests, calling the faithful to prayer, intertwined with the call of prayer in the citadel of the Moors, a song like a cry echoing down to the queen's encampment. Every day the call competed with the Christian bells. Christian and Moor mirrored one another in their worship of God.

Each morning, the earth trembled as horses passed their tent, signalling the start of a new day for the queen's cavalry in the field. Battle-drums and war-cries became a normal part of Beatriz's life. The screams of the wounded and dying from nearby tents pierced her dreams, awaking her, bathed in sweat.

One night she opened her eyes, shaking with the remnants of nightmare, fighting to regain the solid ground of reality. Outside, men laughed, fought and sang drunkenly. A chorus of countless cats screeched, as if twirled around and around by their tails. "Santa María, what's that?" she asked in fright.

Their night candle doused some time while she slept, the tent's inky blackness left her dislocated and confused, and still enmeshed in the web of her foreboding dream. She started, hearing the exasperated voice of one of the queen's ladies. "It's the bagpipes, Beatriz. Those English devils run amok again.

Every night they feast and drink, making so much noise I cannot sleep."

Hearing the unholy scream of bagpipes begin again, Beatriz remembered her nightmare, and remembered the terror that had birthed it.

Only the day before bright sunlight had slanted upon Queen Isabel's stout form, glittering the gold in her gown with every movement. From the safety of the highest house in the village of Las Zubias, eyes burning with zeal, the queen stood at the un-shuttered window of a chamber on the upper storey, watching the brave and noble Cádiz routing the Moors to savage defeat on the plains of Granada. Close to his royal mother, his three young sisters and little María, Prince Juan pointed out the king coming to the duke's aid.

María's father, Martin de Salinas, recovering from a head blow and forbidden the field this day by both physician and the queen's command, kept his royal kinswoman company. Overlooking the battle as if a bullfight, he explained the battle manoeuvres, and their strange dance between life and death.

Steel clashed and sparked against steel, man clashed and sparred against man, sword-to-sword, dagger-to-dagger. The wind carried the screech of metal, often followed by the shriek of death. Red dust billowed and swirled, spreading through the air a thick, undulating curtain, veiling warrior and horse from one another, causing a state of confusion, disaster and more violent death.

Galloping horses drummed a rhythm to the sway of war. Their manes whipped by speed and wind, some steeds crashed to the earth, their bellies torn apart by spear poles fixed into the ground. Death whined for prey in the high-pitched wind. Again and again, clouds of black arrows soared, arching into the sky, marking many with death, and maiming just as many.

Not wanting to watch, Beatriz gazed around for water. Her lips and mouth dry, a poem drummed continually in her head – a poem of a great leader, a leader once both Vizier and Nagid of Granada, a man who dared challenge the glory of war. Years ago her father, proud to trace his lineage to him, had read his poems to her from a precious volume handed down the generations from eldest son to eldest son. Now one of its poems came back to haunt her:

The horses lunged back and forth like vipers darting out of
    their nest.
The hurled spears were like bolts of lightning, filling the
    air with light.
Arrows pelted us like raindrops, as if our shields were
    sieves.
Their strung bows were like serpents, each serpent spewing
    forth a stinging bee.
Their swords above their heads were like glowing torches,
    which darken as they fall.
Still, my gallant men scorned their lives, preferring death.
These young lions welcomed each raw wound upon their
    heads as though it were a garland.
To die – they believed – was to keep the faith;
To live – they thought – was forbidden.

Garland on a battlefield? Beatriz saw none here. A man screamed foreign words that meant nothing to her, but she understood his terror, his agony, his desire for life. Martin de Salinas pointed to men garbed in English colours. "They call for Saint George!"

"Mother! See the English archers find their target!" Prince Juan spoke in awe.

The crackle of gunfire, followed by tell-tale wisps of blue smoke, intermingled with the scream of man and horse. Even from this safe distance, Beatriz just desired to cower, seeing one man smote by an arrow straight into his eye.

Tall like his countrymen, an English soldier hacked down a terrified Moor with his battle-axe. From their vantage point, the Moor looked to Beatriz just a boy, no more than fourteen. The axe left him broken and bleeding upon the earth. His assailant swung his axe again, down on the boy's neck, before rushing further into the heat of battle. A wing of Castilian cavalry swept over the slender body, trampling it under-hoof. When the tide of horses swept by, it left nothing of the Moor but a sack of bones, gore and blood.

"Ahmed," Beatriz whispered. It could have been Ahmed trampled to a bloody death. She swallowed back bile. For his own safety the prince remained some distance away until his father finally admitted defeat.

"Oftentimes they're slow to engage, my queen," De Salinas said, "but in full battle the English show their true worth. Your Grace, good soldiers to have on our side."

Thoughtfully, De Salinas fingered his chin before dropping his hand back to his side. The tips of his long fingers possessed calluses from his vihuela. Beatriz found herself staring at them. *Why did men make music as easily as taking up a sword?*

De Salinas cocked his head, looking aside at Prince Juan.

"My prince, did you know the English believe themselves the most perfect race placed upon the good Earth? The English think themselves better than not only the Moors, but also our men. Indeed, they proclaimed their lord commander better than any grandee. My soldiers little desire their fellowship."

The prince chortled, his laughter ringing strange to Beatriz's ears. He leaned out the window, watching his father engage in combat. "Do they, cousin?" The smile masking his lower face failed in its journey to his humourless blue eyes. He suddenly seemed so much older than his years. "As long as they fight for us with courage, I won't tell them any different."

"Civil war in their barbarous country," De Salinas continued, "have given these men a taste for blood and battle. The English wield both sword and battle-axe with great might, refusing to give ground even when defeat stares them in the face. They're good, staunch comrades in arms, as long as they remember to try not to outdo our men in their wish to keep all the glory to themselves."

Beatriz's stomach churned, its hollowness leaving her both dizzy and ready to vomit. Racked by the awful torture of watching men and boys kill one another, she wiped her sweaty hands on her gown, her mouth simmering to desiccation with each quickened breath. She stepped farther away from the royal family. *Please God, pray let this soon be over.*

Swallowing back bile, Beatriz opened her eyes again to the battle. She no longer had a sense of foe or friend or Englishmen. All she saw was a mass of humanity coming together, and then coming away lessened. Men and beasts littered the field – the dead alongside the wounded and the dying.

Countless ravens gathered in the battlefield, fluttering in

short, considered flight, picking at unclaimed bodies where men no longer fought. Drawn back and gone, the tide of war took its deluge of blood to soak elsewhere. The harsh, uncaring, grating caws of raven interwove with the screams of men and beast.

Raven eyes – jet-jewelled and cold – burst into Beatriz's mind and took hold of her scattered wits. No matter how hard she tried to banish them away, the vision lingered, becoming more substantial with every breath she took.

Her breathing quickening again, she took another step away from the royal family, trying to banish her vision. Its cruel form haunted her without mercy. The ravens became as if tailed demons – black like ebony, glistening with a greenish slime, their eyes now red, burning embers withering her soul. They seemed to stand all around, taunting, stalking her as if in a game of cat and mouse.

Beatriz crossed herself and prayed. She looked towards the window – a window revealing not only the bright summer's day and hazy blue hills, but the black emptiness of bloody, violent death.

She turned away from the increasing carnage, her hands no longer palm-to-palm in prayer, but knotted together across her chest – gripped tight enough to hurt. She could no longer thread together the reason, the need, the purpose for this battlefield.

Beatriz owned the queen an intelligent woman, but her utter concentration on this battle only confused her. The queen's dislike of the dance of death between bull and man was known to all those close to her. It was yet another reason to love the woman ruling Castilla with such an iron grip. *Why, then, bring children here to watch this?* This battle seemed as senseless as the bullfights where men tormented dumb animals to their deaths.

She remembered the years she spent as a child in the convent, when she took mice away from the kitchen cats despite the disapproval of the nuns. She had yearned to ask them: "Why kill just for the sake of killing?"

She was of the blood of El Cid and a long line of warriors. Her ancestor Samuel Ibn Nagrela traced his descent from the house of the warrior King David, the same house that saw the birth of the Lord Jesús. Fed a feast in childhood of crusade stories, hundreds of years of battles won and lost, she had realised early in her life that war was no game.

On this battlefield rode the flower of Christian chivalry. Men left the camp enthused with a strange kind of joy. Even when they returned bloodied and broken beyond all hope of saving, their eyes still shone until death darkened them forever. Beatriz's heart throbbed to the words of her ancestor:

These young lions welcomed each raw wound
upon their heads as though it were a garland.

Bewildered, Beatriz shook her head, wondering if men lived just for this one moment, the one moment when, god-like, they dealt out death. She did not understand this war – nor the death of men, Christian or Moor. *Holy war? A war the good God wanted? God wanted men to hate and kill one another?* She could not believe it.

Men believed to die here opened heaven's gates, and took one straight to paradise. There were no angels singing, only the cries of savage death and the cawing of crows. Shutting her eyes,

Beatriz seemed to hear the evil cackle of demons. Their cackle became louder every moment she stayed in this chamber.

Carried by the uncaring wind, the screams of men and beast assailed her, tearing her heart into shreds. In the midst of a wide-awake nightmare, she looked again out the window. Demons swam all around her, red eyes spewing tongues of fire and flame, fangs pointed and dripping blood. They wanted prey. They wanted her. Unable to block out the sounds of war, unable to stop watching out the shutter-less window, she trembled, fighting an urge to scream: *The window! Shutter it! Please! I beg someone! Shutter it! Don't let the children watch this one moment longer. Oh please, someone! Close the shutters!*

Queen Isabel stood at the window as if transfixed. Even Juana and María seemed surprisingly undisturbed, locked upon the crest and fall of battle, the crest and fall of life and death.

Catalina took María de Salinas's arm. "Come." Beatriz saw the child's white, sick face. She knew it a mirror of hers. "Come and play with me."

Uncaring for their rich velvets, the two girls sat on the dusty floor. Motes rose, spun, glittering like flicks of gold in a slanting sunbeam.

Upon her square palm, Catalina offered to María silver-gilded knuckles. Earlier this morning, unaware that her mother would take her where no child should ever go, she had scooped them from the chest in her chamber to put in the pocket of her gown. The two girls had been innocent then. How could they be innocent now? Beatriz winced seeing Catalina's trembling smile.

"You call first," the child said. Tears ran down Catalina's pale cheeks. She met María's eyes, and Beatriz seized on the one light in a far too dark afternoon. From the first moment the two girls had become friends, they shared a kinship beyond flesh.

Catalina tossed the knuckles up in the air and, like the motes just before, the silver knuckles winked and glittered in sunlight. The girls became children again, while Beatriz tried to shutter out visions of Hell.

11

The world and its desires pass away,
but the man who does the will of God lives forever.
John 2:16-17

Dear love,

I continue to wait eagerly for your return. Did you not tell me, love, that you witnessed the king knighting his son in sight of the beleaguered city of the Moors two years ago? Yesterday, Prince Juan had his first taste of battle – a carefully dealt out taste. The prince's life is far too precious for his parents to tempt fate overmuch.

The queen's daughters would prefer not to spend their days at camp, but victory over the Moors is so important the entire royal house must witness it. They are guarded well – perchance, too well. The lives of the girls are more confined here than when we live in the great comfort of a royal alcázar. We are crowded together in a tent, although the infantas take turns to sleep with their mother in the magnificent tent loaned to her by the Duke of Cadiz...

A peculiar red-tinged orange light flickered against Beatriz's closed eyelids. Drawn out of the eddy sucking her into sleep and dreams, she opened one eye and then the other. Her eyes stung, watered, blinked. The orange glow wavered, illuminating the tent. The light grew stronger until – moment-by-moment – it eclipsed the amber light of the tent's lone candle.

Surfacing from her drowsy haze of confusion, Beatriz coughed –signalling a sleepy chorus of coughs from the infantas and their attendants. Beatriz's throat and lungs started to hurt. She wheezed, and the reason hit her like cold water. She bolted up in bed, her heart racing. Fear opened in place of her stomach. She breathed smoke – not the smoky air of a camp numbering hundreds of tents, but increased a thousand-fold, and more. A woman screamed. Drums and trumpets sounded the alarm. Voices shouted. More screams cut through the air, closer this time, cries of women intermingled with squeals of terrified horses.

Outside the tent men yelled and swore. Heavy feet crunched upon earth, stumbled, ran. The queen, her deep voice heightened by rare panic, screeched, "...leave me! See to the prince and my daughters. Make certain they're safe."

Fearing the camp attacked, Beatriz shook her two charges awake. At almost the same moment soldiers, some dressed only in heeled hose and shirt, rushed into the tent. One carried a torch and pointed to Catalina and her sister María. This night saw Juana sleep in her mother's tent. Without any concern for decorum, ignoring the girls' startled cries, the men bundled the two infantas and small María in blankets from their beds and carried them into the night. The other occupants of the tent had only the fire's light to help them to safety. Drawing a blanket around her shoulders to cover her shift, Beatriz hurried after the men, coughing every step of the way.

She gazed over her shoulder. The other women emerged and ran from the tent. Turning slightly, she saw the queen's pavilion. Glowing bright like a blazing funeral pyre, its red and orange flames lit the night sky.

The wind gathered strength. Embers flared out, catching the top of the infantas' tent. Flame-tongues licked until the blaze took hold. Metal gleamed then turned into molten rivulets. The pavilion she had just left became buckling walls of flames. The fire ate and ate, its sparks spreading to yet another tent, gorging upon the silk and metal.

Making her way to Catalina and María, Beatriz shivered, iced both by terror and cold night. Her naked toes curled in pain against the hard, stony earth. She limped in agony by the time she reached her royal charge. Nestled under the queen's arm, engrossed in watching the night spectacle, Catalina reached to clasp Beatriz's hand in hers. Little María ran to her, taking her other hand.

On the other side of their mother, the infanta María stood beside her older sister, Juana, who held Prince Juan's hand. All of them were robed in blankets. Even King Ferdinand seemed to have had a close escape. Marching back and forth, directing soldiers fighting the fire, he wore just his white shirt and hose and held his sword, buckler and cuirass, as if ready to do battle.

He scanned the efforts of his men, the fire flames flickering in his dark eyes.

Hearing a cry of warning, Beatriz glanced over her shoulder. The fire gorged everything in its path, enveloping the nearby sleeping booths made from tree branches, rough and ready protection from the elements for many soldiers. Compassion tugged at Beatriz's heart. They would be left without sleeping places this night. They would not be the only ones.

The fire continued to feast. The night air filled with the crackle and snap of a ravenous beast. Unsatisfied, greedy for destruction, the beast grew in size, becoming grotesque, a monster on a rampage. A hoard of soldiers formed bucket lines and struggled to quench its advance.

"Men, let not the Moors benefit from this night's work and discover us with our guard down! Cavalry!" the king yelled. "Mount your horses! Ring the camp and protect the queen!"

Answering his command, a battle-horn swelled its long call into the night. The thunder of a thousand or more horses stormed around them, the queen's cavalry rushing into the black of night. Gathered together and safe, as if on an island of calm, chaos and darkness lapping at its shores, Queen Isabel and her children stood close to one another. The gusty wind radiated a wall of heat in their direction. They had made their escape just in time. Good fortune had robbed the blazing pyres before their eyes of the dead.

A dismal dawn broke over the camp the next day. Low grey clouds intermingled with mist and lingering smoke. Exhausted soldiers salvaged through the smouldering ruins, carefully sifting the remains of the queen's tent for any signs of evil intent or for anything worth saving. The exquisite pavilion of the Marques of Cadiz destroyed, Queen Isabel, her three unwed daughters and their closest attendants shared a large tent undamaged by the fire, wearing upon their backs clothes given to them by those still with possessions after the dreadful night.

Garbed in borrowed gowns too big for them, Catalina and María stood with Beatriz on the edge of the destroyed camp, watching the soldiers at work. Over-tired from a sleepless night, long moments passed before anyone spoke. Catalina stepped onto the scorched encampment. She dug into the ground with her slippered toe, examining the little pile of earth as if wishing to make sense of it.

"Jesu'. The very earth itself is black and seared." Catalina lifted her head. "You spoke to my mother? Do they know how it happened?"

Beatriz joined Catalina, studying the scorched earth too. Sunlight broke through the heavy cloud and glinted off some object half-buried in the soil. Cleaning it with her foot, Beatriz picked up a small mass of shapeless metal. "Whatever this was once, none now can tell." She sighed and dropped it back on the ground. "So much destroyed in a single night – our clothes chests and furs the least of it." She pushed back a strand of hair blowing in her eyes. "How did it happen? My infanta, last night, the queen prayed alone for the safety of the king and the prince. When the pavilion filled with smoke, Queen Isabel wasted no time taking flight with your sister."

Catalina took Beatriz's arm. "Was it treachery?"

Beatriz tried to smile her reassurance, but a nasty taste was in her mouth. When she looked at Catalina she shivered. God knew she would always protect the queen with her life, even if it risked her soul. "Treachery is always a possibility," she sighed, not wanting to think about it. "But the queen believes the fire was an accident."

"Can you be certain?" Catalina asked.

Beatriz shrugged. "The queen commanded a taper be taken from near her couch and placed elsewhere. It appears the attendant placed it too near the hangings and forgot the strong wind last night. Thank God only our possessions were destroyed. It could have been far, far worse. Our good queen came too close to death here."

While the queen and her court escaped a fiery death, the wheel of fortune turned elsewhere, giving with one hand, taking with the other. One month after the fire, when the sun was high in the sky, a horseman rode into the camp, his horse – rolling-eyed and frothing blood – ridden to the ground. Rumour of his grim news spread around the camp as fast as the blaze that destroyed the queen's camp, but 'twas not until the next morning that their grieving queen told her attendants the story come from Portugal.

A week before, Prince Alfonso hurried home to his wife at nightfall, galloping his untried, half-broken stallion, a recent gift of King Ferdinand, on the uneven ground of the Tagus riverbed. It was to be the good prince's last twilight before night fell on his mortal life forever.

The queen told her women a swooping owl had spooked the

prince's horse. The animal wheeled from the rough track into rougher terrain, an unseen hole snapping the horse's leg. Alfonso was tossed from his mount, then the animal crashed down on him. Alfonso's Castilian groom took him to a fisherman's hovel before going for help. By the time the king's physician came to the prince's aid it was too late to move him. Alfonso lay for two days close to death. The King of Portugal, the Queen of Portugal, his mother and his wife remained by his side. Both women held on to him as if that alone held him to life, but he never regained consciousness.

Death came for him on the second night.

Queen Isabel and most of her inner court now resided in a new and more comfortable dwelling, a small Moor alcázar taken in conquest, half a day's journey from the battlefield. The queen waited there while her soldiers built for her a half city and half camp, naming it Santa Fe: Holy Faith. Santa Fe would offer her better protection and comfort than the king's camp. Beatriz spent much of her time in the queen's chamber, teaching Catalina and María their lessons. With Queen Isabel unwell, full of unrest and worry about her eldest daughter, Beatriz knew Catalina's presence helped to lighten her mother's mood. Often she wondered if the queen really noticed them at all, especially the day when the message arrived from Portugal.

Reading it the queen gasped. "My Isabel has locked herself in a dark chamber. She has not slept or eaten since Alfonso's death. She weeps and weeps and refuses to wear anything but sackcloth." She read a little more. "Sweet Jesu', she's cut off all her hair! Her women fear for her. They think she may try to take her own life. Queen Leonor fears the same. She writes that they have taken Isabel's dagger from her. My daughter must return. I shall write so now!"

Thus, the King of Portugal sent Isabel home.

Beatriz abandoned any hope of teaching the girls when outriders brought them news that Isabel's cavalcade was but a day away. The next morning she took them to the balcony overlooking the winding road ribboning its way to the alcázar. Grateful for the balcony's stone bench, Beatriz read a book as Catalina chewed at her thumbnail, looking down at hills and valleys, spreading out to become the blue mist of distance.

The sun passed its pinnacle while María strummed her vihuela. At times, Beatriz scrutinised Catalina. The child stayed at her post as if she could not move. Her book unexpectedly boring, time trudged slowly onward like a spark igniting a damp log.

At last Beatriz heard a fanfare of trumpets. Catalina let out a cry. Half sobbing, half laughing, she picked up her skirts, running from her chamber. María put down her vihuela and raced after her. Beatriz followed until, breathless, she reached a large gathering of courtiers come hither to welcome the queen's eldest daughter.

The andas halted before the steep, narrow stairs and the king helped his daughter out. A ghost-woman emerged from the andas, shrouded in black veils billowing in the gusting wind, overtop a widow's white headdress. Sheer black gossamer veils did little to conceal Isabel's haggard, ill face.

Her women kneeling behind her, Isabel curtseyed. The king raised her up, kissing her cheek in welcome. He took her up the steps for her mother's greeting. Isabel pulled back her veil as a sign of respect. With exhausted grace and lowered eyes, she dropped to her knees and kissed the king and queen's be-ringed hands. Queen Isabel bent to speak to her daughter. Despite her closeness, Beatriz could not hear Isabel's reply, only softly mumbled words.

The king and queen gazed at each other before they assisted their daughter to her feet. Isabel kept her head bowed as her mother kissed her. She did not look at either parent, she did not look at anything. The long trail of her gown dragging behind her, she stumbled up the steps like one blind.

Catalina shifted from one foot to the other. Unwilling to wait one more moment, forgetting protocol, she rushed down those last few steps to her sister. Blanching, Queen Isabel swung an alarmed glance to the king, reaching for her youngest child. Too late. Catalina flung herself at Isabel, wrapping her arms around her sister's body. Her older sister took a backward step and stood like stone, her arms stiff at her sides.

"Isabel!" Catalina cried, hugging her again, this time tighter, almost pushing her sister back another step. Isabel stared ahead, far too lost within her own grief to be conscious of the grief she herself caused, unaware that her youngest sister's mouth trembled, or that Catalina's tears welled, running down flushed cheeks. Grim, his eyes hard, the king separated Catalina from his older daughter.

The princess returned to them a stranger. Over the coming days she wafted through the court, her drawn, sorrowful face hooded by a mantle, garbed in mourning from head to toe, speaking little, and only when spoken to.

There were moments when she resumed some semblance of her former self, but a misspoken word or deed soon caused Isabel to disappear like a genie into its lamp. The light extinguished from her eyes, she withdrew into the shadows of her deep hood. Ever protective, the queen kept her eldest daughter close and even insisted the girl sleep with her at night.

Two weeks after Isabel arrived home, Beatriz and her two small charges slipped passed the queen's attendants. Either gossiping over their sewing or playing chess, the women paid them no mind. Catalina pushed open the heavy oak door to her mother's bed-chamber and froze. Isabel knelt at her mother's side, head cradled upon folded arms on the queen's lap, sobbing and sobbing. Never before in Beatriz's life had she witnessed such grief, not from man, woman, or child. Isabel's sobs tore out of her and cut deep like a dagger.

Free from layers of head-dressings, Isabel's naked head showed no longer the silken, glorious red-gold hair once envied by so many at court, but a skullcap of reddish bristles pressed against the breast of the queen's black velvet robes.

Beatriz strangled back a cry. Jagged, ugly, half-healed scabs scored Isabel's scalp. The rumour then was true. The princess had slashed her head with such frenzy she drew blood. Some of the wounds looked already scars. No wonder her women feared for her. No wonder there were mutterings about her sanity.

Beatriz saw in her mind Prince Alfonso standing eagerly at Isabel's gold stirrup, his blue eyes looking at her, lit with love. She remembered Isabel bending to speak to him, her tresses curtaining them in a shimmering veil. A gust of wind had intertwined his hair with hers, and their two right hands clasped, as the young woman and man took an unspoken troth, in love and faith before all, and an unspoken vow to share a life together. Only eight months passed before she returned a broken-hearted widow.

María and Catalina gazed at one another, their faces pictures of bewilderment. *Still so young.* Beatriz sighed. She tried hard to shield the girls from the harsher realities of life. Now Isabel's grief was as if a dark, heavy cloud covered the sun. About to shut the door, Beatriz paused. Isabel spoke, her voice hoarse, drowning in tears. "Mother, oh, my mother, please, I beg you, please let me go! Please let me take the veil. There's nothing left for me here. Nothing!"

Through the narrow crack, Beatriz saw the queen close her eyes. She grimaced in pain and stroked her daughter's shorn head. Grief and unhappiness etched deeper the lines on the queen's face and dragged down her mouth. She held Isabel's face between her hands. "Dear one, you ask for the impossible. I wish I could say otherwise, but I cannot. You are next in line to my throne after Juan and perchance your father's throne, too."

Anger lit fire and life to Isabel's eyes. "I never wanted any other crown other than that of Alfonso's consort. Father never wanted me to marry him. Time after time he delayed our match, or suggested Alfonso wed María instead, even knowing Alfonso and I already loved one another! Mother, you never told me Father attempted to bribe the pope to dissolve our betrothal. Alfonso's father spoke of it to me."

The queen blanched. "Your father believed he was doing

right. I too was not in favour of this match, but I knew you'd set your heart to it." Queen Isabel lifted her daughter's chin, forcing her to meet her eyes. "Fortune did not look kindly on it. It was not meant to be for you to remain long Alfonso's wife. It must be as it was before."

Isabel jerked her face away, as if burnt by her mother's touch. "I have three sisters. You don't need me. Let Juana take my place. She's old enough. More, Mother, she hungers for it!"

The queen rubbed her temple. "Isabel, 'tis not as simple as that. Your life is given by God for the good of Castilla and Aragon. It is your duty to serve, just as it is mine. Nothing changes this. Not even Alfonso's death."

Clasping the sides of her shorn head with her hands, Isabel collapsed onto her mother's lap, and the floodgates opened to even rawer grief. The queen, appearing torn apart herself, rocked her daughter, attempting to console her.

Catalina grabbed Beatriz's hand. She pulled her from the door and closed it, shutting away the darkness within. "No more!" The small infanta stamped her slippered foot. "No more, I say! Let's go somewhere else. Let's go now!"

Dragged along by Catalina, out of her mother's ante-chamber and into the corridor, Beatriz's stride quickened to keep up with her. She looked at Catalina – not knowing what to do. She felt swept into Catalina's whirlpool of unhappiness.

Catalina no longer seemed to see the long corridor before them, and not just because of her short-sightedness. Without warning, she dropped Beatriz's hand, picked up the skirts of her black velvet habito, and ran.

Gathering up her own skirts, Beatriz sped after her, catching up when she reached the library. Catalina leaned her face against the wall, her hands on either side of her. As if fighting for air her breaths rasped fast and uncontrolled. Beatriz gripped her shoulder. "Child…" She swallowed. "I am here. I am here." *Oh dear God – what else can I say?*

Catalina's hot tears dripped onto her hands. Beatriz's eyes blurred with tears too. She remembered writing in her yet unfinished letter to Francisco: Queen Isabel's daughters wept with good cause. Yes – they wept for good cause, and left those who loved them feeling helpless.

A few days afterward Beatriz saw Isabel smile at last at her youngest sister. True, a faltering smile, but a faltering smile was better than none. By the end of the month, Isabel had resumed the long habit of older sister caring for the younger members of the family. Isabel never realised how many times it was her younger siblings doing the true caring.

Prince Juan spent all his free time at his sister's side, often playing his vihuela for her ears alone. Almost every day her three sisters requested Isabel's company while they sewed or embroidered together. When the princess took her needlework, either outdoors or indoors, to sit with her sisters, María, Juana and Catalina gently drew from her stories about her time in Portugal. The stories she told often diverted Beatriz from the book she brought to read. So many times Isabel seemed to speak of her months away from her mother's court as if of a story of distant legend in which she played no part. She rarely spoke of the young prince she had given her heart to. Those memories she locked away with her ability to reclaim joy.

"This story is for our chiquitina," Princess Isabel said one warm, blue-skied morning. Lifting her eyes from her almost completed eagle of Saint Juan, she resettled against the cushions on a large rug flung out to cover the grass. With Juana summoned to her mother's this day, to talk over her betrothal to Philip the Fair, the remaining infantas, accompanied by their more favoured attendants, took their leisure by doing needlework.

Beatriz dropped her book to her lap. Now returned to sewing, Isabel's needle flew through the fabric without one mistake. Under the princess's deft and experienced hands, the bold lines of the eagle took animated shape, wings spread wide, sharp beak opened as if about to swoop down on its prey. The warmth of the day made her drowsy and Beatriz drifted as if in a dream.

"There was a hidalgo at the king's court, an adventurer called Hatchet-face. His true name was Pedro Vaz da Cunha, the victor, so he boasted, of countless battles. He must have come close to losing his life in one, for it left him with one eye and his face badly scarred, thus earning him his nickname.

"When I first met him, Hatchet-face had with him a page, a pretty youth of some seventeen years who answered to the name of Perkin Warbeck. Pedro claimed to his friends that the page was in fact an English prince. Dressed in rich brocade and silk, the page truly gathered to himself the presence of one. More bewildering and strange, some foreign men at court behaved unto him as if indeed in the presence of royalty."

"A page treated like royalty? How can that be?" Perplexed, the infanta María reached into the shared sewing basket for a card of scarlet thread.

Isabel gave a small smile. "'Tis strange, my sister. But not as strange as the rest of this tale. Hatchet-face and his page accompanied the king from Lisbon to Evora and finally to the king's favourite hunting grounds at Setubal. Hatchet-face also had with him Edward Brampton, a man I once met with our mother when you were but an infant, Catalina. He came as part of the English party negotiating for your hand in marriage to Prince Arthur. Brampton's name and adoptive country well hid his tangled history. Whilst sponsored to the true faith by Edward IV, the man was a lowly born Portuguese Jew and, I believe, a bastard. I spoke to Brampton one day…" Princess Isabel's lips tightened, her eyes slanting sideways from her sewing. A frown deepened lines between her fine brows. She gazed at the nearby budding white roses, her pale face strangely composed.

Isabel turned glazed eyes back to her sisters. Beatriz thought of still, deep waters that hid so much. Uneasy, she shifted on the rug. *Is Isabel keeping a secret from her sisters? Why do I feel a threat of some kind?*

Isabel started sewing again. "I thought Brampton treated his page strangely – sometimes like a son, sometimes with deference, but also like a man burdened by a responsibility he no longer desired or wanted. At those times, his eyes simmered with resentment. Once I asked him why the page distressed him so." Isabel laughed briefly, noticing Catalina widened eyes of surprise. "I am a grown woman, Catalina…" Isabel took in a deep breath, "… and a woman then happily wedded. I can speak to men if I wish, and knowing Brampton in the past gave me the liberty to address him directly." Seeing Catalina's confusion, Isabel leaned towards her. "Believe me, my sister, there are times when women must question men, otherwise we risk knowing nothing at all.""

"And Brampton? What did he say, my lady princess?" asked little María.

Her face no longer clouded, Isabel smiled. "Nothing that day. But another time we were out hunting and I found my horse alongside his. He told me then his tale. I have repeated it to the queen since coming home." Coming to the end of her thread, Isabel gazed at her sisters. "Mother said it was ludicrous – spun from moonbeams and an addled brain of a mad man." With a flicker of annoyance, she pushed back a few strands of hair. Since her hair started to grow again, it often escaped from beneath her head veils, tickling the hollows of her cheeks.

"Brampton's story was that the last York king put his nephew Richard into his care, making him vow to take him to Flanders if he lost the battle with Henry Tudor. When King Richard was no more, Brampton said he could do no other than keep his promise to his dead sire. Thus, Brampton claimed the page with Hatchet-face was the White Rose himself and the rightful King of all England."

The full implication of her words spun around them a net of silence. Beatriz saw Catalina narrow her eyes. The child looked over to the same bush of white roses that had captured Isabel's attention just moments before. The flowers trembled in a sudden gust of wind, and petals swirled in the air, drifting to the ground. She turned back to her older sister. "There were two sons of King Edward. What of the older one, the one named for his father? Wouldn't he be the rightful heir? How did Brampton explain that?" "Mi chiquitina, you're learnt well from Latina. I did think to ask this question of Brampton. He said it was believed someone poisoned the older boy. Believing he protected the boys by placing them in the Tower, King Richard took the news of his nephew's death to heart. The suspicion of poison just made it worse.

"King Richard hid the younger boy in the home of a man he trusted and made Brampton vow that if all went wrong for him, he would take his nephew to Flanders and to his aunt, the Duchess Margaret. This Brampton did, but with Flanders so close to England the duchess feared discovery by Tudor spies. She, in turn, entrusted Brampton on another mission, to take the boy to Portugal, and she placed him in the care of Hatchet-face. Proven loyal in the past to those who paid him well, this man's protection would cause those wanting to capture the youth to think twice before treading on dangerous ground."

"You don't think the story is true?" Catalina asked, her sewing forgotten on her lap.

Isabel shrugged and rethreaded her needle. "Like I said, Catalina, our lady mother says no. But when mystery surrounds the death of princes, there will always be fables following soon after. I doubt we'll ever sift the truth from this story, but what's important for us to know is that the king who sits on England's throne made it his by sword and conquest, and he's the rightful king in our parents' minds. Henry Tudor is not likely to welcome back one claiming to be the son of the York king, especially when he now has sons of his own." She sighed. "As for this youth. He disappeared from the Portugal court not long after I first saw him. Mother now tells me he reappeared in Burgundy and declared himself Richard IV of England. If this young man is who he claims to be, I think he would be far wiser to forget all about England's crown. It would be shrewder of him to make a new life elsewhere and just disappear, especially from those hoping to use him." Her fingers paused, and Isabel gazed into nothingness. "If those of royal blood are fortunate to escape their fetters, let them stay that way."

Later that same day, Beatriz made sense of Isabel's sudden unease. Ushered from the room where the queen's attendants sat and sewed together, once again Catalina pushed open the door of her mother's bedroom to hear the faint voice of Isabel.

"Will you tell Catalina about what you ask of the English king?" Beatriz peeped through the crack created by the open door. At the other side of the room the queen and her eldest daughter, heads bent over their sewing, sat close together, facing the shutter-less window.

"No. I want her to be a child a while longer."

Isabel turned her head. In fright, Catalina almost shut the door, but not enough to prevent them from hearing further.

"Do you really think it necessary, Mother? All speak of Warwick as if he is an innocent, even weak-minded. No one, surely, would seek to place a crown on one such as he?"

"The weak and innocent are used and shaped to the purposes of the strong, my hija. I do not like asking for his death, but your father convinces me of its need. Warwick is now a young man of seventeen and is looked on by many as a strong claimant to the English crown. I will not allow my youngest child to leave me until I know this particular problem has been dealt with. Our chiquitina will go to England in safety – as safe as I can ensure – or not all.

"We have been long in secret talks with Henry VII about this matter, but the English king refuses to do what we ask, even when we point out Warwick alive only places in danger Henry's own sons. While I understand the queen cares not to forget her close kinship with the youth, she must understand I simply cannot send Catalina to England while he lives. Henry and his gentle queen must own the difficult responsibility in wearing a crown and the painful decisions that accompany it."

Softly closing the door, Catalina almost dragged Beatriz away. Feeling like life repeated itself, she allowed Catalina to lead her, this time to the safety of the infanta's bedchamber. Once there, Catalina collapsed on the clothes chest at the end of the bed and looked at her. "Warwick? That's the son of Richard III's older brother, the one Edward IV executed for treason. He is in the Tower of London, isn't he?" she asked.

Many of Beatriz's lessons included long study of the court and nobility the infanta would one day rule. She eyed Catalina and shrugged. "Like your sister said, most believe him simple-minded and no threat to anyone."

"But Mother thinks he threatens me?" Catalina chewed at her thumb. "My mother said she asked the English king for his death. You heard her say this too?"

Beatriz nodded. The horror she saw on Catalina's white face made her blink and glance away from her. She tightened her lips and inhaled her deep breath. "She does it for your safety, Catalina." She dared look at the child again. Her horror hadn't lessened, rather she trembled and held herself, as if stricken with fever.

"Someone to die? To die for me, Latina? I did not ask it. I do not want it!" Catalina burst into tears and flung herself on the bed.

Beatriz stood by her. Lying on her back, staring at the ceiling, Catalina no longer cried, but heaved in deep breaths as if struggling for air.

'Let her be a child a while longer,' Queen Isabel had said. *A child a while longer?* Looking down at Catalina's pale, still face, Beatriz wondered if the queen wished for the impossible.

12

'Allah has grievously visited my sins upon my head. For your sake, my people, I have now made this treaty, to protect you from the sword, your little ones from famine, your wives and daughters from outrage, and to secure you in the enjoyment of your properties, your liberties, your laws, and your religion under a sovereign of happier destinies than the ill-starred Boabdil.'

Granada fell at last, cannon crumbled its final walls of defence before winter brought its own desolation and famine. Ravens circled the skies. Flocking and fluttering on the broken city's walls, the ravens seemed an edge of black lace on the fabric of reddish stone.

Knowing many hated the defeat, and fearful of his people's unrest, Boabdil set the second day of January as the date for the final surrender. Waiting for that time to come, Queen Isabel and her court no longer dwelled in the alcázar found for her after the fire, but at the newly readied Santa Fe.

Messengers went to and fro, exchanging a flurry of letters between the two courts, royal protocol the main matter of concern. Boabdil's mother refused to allow her son to humble himself to the king and queen, insisting the ceremony not include the king of the Moors kissing the hands of the victors.

Suspecting that Boabdil's mother might yet disrupt the smooth transition from one ruler to another, King Ferdinand and Queen Isabel chose to gentle the way of the vanquished. Word was sent to the Moorish king to come forth on horseback on the morning he was to give them the city keys. An offer of homage was all that King Ferdinand and Queen Isabel desired and expected from him, homage they agreed to decline on the day.

The promise that Boabdil would be treated with all due respect to his rank at last satisfied his mother. The final terms of surrender now agreed, Boabdil swore his loyalty to the Castilian crown and freed the city's captive Christians. The queen summoned those caring for Ahmed to bring him to the Santa Fe.

The last night before the city's hand-over, Beatriz stood with Francisco, watching together as the sun set behind the mountains, both of them relieved of duties for a time. The royal family wanted to spend this night with Ahmed, saying farewell to a boy brought up like a beloved son and a brother. There was no certainty any at court would ever see him again.

Grieving too about Ahmed's approaching departure, Beatriz studied the sun-kissed mountains and then the hill of La Sabica. *How the walls of the Alhambra ringed it in a fit marriage.* The setting sun turned the walls a deeper red, giving it glorious luminosity. The Alhambra meant crimson alcázar – crimson, the colour of blood. The colour of fire and war.

Surrounded by the jubilant expectancy of the camp, Beatriz listened to the cold, cutting wind, tinged with death, defeat, and despair, bringing down to Santa Fe the lament of the Moors.

"Why so downcast, love?" Francisco asked, putting his arm around her. "Believe me, there's no reason for pity. The terms given to the Moors are generous. After a war lasting so many years, the victorious do not usually allow the defeated leave to keep so much." "But, Francisco, how can you say this when their city no longer belongs to them?"

Francisco frowned. "The queen has been more than fair to the Moors. She promises to allow those who wish to stay to keep their religion and laws, governed by cadis of their own faith, men overseen by governors trusted by the queen and king. For three years they will be exempt from tribute, and those wishing to return to Africa have free passage to do so."

"And the secret promises my small infanta heard her mother speak of?"

Glancing around in alarm, Francisco took her arm. "What secret promises?"

"The queen assures Boabdil and his descendants of lands that will replace this city not only for a short time, but for all time. The king and queen will also pay him thirty thousand *castelanos* of gold on the day he leaves the city."

A grim smile tightened her lover's mouth. "Thirty thousand castelanos… more like thirty pieces of silver. 'Tis the final betrayal of a weak king. His signing of the treaty broke the heart and spirit of the city. Many Moors would rather die than see this day finally come. Many believe they have lost so much they might as well lose all. You remember the recent rebellion, when one of their prophets provided the spark for the city's populace to burst into flames? That man declared the king and other Moor leaders cowards and no longer true Moslems. Thousands and thousands, women as well as men, armed themselves, paraded in the streets and shouted for the fight to continue. One leader said, 'We are men. We have hearts, not to shed tender tears, but drops of blood. Let's die defending our liberty.'" Gazing up at the city, Francisco gripped his sword's hilt as if thinking of battle.

Disturbed by his action, Beatriz gnawed her bottom lip. "I thank the good God those words fell on deaf ears."

Francisco continued. "For a day and a night the king dared not emerge from the Alhambra until the prophet, perchance murdered by the king's own men, disappeared. The King of the Moors knows there's nothing more to be done but admit defeat. He is a beaten man, full of despair and guilt. He blames all his misfortunes on coming to the throne in rebellion against his father."

The setting sun spilled a crown of gold over Francisco's black hair and made his face difficult to see. Some distance away, soldiers lit night torches, cutting around the camp a trail of light to follow as dark fell. Very soon, the red fading from its walls, the city's stones would be silvered by starlight.

Her eyes on the guttering torches, Beatriz combed her fingers through her untidy hair, remembering the tale of how men built the Alhambra by torchlight. Now, when the Moors owned their beautiful city this one last night, the light of the torches seemed to throb out a silent dirge to her that the city's very beginning predicted its end. Perchance 'twas true of everything. Life was an unending circle of birth and death, beginnings and ends. Her own mortality opening before her like a black hole, she swung her gaze back to Francisco.

As if catching her mood, he gripped her shoulders. Kissing her, his fingers dug into her flesh. Usually so gentle, she knew he didn't mean to hurt her, but was forgetful due to his unspoken fear. Tomorrow Francisco would be gone again – once again risking his life as one of the few who understood gunpowder and its myriad uses in battle. Si – war ended here. Tomorrow the Moors would yield up all their artillery, their city gates, towers and fortresses to the king and queen. But there were still battles to be fought and won before peace could truly be claimed.

———

The hours sped by to the city's handover. In the dark of night, leaving their king behind, Boabdil's family stole out of the city, going a way determined in great secrecy when the last treaties were signed. They said his mother rode in haughty silence, while the sobbing of his wife and concubines invaded the dreams of those fortunate enough to find any sleep that night. Boabdil's household went to a hamlet overlooking the city, and there they stayed in wait for their vanquished king.

Dawn broke to the boom of signal guns from the Alhambra. The snow peaks of Sierra Nevada glowed blood-red, as if nature took upon itself the duty to spread out the Moors' banner of defeat. Under countless standards, the Christian multitude gathered, garbed in their finest. The queen even convinced Princess

Isabel to put aside the colour of mourning. From Santa Fe, led by the king and queen and their two courts, an army trekked across the Vega to halt at the village of Armilla, half a league from the city.

There was already one there who was important in these happenings despite his tender years, the childhood companion of the royal children, Ahmed.

King Ferdinand went on ahead to meet the Moor king. The queen later relayed the day's happenings to her attendants who didn't see for themselves.

Before the advance of the queen and king, their armies and cavalry, old Cardinal Mendoza, accompanied by Don Gutierrez de Cardenas, entered the city via a road outside the walls. A horn swelled its long note in signal.

Accompanied by fifty of his companions, Boabdil rode forth from the Tower of the Seven Floors. Once outside the city's walls, he swung from his horse and approached the cardinal on foot. Mendoza dismounted to meet with him. For a few minutes they spoke so none could overhear. Then Boabdil lifted up his voice: "Go, senor, and take possession in the name of the powerful sovereigns to whom God has been pleased to deliver them in reward of their great merits and in punishment of the sins of the Moors."

Boabdil took a gold ring from his finger and gave it to Don Inigo Lopez de Mendoza, Count of Tendilla and kinsman to the cardinal, the new governor of the city. "With this ring Granada has been governed. Take it, govern with it, and may you be more fortunate than I."

Boabdil rode on to King Ferdinand – who now approached

the city. He offered to dismount and kiss the king's hand, but, as promised, King Ferdinand prevented him from doing so. The Moor king leaned across and kissed the king's arm, while at the same time delivering to him the keys of the city.

"These keys are the last relics of the Arabian empire in Spain. To you, oh king, we give our trophies, our kingdom, and our person. Such is the will of God. Receive them with the clemency you have promised, and which we look for at your hands."

At the village of Armilla, Boabdil rode in on the wind that brought also to their ears the music from the city, the music of Christian victory.

"My father comes," said Ahmed in a small voice. Holding their hands, he stood between the infantas María and Catalina. Wondering how Ahmed recognised his father, Beatriz noticed the Italian, Cristóbal Colón, watching them closely as he stood with a small gathering of the queen's inner court.

Queen Isabel waited for the Moor king to make his way to her. Seeing him about to kneel and offer her homage, she put out her hand and stopped him. "There's no need for that."

The queen turned, beckoning to Prince Ahmed. When he reached her side, she rested a reassuring hand on his shoulder. Her eyes shut for a heartbeat, and her mouth trembled. "Kneel, infantico mine no longer, kneel for my blessing." The prince's eyes were huge when he fell to his knees. "God bless you, Ahmed, and keep you safe from all harm." Queen Isabel raised him up. "You've been a good son to me, a beloved son, and a beloved brother to my children. I and my family will never forget you. Go with my love." She turned from him without saying one more word. Mounting her horse, Queen Isabel jerked savagely on its reins. The animal half reared in protest, the queen wheeling it towards the Alhambra. Beatriz saw her slowly ride and a gust of wind gathered strength and began to whine. It seemed she heard the wings of time rush by.

Boabdil embraced his son. Ahmed gazed at the royal children one last time before, accompanied by a few companions of King Ferdinand, he rode off with his father. The king's men witnessed the Moor king re-joining his family on the bridge just outside the hamlet.

That same night, the grandees recounted their last sight of Boabdil. The Moor king stopped at the bridge and looked back at the royal banners unfurling from the highest towers of the Alhambra. The great silver cross of the crusade rose on the Torre de la Vela, the pennon of the Apostle of Saint James flapping beside it. Despite the distance, all could hear, rising to the heavens, a shout of "Santiago! Santiago!" A Christian multitude sang *Te Deum Laudamus*. Then there was a roar for King Ferdinand and Queen Isabel. Boabdil wept.

His mother looked at him in contempt and snarled at him, "You do well to weep like a woman for what you failed to defend like a man." Thus, Boabdil and his family departed for their life of exile. Never did Beatriz or the royal family see Ahmed again.

<hr>

While the main war was now over, here and there many Moors still refused to admit defeat and chose to battle on. For years rebellions broke out in the mountains where the last insurgents fought to their deaths and the deaths of others. Sometimes insurgents came to the city itself.

Life at the Alhambra often caused Beatriz to forget this. Si. The Alhambra. A place of perfect beauty – and a homecoming like none other. The place where Catalina's childhood ended, swiftly, violently, like an eagle swooping down on its prey.

13

*'To order the said Jews and Jewesses of our
kingdoms to depart and never to return.'*

~

Mouth of ancient woe
~ Castilian proverb

Beatriz loosened the reins in her hand, reaching down to pat the neck of her patient horse. *Such a pretty chestnut mare. How I love to ride.* On a horse, she felt free, all the constrictions of her life falling away. Next to two horses, one white and the other black, Prince Juan waited for his sister, his hooded peregrine upon his wrist. As was often his wont when riding forth with his sisters, Juan robed himself in simple, though still costly, garb. He sought anonymity rather than proclaim to all and sundry his rank. Watching and waiting a short distance away, the prince's companions, six noble born youths, sat on their own horses.

Hunting dogs lolled and scratched, brave and silly ones darted and gambolled in game between the horses' legs, gaining curses from the young men each time they unsettled their mounts. The companions talked amongst themselves, remaining at the ready to ride at Prince Juan's spoken command.

Behind Juan there was a sudden flurry of movement, flash of sleek colour, toss of chestnut head and canter of hooves. A stable boy rushed out with yet another saddled horse. Despite its leather hood, the falcon flapped its wings in fright and screamed. The stable boy reached the prince and fell to his knees, holding out the reins as if offering a gift of gold.

Murmuring his thanks, Prince Juan took the reins from the boy before stroking and calming his bird. The prince shared a smile with Diego, the horse-master. Catalina hurried to his side, with María de Salinas a few steps behind her. "What did I tell you, good Diego? I ask my sister to ride with me and again she brings her shadow."

Dipping her head to Juan's words, his sister beamed at him, tying the ribbon of her wide straw hat more tightly beneath her chin. "Shame, brother, you steal our mother's own nickname for our cousin!" She glanced at Beatriz. "Latina told María to come. She would have been lonely otherwise."

Glad of her hat's deep shade, Beatriz grinned at Prince Juan. At fourteen he already dwelled in another world to the one her two charges knew at seven. But then he was the queen's only son and heir to two kingdoms. Only within the inner circle of family and a trusted few did Juan show the boy he still was.

Seeing María falter and struggle for composure, Beatriz beckoned to her. She leaned from the horse and whispered close to the child's ear: "Rest easy. He is only teasing because he loves you."

María beamed and shuffled a little dance – knowing the truth of this.

The prince gave his falcon and his horse's reins to his waiting page. From one wrist to the other, slate-grey feathers ruffling in protest and flecking with shimmering rainbows, talons seeking a perch, the hooded falcon screamed its long and piercing *kek*.

Prince Juan mounted effortlessly. Mane bristling, the horse arched its neck and wheeled in a half-circle, ready at the lightest touch of a heel to burst into a gallop. The prince pulled the reins, bringing his stallion under control. Prince Juan's black hose already showed a shapely, well-muscled leg from hard hours of dedicating himself to physical activities. Despite times of ill-health, his shoulders became broader and less boy-like day-by-day. The horse-master stood with thumbs hooked into his wide belt, chewing mint loudly, watching the prince contain his spirited beast. Diego nodded and smiled with pride. As if as an afterthought, he gave a brief bow, spitting out mint leaves to the ground as he turned to help Catalina onto her horse.

Astride and settled, she gathered the reins in her tiny hands and straightened her back. Eager for her turn, María took the reins of the spare horse from the stable boy. Beatriz suppressed a smile, noticing the stable boy still gazing at the prince with unhidden adoration.

Snorting, the horse nosed María's hip, pushing her back a step. The child looked into the mare's liquid brown eyes, as if gauging its character, giggling when it nosed and pushed her yet another step. Warm brown eyes with long, thick eyelashes wooed little María closer. She patted its nose and rubbed the side of a hand between her gentle eyes, murmuring words of pleasure.

With a friendly nicker, the horse pranced and pricked her ears. María laughed again and stroked her neck. Closing her eyes, she fanned her fingers, stroking backward and forward on the mare's neck. Her feet jigged in excitement, her hand on the mare's neck, waiting for the horse-master to finish with Catalina and come to her. Beatriz shortened her reins, bettering her hold, also impatient and eager to begin their outing.

Diego expertly re-adjusted the saddle straps for Catalina's shorter leg. Her feet, booted in soft leather, bore down in the gold, ornamented stirrups.

"You ride today Isa, my infanta. She's more demanding than your usual mount, but you're ready to meet the challenge. Now, let me see how you sit on her." Diego, one of the best horse-masters in Queen Isabel's kingdom, circled the horse, making certain Catalina held her reins not too tight or too loose. Bow-legged from a lifetime on horseback, he stepped back, his dark eyes going from horse to infanta. With a short laugh he relaxed, giving a gap-toothed smile before dipping his head to her. "Brave infanta – our noble queen will delight when I tell her what a good horsewoman she has in you. Take Isa around the yard, my infanta. See how she feels, while you let her get used to the feel of you in the saddle. Remember, don't let Isa act outside her place. You're her mistress, not the other way around."

Diego lightly smacked Isa's rump. The horse arched its neck and flicked its mane, edging forward and then a little backwards, its hoofs crunching into the stony earth. Laughing, Catalina leaned over and whispered in its ear. With a jubilant neigh and a shake of its head, the horse shifted and shuffled, cavorting almost on one spot.

The olive skin around his dark eyes crinkling, Diego laughed. As if remembering Catalina's rank, he dipped his head, but then became master again. "Stop her playing, infanta. I'll get Doña María onto her mare." Keeping an eye on Catalina, Diego stepped over to María.

Beaming, Catalina firmed her seat and pulled back tight reins. With a loud "Yah!" she dug in her heels, the horse answering the command with a sudden gallop.

Diego watched as Catalina concentrated, using all her strength to gain full control of Isa. She seemed so tiny on a horse standing at least fifteen hands. Beatriz released her breath when Isa tossed her mane, let out a joyous neigh, and settled into a steady trot, finally giving herself over to the fearless girl on her back. Diego turned, grinning up at Beatriz.

Away from their riding lessons, Catalina and María giggled at Diego's green teeth. Whatever the season, he always chewed leaves of mint growing near the stables. He told the girls it kept him in good health. But the girls never laughed about what Diego taught them. He knew the name of every horse in the stable as if it was his beloved child. No matter what its temper, any horse, in the first hour or so of meeting Diego, became gentle, wanting to eat out of his hand. Whenever he rode, it was to see a centaur come to life. Beatriz doubted there was a horse alive that could or would throw him.

Queen Isabel employed the best teachers for her five offspring. Catalina and María were only seven, yet more than a year had seen them no longer needing their horses tied to training ropes, or riding their mounts around a pole in the stable yard.

Grinning at Diego, Beatriz clicked her tongue to her mount in encouragement, her eyes still on Catalina. The girl now cantered Isa in wide rings around the yard. Catalina's smile of deep pleasure caused her cheeks to flush and her eyes to shine. Always, riding added to her natural prettiness.

Diego patted María's mare. Nickering, the horse nosed his shoulder, greeting him with affection. He laughed, giving the mare another pat. "I see you've made good friends with Bela, little Doña. I thought you would. You go well with her. She ate the grass of your birthplace as a foal, and the best of your father's stallions was her sire."

"Not Hector?" María looked more closely at the animal. "Do you know her mother?"

Planting his calloused hands on his hips, Diego barked out a laugh. "What other mare would it be but the queen's favourite, gifted to her by your good father?"

María almost danced with excitement. Diego winked and smiled again at Beatriz. "Up you go." He gave María a leg up onto her mount.

Beatriz pulled down at the sides of her gown, ensuring her lower legs and ankles remained hidden, keeping her eyes on her two charges. María watched from her horse as Catalina reined in her mount, coming to a halt next to the waiting Diego. The horse-master rubbed the mare's ears while murmuring love words to her. He nodded at Catalina. Grinning again, the lines around his eyes crinkled and deepened. "As I thought, Isa's a good match for you, my infanta. You and she possess a similar spirit. She is loyal, brave and always protects those she loves."

Juan trotted his stallion over to Catalina. "Where to today, my sister?"

After a moment, Catalina smiled anew. "Our good horse-master Diego has given me a demanding horse. Brother, what if we go for a demanding ride today?"

A demanding ride? Beatriz sighed again. It promised to be another day when she would have little time for her books or study.

Away from the stables and prying eyes, Beatriz slowed her horse to an unhurried canter, trying to keep behind María, the prince's companions and well behind Juan and his sister, allowing them to be alone together. Three of Prince Juan's large hounds bounded past her.

Prince Juan half-wheeled his mount, looking across the green fields. Catalina did likewise, her ribboned sunhat slipping off her head, bouncing against her back. Juan pointed over to a low, green hill, a good ride from the earthen track they now followed. Holding her reins in one hand, Catalina stood up, balancing in her stirrups. She shielded her eyes and gave him a quick nod. The pair galloped off the road, heading across the fields to the hill, the prince's dogs barked and followed after them.

One of Prince Juan's companions swore. Another yelled, "Follow him." Horses neighed, protesting as men kicked them into a gallop. Hooves pounded the earth, stirring and flicking up dust and dirt.

Beatriz's frightened horse snorted and half reared, circling one way and then the other. By the time she had calmed it, she found herself left well in the wake of the other riders. She dug in her heels. Up ahead, a dust cloud was the only sign of her companions. *How fast they move across the fields!* Harder this time, she dug in her heels again and surged ahead with greater power. The valley dipped and a path opened up before her, long years of man and beast cutting the way clear.

A short distance away, horses and riders gathered close together. The race seemingly over, Beatriz saw why upon reaching her party. Dismounted from their horses, the prince stood protectively at the back of his sister and María. He held two snarling dogs by the leather of their jewelled collars while Catalina waited for an old woman to finish drinking from her flask. Nearby, a young woman, hair hidden under a matron's veil, her tiny frame showing the swell of pregnancy, sat on the edge of a wagon's broken wheel. Semi-shaded by the loaded cart, she wiped her wet mouth with her sleeve. Her worried eyes, large and blue, stayed on the men and their horses. Tied to the cart, a mule pulled tight its rope, backwards and forwards in a half-circle, hee-hawing at the sight of strangers.

Beatriz rode close to Catalina's mount and slipped off her horse too. Getting her land legs back and grabbing her horse's reins, she hurried over to her infanta.

"Do you need food?" Catalina asked the women.

"God bless you, child," the older woman said. "There's plenty for us to eat, just nothing left for us to quench our thirst. Our drinking jars broke when the cart fell into the ditch."

Concern fluttered over Catalina's face, darkening her eyes. Giving his dogs to his page, Juan came to her side. He tossed back his black fur cloak, freeing one shoulder. "You say your men went to the village for a new wheel?"

The young woman stared at the prince, her mouth wordlessly opening and shutting. Gazing fully at her, Beatriz realised her youth. Her skin, eyes and mouth, even the shape of the face seemed unformed and childlike. She seemed no more than a maid of thirteen, not much younger than Prince Juan himself. "My man, he –"

With the suddenness of an angry snake, one of the prince's companions jerked his head to another and hissed, "Don't they know whom they address? Why do we waste our time here?"

Fear widened the whites of the girl's eyes. Someone spat, the explosion of sound breaking into the brief silence. Diego de Deza, Juan's tutor, came to the prince's side, speaking swift, soft Latin meant only for him. Beatriz listened, disturbed. "You think this wise, Your Highness? Our blessed queen, your most prudent and noble mother, gave the Jews a chance to do right by our land. These ones have clearly chosen exile. It is not for us to meddle."

Men shifted and muttered angrily. The prince glanced over his shoulder and frowned, gesturing for them to desist. "Go, leave us." Loud grumbles swelled before another dark glance from Prince Juan caused his companions' protests to tamper off into silence. A few men shrugged and laughed. Behind Beatriz, one man murmured, "It is good he cares. A good king he'll be one day."

Two companions broke away from the group and returned to their horses. The rest soon followed. A flurry of vaulting feet, grunts and groans interwove with that of horse neighs and wickers, hooves shifting in the dry earth, as the prince's companions and his small troop of guards remounted. One of the older men gave a jerk of his head. He whistled, wheeling his horse around. His fellows trailed after, moving farther away. The clearing now filled with a smaller number, Beatriz clasped María's hand and Prince Juan again addressed the girl.

"I promise you my sister and I only want to help. You were saying?"

"My son went, my good lord. We were with others, but they feared to wait for us when the wagon broke. This path took us too close to the alcázar of the queen and none of our company could help us, for none possessed a spare wheel." Fingernails broken and dirty, the old woman twisted her gnarled, bare hands. "They wanted us to leave all our belongings and walk behind them, but this is all we have. Young lord, I am old, and my son's wife is weary and ill with child. We cannot carry much."

Catalina stepped in closer. "Tell us what my brother and I can do. Our mother teaches us the meaning of charity."

The old woman gave an almost toothless smile. "God bless her good heart, and you and your noble brother. Sweet children you both are, that I can see. A shame others do not teach their children like your lady mother."

Fidgeting, Prince Juan fingered the dagger tucked in his belt and the sun glinted off the rubies embedded in its hilt. He studied his feet before gazing again at the women. "Are you Jews?"

The girl cowered, and moaned softly. The old woman tightened her mouth. "Be calm, Raquel, and don't carry on! You're overly taxed, that's why you are having some pain. The babe's months away yet."

The woman held out her other sleeve. Sewn upon it was the badge all Jews wore.

"My poor dead husband called us God's elect." Her face crumbled. "God's accursed more like. I give thanks that death came for him before he saw his whole life's work sold for little more than a song and his wife and son driven from their homes, with nowhere to go. It would break his heart to see his first grandchild born in the open, as is now like to happen."

The girl rested her head on the woman's shoulder.

One of the prince's companions brought his horse closer to us. "My lord prince, more Jews approach."

The woman's eyes opened wide, her face blanched grey. Juan's eyes met hers. His mouth pursed and he nodded, holding out hands palms up, as if showing them empty of weapons. Beatriz's heart missed a beat. *He came in peace? The prince came in peace? Is this what he is trying to say?*

Bewildered by his action, she felt cast adrift in dense fog. When Juan and the old woman gazed silently at one another, Beatriz felt more than simply adrift. All the tales of sailing to the end of the world became all at once true. Tottering on its edge, she couldn't see what lay beyond it, but she knew, whatever it was, something slithered and hissed, hissed of everything in this world that was evil.

Trembling, Beatriz shook herself, mentally stepping away from her dark thoughts. She returned to the bright, hot day, only to be reminded of the reason for the darkness. She gazed at the path winding and cutting its way up the hill. Some distance away two young men and a far older one strode fast towards them. The two younger men dragged behind them a frame made of tree limbs with a wheel and saddlebags roped to it.

Hand to her belly, the girl lumbered weakly to her feet. Her face lost all colour. She moaned louder this time, half bending forward. The other woman's eyes narrowed in concern. Getting her breath again, the girl straightened and rubbed the sides of her belly. "David," she called.

Beatriz stared at the girl's slender hips, remembering the queen's arguments one year ago when the king wanted to finalise Juana's marriage. "Do you want to give us cause for uncalled grief? Husband, she is barely flowered. Speak to your mother if you need to, but I don't need a midwife to tell me we'd see our Juana dead within the year if we give her to her husband now. She's still only a child. Have you noticed her hips? Narrow like our son's."

Just like this girl in front of her, who now shielded her eyes with her right hand. Beatriz sucked in her top lip, disquieted. Her eyes searched the track. A young man hollered, trying to enunciate his words over the distance. One man waved. They quickened their stride, almost to a run. The girl stepped forward as if to go to them, but the woman grabbed her back.

"Wait! They're almost here. I beg you, Raquel, let us not have any more mishaps we can avoid by patience."

The girl bowed her head like a censured child, returning to her mother-in-law's side. Once there, she squeezed shut her eyes and groaned again. The older woman's mouth pursing into fine wrinkles, she looped her arm around the young girl's shoulders, hugging her. She looked towards their menfolk, swallowing hard.

"See, Raquel. I told you all will be well. David would never abandon us. And look! He brings back my brother and his son." She glanced at the prince, her head dipping in acknowledgement. "My lord prince, I thank and bless you for all your help. God will remember your charity. But please leave us now. Go in good conscience." A smile burst across her lined face, hinting at the once handsome woman of long ago. "My son returns, and we must be on our way."

Catalina stood, shaking dust and leaves off the bottoms of her skirts. She gazed at her brother, but he refused to meet her questing eyes. Wringing her hands, she faced the old woman. "You don't want us to find you a place to give you shelter? Your son's wife looks in sore need of it."

The girl's eyes opened, her pupils so large they made her eyes seem black. Her tears welling, she bit her lower lip.

Juan took his sister's arm. "Come away, Catalina. Their men are almost here. I promised our lady mother I would have us both home before it becomes too hot. We best go."

Confusion clouded Catalina's eyes. "My brother, the girl's in pain!" Prince Juan looked helplessly at the woman. She smiled gently, then lowered her gaze to Catalina. "Good Doña, we cannot stay. Our broken wagon has forced us to tarry overlong. By nightfall, we must journey as far as we can while we still have our donkey –" She glanced at the beast pulling up grass near the cart. "At the border we must give him up, too, God help us..."

Another groan came from the girl. Breathing hard, her face frightened, she crumbled against the cart's frame. Beatriz saw her stare ahead, her youth leaching away to nothingness. The woman gripped the girl's shoulder and turned to Prince Juan. His eyes glimmered bright in his white face.

"My lord prince, take your sister away. We'll look after our own, but I beg you, take your men and the two little maids from here now. Our fates rest in the hand of the good God."

Only a short distance away their men strode toward them. Seeing fear stamped on their faces, Beatriz tightened her grip on María's hand and stepped over to Catalina. Sunlight turned tears on the girl's eyelashes into tiny diamonds. Taking her hand, Beatriz walked with the girls back to their horses. She gazed at the two women and then more searchingly at Juan. He marched swiftly away from his small sister, his back rod-straight and his hands at his sides in tight fists. A grey, large cloud covered the sun, dimming the colour of the day.

"I don't understand," Catalina whispered.

Beatriz licked her dry lips. "Your mother may know the reason for it."

She looked back. The woman crooned, cradling the girl's head on her lap. The girl writhed and moaned, her legs continually bending, unbending. In the dark earth, rivulets of blood gushed from underneath the girl's skirts. Utterly chilled despite the afternoon's heat, Beatriz felt touched by a finger of death. She gazed at the girl. No – death touched not her.

Beatriz met Catalina's terrified eyes. Si – childhood ends so quickly. One moment a rabbit bounces and leaps, unaware, free, heading for the safety of its hole, weaving a streak of amber life through the long, green grass. The next moment, it is only torn flesh, blood and bone. Just a memory of blithe beauty glimpsed and then, like a falling star, gone forever. Beatriz took the child's arm and quickened her pace to their horses. Nothing remained of the day's joy.

14

The beginning of health is to know the disease
~ Castilian proverb

Riding with María behind Catalina, Beatriz pondered about Prince Juan's behaviour. Meeting those poor Jews had left him unnaturally silent and brooding. The change altered him so much from his usual companionable self. Juan rode slouched in the saddle, as if a great weight burdened his spirit. Catalina questioned him, trying to untangle her knot of bewilderment. Over and over she asked her brother for answers until he swung around, blue eyes blazing, and snapped, "This is none of your concern." Savagely, he dug his heels hard into his horse, making it protest and half-rear before it bounded away, leaving those behind in the wake of its dust. Soon, only two of his companions remained with them, the rest galloping after their prince. In silence, they herded Beatriz and her two small charges back the way they came such a short time ago.

At the entrance of the alcázar, Beatriz saw Juana and her sister María. Juana, white-faced and eyes glittering, stalked up and down the hallway. Their duena stood some distance away, as if she sought to stay away from the infanta. The infanta María watched on, her face tense and unhappy.

Seeing them enter the alcázar, Juana rushed over. "Why did you not tell me you were going riding with Juan?"

Catalina blinked. "You didn't tell me when you went with him yesterday."

Juana grabbed her sister's arm, shaking Catalina so hard her wide sun hat, with its loosened ribbons, fell to the ground. Her fine dark hair loosening from its net, Juana wiped tears from her eyes. "And I would have gone today too, if you sent me word. What right have you to ride alone with him? He is closer to me than you."

Their eyes locked. Whatever Catalina saw there made her lower her head. She attempted to free herself from her sister's hold. "Stop it, you're hurting me."

Flinging Catalina away, Juana burst into passionate tears and ran in the direction of her bedchamber.

Taking the hand of one charge, Beatriz hurried over to the other. Catalina rubbed her arm and wiped her eyes. Beatriz wound her arm around her in sympathy. Nearby, the infanta María fanned out her fingers on either side of her wide girdle, staring after Juana. She stepped towards them, picking up Catalina's hat. Frowning, she handed the hat back to her sister, her long fingers fluttering up and down Catalina's arm, as if not daring to touch. Hooding her eyes, she heaved a long, sad sigh.

"Mi chiquitina..." She sighed again, and eyed her sister. "Juana sometimes thinks Juan belongs only to her and that he should never give any mind to his other sisters; especially on a day when our father lashes her with his tongue. She does not mean it, my sister. She strikes out only because she is hurting." María touched Catalina's wet cheek. "Do you want me to tell Mother?"

Catalina lifted and dropped her shoulders. "I don't know..."

María shuffled her slippered feet and frowned. Disquiet darkened her eyes. "When Father shouts at her like today, calling our sister unworthy of both him and our royal lady mother, Juana turns into another person. Sister, it might be best to tell her when you next ride with Juan. While Juana loves him dearly, as we all do, she fears making him angry too. Thus, she accepts it when Juan tells her she's not included." María frowned and bit her bottom lip. "I will go to her now. I'll get her to apologise to you."

Juan rarely asked his sister María to accompany him on his daily ride. Less pretty than her sisters, and often taken for granted by many – sometimes even by her own mother – María shone with an inner sweetness and truly deserved her nickname of Joy. Bestowed with common sense, content with her lot in life, her calmness offered others a green oasis of peace in the midst of a family made up of emotive and complicated individuals.

Catalina stood on tiptoes, kissing her sister's cheek. "Thank you. I'll remember. Is Mother busy?"

Starting down the corridor, the infanta chuckled over her shoulder. "Mother is always busy, but she sees us even so."

Catalina chewed her thumb, watching María stride away. "Is this a good time, do you think?"

Beatriz pushed back strands of hair from her forehead. "I cannot say. No time is ever a good time when you are a queen –"

Catalina took her hand. "But Mother will speak to me."

Beatriz nodded, taking Catalina and María's hands. They slipped through the stone arch into the Court of the Lions, edging close to the narrow path of water dividing the court. Twelve stone lions supported alabaster basins, into which crystal jets of water poured and sparkled.

East, west, south and north, triangles of well-tended flowerbeds marked the corners of the courtyard. Fronds from various climbing plants festooned their own nimble design. Slender columns of the purest white marble supported archways of open filigree. Delicate fretwork covered the walls.

Wherever Beatriz looked, light dappled and water sparkled in a constant exchange between one and the other, the exquisite art of nature adding to the fine art as man had ever wrought. The Alhambra, Heaven reflected on Earth. Surely little in their mortal world compared with the beauty found here?

Beatriz's pace slowed, drawn again by the seductive beauty of this place. Catalina grabbed her, heading into the Hall of the Two Sisters, going straight to its secret staircase taking them to the queen's chamber in the highest tower.

Out of breath by the time she entered, Beatriz covered her surprise at finding Prince Juan also there. He sat at his mother's feet, in front of her high-backed chair, arms around one bent leg, leaning his chin upon his well-formed knee. Seeing Catalina, he blanched, straightened his shoulders, looking up at the queen. "Mother, I tried to tell her it was none of her concern. Still, my sister must know everything. Isn't that right, Mi chiquitina?"

Stepping out of the grey shadows in a window embrasure,

Princess Isabel padded over to the rear of her mother's chair, garbed in one of the black habitos she wore, day after day. The coarse fabric left behind patches of red, irritated skin. Hollows pushed deep into her cheeks and dark rings circled her huge eyes. Some days, especially when she fasted overlong, her grief ate away at her – soul and flesh. Those days the princess seemed a beautiful rose placed in a dark place, wilting for lack of sun and water. Then they needed to beware her thorns.

Mouth hard, nose pinched, Isabel glared at Beatriz. "Go. My sister must speak to the queen. Alone."

Beatriz faltered. She felt struck. Once she had thought of Isabel as a friend.

Starting to leave, Beatriz saw the queen shake her head at her, gesturing to her to halt, her grim eyes on her youngest daughter. "Latina will stay, Isabel," the queen said. "She can take Catalina back to her chamber once I finish speaking with her."

Looking at her youngest daughter, the queen's face wore almost the same expression as when she had scolded Gonzalo, one of her most powerful grandees. "Stop squandering all the honour you earned through your victories by misgoverning," she had told him. The queen's words reduced him to abjection and fervent apology.

As if fighting against a sea rip, Queen Isabel's confessor, Hernando de Talavera, trudged his way through the deep gloom of the recesses bordering the queen's chamber. His head popped out from the cowl of his dark monk's mantle. Beatriz took hold of María and led her back a few steps. The grim atmosphere in the room entangled her tighter in its net. She sought refuge in humour, remembering the turtles Prince Juan had received from his father on his last birthday. Re-emerging to the world after being frightened, their heads popped out of their shells in almost the same manner as the queen's confessor. But her refuge crumbled when she noticed the red eyes of the cardinal. Mouth trembling, tears still dripped down his winkled, hollowed cheeks. Bowing very low, the priest fell to his knees, clutching to his breast his heavy, gold crucifix, a recent gift from Queen Isabel. "My noble queen, pray, I beg you. This a great sin and an act of infamy. I agree with Abravanel, your grace, what you and the lord king now do risks divine punishment. Your Majesty, 'tis not too late, I beg you, withdraw the order."

The queen rounded on her priest. Beatriz shivered at seeing her white, stark face.

"Dare you question us, my lord cardinal?" She spoke a voice Beatriz rarely heard from her – soft but threatening, underlined with steel. "Did you not once advise me to be a model to my subjects in the service of God? I remember your words, even if you do not. I need your prayers and support, confessor, not your ill-considered doubts. God gave me this crown, and I mean to do what I believe is right."

Queen Isabel swung a scorching glance at Beatriz. "Bad enough that Latina argues with me too."

Beatriz looked down at the floor, feeling like a roped felon. She gazed over her shoulder at the arches opening to views of the palace grounds. Up high, engraved in the delicate stone-work, were the words: *I am in this garden, an eye filled with joy.* In this sunlit room, there was nothing of joy.

"My queen," pleaded the cardinal, "I once also told you that you were an eagle, placed on the peak of honours and sublime dignities." The priest choked and wiped his hand across his mouth. "Never would I believe the eagle capable of ripping and tearing her kingdom to shreds."

The queen lifted her chin. "I vowed to my first confessor, Torquemada, to devote myself to the extirpation of heresy. I must do what I must. Enough, I say. I have heard enough." Furious, her eyes glittering like aquamarine stones, Queen Isabel rounded on Beatriz. "I've changed my mind. Go with María and I will send my daughter back to you once I speak to her. Leave us."

Relieved at the queen's dismissal, Beatriz re-clasped María's hand and curtseyed as she backed to the door. Before she closed it behind her, she made another curtsey, a curtsey that almost buckled when she saw Catalina's wide, scared eyes. She couldn't smile at her, couldn't offer her any comfort. She could do nothing but leave her all alone to face whatever this was, what the priest called an act of infamy.

Trembling outside the chamber door, Beatriz found herself weeping with María. Drying her own tears, she took the child in her arms, giving her the comfort that she couldn't give to her other charge. Sweating now in the mounting heat, she led María to the infanta's bedchamber, and they waited for her. María too upset for lessons, Beatriz took up a book to read while the child took up her sewing.

For once even Aristotle could not hold Beatriz's interest, and her threads of thought unravelled. So much stayed knotted and tangled like the uneven stitches María now needed to unpick and redo. The hours passed, the bright afternoon light growing dim and grey, as day approached night.

Drawing the curtains on the remains of the day, Beatriz lit the candles in the room. She sat on the red velvet-covered stool closest to the unused fireplace, near María. From the open wicker basket at her feet, the child picked up a small canvas frame. She rummaged in her basket, and then settled back on the stool and sewed, more clumsily than ever. She dropped the frame to the floor and took out from the basket a small square of saffron silk. Traced on the silk there was a small, wine-red butterfly, with half of one wing still unstitched. María started sewing again and gave a cry of dismay when she stabbed her finger, soiling the embroidery with blood. The wide, terrified eyes of the girl they met today flashed in Beatriz's mind, a terrified child-woman feeling birth pangs upon her. She remembered the prince almost breaking down before them. How the old woman had looked at him – full of... knowing... forgiveness... compassion... pity.

María sewed a loop and pulled too hard, puckering up the scrap of saffron silk. The butterfly wing close to ruin, the child looked about to burst into tears. She tossed the silk onto the already abandoned canvas. The silver needle spun in the air, a filament of candlelight caught it and glittered it with light.

The child picked up the precious piece of silk again and smoothed it out on her lap. *Such awkward stitching for a girl with a mother and grandmother who sewed with such great skill.* Beatriz almost smiled at the girl's look of tragic despair. María was yet to learn that to capture beauty was the work of a lifetime. She too yearned to hold beauty in her hands, make it stay for more than just a heartbeat, a breath of time.

The eyes of the old woman flashed in Beatriz's mind. They merged with Catalina's, the gaze turned towards her when she closed the door of her mother's chamber. She trembled, chilled, the afternoon's heat all gone. She knelt on the floor and threw kindling into the fire's hearth and started to ready it for lighting. She heard the door open and close. Catalina leaned against the door, her eyes and hair lit by the light of candles.

The child released a moan, odd and ragged as if contained overlong, and ran over to Beatriz and into her waiting arms. María came to join them. "You've been so long!" she said. Beatriz shook her head at her, hoping she would not ask any questions. The distress on Catalina's face slammed the door upon that.

Catalina reached out and clasped María's hand. Beatriz studied their interlaced fingers – chubby and thin, one hand with broken fingernails, showing evidence of morning gardening, the other the well-kept hand of royalty, both hands still those of children. She sighed.

"I've been praying with my mother. We all were." Catalina swallowed, chewing at her bottom lip.

María stared, her eyes wide in her pale face. Time for prayer came for the girls from morning to night, but they had never prayed away a whole afternoon. Lowering her eyes, Catalina pulled at her riding gown, straightening its folds.

"I am not allowed to ride with Juan until Mother tells me." She shook her head a little as if to clear it. "I am not allowed to go riding. I mean, we're not. We're to stay inside, unless told otherwise."

María blinked. "But why? Did we do something wrong?"

"Not us. We've done no wrong..."

"Then why can we not ride?"

"We're in danger from the Jews..."

The two girls looked up at Beatriz. They looked more lost

than ever. Beatriz rubbed the side of her face, uncertain of what to say. "Did the queen tell you this" she asked Catalina.

"Si." Her grip tightened on Beatriz's hand, and her eyes fell. "They are bad people. They have done bad things, evil things…"

Beatriz shivered, and the words of a poem beat like a heartbeat in her mind. A poem written by a Jew:

Hand of its clouds, winter wrote a letter
Upon the garden, in purple and blue.

Upon the garden, in purple and blue Now she feared what happened this day would shadow winter's clouds upon these two young lives. Forever.

Yet again haunted by the girl and her mother-in-law, Beatriz remembered the old woman's compassion, her tender care for the child-woman. She remembered the girl's terror.

"Those people we saw today? Truly them?" María asked.

Catalina's mouth trembled. "Perchance, not them, but their people bear the guilt of wrong doing "

María blinked and shook her hand. "What have they done?"

Catalina swallowed again, her eyes travelling around the room before returning to stare down at the hand clasped by her friend. Once again, her hand tightened on Beatriz's.

"I don't want to speak of it."

"But," María injected, "we vowed to tell each other everything!

Everything!"

Beatriz felt it was time to interrupt. "Did the queen tell you not to speak? If she did, you must do what she says."

Catalina rubbed at her eyes. "No, Mother said nothing about that." "Then please tell us," María said.

Beatriz shivered at what she saw in Catalina's frightened eyes. "Why do you always want to know?" the child said.

María wound her arms around her and hugged her tight. "Because I love you."

Catalina let go of their hands and stepped away from them. When she faced them again, tears ran down her face. "The Jews crucified a baby! An innocent boy! Cut out his heart and asked the Devil to kill us all. The Jews desire our deaths – the death of Christians."

Beatriz felt sick. Putting her arm around the horrified María, she whispered, "By all... who said this?"

"Mother." Her eyes challenged Beatriz. "Do you doubt her word?"

Hand of its clouds, winter wrote a letter
Upon the garden, in purple and blue.

The garden, their childhood. The two girls looked dazed, as if their whole world had darkened, and been ripped apart.

Beatriz remembered her grandfather, son of a converto descended from the great Samuel ibn Nagrella himself. Her mother's great-grandfather stayed a Jew to the day he died, as did so many of his kin. Her kin. Jews. And not too many generations away Catalina's own father and mother lay claim to sharing the blood of a converto. Learning lessons of history in their schoolroom, they often delighted to own these men as kin. Sometimes, even the queen spoke of them to her daughters, telling stories that fuelled their pride.

Rubbing the tears from her face, María spoke. "If the queen told you this, then it must be true. But all the Jews? How can it be all the Jews, Catalina?"

Returning to the stool, Catalina sniffed. "Mother said she gave the Jews three months to become convertos. That time has ended, and now all the Jews not Christian must go.

"That old woman and her family were leaving Castilla, as my mother commanded. Surely if they were truly good people, they would convert and stay. Mother says those people we saw today not only have the blood of Jesús on their hands, but that of the child's. She thinks only of her kingdom's safety. That boy was her subject, and Jews murdered him."

"My mother says there are bad people everywhere, calling themselves Jews, Moors or Christian. Just because a few are bad doesn't mean all are," María pleaded.

Catalina appeared deaf to her friend. "The Jews refuse to turn from their evil life. They refuse to see Jesús Christ as their Messiah. Mother says as long as she allows Jews to stay, she's endangering the unity of her kingdom, failing her duty to her subjects and service to God. God made her queen, and her conscience tells her she must clean Castilla of... this contamination. Father thinks likewise. God stirs them to do what is right for all."

She spoke a lesson learnt by rote. For the third time today, Beatriz saw in her mind the virgin-faced girl, labouring far too early with her child. Kept silent because of her loyalty to the queen, she wanted to weep. She felt the prescience of death, casting its shroud upon her, the girls, the winter clouds that shadowed them all and made their world black.

"Contamination... What do you mean?" María asked

Catalina sniffed again, gnawing at her mouth. Another milk tooth came loose. Catalina's eyes continued their restless search around the room. It seemed peace eluded her. Beatriz felt sickened. Surely a child of seven should not be burdened with such things? "The Jews are a stain on Castilla and my father's kingdom. God wants us to rid ourselves of them – my mother told me so. Please, let's not talk of this anymore."

She fell on her knees, pulling María down alongside her. "Pray. Pray with me. For our sins."

Beatriz could not look away from the child's tear-streaked face as Catalina said one of her mother's most loved prayers. "I praise the Virgin Mother and her son Jesús. Vehemently I mourn my sins, constantly hoping in Jesús."

15

He who inherits a hill must climb it
~ Castilian proverb

The days following, Beatriz found Catalina glum and silent, not even responding when it came to her studies. For hours the child prayed in her mother's private chapel, leaving Beatriz with María as her sole scholar. Miserable too, María longed to go home to her own mother. With darkness surrounding them – a shroud of miasma hiding some nameless horror – suffocating and ill, Beatriz decided to grab their sunhats and take María out into the garden and wait for Catalina there.

Encouraging María to do the same, Beatriz fell to her knees and started clearing the weeds from the herb garden. An hour sped by before a shadow fell over them. Beatriz straightened, rested her dirty hands on her lap and peered up at Catalina. Beside her María gave a yelp of joy, going to embrace her friend.

"What happened to today's lesson?" Catalina asked,

narrowing her eyes against the morning's glaring light. Not waiting for an answer, she sank down to her knees and picked up a spare hand fork. "Let me help you."

Catalina cocked her head, and pointed to a small shrub. "What's that?"

Beatriz dug into the earth. "Sage. It's used in salads and sauces. And to protect us from restless spirits, and even for wisdom."

Catalina inhaled a deep breath and sighed. "I pray to be wise."

Beatriz jabbed deeper around the rosemary bunch, careful to avoid its spiky branches, tidying the patch of earth in front of her. "Time will give you that wish," she said.

"Mother is so unhappy."

Beatriz gave a vicious tug to a healthy dandelion growing overtop a wilting feverfew, and tossed it to the pile mounting at her side. "I must speak to the queen about the good sisters here. By all the good saints, either they possess a great need for diuretics or they neglect this garden. The dandelions win the victory here." With a sigh, she sat back on her haunches, contemplating Catalina. "You know your mother's position is not one to encourage happiness?"

Beatriz carefully eased up a small seedling of angelica too near to the comfrey and replanted it farther away so it would not fight for ground as it matured and grew its tall stalk. She perused the garden, naming the herbs. Yarrow, the awful tasting horehound –what she used to becalm Juan's coughs – rue, rosemary, balm – to attract the bees – and the low, grey-green leaf of creeping thyme. "Si, a ruler's life is not an easy one," Catalina murmured.

"You don't know the half of it, child. Times like these dagger the queen's good heart." Beatriz pulled out another dandelion. "Child, I do not mind dandelions. As I have told you, boiled in water and left aside to sit for a time, they make a useful drink that helps us void our bladders." She grinned at both Catalina and María. "The French call dandelion not only Lion's teeth but also Piss in Bed – a good name too. They do their job that well. But this plant needs controlling otherwise they'll take over an entire garden. If I left this any longer, I fear all the precious herbs used for doctoring would be in a bad state. Already, dandelions draw to themselves all the moisture in the earth."

Catalina planted her hands on the warm, rich earth. "You talk of other than simply dandelions, Latina..."

Beatriz grinned at her bright student, yanking another weed out from the earth to add to her pile. "More things grow in the garden than the gardener sows or desires. Child, a good ruler is a little like being a good gardener. Gardeners are often called on for decisions that bring them pain. Not long ago at my home at Salamanca, I gave permission to cut down a dozen good trees in my orange grove to give the remainder a better chance for a longer and more productive life."

Catalina absorbed her words while the eyes of the old mother flashed into Beatriz's mind. What real harm did she hold for them?

The words she spoke to Catalina seemed so hollow – so wrong.

Beatriz rubbed her face. *Do not cry, do not cry.* How many times she had spoken to the queen in recent times? Reminding her of the golden age, when Christian, Moor and Jew all worked together for the advancement of all. It was not perfect, nothing ever is, but it showed what could be done. "God Himself tells us a kingdom divided against itself cannot stand," she said, trying to remind herself, as well as offer some comfort to Catalina. "Your mother has tried hard to solve her kingdom's troubles ever since she first came to the throne. Now she is ill and worn out. She fears for your brother, Prince Juan. She wants him to inherit a strong and unified kingdom."

"So she commands the Jews to become Christian or else leave Castilla."

"Believe me, 'twas not an easy thing for her to do. The queen realises she is indebted to many Jews. From the first days of her rule, powerful Jews formed an important part of her government. She knows the debt she and Castilla owes to them, especially men like her finance ministers, Abraham Seneor and Isaac Abrabanel. She begged them – so many times – to convert. Some Jews have –the loyal Andrés Cabrera for one. It is my thought that being the governor-general of Segovia and married to Doña Beatriz de Bobadilla helped here. The queen rewarded him richly. She would have done the same for the other Jews, if only they converted."

Catalina bit her lower lip. Beatriz lifted her eyebrows and heaved a sigh. "Your question, child?"

The girl looked all around, as if making certain there were no others in the garden. "Do you think she's right to do this?"

Beatriz attended to the herbs for a moment, hoping to hide her sudden tears. "Your mother believes herself right, that God Himself means for her to do this. You know God's will is the stone on which her whole life is built." Beatriz pulled out another weed, another, and another. "For your mother, and for so many others, the divine right of monarchy is as real as this garden we see here. To doubt it places doubt upon her entire rule. But I see the woman behind the queen and know, even if she refuses to own to it, how this daggers her brave heart."

Straightening up again, Beatriz heaved another sigh and rubbed her hands from the top of her thighs to her knees. "My whole life revolves around questions." She reached for Catalina's hand. "I trust you with the truth. I want to speak to you as I would to one full-grown. Infanta, my heart tells me that only time and God will tell us whether our queen judged right for her kingdom.

"But I give thanks to our Almighty God. I'll never be forced into a position like my queen. In my life I can expect to cast out just weeds and other unwanted plants from a garden such as this. I can sleep at night and, if not, a hot elixir of Valerian will soon put me to right. Not so with your mother. She sleeps hardly at all."

Weeks plodded by, and the royal family remained at the Alhambra for the hottest weeks of summer. Despite the sunlit season, recent events still darkened the infanta's spirits. Catalina's capacity for joy was such that she usually surmounted her sadness during the day, but her nightmares increased at night. Beatriz tried to keep her occupied with new books, but it seemed her nightmares began to keep her company during the day too. Even her companion María could not console her. Depressed, Beatriz felt as changed as both girls.

One day, Beatriz brought Catalina and María to one of their

favourite places, the seats set near the fountains in the Hall of the Lions. For a time, Catalina just sat, saying nothing and staring out ahead. Sighing, Beatriz read again the lines engraved around the fountain. Hoping to raise a smile from Catalina, she read the poem aloud. Like the water pouring down in the huge marble bowl, her words flowed in musical rhythm:

In appearance water and marble seem to confuse
themselves, not knowing which of each is flowing.
Do you not see that the water spills into the basin
But its drains hide it immediately?
It is a lover whose eyelids brim with tears,
tears which hide in fear of a betrayer.

Catalina groaned, as if the poem tore down her fragile defences. Beatriz turned. She clasped Catalina's hand when she saw her sorrowful face. "Speak child. Tell me what disturbs you," she said.

Catalina lifted her chin, sucking in her top lip. She shook her head as if in sudden anger. "I cannot tell you..."

Beatriz gazed all around – only wide-eyed, listening María and the growing shadows kept them company. Beatriz squeezed Catalina's hand. "You can." She called María to her side. "Child, go to my chamber and get the book on my table. We might as well do our lesson here."

María gone, Beatriz turned back to the infanta. "Tell me what troubles you."

The blue shadows under her eyes speaking of her broken nights, Catalina took a long breath through her nose, and lowered her gaze. "My father is a liar," she muttered, before clamping her mouth shut, screwing up her face, as if she tasted something vile.

Beatriz rubbed the side of her head. *So she knows. But what lie does she speak of?* She wondered if this intelligent child finally acknowledged her father's mistresses. How could she not? At court, his bastards outnumbered those of his children born in wedlock. Beatriz shivered. She would rather not think about the king, ever. But she caught Catalina's restless, unhappy gaze, and took a deep breath before posing her next question. "Are you talking about your father's women?"

Catalina winced. "No. 'Tis more than that, Teacher," she whispered. Bowing her head, she gnawed back and forth at her thumb knuckle.

"More? What more, child?"

Shielding her face with a hand, Catalina shook her head, making a tortured sound. "My father is a liar." She gazed up with desperation, her eyes begging Beatriz to say otherwise. Beatriz looked away, fighting a temptation to lie herself, but unable to. "Why do you say this, Mi chiquitina?

Without meaning to, Beatriz called the girl the name used by the royal family. As the child's tutor, she avoided using it. Catalina didn't notice Beatriz's slip of the tongue. Perchance it no longer mattered, and she didn't care.

"It is not because of God he wants the Jews gone. My father wants the Jews' gold."

This did not surprise Beatriz. "That could not be your mother's reason," she said quietly.

Catalina shook her head. "My mother does this because she believes it's God's will, but not my father." Catalina snatched Beatriz's hand. "He must have good reason. Perchance he believes he does do it for God too, if pushing the Jews out makes his kingdom richer and stronger. 'Tis right that they do this for my brother – one kingdom is hard enough to rule, let alone two."

"It could be that..." Beatriz chewed over what she knew of the king. Si, he hated the Jews. Si, wealth was important to him. He loved the power it gave to him. Whilst the queen built her whole life on serving God, the king built his on gold. No, she didn't think King Ferdinand used religion for any other reason than as an excuse to achieve his own ends. But looking at Catalina, seeing how the child trembled, Beatriz stayed silent.

Not many days after this, an awful event caused Catalina to lock away her doubts about her father.

"Catalina!" With only one attendant behind her, Princess Isabel burst into the school-room. "Catalina!" Princess Isabel rarely raised her voice, but now she almost screamed. The princess looked white, her huge eyes wide with fear.

Catalina bounded up, her haste toppling over her stool. Wood resounded against the floor, the sound punctuating a moment of silence.

"Come." Princess Isabel struggled to catch her breath. "'Tis Father... they have bought him to his chamber..." Isabel closed her eyes, her mouth moving as if in silent prayer, before looking again at her youngest sister. "An assassin tried to kill him. He is alive..." Princess Isabel raised her hand to rub at wet eyes. "Sister, our father is gravely wounded. Mother wants us with her. We must go."

Deciding her place was with Catalina, Beatriz told María to stay in the library and practice her writing, Beatriz followed after Catalina and Isabel. The closer they came to the royal apartments, the closer to turmoil. Men scurried about and ran down the long corridor. Passing one of the royal physicians, Beatriz glanced into the silver bowl he carried. A blood soaked white doublet lay within it.

Outside the door of the king's bedchamber, a crowd of courtiers stood close together. Seeing the daughters of the queen, they bowed and cleared a pathway to the closed doorway of the king's most private room.

Beatriz gazed over her shoulder. *Should I go back?* She wished she could but, despite her hatred for the king, she couldn't forsake Catalina. Following them, she closed the door after the princesses and froze. Beside the unconscious king the queen knelt holding his hand while her children huddled in a frightened knot behind her.

Arms up to his elbows covered in blood, Guadalupe, the king's favourite and most trusted physician, bent over the bed, tying the bandage firmly across the padding on the king's right shoulder and chest. A smaller, similar padding covered his neck. Blood seeped through the cloths. Guadalupe stood to his full height, rubbing his face with blood-spattered hands. "The wound's serious, my queen. Four inches long and almost as deep. But I don't believe it has touched the nerve and spine."

The queen, keeping her eyes on the king's face, whispered, "I must pray." She clasped her hands. "Dear God, it is true kings die by accident like others. We believe we are ready to face death, but trials like this teach otherwise. God, in your mercy, do not let it be time for your servant, my husband, to be taken from us. God, do not take him from me..."

In the following days the queen and her children stayed by the king. His fever worsened until the day it gripped him utterly. Beatriz remained in the school-room. Never had she felt so conflicted. She did not care if she left the king's physicians without the benefit of her expertise and advice. When she tried to pray with the court, knowing the crisis had come at last, the words were ash and meaningless in her mouth. She wanted to curl up on her bed and hide from the world.

Like most mornings the dawn song of birds woke Beatriz to a new day. For a time she lay in bed, fearing what this day would bring. Dressing, Beatriz stepped lightly to Catalina's chamber. Disturbed at seeing only María sleeping in the bed with Catalina's side untouched, she made her way back to the king's apartments.

A courtier outside the king's chambers told her the news. Hours before, King Ferdinand's fever had finally broken and he had asked for food. All the royal family remained with him.

She entered the large, inner chamber next to the king's bedchamber. Before she reached the door of the king's most private room, she paused, hearing the pure voice of Prince Juan close by, singing like an angel:

> *Glorious king, true light and clarity,*
> *Almighty God, Lord, if it please You,*
> *Be a faithful aid to my companion,*
> *Because I have not seen him since the night came,*
> *And soon it will be dawn.*

Beatriz looked towards the room's embrasure. A haze of golden light enveloping both their forms, the prince sat with his sister Isabel across the other side of the room in the deep window seat. Isabel gazed out the window, her long, golden hair uncovered, knees drawn up, as her brother, his head lowered, played his vihuela and sang. They were so engrossed in their own private worlds they didn't notice Beatriz across the room. Like a bee to pollen the prince's beautiful voice drew her in. She leaned against the wall, letting the dark shadows cloak her, listening to the prince:

Fair companion, are you sleeping or awake?
    Don't sleep any longer, but softly rouse yourself,
    For in the east I see the star arisen
    Which brings on the day, I know it well,
    And soon it will be dawn.
    Fair companion, I call you with singing:
    Don't sleep any longer,
    because I hear the bird sing
    Which goes to seek the day through the woods,
    And I fear that the jealous one may attack you,
    And soon it will be dawn.

Prince Juan looked out at the breaking day with his sister. "I wish my songs were as good. To write one song to last down the years, as this song has, is to have immortality."

"Father will be soon well enough for you to sing to him." Isabel spoke automatically, as if not really attending to his words.

Juan lowered his head and let out an odd sound. He put the

vihuela down beside him, his hands gripping his upper legs. "Well or unwell, Father has never liked me singing to him."

Isabel swung around. "Is that important when we praise God for giving back our father? What is a song, brother, long lasting or otherwise, compared to Father's life? At least this hasn't proven to be a death-watch like when I lost Alfonso."

Juan reached and clasped her hand. "Isabel, you mistake my meaning. It goes without saying, I thank God for our father's life. Perchance I have true and better reason to thank Him. For days I have feared I might be called to take Father's throne."

Isabel turned back to the window. "And if you were so called? Fear or not, 'tis your place to take up our Father's crown. 'Tis your duty. Just thank God that you've more time to ready yourself for it."

Juan picked up his vihuela and stared at it. "What if I am never ready for it?"

The prince looked drawn, pale, fearful. Beatriz began to steal away, going closer to the bedchamber of the king. All the time Beatriz kept her eyes on the prince, hoping his sister would offer a word of comfort and chase his sadness away. Isabel did not move, but kept looking out the window.

My love,

Pray, forgive my evil writing – my hand cramps from an afternoon spent translating a book I discovered in the library. A very difficult task it proved, too. The book is old and written in poor ink – some of the pages are almost impossible to read. But it is a valuable book, all about disorders of the blood. It is far too important not to try to save.

We have moved to another alcázar *– one better suited for King Ferdinand's convalescence. He recovers slowly. Queen Isabel told me she feels like she has been to Hell and back. She prays daily for her family to be spared more grief. She does not think she could withstand any harder trials.*

Like many men forced to remain inactive, the king is often short-tempered with his family. The other day he muttered angrily, "Isabel. I am not Lazarus. Do not treat me as if I have been raised from the dead!" He was angrier still when she replied, "To see you suffering, my husband, was more than I could bear. I deserved to suffer in your place... I would have, if God had allowed." Forgive me, love. I know you respect the king, but I wish he could look beyond himself and see how ill his wife is – and the great distress and fear of his children...

Beatriz lifted her head. On her table, the candle flame flickered and danced in a draught, and wax dripped down the length of the thick candle. She sighed. Catalina was an utterly altered child since the threat of death touched her father. Normally a child who claimed happiness in the school-room, now she just came and attended silently to her books. She never brought up again that her father was a liar.

16

How beauteous is this garden where the flowers of the earth vie with the stars of heaven! What can compare with the vase of yon alabaster fountain, filled with crystal water? Nothing but the moon in her fullness, shining in the midst of an unclouded sky!
~ Arabic inscription on the walls of the Alhambra

Beatriz drooped and panted for breath, the heat of the day stifling her in the school-room. Seeing the pale faces of Catalina and María, she decided to end their Latin lesson, packing up their books, quills and writing equipment.

"Pray, could you not tell us a story?" entreated Catalina. Locking up her moveable desk, Beatriz thought longingly of an afternoon siesta. All she wanted was something to eat, and then to fall into bed, whiling away at least one hour of summer heat in slumber. But still she laughed. "Do I need to ask which one?"

Catalina's eyes lit up, her tiny feet jigging on the tiles before doing a dancer's turn, with one arm flung up, the other across her waist. Beatriz gave a sleepy laugh followed by a longer yawn, envying again the children's boundless energy after hours of study, and pleased to see Catalina's zest for learning making her happy and zestful in other ways.

María interjected. "Please, my princess, could it be my favourite story this time? The one about the three princesses locked in the tower?" Since listening to stories meant keeping their hands busy in other ways, María skipped to collect their embroidery frames from their exile at the side of the closed door.

Catalina tapped her mouth with a bent index finger. "All right, my choice of story for another time. But remember, my turn next. Shall we take our embroidery to the Hall of the Two Sisters?"

Beatriz forced herself to stop yawning. "A most fitting place for storytelling." She gathered up the books about Alexander the Great and Charlemagne from the table. Tossing back her head, she laughed. "So we go from the tale of the king gifting his beloved wife a field of almond snow to that of a faithful daughter. Perchance my next lesson should not be history but give thought to the use of metaphors in fable." She took care to place the books in their rightful places on the library shelves. When she faced the girls again, she smiled at them teasingly. "Did I say I agreed to this?"

Catalina and María laughed, and Catalina grinned. "Good teacher, have you ever refused us a story?"

Beatriz planted her long-fingered hands on her narrow hips and pretended to think. "Now, give me a moment to cast my mind back." Catalina and María exchanged looks, grinning at one another. Drumming ink-stained fingers on the soft folds of the black velvet habito, she pursed her lips, as if preparing to whistle. "I have been your teacher for three years. Surely there has been one time when I told you girls no?"

Chuckling with mirth, Catalina shook her head. "Never! And for that, Latina, we're both grateful. No other compares with you as a storyteller. We never get enough of your stories. They're a perfect reward after a hard morning's lesson, si, María?"

María nodded vigorously, turning begging eyes upon Beatriz.

Beatriz tilted her head to one side, fighting laughter. "You never get enough? I would have never guessed! But with praise like that from you, my infanta, Doña Catalina, one day Queen of England, how can I refuse?"

From the library, Beatriz walked with the girls to the Hall of the Two Sisters. Soon, the murmur of water fountains melded with the soft pad of slippered feet upon the tiles of paved coloured marble. The cheerful chime of running water returned Beatriz's thoughts to the Moors, awed anew by the creation wrought by their skills and labours. Here, as in so many of their alcázars, they created a paradise on Earth, rendering beauty from word to reality.

Water came down from the surrounding high mountains to the River Xenil. Building the Alhambra, the Moors had drawn from myriad tiny streams to make a system of aqueducts throughout Granada. Another alcázar of gardens and fountains and the most glorious alcázar in all Castilla, high-ceiling chambers, honey-combed walls and archways melded together water, light and shadow, rendering the Alhambra a place of wonder, a place to nurture their very souls.

Beatriz eyed the inscriptions on the nearest wall: "There is no conqueror but God" and "Your God is one God". Similar sentiments echoed upon the other walls too. Everywhere she looked the walls of the Alhambra gave voice to man's reaching out to God, man's love of God. The words built a bridge of man's faith to a God of love and seemed as real and solid as the tangible stones that built the Alhambra. Years of long study had brought her to the belief the Moors worshipped the same God as Christians. Heavy of heart, she sighed. What right did they have to believe the Moors wrong? Did God really belong only to those who called themselves Catholic? A cold finger smote her. If she ever spoke her thoughts she knew what people would call her: Wicked! Evil! Sinner! Blasphemer! Repent, or you'll end in Hell.

The light showered upon her and she felt disembodied, as if her spirit broke free from her body and she became one with the haze of light, seemingly veiling the air itself. She shook her head and returned to her body, back into the moment. She had no sense of evil here, rather the Alhambra deepened her awareness of God. Slow, reflective weeks at this citadel of the Moors made her feel whole.

She remembered her father telling her of his grandfather, a son of a learned rabbi, himself a descendant of the great Samuel ibn Nagella. Converting to Christian faith in young manhood, he had told his grandson that God was God whatever name man —whether Jew, Christian or Moor – gave Him. Many roads journey to the same destination, to God. Gazing around Beatriz pondered this, wondering whether men able to create such beauty truly deserved condemnation. The Alhambra sang a song of love and praise to the inner life of man, and spoke of eternity. Many times, walking along this same way, through the shadows of the arches, Beatriz sensed the watching ghosts of Moors, as if they held her presence somehow accountable. Perchance, this was the truth. She belonged to a people who had robbed this beauty from others. What gave them the right, when the Moors had wrought this beauty with their own hands, hearts and souls? Her people lived here only upon sufferance. They had no right to call this home. Beatriz felt a darkness falling on her spirit – a darkness as black as crow wings. In her mind flashed the memory of crows picking at death's leavings on the edge of battle. She shivered, her heart as cold as the marble chilling her feet through her thin slippers.

Around the Hall of the Two Sisters exquisite tiles decorated the lower walls. Each one a work of art in its own right, some bore the escutcheons of former Moorish rulers. Above the tiles, interwoven with rich gilding and lapis lazuli gemstones, stuccowork formed large plates of arabesques. On the plates was written text from the Koran or verses from Moorish poetry. Sometimes she read the words out loud to the girls. She prayed that Catalina would one day understand:

> *My heart has become capable of every form:*
> *it is a pasture for gazelles*
> *and a convent for Christian monks,*
> *and a temple for idols and the pilgrim's Kaa'ba,*
> *and the tables of the Torah and the book of the Quran.*
> *I follow the religion of Love.*

Beatriz brushed tears from her eyes. All she ever wanted was to understand. She gazed up at the cupola. Gentle golden light imbued the Hall of the Two Sisters and rendered it restful, but it was a serenity her conscience refused. No matter where she looked, voices of the former owners spoke from the walls of the alcázar, proclaiming loudly, *What you take, you never own.* To live in such ill-gotten beauty, tarnished by years of war and destruction, so often stole away her peace.

She led the girls to the far side of the chamber. They sat on a low ottoman, directly below an inner balcony belonging once to the harem. She gazed up, once more disturbed by fleeting shadows. Phantoms lingered there, up in the balcony – ghosts of beautiful, jewelled women, with slender wrists, ankles and waists encircled by chains of gold.

Half shutting her eyes, she imagined them gathered on the balcony, brushing and braiding each other's hair, threading tiny jewels in their long dark or fair tresses. One ebony-haired woman turned her way. Spreading out long, henna-stained fingers, the woman's deep-set, dark eyes stared down, her mouth clamped shut in a thin, straight line. Beatriz blinked, and saw a black skull, eye sockets embedded with fiery jewels. Hatred touched her soul. She blinked away the vision and trembled.

The girls waiting for their tale, Beatriz shut the door on her thoughts and lounged back on the cushions of her ottoman, closing her eyes. "Years ago, there lived in Granada a king named Mohamed El Hayzari, meaning Mohamed the Left-handed. His people named him thus because he used his left hand rather than his right, or perchance because he always conducted his life the wrong way around and was continually in some kind of trouble."

"Your sister Juana is left-handed, too," María whispered to Catalina. Frowning in annoyance, Catalina shushed her.

Beatriz opened her eyes. "Shall I go on, María?"

The rebuked child wiggled in discomfort. "Forgive me, Teacher.

I will be silent."

Beatriz smiled, all lightness again. "I am but teasing, little Doña. Now, where was I? Si, he was a brave king and managed to keep himself upon his throne no matter the trouble he brought on himself and his people. And not forgetting us Christians. When Mohamed was an old king, he rode with his people in the foothills of Elvira. It was spring and even the old find it difficult to stay always within stone walls..."

As she told the story, she found herself drawn to the cupola. Light. There's always light. She looked at the girls. Si, light. Both the girls were that. Lights piercing through the darkness of her life.

17

We do not easily suspect evil of those
whom we love most.
~ Peter Abelard

Not long after the fall of Granada, Beatriz discovered the reason the king detested his second daughter Juana. That same year, María had returned home to welcome her newly born brothers, Pedro and Ferdinand – twin boys, as if God gifted back to her mother two of the babes lost to her while in service to the queen. María's father, with Francisco, still fought Moors who refused to admit defeat. When María joined her family to celebrate the births of her brothers, the queen sent Beatriz to accompany her, knowing she missed her friend too.

She came for another reason. Queen Isabel had also brought forth twins into the world and almost died in doing so. The first twin, her daughter María, came into the world easily, but not so her sister. It took two days of dreadful agony before the queen, near to death, brought forth her dead babe. Queen Isabel, remembering that experience and how close her cousin came to dying three years ago, wanted Beatriz to assure her all was well and remained well for her cousin.

Arriving home, little María found her mother and grandmother ready with gifts for her – for the most part, additions for her clothes chest, gowns or undergarments to replace those outgrown since the child's last visit home. Largely, the clothes were once worn by her older sisters – made anew by a new collar, girdle or sleeves – but amongst the gifts were two garments made especially for her by her mother and grandmother. María's grandmother gave her a chemise, one so sheer Beatriz wondered if she had made it from silk. Seeing the fine, skilful embroidery at neck and hem, she thought it fit for the queen or her daughters.

María gasped with happiness when she opened her mother's gift. Josefa had cut down one of her favourite court gowns to her daughter's size, making it a smaller copy of the original, yet leaving seams for room for the child to grow. The last cords tied on the gown, María turned to her mother's mirror. Beatriz recalled Josefa in this gown, her long, thick, black hair adorned with pearls, hanging in a plait down her back, one of the few times she ever did so, going against her usual choice of keeping her hair veiled under the toca. Black hair, dark eyes, olive skin, all melded with the red velvet gown and made her a paean of beauty. Now, Beatriz saw the same promise in Josefa's daughter.

Day-by-day, Josefa recovered her strength. Beatriz and María spent much of their time in her chamber, keeping her company while she lay abed, wet-nurses now attending to the needs of her sons. Early one morning, María asked what was often in Beatriz's mind. "Mamá, why does the king hate Juana?"

Working on a new chemise for the queen, Josefa stitched with care, her needlework a labour of love, readying it for when Beatriz and María returned to court. Her dark eyes rose again, considered her daughter, then fell to focus on the seam. Shifting closer to the candle near the bed, Josefa squinted at her sewing, leaning against the pillows.

"Do you think it hate?" she murmured.

Shrugging, María thoughtfully traced the thick lines of black embroidery on the scarlet brocade covering her mother's bed. "The king's cruel to her, Mamá."

Beatriz lifted her eyes from her own slow sewing, watching Josefa's needle dart almost as fast as a hummingbird in search of nectar. Her friend's needle flew in and out of the silk chemise, in and out of the sheer material, the white fabric so fine she saw Josefa's hand moving underneath it, every stitch tiny and neat. Beatriz shook her head, overwhelmed by the speed with which she sewed the seam. Her friend came to the end of her thread and sorted through her cards, seeking the same colour. "I am growing careless in my old age. Where did I put it?"

María picked up the card from the edge of the bed and handed it to her mother. Josefa beamed a bright smile that restored youth to her pale face.

"Thank you, hija. You asked about the king and the infanta." Josefa considered her daughter. "We shouldn't question the rights and wrongs of the family we serve."

María nodded, but grinned teasingly at her mother. "But you told me to keep my eyes and ears open to serve them better." Smoothing out the brocade of her mother's bed, María appeared all at once saddened. "Sometimes, my princess cries at night because of her sister. I don't know what to do."

Threading a needle, Josefa glanced at María, her eyes full of compassion. "From the time you toddled around my feet, you found something to mother – a kitten, a rabbit, and let's not forget all those half-dead mice you saved from our kitchen's cats – and then you were only scratched for your trouble. I'm not too certain if it wise to also wish to mother the infanta."

Not waiting for her daughter to answer, Josefa rubbed the side of her head. "Child, life is full of unanswered questions. Men and women are the same in this – none of us ever find all the answers we seek. Methinks, I agree here with the priests, only by suffering do we truly gain understanding. But suffering also means casting aside innocence about life. I do not wish that for you yet."

María clasped her mother's hand. "I see it in your face – you know the answer. Tell me, I beg you."

Josefa frowned, bringing her dark brows together that they almost seemed one. "I do know." She pursed her mouth, her eyes darkening. "A simple thing, my María, and a great misfortune for the infanta. Juana inherited too much likeness to the king's own mother."

María stared, startled. "The king speaks well of his mother. I have heard him many times. He speaks words of love."

Not looking at her daughter, Josefa lifted her chin and shook her head a little before exhaling a longer breath. "Santa María, must I really explain?"

"Please, Mamá."

Josefa raised pained eyes. "What can I do with a child who

asks such questions?" She sighed again, and leaned closer. "This is something you really must know?"

María stood there, a knuckle at her mouth. "I think so, Mamá," she said slowly.

Josefa smiled at her daughter tenderly. "You're right. You should know the truth. Words, hija. Beware of words. Just because the king speaks, that does not mean he speaks the truth. Juana is too alike her grandmother, in looks and intelligence. The king can hardly bear it. He stifles her, perchance because it seems to him he finally has power over his mother. You are right to say he is cruel. In the right soil, Juana could grow into the best of both her parents. As it is, her own father twists her spirit into deformity. I fear for her."

Beatriz dropped her sewing in her lap, staring at Josefa, horrified at her friend's words. Also floundering, María swallowed, saying what Beatriz was thinking. "That's not fair. She is not his mother!"

Josefa twisted her heavy gold thimble around her thumb. One of the presents Beatriz had brought for Josefa from the queen, the arrows of Isabel's regalia engraved the thimble's circumference.

"We know that. But I do not think the king cannot stop himself recoiling from the constant reminder that Juana presents to him. It is hard for a man, especially a man like the king, to know he will never measure up to his own mother, her strength and intelligence makes him seem small. He is intelligent, but good, sound cloth does not compare to cloth of gold. He has few of his mother's gifts to call his own, then he marries a wife also more gifted than him... With his hijas, the king ensures he keeps an upper hand and they remain well and truly in their proper place. Perchance, child, the king deserves our pity and our prayers."

"But, Mamá, he is cruel... and always to Juana. Always to her!"

Josefa reached for her daughter's hand. "Si, I know, my child. Remember, I saw it for myself when I lived at court."

María shook her head, snatching back her hand. "Why does the queen not stop it? She could if she wanted to. Juana cowers whenever her father looks at her."

Josefa's well-shaped brows came together again before she resumed stitching. Moments passed, and then she lifted dark eyes brimming with sadness. "The queen cannot."

Blinking, María scratched her head. "Mamá, you become cross with Papa when he is angry with us for no good reason."

"By God's good grace, your father and I agree too well for that to happen often. But I am not the queen. Queen Isabel must present a united front with her husband – not only for the reason of their family, but also for the well-being of their kingdoms." Josefa took a deep breath. "Know this well, my hija, great woe falls upon a house divided. An enemy within is more dangerous than an enemy without." She glanced at her daughter. "Do you understand my meaning?"

María nodded, the explanation continuing to pour forth from her mother without her needle stopping once. "If people ever saw cracks in their relationship, my hija, that would be enough to plant the seeds of rebellion in men's minds. Always the queen remembers the road she must walk to ensure the survival of her marriage. So much depends on it.

"I know the queen's heart desires not to sacrifice her children for any cause, not even to safeguard her unity with the king, but she always has to think of the greater good. She first must be queen. For that, 'tis the mind that must rule over the heart. Believe me, she tries hard to be a good mother to all her children."

"You speak the truth, Josefa," Beatriz said quietly, moving to the table close to the draped window.

Josefa threw up her hand to clasp the side of her head. "Good Madonna, help me, you've that look in your eyes. Pray, not another of your vile concoctions you want me to drink?"

Beatriz laughed, holding up a wide neck urine flask. "And here I thought I pleased you by putting honey into all your medicines. Your complexion's far too pale for my liking, Josefa. I would like to see your urine."

Josefa settled against the pillows, her gaze rising to the ceiling. "By all the good Saints in Heaven! I am only pale because you refuse me permission to leave this chamber. I grow stronger with every new day."

Beatriz laughed. "Because you follow my instructions." She placed the urine flask on the chest near her friend's bed. "There's no hurry, but just give me a fresh sample when you next void."

Josefa grimaced. "I don't know what you expect my urine to tell you."

"Nothing, I hope. But many years of peering into urine flasks and using my nose and eyes has taught me a great deal." She smiled, glancing at María. "One day, I hope to share with your daughter some of my hard-earned knowledge."

"Me, Latina?" the child piped.

Beatriz lifted up the child's chin with her ink-stained fingers, and smiled. "Your eyes are round as twin plates."

Gathering her sewing on her lap, Josefa studied her daughter before turning back to Beatriz. "You know María's tender heart. We may be wrong, Beatriz. She may not be the wisest choice for this. She hates the sight of blood."

María's eyes darted from Beatriz to her mother. "Blood? I don't understand."

Josefa returned to her sewing, her needle neatening the neckline of the chemise, and spoke softly. "Latina wants you to learn from her to be a healer, and I have agreed."

María blinked, and her mouth fell open. She gazed at Beatriz and her mother, bewildered.

Glancing at Josefa, Beatriz laughed. "Child, why the surprise? Your mother and grandmother are both skilled healers. They have already taught you a great deal, more than you know. But, si, I plan to teach you. When the infanta leaves for England, it will relieve the queen's mind to know you safeguard the Princess Catalina with such skills. "

Josefa's dark eyes became deep wells of anguish. She gazed long at her daughter before glancing back at Beatriz. "I do not wish to think of this – my youngest hija forever gone from me, far away from her family, alone and exiled in a strange land..."

Beatriz sat on the edge of the bed and clasped her friend's thin hand. "You know the day will come."

Josefa tossed her head back as if combating something unseen. "But not yet for many years." She spoke so quietly it forced Beatriz to lean closer. "Too soon she will be gone from here, and I will see my child again only when the good God and the queen permit. Let me enjoy her while I can without remembering there will come a time when she is gone from me in this life..."

Beatriz stilled, her thoughts caught between one moment

and the next. She stood, going to the chest with a selection of her glass medicine bottles. She straightened them in a row, exhaled a deep breath and pulled at her girdle. Turning to Josefa, compassion filled her heart. "Change is one of life's realities, and farewell is just a part of it, the long and the short." Beatriz gazed at little María. The child seemed all ears and eyes. "Like you and the queen, I do my best to prepare the children to deal with change. That's all we can do."

María turned back to her mother. "Mamá, but what of the infanta Juana? The queen must help her."

Beatriz eyed her friend. Josefa gnawed with worry at her lower lip, turning it cherry red, but gave a brief nod. Beatriz rested a hand on María's shoulder. "She cannot. The queen shamed the king once and she promised him never again."

Her face bewildered, María raised her thumb to her mouth. Josefa glanced at her daughter and pulled the thumb away. "Beatriz, tell her," she murmured, returning to her sewing.

Stepping into the light streaming from the un-shuttered window, Beatriz picked up one of the medicine bottles, put it down, picked up another, put that down. Rubbing the side of her face, she sighed. "You know the queen's word is sacred to her, si?"

The child nodded.

"What I tell you happened when your mother and I were younger than you... I heard it from my father so many times, sometimes I see it in my mind as if I witnessed it myself."

"You speak for me too." Josefa shrugged. "It's such an important story in our good queen's reign, likely we're not alone in this."

Beatriz grabbed a stool near the bed and sat down. She

clasped María's hand. "You know our king and queen are cousins, si?"

María nodded. "Mamá told me."

"Did she tell you that the king also had the right to claim the crown of Castilla?"

Shaking her head, the child seemed to ponder this. "But the queen is queen…"

"Si, the queen is queen, thank our good God for His great mercy, but the king offers no thanks to God for it. When King Enrique, her brother, died, our queen found herself alone, her husband gone to aid his father in his wars. As soon as she knew of the king's death, she acted without hesitation, seizing the throne in her own right. King Ferdinand, still yet a prince of Aragon, was with his father when word came to him of the death of the King of Castilla. By the time he joined his wife, she had already had her coronation, a magnificent coronation when all the nobles of Castilla recognised her as queen."

Josefa spoke. "Our queen rode a white horse given to her by your grandfather; your father's own favourite war stallion comes from the same bloodlines. Mounted on his horse before her, don Gutierre de Càrdenas held forth an upright naked sword, the ancient symbol of the ruling monarch's judicial power over all. Si, the power of life and death, set in a young woman's hands." She shook her head in wry amusement before cutting the thread from the chemise with her teeth. "Furious, the king arrived back from his father's wars, ready for another kind of battle. Your grandmother attended Queen Isabel then. She told me he hurled at her the words of homage he owed to her as queen like ringing stones, asking through stiff lips to be alone with her. Once alone, the shouting began.

"Mother said all the court would have heard the king's anger if there had not been two chambers before the Queen Isabel's bedchamber. Your grandmother, alone and close by in the next chamber, feared for the queen's safety. The king was that angry."

Discomforted, Beatriz crossed her arms, pressing her fingers into her forearms. "The king likes not to be crossed…"

Josefa's head snapped up. "Nor does the queen, Beatriz." Beatriz met her friend's eyes, feeling as if she had been slapped.

"I did everything to keep him at a distance." Brushing away tears, she lowered her head. "I have no power in this. Everything I do works against me, Josefa."

"Why are you crying, Teacher?" María asked.

Josefa stared at Beatriz. "By the sword – the fields have eyes and woods have ears." She lifted her chin and looked at her daughter. "Your teacher weeps for a matter that does not concern you, María."

Beatriz swallowed and then spoke quickly. "María, do you remember what we discussed before we left court? 'Man is active, full of movement, creative in politics, business and culture. The male shapes and moulds society and the world. Woman, on the other hand, is passive. She stays at home, as is her nature. She is matter waiting to be formed by the active male principle.'"

"Aristotle's Politics!" María squealed with delight, looking over to her mother for her approval.

"Si, we spoke about the power of such works, and the great power they have upon our poor female lives." Beatriz crossed her arms again. "Sometimes, I think I am drawn to Aristotle's writings because it gives me much cause for dispute and argument." She laughed a little. "If only to myself. But think, child. What must it have been like for the queen to seize her rights when men have had such thoughts and still have such thoughts? And not only men! Most women, lacking the education to know any better, submit wholeheartedly to them too. When the queen married her cousin, I feel certain he believed he strengthened his own claim to the Castilian crown, not that his wife would see her marriage to the Prince of Aragon strengthening her stronger claim, and decide to act upon it quickly when the opportunity presented itself."

"But the queen is the rightful ruler..." María looked bewildered.

"Si, we see it that way now, only because we know what kind of queen she is, but at the beginning of her reign, nothing yet was proven except the queen's great determination and ability to draw the right men of power to her. Even as a young woman, many knew she possessed a lion's heart. She needed that and more to convince her husband she did what was right."

Josefa rested her sewing on her lap. "The king knows that now, I am sure of it. He respects her more with every passing year even if his passion for her is no more. He is a good king in that regard –able to recognise that he is stronger because of their partnership."

María shook her head, gazing at her mother and then at Beatriz. "But the infanta Juana? I don't understand why the queen cannot help her."

Beatriz leaned closer to the child. "Believe me, I speak only truth when I say she does all she can. But the queen's marriage ran afoul of rocks when she sailed ahead and seized her throne without her husband, without waiting for him, and not wanting to wait for him. She gained a kingdom, but almost at the cost of her marriage. It took months before he calmed down and saw reason. By then, she promised him he would always have the final say when it came to their children."

Josefa started sewing again – this time, beginning an edging of red arrows around the queen's chemise. She spoke without looking up. "Our good queen keeps her promises to those she loves, even when it causes her pain."

Later that day, Beatriz was alone with her friend. "You must stop the king," Josefa said.

"Don't you think if I knew a way, I would?"

"Amiga, if it was me, I'd leave court. While you stay there, you are far too close to the fire for your own safety."

Eyeing her friend, Beatriz sat on a stool near the bed. She rested an elbow on its edge and cradled the side of her face. A miasma of morning light stripped Josefa of all colour.

"Why should I go? I've done no wrong. In any case, both the queen and Francisco would want to know why. They would not understand me leaving when they know how much I love teaching María and the infanta." Beatriz shook her head. "And how can I tell Queen Isabel the reason? I never want her to know – it would kill me. 'Tis bad enough that he always threatens to tell the queen the truth about me." She laughed bitterly. "A truth he forced on me."

"He lusts for you more because he knows you have no lust for him. It crazes him, causing him to burn for you even more."

Beatriz rubbed her wet eyes. "You think I don't know this? When he raped me the first time, his threats and strength backed me against a wall, and I mean a wall, until I could do no other but submit. He has made me into his whore, Josefa, except it is I who pays. I the one to live with shame."

"End it, amiga."

Beatriz clasped Josefa's proffered hand. "'Tis not as simple as that. I wish it was."

"We are women, si? You're intelligent. Don't tell me at your age you do not know how to make a man stop lusting for you."

Beatriz shrugged, defeated. "I am a woman, si… I curse that almost every day of my life. But what of his threats? How can I ignore them? What if he follows through with them?"

"Threats? What threats?"

"Si, his threats to remove me from teaching the infantas, prevent me from teaching at the university. These positions are everything to me, Josefa. God forgive me for my weakness, but take away those two things, and you might as well take my life too. He took my body, my virginity, and I prayed he'd leave me alone. It wasn't enough. Whenever he wants to pull the string, he reminds me he has the power to strip everything from me, and this puppet must dance. I thank God I am not his only woman. Most of the time he finds another mouse to play with, and he leaves me alone. Thank God too I have never conceived his child."

Josefa sniffed. "My amiga, have you thought to speak to the queen's confessor? 'Tis possible he might help you."

"Si, I've thought of this."

"Then why not go to him?"

"A simple answer: Hernando de Talavera does not like me. I asked him why and he told me bluntly I am a weak woman, greedy for knowledge, one of the greediest he has had the misfortune to ever meet in his long life. He disapproves of me so much, I hesitate to give him true cause."

Josefa tightened her grip. "Si, like so many men cut from that cloth, he never forgets we are hijas of Eve, but I am surprised you have taken upon yourself his disapproval of all women. Do not let yourself be hurt by this. You should know the queen is the only female he allows himself to like and respect. Still, Beatriz, the father is a good priest, and I believe he would help you, if he can." Josefa spluttered out a strange laugh. "The good father has a tender heart when it comes to sinners. The more we sin, the more he loves."

Beatriz tried to smile. "I will think more of it, amiga. My father knew Talavera well when they taught together at Sala-macha. They were good friends. He remembers me from when I was but an infant, in my mother's arms – more memory of her than I am blessed to remember. My father told me Talavera gave him much comfort when she succumbed to the plague."

"Surely that gives you even more cause to go to him for help?"

Round and round, Beatriz traced with her index finger a spiral on the bedcover. Unchecked, her tears fell, spattering their pattern as if following the finger's wake.

"What is it, Beatriz?" asked Josefa.

Beatriz raised her hand and wiped her face. "I'm not sure if knowing him from childhood would help me here. I remember too well the many harsh words he and my father had over my education. He believed my father was very wrong and misguided in his desire to teach me as he did."

"The good father would not have been alone in this. Very few women are brought up to be prodigies of Latin."

Bitter, Beatriz gazed at her friend. "Even you expressed strong disapproval of this."

Josefa heaved a sigh, shaking her head slowly. "'Tis not that I disapprove… I have told you this before too. I believe women walk a hard enough road without walking a road where there are pits at every step. As my mother often said to me, since we cannot get what we like, let us then like what we can get. Tell me truthfully, Beatriz. Do you think you'd have this awful hole dug for you, as you do now, if your father had not set your feet on this journey to become a scholar and professor of the university?"

Beatriz pondered Josefa. "Si, I am in an awful hole, as you say. But, Josefa, I know there are more terrible and darker holes. I will always be grateful to my father for giving me the key to escape ignorance, even if it only came from his great need to console himself after losing my mother."

Josefa placed her hand over Beatriz's. She gave her a wry smile. "Escape ignorance? You know many ignorant women, si?"

"Josefa, you mistake my meaning." Beatriz stared at the coverlet of Josefa's bed. "All of us must walk our own roads, but 'tis wrong to prevent women from walking so many roads just because we're women. Even Plato said, 'Nothing can be more absurd than the practice of men and women not following the same pursuits with all their strengths and with one mind, for thus, the state instead of being whole is reduced to half.' I so agree. Our world cuts off its nose to spite its own face by insisting the only purpose for women is to bear children and perpetuate the human race, as also said Plato. Surely 'tis far too hard a view to forever blame women for Eve's sin."

Josefa frowned. "But, Eve's sin brought death to the world and condemned women to suffer."

"Perchance you can see it that way. But our Lord Jesús welcomed women as his followers. Whenever I feel defeated, I keep that in mind and remind myself that the good lord knew women possess minds as well as hearts and encouraged them to use them. If our saviour believes this, then it must be right. That's why I believe learning for the young to be so important. For not only do most of us then discover the road we are meant to walk, but good learning also hands a child a light to guide them all their lives. Just because a child is female, does it mean she should walk in the dark?"

"Si, I understand, Beatriz. But perchance my feet are more on the ground than yours. I am not at all certain that learning, as you give my María and the queen's hijas, will make their lives any easier."

Beatriz laughed. "Easier? My good Josefa, have I ever said learning makes living any easier? But to be taught to think is to be taught to truly live."

Josefa lifted her dark eyes. "And I believe he who knows how to live, knows enough. 'Twas not until I was a grown woman that I began to have the learning you speak of. 'Twas not because I doubted the fullness of my life, but because the queen asked me to learn alongside her."

"Do you regret it, amiga?" Beatriz asked.

As if weighing her answer, Josefa slowly shook her head. "No... I appreciate having now the words to describe so much that once eluded me like a mirage eludes us in the desert. But still, my amiga, I remember the prayer of the good Saint Francis,

'Lord, grant me the serenity to accept the things I cannot change.'"

Beatriz laughed. "Perchance you, Josefa, are the wisest of us two. I cannot tell what must be changed and what must be accepted as unchangeable. I just charge ahead into the dark, carrying my little bit of knowledge before fear gains an upper hand, pulling me back. But despite the winds of life often pushing me the wrong way, I am farther along the road than I was when I first started my journey."

Rubbing her forehead, Josefa sighed. "And we are no further along than when we began this conversation, to no good purpose, amiga. You must find a way out of this cesspool before the dam breaks and carries you away with it. I fear so much for you."

Beatriz reached for her friend's restless hand. "Don't. I tell you truly, talking of bulls is not the same as being in the bullring. Life has taught me well how to survive my dance with my particular bull. Even if I must humiliate myself to do so, I will extricate myself from the mire before the flood comes."

18

The male is by nature superior and the female inferior; one rules
and the other is ruled.
~ Aristotle: *The Politics*

"I require and charge you both, as you will answer at the dreadful day of judgment when the secrets of all hearts shall be disclosed, that if either of you know any impediment, why you may not be lawfully joined together in holy matrimony, that you confess it. For you be well-assured, that so many as be coupled together otherwise than God's word doth allow are not joined together by God, neither is their matrimony lawful."

Sunlight struck Beatriz's indigo wedding dress as the priest's words drummed in her ears. Clutching at her cloak to cover her gown, she looked aside at Francisco and consoled herself. *One of us is happy. Pray God, Francisco would always be this happy. Let the ceremony end before I run away.*

Standing near the church door with Francisco, his grown

children and a few of his friends as witnesses to their wedding, she once more confronted her uncertainty about marrying him. Si, she loved him, but could marriage change her life just like Francisco's artillery changed the landscape of the war? *Pray God, I am barren.* She stared at the elderly priest and then at Francisco. *Did I speak that out loud?* Swallowing, trying to slow her breathing, her rising panic became difficult to contain. *Surely Francisco's three children means he would not miss having more?*

"Will you have this woman to be your wedded wife, to live together after God's ordinance in the holy estate of matrimony? Will you love her, comfort her, honour and keep her, in sickness and in health, and forsaking all others, keep you only unto her, so long as you both shall live?"

Francisco's smile after he said his firm "I will" began to calm her. He doted on her, was proud of her. He promised to place nothing in her way to prevent her from keeping her position at court, and the university. He would not make that promise to her unless he meant it. His years of patience, waiting to marry her, surely proved he was a man of his word.

"Will you have this man to be your wedded husband, to live together after God's ordinance in the holy estate of matrimony? Will you obey him, and serve him, love, honour and keep him, in sickness and in health, and forsaking all others, keep you only unto him, so long as you both shall live?"

"I will," Beatriz murmured. Gazing at Francisco, she swallowed, speaking the words louder. Wedding Francisco offered the best solution to her problem of the king. The king admired Francisco. He was not likely to pursue a woman married to a man he called friend. The rest of the ceremony seemed a dream. It still felt like a dream when they feasted with his family and friends at Francisco's home. The little she forced herself to eat lacked taste and made her nauseous. Hiding her disinterest in the festivities, her eyes kept returning to her wedding ring. A plain band of heavy gold, it fitted tightly around her finger. *Don't be a fool. The ring is not already leaving its mark on you.*

It was after midnight before she was alone with Francisco in his candlelit bedchamber. The night was cold and the fire in the hearth burned sluggishly. Francisco, now in his shirt and hose, went to the fireplace to stir it back into life. The embers glowed red and he carefully arranged twigs before placing a small log onto flames. Mindlessly, Beatriz began to undo the cords of the low neck of her gown. Glancing up, Francisco grinned, rose from the fireplace and came over to her. "Let me do it, love."

Standing with him so close, watching his busy fingers, Beatriz felt a lump in her throat. Francisco was a good man. A good, good man.

Her untied gown fell to the ground. She shivered in her thin shift, and crossed her arms over her chest. The neck of her shift was so loose it threatened to drop from her shoulders and expose her breasts. Francisco grinned again. "We are married, love," he said.

Gently, he took her arms away from her body and the shift fell almost to her waist. Cold air puckered her breasts with goose bumps before Francisco's warm hands cupped them. She stood there, gazing at him, aware of her partial nakedness, his hands on her body. He pulled her into his arms, kissing her mouth, first one side, then the other, his tender lips slowly claiming hers. *Thank God, thank God, the king never sought to possess my mouth. Don't think of the king. Don't let him destroy your wedding night.*

Just think of Francisco. It is time to experience what it is really like between a man and woman.

Francisco released her, loosening the drawstrings of her shift so it dropped to the floor from her naked body. He studied her for a long moment, and Beatriz raised her hands to her hot cheeks. As if she weighed nothing, Francisco gathered her in his arms and carried her to the nearby bed.

He put her down gently on the bed and pulled his shirt over his head. Stepping out of his hose, he almost bounded on the bed beside her. Lying on his side, keeping a little distance between them, he turned her to face him. Francisco traced a finger from her temple to the side of her mouth. "My beautiful wife," he said, before kissing her again. This time, she kissed him back, first experimentally, then with greater confidence. He tasted of honey, and a hint of good wine. When his tongue went into her mouth, she drew her head away in surprise and looked at him, lifting an eyebrow. "You've never done that before," she said.

"If I had, I would have found the years of restraint too hard. You didn't like it?"

"I don't know." She moved her face closer to him. "Pray do it again and let me decide."

Kissing him again, she found her mouth opening to his. The feeling of his tongue in her mouth stirred her. Without thinking, closing her eyes, she began to do the same to him. Her heart drubbed fast in her ears.

Francisco pushed her back down on the bed. He must have felt her tense up because he smiled, caressing her face again. "Don't worry. I have waited too long for this day to spoil it now by hurrying. We have tonight, tomorrow night, all the nights of our lives. I want you to want me as much as I want you."

Francisco stroked from her cheekbone to her neck, his finger following an unseen line to her breast. Smiling, he traced its large areola, and her nipple hardened. Francisco lowered his head and kissed her breast, before sucking the nipple softly. She moaned a little, a strange feeling beginning to course and pull in her woman parts, making her move closer to him. He gazed up at her, grinning like a youth. "You like that, love?"

Trying to chase away her shyness, she smiled back and reached up to touch his face. "And what do you like, Francisco?"

He smiled again. "That answer can wait for another night. We have weeks before us for you to learn what I like." He cradled tenderly the side her face with his broad hand. "Tonight... tonight let me show you men do not always hurt. I want you to know true lovemaking is about mutual pleasure, not pain. I want tonight to forever cast from you the memory of being ill-used."

She placed her hand over his mouth. "Shhh – do not speak of it." Her hand going behind his head, she pulled him closer to kiss him. Her mouth seemed to dissolve into his. She felt his hand go between her thighs and opened them up to him. She froze when his fingers slipped into her, but became relaxed and loose-limbed at his gentle touch. She laid back, letting his skilled fingers give her sensations she had never known before.

"Is this the sin the priests warn against?" she murmured, her blood coursing with sweetness and delight.

Francisco laughed. "The priests can go hang. I will never call loving my wife a sin." His lips went to the side of her neck, kissing from just under her jaw to where neck and shoulder joined. She gave a moan, and he kept kissing and sucking gently at her neck until she embodied pure pleasure. His erect penis pressed into her side when his gentle fingers entered her again, this time with greater ease. Aware of wetness between her thighs, she tossed her head back, shut her eyes and moaned.

"Are you ready for me, love?"

She turned, met his eyes, and took a deep breath. Unable to speak, she nodded.

Francisco shifted his body over hers, and opened up her thighs to kneel between them. Skin touching skin, she felt a moment of surprise at his hairiness but, unlike her past experiences, he only hurt a little as he eased himself into her body. She wound her arms around him, her hands caressing his back muscles. He began to move, and she found herself moving with him. A flash of memory. Strong, vice-like hands tearing at her clothes, refusing to let go, forcing, hurting, debasing. *Hear me. I deny you now. You will not destroy this moment. You are nothing to me. Nothing.*

She began to move rhythmically with Francisco, her pleasure intensifying. Beatriz felt swept on a wave taking her beyond the constraints of physical flesh to where Francisco and she fused, as one.

A lull in the flare ups of fighting between Christians and Moslems meant Francisco expected to stay at court for several months. Beatriz still tutored Catalina and María in the mornings, but now spent most of her afternoons with Francisco. Often, they would go into the countryside. Her hands already ink-stained from teaching, she dirtied her hands even more by helping him experiment with small parcels of gunpowder and small hand weapons he had designed. She had designed something too, thick woollen hats with earmuffs to protect their hearing. Francisco had burst out laughing at seeing them.

"I'm not too certain if I can wear these at the battle-front," he told her. "But I'll wear them here for you."

Their nights were also happy times – when they washed from their bodies the grime and smell of sulphur, and Beatriz began to welcome marriage and the love she shared with her husband. Mornings, she returned to the school-room to share with Catalina and María what she and Francisco had learnt that day from setting off their explosions. There was another reason she roamed far with Francisco from court. Francisco remained at court because the king remained too. Beatriz prayed her marriage would finally end the king's eyes falling on her with lust, but lived in terror lest she discover otherwise.

Birds chorused a morning ode to spring, the silver wash of a young day spilled out into the hall – pooling a path of light, one leading Beatriz to the outside garden. Alone this morning – Catalina, accompanied by María, commanded by the queen to talk with her after their early morning devotions – Beatriz wandered into the courtyard. There, wide archways encased her in a thousand shades of green shadow. Everywhere butterflies flittered and drifted around the flowering vines. Festooning blossoms, coloured pale to deep and bold, adorned a garden already glorying in the first weeks of spring.

Beatriz stepped deeper into the garden, her movements breaking apart the silver light. A few butterflies flew close to her face, the wings of one tickling her nose in passing. A haze of showering light rendered them into flying, living sapphires, their wings edged with bright rubies. Laughing with simple joy, Beatriz spun around, watching their beauty vanish into the dark recesses edging the garden. She stood there, her palms upraised, grieving again for beauty lost. She wanted to rail and weep at her empty hands. *How long must I wait to see them filled?* Then she scolded herself. She had so much more than most women she knew.

A man's laughter frightened her, and she stepped back into the dark shadows, breathing a sigh of relief when she saw, seated on the far edge of the wide rectangular pool, the man called the Italian. His form half in shadow and the other half in light, he lifted a hand and beckoned to her. "Good morrow, Latina. Come. Come and speak to me."

Curious, but also cautious, Beatriz padded closer to him. She kept her gaze fixed on him, stopping when only half a dozen steps separated them.

The man laughed again. Stretching out his long, thin legs, he considered her. "Strange, isn't it, that I have been back at court for months now, and this is the first time we have really met? I remember seeing you with the youngest daughter of the queen, the day the Muslim king came out of the gates of this beautiful alcázar for the last time. The day the banners of Castilla and Aragon were lifted high on its towers. The day the queen made yet another promise to me. I hear you are the tutor of the youngest infanta."

Beatriz smiled. "Si, since before she was five."

He tossed back his head as if surprised, the moment casting dark shadows on his face. A man in his forties, there also seemed an air of youth around him. He peered at Beatriz more closely. "You know my name?"

Treading on the dry leaves beneath her feet, Beatriz listened to their crackle, and then looked at him, remembering seeing him with the queen before the fall of Granada. "Si, I know your name."

Cristóbal Colón rocked a little, rubbing the heels of his hands on the sides of his black tights, where leg joined body. He took off his black velvet cap and put it beside him, scratching the thinning, reddish-white hair on top of his head. "You have an advantage over me. The La Latina is all I know of you. May I ask you for the honour of your real name?"

"Doña Beatriz Ramirez, recently known as Doña Beatriz Galindo."

Cristóbal Colón considered her again.

"Is your husband Francisco Ramirez? He who serves the queen as one of the men in charge of the gunpowder?"

Beatriz smiled. "The queen calls my husband one of the bravest men she knows. He left two days ago to return to his work."

Cristóbal Colón boomed out laughter, slapping his legs with a resounding smack.

"Why do you laugh, senor? I speak the truth."

A wry look settled on Cristóbal Colón's face. He rocked again before he spoke, crossing arms over chest. "Forgive me. The laughter wasn't directed at your good and most esteemed husband. No, I laugh at myself. Heed my words of warning, Doña. The queen is good in feeding us what we want to hear.

Perchance she means what she says for your husband, but for myself, I am no longer so sure. There have been far too many promises made and not kept, all mixed with too much honey." Cristóbal Colón gazed around the courtyard.

A fragrant place of peace, the arched entrance and the blossoming vine mirrored itself on the quivering pool of water. The drift and flutter of hundreds of butterflies were captured too on the forever-changing water's surface. Cristóbal Colón shook himself, as if ridding himself of his own visions.

"'Tis time for me to leave this place. I have wasted too many years waiting for the queen to make up her mind and keep her promises." He shifted in what seemed to be anger. "Look at me now. Cast aside for yet another morning with excuses, the queen too busy to see me. Si, left to audience with her child's tutor. By God's good name!" Moved into sudden action, he lumbered up to tower over Beatriz. "But all is not wasted. This morning has served to clear my mind about what I should now do. Others in France or Genoa will listen to me. I shall leave for Códoba today." Picking up his cap, Cristóbal Colón turned and bowed. "Farewell, Doña Beatriz Ramirez and thank you. I doubt we'll meet again."

Beatriz stood there, watching him stride away. Oblivious to their beauty, his passing unsettled a crowd of butterflies amongst the flowers flurried into the air, they flitted and interwove a dance around him in the morning light.

Later that morning, Beatriz resumed her Latin lesson with Catalina and María. She selected for Catalina a tract of Aristotle while watching María struggle with Galen. The child squirmed beside the infanta and sighed.

Beatriz placed her quill into the inkpot and turned her full attention to the child. "You have a question, María?"

María pushed the open book away from her. "Too many. He writes of the three principal members – heart, brain and liver – but I cannot understand his explanation about how they control everything in our body."

Beatriz smiled. "You are reading *On Natural Facilities*, si?"

María folded her arms, her face puckering her annoyance. "Of course, Teacher! You told me to."

Catalina, pressed against María's side, piped up, "But Aristotle says 'tis the heart controlling all."

Beatriz clapped and burst out laughing. "First, my student and now the princess." She turned to Catalina. "Aristotle is firstly a philosopher, my young scholar. Philosophers spout theories like the Earth awaking to spring – whether they're right or wrong... that's for you decide. You're free to spout theories in their stead. I would be very disappointed if you didn't.

"María's tract, on the other hand, comes from Galen, a physician from hundreds of years ago. Again, life will teach her to agree with his theories or not." She smiled at the girls. "Believe me, they are only theories. Stepping-stones flung out by men and women from humanity's own journey, for their children to stumble across in search of truth. But I think Galen might be flinging out the right stones. Healers work so much in the dark, we need help to find stones, some substance to set our feet upon."

María scratched her scalp underneath her roundlet. Pulling the book back under her nose, the pages opened to a complicated anatomical drawing inspired by Galen's teachings, the child looked ready to weep. She looked up at Beatriz. "There is so much to learn, Latina. I'll never know it all."

Beatriz twisted on her stool, leaning towards the child. "Do you think I do? I don't – none of us do. But think, and look back at the many hurdles you have now behind you. You've gone over so many since our first days together. Child, let the hurdles behind you now encourage you to go forward. One day, I promise you, you'll thank God you didn't give up. You might even thank me."

The doubt on María's face made Beatriz smile in reassurance. "You learn here the difference between life and death. The queen has every confidence in you, as does your mother. And I, of course, possess no doubt you'll one day be a skilful healer."

María glanced at Catalina, murmuring quietly: "Teacher, is it true the queen feeds us what we want to hear?"

Beatriz stared at her, hearing again the words of Cristóbal Colón. "Who said this to you?"

María lowered her head. "Forgive me, I heard you speaking to Cristóbal Colón in the garden. I did not mean to, but the queen told me to go back to you."

Catalina lifted her gaze from the book, a frown puckered between her brows. "What do you speak of?"

María swallowed in her confusion. "I heard Latina talk with Cristóbal Colón this morning. He told her he has had enough of waiting and will leave the court today."

Beatriz cocked her head to one side, tracing a circle on the polished wood of the table.

She inserted a triangle within the circle, crossed both circle and triangle with a determined line straight through the middle before she stopped doodling and instead drummed the table with two ink-stained fingers. "Cristóbal Colón is a man who wants his own way –and now, not tomorrow." Her gaze fell back on María. "Child, do you think he told the truth? Or was just venting out his frustration?"

María sat straighter, her eyes shining with delight. Beatriz hid her smile, pleased that her question made the child so happy. Scratching her head, María licked her top lip. "He said the words as if he meant them, Latina."

Beatriz remembered the man in the garden, a seated man turned into one of action, disturbing the garden's tranquillity and its butterflies by his sudden departure. She sighed, thinking the child was likely right. She gazed over María's head and rubbed the back of her hand across her mouth. Coming to a decision she stood, the wood of her chair screeching its protest against paved tile, flinging her trailing skirts over one arm.

"The queen needs to know this," Beatriz said. "Keep to your lesson while I tell this news to Santángel. Only yesterday he told me the queen is thinking seriously to sponsor Cristóbal Colón in his quest."

Catalina glanced at María with a shrug of her shoulders, and returned, without speaking, to her book.

Beatriz returned to the school-room near the time they usually ended their morning lesson.

"Did you find Santángel?" María asked her.

"Si, in the queen's chamber." Beatriz swallowed. "The king was there, too, playing chess with Fonseca." She felt her cheeks flush with heat. "The Count of Tendilla, Ponce de León and Gonsalvo of Cordoba watched on while Santángel spoke to the queen alone. You know how serious a game of chess is to the king – I did not dare at first to speak, but then the queen herself directed a question to him about Cristóbal Colón. She wanted the king's thoughts on the matter." She smiled. "Fonseca took advantage of the king's distraction, made his move, saying, 'Your Highness's queen has acted like a rash navigator. She has come too close to the abyss and the black hand is about to seize her.'"

Fascinated by the story, Catalina put down her book, and even María leaned closer. "What did the king say?"

Beatriz shrugged. "What do you think the king said when he came close to losing? He asked the Devil to take the Genoese. But by then I had told the queen what you told me. Once the king had won the game, she told him there would be no great risk in granting Cristóbal Colón his desire. When the king agreed, the queen summoned a page and told him to mount his horse and ride until he overtook Cristóbal Colón, and tell him she had appointed him Admiral of the Ocean."

Time passed. In summer of every year, Beatriz attended her duties at the University of Salamanca. Gone for over two months, she missed Catalina and María, and her husband, although he was often not at court, but at the battlefield. The long weeks at Salamanca returned her to her two charges full of zest and fire. Distracted with writing new treatises, she sat the girls down and read her work to them, treating them like true scholars. She knew this was true for Catalina, but María often struggled with boredom, especially when they detoured into areas of no interest to her. But Catalina was still determined her friend would learn, whether she liked it or not. Sometimes, Beatriz thought María's Latin and knowledge improved simply because of that, rather than because of her skills as a teacher.

Now that the girls were older and able to read and write Latin and their mother tongue with ease, Beatriz handed over some of Catalina's learning to the Italian Geraldini brothers, scholars of high calibre who the queen employed to teach her children.

Catalina enjoyed the younger Geraldini's lessons. One day, Beatriz found them at a table spreading out a large map, Geraldini's black eyes flashing in excitement. "Princess, this is what we knew of the world yesterday, but today?" He stood tall, waving dismissively over the parchment. "Princess, the return of Cristóbal Colón changes the world as we know it. This map is worthless now. Remember this day always, for 'tis not every day man discovers a new world and transforms the old forever." He barked out a laugh. "Thank the good God the noble queen, your mother, honoured me by allowing me to speak to her of my countryman."

Less than one year ago, Cristóbal Colón had sailed to what many believed promised certain doom. Most called him loco, but from the day of his return, Geraldini never let them forget he was one of those to gain the queen's ear, helping Cristóbal Colón obtain what he most desired – the money for his ships. When he returned, he more than paid his debt to his royal patron. He opened the door to a new world of unbelievable wealth.

That very morning, wagons full of treasure struggled their

way to the old alcázar at Barcelona, perched high over the city. The donkeys' high-pitched screams, men whipping then to pull them up the steep road, ripped apart the quietness of dawn, and heralded later events. Not long after noon, the queen and king commanded the court to their presence chamber.

Unusual smells greeted Beatriz when she entered the chamber – sweet, rich and spicy, thick and heady, all wafting towards her. Set against the walls, squawking monkeys threw themselves against the wooden frames of their cages whilst jet-eyed, rainbow-coloured birds, their bright colours putting the colours of the court to shame, cawed incessantly and competed with cries of excitement from men and women.

The royal family gathered below the dais of the queen and king. Her widow weeds making her slenderness painful to see, even the Princess Isabel seemed full of wonder as her mother relished the tangible harvest of Cristóbal Colón's voyage, strange animals, strange food for her to taste, and much, much gold.

Six silent, strange men, strange men with red skin, caught Beatriz's eye. Bathed in golden sunlight streaming through the colonnaded arches, the men wore nothing more than scanty loin cloths and painted skin. Wild looking, lithe and wiry, the men had heavy gold rings in their ears and nostrils, feathers and ornaments decorated their long black hair that gleamed with oil. They appeared forlorn, frightened, alien, but still unshakeably proud.

Grinning, Catalina took María's arm and pointed to the men, and María laughed. Beatriz could only see the men's great unease and almost tangible fear. She looked again at the girls. They were so young – so young they forgot that one day they would be just like these men – these men fated to die far from their homes, in exile.

My sweet Francisco,

Has the news come to you about Cristóbal Colón?

Imagine, my love, a discovery of a new world. Two weeks ago, he returned to court, bringing with him great bounty. Birds, treasures from a strange land, even food stuff. The queen gifted me with a necklace from the treasure chests. Its wooden beads, smooth and polished, stained deeper than the colour of blood, reflected back my face like tiny mirrors. My student María received a similar necklace. The older infantas each took into their possession the best of the caged birds, while the infanta Catalina was given a very young monkey. It clung to her as if to its mother, while Catalina cooed and sung to it.

The animal soon became a great nuisance. It was only in the princess's care a day when it snatched María's necklace from the small chest in their bedchamber. Hearing shrieks coming from the infanta's room, I rushed in to discover the animal whipping the beads this way and that way. I tried to rescue the beads for María, but the string snapped, and the beads flew far and wide.

The next thing I knew, the monkey had scurried up the bed-head, and started swinging on the bed-hangings. It screamed like one possessed by demons. Poor María scrambled on the floor, gathering the beads together. The animal must have thought it was game. Dropping to the floor beside her, the animal fought with her for the beads. It became a race between them to see who could pick up the most. At last, the race over, the monkey scurried to the bed to innocently groom itself. María disliked the animal as much as me. I did not envy the girl sharing a bed with not only the infanta, but also her new pet and its fleas.

Day after day, the animal disrupted my lessons. When Catalina answered her mother's summons, María became the animal's lone attendant. Thank God we could call servants to clean up its messes.

Catalina loved the small monkey and took pleasure in its antics. What else could I do but bite my tongue and care for the animal as well?

María found it cold and dead in its basket one morning, no more than ten days after the princess claimed it for her pet. How I regret all my ill thoughts about the animal. How I wish the annoying urchin was returned to life and back in Catalina's arms...

Remembering the death of Catalina's monkey made Beatriz wonder later whether Juana acted wisest of the four sisters about her wild pet. After Cristóbal Colón's return to court, the king found Juana laughing and dancing with her two female blackamoor slaves – and banished her to her rooms until the next day. The king always told her she was far too free with her slaves, but they were her truest companions beside her sisters and brother. Without her siblings and slaves, Juana would have been very alone at court. The king's constant distaste for Juana caused others at the court to shy away from her. Even her mother's attendants did not serve her with the same devotion they offered to the other royal children. Many feared to befriend her because they feared the king.

Summoned to her mother the next day, Catalina gave a

sudden cry of dismay in the school-room. Coming to stand beside her, Beatriz glanced down at the open volume of *The Consolation of Philosophy* on the table, reading: "But now is the time for the physician's art, rather than for complaining." Beatriz gazed at Catalina and recited: "Are you the man who was nourished upon the milk of my learning, brought up with my food until you had won your way to the power of a manly soul? Surely I had given you such weapons as would keep you safe, and your strength unconquered..." Catalina grinned at her before looking crestfallen. She snatched the book from the table. "Latina, this must go back to Juana. Her new tutor, Doctor Miranda, gave it to her for her study and I've kept it too long. I am forbidden to see my sister. Could you please take it for me?"

Beatriz heaved a sigh. If she were Juana's tutor, she would just locate another copy of the book from the queen's well-stocked library. After borrowing it from her sister, Catalina hadn't stopped talking about it or reading its pages aloud. Already, the girl knew passages from the book off by heart. Like many before her, Boethius's doctrine spoke to her. Catalina wanted to believe she also had the capability to survive the ill winds of fortune, and often talked about how God used fate as a tool to shape them. Of all the queen's daughters, Catalina was the one to truly love knowledge for knowledge's sake. Her intellect grew apace with her age and more. Knocking on the heavy wooden door of Juana's bedchamber, Beatriz heard no answer. She opened the door. Deeper in the large chamber, the inner doors opened wide to the balcony. Padding inside the room, she saw Juana looking out on deep valleys awash with pale oceans of mist. Dawn's light tempered the girl's form in soft light.

The wind blew stronger and whined, twirling Juana's long,

dark hair, up and down, the thin strands of her tresses slithering snakes around her white face like Medusa. The wind's power pulled taut the folds of Juan's red *habito*, accentuating tiny waist and maiden breasts, lifting the gown skirts to reveal narrow, naked feet. Between her breasts, hanging on a black ribbon, a red ruby flashed and winked with light. Passed down many generations, her grandmother had given the ruby to Juana on her twelfth birthday.

Juana's air of grief halted Beatriz halfway into the chamber. The girl opened the golden cage of her small parrot. Beating rainbow wings against the cage, the bird squawked.

"'Tis wrong to keep beauty caged, 'tis wrong to cage living things," she said, stroking its feathers. Calmed by her touch, the bird perched on her hand, fluttering a little. Tenderly, she drew it out of the cage. The parrot ruffled feathers and fluttered wings.

Juana let out a cut-off sob.

"I can no longer bear to see you so unhappy. God gave you the gift of flight..." she flung out her hand in half an arch, "... be free and fly."

Flying a short burst, the parrot first settled on the half wall of the balcony. Juana rushed towards it, weeping with heartbroken abandon, waving her hands. The small bird spread its wings and flew away.

Juana sobbed, clinging to the lace stone rail of her balcony. In the skies, a small bird flapped its rainbow wings higher and higher until, at last, it disappeared from view. Beatriz stepped softly back to the door, not wanting the infanta to see her, desiring to intrude no more. Her heart sad, she left the room still holding the book. Its return could wait for another time.

19

'El vencido vencido, y el vencidor perdido'
The conquered conquered, and the conqueror undone
~ Castilian proverb

The midday sun beat down without mercy. Light-headed, Beatriz wiped the dripping sweat from her brow, sweltering in her heavy clothes. Her mule sidestepped upon the uneven, sun-parched ground, rocking her violently in the saddle-chair. She tightened her hold on the reins, and heeled the mule to canter to sounder ground. She bit back a curse and then another. The wind gusted strong on the summer-seared banks of the River Tagus, blowing dust into her eyes, offering no relief from the heat.

Juana, the last of the royal family to do so, rode her mule to the other side of the wide river. Waiting for her own turn to cross, impatient for their journey to come to an end and finally to arrive at Alcántara, Beatriz noticed Juana's pale, tense face, and recognised the girl shared her impatience too. The infanta reached halfway across the river. She stiffened in the saddle-chair and swung her mule whip to hit its flank, as if urging her mule to greater speed. Beatriz's heart almost stopped when the animal stumbled into stronger currents. Deep water swished and splashed at the bottom of Juana's saddle-chair. Swaying on her panicked mount, she looked down, then back towards her parents. Juana straightened up in her saddle-chair and tried to regain control of her mule. That very moment, the situation worsened.

"Mother of God!" gasped Juana's duena. Mounted next to Beatriz, the woman watched the infanta, horrified. Out of the river's safe depths, Juana's mount had lost its footing. It staggered, stumbling again, throwing the infanta head first into the deep water. For a terrifying moment, she vanished from view. In the rush of water, her dark mantle billowed like an overblown rose, with its petals about to drop.

Voices shouted out from both sides of the river. Beatriz's young mount surged forward, threatening to bolt. It took all her strength, and two stable boys snatching its bridle, to keep the terrified mule from hurling itself from the bank into the river.

Beatriz swung her gaze back to the river. Juana, her veil and mantle lost in the currents, now clung for dear life to her saddle-chair, angled and tottering on the mule's back. Her huge frightened eyes rendered her a child again, rather than a fifteen-year-old princess preparing to leave her family to become a consort of a prince. The rolling-eyed mule appeared too shocked to move, other than to give way, slow step by slow step, to the pull of the currents. A swirling torrent of water rushed and smacked around its body.

On the other side of the river the queen and king galloped their mounts back toward the water's edge, their three remaining daughters and son close behind them. Catalina bowed forward in her saddle-chair, a hand fanning across the lower part of her face, watching her sister struggle frantically in the river.

Too far away for Beatriz to hear, the queen spoke and gestured to King Ferdinand. Motionless, he seemed to watch some play-acting, rather than the life and death struggle of his own daughter. Turning from her husband, the queen twisted on her mule and lifted a hand. In answer, a stable boy broke from the crowd of men and women of the court and rushed to her side. The queen spoke a command and the boy whipped his mule, charging into the river, hollering out a cry fit for the battlefield.

On the two banks of the river, silence settled over the crowd of courtiers. Everyone watched the youth head toward the infanta. Time stilled, and it seemed to Beatriz that they all took roles in a painting, people in various stances, frozen together, locked in a moment, a breath, that might yet unfreeze to the reality of grief and loss.

The youth wrapped a rope around his waist and attached it to his own mule, and then swam the short but dangerous distance to Juana. He seized the bridle of her baying mule, tugging with all his strength and that of his mule towards safer river depths. Cheers echoed from both riverbanks. A few more heart-stopping moments, and Juana and her mule came close enough to the other bank for a group of courtiers to go in after her. They carried the fainted Juana from the water.

The queen rushed to her daughter's side while the king rode

over to speak to the stable boy. Later that day at Alcántara, the court coming to rest like a stork to its nest, Beatriz heard the king rewarded the stable boy by promoting him to keeper of the silver.

Female voices murmured close by. Hastily making her way back to the queen, Beatriz turned into the hallway and almost ran into Juana, half-in and half-out of her chamber's doorway. Fully recovered from her near drowning three days ago, she huddled with her blackamoor slave over an open scroll. Seeing Beatriz, the slave's head ducked as if a whip threatened her. Christened Catalina by the queen, in honour of her daughter, the Moor took the parchment from Juana, fast closing it before Beatriz saw more than a few well-drawn astrology symbols.

Juana smoothed down her gown, visibly relaxing, and clasped her hands before her. "'Tis but our La Latina. There's no need to worry," she said quietly to her slave. The slave Catalina licked her lips, holding the scroll tight to her breasts, underneath crossed-over arms. Her thin shoulders shook as she glanced around. The terror on her face rendered her far older than just fourteen.

Footsteps echoed down the corridor. Juana grabbed Beatriz's arm, her fingers digging so deep Beatriz yelped with pain. She pulled Beatriz through her doorway. Catalina followed, shutting the chamber's door behind her. Closing her eyes, she leaned against it, the parchment still held to her chest.

"Don't worry, Latina keeps our secrets." Juana glared at Beatriz. "She knows what would happen if she did not."

Beatriz stared at the roll of parchment in the slave's arms. "What is it, Infanta?" As soon as Beatriz spoke the words, she wanted to call them back, wanting to go. For the first time in her life, the infanta frightened her.

Juana took the parchment from the slave "Did you see anything?"

Beatriz shook her head. "Symbols of the zodiac, that's all." The slave released a long, held-in breath. Juana glanced at her. Taking the scroll from her, Juana turned to Beatriz in decision. "I trust you to say nothing of this. If you betray my trust, you'd be responsible for whatever happens – my slave being whipped for one."

Beatriz gazed at the closed door, and then back at Juana. She lifted her chin. "I don't want your secrets, Infanta. Keep them." She curtseyed. "With your permission, I must go to the queen."

Juana took Beatriz's arm again, but gently this time. Her tight smile offered her an apology. "Forgive me, but I do no wrong here." When she glanced at the slave, Beatriz wondered whether to believe her.

With a deep breath, Juana whispered close to Beatriz's ear, "My father has always forbidden me to cast my own horoscope, but coming so close to death the other day, I asked my slave to do it for me. So, I haven't disobeyed the king, my father, have I? My slave did it for me, not I."

Beatriz stared at her in horror, knowing what the king would think. She hoped for Juana's sake the king stayed unaware of that parchment in the slave's hands. Not only did she risk punishment for her slave, but she risked it for herself too. "He forbade you to do this?" Beatriz gazed at the slave. She held the parchment to her as if it somehow protected her. "Why? There's no harm in looking at the alignment of our birth stars. All do it."

Juana lowered her eyes and shrugged. "I know not the reason why my father commanded this, only that he has." She nodded to her slave. "Open the door. Latina will not betray me."

Dearest One,

Pray forgive me for the delay in replying to your last letter, but much has happened since last time I wrote. We have had important visitors at the queen's court. A weary group of Englishmen arrived almost a month ago. After their first welcome, they barely had a day's rest before torchbearers brought them to stand before the king and queen in the great hall. I stood near the royal children, while other attendants spread out at distance from the dais of the queen and king. How the eyes of the men widened at the sight of our two monarchs in their jewels and rich clothes. Upon the dais, sitting close together on their thrones, the queen and king were garbed in cloth of gold edged with sable. Cloth of gold hung behind them too, quartered with the arms of Castile and Aragon and the words of their motto: Tanto monta, monta tanto – Isabel como Ferdinand, *as much as the one is worth so much is the other – Isabel as Ferdinand.*

The queen draped a black velvet cloak, edged with gold and rubies, over her golden gown. With every movement, the queen's jewels shimmered and flashed in torch and candle-light. That night the English fell on their knees and bowed low, greeting Queen Isabel and her husband as "kings". I could not help smiling when my infanta lifted her head with pride.

Much feasting, costly entertainments and long, private meetings with the king and queen followed over the coming days. There is news of more unrest in England. With the support of the Scottish king, the young man claiming to be Richard IV invaded England with his army. He was little welcomed by the English and soon was pushed back into Scotland.

In recent days, the Duke of Milan has written to the queen, asking her and the king to broach Scotland and negotiate with them a peace with England. When the men departed, they took back with them not only gifts for their royal family, but also what the King of England desired: a new treaty for Catalina's marriage.

The infanta Catalina is now formally betrothed. Catalina stood in her mother's presence chamber, and appealed to the papal delegate to allow her to wed before reaching legal age. She then wed England's prince and heir by proxy. Si, still only in her tenth year, my princess's life now belongs to England, and a prince she has never seen...

Their backs slouched against the wall, Catalina and María sat on the wooden bench in the library, listening intently. "How Sir Tristram and La Beale Isoud came unto England," Beatriz read, "and how Sir Lancelot's brought them to Joyous Gard. Then La Beale Isoud and Sir Tristram took their vessel and came by water into this land. And so they were not in this land four days but there came a cry of a jousts and tournament that King Arthur let make –" Hearing Juana call out to her sister, Beatriz stopped reading.

Even so, María's gaze adhered to the illumination of Beale Isoud and Sir Tristram and a dreamy look settled on her young face. The knight and his ladylove was so vibrantly painted, the picture seemed lit from within by myriad candles. *No wonder they name such things illuminations.* The girls had asked her to read to them the story of Isoud and Tristram. She pushed down her discomfort. Perhaps she should have chosen something to help them deal with real life, rather than see them take to heart stories of courtly love.

Catalina glanced aside at her friend. "You need not come." Laughter bubbled in her voice.

"No, no, I'll attend you," María said. Beatriz smiled, shutting the precious book. At ten, the girls strived to act adult.

With her usual impatience, Juana stepped out of the open doorway and into the sunlit corridor. Beatriz studied Juana. Whitewashed walls on either side seemingly caging the girl, Juana's fine black hair was precisely parted down the middle, arranged so carefully, so tautly, conflicted with the flashing, midnight blue eyes and a passionate mouth. Not yet sixteen, Juana was the fairest of all the queen's four daughters. Aware of it, she held this knowledge to her as a shield, sometimes acting condescendingly to her less beautiful sisters. The other royal daughters, content with their own measure of beauty and rarely victim to their father's darker side, understood. The four sisters loved one another. Sharing these last days together, Juana readying to leave her mother's court and sail across winter seas for her new life in Flanders, the sisters seemed closer than ever.

María shuffled her over-large feet away from her skirts, her black, tight slippers doing little to disguise their true size. She looked at Juana with jealousy. Beatriz could not help wondering if María was remembering the painting in the book. The artist had depicted the knight's ladylove with tiny, graceful feet, so alike to Juana's. The infanta, on the threshold of young womanhood, made Catalina and María but pale moon slips set against the bright noonday sun. Juana's zenith was here and now, whilst they still lingered in their dayspring. Beatriz thanked God for it.

"Hurry!" Juana called, looking back over her shoulder. "Mother wants to walk with us while the fair weather lasts."

Stretching like a waking cat, Beatriz arose a trice after her two students, returning the book to the table in the schoolroom. She set it carefully between the other two volumes telling of King Arthur's court. A well-thumbed volume of *El Cid* rightly crowned the three books.

Down the corridor she saw the two infantas and María, waiting for her to catch up. Standing side-by-side, Juana towered over Catalina. Tiny in size... gazing at her small princess, answering her wide smile with her own, Beatriz couldn't deny Catalina was surely that. But she made up for her lack of height in many ways. Already greatness blazed its promise around her – a promise beyond the fleeting beauty of soon corrupted flesh. Si, Juana may be the noon-day sun, but already a new star rose in the dawn's horizon and shone.

A ribbon of unending gold, the sandy beach stretched and curved towards the land-locked embrace of smoke-blue mountains. The setting sun dyed the sea pink and orange. Luminous, it shimmered and swelled, the white froth, streaked and flecked by the sun, going in and out, in and out, onto the beach.

Seabirds flying out to sea changed from white to orange to pink and finally to spots of darkness on the horizon before disappearing from sight.

Despite the evening's chill, Beatriz walked barefoot, holding up her habito from the packed, wet sand. The infantas had also kicked off their slippers. Catalina and María walked together, hand-in-hand. Far behind, her grumbles no longer heard, the infanta María's newly appointed duena carried the girl's silk slippers, protecting them from ruin. Exchanging a quick look with one another, Catalina raced against María de Salinas. Despite her shorter legs, Catalina made it difficult for María to win.

Catalina swung around and grabbed María's hand. Holding up their gowns, the girls danced around and round, making a circle in the sand. María laughed and laughed. Letting go of Catalina, she collapsed on the ground. Half-lying on the sand, rubbing her belly, María gazed up at the clouds and pointed. "Look. A galleon sails in the heavens."

Catalina sat beside her friend, drawing up her knees. Her eyes scanned the skies. "No longer a galleon, see. The wind breaks it apart and turns it into two angels." Her eyes shone. "'Twas a ship of God you saw."

María looked at the clouds, and then glanced first at Catalina and then Beatriz. Shyly, she grinned. "Let me try a poem." She looked back at the clouds, gnawed her lower lip for a moment. "All right. Tell me what you think:

Scattered clouds,
Wisps of cloud
White, billowing clouds
Pregnant cloud,

Life-giving clouds.
Thin streaks of cloud,
Banner cloud,
Shape-forming cloud,
Storytelling clouds.
Clouds made golden,
By bright sunlight
When the sun
Beats against
Dense grey veils
Of cloud."

Catalina giggled. "Far better than your last attempt. We might yet call you a poet." The girls helped one another up, still searching the skies. Beatriz knew it distracted them from what happened now, upon this beach.

A fair way ahead, her arm threaded through her daughter's, the queen walked and talked with Juana. Loosened and lifted by wind, the infanta's ebony locks gleamed with the blue shine of a crow's wing. The low murmur of their voices drifted to them whenever the brisk, chilling wind dropped or the surf pulled back to a quieter roar.

Early next morning, if the weather continued to be good, Juana and a large party from her mother and father's courts would board the ships now waiting in the royal bay of Laredo, the ships that waited to take Juana to her marriage to Philip of Flanders. Before the infanta boarded her ship, the queen would bid the girl farewell, leaving her second daughter to face her future.

"Come," Catalina said. She pulled María along for another

race, their feet sinking into the sand. They faltered when Juana crumbled against her mother. The wind carried to them her unconstrained sobs. Holding her daughter, grief carved upon the queen a stillness none dared near.

Catalina and María clasped hands, looking back the way they had come. Water filled their small footprints, making tiny pools reflecting back the vivid colours of the setting sun.

A few steps away, Prince Juan, the gloaming burnishing his tousled hair gold, coughed behind his hand. Standing with his sisters Isabel and María, Juan, like his two sisters, gazed out at sea, pretending unawareness of Juana and their mother's grief.

Overlooking the bay, upon sandy hills, tall tufts of green grass growing here and there, the family guards stood at watch, archery bows at the ready. Beatriz wondered what they thought, watching this drama enacted on the beach. Queen Isabel held her daughter as if she would never let her go.

Catalina dropped María's hand and looked at Beatriz as if for reassurance. "My mother's afraid. I have never seen her so afraid." She picked up a shell from the yellow sand, tossing it out towards the surf. The white shell arched far in the air before disappearing into the water. Dark storm clouds on the horizon-edged sea and crimson cloud ribbons streaked the sky.

"'Tis being forced to send your sister at the beginning of winter," Beatriz said, gazing again at the ocean.

María spoke the words she dared not voice. "They say the sea crossing is not for the weak-hearted."

Catalina laughed as if discomforted. "Juana isn't weak-hearted. Father says Juana's heart rules her head. She is a slave to her emotions. That's Juana's weakness, my father says." She gazed at Beatriz. Clearly guilty for saying so much, Catalina blustered out, "If only he was here to lift mother's heart. Alas, his soldiers have great need of him."

Beatriz gazed at the grieving daughter and mother and pondered Catalina's words. No more did the child express doubts about her father's motives. It had taken the king many months to recover from the attempted assassination, that and his frequent absences returned him, unquestioningly, to Catalina's loving heart. Far better, Beatriz thought, the king remained with his soldiers. She could easily imagine his black-froth fury at both his wife and daughter for their public display of emotions. On the eve of her departure, Juana especially did not deserve his contempt for her unchecked tears.

Staring down at the sand squeezing through her toes, Beatriz's thoughts pounded in her mind like the surf on this beach. The queen was so alone, so miserable – bereft of the comfort of the man who held her heart in the palm of his hand. He failed her as he did his daughters. Beatriz glanced up at Juan, still struggling to stop coughing. He even failed the prince, giving him a poor example of manhood to follow. Rather than uncompromising, so often pitiless kingship, King Ferdinand would be better to show the prince a loving, compassionate and noble heart. But how could he do this when he lacked those very qualities?

Wretched for the queen but helpless too, Beatriz stepped away from the royal family, picked up two scallop shells from the sand, and studied them. So alike, yet so different, each one shaped by the elements to their own special uniqueness.

She slipped the more perfect shell into the hidden pocket of her gown, and traced the fan of the other, beauty etched in simplicity, humbled at the art wrought by God. It was no wonder pilgrims of Santiago took the shell for their symbol. Not only did Christians love the shell, but once pagans did too. The scallop shell, coupled with the sea, symbolised eternity and rebirth.

Beatriz held the shell up to the light. Watching the translucent fan draw in the colours from the lowering sun, she wondered if she could do a painting of it. She walked slowly alongside the sea, looking at the meandering trail of shells marking the tide of the surf. Why just one? Why not a whole border of shells? White shells emblazoned by light.

In her mind, Beatriz saw her painting take shape, the canvas edged with scallop shells, all of them unique. She looked back at Catalina, seeing her beside Prince Juan, his arm protectively around her. Like the shells, her students too were unique. She made her way back to them, hearing the prince speak: "Is it any surprise our mother's heart breaks? She is worried she sends Juana into danger or worse. But she is queen. 'Tis her duty to let her go, as she will do with all of us."

Without warning, Princess Isabel strode towards the sea, the trailing hem of her black habito becoming drenched by the outgoing tide. She gazed all around, as if seeking a way to escape. She looked aside at her siblings, her huge eyes welling with tears. "Soon, it will be my turn again."

For the last five years, Isabel had devoted herself wholly to God. For five years, she clung onto the hope of taking the veil, despite the continual refusal of her mother and father. Isabel gazed at the sky, closed her eyes, and swallowed. The pulse in her neck beat hard and fast, like a caged, wild bird. She opened tormented, haunted eyes. In spite of the passing years, she had never stopped sorrowing over the loss of Prince Alfonso. It was a grief darkening and eating away at her spirit.

Beatriz clasped the shell in her fist, its sharp edge almost cut into her flesh, and a cold finger stilled her heart. She thought of Francisco. He was so far from her, living day-by-day a life flirting with danger and death. Loving always carried with it such burden, the danger it could destroy as well as give joy. She remembered her father once telling her that love was a two-edged sword. He had never recovered from losing his wife, and died only months after Beatriz left their home. But he also told her when you love – really loved – it becomes part of your whole being, something you never lose. Surely, that was true?

Princess Isabel stepped further into the surf. For a moment, Beatriz feared she wanted the sea to sweep her away. "No more I say! I don't want this duty." Isabel's words were like a scream that competed with the surf.

Prince Juan reached out and enfolded her hands with his own. Coughing, he pulled her back to drier sand. "Sister, sister. Please, I beg you, don't let grief destroy you. Leave this darkness, Isabel, I beg you, and take joy in life."

Tears fell down Isabel's cheeks and dripped onto her neck. She inhaled a deep, ragged breath and shook her head. "Juan, you don't know. You've no notion of how I fight every day to live – and how I hate it when Father and Mother remind me of my duty to marry again. One marriage is all I want, and Alfonso my only husband. I don't want to be ever unfaithful to him – even in memory. I sicken at the thought of another man touching me." Isabel bent her head. "Our lord father tells me Portugal has again said no to María. I'm to marry Alfonso's cousin. Father refuses to listen to me... refuses to give me more time." Isabel closed her eyes tight, wrapping her arms around her body. The coarse black habito, pulled tight about her form, revealed Isabel's years spent in fasting and vigils. Her body was simply taut skin over far too slender bones.

Isabel muttered, her voice tear-drenched, "Castilian princesses never cry without good cause. They do their duty. Duty!" With a savage cry, she opened her eyes and kicked at the sand. "How I hate that word! Hate it, hate it, hate it!"

She whirled back into the surf, stumbling to her knees. The foam licked, eddying froth around her skirts.

Juan lost all colour and left Catalina standing alone, taking his older sister in his arms. Waves splashed their lower bodies, soaking the silk and velvets of the prince's rich robes and Isabel's chosen nun-like gown. They took no notice. Juan, coughing, hugged his sister tight, his own eyes awash with tears. "Hush, sweet Isabel. You who have so often been like a second mother to us four coming after. I wish I could give you true comfort. I cannot. You are the eldest child of our parents. Look into your heart and tell me you never knew this day would come."

Her face hidden in his doublet, Isabel clutched at him like one drowning and spoke with a muffled voice. "I prayed so hard, so hard every day, for this cup to be taken from me."

Beatriz trembled, her heart full of pity, unable to take her eyes away. Isabel had so hoped her parents would relent and allow her to become a nun. Perchance the hope had increased because the queen, who loved her daughter dearly, stalled her husband whenever he suggested it was time for Isabel to face again the marriage bed of diplomacy.

Juan shook his sister gently, helping her to her feet. "Think what your marriage will do – again unite Portugal and our parents' kingdoms. Our parents worked hard and sacrificed much to make their two kingdoms united and strong. You wedding Portugal's king is but another of our mother's sacrifices."

"Mother's sacrifice, Juan?" Isabel laughed with bitterness. "What about me? Brother, it is I who our mother sacrifices." She gazed towards Juana and her mother, and then back at her two sisters who stood nearby, listening, still as statues. "All her daughters are! We are the lambs our parents sacrifice upon the altar of power. Sometimes I wonder if the profession of our parents' love is but the Judas sheep leading us to our fate." Isabel shut her eyes, as if struggling for composure. Catalina's companion, María, edged closer to Catalina's side, clasping her hand.

"I knew Alfonso and loved him. Loved him, Juan! Do you know what that means? I still love Alfonso. My heart belongs to him. Only to him! His cousin Manuel – I barely know him. And I don't want to know him! I curl up inside and die a little whenever I think about another marriage."

Juan gazed towards his mother and his other sister. Smaller in the distance, they walked hand-in-hand, leaving a trail of footsteps behind them. Grimacing, he glanced back over the long way they had walked this evening, to the other side of the harbour where a fleet from the king's navy, two carracks and one hundred caravels and more, rocked in the bay. Even at this distance the wind carried to them the complaint of wood groaning in the sea and sailor songs. Tightening his embrace on his sister, Juan kissed the top of her head, cushioning his chin there. Beatriz gnawed her bottom lip, concerned about the Prince. He was so pale. Taught from birth to take his burden of responsibilities seriously, in recent years

Prince Juan was less inclined to venture out to ride with his sisters. Ritual cloaked almost every moment of his life. From morning to night, it choked his spirit, leaving him increasingly rigid in public and stripped of every ounce of spontaneity. Royalty robbed him of a true season of youth, leaving him far older than his years.

"Sweet sister, Juana goes to a man she has never met. As will María and Catalina. I too wed a stranger, who comes with the return of our father's ships." He turned his face, coughed again, and shrugged. "'Tis the destiny of princes. Look to our parents – they wed only days after meeting one another for the first time. Yet they love truly. We must hope for the same for ourselves. Hope eases our journey in this world. I beg you, Isabel, try to hope, try to believe you can be happy again."

20

And I beg you to be served
By the present treatise
Very perfect infanta,
Furnished with virtues
And prudent at a very tender age;
In much you follow the shining
Great Queen of Castile
Who is the fountain of virtues.
~ Pedro Marcuello's ode to Juana

Beatriz sat in the embrasure with Catalina and her sisters, all of them watching the queen read the letter, the dry parchment crackling as it moved in her eager hands. Concentration scored a frown between her greying, thin eyebrows. Lifting her eyes from the letter, relief lessened the worry lines on her face, and Queen Isabel smiled. "All's well with Juana. Thanks be to God."

The king strode across to his wife, taking the letter. Closing the weak eye inflicted by a cast, he skimmed the page with his good eye. He glanced aside at the queen, his poor eye blinking, readjusting to light.

"More pleasing news, wife. The fleet lost only two of its vessels crossing a winter sea. All is as I hoped, and expected. The ship carrying our hija had the best captain to ensure she arrived safely in Flanders." His eye squinting again, the king smiled and pointed out a line. "Note here, Juana writes they praise her beauty."

Queen Isabel held his arm, glancing back at the message. "And her suitability for motherhood." She swallowed and looked away from the missive, her mouth clenching shut.

The king, his eyes and mouth no longer merry, placed his hand overtop the one on his arm. The queen's fingers clutched his, keeping his hand imprisoned. He frowned.

"Why so glum, Isabel? Be easy. There's no better mother than you, and Juana is your hija. With little time, she will prove these words right."

Any suggestion of healthy colour fled from the queen's face. "Husband, I have told you this before. Juana reminds me too much of my dear mother. She lost her mind after my brother's birth. I am fearful, my lord. What if the same fate awaits Juana? I pray to God we did right to send her so far from us. She needs love and understanding. What if she finds that lacking in Flanders?"

Carefully the king folded the parchment in half, setting it upon the table beside him. "Pray, forget it, wife. You worry over-much for her – for all our children. What will be will be. Making yourself ill isn't going to help matters. Think of the stronger ties we've gained by sending Juana to Flanders. Very soon our son's wife comes, and the ties will be stronger yet. Smile. 'Tis long since I've seen you smile, my Isabel."

The queen leaned on him. Her beautiful green/blue eyes liquid pools, she offered him a tremulous smile. "I am becoming out of practice, my lord. 'Tis good and well I have the company of our children. You're away far too often, and for other causes than ruling our kingdoms and leading our armies. My lord, I beg you, stay at my side…"

Eye to eye with his wife, the king kissed her slack cheek.

"You know I want that too. I am your slave, now and always. But you know our service to God means there's much to do. We're so close to achieving our dream of two united kingdoms for Juan to rule after us. With God's help, the day will soon come when I never need to leave your side again."

"I pray God that day is close at hand, Ferdinand." Espaliered against the king, the queen crossed herself.

Beatriz looked across at the queen's hands, troubled. She wore no rings – gout swelled her fingers to almost double their natural size.

"And our eldest? Is she now ready to show the face of a willing bride? We cannot stall the Portuguese for much longer. Their patience wears thin, as does mine. We have allowed her five years of widowhood – surely that is enough time for Isabel to put the past behind her. The girl gets no younger."

Queen Isabel's anguish shadowed her eyes. She lifted her chin. "Isabel knows her duty. I pray to God we do right in this too. My heart hurts every time I see my daughter's unhappiness."

Shrugging, King Ferdinand removed himself from his

clinging wife. For a breath, she stood alone, holding out empty arms, before wrapping her arms around herself.

"You make too much of it. Marriage and children is what she needs."

Queen Isabel gazed at the king, her brow knotting into a brief scowl. "I pray God you are right, husband," she muttered. Seemingly without any awareness, she dug her heavy crucifix into her breast.

The king turned from his wife and strode to the table, opening another letter. Reading it, his eyes widened, his face loosening and greying to sudden ugliness. His mouth clenched shut and hardened into a thin line. Beatriz met Catalina's wide eyes as the queen rushed to her husband's side. "What is it?"

King Ferdinand folded the letter and put it back on the table. He covered it with his hand. "'Tis no matter. Just a letter from Juana's confessor."

The queen held out her palm, "Let me read it."

They stood there gazing at one another, battling out wills, whilst all in the room watched. King Ferdinand passed the letter to her, glancing across at Beatriz and his silent daughters. "Leave us," he commanded.

Hurrying after Catalina, Beatriz left the room just as the queen gasped. She looked back over her shoulder. Queen Isabel sat on her chair as if her legs suddenly lost all strength, one hand clasped behind her bowed head.

King Ferdinand rested his hand on her shoulder. "I tell you 'tis no matter, Isabel. The girl is safely wed now."

A terrible, raw sob tore from the queen and the letter fluttered to the ground. "Juana. Oh, my Juana! Why can you never think before you act?"

Early the next day the story came to Beatriz. Not from the king and queen – if they still spoke of it, they did it behind closed doors, well away from other ears. But the infanta María overheard the gossip of her mother's women. Distressed, she whispered what she had learnt to Catalina, and Catalina brought the tale to the school-room.

"Do you think your sister has the right of it? How could Philip bed Juana within just one hour of meeting her and before the final wedding vows?" María de Salinas looked a picture of confusion.

The day already warm, Catalina wiped at her sweating face. Sunlight coloured her cream habito saffron and rose, and transmuted her hair to gold. "All speak of it. Your lady mother's so discomforted I think there must be truth in the story. They also say this is what Juana and Philip wanted, and the clerics blessed their marriage," she said.

"But the final wedding ceremony wasn't until the next day. They named it an act of love... of great passion..."

Catalina gazed aside at her friend. "You believe that? My sister says Juana arrived in Flanders very ill. You know what she is like then. Speak one word to her and she growls. Philip and Juana don't even speak the same language. Si, she reads French well, but her spoken French is... impossible. She does not understand the language when people speak too fast."

Beatriz stared at her. "What are you trying to say, princess?" Catalina swallowed, glancing first at Beatriz, and then at María.

"I don't believe this of my sister. Mother thinks she should have used her woman's wit to make him wait until at least the next day and the proper ceremony. But think you, what woman's wit has Juana in this? My sister's not yet sixteen and gently brought up. Now Juana is surrounded by strangers. What choice did she have but to do what Prince Philip wanted? Did she even know what would happen when he took her to the next room – without even the priest coming with them to bless the bed?" She swallowed again. "Seems to me... seems more... like rape..."

She murmured the last words under her breath. Beatriz studied her. In this school-room, she did not avoid telling the girls terrible events from history when royal women had met the refusal of virgin martyrdom, tossing in unbridled legends of lustful Greeks for good measure. Still, she would have expected twelve-year-old maids to shy away from saying the very word. Beatriz shifted with discomfort on her chair, staring at the high ceiling. The gold swirls decorating it made her head spin.

She closed her eyes and saw Juana sobbing like a child in her mother's arms the morning before she boarded the ship taking her to Flanders. Catalina was right. How would Juana have known what Phillip intended? Ah, how she pitied Juana. She no longer had her mother's protection. Her fate was now in the hands of her husband.

"Mother says it hurts the first time, and for some time after," María muttered.

Now Beatriz stared at the blushing María, glancing with apprehension at the wide-eyed Catalina. "She has spoken to you of such matters?" she asked.

María looked at Beatriz in silence.

"María – please answer me."

The young maid squirmed. "My sister wed last year. Mother told Isabel."

"You never spoke of it to me," Catalina said.

Blushing again, María eyed Catalina. "I thought you knew."

"How would I, María?"

"The queen? Your eldest sister?" María offered. The maid glanced at Beatriz. "Latina?"

Catalina reddened now and shook her head. "I could never ask my mother. I can talk to her about so many things, but my tongue ties into knots whenever I think of asking her about what happens abed between a man and a woman. And now she spends all her free time in prayer. How can I ask her?"

"What about the Princess Isabel?"

"Oh María! When I asked Isabel, she bolted from the room. Later, my sister suggested I borrow Juan's copy of Julius Caesar commentaries – written, she said, in very pure Castilian. Like I should strive to be. She told me to exercise my mind by attending to my studies and confess to the priest about thinking of such matters."

María giggled while Beatriz turned away her smile.

"And did you?" María asked.

"Did I what?"

"You know what I mean. Why borrow your brother's book when a copy is in this library? Did you confess to the priest?"

"Of course. He told me to fast and pray with Isabel for God's help to keep a clean and chaste mind." Catalina looked across at Beatriz. "Teacher, could María please tell me what her sister said."

Beatriz looked out of the un-shuttered window. The sky was blue, cloudless. A bird winged to land on a nearby tree and sang its courting song as the tree's green leaves trembled in the breeze. She felt like laughing – in minutes the conversation had gone from disaster to comedy. "We all would need to confess then."

"We confess always. At least this would give us something new to tell the priests," Catalina argued.

Beatriz met María's eyes and they both laughed.

"All right. How about if I leave you two girls alone for a time while I go back to my chamber to find that copy of the Commentaries. I borrowed it from the library yesterday." Beatriz grinned at the two girls. "If there are any areas of confusion, I am certain in my role as your tutor I am allowed to provide answers." Beatriz left the room, not heading to her chamber but to the garden. She heard the call of spring.

Two weeks later, Beatriz hurried with Catalina and María in answer to the queen's summons. They entered the curtained-drawn chamber, one lone candle guttering and smoking in a high sconce. Her daughters Isabel and María trying to comfort her, Queen Isabel wept by a cold, unswept fireplace.

Closing the door behind them, Beatriz took María's arm, leading her deeper into the chamber and farther away from the queen and her daughters. Stepping with María into the window's embrasure, she whispered close to the girl's ear. "We'll stay. Catalina might yet need us."

The infantas María and Catalina now knelt by the queen's side. Isabel gripped her mother's shoulders, her pale face pinched, her eyes flashing with annoyance. "What has Juana done this time?"

The queen sniffed, blowing her nose. She leaned against the intricate carving of the chair's high back. "Not Juana, 'tis nought to do with my Juana…"

Dressed in hunting clothes, Prince Juan broke into the room, his blue eyes searching for his mother. Beatriz started, gulping back a bubble of laughter. Struck in various poses, the prince's men took one look at the scene within. The closest man unfroze and shut the door fast between him and the royal family.

"What's wrong?" Juan cried, his long legs bringing him to his mother in no time. Queen Isabel reached out her arms to him, her eyes welling with tears. "Son, my Angel."

Falling to his knees, he took her hand, gazing up at his older sister. Expressionlessly, Isabel shrugged. The younger infantas nestled closer to their mother, holding her tighter.

Hooking a finger under his belt, Juan frowned. Unnoticed next to María, Beatriz almost forgot the queen's sorrow for a moment. For the first time she saw Juan as a grown man.

"Mamá, you're frightening us. I beg you, what has happened?" "My beloved mother…" The queen pulled Catalina and María closer. "She's dead."

"Mamá!" Isabel gasped, the younger infantas looking up in shock. Prince Juan massaged his mother's hand. Beatriz could easily guess his thoughts. The younger royals dreaded the times when the queen visited her sixty-eight-year-old mother. The queen's mother's black moods and sudden bouts of inconsolable weeping frightened them. Living a life of enforced isolation, their grandmother only recognised her daughter, gazing at her grandchildren with glazed bewilderment. The old queen knew them somehow connected to her, but Beatriz had long stopped counting the times she called Prince Juan by the name of her own long dead son.

For months the queen's mother loosened her hold on life, no longer wanting to eat or drink. On her last visit, Queen Isabel sat down beside her mother and fed her with her own hands. Perchance, Beatriz thought, the queen's mother's death should be regarded as a blessing.

Prince Juan kissed his mother's hand. "Mamá, no more weeping. Your mother is now at peace, and with God," he comforted.

Red rash splotching her face, Queen Isabel flailed out her hands, snatching at Juan and Isabel's clothes. "Si. With God, and my poor, poor brother, Alfonso. God bless both their souls." Queen Isabel gazed at her eldest daughter. "I named you for her. Despite everything, every day we were together I knew her love. She called Alfonso and me her gifts from God – as you five are to me."

The queen crumbled, her sobs tearing from her as if something broke irrevocably within her. Her four children tightened their knot around her, helpless to stem her wild grief.

21

How beautiful it is to do nothing,
and then rest afterward
~ Castilian proverb

My love,

I beg your forgiveness, but I write to you with a sad heart. Everyone is sad. No – not everyone – those who hate the queen no doubt gloat at the signs of the queen's weakness, her woman's tears. They do not pity her for the loss of her mother.

Once I would have said there was no one more certain of her actions than our queen. No more. She is often lost, and disturbed by little things. She worries all the time about her children. Every morning, she goes to visit her mother's tomb. On her return, I see she has cried.

The king seeks to distract her by the plans to celebrate the arrival of Prince Juan's bride...

All night the snow fell heavily at Burgos. By dawn, the flurries lessened and a messenger rode in before the snow fell again at the palace of the Constable de Velasco, where now stayed the king and queen. Soon, all the court knew his message. Her sea journey safely over, Prince Juan's bride and her party slowly rode to Toranzo. King Ferdinand and his son broke their fast and set off to meet them, accompanied by a strong gathering representing both the nobility of Aragon and Castilla.

Beatriz stood outside with Catalina and María, watching them prepare to depart. María drew her thick fur mantle around her thin body. As yet she still had the body of a child. "How will they find her, I wonder?"

With the lightness of a dancer, Catalina stepped quickly backwards and forth, making it a game to keep warm. She shrugged. "As well as can be expected after such a rough sea crossing." Catalina's laughter sounded grim. "The messenger praised the princess, she kept up everyone's spirits, but it must have been truly terrible. Mother told me my new sister came to shore bearing upon her a verse she had written when she thought they were all doomed to a watery grave."

"A verse? She wrote a verse?" María stared at her, amazement widening her eyes like saucers in her face.

Catalina giggled. "Not just a verse, but her own epitaph." She closed her eyes, screwing up her face in concentration. "'Here lies Margot, the willing bride. Twice married, but virgin when she died.' My new sister has a good sense of humour. And she's brave. She wrote that despite her terror. Mother told me my brother's bride was so certain she was going to die she tied the verse to her hand with a purse of gold for her burial."

Beatriz smiled at the story, gazing again at the king and

prince. Juan brought his mount alongside his father's. Gay and eager, and now fully grown at nineteen, Juan's leanness was noticeable when compared to his shorter, stockier warrior father. Even from their distance the definition of the king's leg and arm muscles was apparent. Prince Juan tossed back his head, laughing at something the king said. King Ferdinand looked at his son as if seeing him anew, joining in his laughter. Prince Juan was joyful that day –going to his bride.

Margot, fickle the ways of kings, was an unexpected bride for Prince Juan. The girl had spent most of her childhood in France, learning to be its queen, but the man she called her husband, Charles VII, cast her aside for a far bigger prize. He married Anne of Brittany instead. The shift of power to the side of the French caused a sudden scramble by her father and Queen Isabel and King Ferdinand to balance it, and Margot boarded a ship to wed Castilla and Aragon's golden prince.

Beatriz shivered with cold despite her thick, fur mantle, beating leather-gloved hands together. Overhead, luminous clouds readied to burst forth more snow upon the already thick layer covering the ground. The long cavalcade, king, prince, grandee, soldiers and slave became smaller in the distance, as the snow's bright, reflective light hurt and watered her eyes.

"Prince Juan at last to marry," María murmured distractedly. Troubled, Beatriz glanced aside at her. *Not her, too?* So many maids at court dreamt of becoming Juan's beloved, if only for a single day, a single hour. The unwed girls at court wept jealous tears on hearing of his approaching wedding. Handsome, noble and gifted, Prince Juan sang with a voice to make any maiden swoon. Plucking the strings of his harp, he strummed the cords of the hearts of many young girls to hopeless misery. Shadow, he called María. He cared for her as his cousin, but nothing more. Surely she had not allowed herself to hope for his love?

The years fell away, and Beatriz remembered the first time she too had loved without hope. She had been only thirteen when she awoke from a dream of bewildering desire, a dream when she had been naked with the boy, alone in a white bed, their bodies, a confusion of limbs, writhing together in a mysterious, rhythmical dance, coursing her with sweetness as thick as honey, and awaking her to guilt. Terrible, terrible guilt, trepidation and shame. Her heart beating fast, she had swung out of bed and fallen to her knees to pray.

Beatriz gazed at Catalina and María. The girls were almost the same age when desire first fired her heart and body. María's eyes stayed locked on the prince. Beatriz gazed at her with pity. Twelve was very young for María to face Prince Juan embodied a dream of love and only that. Beatriz had no doubt that, for the girl, it would stay an illusion, a wisp, a daydream, a vapour dissipating like a morning frost in the harshness of cold reality. It is well to dream of love, above all at only twelve, but the grail of one's heart often proves something else entirely. Her sweet, green passion for the prince was likely but the forerunner of the love one day to come, the love to flourish like a pomegranate tree, bearing fruit both

bitter and sweet.

Threading her arm through her friend's, Catalina sang softly the words from a song about Montserrat:

Resplendent star on the mountain.
Like a sunbeam miraculously glowing,

All joyous people
Come together
Rich and poor
Young and old
Climb the mountain
To see with their own eyes
And return from it Filled with grace.

Beatriz went back to fetch the bucket she had left earlier at the entrance of the alcázar. Holding the rope of the bucket in one hand, she clutched her dress with the other to keep it from the snow. Already the sodden bottoms of her gown and mantle showed the ill effects of the winter day. A ruby and sapphire brooch, pinning together her mantle, sparkled in a haze of silver light. A gust of strong wind flapped open her cloak, revealing the gown of rich brocade with a pattern of red thread. About to enter the alcázar, Beatriz saw just inside the building a knot of servants waiting for Catalina's return. They grumbled, pounding their hands and feet for warmth.

"Princess! Doña María!" Beatriz called. "Come quickly. If you're not careful, you'll find yourselves with colds on the morrow."

Catalina dimpled with amusement. María laughed, stamping her feet in her own dance against the cold. "What about you, Latina? You're more wet than us!"

Beatriz glanced at her dragging skirts, yanking them up from the steps and holding them away from her honey-brown leather boots.

"By all the good Saints, you're right." She shrugged her

shoulders, shaking off flakes of snow. María glanced at the packed

snow in her bucket, and then back at Beatriz. Dimpling again with quiet laughter, Catalina picked up her skirts and padded back inside. Beatriz and María followed her. Servants rushed all around, relieving them of their mantles. Beatriz passed the bucket to one of the women, murmuring low her instructions. The servant nodded, hurrying towards the private chambers, while other servants sped off with their damp mantles, disappearing in the opposite direction. María gazed at Catalina. Their eyes mirrored unbridled curiosity.

Without need to hasten elsewhere, Beatriz took the girls to the hall's fire. There, the three of them warmed their icy hands back to life. Catalina lowered herself onto a stool. She pulled up her thick layers of clothes to her ankles, directing her feet to the fire's heat. María seated herself beside her. María acted as her friend's body servant. She undid the laces of Catalina's wet boots, pulling them off with a plop. Twisting one side to the other, Beatriz studied her wet hem.

"Si, I wear one of my best gowns today, when we go out to stand in the snow." She sighed. "The queen gifted this to me only two months ago. I don't think she'd approve my lack of care." She held the hem of the wet brocade out to the warmth of the fire. The red threads of its drenched embroidery seemed rivulets of blood.

The firelight flickered on her hands and the heat began to make her feel drowsy. Yawning, she turned back to the girls. "To be truthful, I am glad we went out to watch the prince make his departure. It offered us a pleasant escape for a time and gave me the chance to gather what I need to test an idea."

María glanced askance at Catalina. "And what idea was this, Latina?"

"Si." Catalina laughed. "Pray, tell us the reason for the bucket of snow."

Beatriz pushed aside the two separate pieces of the brocade skirt from her legs and sighed, plucking at the layers of clothes underneath. "Saint Michael's sword – even my stockings are wet. I must go and change." She smiled at the girls. "Why don't you both come with me to my chambers and see what I do with my bucket of snow? Hopefully the snow hasn't all melted."

The girls exchanged a look and let loose a short ripple of laughter. Catalina broke into a wide, unrestrained smile. With Beatriz and her friend María, Catalina slackened the knots tied upon her by her position as a royal daughter. "Si, why not? It will give us both something to do while we wait for my brother's return."

Yanking off her own boots, Beatriz grabbed their slippers by the fire. With foresight, she had left them there to warm before venturing out on the cold morn.

Beatriz led the two girls to her chamber – conveniently not far from the queen's rooms. Valuing her opinion, morning and night, Queen Isabel would often call on her to speak over matters of state. The passing of years had made her one of the queen's most trusted advisors, rivalled only by the cardinal, the queen's confessor.

A roaring fire and half dozen or so lit candles gave the large, spacious room as much light as could be expected on a winter's day. The court had settled at this alcázar for all of winter – long enough for Beatriz to set up the room to her liking. A wide wooden screen, so dark it appeared black in the dim light of the far end of the room, was placed near a wall. A large bed, a table, a stacked bookshelf at one end, Francisco's second best vihuela, two stools set by the fireplace and a high-backed chair by the long table furnished the room. In the huge fireplace, over a thick bed of red-hot embers, a large steaming pot simmered.

Beatriz picked up the bucket of snow left at the side of the door and smiled, seeing the snow still packed tight and little melted. "María, please bring me my box from the table."

Beatriz pointed to the long, wooden box lying across the end of the table, its wood blended so well with the dark wood beneath it. María padded over to the table and picked the box up, bringing it to her. A sweet, musky fragrance from the box brought to Beatriz's mind hot summer days.

Beatriz pulled the cauldron away from the fire's flame on its hook. Simmering water lapped halfway up an empty metal bowl. She held out her open hands to María. "Pray give me the box." Releasing its sliding panel, Beatriz showed to the girls the rose petals filling the box almost to its brim.

"From my best roses this last summer," Beatriz said. She scattered rose petals in the simmering water, all around an empty inner bowl, and then picked up the cauldron's lid, placing it upside down on the pot. She gazed back at the two girls. "I thought this morning of another way to make rosewater. Now for my snow." Reaching for it, she scooped handfuls of snow until the concave of the lid became almost full, then swung the black cauldron back over the burning embers. "We wait now and see if this works."

Catalina peered at the snow filled lid. "Why the snow, Latina?"

Beatriz grinned. "Cause and effect." Taking a chair from the table, she half-lifted and half-dragged it closer to the fireplace. "I beg you, princess, please sit down here. With permission, María and I can make use of the stools. But I am in need of a change of clothes first. Once I do that, you both can ask me whatever questions you want."

Beatriz slipped behind the screen, tossing her wet garments over its top and ensuring the brocade gown hung straight. She chose a deep moss green velvet habito from her clothes chest and re-plaited her hair so it fell over her shoulder before covering it with a transparent toca. She strode back to the princess and María, and sat on the stool, holding her hands out to the fire.

"I must ask my servants to find a brazier for this room. Jesu', the day's so cold!"

Beatriz winced at her distorted reflection on the side of the cauldron. She looked pale and weary, her large eyes with dark rings beneath them. María must have caught her thought. The girl shook her finger at her, just as she did with the girls, on the rare occasion when she scolded them. "To get yourself in such a state, my good Doña! I'm surprised at you! Did not the ancients say a healthy mind in a healthy body? Wasn't it enough to go outside to watch Prince Juan make his departure? Did you have to get a bucket of snow too?"

Beatriz laughed, turning aside to Catalina. "See, princess, my time spent with María is not wasted. Already she sounds like a healer, although a trifle disrespectful to her elder, and not forgetting the one who teaches her too."

Catalina grinned. "Blame the disrespect on me. I tell María to always speak her mind in private, but she has right to be concerned. You look none too well…"

Beatriz shrugged before swinging the cauldron under her

gaze. The snow mostly by now melted, she scooped the water back into her bucket and grabbed a thick towel from the floor. When her hand hit the lid to raise it, the sudden movement caused the heavy lid to clang upon the floor. A few droplets of water left over from the snow dropped like rain on the floor. Liquid filled the metal bowl almost to the brim. Beatriz smacked her lips. "Rosewater, my young scholars. When the pot cools, I'll pour the water into flasks." "And the snow? You haven't told us about the snow?" Catalina asked.

Beatriz turned to María. "Can you give the princess an answer, child?"

María blinked, shaking her head with such vigour her roundlet became lopsided.

Beatriz pursed her lips. "María, if you thought long about it, you'd know the reason."

Catalina giggled, fanning short fingers at her hips. Firelight twinkled the large ruby in her new thumb ring, a recent gift from the English king, given in the name of his son. "I don't think María wishes to think about anything today. Surely you know cold days turn her into a cat wanting only a warm spot near the fire? You had better just tell us."

Beatriz stretched out her hands again to the fire's heat. The cold of the day seemed to be seeping into her very bones. "A simple thing really, and most likely thought of before today," She shrugged again and faced the girls. "Perchance I may have read or heard of this already, but I cannot recall it. Perchance from Aristotle..." She grinned. "Putting snow on the inverted lid caused condensation to form inside the pot and then rained rosewater in the waiting pot." All at once, Beatriz felt dizzy and ill. She put one hand on the swell of her belly, and the other over her mouth. "Pray, excuse me –" She hurried behind the screen, grabbed her chamber pot and vomited. Dry retching, she heard the girls speaking.

"She must be with child," María said. Beatriz retched again, overlaying it with a few choice words she had learnt from Francisco.

"With child?" Catalina asked. "Isn't she too old?" Still dizzy and retching, Beatriz now fought back the urge to laugh. "No, not too old," María said. "But didn't she tell us that she did not believe her marriage would see the blessing of children?"

Someone clapped, and the princess spoke. "'Tis like the story of Saint Elizabeth. How pleased she must be."

Still nauseous, Beatriz returned to the girls and sat on the stool again, avoiding the eyes of her students. An uneasy silence fell.

Catalina cleared her throat. "Does Don Francisco Ramirez know?" Beatriz licked her dry lips. Francisco still served the queen, spending long weeks away from court fighting against the Moors who still resisted the queen's yoke. "No – he doesn't know. Can I beg you both to say nothing? To no one, please." Catalina gazed aside at her. "Not even my mother?"

Beatriz reached for Catalina's hand, clasping it in both of hers. "Especially not to her, my princess." She licked her dry lips again. "I do not want to be the cause of giving the queen needless worry. She doesn't know, and I don't want her to. Not yet."

María blinked, and turned a look of bewilderment on Beatriz. "But she'll know sooner or later, si?"

Keeping hold of Catalina's hand, she now reached for María's "You must both promise not to say a word of this to the queen. I cannot tell you how important that is to me."

"But the queen will know –" María interjected.

Beatriz shook her head. "By all the saints in Heaven, not for a long while if I can help it," she muttered, as if vowing to God Himself. She gazed first at Catalina and then at María, feeling like a trapped animal, desperate for escape.

"Princess. Doña María, if the queen knew..." She swallowed hard, lifting her chin. "I am not certain if the queen would want me to continue as your tutor if she knew I'm with child." She pressed her fingers into her temples. "Pray help me hide it from the world a little longer." Beatriz glanced at them, her tears blurring her sight. "Have I your promise not to say a word to the queen, not to anyone? Let me have more time to work out how to convince the queen that I can stay at court and teach, without her thinking she needs to send me away from here to be a wife and mother."

22

Have patience and the mulberry leaf will become satin.
~ Castilian proverb

Later that day, Beatriz made out the first hazy glimpse of the returning party as they crested a near hill. She pointed them out to Catalina. "Look! The princess rides between the king and prince."

Shielding her eyes, Catalina leaned on the balcony. "Is she pretty?" Beatriz laughed, lounging beside her. "How can I tell? At this distance she could be Helen of Troy brought back to life. All I can tell you now is the honour bestowed on her by the king – she rides beside him – and that the princess rides like a true horsewoman." Catalina bent forward for a better view. "I see them now."

The royal party close now, the girl between the prince and the king twisted in her saddle-chair, turning in the prince's direction. The gloaming light illumined her strawberry blonde hair and profiled her pert, turned-up nose. Prince Juan twisted in his saddle too. It seemed their movement towards each other strummed the notes of a song, echoing bird songs in spring. Beatriz grinned. "I think the prince and princess already like each other very much."

At her table in the library, Beatriz pretended to read a book. María and Catalina, sitting close together in the nearby window-seat, had clearly forgotten her presence – or perhaps they did not care if she heard them or not.

María read out loud: "Without permitting anyone else to lay a hand on him, the lady herself washed Salabaetto all over with soap scented with musk and cloves. She then had herself washed and rubbed down by the slaves. This done, the slaves brought two fine and very white sheets, so scented with roses that they seemed like roses; the slaves wrapped Salabaetto in one and the lady in the other and then carried them both on their shoulders to the bed."

Catalina leaned back, glancing out at the bright morning. Threads of bird songs looped an embroidery of sound, thick, thin, bold and sweet. The girl closed the book on her lap, chewing at her bottom lip. Beatriz knew that look – the child brimmed with questions she wanted answered. Cupping her cheek with a hand, she sighed. "Do you think our wedding nights will be like that?" María shifted restlessly, and the girls remained silent for a time.

Beatriz suspected their choice of reading and conversation was sparked by recent events at court. From their first meeting, when Margot's humorous dismay at the court musicians' over-loud welcome had brought the prince to laughter, she gifted to Prince Juan happiness. Those who loved Juan thanked her for it. Si – the marriage of Prince Juan and Princess Margot was a great success. Since their wedding, Prince Juan gazed at his bride as if unable, si, unwilling, to draw his eyes away. They found every excuse to touch and caress the other, disappearing for hours into their private chambers at every possible opportunity.

Sitting crossed-legged, María moved deeper into the window-seat. "'Tis a long time before that day comes, for both you and me." Catalina sighed, her words rushing out as if in pain. "Amiga, you know the English demand Mother stop delaying and send me to their country now?" Her eyes glowed with unshed tears.

María reached out and clasped her hand. "Si, but the queen plays them for more time. Why should this be any different than what happened with Isabel and Juana? The queen will not let you leave until you are at least fifteen."

Beatriz winced at Catalina's bitter laugh. "Father says differently. He's more than willing to see me go."

María released Catalina's hands. She gathered herself up in the corner of the window-seat, hugging her legs.

Beatriz listened to the birds twittering and chirping outside. *How happy and carefree they sounded.* How many times in her life had their song of joy to morning's glory lifted her heart and filled it with hope? What would she do if she were forced into a life of exile? She heaved a long breath and gazed at the girls. Should she remind them that Christ cared for the least of his creatures?

María settled her shoulders against the stone. "Has your

mother allowed any of her hijas to leave her side before she knew them ready to do so?"

Rubbing her temple, Catalina averted her face to the shadows. "The day comes."

Beatriz blinked away sudden tears, relieved to see María lean towards Catalina and take her hand. "I say again the day is still a long way from today. Listen to the whistles of the larks, my princess, and please, like them, welcome the spring morn. Joy is here for the taking, amiga. Worrying about what will befall us in the future won't change it. Whatever will be will be. And my princess, whatever the future might bring, rose petals will adorn your wedding sheets." María giggled. "But not until your mother allows."

Catalina held María's hand in both of hers. "You will be there –you will come with me?"

"Do you doubt it?"

Catalina shrugged, a slight smile tugging at her lips. "I don't doubt it. But tell me true, is it what you want, really want?"

As if she made a vow, María placed her hand over their linked hands. "My life is with you. Don't you know that yet?"

"You haven't answered me. Is it what you want, María? You don't need to leave Castilla..."

María leaned towards her and spoke the words of Ruth. "Whithersoever thou shalt go, I will go: and where thou shalt dwell, I also will dwell. Thy people shall be my people, and thy God my God. The land that shall receive thee dying, in the same will I die." María rubbed at her eyes. "It is as simple as that. If you go, I go too. I cannot lose my sister. Not now, not ever."

The light from the window glittered on the tears on Catalina's thick eyelashes. "If you come to England, you'll likely marry an Englishman. Have you thought of this?"

María rolled her eyes. "An Englishman," she giggled. "I have thought of this. Can you promise me something?"

"You know if I can, I will."

"Promise me that I can choose my own husband. Grandee or English lord, I would like to think I could love him."

Catalina rested her head on her friend's shoulder and clasped her hand. "I promise, my sister. That's the least I can do for one who is willing to be my fellow exile."

Beatriz stared down at her book, and the page blurred. Blinking away her own tears she felt so helpless. All she had was books to help ready her students to leave their home, forever.

My love,

We have a son. He was born three days ago – a healthy, beautiful boy. The wet-nurse cannot believe how lusty he is – I tell her he takes after his father. Josefa looks after us very well. I am so blessed to have her as my friend. That she has agreed to take care of our boy when I return to court – I cannot say how grateful I am.

The queen is happy about this arrangement too. I cannot believe how I feared to tell her of my pregnancy. I thought it would be the end of my position at court. Strangely, like you, my love, she wants to support and help me continue to walk this road that is so different to so many women. Our baby is a miracle. He deserves a woman who will devote herself to him with full joy, not a mother who desires to devote her days to study and teach-

ing. I own it a selfish devotion – but here at court and the university I can give more to the world than to a home. I am what I am, and it is too late to change that. You say you do not wish me to change. For that, I love you.

Every day I thank God for you, Francisco. And now there is another Francisco. Josefa will raise him well. She has even promised to do the same if we have more children. I cannot believe my good fortune.

When I left the court three weeks ago, Queen Isabel was dreading farewelling her eldest daughter, Isabel. As you know, my love, the queen blocked Isabel's new Portugal marriage for years. She played a hard game of chess against the king in his efforts to pressure her into agreeing to their eldest daughter resuming her position as a pawn to be moved for the sake of power. But the passing of five years has now shut the final door on both mother and daughter, leaving them no more excuses of avoidance.

Once more Isabel retreated to the shell she had built around herself after her husband's death, ignoring the preparations for her wedding. She even cut her hair short again, as if proclaiming her unwillingness to marry, and her desire to take the veil of a religious order. Soon the season turned and time neared for Isabel to leave her mother's court for her new life in Portugal. The queen became increasingly desperate to see Isabel show some sign of happiness before her wedding.

"My hija, Manuel has done as you asked," Queen Isabel said. "He has commanded the Jews to convert or leave his kingdom. He has given them three months to do so."

Without expression, Isabel lifted her eyes from the altar

cloth she was embroidering, glancing at her mother. Despite her extreme slenderness, her beauty at twenty-five seemed far greater than Beatriz's memory of her at twenty. Isabel's pale, thin face possessed the delicacy of a sorrowing angel. The young woman looked back at the embroidery. "Then in three months I wed."

A frown deeply furrowed between the queen's eyebrows. She watched her daughter add the final threads to a red cross. "You go to be queen, Isabel."

Isabel's head cast a shadow over her embroidery, dimming the colours of her intricate work. She sewed on for a few moments in silence.

"Si, Mamá, Manuel's queen." She pulled too hard at the red thread, puckering the material. Her fingers stilled over the ruined cross. "Do not fear, my mother and queen, I know my duty."

Queen Isabel winced. Catalina swung from the window-seat, as if to go to her mother. Beatriz grabbed her arm, shaking her head in warning. At Catalina's cross look, Beatriz stepped into the shadows beside her, whispering close to her ear, "This is between your mother and your sister."

Catalina drooped back onto the cushions, her eyes fixed on her mother and sister. The queen reached out to her oldest daughter, but Isabel, her head lowered, ignored her mother. Spoiling her embroidery even more, she jabbed and jabbed at the cross, ignoring her mother's trembling hand. Beatriz almost wept seeing Queen Isabel's fallen face. For a long moment, the queen's mouth seemed to struggle for firmness before she turned away from her daughter.

Beatriz recalled Josefa, María's mother, saying to her, "Princess Isabel is the daughter most precious to the queen, perchance because after her birth there was no other living child born to the king and queen for nearly eight years. By the time of the prince's birth, our queen more than simply doted on Isabel. Isabel became the glory of her mother's life. Whilst Juan is his mother's angel, his older sister reigns in her mother's heart like the Queen of Heaven." But Queen Isabel was first a queen. Like Abraham sacrificing Isaac, she sacrificed Isabel's desires for what she believed right for her kingdom.

Summoned by the queen to her private chamber, Beatriz slipped into the shadows of the embrasure. Not far away two physicians knelt before the king and queen. "We advise a time of separation," one said.

Prince Juan, sitting on a large cushion at his parents' feet, jerked up to balance on one knee. His eyes fired with anger. The king rested a hand on his son's shoulder, meeting his son's eyes, shaking his head. His hands clenched at his hips, the prince settled back onto the cushions.

"Let them be," the king laughed. "They are young. 'Tis only right the passion waxes strong between them. I remember too well how it was when I first wed you, wife."

Beatriz raised a hand, touching her hot cheek, feeling ill when she saw Queen Isabel's face. Her eyes glowed with love meant only for one man. For a moment, the ghost of a young woman settled upon her. The ghost still lingered when she beckoned Beatriz. "Good friend, what is your opinion? Are the physicians right to ask this?"

Beatriz gazed at the cowering physicians, and then at Prince

Juan. There was no trace of the boy he once was, only a furious young man. She sighed, thinking of the vein of melancholy running deep in this family, and the link between body and mind. "My queen, your son loves his wife. For what my opinion is worth, I say a separation could cause him great unhappiness, and may do more harm than good."

The queen nodded decisively, turning back to the physicians. "What God joined together let no man rip asunder. There will be no more talk of separation. You're dismissed."

Fidgeting as if sitting upon sharp rocks rather than soft cushions, Prince Juan scowled, watching the men leave the room. Utterly mother now, the queen bent low to her son. "Did we do right, my Juan?"

"Mother, those men are fools!" The prince's blue eyes flashed in his pale face.

She gripped his shoulder. "'Tis true what they say. You've lost flesh since your wedding..."

The prince bounded up to his full height. "Mother! There's nothing wrong! The physicians have brought you worry every day of my life. I am fed milksops and forced to stay abed at the least

sign of illness. I am a man, Mother. Pray, as God intended, let me act the man."

The king grinned with pride. "Listen to our son. Can we doubt this marriage is good for him? Juan is right. 'Tis time for our son to live his own life. How else will he learn to be king?"

The queen's mouth tightened. When she gazed down on her son, she seemed, to Beatriz, mouthing a silent prayer.

The three expected months to Isabel's wedding stretched to four. Time enough for all to grow to love the Archduchess Margot. That she loved the prince was apparent to everyone. She wanted to please him in every way. Margot was a good wife, a good daughter, a good sister, embracing Prince Juan's family as her own.

Outside the library, Beatriz listened to Margot's sweet, melodious voice singing and the soft notes from a vihuela:

"The time is troubled, but the time will clear;
After rain fair weather is awaited: After strife
and cruel contention
Peace will arrive, misfortune cease to be,"

Both vihuela and voice dwindled off when Beatriz entered the room, Margot and Juan sat with Catalina and María, the prince holding his vihuela as if he was about to play again.

"Come," Catalina said, smiling in welcome. "Join us." Gesturing to the space beside her on the bench, she turned to the princess. "Latina writes poetry too."

Bobbing a curtsey to the three of them, Beatriz laughed. "I don't think my poor verses compare with Princess. I've heard enough to recognise the better poet."

Margot smiled impishly, and her blue eyes twinkled. "You flatter me. But don't you agree any poetry sounds good when set to music?" She took her husband's arm and looked up at him. "This poem is still far from finished. I only have to scribble out a few words and my lord husband must make it a song."

The prince kissed herc heek and then, more lingeringly, her

mouth. "And why not? Finished or not, your words are music to my ears."

Bestowing another kiss on him, Margot threaded her arm through his. "My sweet lord, you distract me from my task." Holding his face between her hands, the girl kissed him again. Her body seemed to melt into him. She sighed, and playfully pushed him away. "I must not forget your mother sent me here for a purpose. My sister Catalina must become fluent in French, and who better to teach her than I, once called Queen of France?"

The prince scowled. "Do you regret the loss of that title?"

Nestling into him again, Margot pealed with laughter. "You're jealous? How can I regret it when I am your queen, my King of Granada?" She took his face between her hands and showered it with kisses. "I love you, Juan. Love you, love you, love you." Her arms winding around his neck, she kissed his mouth. Prince Juan enclosed her in his arms and kissed her back, deep and long.

Catalina picked up a letter on the table. Ignoring her brother and sister-in-law, now whispering love words to one another, she stared at the parchment. "Elizabeth of England advises I come to England speaking flawless French. 'Tis the second most spoken language at their court. My mother asked my good sister to help me."

Beatriz looked at the embrace-locked two young lovers and laughed. "If the princess really wants to teach you, I think she best leave your brother elsewhere."

But as the months sped by, Margot rarely taught Catalina her French without the presence of Prince Juan. Despite her constant love games with her husband, she still managed to tutor

Catalina, helping her improve her French. By the end of four months, Catalina's grasp of the language was one the English would find difficult to fault.

Beatriz was pleased to see this time also teaching María to lose her jealousy of Margot. The girl's sweetness, her impish sense of humour, her intelligence that sparred and grew equally with the prince's, helped the child let go of her dreams – whatever those dreams may have been – but she seemed to let go of childhood too. The girl appeared to have learned one of life's lessons: to accept with good grace what she could not change. To be happy that others could be truly happy – even when their happiness was not hers.

At Alcántara, close to the Portugal border, the queen and her court celebrated Isabel's wedding to the Portuguese king. Just a year older than his wife, King Manuel treated Isabel tenderly, gazing at her like one love-struck. The queen told Beatriz that the king had fallen in love with Isabel when he met her during her marriage to his cousin. After Alfonso's death, he never gave up hope that she would agree to marry him. His unhidden love gave the queen hope that Isabel might yet find again happiness as a wife.

My dear one,

Princess Isabel will soon be Queen of Portugal. Her final days with her mother come hard on the heels of another farewell, one causing Queen Isabel less pain, if not less worry. Prince Juan and his now pregnant wife have been cut loose from his mother's court to set up their own in the city I call home: Salamanca. If only the desire for greater independence was the only reason for this decision. Alas, Prince Juan has been once more struck down by a serious malady. Whilst he is mercifully recovered from his illness, the queen wishes him in the care of his former tutor. Diego de Deza is a man both trusted by the queen and her son, a man who Prince Juan can never mislead about when he sickens and knows how to deal with the prince in such times.

Thus, on the slow, long journey to Alcántara, the royal courts detoured to Salamanca and we remained there for two weeks. The queen and king were greeted with joy, the citizens of Salamanca happy and proud they chose their city for Prince Juan's court. The city's celebrations showed no sign of abating when the king and queen and their courts farewelled Prince Juan and his wife...

God have mercy, the stop of one heartbeat turns joy into sorrow in a blink of an eye. That day Queen Isabel, the unending celebrations for her daughter's wedding proving too much for her failing health, dozed in bed. As was often her custom when the queen sickened, Beatriz brought Catalina and María to the queen's chamber after their morning of study, and they took turns reading to Queen Isabel, or playing chess or sewing together. Beatriz was not certain if the queen really desired their company, but Catalina always found a way to comfort her mother.

Whilst the queen slept on this day, Beatriz read her book and Catalina and María embroidered, talking softly to one another.

Their conversation stopped when the king entered the chamber, hurrying to Queen Isabel's side, oddly followed by Cisneros, the queen's confessor, and Guadalupe, her most favoured physician.

"Isabel."

The queen awoke, starting at her husband's voice. Catalina and María gazed at one another. Beatriz could see they, like her, wondered what was afoot.

Queen Isabel half rose from her pillows. She rubbed her eyes, straightening with difficulty. Her eyes widening at sight of her confessor, she turned to her husband. "What is it?"

The king almost spat the hateful words: "A messenger's come from our son's wife… Margot… She says Juan's dying!"

Catalina dropped her sewing onto the floor. Beatriz stared at it, mocked by the almost finished summer's garden, the silks chosen for their bright beauty to celebrate abundant life. Beatriz picked it up, pricking her finger on an unseen needle. The sharp, sudden pain brought tears to her eyes – or was it from hearing the king's words? They pierced her heart far more than a simple needle.

"Ferdinand," Queen Isabel cleared her throat, "there's some mistake."

The king shook his head, his shoulders slumping in defeat. Sitting on the edge of her bed he gazed at his wife. "The messenger also brought word from Juan's physician. He says the same."

Queen Isabel opened and shut her mouth. For a moment she seemed deprived of all speech. "How can this be so, Ferdinand?" she asked at last. "Juan was well when we left him."

King Ferdinand laid his broad hand over his wife's. Like a claw of an old woman, the queen's hand curled and trembled beneath his. The king sighed, took his hand away, rubbing at the top of his leg hose with the heel of his palm. "For not long after, my Isabel. Our son refused to listen to the entreaties of his physician. He begged Juan not to further exhaust himself by following day revels with night-long banquets. Knowing our son, Juan probably didn't want to disappoint both the city and his wife, but it proved too much for him. The physician says he has done everything, but Juan's fever gets no better. Our son is too weak to fight."

The queen moaned. Her hands flailed out, her body writhing with no true purpose. She sounded and looked mad.

"Help me up – I must go to him." She attempted to right herself, pain distorting her face. Shutting her mouth and eyes, she slipped back upon the pillows and her moan became one of anguish. Beads of sweat ran down her forehead, over her closed eyes, dripping over the straight, thin line of mouth and slackening chin.

On the other side of her huge bed, the physician picked up her hand, checking her pulse. With considered gentleness, he placed her hand back on the bed and shook his head at the king. He gazed back at the queen with grave worry. "Your Highness, you're far too ill for travel. Going to the prince would only place your life in great jeopardy. I cannot in good conscience allow it."

From the shadows, Cardinal Cisneros stepped forward. He stood by the physician's side. "My queen, think what's right for your kingdom."

Queen Isabel's agonised eyes flew open at the priest's words. Anger sparked a fiery renewal of her familiar majesty.

"Always I think what's right for my kingdom. That and only that has been my first concern from the time I first became queen." Raising her hand, she brushed tears from her eyes. "Sweet Jesús, I am a mother, too." The queen glared at her physician. "And pray tell me, little man, what gives you the right to say what I can or cannot do?"

The king dismissed the recoiling physician. He reached for the queen's hand. "Hearing his beloved mother is at her death door because she hurried to his side will not aid our son. I beg you, listen to reason and heed what I say. You're too ill to leave here, but I will go and act for us both in this, just as we have done for one another in the past. I can reach our son's side with greater speed if you remain here. With my best riders I make this vow to you. I will reach our son in less than a day."

Queen Isabel eyed her husband. As if passing all her remaining strength to him, she wilted against her pillows, her trembling hand spreading over the lower half of her face before dropping it to the bed's coverlet. The queen lifted her chin again, inhaling a ragged breath. "God speed, husband. God speed. Tell my son I love him. Tell him I pray only for good news of his recovery." She averted her face, tears trickling from her closed eyes. "Pray God strengthen me..." She spoke in a whisper, her quiet words pulsating in the room's uneasy, unearthly silence. "For I do not think I could withstand the loss of our boy. God – please God, if you love me, do not take him from me... do not take Juan, do not take my angel."

Dear Francisco,

I do not even want to put this down on paper. If I do – I deny all hope of rumour, and rather confront truth: word from Salamanca tells us that Prince Juan

is dying. Receiving the message from his son's physicians, King Ferdinand rode to the city that very day. We hear he rode all through the night and into the next day. The court waits, tottering on a dagger's point, for news.

One day. Two days. Three. Four. Five. Six. The long days drag from waking to sleeping – if any of us are fortunate to find sleep. All close to the queen live in hope of a messenger from Salamanca, living in fear of that message. When the messenger comes, the court hears the prince is better, and then worse, then better, but none tells the queen what we all pray to hear: that Prince Juan overcomes his illness and is well again.

It is now two agonising weeks since the king left for Salamanca. Two weeks of sorrow and helplessness. The queen is distraught. Princess Isabel, now the Queen of Portugal, walked like a sleep walker into her new marriage. Joyless, she wedded the King of Portugal loving life not at all, resigned to fulfil her duty. But I think only with her body – the queen's eldest daughter turns her gaze so much to the Kingdom of Heaven she cuts herself adrift from the mortal world.

Queen Isabel masked a brave face for her daughter's sake. She left her sickbed, calling upon all her powers of persuasion, convincing Isabel the right course of action meant she must go with her new husband as planned and wait in Portugal for news of her brother. Farewelled by the queen's court one more time in her life, Isabel departed yesterday for her husband's kingdom, not knowing whether her beloved brother would live or die. Her eldest daughter gone, Queen Isabel lives now for her husband's messages.

My little infanta no longer enjoys her daily lessons. All she wants is the comfort she finds in the chapel when she prays with her mother...

For days, the entirety of Beatriz's life seemed that of dark, shuttered rooms and the strong smell of melting beeswax in the chapel. But closed shutters did not shut out the sounds of the day. Sunlight peeped into the chamber through every crack. Pulsing air caused the lit candles to wisp with smoke. The crisp smell of autumn awoke in Beatriz the desire to come away from the dark oppressive air that lingered everywhere. One day Catalina refused to consider doing anything other than pray. Unable to stay indoors for one more moment, Beatriz asked for release and took herself into one of the most beautiful court-yards of Alcántara. Once there she sat by the pool, staring into the water, feeling as if swept into a maelstrom. A sudden breeze blew loose strands of hair into her eyes, forcing her to push it away.

An uncertain pale face wavered in the pool, breaking apart when another gust of wind blew across the rippling surface. Beatriz turned to see María beside her. No longer a child but still far from womanhood, María looked more and more like her beautiful mother. Beatriz sighed. And when time fulfilled that promise? What then? Passing time would only steal beauty away again. Time was as indefinable as the water passing through her trailing fingers. Unable yet to trust her voice, Beatriz brushed away her tears. Sorrow seemed to drub with every heartbeat – a painful cadence echoing loudly in her ears.

A dragonfly flashed its shimmering, rainbow wings over the silver, now still water. In the tree growing in the corner of the garden, a bird trilled a short burst of song. Another bird answered, and then another, until the air throbbed with bird-song. Comfort settled upon her like the sun's mantle of autumn warmth. Her heart swelled feeling, somehow, that this comfort came from the prince.

Beatriz saw him in her mind's eye – lean and straight, fair and handsome, smiling his teasing and quirky smile at his sisters and María, who he always treated as another sister. She remembered the first time she had ever seen him playing upon his harp in his mother's chamber. Barely a youth he was already a skilled harpist. Whenever he plucked the strings of his harp or vihuela – whether as a boy, a youth or a man – he wove his passion for music into the melodies he played, melodies he composed from his loving, noble heart. They were memories that would stay with her forever. Not even death possessed the power to rob them from her.

Beatriz reached for María, putting her arm around her shoulders. A breeze teased the pool, rippling it alive and flecked with silver stars. The dragonfly winged close to them. The beauty of the moment left her breathless, aware of the sweetness of life. Surely nothing once loved is ever truly lost? Love, even if as brief in life as the ethereal, darting dance of a dragonfly flying across water, outlived time itself. Love held the pomegranate seeds of immortality. Beatriz glanced at María, seeing her gaze down at her reflection.

"Avoid the mistake of Narcissus, child," Beatriz said automatically, then scolded herself for stupidity. María wasn't being vain, just contemplative, like she had been just seconds before. She wasn't surprised when she heard María's reply.

"I wasn't admiring myself, Latina. The whole world drifted

away to nothingness. I felt at peace, like I was in a dream, looking down at my face in the pool."

Suddenly cold, Beatriz drew her mantle around her. "What's wrong?" María whispered, her eyes frightened.

"Your words remind me of an old belief of the long ago Greeks." Beatriz took María's hand onto her lap, saying no more. Their faces wavered together in the water, sparking with diamonds of light.

"What old belief, Teacher?" María directed her question at Beatriz's reflection.

Beatriz considered the girl, biting her bottom lip. "Tell me," María begged.

Beatriz turned to her, her fear widened its jaws. Once again scolding herself for stupidity, Beatriz held María's hand tighter, and inhaled deeply. "The Greeks once believed to dream seeing your reflection in water omened your death."

María sputtered out laughter. "Fear not, teacher. I daydreamed of what might one day befall me, all my hopes for a marriage like my mother's. There was no dream, daydream or otherwise, of my reflected face upon the tranquil water. Pray, don't worry about me. God willing, I don't plan to die, but to live a long, long life."

"No one plans to die." Beatriz cleared her throat, not daring to look at María. She tugged at her girdle, thinking of the prince. "Speak never thus aloud, for perchance we tempt fate."

The low shadows of autumn lengthened. Beatriz shivered, the sunlight no longer warming her, but thin like Lady Lent. Downy clouds gathered above, blocking out the sun, dulling the pool to burnished steel. She trembled again, unable to stop the flood of memories. So many, many precious memories of the prince, glittering jewels strewn along a beach stretching back for years and years. Without Prince Juan the court would be a place dark and bereft. Already the threat of losing him buffeted them without mercy, tossing them like a ship floundering on storm-swept seas. If the prince died, it diminished them all.

"I prayed for the prince," María said, lifting shining eyes. Beatriz sighed. "We all are."

"Do you think God will hear us?"

Beatriz reached again for María's hand, shutting her eyes. "He hears us." Helplessly, she shrugged. "But, always, there's a time to be born and a time to die. Whether the time has come for Prince Juan we don't yet know..."

Beatriz gazed back at the pool. The wind blew gently on its surface, and moved the clouds away from the sun. Light danced upon the water. Swaying backward and forth, the shadows of the surrounding trees lengthened as time moved forward. She closed her eyes, her skin tingling in the cool air. Death did not belong here, not in this garden, and surely not with Prince Juan. The happiness of so many depended on his life.

The garden seemed an Eden untouched by death – all that Beatriz loved safe within. The prince's death would mantle them with cause for sorrow until the end of their days. Like blind bats, her twirling thoughts and prayers circled in her mind without mercy. Her head pounded when María asked, "Why didn't the queen listen to the physicians?"

Beatriz stared at María, feeling the colour drain from her face. "What do you mean?"

"The prince was not well."

Beatriz swallowed. "All close to him saw that. The queen also owned it in her heart."

María grabbed her arm and shook. "If we all knew, why was nothing done?"

Beatriz lowered her head, retying her girdle. "María, 'tis hard to explain –"

"I beg you, tell me. I am no longer a child."

Beatriz found it hard to look María's way. "We are often blind when it comes to those we love. We only see what we want to see." Beatriz thought over the last five months. The prince and princess's passion for one another resulted in disapproving and worried mutterings from many, not just the queen's physicians.

María shook her arm again. "I have learnt enough from you, Teacher, to recognise illness when I see it. The prince was not just frail... his recent malady was not the cause of this but just a small part."

"Si." Beatriz put her hand on her aching temple. "There was a translucent sheen to his skin; his eyes glowed with constant fever. He had lost much weight since his wedding."

María stirred in anger. "I do not understand. You've told me to use my eyes and instincts, and act on it. Did not the prince's physicians care enough? Why did no one do anything until now, perchance when 'tis too late? I am but a maid and of no importance, but the months since his wedding... Every time I looked on him, I felt anxious, scared for him. Passion did not cause this."

Beatriz played for time by tightening her girdle. She sniffed. "No, you are right, my bright young student. There was another fire eating away at the prince. He fevered, not enough to bed him, but enough to drain away his strength."

"Then why did no one do anything to stop it? Why did no

one take good care of him? Bar for lots of mutterings in corners and the few physicians brave enough to speak to the queen, everyone kept a conspiracy of silence about him. And now look at what has happened."

Beatriz bent her head and rubbed at her wet eyes. "You have known the prince since he was but a boy. You can answer this question just as easily as I."

Tears falling down her face, María stared across the expanse of water. A steady eddy of wind blew a few stray autumn leaves into the clear pool. They drifted towards them, their colours, red, gold and almost purple, brought to brilliant life again by water and the gloaming. Beatriz rubbed her eyes again, her sight blurring. She took a deep breath, trying to keep in control. If she started to weep, the tears would never stop.

Juan's fire of life had blazed bright alongside the bright light of his wife. Whereas Margot's fire ate to its content from a healthy body and spirit, the prince's stalwart spirit alone fed his. Others at the court saw this better and clearer than his family. They all wanted to believe the same as him and, God have pity, allowed Juan's pretence of health, his desire to be worthy of the love of his wife and not prove a disappointment to her, to his family, to blind them all. Love, or perchance the great fear of losing what they love, often stopped them from seeing what they should see. "What God joined together let no man rip asunder," the queen had said months ago. But what no man rips apart, death finds a way to do.

Almost two weeks passed, the queen still under strict instructions to rest in her chamber. Along with the infantas and María de Salinas, Beatriz was one of the few who daily attended her. Beatriz and the girls were with the queen when the king entered her chamber, unannounced. Before dropping to a low curtsey, Beatriz saw his defeated face. Her heart fluttered to her throat and seemed to strangle her. Watching him approach his wife, Beatriz wanted to disappear, to close her ears. His red-rimmed eyes told her his news before he said one word.

"Juan?" Queen Isabel attempted to lift herself out of her chair, but fell back, seeing the despair, the sorrow newly carved upon her husband's face. She stared at him, her mouth moving silently. All his attention on his wife, he strode to the chair facing her and sat before taking hold of her trembling hands. His bottom lip jutted over the top one, a muscle in his chin jerking, tightening. Tears welled and overflowed down his cheeks. The king's hollow voice echoed grief and hopelessness. "Our son is dead."

Beside Beatriz, Catalina gasped as if knifed, and the infanta María let loose an awful cry. *The prince dead? Prince Juan dead? Their golden prince, dead?* Beatriz found Catalina in her arms, not knowing how it came to be, no longer able to make sense of anything. Time and life tangled into a knot, tightening around her heart. Hugging Catalina to her, she knew she was not the only one in shock. It felt like a dream – a horrible, pitiless dream. The infanta María, her skirts gathered before her, sped from her mother's chamber, leaving the door wide open. Her gasping, broken sobs and stumbling footsteps petered away. Time remained still, and strangely at rest.

Queen Isabel, her high cheekbones splotched with

unhealthy colour, the rest of her skin chalk-white, snatched her hands away. Recoiling in her high back chair, she gripped its carved armrests as if holding onto life itself. "No, no! It cannot be! Your last message said Juan was better."

The king muffled a ragged sigh with his hand. Hooding his eyes, he leaned against the back of the chair. Grief and exhaustion left him grey. More tears fell down his cheeks. Beatriz had now lived at court for over a decade. This was the first moment in all that time when she saw the man emerge from the king, a vulnerable man unashamedly exposing naked, raw emotions. He leant towards the queen, clasping her hands again.

"My love, I am your slave all my days... mine own beloved, I beg for your forgiveness and understanding. When I sent that message, our son was already prepared for his tomb. He died in my arms, on the Feast of Saint Francis."

The queen's eyes bulged, not focusing on anything, tears running down her face. Standing, she gripped the arms of her chair. Slowly enunciating each word as if she dipped them in venom, the queen asked, "My son... he died days ago, and you did not send word to me?"

The king clasped her clenched hand and bowed his head. His tears pattered like heavy raindrops upon their linked hands. Swallowing, he licked his chapped lips. Eyes swimming with more tears, he gazed at his wife. "Beloved, such news should not come other than from one able to grieve with you. I commanded no one to speak to you of our son's death until we could console one another."

Her eyes breaking from his, Queen Isabel swayed, fighting for breath. She raised her chin, breathing through her nose as if forcing back half-born sobs. Sitting back on her chair she shook her head, as if wanting to clear it, speaking in a voice hoarse with grief. "How did he…" Her trembling hand framed her face. Once again she shook her head. "How did my angel die? Did Juan… did he suffer?"

The king averted his face from his wife, a rapid pulse twitching the eyelid of his weak eye. Anger flared a flush of normal colour to his grey face. "We must give thanks to God." The king spoke bitterly. "He suffered but a little – and died confessed of all his sins."

Queen Isabel leaned closer, gripping his hands. "What is it, Ferdinand?"

The king's full, sensual mouth disappeared into one straight, hard and vicious line. Fearful, Beatriz recognised this look so well from the past – the need for the king to lash out at whatever stood in his way. "Juan resigned himself to death." His teeth gnawing at one side of his mouth, the king shook his head. "By the time I arrived, he had lost all heart. Juan fought a little harder knowing I was there, but I could do nothing but watch our son die." He glared at his wife. "I begged him to live. I reminded him of his wife, of his unborn child, the two kingdoms he would one day rule, joined together to their full glory. I do not understand why he gave up his battle for life so easily. He had so much to live for. Except for a too often frail body, he was the best of us…"

The king wiped the side of his hand under his dripping nose. "I cannot help remembering how we rejoiced at his birth, thanking God for him. Or how much I rejoiced knowing the man he grew to be and the strong kingdoms we were to pass to him. His death makes no sense to me – no sense at all. There's no purpose in it other than to destroy all our hopes. It mocks at everything we have worked so hard to do. 'Tis God Himself who mocks us."

The queen lowered her head. "Ferdinand, don't." Swallowing, she licked her chapped mouth. "You speak through grief. 'Tis pointless to go down that road, my husband." She lifted desperate eyes. "God gave him to us, and He has now taken him back. My angel is with God, amongst God's own angels."

The queen crumbled, her fragile bridge of comfort collapsing. Taking her hands from her husband's, she wound her arms tight across her chest. Bending forward, she wept.

King Ferdinand groaned. Violently shifting in his chair, he clunked his head against its back, bone against wood. Awash with tears, his eyes flew open. The king half stumbled, half tossed himself, kneeling beside his wife, gathering her in his rock-hard, muscular arms, befitting a soldier-king.

Man and woman sobbed, rocking together, united by mutual anguish, unaware of anyone or anything. Her arm around Catalina, Beatriz led her from the queen's chamber. In the long hallways outside, shock and sorrow weighed down both their steps. Beatriz wanted to wake from this awful dream. But it was too real to be a dream. Everywhere she looked she saw and heard the mirror and echo of despair, of sorrow.

Beatriz slept in the princess's chamber that night, knowing María out of her depths to comfort the Catalina. They prayed for the prince, prayed for God to comfort Juan's grieving wife and parents. They prayed for themselves, for God to give them strength to bear this loss – a loss that seemed so insurmountable. Well into the night, the three of them wept together until, exhausted, they fell asleep.

Dagger-sharp grief pierced Beatriz's dreams and she awoke

to her tears chilling upon neck and face. Set close to the bed, the tall, guttering candle showed she had slept only perchance one hour or two. She wiped away her tears with the sleeve of her chemise. Still tears fell and fell. *Do I breathe only to weep? Our golden prince dead. Juan, dead... dead... dead...*

Half-rolling onto her back, she stared into the darkness, the awful nothingness above suffocating and oppressing her. Silently she railed at fate and the injustice of life. Like the king she hated, Beatriz did not understand God's purpose. Catalina and María both restless but still sleeping, she swung from the bed and lit another candle to leave at the door before going outside.

The inner doors of Catalina's chamber opened into the walled courtyard, shared with a few, fortunate others on the women's side of the royal chambers. Beatriz pushed open the heavy door, stepping into the black velvet night, seeking its embrace and comfort.

All her life, nature lifted her moments of sadness. The sudden trill and thread of birdsong, rain soughing after the heat of a summer's day, the gold-spun gloaming cast upon a garden. Nature renewed her and strengthened her faith, for in all such moments she felt God Himself holding her in his embrace.

Beatriz had never before doubted or questioned God, only owning the truth of human fallibility. But tonight her despair was such she entered a black valley of doubt, doubt leaving her tottering at its crumbling edge. Blinded by grief and anguish, she desperately sought for light to show her the way to step away from the edge.

Barefoot, almost welcoming the cold piercing the soles of her feet, she trod carefully on the night-damp, mossed-covered stone steps to the thick carpet of grass edging the courtyard's garden. She found herself in another world – a grey world lit by moonlight that, even so, was beautiful.

The huge full moon painted the stones of the palace's walls, grey by day, to luminous white and delineated the grove of tall poplars as if brushed white by an artist's hand. She halted on the steps, the moonlight pooling over her its scorn. How dare she recognise and acknowledge beauty with Prince Juan dead, and his young body food for worms?

"Latina!" Barefooted too, Catalina approached her, her mantle's hood settled upon her shoulders. Upon it, her unbound hair curled in heavy ringlets before disappearing down her back. Hair and mantle billowing out in a gust of strong wind, she moved towards Beatriz. Suddenly the bright moonlight outlined her naked, childlike form beneath her white shift. Beatriz was suddenly aware of freezing feet, and shivered. The thinness of her own shift offered no protection from the night.

Reaching Beatriz, Catalina took hold of her hand. She tutted, wrapping her thick mantle around them. "Latina – out here alone, on a cold night like this! You should know better. We need no more illness." Letting go of her attempt of maturity, Catalina lay her head upon her breast. Beatriz felt her chemise become wet with the infanta's tears.

Beatriz tightened her hold. "You're not alone in your sorrow. We all loved your brother."

Moonbeams cast Catalina in blue light, turning her into a living, moving statue of marble. "Why did he have to die?"

Beatriz sighed. Of all the questions Catalina had asked her since she was five, this one was the hardest to answer. "Mi chiquitina, who is not neustra chiquitina anymore, I wish I had the words to comfort you. But 'tis a hard lesson we learn, so many times – life gives to take away."

Catalina shifted as if in anger. "Then life is cruel," she sobbed.

Beatriz kissed the top of her head. "Well and good, my child, you learn that at twelve. I learnt it long before that, before I could barely speak. But there's another side to life giving comfort. Surely all of us are richer for having had the prince in our lives, even if it means bearing his loss."

Catalina wiped her cheek on Beatriz's chemise. "That's no comfort, not when I will grieve for him for the rest of my days."

Beatriz let out a ragged sob. "You're such a young maid. Time will dull this grief until it becomes as distant as the moon that shines down on us tonight." She sighed. "I cannot say the same for the queen. Joy has left her forever. I am so worried for your mother."

"Father is broken-hearted, too"

"Si. The king too." Beatriz threaded her arm through Catalina's, leading her back up the steps to the royal chambers. "But he has other sons, all bastards, si, but soon this knowledge will console him. Shortly he returns to the battlefield. Action – dealing out life or death – will make him put aside his grief. But your poor mother... She has lost her only son... a son who died lacking his mother's final kiss. She was not even there when they laid his body in its tomb. I think we will find all her mortal joy lies entombed at Salamanca. Come, let us leave the chill of this sad, sad night."

23

Seeing as God made you without peer
In goodness of heart and goodness of speech, Nor is your
*   equal anywhere to be found,*
My love, my lady, I hereby tell you:
Had God desired to ordain it so, You would have made a
*   great king.*
~ King Dinis of Portugal of his wife Isabel, d. 1325

Dear love,

Pray come soon. I need your strength – and your arms around me. I do not know how to bear these sad days. The loss of Prince Juan strikes us all deep, the sorrow for his death like a strangling winding cloth on all our spirits, the family I serve most of all. I so yearn for your comfort, Francisco…

Juan's heart-broken wife returned to court very changed from the gay, vibrant princess farewelled at Salamanca. She came not only bearing her own heavy, sorrow but also the hopes of Castilla and Aragon in her swelling belly. Hopes too soon come to nought. Two months after the prince's death, Margot's labour began.

Too early for the birth of a living child, the princess fought her pangs of childbirth like a crazed woman. Helping the midwives in the birthing chamber, when nothing more could be done to prevent the inevitable, Beatriz turned her face and wept, hearing the princess beg and plead, "Do anything!" she sobbed. "Oh God, oh God! Don't take our child away too!"

On the morning of the third day, as dawn broke, Beatriz came to the queen's chamber. Still spattered with blood, she wobbled an exhausted curtsey. When she stood, she gripped her forearms, trying to hold herself her together. The queen waved a hand towards the stool near her. Sitting, Beatriz met the queen's eyes.

"Speak, Beatriz."

"'Twas a girl-child, Your Grace..." Beatriz swallowed, realising how long it was since liquid had passed her lips. "My queen, there was never hope to bring forth a living child, not at six months. The babe's heartbeat stopped in the womb last night. We said nothing of this to Princess Margot, but she knew. The princess lost all heart and went into a stupor. It forced us to act for the princess's only chance for life this morning. We pulled the dead babe from her womb. God help and forgive us, 'twas the only thing we could do. My queen, if the princess survives and marries again, 'tis doubtful she will bear another child."

Sweet Francisco,

Will these dark days ever end? The loss of our princess's child was terrible enough, but it resulted in a dreadful power struggle, after the husband of Juana seized the opportunity to proclaim them both the queen's heirs. Such a despicable action of Philip the Fair – a man whose nickname seems more and more an ill-thought jest.

Queen Isabel summoned her daughter Isabel to come in person and ensure her rights of succession. Isabel was then five months gone with child, and it upset our queen greatly to have to beg her daughter to journey such a distance.

At Toledo, Queen Isabel's Cortes, the parliament of her nobility, proclaimed Isabel the heir to Castilla, but the Cortes of Aragon still stubbornly holds on to its desire for male ascension. To persuade them otherwise, the king and queen sent again for the young Queen of Portugal. King Ferdinand believed this was the only course of action to convince the Aragonese. How the queen hated to summon her daughter back to her court. Since Isabel's return to Portugal, the reports of her health have gone from bad to worse. Now the subjects of her father forced Isabel to endure yet another hard, long journey, this time to Zaragoza, far from the Portugal border, when all her physicians advise otherwise.

"My hija must conserve her strength. It would be more glorious and would cost me less to bring these people to the right by force of arms, rather than suffer their insolence," my queen fumed, her voice as cold as steel, to the kneeling Alonso de Fonseca, after he brought word from the king.

I saw Fonseca cross himself. His long, narrow face harden-

ing, he lifted his chin and said: "Your Highness, if the Queen of Portugal wishes to be recognised as her father's heir, she must come. The Aragonese will prove constant to the monarch to which they swear."

We leave soon for Zaragoza, my love...

Two weeks later, Beatriz rode her mule behind the royal family to the Aljafería, leaving Margot behind in Sevilla. Still grieving for the loss of both husband and child, she had yet to find reason to regain her health after the birth. She was so unwell the queen and king put off all decisions regarding her future, not knowing if she would ever recover.

The summer alcázar of the kings of Aragon spread out its certain claim upon the highest hill in Zaragoza. Struggling up to reach it, Beatriz's tiring mule refused to lumber forward beyond what seemed a snail's pace. Exhausted too from the long journey and disinclined to use her whip on her poor beast, Beatriz studied the beautiful alcázar. Two circular greyish white towers at either side its entrance and similar round towers broke up the curve of strong walls. The alcázar seemed strong and impregnable, yet Christian victory had banished the Moors hundreds of years ago. On a far smaller a scale than other residences of the king and queen, this had once been the home of Saint Isabel. Eager to come to the end of her journey, Beatriz shivered, touched with forewarning.

Afternoon light crowning their veiled heads anew with gold, two black-robed queens walked arm-in-arm in the walled courtyard. Sunlight filtered through the decorative stone of the high arches and their filigree collars of lace, throwing out a dappled design of shadows upon the ground and into the building's interior.

Not long come from devotions in the tiny church belonging to the alcázar, once used as a mosque centuries ago, Beatriz sat with the infanta María, and her duena on the stone bench sewing, while Catalina and María sat on another bench close by. The girls no longer even pretended to read the books selected for their study. Beatriz heard Catalina speak to María. "What do you think they're saying to one another?"

María shrugged, kicking the dead leaves in front of her, as if attempting to clear the paved footpath. "How would I know?" Putting out her leg, she rolled her ankle, looking at her new black slipper, its thin red ribbon criss-crossed her ankle before the final tie. Both slipper and ribbon made María's foot and ankle seem narrower, perchance even dainty. María eyed Catalina. "Whatever it is, they don't want us to overhear."

Catalina lifted her eyebrows as if surprised. Her eyebrows recently thinned like the older women at court, it gave her face a strange flicker of maturity. Beatriz finger followed the high arch of her own eyebrow, courtly camouflage veiled both youth and age.

"You were not the only one dismissed by my royal mother. Isabel is my sister and I have missed her every day since she left for Portugal. I have hardly spoken to her since she arrived."

Beatriz gazed at the two queens, their backs turned towards her. The paved, narrow footpath led around the courtyard's whole circumference as well between the twin rectangular gardens. Queen Isabel and her eldest daughter reached the other side, changing her view of them. Too far away to hear other than the murmur of their voices, Isabel's huge eyes locked on her mother. She nodded at something the queen said.

Beatriz worried again about Isabel's thinness. With the young queen so slender, her huge belly appeared grotesque. Chilled despite the warmth of this spring day, Beatriz returned her gaze to Catalina. Beside her María was kicking the leaves again.

Catalina shook María's arm. "What's wrong?"

María met her eyes, looking like she wanted to weep. The prince's death, soon followed by that of his child, swirled everyone's emotions too close to the surface. For months now they had struggled to reclaim and piece back together their lives after grief and more grief tore it into shreds. Beatriz sighed. *How many times is life's fabric undone?*

María stared at the ground. No leaves left for her to kick, she gazed back at Catalina. "I wish we were not here – anywhere, but here."

"But why? You've always liked it here!"

Perturbed, Beatriz wondered if María too had caught the same sense of impending disaster she had felt on coming here. She turned her attention to the courtyard. Sunlight slanted over the roof, deluging the small trees sculptured like huge globes. Losing none of its power, the afternoon light struck the water fountain at one side, sparkling the jets of water into crystals. Backed by a sapphire sky, a small bird, with a flutter of brown wings, hopped along the edge of the roof, stopping now and then to look around for foes, raking its beak upon stone. Nothing seemed to threaten them here. But Beatriz felt threatened. Day-by-day, she felt threat's shadow deepen and lengthen.

"Our ancestress haunts this place," María said. As if shocked at her own words, the girl's teeth clamped down upon her bottom lip.

"What's wrong with you today? You talk like a fool. And which ancestress do you speak of? So many of our family lived here." "You should know. This courtyard was once hers, the place she spent her childhood. Always the queen has held Isabel, so long ago Queen of Portugal, up to you and your sisters. Always, it made me uneasy."

"Uneasy? Why uneasy about Isabel of Portugal? Surely a saint amongst our forebears is reason for pride. She would not haunt us. Why should she?"

María tossed back her head. "If she does not haunt you that does not mean she doesn't haunt someone else. You know as well as I, since her first husband's death, all Isabel has wanted was to be like this other Isabel..."

Catalina paled. Studying her older sister she shook her head. "Maybe once, but you forget that our ancestor was an old woman when she took the veil, after her husband's death. Her children were grown. Now, thank God, my sister has the same chance to become a mother."

Beatriz also lifted her eyes to the young queen. Yet again, with her back towards her, she reminded her of a thin, straight stick. There was nothing to her but black robes and huge belly.

"Cannot you see?" María asked, holding her friend's hand. "Nothing really has changed for her. Too many times she smiles at us as if she is not really here, even to the queen, your mother. 'Tis as if she moves through life just to reach the day of death."

Catalina snatched her hand away. "Don't say that."

María lowered her head and shrugged. "You said you always

want me to speak honestly to you. I know your sister almost as well as you. She has never hidden from us what is in her heart."

Catalina rubbed at her eyes. "There's the babe. When Isabel holds her child, she'll no longer think of death."

María clasped again Catalina's hand. Feeling cold, Beatriz sat in silence, left to the harsh mercy of her thoughts.

***

Am I a fool with all this disquiet about impending doom? Beatriz wondered the next day. For in the garden the young queen sat and smiled amongst them, busily sewing a baptism robe for her unborn infant. Talking about her new life in Portugal, she reminded Beatriz of the less dark-spirit Isabel at the onset of her first marriage to Alfonso. Her free hand resting on her swollen stomach, Isabel smiled tenderly. "My little son is restless. He knows his father will arrive here soon. Manuel will not miss our boy's birth."

Catalina and her sister María lounged against large cushions set upon a rug near Isabel. Beatriz sat with María de Salinas on the thick, lush grass. The infanta María reached over, plucking a few camomile daisies. Crushing the flowers in her hand, she brought them to her nose and closed her eyes.

Beatriz plucked a daisy too. Placing it face up on her palm, she spread out its petals, reminded of a golden sun, its centre gloriously yellow, rays white with heat. Hearing the infanta María's sudden bell of laughter, she raised her eyes. The girl knelt at Isabel's side, their heads close together, comparing the tiny baby clothes they made. Flowing free from under her black, unadorned roundlet, María's long blonde hair gleamed with red lights, contrasting vividly against her sister's black veils.

Seeing them close together always made Beatriz very aware of their similarities. Isabel's veils hid a similar glorious hair colour to her younger sister, and their eyes were of the same deep green/blue. Except for Juana, all the queen's daughters bore the strong physical stamp of their mother. As for the mental stamp... Beatriz thought again about the infanta María. Happy just to be and live, María never seemed to share the same stubborn fire of faith of her three sisters and her mother.

Catalina shifted, righting herself to her knees. Leaning closer to her older sister, she touched the swaddling clothes in Isabel's hand. "They're so small, sister. You forget how little babes are until you ready garments for their birth." Catalina glanced at the blanket held in her hand. Hours of painstaking embroidery brought the coat of arms of Portugal nearer to completion, a red shield with yellow castles all around, set in the midst of a yellow circle. Now she sewed the final smaller blue shields upon the white shield in the centre. "Would it matter so much if your child is female? I would welcome a niece as much as a nephew."

Isabel laughed, shadows deepening the hollows of her face. "You would be singing a different tune if you were the one awaiting childbirth. I would not be too pleased to go through all this trouble, all the days of illness, just to bring forth a girl-child. Especially remembering how much trouble being a girl-child brought me. Being female is not something I would ever wish for my child."

María narrowed her eyes against the light. "You seem so certain the child will be a boy. Surely, 'tis not for us to know the sex of our children before birth, and girls must be born, no matter our desire." Isabel considered María, drumming fingers against the side of her taut gown. "You're right, girls must be born. But I feel certain I bear within me a son. I have felt like this ever since I first felt the child quicken with life." She laughed a little. "You know I am rarely wrong."

Catalina laughed the gruff laugh so alike her mother's. Peering at her sister, she smiled mischievously. "And the times you were wrong, our Isabel? I remember not so long ago you said you would never be happy again, yet here you are today, making merry with your sisters. It gives me joy to see you thus."

Isabel drooped forward over her big belly like a flower pushed forward in the wind. She sighed. "Mi chiquitina, I know now we are fools if we don't take joy when it is offered and revel in happiness while we may."

Isabel became silent, spreading out her baby's robe upon her lap. She lifted shining eyes. "I have done much soul-searching ever since our brother died. It took his death, rather than all the years Juan tried so hard to comfort me, to awake me from the darkness of my half-life, never seeing the woman I so sinfully allowed myself to become.

"I caged myself in my grief, selfishly shutting out all those who loved me. When Juan died, in my mind I heard his voice encouraging me to seek out joy... I felt again the warmth of his love that I often turned from while he lived.

"I know now my self-pity cost me much, years and years when I could have been a better sister, not only for you, María and Juana, but also for him. Juan hated the thought of being king, yet few he trusted with the burden of this knowledge. He trusted me – tried to talk to me about his fears of not being the king our parents hoped and wanted of him. I will regret to my death how I failed him. I should have listened to him rather than wallow in self-pity." Brushing away her tears, Isabel smiled, looking at the sunlit garden. "But I try hard not to fail him now. I have had enough of unhappiness."

Catalina and María gazed at one another. Without a word, the sisters knelt on either side of Isabel, nestling in close, each taking one of their sister's hands. Despite their smiles, grief marked their faces. The months since the tragedy of the prince's passing had not lessened the gaping hole of loss. Beatriz brushed away tears. Her heart ached too. She doubted time would ever heal the loss of their golden prince.

As predicted by his wife, Queen Isabel's court was soon joined by the King of Portugal. Arriving with little fanfare, none knew of his presence until he burst into the garden, looking for his wife. "Isabel," he cried, his unhidden anxiety turning into joy.

Surprised to see him race to his wife's side like a boy, Beatriz stood and then curtseyed with the infantas and the other attendants. The king did not notice. He dropped to his knees, threw his arms around Isabel, laying his head on her breast.

Kissing the top of her husband's dark head, Isabel laughed. "I fear your son must learn courtesy. Our boy has kicked you."

Hands on Isabel's belly, the young king hooted out a laugh that made all smile. His eyes alight, the adoration he showed during their wedding celebrations had not changed since the months of marriage. He rose to kiss his wife. Beatriz smiled. It seemed their months of marriage had only served to increase his love. Isabel too lifted to him shining eyes. Whilst they blazed not with the deep, first love she once showed to Alfonso, they still glowed with something near.

The final weeks of her pregnancy passed slowly. Soon, Isabel's belly became so large she needed the assistance of those around her to help her rise from sitting to standing. Her husband was often the first one to help. Bringing out his harp to make music while she sewed the baptism gown for their child, the king spent all his free time with his wife enjoying the lovely spring days in the garden.

Two weeks after King Manuel's arrival, Beatriz knelt on the grass in the courtyard, picking camomile daisies to make a soothing tea for the queen. Lessons over for the day, Catalina was again with her mother, playing chess with María. No doubt the girls were talking about the latest communications from England. The English king grew more and more impatient for Catalina's arrival.

Feeling too warm, Beatriz righted herself, her eyes drawn to the beautiful staircase leading to the royal chambers. A coffered ceiling overtopped the staircase. On one side, the interior of the alcázar opened up. She leaned against the Corinthian column that formed one end of an arch, looking up at the ceiling. The throne room also possessed a ceiling worthy of note, an over-ornate carved and painted artesonado ceiling, the rich wooden panels very alike to that of a ceiling at the Alhambra. All feasted the eye.

Heavy footsteps crunched gravel. Beatriz looked through a crack between wall and the jutting Corinthian column hiding her from view in the garden. The young queen and her husband walked along the garden path, talking animatedly to one another, but as yet too far away to hear.

Beatriz gazed at Isabel's husband. The complicated web often spun out by kinship, especially that of royal kinship, very little suggested the blood ties between this short, slight man and his nephew, the long-dead Alfonso. King Manuel's much older sister was Alfonso's mother. Isabel's distressed voice stopped her thoughts. Through the crack she saw Isabel push her husband away. She spun around, facing the path leading in Beatriz's direction. Her eyes blind and wide with horror, she ran awkwardly. The short distance left her gasping for breath.

Beatriz stood and stepped back, tight against the wall, keeping herself out of sight. King Manuel reached his wife and took her arm. His black eyes beseeched Isabel. "My love, forgive me. I thought it wisest to keep this from you, but how could I when we vowed to speak truth to one another? Now we are here... a voice from the grave does not give me any peace. You needed to know, my Isabel."

"You lie," she sobbed. Hiccupping through her tears, she sagged against him. "Why do you tell me this? Why now? Manuel, why now?" His face the colour of ash he lifted his chin, the angles of his face sharpening in his finely drawn face. "Love, believe me only fear for our child moved me to speak. I would not have told you this for the world, but my cousin João would never have spoken to me of such matters unless he thought it true."

Isabel pulled away from him and stood rigid, her hands tight fists at her sides. "My father is not a murderer!"

Beatriz's heart stopped, freezing her to absolute stillness.

King Manuel reached out to Isabel, dropping his hands to his sides at what he saw in her face. "Forgive me. Put it from your mind, my Isabel. I promised your mother our son can be raised at her court. I know he will be safe with her."

Isabel stared at her husband. "Our son... remain in Mother's care? When was this arranged? Why am I the last to know that my child is to be taken from me?"

The king took hold of her shoulders before slipping his arms around her. "Sweet love, my own sweet love. This is why I had to tell you. Treachery has been my companion all my life. I smell it, as if I smell a decaying corpse. My love, that smell follows your father, wherever he goes. Marrying you, I never wanted to believe what my cousin told me, but if our child is a son... I cannot risk his life by acting blind and deaf. Placing our boy in your mother's care

ensures him of life. I believe that. And your father will not rid himself of a grandson he comes to love or trains to be king after him. I have to believe that, have to believe he'll grow to forgive our boy my blood."

Isabel slumped into his arms, holding onto him for support. She stared up, breathing heavily. "Manuel..." All life drained from her face. "You truly believe my father murdered Alfonso?"

The king groaned and tightened his arms around her. "Love, you must know political expediency is your father's only catch-cry. For years he has pushed the English king to do what he would have done years ago, rid himself of a harmless, imprisoned man, just because his blood makes him too close a claimant for the throne."

Isabel shook her head. "No, no – you do my father grave injustice." Her hand gripping her throat, she swallowed. "To say such things about my father... As for Warwick, he just wants to make England safer for my sister when she's queen."

King Manuel's face became ugly. "Si, safer for your sister. All should have such fathers..."

"Is it wrong that he cares about my sister's safety?"

He stared over her head. "I don't believe it is just for your sister's safety, but rather looking to the future and ensuring she becomes queen and stays queen. Power means all to your father.

"With Alfonso, your father feared your mother's worsening health would bring Juan to her throne too soon. Your brother was untried and often unwell, when Castilla needs a ruler with a strong hand. With you married to the heir of Portugal and next in line to your mother's crown, your father worried João might be tempted to reach for the apple itself. Many in Castilla respected my cousin João, knowing him a strong king with a strong son.

"Your father hates us. The turd Portuguese he calls us behind our backs. I don't think he cares over-much that his insults come back to me. He did not trust the uneasy peace your marriage to Alfonso brought with it. Your father never wanted your marriage, but the queen, your mother, knew you loved Alfonso. What she can do for you she does, even at the cost to herself."

Isabel's fingers squeezed her husband's hands, as once before on a beach at sunset, before the beginning of so much grief, she held onto her brother, begging release from the fetters of duty. "My mother... does she know?"

The king shook his head. "No, no, my love. João was certain it was your father's hand that set in motion Alfonso's death. Remember, it came at a time when your hopes of bearing Alfonso's child had just come to nought, followed by the fire that almost cost your mother her life. A short time afterward,

Alfonso received a gift from your father, the stallion that took his life."

Her mouth open, Isabel stared. "But it was an accident."

Manuel shook his head. "Made to look like an accident. My cousin learnt later that the horse hated the touch of man and was easily spooked. And if that was not enough, a Castilian groom was Alfonso's only companion that night. Who knows what really happened that evening.

"King João went to his grave believing the tragedy was no accident. It bore too much the wily, underhanded stamp of King Ferdinand. He believed that after the camp fire your father decided to take no more chances of Portugal threatening the smooth succession of your brother. He wanted Juan to assume the throne without any threatening him."

Her face wet with tears, Isabel shook her head and hiccupped. "Father killed Alfonso." She stared up at him. "You are certain my mother does not know?"

The king tightened his arms around her. "Your mother loves God too much to ever design to kill the beloved husband of her daughter, whom she loves more than life itself. But my love, when I spoke to her about our child... Isabel, my heart tells me she suspects your father, but is too loving a wife to ever voice these suspicions."

As quietly as possible, Beatriz stole away in the direction of the staircase and, once up them, to her chamber. She closed her door and sat on the closest stool. She wished she had never been in the garden. Now she possessed knowledge of such magnitude it could have her killed. She gazed towards the fire-place. The hearth black and dead, yet she felt she stared into Hell. She knew the king was capable of murder, but whether he had Alfonso's blood on his hands she did not want to know.

***

Her husband's suspicions destroyed Isabel. She no longer sat with her sisters in the garden, enjoying the warm days of spring, but remained in a darkened chamber, waiting for her baby to be born, waiting to die. Blaming himself and increasingly desperate, despairing, King Manuel only left her chamber to walk around the garden.

Isabel told her mother she no longer wished to live. She wanted to be with Alfonso and Juan, where nothing and no one would hurt her again. Whether she told the queen the reason why, Beatriz did not know. But she suspected she did. Queen Isabel, when she emerged from her daughter's chamber, seemed an utterly broken woman.

All day long, hour by hour, back and forth, her confessor, her mother and her husband visited Isabel in her darkened chamber. None turned her from her quest to seize death in childbirth. Thus, Beatriz joined the midwives, preparing to battle for her life.

Catalina could not understand why her sister no longer wanted life. Listening to her, consoling her, Beatriz locked her awful knowledge away, praying to God for the strength to always keep it from her. Catalina loved her father. It would not help her to know the truth of the shallowness of his love for her, that her happiness meant nothing to him before his ambitions.

Spring no longer ruled their days. The knowledge Isabel turned her face from life darkened everything. They prayed and prayed, but Beatriz knew in her heart of hearts that Isabel's last chance for life died when Manuel told her the truth behind Alfonso's death.

King Ferdinand returned from his discussions with his Cortes on the day Isabel began her labour. Still unhappy with the thought of a woman ruler, his grandees asked to delay their decision until the birth of Isabel's child. They hoped a son would solve the problem of succession. The king never realised his daughter no longer cared who ruled Aragon, or Castilla.

Isabel gave birth to her boy, held him for a moment, and died. Beatriz brought the news to Queen Isabel, leaving the midwives to deal with the weak infant.

Beatriz entered the queen's chamber and the queen rose from her chair, hands gripping tight the armrests, her face so bone-white and ill-looking Beatriz feared for her life too. The king stepped out of the shadows, standing next to his wife. Beatriz couldn't speak but shook her head, holding out her hands in defeat.

As if she defended herself against life, against grief, Catalina bolted up from the cushion beside the queen's chair. She whispered, "Mother –" Beatriz did not know whether Catalina cried for help for herself or in worry for Queen Isabel. She wound her arm around the now weeping girl.

"Isabel's son lives," Beatriz said, desperate to say something of hope.

"Our hija has left a son," the king repeated.

Queen Isabel stared at him, her mouth snapping shut. She groaned, falling to her knees, arms tight around her body, chest heaving, rocking to and fro. Blinking back tears, Beatriz winced. The queen moaned and moaned like a woman in the throes of agonising childbirth. The king gazed at her with distaste, and then searched the room as if seeking escape. He heaved a shuddering breath, pain and grief carving deeper lines on his face. Straightening his shoulders, he strode over to his wife's side.

"My Isabel –" He tried to pull her up from the ground. Again, he gazed around the room, this time at the queen's weeping attendants. Pulling once more at his wife's arm, King Ferdinand gathered back to him the guise of a king. "Let us go your bedchamber, and grieve in privacy."

She shook off his hand. "Don't touch me!"

The king took her arm again, speaking so softly that only those close enough to him could hear. "Wife, remember where you are. I say again, let's us go to your rooms together and there grieve for our daughter."

The queen shook her head, refusing to meet his eyes. "I don't want you here. Leave me. Please, please, leave me alone."

Bewildered, his mouth trembling, he stared at her. The king almost appeared like a child suddenly abandoned by his mother. "Isabel. Isabel –"

"Ferdinand –" The torments of Hell blazed out of the queen's eyes.

Beatriz licked her dry lips. *Dear God. Pray, this latest tragedy does not drive the queen to madness like her mother.*

"Leave me now if you don't want our love destroyed."

Fear alight in his eyes, the king stared at his wife. He bowed, backed away, and left the queen to her women.

Beatriz thought, *She knows! She knows everything.* Next to her, Catalina began to weep. Murmuring, "I am here," Beatriz led the shocked girl into the courtyard. Spring still embraced the season, but it seemed the bleakness of winter chilled all their hearts.

My love,

You are away from me too long – how I look forward to the day when I welcome your return. I received a letter from Josefa yesterday. She tells me our son is well and happy, and invites us to stay with her when our duties allow.

The queen is sadly changed from the woman we knew years ago. Her sorrows weigh her down until she almost drowns under their weight. She closets herself with her priest for the hours and worries about dying well. Since her daughter's death, she has placed her house in order and paid many debts.

The infanta María is now married to the King of Portugal. With his daughter Isabel securing the succession of Aragon by the birth of a son, the king was happy to see another of his daughters become a consort to a king. The queen told me that it was seeing the tenderness and devotion of Manuel for her Isabel that swayed her to marry him to María. Pray to God, may María have the happiness denied to her poor sister...

That tragic spring frittered away to autumn, to winter and then another spring. Spring restored verdant life to the land, but not to the spirit of Queen Isabel. Fighting her own battle against despair, Beatriz felt bereft of any words offering any real meaning as the increasingly fragile queen spiralled deeper where none could help her. But she tried to talk to her, tried to get her to open her heart to her. One day, she was more fortunate than on others.

"God's wounds, Beatriz," the queen said to her. "There isn't one day or night when I do not doubt. Every day my doubts pull me down like hunting wolves in winter."

"My queen, doubt is a part of life."

"Part of life... Once life was not the dark world I find myself in now. Once, doubt never ruled me. Once, with all my heart, I believed I had to ensure the succession of a strong kingdom for my son. I believed I did it for God. I believed I did it for my son. Juan's death showed me the error of that belief. What I believed came from God was but the drub of my own desire, my own fear and lack of true faith. Was it all for nought, Beatriz? The last few years have seen me like Job."

"Your Grace, your losses would test the strength of saints. But cannot you think your hard trials prove God's love for you? Suffering turns us to God and the truth of our existence. The labour pains of our Earthly life birth us into Heaven. Remember, sorrow comes in order to test faith."

The queen sputtered a grim, bitter laugh. "You speak like my confessor. Perchance on another lighter day I'd give your words better credence. Today I am just too tired, too heart-sore. I have tried my upmost to be a just queen. I never wanted to be called a tyrant. I came to the throne believing with all my heart that Castilla was mine, that the deaths of my two brothers left me the rightful heir to our father's crown. I never wanted to see Castilla endangered by passing to the rule of a foreign lineage. God, I truly believed, placed me in this royal state as rightful queen. All I thought was to do right by God and my country, to bring my subjects peace after years of so much evil and destruction."

"And so you have, your Grace. You are a good queen."

"I remember well the times you told me otherwise – if not in words, then a look I could not fail to understand. You were right. I made too many mistakes thinking I acted for God when it wasn't that way at all. I only listened to myself, or my husband. I wasn't listening to God at all."

"My queen, please don't torment yourself. We all make mistakes. We are human, after all."

Queen Isabel laughed bitterly. "My husband assures me queens and kings do not make mistakes... But I have made them, Beatriz. I vowed to bring peace and prosperity to Castilla, only to bring the harbingers of death and destruction. I lie awake at night and think that the loss of Isabel and Juan is more God's punishment for the evil of my mistakes. Remember, Abravanel promised divine punishment if I expelled the Jews. Perchance that's the root for all my grief.

"My thoughts at night suck me into a black void of nothingness. I wonder then if this is Hell, for all my days seem Hell already." Her heart heavy, Beatriz thought, *Was the victory of the Holy War paid in sorrow? Did the queen reach for glory, only to find it hollow and worthless?*

"Isabel, how I wish I knew the words to comfort you. If I was a priest, I'd probably say 'tis not for us to question the way of the Lord."

"Those words do not help, Beatriz."

"Then let me speak of what's in my heart. Life means more than simply waiting for death. I believe everything in life happens for a purpose. I believe we are here to learn – and the lessons are so often hard. Sometimes, it would be far easier to let ourselves go under than keep on fighting. Yet this is what we must do. It is the only thing we can do."

24

"There is no one in the city who is not
Christian, and all the mosques are churches."
~ Cisneros

In the Hall of the Two Sisters, the overhead cupola tempered forth a muted light – a light birthing another day, a light that conjured the imaginings of wide awake dreams. Beatriz wrote beside Catalina. The girl read *The City of Women*, while Beatriz wrote notes concerning her favourite tract of Aristotle.

María plucked notes on her vihuela, singing a slow song of love, betrayal and death. Catalina put her book down and rose from the bench. She began to dance, her movements flourishing the song's lyrics with measured movements. Catalina was still tiny, but she danced in perfect harmony with her height.

Beatriz sighed. The girls were now thirteen and no longer children. Their bodies took on womanly forms and flowered to the promise of spring. Already small apple breasts pushed against their chemises, waists nipped in, widened hips boded fertility.

Months ago the queen had wept when Doña Teresa Manrigue murmured of the start of Catalina's courses. Discussions then became frequent about the right time for her to leave her mother's court for England and make a true marriage. While the queen conceded these talks to the English, all knew she would not let her youngest child leave her court for some time yet, not only because Catalina was just thirteen. Queen Isabel needed her youngest child at her side.

Si, both her girls were no longer children. The presence of Doña Eliva Manuel, elected the duena who would one day go with the princess to England, now became a constant shadow on their day.

Overly efficient in her duties she strived to please Catalina, even biting back in the presence of the princess her dislike and jealousy of Beatriz. This morning Catalina escaped her watchful eye by asking her to oversee the selection of gowns for the expected arrival of English diplomats.

Lifting her head, María closed her eyes. Her beautiful voice soared and throbbed like the notes of her vihuela, touching Beatriz's heart. The page she wrote on blurred, and she saw Francisco in her mind. They rode together on his horse from the abundant, colour rich gardens banked against the walls of the Alhambra. The river of Darro wound before her eyes, like a thin ribbon of silver, alive, pulsing, glittering and glinting, as if the morning light jewelled it with countless diamonds. The hills and plains of Granada stretched out as far as the sight of an eagle in flight. Sunlight seeped into the very air itself. The brown, flower-rich land swelled with life and passion, a land feeding and nourishing heart and soul.

Astride, mantle-less, skirts tucked up high, thighs pressed tight against the sides of the mount, Beatriz wound her arms around Francisco's lean waist. Her long black hair streamed loose in the wind. Like Adam and Eve, they were the only man and woman in an innocent world. A world untouched by sorrow.

A string broke and woke Beatriz from her trance and daydream, desire firing her heart and coursing in her veins. She gazed at María. Still an awkward maid, the girl was like Catalina, protected from the gaze and touch of man. The girl looked bewildered, as if her song had stirred her too. Beatriz knew from their conversations that María yearned for adulthood, but feared it, too. Catalina also seemed disturbed, breathing hard from her dance, hands planted on her hips, she shook her head, as if shaking away the remnants of a dream.

Beatriz smiled and clapped her hands. "Your song goes well, María. It is finished, si?"

The girl blushed, her fingers strummed the unbroken strings, they made a jarring noise. "My infanta thinks it finished. But I'm not certain."

Beatriz laughed. "In all the time I have been your teacher I have never seen you entirely satisfied with what you do. That makes me content because I know you'll always strive to climb higher. All teachers should have such students."

"And me?" Catalina asked. Standing beside her friend, a wide smile spread on her face.

Beatriz reached for the bowl next to her with pieces of dry apricot. Taking a piece, she put it in her mouth and chewed, thinking out her answer. "I never hide from you the great delight you give me. Often I regret I cannot train you to take my place as professor at Salamanca. You have so many skills and talents, just like the queen."

Catalina bit at her bottom lip and blushed. "If I am just a little like my mother, I'll be content."

Her eyes staying on Catalina, Beatriz pulled her earlobe. "Infanta, don't mistake my meaning. You bear the seeds of great promise, but they are different seeds to that of our noble queen. You are unique, we all are. If life teaches us anything it is to know ourselves, our strengths and weaknesses. Do not fall into the trap of yearning to be someone else. We praise God for much, but our greatest praise to Him must be to gift Him with our true selves.

"Be thankful, my princess, that God has given you the learning the queen lacked as a young girl. Most importantly, God places you where you can observe a woman ruler able to rule men. No lesson I could teach you has as much value as that."

***

Another day, another sweet, pure voice sang another song:

For ever there remains with me one longing,
Ceaselessly, day and night, at every hour,
Tormenting me so I would gladly die,
For my life is nothing but a pining,

And in the end I'll have to die of it.
I thought myself quite sure against misfortune
When that accursed longing in which I dwell
Overtook me, intent that I should die,
For my life is nothing but a pining,
And in the end I'll have to die of it:
Forever.

Margot's fingers plucked the final note. "Forever," she repeated. The young woman stared as if at nothing, her tears dripping onto Juan's vihuela. Beatriz met the miserable eyes of Catalina and María. What comfort can be given to one so full of grief, especially when you too share that grief?

María turned, rubbing at her eyes. The girl had grown up watching Juan play his lute or vihuela, his beautiful voice wooing her from childhood to a sadder and more uncertain time. It was no wonder his wife begged the instrument from his mother. María probably wished she had the same right to ask for something, anything, once belonging to Juan. She had only the vihuel he gave her in childhood. She had nothing else of him but the memories they all shared. Somehow that thought comforted Beatriz. She gazed around so certain of Juan's presence.

Despite the tears lighting her eyes, Margot seemed comforted too. "The queen and king have given me many gifts to take home, but none is more precious than this."

"You will write, my sister?" Catalina asked.

Fresh pain thickened Margot's voice. "I cannot promise you that, mi chiquitina."

Catalina turned a face furrowed by distress. "But why?"

Margot got up, placing the vihuela carefully on the stool's

cushion. She sat next to Catalina and wound her arm around her.

"Not because I don't love you. Never think that. I will always love you. But you forget, I go back to be a pawn again. My father hates your father – and so does my brother. I do not believe we will be allowed the consolation of letters." She gazed sadly at the vihuela. "Perchance that is for the best. I must stop myself from looking behind, otherwise my poems will come true and I'll die of grief." She rested her head on Catalina's shoulder. "Juan..." Margot swallowed hard. "My sweet Juan would not want me to pine my life away."

There was one more royal death during these dark years. Writing of it to her husband, Beatriz recalled the gossamer-winged dragonfly she had seen, just days before knowing Prince Juan was lost to them forever in this life. Across the water it darted, in an eye-blink of time, its shimmering, rainbow-hued wings flashing over the water's surface before clouds blocked out the sun. A moment of beauty gone forever, but even though grief tore once more at Beatriz, she held onto the one thing she believed with all her heart: you cannot really lose what you love, for loving renders eternity.

Two years of life was more than enough time for love to bridge eternity. And how could any not love a little bright-eyed boy so filled with joy? Every day of his short life, he stretched out his arms for his family's embrace. How could any ever think of him as a promise never fulfilled, a flower pushing through the winter snow to never bloom?

The boy made his grandmother smile again, sitting on her lap, one hand patting her face and the other playing with the heavy chain of her crucifix, chattering a mixture of real words and ones he made up in his attempt to tell one of those he loved the great story of his small life. The little one gave them the delight of hearing the queen laugh once more.

If not in his grandmother's arms he was in the arms of those who attended her. Not a day passed after Isabel's death when Catalina and María did not hold him, kiss him, play with him. Before they knew it, he grew from tiny infant to active child, wriggling out of arms, demanding to be let down, wanting to toddle around his world in his impatience to seize it.

Dark-haired like his father but with his mother's sea-blue eyes, in his tiny palm he captured so many hearts during his brief life. With great pride, he spoke his first full, clear sentences the day the fever struck. Death again stole away the darting dragonfly of beauty and left them bereft once more. But that was not the end of grief.

***

Beatriz sat with Francisco by the hearth. Leaping flames of a famished fire flickered its reflections on the polished wood of his vihuela. His fingers plucked the strings, the ruby in his heavy gold ring flashing in the firelight with each note. "Time for one more song before we go to bed?"

Her hand going to rub her throat, Beatriz laughed. "I think you said that about the last song. I am likely to be hoarse if I sing more."

Francisco laid his hand over her hand. "Sing for me. You

don't know how much I dream of evenings like this when I'm away from you. I hate and curse these unending skirmishes. I hate and curse those Moors who refuse to admit defeat. I resent anything that keeps me from your side. I'm an old, weary warhorse who only wants to be put out to pasture."

Beatriz shook her head. Taking her hand from his, she placed a finger across his mouth. "Shhh – not old – never that. We can only pray that soon all the fighting will come to an end."

Francisco averted his face and gazed at the fire. He sighed. "Don't waste your prayers on something that never will happen. I have lived long enough to know to talk of peace and men is but a children's fable."

Beatriz clasped his hand. "Remember – we promised to speak of only happy things tonight, and all the nights we have together before you must leave me again."

Francisco grinned at her like a young man. "So we did. And for me to play my vihuela and for you to sing."

Beatriz laughed at him. "All right – one last song. What will it be?"

Francisco brushed his fingers against the strings of his vihuela and a familiar chord took shape.

Beatriz laughed again. "Will you sing it with me?"

Francisco leaned across and kissed her lips tenderly. "I am so happy," he murmured.

Beatriz stroked his face, her finger tracing around his mouth. "While you are with me, love, so am I."

Beatriz cleared her throat, and sang with her husband:

"I am so happy!"
All of the birds of the world of love were singing;

It was my love and yours that they had in mind.
"I am so happy!"
All of the birds of the world of love were chanting;
It was my love and yours that they were naming.
"I am so happy!"

In the school-room the next day, her own father also soldiering again, María hounded Beatriz mercilessly with her questions, trying to understand why her father must again go forth into battle when she knew he had so hoped to go home. Loud rumours at court blamed the most recent rebellion on the queen's new confessor.

"You must know the Franciscan Cisneros is a man of deep convictions," Beatriz at last answered. She bent over her desk, sorting through a thick pile of untidy papers.

"My princess tells me he once lived a hermit life in a wooden hut he built himself. He did not want to be confessor to the queen."

Still searching amongst her papers she glanced up, relieved María was now thinking about other things. "Si. The dying Cardinal Mendoza thought Cisneros the right man to take his place." She shrugged and tried to laugh. "Cisneros had his own doubts about this. He believed being the queen's confessor would only bring him in too much contact with worldly matters. Cisneros understood confessor to the queen also meant political advisor. He did a great deal of soul-searching before accepting."

"You mean Cardinal Cisneros ran away." María giggled.

"Remember when Cardinal Mendoza died? The queen wanted Cisneros to take upon the now vacant Archdiocese of Toledo? He raced from her chambers as if in fear for his life. The guards had to bring him back to the queen to accept."

Beatriz placed one heap of papers to the side of the table, her hand weighing down the greater pile. She eyed María. "I'm not sure I blame him for doing so. The archdiocese brought with it the office of chancellor to the kingdom and all that entailed."

Returning to their conversation about the new battle, María blurted out, "The king believes the cardinal is at fault at this latest rising at Granada."

Beatriz cried out in delight, unfolding a paper and laying it flat on the table. It was a recipe to treat burns, something she wanted to give to Francisco before he left again. Francisco commanded another team of men in these last days of Queen Isabel's Holy War, helping douse out the last flaring fires of resistance.

"The king is likely right. I also thought Talavera's gentle approach wisest, and said as much to the queen. Talavera believed time, education and example would solve the problem of conversion. But when Cisneros joined him, all his work went to ruin. Cisneros forced Moors to convert, not only lapsed Christians. Can you imagine how the Moors must have felt when Cisneros burned countless and priceless manuscripts?" Biting back her own anger, Beatriz shook her head. "What utter stupidity – books we will never be able to replace. Thank God he didn't burn books important to our knowledge of medicine."

A recent memory flashed into Beatriz's mind. The king, revealing again his dark side, had rounded on the queen and snarled, "What do you think, Lady, of the situation your archbishop has put us in? What our kings, our forebears, won with so much zeal and blood, we have now lost in an hour because of him."

"Is this the reason for the rebellion?" María asked.

"No..." Beatriz sighed. "Cisneros believes force necessary, if it means gaining converts for God. He imprisoned a Moorish leader, placing him in chains until he yielded to conversion. Before we knew it, all hell's let loose, and rebels besiege the cardinal's residence. Cisneros refuses to leave for the safety of the Alhambra. That's why your father finds himself wielding his sword again, and my husband must again serve the queen in war."

María punched the air. "'Tis not fair – none of it is. Not fair for us, nor the queen. The king is as furious at her as he is at Cisneros." Beatriz picked up her paper. "María, the king is very jealous of the power the queen has given to her new confessor. She struggles to keep the peace between them."

Beatriz recalled the queen's reply to the king: "My lord husband, I beg you, give him the benefit of the doubt and do not listen to rumour until we have all the facts before us and hear what he has to say. Let's wait until we know the full story before we point fingers of blame."

Thus, before the end of another week María's father and Beatriz's husband accompanied the king to put out the fire of this new rebellion.

The sky still streaked with the colours of dawn, Beatriz and María stood close together, watching them go. María's father hurried after his lord, King Ferdinand, his long, black hair now streaked by grey. Years of soldiering out in the field bronzed his skin to dark leather, etching deep and permanent lines upon his face, but still he strode to his waiting horse with all the loose-limbed grace of a far younger man.

But Beatriz really had eyes only for one man. From their vantage point, Francisco seemed little changed from the handsome man she had fallen in love with years ago. Wise when she first met him, time only deepened that well while gently changing his physical shell. Her forever merry husband appeared to possess not one worry in the world, taking charge of his men with power, energy and confidence.

Seeing his brown hand on his sword, Beatriz thought of his long, calloused fingers making music and touching her with love. Her heart started to hurt. She heard him saying again, "I'm an old, weary warhorse who only wants to be put out to pasture." But there was no other choice for him. The passing of years only made Francisco more devoted to the queen, and more expert with gunpowder. While the queen needed his skills, he would never ask for release from her service.

Francisco took the reins of his horse from one of his waiting men. It was his favourite stallion he rode that day. Later, much later, Beatriz was glad of that. A man going unknowingly and so nobly to his death should have with him at least one thing he loved. Placing his hand on the saddle, he effortlessly bounded onto his horse's back.

Astride, Francisco half-twisted towards her, a wide smile stretching across his face. The steady wind ruffling his greying hair, he flung out his arm wide in farewell. Beatriz would never forget the pride in his eyes, the pride that seemed to shine brighter than the sun. How could she forget? That day, for the last time, she saw his pride in her.

Beatriz lifted her own arm in farewell. Francisco wheeled his horse. Half-rearing, it neighed, as if welcoming the coming battle, and galloped away, out of sight. For a long while Beatriz stood with María until they could watch no longer, and then went back to the royal chambers. Before that week's end, both of them would have reason to comfort the other.

25

A word from the mouth is like a stone from a sling.
~ Castillan proverb

The king backed Beatriz against the wall, tearing off her widow veils, roughly dragging down her bodice to bare her breasts. His other hand disappeared under her skirts, his arm levering up her gown. A beam of light struck the naked skin of her legs as he elbowed them apart.

"No, please, no. I beg you, my lord… my Lord King, please! I am in mourning."

The king kissed her hard, all the while loosening the drawstrings of his black leggings, ramming her against the wall with his soldier's strength. Helpless to fight back, Beatriz put out her hands on either side of her, feeling like one crucified.

"Mourning? I'm sick of mourning, Beatriz. Sick of women who mourn. Sick, do you hear? I want to forget grief and what better way than this. Beg again, my dear, I like women who beg…"

With a violent movement, he pushed her legs apart, wider. He ground into her, one hand squeezing her breast and the other beneath her buttocks. He grunted and grunted to rhythmical movements, while Beatriz crumbled against him, beaten by pain, defeated by life, and turned her face away. She wept. Birds chirped to the sound of his heavy breathing. She wept. The king's awful animal sounds went on and on, assaulting her almost much as the physical assault. She wept and wept.

How could she let this happen, couldn't she have done something to stop him? Why now? Why again? She wanted to die.

***

Selecting her book from the pile on the table, Beatriz sat there, leaving it unopened before her. It was still unopened when Catalina turned from her half-filled parchment to resharpen her quill.

"Thinking of your husband?" she asked.

Beatriz shrugged. "I will always think of him." She rubbed her wet eyes. "My books give me little joy today."

Her face empty of expression, Catalina gazed at her quill. "Do you want to talk about it?"

Beatriz bent her head. "Is life a jest that God plays on us?"

Catalina bent forward with widening eyes. "Teacher!" she gazed all around, as if wanting to ensure they remained alone. "What has happened for you to say such a thing?"

Unable to look at her, Beatriz put her head in her hands and wept. She felt the warmth of Catalina's hand, touching her head. "Forgive me," she sputtered. "I am just raw today."

Before her marriage, Beatriz had sometimes thought it would be far easier to die by her own hand, like the Roman Lucretia, rather than live with dishonour. Marriage to one of his favoured men had protected her from the king's lust. In her first years at court, she had believed his threats – that he would take almost everything she valued away from her. She could not bear the thought of not teaching, but then she had found herself in a mire almost impossible to get out of – the more she tried, the deeper she sunk. Only marriage to Francisco had saved her. Now she wondered how she would bear it for it all to start again. She lifted her head and tried to smile at her princess. She had to tell the queen, no matter the consequences. She could not live like this again.

"You asked to speak to me, Latina?"

Beatriz rose from her curtsey and lifted her eyes. Seated by the open window, Queen Isabel bent her head over her embroidery, the harsh afternoon sun showed all the lines on her face. She looked so much older than her years. But was that surprising? The last years had been grief after grief.

Beatriz licked at her dry mouth. All her life she had never struggled to begin a conversation. She thought of words as stones – things she used to build, not to destroy. Now? Now she was terrified of what her words could do to her queen.

"Beatriz?" Queen Isabel waved a hand towards a nearby

stool. "Pray, sit. I have seen that look too many times over the years to not recognise trouble."

Sitting on the stool, Beatriz took a deep breath. "Your Majesty –what I have to come to say is painful – not just for me, but for you." Queen Isabel blinked. Cocking her head to one side, she narrowed her eyes. "Painful? My friend, pray come to the crux of the matter."

"You called me friend, my queen. Do you really see me that way?" "Beatriz – I have never known you to make no sense. Of course we are friends. Good friends. How can we not be, after all these years... you are one person who I thank for stopping me from going mad. Never doubt my friendship – never doubt you can speak to me about anything."

Beatriz swallowed. It was the opening she wanted. This was the moment when she would discover the truth of their relationship. "Pray, I must talk to you about the king."

"The king?" Queen Isabel stared at her. "You say the king?" "Oh, Isabel, I must call you Isabel or I cannot speak of this." She swallowed again. "Your husband..." She bent forward, her head between her hands. "Oh, God, dear God. I cannot say it..."

Beatriz wiped the tears from her face, aware of the other woman's silence – a silence that seemed endless. She raised her head, rubbing her wet eyes. Isabel sat very still, her white face averted to the window. At last she turned, breathed deeply through her nose, and looked sadly at Beatriz.

"I think I know what you cannot say. I think I have always known. My husband hates you, my friend. When he hates, he acts on it." Isabel placed her arm on the armrest of her chair and cradled her chin in her hand. She pursed her lips. "How long?"

"For years – but never often. And never while I was wife to Francisco. But it has started again…"

Isabel lowered her head, placing her embroidery on her lap. "You should have told me, Beatriz. To suffer in silence for so long –my friend, did you not think to come to me?"

"Not when it began. I did not know you then, not as a friend. All I knew were the king's threats, and his promise to see me removed as tutor to your children and teacher at the university if I refused him. I am no longer a young woman. I believed I was no longer in danger of the king's unwanted attention. But now, to my great shame, I know otherwise."

Turning again, Isabel looked at the window. A lush green pomegranate tree grew close by – its branches heavily laden with unpicked fruit, so heavy, the luscious red fruits weighed down the branches. Bright green leaves and bright red fruit against bright blue sky – the tree was a reminder that spring was almost at an end. Isabel heaved in a long breath and let it out. "The shame is not yours, Beatriz. Do not think that. It is not my place to beg you to forgive him, but we can guess what lies at the root of his actions. He is a man with a powerful wife, a wife far more powerful than him. All the years of our marriage I have tried so hard to not remind him of this. But I am Queen of Castilla. Sometimes, Aragon must remember its place. I make my husband very angry when that happens.

"He knows I love you. By hurting you, he hurts me. This does not excuse him. And in this instance, I am glad I have the power to remind my husband how much he needs my partnership… even if it is but the wealth of Castilla he needs. This is why you are here? You want me to speak to him?"

"Isabel – please. I know I ask of you a great boon, but I cannot remain at court if I am forever avoiding the king."

"You'll not leave the court. I say this selfishly. I do not want to lose my friend. I will speak to him tonight and warn him. If he touches you again, do not fear to come and speak to me again. I promise you, my husband will live to regret it."

Another year wore on, a far, far kinder year. The queen kept her promise. She never told Beatriz what she said to the king, but he avoided her from that time. Just when she started to believe they had finally emerged from the years of darkness, Beatriz found Catalina sitting on her clothes chest, weeping. Hands planted on either side of her, she held herself straight, taking quick breaths as if in shock.

Beatriz sat beside her "What is it?" she asked, her heart in her throat. Whatever upset her must be dreadful. No longer a girl who wept easily, Catalina was a maid who knew well the burden of grief.

"He's dead," she whispered.

Beatriz's heart missed a beat. "Who?" *Death had smitten again a man or boy in their close circle – someone to give Catalina cause for sorrow?* Only her father was left for her to grieve over. Beatriz had gone the other way when she saw him, hale and vigorous, coming out of the queen's chamber less than one hour ago.

Catalina wiped her pale face with the sleeve of her chemise. Several times, she inhaled and exhaled deeply. "Forgive me. The news has come of Warwick's execution. He tried to escape with the traitor Warbeck – and now they are both dead." Catalina took another long breath. When she spoke again, Beatriz could almost hear the voice of the queen. "It is for the best. Henry Tudor has done right by his kingdom. There's now one less cause for rebellion. I shouldn't let it disturb me."

Beatriz swallowed, clasping Catalina's hand. The girl had dreaded this news for years. "It is not your fault," she said.

Startled, Catalina stared up. Fresh tears fell down her white face. "Not my fault? How can you say that? Our ambassador told King Henry in great secrecy my parents would not let me go to England until Warwick was dead. Latina, they killed him for me."

Tightening her grip on Catalina's hand, Beatriz leaned closer. "Listen to me – I say again it is not your fault." *What to say – what can I say to her to chase the demons away?* She swallowed again.

"Terrible things happen in this world…" She shook her head. "Evil things, Catalina. But think, my princess – Warwick was a catalyst for greater evil –" Seeing Catalina about to speak, Beatriz placed a finger on the girl's lips. "Let me finish. Yes – Warwick was not evil, only a young man whose great tragedy was his birth. But by allowing him life, others would have been tempted to use him for evil – and start another English civil war." *Oh – the emptiness of my words.* She took a deep breath. "We live in a world where it is wiser to enact a lesser evil to prevent a greater. Dear God, Catalina –" Beatriz cradled the side of her head. "It is not your fault, but the world we live in. All we can do is strive to change the world by our own lives, and to remember we never come to the Kingdom of Heaven but by troubles."

Too full of thoughts to desire company, once again Beatriz sat alone in the courtyard where, years ago, she had spoken to Admiral Colón. Then, as now, early morning sunlight hazed forth the verdancy of spring and countless butterflies dappled her with their fluttering shadows as they danced in mid-air. She gazed at the sky. Blue and cloudless, it mattered little when the departure of her princess and María loomed like storm clouds on the horizon of her life. Thinking about all she would soon lose, and all she had already lost, Beatriz thanked God for the intertwining of good with bad. The constant flare of Moorish rebellion close to Granada ensured the king and queen remained at the Alhambra beyond just one summer season. Content to stay at their favourite royal place of all, they still dwelled there when time approached for Catalina to start her long journey overland to the ships that would take her to England.

Days kept them busy with making and packing, ensuring the dowry chests the princess took with her included everything she needed to begin a new life in a new land. And, likewise, her attendants, those the queen chose to accompany her daughter, prepared for their new lives, too.

These busy days of preparation brought María's mother to court for a rare visit. Not yet forty, once constant childbearing softened and rounded her form. Now a year and more had passed since her husband's death. Sorrow left her thinner whilst not lessening her attractiveness. The last months had cried rumour of another grandee wooing her, desiring not only the great wealth she inherited after her mother's death, but also her mature beauty and proven fecundity. She soon sent her suitors away. Josefa refused to consider another marriage. In truth, while no other man ever threatened her husband's place in her heart, nine hard childbirths, and one that of twins, would leave few women lusting for more.

Even so, Josefa was lonely, a palpable loneliness that Beatriz knew too well.

When María told her mother she wished she could find some other man to love, Josefa had smiled at her daughter. "My María," she answered. "There's no reason for you to feel pity for me. Few in life experience the love I knew with your father. Hija, 'tis a love bridging between life and death, me on one side and your father on the other. How could I marry again feeling like that? I'm content to wait for the sake of our children, knowing when I cross that bridge, I return to his side, this time forever. I know your father waits for me."

Her way of dealing with his loss meant leaving herself with not one idle moment from dawn to dusk. María's twin brothers, now seven, as well as Beatriz's growing son, came more and more under her older brother's guidance, and her two older sisters were married to well-placed grandees. María's baby brother, the child her mother bore four months after her father's death, seemed to live with her two sisters and their children as much as he lived with his mother.

Si, Josefa was a grandmother now, but like her own mother before her she refused to just sit and sew or weave by the fire. Be that as it may, María's mother still sewed and weaved. In the school-room, Josefa threw over her daughter's shoulders a deep red woollen mantle.

"Red suits you." She drew it around María, pulling the hood over her head and straightening its folds. "I dyed it until I got the colour right. Others wanted to help me with it, but I refused. Every stitch is from my own needle. It will last you many years."

Gazing wordlessly at her mother, María gathered its thick, soft folds against her chest. From another full saddlebag, Josefa took out a tied canvas bag. "Take these too."

Standing next to them, Beatriz breathed in the smell of earth and glanced inside the bag at the small brown bulbs. There were too many to count.

"What are they?" María asked.

"Saffron. Look after them and keep them safe from frost. That's certain to kill them and prevent them flowering. They take a lot out of the earth when they grow. Take the bulbs out every year or so after they have done with flowering, then feed the earth before you plant the bulbs back again. Do this and they will multiply and give you much cause for pleasure. You know their many uses?"

Holding the precious bag to her chest, María beamed. "Gracia, Mamá, si. I shall find a place in England to plant them." The girl glanced at the bundles already piled high on the bed – amongst them apricot and peach kernels and apple seeds from her mother's best trees. María bit her lower lip. "As I will do with the other seeds from home."

Josefa fixed her gaze on her daughter. "When you're married, I'll send you more. I will also send you young saplings from our orchards by ship."

María offered her mother a trembling smile. "Mamá, I am grateful." She touched her mother's hand.

Beatriz thought Josefa somehow diminished. Beside her towering husband, her friend's huge spirit more than made up for her tiny size. Somehow, Beatriz felt as if Josefa's inner core of strength had passed from her to her daughter, like the mantle she had placed over her shoulders. Beatriz heaved a deep sigh.

"But it might be best to send them for my princess's wedding,

not mine. Who knows when I will marry," María said.

Alarmed, Josefa blinked. "The princess will find you a good husband."

Turning to her mother's distress, María clasped her hand. "Si, Mamá."

Beatriz studied the girl. María was likely wise to keep silent about Catalina's promise to let her first seek out her own. The knowledge would worry her mother.

Gazing at Josefa in her widow's weeds, Beatriz remembered her in her husband's arms. Like her and Francisco, Josefa and Martin's love blazed dazzling white-gold like a well-stacked fire. She did not blame María for wanting the same as her parents, for wanting abiding love and passion, a true marriage, not a sham. Josefa's eyes drowned in tears, running down her aging cheeks. Beatriz touched her loosening cheek. *Si. Like mine.*

Josefa cradled María's face between her hands. "Promise to write?" Her voice choked. "If you send your letters home with the princess's letters, the queen will ensure I get them."

Beatriz thought she could be strong, now watching her friend weep showed this only make-believe. A tidal wave swelled within her, and she rubbed at her wet eyes.

"Mamá mine, I vow to you, I shall write. As many letters as I am able." María wrapped her arms around her mother and kissed her. The girl seemed to be breathing in her mother's smell. "Mamá, if the letters come slowly, please remember I will pray to God every day of my life to keep you and my brothers and sisters safe."

Josefa smiled, reaching to give María her kiss and blessing. The girl crumbled in her mother's arms and wept, holding her tight.

"Dear one, I am here. I am here. Always," Josefa comforted.

Beatriz rubbed at her eyes. Soon María would never hear again those words from her mother's lips.

***

Beatriz witnessed another farewell, this time in the royal baths at the Alhambra. Both now finished bathing and in their dry shifts, Queen Isabel stood behind her seated daughter and brushed Catalina's hair before a body-length mirror propped against the tiled wall. Beatriz leaned back against the marble bath, going deeper in the hot water. The white shift she wore billowed. She lifted a hand and studied her wet, water-shrivelled fingers. She wondered if she should get out of the baths too, but it was so pleasant to just be at rest and linger in the heated water. Overhead, light beamed down from the star-shaped skylights of the cupola and created a constellation of twinkling stars around her in the water. She raised her head when she heard the queen say, "Mi chiquitina…"

Catalina glanced at her mother, then lowered her gaze to her lap. Queen Isabel straightened her stance, not missing one brush stroke. "I shall write to you every moment I can. My letters to you will make you feel you are with me and never, ever lonely for my love. I tell you true, love makes of distance nothing. Nothing, I tell you." The queen swallowed, shaking her head. She sniffed. "Catalina, I am a good judge of character, si?"

Catalina lifted her grey/blue eyes again, glistening bright in candlelight. The mirror reflected her mother's sorrowful smile. From her earliest years, Queen Isabel told Catalina her English great-grandmother and namesake possessed such eyes. Beatriz inwardly shrugged. Catalina of Lancaster was the daughter of John of Gaunt – also the ancestor of Henry VII of England. Queen Isabel regarded the English king as kin, but she was a crowned queen, the daughter of a crowned king. King Henry's background was like a shabby, half-made blanket compared to the gold-cloth of her queen's.

Catalina chewed her upper lip and cleared her throat. "Si, Mamá."

"Mi chiquitina, you know letters have gone from me to Elizabeth of York since her firstborn wore swaddling cloths. The queen is a good, wise woman and devoted to her children. She will care for you as one of her own. Always listen, Catalina, to her. Her husband, the king... Hija, I am not as certain of him."

The chamber became so quiet Beatriz counted the strokes of the brush, so many it transmuted Catalina's hair into what seemed liquid gold. The queen's eyes fell upon her daughter's reflection.

"Hija, I believe King Henry to be like most men – desiring his women to make him believe himself better than other men. I have not enjoyed the marriage negotiations he has forced on us. Our arguments over your dowry have made me feel like a shopkeeper. But to be fair to him, he is a man who has learnt the hard way to value gold. Never forget he is a king not long secure in his crown."

Catalina blinked. "But he has been England's king for sixteen years."

The queen paused, tightening her lips. She lost the vibrancy sometimes making her seem ageless. "Si. More than your whole lifetime. I understand it seems a long time to you." She bent her head, and began brushing again. "But sixteen years is nothing for a king such as Henry Tudor... and an English king..."

Her hands stilled. "There are those in England with blood more deserving of England's crown. Henry won his throne by killing in battle England's last king. In truth, King Henry, descended from bastard, albeit royal blood, only became king through the ancient right of conquest." The queen glanced and smiled at Beatriz. "I know your teacher has told you this."

Catalina's eyes narrowed, a line puckering deep between her eyebrows. The queen rested a hand on her daughter's shoulder.

"Your father and I have watched the English king closely. Never would we send you to marry his son if, for one moment, we harboured any doubts of Henry Tudor's capability to stay upon his country's throne. Just know my assurance, mi chiquitina, all you need do is enjoy your wedding day and be Prince Arthur's good wife and consort."

Placing the brush aside, the queen lifted Catalina's thick hair, now gleaming with red-gold lights, away from her neck. The long minutes of brushing had chased away most of its natural wave. Queen Isabel took up a tendril, curling it around a swollen finger. She sighed, patting the curl back in place, smoothing the brushed hair behind her daughter's ear. The flowing hair fell like a silken, golden-lit mantle down Catalina's back, reaching beyond the seat of the stool.

Fingertips touching the sides of her daughter's head, the

queen spoke again. "As a girl my hair too was thus. You are my true daughter. My heart knew this from the first moment I held you after your birth." The queen inhaled a deep breath. "All last night I found myself thinking of that time at Alcala de Henares, you in my arms, your sisters and brother by my bed. You made Juan annoyed, child, by being another sister, but Isabel took you from me and fussed over you like she was your mother. At fifteen she wanted to be a wife and mother very much." She heaved another sigh. "Your birth was such a happy time – all my children close to me, the blessing of a new hija."

The queen lifted Catalina's chin. "You are strong, strong and brave and intelligent. There's a great queen in you, a true lioness. How you'll surprise men with your roar. You'll make them quake, just as I do. How could you not, my hija, born in the middle of a Holy War? Catalina, you make me proud. Every day of your life you've made me proud. The English do not know yet what I send to them, but they soon will. One of my greatest, and most precious jewels." Queen Isabel rested her hands on Catalina's shoulders. She gazed with her daughter into the mirror– a picture of hopeful youth and sorrowing maturity shining together in the amber glow of candlelight.

Queen Isabel bit her lower lip, leaving behind the mark of teeth. When next she spoke, her deep voice trembled. "Always, always remember this: drink nothing without first seeing it tasted by someone else; sign nothing without reading it thoroughly. Be careful where you give your trust." She swallowed, gazing at Beatriz. "Latina would give her life for me, and my heart tells me this is also true of our María for you. But other than María... Hija, I know you like and trust Geraldini, who I send with you as your confessor. He will also keep you company in your studies. But even with confessors you must be very careful. Only trust the good God." The queen gently caressed Catalina's cheek, heaving a deep sigh. "Hija, always remember the mask we wear when the doors open from our private chambers to the court. That's your armour behind which you hide your heart. Reveal that, and you give a weapon into the hands of your enemies. You will have those, and many. Our place in the world makes it so. But you're my child. You'll know what to do. I have won countless enemies to me, and do not doubt you can too."

The queen's arms slipped around Catalina's neck, her chin resting on her head. Beatriz huddled deeper into the shadows of the pool, her presence forgotten, feeling like an intruder.

"Next week, you shall leave us. Next week, my letters to you shall begin. Every free moment I shall write to you. I vow this as the mother who loves you."

"I promise too, Mamá." Catalina's eyes glowed brighter, brimming with liquid gold.

The queen gently shook her. "Mi chiquitina, you promised me. You are a princess and one day will be queen. There have been enough tears in recent years... Your marriage gives us reason to rejoice."

Catalina blinked, nodding.

Sitting far from them, Beatriz remembered Catalina's daily prayers. She so wished to postpone this departure for the sake of her ailing mother.

The queen reached for her cloak. From inside its deep, hidden pocket, she pulled out a chain with a heavy gold cross. "Take this with you."

Catalina stared. "Mamá! Your fragment of the true cross?"

Queen Isabel smiled, passing the golden chain over her daughter's head. "I always planned to give this to you. I have another gift too." Again she reached into the pocket, drawing out a small gold book. "I had this made for you, mi chiquitina – a private parting gift from me to you."

Catalina took the book from her mother. She turned the pages.

Beatriz saw her swallow hard, gazing with tear-bright eyes at her mother. "Gracia. 'Tis beautiful, Mamá."

"I agree, child. I wanted you to have an hour book like the Flemish one I treasure. The painter did well with it. This annunciation scene – he made our good Virgin look somewhat like you, si?"

With a wry smile Catalina gazed down at the book. "She's very pretty."

The queen laughed a little. "You're just as pretty. When I saw the red-gold hair and grey eyes of this young Madonna, I realised what had happened. The painter, knowing it was for you, looked to you for his inspiration. He painted it with love, Catalina. Mi chiquitina, so many love you. Mark my words – the English will love you, too."

A week later, at dawn, Beatriz stood with Catalina and María on the terraced roof of the Tower of Comares. Rivulets of white gold streamed through feathery clouds, the deluge of light from a rising sun turning the snowy top of Sierra Nevanda aflame, continuing to the near fortress hill. On the last morning with her girls at the Alhambra, the scent of oranges and pomegranates, and a silver morning wove together a vivid design of poignant farewell.

Morning light struck the paved, narrow, winding streets and buildings of Granada, dawn's light gilding red stone gold. Gardens hugged the stone walls of the city, forming a lush, green belt, spreading out wide to the near valley of the Darro. The morning breeze wafted a heady perfume of summer flowers from the gardens. In the valley, crops of grains began to yellow, ripening for the harvest. The same breezes caressing their bare skin on the tower's roof also played a gentle game of back, forth, and back again through the tops of the long green stalks. Stretched out as far as their feasting eyes could see, fruit orchards and mulberry trees rendered a canvas of vivid colour. Festooning vines climbed as if from tree to tree, their yet unripe grapes hanging in plump, glistening clusters.

Beatriz inhaled a deep breath. The aroma of nearby orange groves invigorated and soaked into her soul. She straightened her shoulders, almost feeling the presence of her ancestor Samuel Ibn Nagrela. Unable to take her eyes away from the view, she wondered if he had once stood here, just like the three of them, to greet a new day. Perhaps this was the place that had inspired him to write:

Hurry and give me drink,
Before the rise of dawn,
Of spice wine and juice of pomegranate,
In a cup held by the perfumed hand of a young maid,
Who will sing to me of many things
Both life giving and death dealing.

As if in answer to her thoughts, Catalina's voice returned Beatriz to the waking city. "Of all the places I've lived, I love here the best. 'Tis my heart's true home."

Beatriz squeezed her hand. "All will be well."

"I pray to God that it will be so." She gazed towards the palace. "How will my mother be with the last of us gone?"

Letting go of her hand, Beatriz listened to the bells calling to morning mass. María folded her arms on the top of the wall, glancing at the tiles near their feet. Sun rays spilled through the delicate stonework etching its lace design upon the ground.

Turning to Catalina, María sighed. "God will give the queen strength, as He does for us all, my prima hermana."

Catalina moved closer to her friend. "All her strength comes from God. Her faith is all the certainty she has left now." She lifted her chin, eyes welling with sorrow. "I don't want to leave her, not while she needs me."

Beatriz looked over the city. So far away it appeared so tiny, and almost dreamlike. A loaded wagon headed slowly towards the gates. Time moved them closer to when it would be the girls' turn to follow the same route. Her girls. How she wanted to weep.

"The king says there have been too many excuses, too many delays. You know when the king speaks thus your mother bows to his will," María said.

Tears shimmered gold in Catalina's eyes before she blinked them away. "Why can't he see how much she needs me?"

Beatriz clasped her hand again. "The king sees that every new day you remain makes it more difficult for the queen. Perchance he does only what he thinks right. I promise you, I will never leave your mother. I can never replace you, but you know my devotion to the queen."

The girl rubbed her face. "That gives me some comfort, my teacher." She sighed. "Mother tells me she will not journey with us. She says she will not say goodbye. She cannot." Catalina looked at the sky. "Will England have dawns as beautiful as this? I want to imprint it on my memory so I never forget. There is so much to say goodbye to. Too much." One tear and then another tracked down her cheek. "I told Mother I shall take the pomegranate as my token." Her eyes looked first at María, and then at Beatriz. "Do you want to know why?"

Beatriz gazed down at the city, the well-paved, winding, narrow streets, its golden domed alcázars, the close-placed homes of the city dwellers, some like the rich grandees, but on a far smaller scale, designed for beauty as well as homes in which to live. Courtyards, festooned with flowering vines and water-singing fountains, pomegranate trees with turning leaves of red, already laden and pregnant with fruit. Joyful bells – north, south, east and west – they rang out this fair city's abundant life and vitality.

"An easy riddle, my scholar." Beatriz waved her hand over the city. "Granada, the pomegranate itself. Your parents laboured long for its conquest."

Catalina smiled tenderly at the clouds. No longer wisps of feathers sweeping across the sky, they reminded Beatriz of the latticed stone at her fingertips.

"You guess wrong, my teacher, you who is so rarely wrong. I chose it because of the legend of Proserpina... it is what I want my mother to remember and keep always in her heart. One day I shall return to her, as Proserpina did for her mother." Catalina's gaze lifted to the morning sky. "One day, in Heaven, she and I shall be together, but with no more sorrow and with no more farewells."

Beatriz rested her eyes again on the city. Birdsong scored the bright morning, twittering whistles answered by the warble of bolder birds in an unshaped, musical concert. Carried high and thin in the wind, a cockerel crowed and crowed its pride and delight at the new morn, brooking no rebuttal. Someone on a balcony below plucked the strings of a vihuela. A young boy and girl laughed and tossed a ball, playing with their dog. Heading to the city gates with little hurry, a straight-back, broad-shouldered grandee rode his white stallion as if he owned the world.

The splendour of the morning strummed her like a harp. Wind, light and the warmth of morning sun resonating deep within her, her whole body throbbed with the sweetness of life. She gloried in the day, her whole spirit singing like a bird its own sweet ode. Beatriz squeezed Catalina's hand. "Remember to take joy in life too. Remember, there always will be light, even in the darkest days." She smiled through her tears at her girls. "The love you two share is one such light. It will guide you both through all your days. While you can, live and be happy."

THE END

WRITING FALLING POMEGRANATE SEEDS

First published at *www.tudorsdynasty.com*

A footnote. Sometimes it takes just a footnote to set my imagination alight. Years ago, I found such a footnote, in Isabel la Católica, Queen of Castile: critical essays, a book of academic essays about the times, influence and mythology of Isabel of Castile[1], the mother of Katherine of Aragon. Katherine, of course, was Henry VIII's wife, and went to her grave calling herself that. Really, that's not surprising considering that she was a devout Catholic, and had been married to Henry for over twenty years, and let's not forget their five dead babies and one living daughter, before he decided to replace her with Anne Boleyn. But back to my footnote.

This footnote introduced me to Doña Beatriz Galindo (1465/75?-1534)- a woman who taught not only Katherine of Aragon, but also Latin to Queen Isabel herself. Latin was the necessary language of Medieval diplomacy for the Christian world, but, because she was 'female' and an unforeseen successor to her half-brother's throne, Isabel was not schooled or expected to learn this language in her childhood and early youth. As a mother, Isabel remembered how her own education did not prepare her for her future life. She ensured her five children received the best education possible by employing the best teachers for them.

When I decided to explore in *Falling Pomegranate Seeds* the forces that originally shaped Katherine of Aragon (or Catalina as she was known to her family) during her time at the court of her mother, I turned to Beatriz Galindo to tell this fictionalised story of Katherine's early years. Beatriz was a perfect subject for me as a writer of fiction. I could only find the barest bones of her life story, which offered me a huge gap to fill with the use of my imagination; but what fascinating bones I had to play with. Beatriz was a scholar, a poet – sadly, like so many talented women of the past, her work is lost to us – and such a gifted Latin teacher that she lectured at the University of Salamanca. She also lectured on Aristotle, medicine and rhetoric. And did I mention she was a wife and mother as well?

I felt in awe of Beatriz when I started writing Falling Pomegranate Seeds. I could not help wondering how it must have been for her – a woman who lived a life denied to most women in the Medieval period. Did it come at a personal cost? That question opened up a lot of 'what if' questions that acted as midwives to my imagination.

My imagination constructed Beatriz as a woman who lived a life that challenged the status quo. In a male dominated society, Beatriz somehow, and extraordinarily so, rewrote her life story. She appeared to have both worked with and resisted a society that could have easily prevented her from reaching her true potential.

A recognised scholar and a respected advisor to Queen Isabel, wife of King Ferdinand of Aragon, a kingdom of lesser importance than Castile, Beatriz lived in a time of great change and upheaval -accompanying her Queen during the 'Holy War', Queen Isabel's campaign to 'cleanse' her country of the Moors, which closed the door upon hundreds of years of Islamic influence in Castile. Beatriz Galindo was also a personal friend to the Queen. As a member of Queen Isabel's court, she frequently accompanied the queen in her court's peripatetic journey around her kingdom while employed as Katherine of Aragon's tutor, and likely the tutor to Katherine's three sisters.

Beatriz Galindo seems almost forgotten by world history, yet she deserves to be remembered. Her one and only biography, written in Spanish, is still untranslated and thus unavailable to the English-speaking world. As a tutor of Katherine of Aragon, a woman known and respected for her intelligence and learning, I believe we can say that Beatriz's influence continued into the reign of Henry VIII of England and beyond.

History tells us that Beatriz Galindo was a scholar of the Greek philosopher Aristotle. This philosopher spoke loud and clear his views concerning women who he saw as "unfinished men" and vessels simply designed for childbearing. It intrigued me that Beatriz Galindo studied Aristotle and wrote commentaries about him. Did her resistance to and questioning of his beliefs result in her own empowerment and reshaping her life to one that allowed fulfilment? I could not help thinking about how such a teacher could have influenced Katherine of Aragon.

Falling Pomegranate Seeds is set during the time that saw

Cristóbal Colón discovering the "New World" and Isabel and her husband Ferdinand engaged in their Holy War. Married to Francisco Ramírez, master of the King Ferdinand's artillery, Beatriz Galindo was an eyewitness to the fall of Granada. Later, she saw Isabel send into exile her Jewish subjects, after giving them an ultimatum to convert to Christianity. With her passion for learning and knowledge of medicine, I suspect the expulsion the Moors and Jews would have shaken Beatriz's identity to the core, as would have had a later happening: the burning of countless and priceless Islamic manuscripts, which erased knowledge that had come down the centuries.

Envisioning Beatriz made me wonder what it may have cost her to claim her own life. My imagination posed one possible scenario. My imagination also opened the door to Katherine of Aragon, as both child and girl. Katherine was a woman who loved books and learning. As England's very loved Queen, she was the patron of scholars and of the arts. It is not hard to imagine her then as a child who loved to learn. It is not hard to imagine that she would have loved her tutor, Beatriz. The youngest child of five children, Katherine suffered sorrow after sorrow before she left England to begin her life of exile. But she came to England trained and ready to be a queen. *Falling Pomegranate Seeds* imagines how that happened.

BIBLIOGRAPHY

Boruchoff, D. A. 2003, *Isabel la Católica, Queen of Castile: critical essays*, Palgrave Macmillan, New York.

Denzin, N. K. and Y. S. Lincoln 2003 *Collecting and interpreting qualitative materials*. Thousand Oaks, Calif., Sage.

[1] Studying that book is also the reason why I call Isabel of Castile Isabel rather than Isabella. One of the essays strongly suggests that Isabella originated as a form of belittlement of this strong Queen - who was referred to as 'King' during her long and world changing reign.

THE ALHAMBRA

I decided to first visit Spain in 2007 after writing a scene in the first draft of *Falling Pomegranate Seeds: The Duty of Daughters*. The scene set in The Alhambra of my imagination, I had a vision of white butterflies, countless white butterflies, fluttering a graceful dance in a garden where sunlight flittered through pomegranate, orange and cypress trees. I had no idea if the vision had any similarity to the reality of the gardens of The Alhambra, although an internet search reassured me that butterflies are indeed a part of the natural environment of The Alhambra. In fact, The Alhambra is famed for its butterflies.

My problem with imagining places still in existence today is that I begin to yearn to see them with my own eyes. I live in Australia, but my imagination has never really latched onto the history of my beautiful homeland. My ancestry is British. My children, born and raised in a multicultural country, have always declared their British ancestry as "boring". Two years ago, for my birthday, they gave me a DNA test, hoping to discover ancestral lines far more interesting than those belonging to the British Isles. Alas, my DNA results proved I am more British than the average Brit. For many years now, I have wondered about ancestral memory – and if that may explain why my imagination is so fixated on England. I have in my lifetime somehow managed five trips to the United Kingdom, three of them including time in Europe. One of those times saw me on a tour of Spain for seventeen days. At that time, I was working on my first vision of Falling Pomegranate Seeds: The Duty of Daughters, and had fallen in love with the descriptions of Spain through my research. I wanted to see for myself the places important to the early life of Catalina of Aragon.

My time in Spain enriched and fed my imagination. I saw in my mind Beatriz Galindo sitting and talking with Catalina and María de Salinas, in sunlit courtyards edged by well-kept gardens and shaded by cypress and orange trees. I closed my eyes and smelled the perfume of flowers and heard in my mind the song of water

cascading into stone water fountains. My then eleven-year-old son, who accompanied me on this wonderful adventure, was so impressed with all the water fountains we saw on our travels he was determined to convince his father to build one in our small front garden back in Australia. Alas, that never happened.

What did happen is I fell in love in Spain – not with a person, but with a place; it is a love I share with many. I only had one day at the The Alhambra back in 2007. I remember well the grey sky, and my anxiety that my long awaited day would be spoiled by a downpour of rain. The rain held off until we left – long enough for The Alhambra to soak into my heart and psyche.

Once again, water fountains delighted my son, especially the stone lion protected fountain, which aptly named its courtyard: The Courtyard of the Lions. For myself, I delighted in Moorish architecture, water features and gardens designed to feast the eye. The Alhambra was built by Badis ibn Habus, the Berber King of Granada, in the 11th century. There is a romantic legend that The Alhambra, meaning 'red castle', was built at night, under torchlight. The family of Catalina of Aragon took possession of it from the Moors in 1492, and her parents Isabel and Ferdinand used it for their royal court. It was home to Catalina from the time she was seven to fifteen.

Strolling in the gardens, it was very easy to imagine Catalina there, growing up in this place of great beauty, until the day came when she would leave her parents forever. My time at The Alhambra helped me describe the palace and its surrounds in Falling Pomegranate Seeds: The Duty of Daughters. To my eye, the stone interior and exterior seemed like delicate lace work – allowing light to filter in and out, dappling over floor and wall. The architecture of *The Alhambra* is married to water and gardens. One water feature is very famous, and has been the subject of countless photographs of tourists and the inspiration for artists. A long rectangular pool mirrors the arches of the Partal façade in the Patio de los Arrayanes, or the court of the myrtles.

I was at The Alhambra for only about five hours. It did not feel long enough, but it was long enough to embrace The Alhambra in my heart for ever as one of my favourite places on Earth. I will never forget my time there, or its unbelievable beauties. It was also long enough to fire my imagination. I saw Catalina and María practicing their dancing steps in The Courtyard of the Lion. I imagined them bathing together in the bath of the Comares Palace, under a small stone dome cut with stars to let the light flicker on the water. I saw them in the garden with Beatriz Galindo, sitting at her feet as she read them stories. I saw them preparing to say their final farewells before they started their long journey to England.

Leaving The Alhambra, I promised to return one day. I was lucky enough to do that in 2019 – and I hope one day to make another return.

ACKNOWLEDGMENTS

First and foremost, I want to acknowledge my dear husband for supporting my writing obsession. I sincerely thank him for putting up with our very untidy house and for financing a research trip for this novel. He is often forced to push aside a pile of books to get into bed at night, helpfully locating my missing pens when he tries to sleep on them. Despite everything, he has always encouraged me to pursue my dreams.

Writers need people to believe in their writing. I'm lucky there too. Glenice Whitting, author of the award-winning *Pickle to Pie*, and a darling and long-time friend, never let me forget about this novel. One of my important beta readers, I thank Glenice for always believing in me. I also thank my dear friends Valerie Clukaj and Kristie Dean for their encouragement.

The first version of this work saw Cindy Vallar giving my work the benefit of her red pen and her talents as a gifted editor. This overhauled and reworked version benefited from the red pen of another gifted editor: Rachel Le Rossignol. I express my sincere thanks to you both.

I also want to thank Jan Crosby, who has also read this work in its early life. I am also grateful to Sandra Worth, C. W. Gortner, Barbara Denvil, Nerina Jones, Eloise Faichney, Helen Barnes, Professor Josie Arnold and Adrienne Dillard for their willingness to read and offer feedback on *Falling Pomegranate Seeds* – whether it was years ago for the first version, or this completely reworked version. I also wish to express my gratitude to Dr Carolyn Beasley –who does so much to support me in so many ways.

One lovely memory I have of writing the first version *Falling Pomegranate Seeds* involves my youngest son, David, who was then still a child. As I wrote in bed, David would nestle up beside me and ask for the latest word-count. I will never forget the light of pride in his eyes as the novel grew and grew. That light of pride kept me writing.

Thank you all!

READING GROUP QUESTIONS

Thank you for taking the time to read my novel. As with all novels, there are a number of themes which run through the narrative. I hope that you enjoyed the book and that the following questions help you to get a deeper understanding of the novel.

1. Falling Pomegranate Seeds takes place in Spain as Isabel and Ferdinand finally capture the regions still occupied by the Moors. What did you discover about Spain at this time?
2. Who were the major players in the book, and what were their motivations?
3. How does Beatriz find herself conflicted in her role as tutor to Catalina?
4. Some of the story revolves around the Alhambra palace in Granada. Have you been to the Alhambra or seen pictures of the Nasrid Palace? Even by

today's standards, it is a beautiful place. What do you think it must have been like to live in or leave such a place?

5. Beatriz hides some secrets of her own. What are they? Do you understand and agree with why she kept them secret?

6. What does Beatriz's character tell us about the role of a woman at this time in history?

7. We know that Catalina eventually becomes Katherine of Aragon, the first wife of Henry VIII of England. Do you think that she was prepared for such an important role by her upbringing?

8. Do you think that court life was easy for Isabel, Ferdinand and their children or were the pressures of being a royal family very great indeed?

9. Was life different for the king and queen compared to those who surrounded them?

10. How much did the attempt on Ferdinand's life change Catalina? Was this a key moment in her life or just something she accepted?

11. I have described this book as "a tale of mothers and daughters, power, intrigue, death, love, and redemption, in the end, Falling Pomegranate Seeds sings a song of friendship and life." Do you think this is a good description of the themes running through the book? Which theme is the strongest within the book?

12. Who was your favourite character in the book, and why?

13. Are there any characters you particularly admire or dislike, and why?

14. There are strong emotions throughout the book. Can you pick out a passage that you found particularly profound or interesting? Did it make you think about your own life?

Falling Pomegranate Seeds
All Manner of Things
Wendy J. Dunn
THE FINAL PART OF THE KATHERINE OF ARAGON STORY

Forgiveness frees you from the past.

I dedicate this novel to my son Tim and my sister Karen. Both of them returned me to following my heart.

I also express my immense thanks to Rhys Delios Callanan for designing the cover of this novel.

PROLOGUE

When I investigate and when I discover that the forces of the heavens and the planets are within ourselves, then truly I seem to be living among the gods.

~ *Leon Battista Alberti*

Daylight began to ebb, pulling back like the tidal Thames. María de Eresby put down her unused quill and rose from her seat to light the candles in the tiny room she used for her private study. Returning to her writing desk, she half-twisted in her seat to peer out the window at the oak trees in her garden. The trees, brushed by the falling snow, seemed dream- like through the thick glass, their bare branches darkening to almost black in the dim light of day.

The fire burned bright and hungry in the nearby hearth, but still she shivered. She shook herself and gathered her old mantle closer. *But I've been cold for years.* Ignoring the hard seat, and the whine and whistle of winter wind, she gazed back at the cream-coloured parchment on her slanted writing desk. The shape of her uncovered head casting its shadow on the vellum, the parchment's barrenness taunted her, confronted her. It challenged her to begin.

María sighed, glancing at the matrix seal of the Barony of Willoughby de Eresby beside the full ink well, placed at the top of her desk. She leaned forward, caressing the seal with the tip of her index finger. Her cherished husband, dead these twelve years and more, had given it to her on their wedding day. Now the seal seemed to wait for her to write this letter to their daughter. It would be her truth. In these desolate days, it was the only truth left to her; the only truth which mattered. She picked up the quill and, with practised skill, stroked out the first words, pausing to dip her nib to re-ink it.

Written at my London home on Saint Agatha Day, in the twenty-seventh year of the reign of Henry VIII, for my daughter, the Duchess of Suffolk.

Daughter, my Catalina,

I write this letter to request a boon of you. Death comes for me, and I welcome it. Daughter, do not pen back a letter mocking me, or entreating me to say otherwise. I have studied medicine too long not to know the signs, and I do welcome them. I have seen fifty-three winters, and I do not ever desire to see another. I am weary. Not with age, but with grief. But before I die, I want you to understand – nay, I need you understand why our lives have turned out as they have. I want – no, need to tell you my story. But it is not just my story... from the beginning, the threads of my life have been woven with that of my beloved queen's...

María wiped away tears – hating her weakness. These days saw her cry too easily. She looked again at the letter. What she wrote now would either make her daughter understand at last her life, and the choices she had made, or fail again to breach the wall built between them since Catalina's marriage to Charles Brandon, the Duke of Suffolk. The girl, well taught, wore a happy face to others, but behind closed doors it was a different story. Her daughter's bitter words before her wedding rang again in María's ears, "You promised me I would wed Harry; I never thought you would be so wicked, so unkind as to make me marry a man old enough to be my grandsire."

She should have never made that promise. She should have known better than to trust Suffolk to care for her daughter's welfare. She should have remembered her own life, and its hard lessons.

On the stool beside her desk, a carefully tied bundle of letters awaited the addition of her own. Returned from the grandchildren of Latina, her long ago teacher, these letters too would need to be sent for her daughter's eyes. Most of the missives she had written to Latina were in this bundle. Letters written from her sixteenth year to before Latina's death three years ago.

Glancing at her unfinished letter, María wondered if it would be her last. Already, it was proving one of her hardest to write. *No. I cannot fail again. I refuse to fail. This letter will make my daughter understand the little power women have over their lives.* She re-inked her quill and, for a time, scratched her pen with purpose down the parchment.

Her fingers cramped. María laid her quill down to rest her hand and stared sightlessly out the window. She could no longer hear the voice of the wind. Apart from the occasional crackle and pop of the fire, the room stayed silent. Silent, except for her memories. They flickered and danced in the fire's flames.

PART ONE

Daughter, I was not yet sixteen when all changed for me. In the royal andas...forgive me, my English daughter, I forget you may not know this word I once used for litter in my homeland. For months we journeyed down roads following the ancient paths of pilgrims to Santiago, every day taking me closer to a life of exile. All of us left behind our families. We knew we would never see them again.

1

...We do not wish that our daughter should be the cause of any loss to England, neither in money, nor in any other respect. On the contrary, we desire that she should be the source of all kinds of happiness, as we hope she will be, with the help of God.

- *Isabel of Castile to Henry VII of England, March 23rd, 1501*

June 1501, Pilgrim road to Santiago de Compostela. Monastery of Guadalupe.

Woken by a hard kick to her leg, María bounded up, banging her head against the unfamiliar bedpost of an unfamiliar bed. "By Saint Michael's Sword!" Her eyes adjusting to the dim light, María rubbed her sore crown.

Beside her, bedclothes thrown off, Maria's princess and long-time bedcompanion tossed and turned in her sleep. Catalina panted as if running for her life and cried out a drawn-out, "No."

María reached down to shake her friend and cousin. "Wake up. You're dreaming."

Catalina shuddered, rolled in bed, her eyes flickering open. The single candle beside the bed revealed her terror. "You call it a dream?" She trembled, crossing herself. "A nightmare more like...from the devil himself."

María crossed, too, and gripped her friend's hand. "Tell me about the dream. Chase your fear away."

Catalina leaned against the bedhead, hugging her pillow to her. "Speaking of it will not help."

"How do you know unless you try?" Tired and grumpy, her head still hurting, María peered at Catalina. In the amber candle-light, Catalina's perspiring face appeared luminous. *Had her fever returned?* Days ago, they had arrived at the Monastery of Guadalupe with Catalina's fever making them all fear for her life, thanking God when it broke at last.

María chewed her thumbnail, staring at the door leading to the antechamber, where their blackamoor servant slept. Fleet of foot, the girl would find and bring Don Alcarz to them in no time. *Would that not be the wisest course of action – to send for Catalina's physician?*

Still chewing a nail, María studied Catalina again. She heard Latina, their beloved teacher, speak in her mind: "I attend to Queen Isabel in her times of illness. I have taught you to do the same for her daughter." But in times like these, she reeled in self-doubt, and cursed what little skill she had; it left her uncertain and floundering out of her depths. *I am months away from my sixteenth year. How I am supposed to know anything?*

María slipped out of the bed, lighting the three tall candles nearby. *Light will help me decide whether I should summon Don Alcarz.* Her body only covered by a thin shift, she shivered in the cold night, and hurried back to bed. She pulled up the blanket, covering Catalina, too. Leaning against the hard bedhead, she wrapped her arms around her knees, waiting for her friend to speak. Catalina's large, shining eyes blinked in candlelight. Shifting, María rested her head against Catalina's. "Tell me," she prompted again. "Tell me about your dream."

"It was terrible," Catalina said. "A man begged for mercy. Estimado Dios, he wanted to live, not die –but men pushed his head down on the block." Catalina covered her face with her hands. "The executioner brought down the axe and held up his head, dripping with blood. He still begged for mercy." She lowered her hands, sputtering a half-born sob.

The candlelight flickered in a sudden draft, the night's dark shadows wavering in an odd dance. María got out of bed again, poured a goblet of watered-down wine and held it out to Catalina. "Drink!" She made her high voice as deep as she could, imitating Catalina's.

Catalina attempted a smile, but one soon gone. "I've dreamt this dream before. But this time...I was there, on the scaffold – watching it happen." Catalina sipped from the goblet and closed her eyes for a moment before speaking again. "His way of dying, the place he died – I have never seen the like before, but I must have remembered it from Latina's lessons. She has told me the English behead their noble traitors." She turned to María. "He died on a straw-strewn scaffold covered with rose petals. Countless white rose petals soaked with blood." Catalina grabbed María's arm. "Don't you see? I dreamt the death of Warwick, the White Rose!"

María trembled, not with cold, but fear. A cold finger touched her, as if a finger of a ghost. *Could it be true? Could the ghost of Warwick be haunting Catalina?*

Less than two years ago, the Earl of Warwick had been executed for trying to escape from his long captivity in the Tower of London. Catalina could not forget, to her unending guilt, the young man who really died to make way for her marriage to Arthur Tudor. Queen Isabel and King Ferdinand made it clear to their ambassador in England that they would not send their daughter until Warwick, considered by many to have greater right to sit on the throne than King Henry, was dead. Well and truly dead.

She shook her head. *I am a fool to think such things.* "It is only a dream..." she spoke to reassure herself, as well as Catalina. Briefly clasping Catalina's hand, she swung out of bed again and lit every candle she could find. Catalina's dream destroyed any hope of sleep this night.

Doña, my dear Latina,

We reside at the monastery of Guadalupe, the Holy place of the Black Madonna. The princess was ill when we first arrived. Praise be to God, she now gives lie to the sick girl brought hither only days ago. I so missed your wisdom during that time.

King Fernando's royal fleet waits for the princess's arrival in A Coruña. Slow day replaces slow day, days snail crawling into weeks, whiling away into months. Each day takes us closer to leaving our homeland. In truth, I find myself grateful for these slow days. I dread the journey ahead. I share the fear of the sea crossing with many of our party...

Her quill dry, María put it down and chewed her fingernail. *Should I write of my concerns about Bishop Geraldini?* Less than one hour ago, he had come to the chamber and heard their confessions, before departing to hear the confessions of their companions. Catalina had been pleased when her mother appointed him, a man who had been her tutor for years, to be her confessor in England. María was not certain of him. Latina had been her only tutor, and her loyalty was undivided. These long weeks made her relieved she had never been schooled by this proud, pompous, pedantic man. In her eyes, he seemed a tedious, arrogant bore who possessed little of Latina's gifts.

Garbed in a loose habito, Catalina sat a short distance away, near the open doors to the garden. Morning sunlight intruded into the secluded chamber like stretched out fingers; within the slants of light, countless motes glittered and danced as if tiny stars spun out of control in a dusty cosmos. Outside, the dawn sky cleared to a cloudless blue.

Catalina showed all the signs of their sleep-robbed night. Dark rings bruised the skin under her eyes, and her head drooped over the small Book of Hours she held on her lap. The farewell gift of Queen Isabel, jewel-like colours illustrated episodes of the Madonna's life. In this moment, Catalina seemed oblivious to the book, but it remained open on her favourite page, the scene of the Annunciation.

"Magnificat anima mea Dominum; my soul hath rejoiced in God, my saviour," Catalina spoke softly the good Madonna's reply to Gabriel, when the angel announced God had chosen her as the pure vessel to bear his son. Her words might as well have been a breath, or a sigh. Slowly, Catalina traced the wings of the archangel Gabriel. His sun-alight wings folded behind him, he stood over the kneeling Mary. Mary – a girl not older than Catalina – appeared alarmed, fearful.

María winced. Was it any wonder the girl in the painting was fearful? She had just been told of her impending, virginal motherhood.

"Behold, the handmaiden of my parents." Again, Catalina spoke quietly, her head bowed. From the cradle, Queen Isabel's daughters learnt to do their duty. It did not mean her friend and princess was not anxious about her fast-approaching marriage. Sighing, María wished she knew what to say to help her friend.

Catalina closed the book and rose from her seat. Her face tight with thought, she placed her book on a bookstand by the unshuttered window and then walked to the arched, colonnaded entrance to the garden.

María pushed away from the chamber's writing desk and stepped over to the door. Sounds from nature chorused together. Babbling water fountains poured into the long, rectangle pool; scolding, thirsty birds dipped into the water for a morning drink before staying to splash and swim. The lace-stoned arches opened to wide pathways of sunlight intermixed with shadows. Gentle breezes wafted into the chamber a bouquet of perfumes from the well-kept remains of a Moorish garden. But it was Moorish no more; the garden belonged to the Catholic Queen of Castile.

Like so many other gardens María had known and loved during her life, the rose held court as reigning queen, and far outnumbered all the other flowering blooms. The colours of the roses created a living embroidery of every hue imaginable. One rose was so dark it reminded her of black velvet.

Close to the enclosed garden's edge, a crimson rose bush, laden with buds, grew in a large ceramic pot. Barefoot, Catalina padded over to it. Taking her small meat dagger from the leather purse hanging from the waist of her gown, she cut off a stem and raised the opening bud to her nose. Pleasure lit up her pretty face, chasing the lines of illness and anxiety away. She closed her eyes, her thick, long eyelashes shadowing half- moons on her cheeks.

Relieved to see Catalina no longer despondent, María moved towards another ceramic pot and brushed the velvet petals of a full-blown rose. To her dismay, its beauty dissolved, its petals breaking away and dropping, one by one.

Come to my garden and pluck
The roses whose perfume is like pure myrrh.
And by the blossoms and gathering of swallows
Who sing of the good times, drink ye
Wine in measures like tears I shed over parting
With friends and as red as the faces of blushing lovers...

María heard in her mind the words of her long-ago ancestor, Samuel Ibn Nagrela. Like her mother, María had memorised many of his poems. He had been a prince and mighty warrior, as well as a poet – and it mattered little to her that he was a Jew. She was proud of her lineage. Whilst Catalina had been influenced by the queen, her royal mother, to view Jews with mistrust, María had learnt from her mother, and Latina. Both women respected everyone who deserved respect.

Her ancestor's poem brought to mind the poem she had written on her last summer at the Alhambra, on a day when she had sat alone amongst the roses. Like this moment, early morning had spread its magic upon the garden, and a soughing breeze had gathered up rose petals into what seemed an eddy echoing her sorrow for leaving her mother.

Returning to the entrance of Catalina's chamber, she picked up her vihuela and sat on the stone bench. *Can I turn my poem into song?* She strummed a scattering of interrupted notes. Not wishing Catalina to hear, she sang softly:

Red like blood
I plucked a rose
grasped its beauty close to me
uncaring of its thorns

The crunch of undergrowth halted her fingers on her vihuela and returned her eyes to the garden. Catalina strolled beside the pool. Wind and sun played a joyous game, speckling shadow-shift and dazzle upon the water, while sunlight dappled its way through the leaves of the tall trees and shadows drifted over tiles paving the ground.

The breeze lifted long strands of Catalina's loose hair, and the low, morning sun turned her red-gold hair aflame. *Sí, the garden is a jewel, and so is Catalina; she is her mother's jewel.* María flinched, not wanting to take the thought a step further. *It is not true. The queen does not think of her daughter as a possession to be bought and sold.*

The garden shadows of the trees wavered, then receded. Like countless times since her fifth year, María waited in the shadows.

She had been Catalina's companion long enough to know when to speak or remain silent. Content with her own company and time to read or write, she never minded if Catalina wished for solitude. She was secure in their friendship. She turned her eyes towards the closed door of their chamber. In her mind, she saw on the other side of the door Inés, the pretty, fifteen-year-old daughter of Catalina's long-ago nurse, María de Roja, the most beautiful of Catalina's attendants, and the dark-haired, spirited and dimpled Francisca. She knew the three girls resented she was here alone with the princess. María inwardly shrugged. Catalina regarded her as a sister; only time would do the same for the other girls. Catalina approached her, and sat beside her on the bench. "Do you think he will like me?" she asked, holding in her hand a well-creased parchment. Before her friend closed the letter and slipped it into the deep pocket of her gown, María read the first lines, recognising it as the letter Arthur had sent to Catalina three years ago:

> *Most illustrious and most excellent lady, my dearest spouse, I wish you very much health, with my hearty recommendation.*
>
> *I have read the most sweet letters of your highness lately given to me, from which I have easily perceived your most entire love to me....*

María wound her arm around Catalina's shoulders. "Have I ever told you worry too much?"

Catalina laughed. "Many times. But would you not be worried too if you were going to marry someone you had never met?"

María took in a slow, deep breath, and released it. "Of

course." She clasped her hands together. "Did you ever ask Latina why she gave us all those books of philosophy to read?"

Catalina raised an inquisitive eyebrow. "No. But your question makes me think you did."

Shifting a little on the uncomfortable bench, María gazed around the garden, gathering her thoughts. "I had a lot more time with her than you in these past years." She laughed a little. "I did not envy your lessons with the bishop."

"You do him injustice. He is a brilliant teacher."

María shrugged. "So is Latina. When poor health compelled my mother to leave the court, Latina became a second mother to me."

"She was like that to me, too. But you have not told me why Latina wanted us to read philosophy books."

"She thought it important." María grinned at Catalina. "I thought I would never enjoy gaining knowledge for knowledge sake, but I do now." She shook her head, thinking about how the years had changed her. "I am not a natural student like you." She chuckled. "I was always asking Latina why I had to learn this or that."

Catalina touched her hand. "I remember. But you have not explained why Latina spent so much time teaching us philosophy."

She eyed Catalina. "She told me it would help prepare us for our lives. Life is never easy, she said, but as long as we continue to learn who we are, we live life as it is meant to be lived. She also told me no one can take from us our interior lives. Knowing that helps me not to worry too much. Whatever life brings me, I will face it when it comes."

A brisk, sharp knock echoed into the garden followed by the

sound of the bedroom door opening. Doña Elvira strode towards them, her heavy footfall warning of her mood.

She curtseyed to Catalina. "Princess, why are you out of bed? You must rest before we start our journey again. Doña María should know better than let you dress and overtire yourself." Her eyes swung to María. "And you – you should not be sitting beside the princess. You always forget your place – and take too many liberties."

Catalina glanced aside at María, then back at Doña Elvira. "Doña, I sat beside María, not the other way around. In these private quarters, I regard María as my sister. Pray, remember that." She shifted to the edge of the bench as if ready to stand. "I do thank you for your concern, Doña, but I am no longer ill. Indeed, today I wish to pay my respects to the Virgin."

Doña Elvira scowled. "Your highness, I think that most unwise. You must return to bed."

Must. Doña Elvira, had used the word twice. María almost rubbed her hands in anticipation of Catalina's reply.

"Doña Elvria, you forget yourself," Catalina said quietly, her eyes hooded.

The woman did not take the hint, but placed her hands on her ample hips. "My princess, you are in my charge. I cannot see you arriving in England too ill to go forward with your marriage. I will send your servant to remake the bed, and you will return there."

María stared at the woman in disbelief. Doña Elvira bullied all of Catalina's women, but usually avoided doing the same to their princess. Surely, she knew Catalina well enough to know her seemingly gentle appearance hid a stubbornness like a solid rock. She almost felt sorry for the woman. Catalina's illness must have frightened her so much she could no longer restrain her tongue.

Catalina lifted her chin. "I will not pass this way again, Doña Elvira. You cannot forbid me to pray at the shrine. You must know this is an important place to my family – to all Christians. My ancestor King Alfonso, one hundred years ago, celebrated his victory over the Moors here. He believed it due to the intercession of the Black Madonna. It is only right I show my respect too. Now, leave me."

"But," sputtered the older woman.

Catalina stood, her eyes alight with rage. "I said, leave me. And do not return until I command it. I have no wish to see you again today."

As if blaming María for Catalina's anger, the woman turned to her a look of pure viciousness before backing to the door. María inwardly sighed. The woman had disliked her for years, resenting her influence on the princess, influence she was desperate to have as her own.

Catalina sat again and shook her head. "I wish my mother had listened to me and not decided to send Doña Elvira to England with us. The woman always desires to have the upper hand." Her eyes widened. Looking beyond María, her face, panic-struck, lost all colour. "You! Why do you plague me?"

María sucked in her bottom lip. She took Catalina's arm, gazing around the garden. "What is it? What do you see?"

Catalina whispered, "Warwick. It must be him. I saw his shade, the man from my dreams."

Disturbed, María crossed herself. The weeks of travel had rekindled the undying embers of grief and sorrow. From Catalina's twelfth year, death had followed death. First Catalina's grandmother, next her brother, Juan, followed by her older sister, Isabel, and then the death of Isabel's little son. But it was not only family deaths to cause Catalina deep sorrow. She could not forget Warwick and how he came to his death.

Brought up with Catalina like a sister, each death tore at María too. Her own father had died not long after the little prince. She blinked, remembering her father riding off to his final battle with the husband of Latina, Francisco Ramirez. They had both wheeled their horses to join the king, and looked back to wave farewell. Then her father rode away, riding away from her life, into the mists of time, and memory. She squeezed the hand of her friend.

Doña, my dear Latina,

Every place on our long journey I have carved into my heart: Cordoba, Merida, Caceres, Palencia; soon I will do the same for Salamanca, and Santiago de Compostela. So many farewells; the last one will be the hardest of all.

With a dangerous sea journey fast approaching, we all look forward to reaching Santiago de Compostela, where we will pray for Saint James's protection. You must already know our noble queen gave our party permission to go as pilgrims and take advantage of the papal jubilee year. Bishop Geraldini tells us this means we will spend no time in limbo when we die.

I am happy to tell you my princess is fully well again. She brooked no arguments and insisted we detour to the Monastery of Saint Thomas, in Avila, even if it meant adding extra days to our journey...

The others were not pleased when Catalina told them to stay

outside the Cloister of Silence and wait for her return. María followed Catalina into the chapel. She stepped forward with caution, her sight adjusting to the dark interior. She raised her eyes to the high ceiling. Far, far above her, the intricate ribbed vault belonged more to a cathedral than to a monastery, even one richly endowed with the patronage of royalty. The generous quantity of candles all around the building and the light coming in from the high windows did little to change the oppressive, depressing atmosphere.

The sight of the choir drove an arrow into her heart. Behind the altar, the white alabaster tomb of Prince Juan could just be seen. Memories washed over her, threatening to break through her resolve to not weep. She hugged her arms tight to her body. *Control yourself. You asked to come because you didn't want Catalina to face this moment alone.* Picking up her skirts, she hurried down the aisle and joined Catalina at Juan's tomb. María's throat closed. The sculptor had done his job well. Juan seemed asleep before her, sleeping like the angel his mother had called him in life. Now he was an angel in death.

From the time she was a little child, he had captured her heart. He had been a sweet and caring youth who had grown into a beautiful young man with a noble heart and soul. Recognising her gift for music, he took her under his wing and spent hours teaching her to play the vihuela and guiding her to compose her first songs. By twelve, she had started to dream of him in ways leaving her disquieted, confused, and grieving at news of his marriage. For weeks, she had fought a hard battle to surmount her jealousy of Margaret of Austria, his wife. Margaret, though, made Juan happy in the last months of his life; so happy, it soon salved her own unhappiness.

Looking back, that twelve-year-old María seemed to her a fool to ever dream he would look her way and make her his bride. But not a fool to love Juan. Never that. Everyone who knew him, loved him. When Juan had died, María wished to do the same as his dog, Bruto, and lay down at the foot of his bier and howl with misery. She knelt beside Catalina, wishing to howl again.

Catalina touched Juan's tomb. "I know he is with God, and at peace, but I still look for him and desire to hear his voice again," she murmured.

María put her hand beside her friend's. There was nothing she could say. The cold stone cut into her as she reached up to his effigy; it was beyond her reach. She sighed. He had always been beyond her reach.

"We have only one night here and then we journey on. I will never visit Juan's tomb again," Catalina said.

Bowing her head, María had nothing to say to this either. It was only the truth. She clasped her hands before her, and tried to pray. But she could not take her eyes away from Juan's effigy, unable to stop thinking of death; of farewell; of all the promise turned into dust and worms.

Tomorrow they would go to Salamanca before going to Zamora where they would re-join the pilgrim road to Santiago de Compostela. María trailed her fingers down one of the carved holy figures on the tomb: so smooth; so polished. She stared at her fingers. It would be more fitting if the stone had cut them into shreds, as Juan's death had done to her heart.

Shifting on her knees, she dropped her hands to her lap. Six weeks or more before they reached the church of Saint James. A few days there, and they would begin the final leg of their journey. With every new day, A Coruña came closer.

At last, they arrived at the river of Lavacolla. Making her way down to the riverbank with the other women, María looked behind at the dense scrubs and tall trees. Hidden behind them, the men waited their turn to follow the rituals of centuries. Garbed only in their shifts, the women accompanied Catalina to bathe.

The young women rushed to the water together, their squeals competing with loud splashes as warm bodies came in contact with cold water. Soon, all the girls seemed like children again as they giggled and chased each other in the almost shoulder deep water.

Glowering at the girls' behaviour, Doña Elvira announced her intention to leave after only a short time, clearly expecting Catalina and the other girls to follow suit, but Catalina merely waved a hand at her in dismissal and farewell. María almost burst out laughing at the woman's furious face.

Washing the long days of travel off her skin, María sank to her knees, immersing her head in the water, and then sprang up again. Small pebbles surfacing the riverbed dug into her. She held out her arms before her, opening and shutting her hands in the water. The morning sun had seemed miserly when they had made their way down to the river. Now, hot air blew all around them and sunrays reached down through the trees and bushes, filtering an eerie greenish net of light over everything.

Nearby, Francisca, standing right next to Inés, burst out laughing.

Rousing as if from a trance, Catalina half twisted towards her. "What is it?"

Francisca reddened, glancing towards Doña Elvira, now too far away to hear them. "Forgive me, I was thinking of what some call the river."

María laughed. "The Lavacolla is a good name for it, and you cannot say we are not doing the same." She laughed again. "Except we use other Latin words for our woman parts." She glanced aside at Catalina, knowing she would agree. "When we are alone like this, we should call a fig, a fig."

Catalina pulled her thick plait of hair across her shoulder. Sunlight caught loose strands, turning them gold. Taking a wet cloth from the other María, María Rojas, she scrubbed behind her neck. "There is no shame in making ourselves clean before journeying on to the cathedral. Rightfully so; we are only doing what all pilgrims have done since Saint James became a place of pilgrimage."

María Rojas squatted deeper in the water, her shift ballooning around her like an opening flower. Lifting her face to the green light, she swirled the water with one hand and then the other. "Pilgrimage or not, I am just thankful for this chance to bathe." She giggled. "Even the jasmine perfume oil the queen gave to the princess no longer helped to disguise our need for a good wash."

María gazed aside at María Rojas. Another close kinswoman to Catalina, she not only shared the same golden colour hair as the princess but also had similar light blue eyes, and pale skin. Her oval face was perfect.

María glanced down at her own reflection, and bit her bottom lip. The English King had told Queen Isabel to select only women of beauty to serve her daughter in England. Not that Queen Isabel would do this simply because he wanted it so, but there were no ugly young women amongst Catalina's party. She studied her image in the wavering water. High cheekbones, large dark eyes, full lips, an oval face like the other María, but with hair so dark it shone with blue lights. *Am I truly beautiful? I am told so. Fool! Beauty of the body dissolves with the passing of time, and can be taken from you in a breath.* She struck the water with her hand, and her reflection vanished. *Beauty does not matter. What matters is to serve Catalina loyally for the rest of my life.*

Catalina looked at her in amusement before wading over to María Rojas. She clasped the hand of her other kinswoman. "I have been thinking…"

María laughed, and splashed water in her direction. "Believe me, the princess is always thinking."

Catalina chuckled, the other girls laughed as well. Catalina grinned. "I'm thinking of the problem of two kinswomen with the name of María serving me." She looked at María Rojas. "The queen, my mother, has always had a liking for nicknames. Did she ever give you one?"

María Rojas laughed, and blushed a little. "Si. Our beloved Queen, your mother, called me Bella."

Catalina grinned. "It suits you. Would you mind us calling you Bella?"

María Rojas smiled at her, nodding. "If that is what you'd like, I am happy to be so called. It will remind me of Queen Isabel, your dear mother, and my noble queen."

Watching on, María swirled the water again, enjoying the coolness of the river as the heat of the day increased. The heady sweetness of her own youth seeped deeply into her heart, and soul. She was content; content to be with Catalina, and the other girls. Catalina also seemed content, all her anxieties about her coming wedding forgotten. She also seemed to desire to befriend her other companions. *Can I make Catalina speak openly to the other girls so they know her better?* "My princess," she said, "are you happy to marry Prince Arthur?"

Catalina rounded on her, her eyes wide with surprise. "Happy?" She inhaled and let out a long sigh. "I am happy that my marriage will strengthen my parents' hand against the French – and lessen the likelihood of war for Castile and Aragon."

"But what of the prince – are you happy to marry him?"

Catalina blinked, and cocked her head, looking at her inquisitively. "You ask strange questions today, *prima hermana*."

Despite the heat, María felt chilled when Francisca gave her a look of jealousy. The other girls often showed their resentment of her close relationship with Catalina. María forced out a laugh, and scrambled for a conversation that would include the other girls. "I was daydreaming about what it could be like to be married to an Englishman." She laughed again. "The French say they have tails."

All the girls laughed, and the moment of unpleasantness dissolved.

"And we say the French have tails," Inés said. Her eyes downcast, she twisted side to side in the water.

Catalina giggled. "Surely that is more likely than the English. All the English I met have been pleasant." She glanced around at the girls. "None of you need to feel you must find an English lord to marry. You can go home if England is not to your liking." Catalina stilled, her face serious. She shrugged. "It is not a choice open to me."

Concerned again about their conversation, María steered it to lighter subject. "Whoever I marry, I want a dozen children at least." She laughed. "My grandmother had twenty who lived to be adults, but she married at fourteen. I am already almost two years older than her, and still unwed."

"Twenty? That seems overmuch for any woman," said Bella. "Can you imagine bearing twenty infants?"

"I do not want to imagine." Francisca shrugged. "I am not too certain if I want to have children."

Catalina turned to her, her face alight with interest. "You plan to enter a religious order, Francisca?" she teased.

Francisca giggled. "Not me." She giggled again. "I like men too much."

Bella shifted closer to them, combing her fingers through her long, wet hair. "Are any of you afraid...?"

"Afraid of what?" asked Catalina.

"Afraid of what happens between a man and a woman?" She half closed her eyes and visibly shivered. "Mother told me..." She eyed Catalina, and bit her bottom lip.

Catalina took her hand. "What did your mother tell you?"

Bella blushed and bent her head. "It is like a knife," she whispered.

Catalina let go of Bella. She put her hand over her mouth for a moment before bursting out laughing. "My mother told me differently." She sank a little deeper into the water. María watched her twirl the water on either side of her into what seemed unending spirals. "My mother said it is one of the sweetest things in a marriage." She smiled a little. "My brother and his wife thought so too." She looked up at María. "Do you remember?"

"Si – I remember," she said. Her heart bled with other memories – memories of envy every time Juan held and kissed his wife.

María swallowed, and turned to Bella. "My sister told me it does hurt the first time, but she grew to like it. A lot, she said." She laughed and caught Catalina's eyes. "Latina, our teacher, told us it is nothing to fear – not when a woman is willing, and not forced by the man." She grinned. "She also told me many men believe a woman can only conceive a child if they enjoy the act. Si." She laughed. "Latina said that was not true, but if men believe it then they are more likely to pleasure their wives. She would not tell me what she meant by that. She told me if I wanted to know more, I had two choices: marriage or to seek out the books which would tell me."

Bella blushed again, and lowered her head. "Do we sin to talk of such matters?"

Catalina shrugged. She lay back in the water to float, blinking against the sunlight. "How else are we to prepare for marriage if we do not talk? Like María said before, when we are alone like this, let's call a fig, a fig. We have enough to face without making some effort to speak the truth to one another, if only to ease the journey before us."

After the men had bathed in the river, all the party proceeded to Mount Gozo. Some of them broke away and dashed to the summit. The first man to reach it called out: *"Mi alegría."*

María wanted to run too. But it was another thing forbidden to her. She turned to the other young women. *Do they look on with regret too?* She let out a long sigh. So many freedoms denied to them, but allowed without question to the men. But for this part of the journey, the women were allowed to act as pilgrims and walk down to the cathedral. For once, they were no longer expected to remain confined in the royal andas.

She reached the apex of the mountain, joining those already on their knees, and raised her voice in song. The city of Santiago and the distant spires of the cathedral of Saint James shimmered in the sunlight. *The basilica of Saint James, the temple of stars...* It kept safe in its sanctity the bones of the martyred Saint James, the man Christ had once called brother, and "Son of Thunder." They would spend five days in Santiago de Compostela – and then make their way to the waiting ships. *Si, my days in my homeland are drawing to a close.*

María lifted her skirts and hurried up the short flight of steps to reach the cathedral. The Portico de la Gloria rose up as if in greeting: hundreds of holy figures, all them carved in stone and realistically painted. In its centre, the statue of Saint James lifted a hand to bless and welcome them to the cathedral. The beauty of the Portico took her breath away, and paused her in awe.

Going to the other side of Saint James, the archbishop

pointed out a statue half her height to Catalina. "It is Master Mateo," he said softly, "the stonemason whose work we see all around us, my princess." He grinned. "They say if you wish to receive some of Master Mateo's wisdom, you must tap your forehead three times on his head. I have done it many times; alas, I am none the wiser. But I trust in the guidance of God."

He had then led the party on, taking them into the dark interior of the cathedral. Before them, at the end of the long aisle, a golden altar glittered with the light of countless candles. They stepped up the stairs behind the altar, the archbishop taking them to a golden statue of Saint James. He wound his arms around it from behind, and turned to the rest of the party. "Before we go down to the holy crypt and visit his relics, we invite all pilgrims to embrace Saint James thus."

At last, her turn, María put her arms around Saint James. She closed her eyes, laying her hand in one of the grooves on the saint's pillar left by pilgrims who had come before her. *Lord God, bring us safely to England*, she prayed, *grant us happiness there.*

María followed the others going down to crypt. The space was so tiny it allowed only a few people to go in at a time. She reached the tomb of Saint James. Within it, the silver casket, revered for centuries, was small enough to be carried by a child – yet the human remains it contained had set in motion the building of this great cathedral. The holiness of this place was tangible.

In the crypt, the archbishop and Catalina knelt beside each other, their heads bowed in silent prayer. Voices of monks, raised in song in the cathedral, echoed almost eerily. Waiting her turn to enter the crypt, María watched a sliver of light flickering weakly by her side. She closed her eyes, listening to the men sing, imprinting in her mind, heart and memory, every moment spent at the cathedral this morning. She opened her eyes to the light flickering by her side again, and the realisation that it was her turn to go into the crypt. She had been awed when she had entered the cathedral, now, kneeling before the bones of Saint James, she felt overcome. She bent her head. *Dear God, help me to keep faith. Help me to be strong, and never regret my vow to share Catalina's exile.* Aware of the others waiting for their turn, she rose and followed after Catalina to the nave of the cathedral.

Sitting behind Catalina, Francisca frowned, but shuffled closer to Inés to give María space to sit beside her. Taking her place, María smiled at Francisca her thanks. Francisca smiled back. Since their time in the river, the girls gave her moments like this, and increased her hopes that one day they all would be friends.

María looked around the magnificent cathedral. Eight red-robed men carried out the famous huge incense burner called the Botafumeiro. The monks attached it to ropes as thick as a man's arms, and took turns to put hot embers into the burner before closing the lid. A dense haze of white smoke escaped and swirled around the burner, its heady fumes becoming almost overwhelming. The eight men worked the rope pulley together, heaving the Botafumeiro up into the main dome. With great effort, and the coordination of the carefully trained, they tugged at the ropes, swinging the burner high, from one side of the church to the other.

Full of wonder, María could hardly breathe, unable to take her eyes away from the swinging Botafumeiro, a sight of power and might. All was well for several heartbeats, but then it swung towards the high window of the cathedral and broke free from its ropes. A tremendous crash reverberated in the cathedral, followed by shattering glass. The enormous burner sailed out of the building.

Shocked, her heart in her throat, María fell to her knees, hearing the noise of others doing the same. Dropping to her knees too, Catalina turned. Her eyes huge and frightened, she whispered, "It cannot be an omen. It cannot be that."

María shook her head, refusing to voice the words in her head. Wanting to be sick, she glanced at the few remaining shards of the stained-glass window. Madness seemed to reign for a time. Monks scurried around in panic, while the men who had swung the Botafumeiro stood close together. Their faces white, they stared up at the high dome.

Monks hurried to pick up the broken pieces of glass. Holding the loose robes of their cassocks like scooped aprons before them, they carried away the glass. All around, people buzzed an under-current of dismay. At last, the archbishop took matters in hand. He returned to the pulpit. "Let us pray," he intoned. He prayed for so long, María shifted from sore knee to sore knee, her body stiff by the time he told them to go in peace.

Later, back at his palace, the archbishop said nothing to them about what had happened. It seemed he wished to pretend it had never taken place. He was not the only one. Everyone was glum at the evening banquet as Catalina sat with the archbishop on the dais, staring out ahead at nothing, pushing her food around her plate, but not eating it.

María waited until they returned to the privacy of Catalina's chamber to speak to her. They undressed and slipped into bed, and she reached for Catalina's hand. "Pray, do not think any more about today's mishap. It means nothing."

Catalina rolled over, facing the other way. "Be quiet. I want to sleep," she grumbled.

María lay awake for a long time before falling asleep. And she dreamed. She dreamed she pulled herself up a mountain, hand over hand, her questing feet seeking out any possible foothold. A cloudless sky beckoned her on to a city of gold glimmering in the overhead sun. *Santiago de Compostela* – high on the mountain's apex, yet more real and vivid in her dream than when she first saw the city only days ago. Despite its distance, the city's brightness blinded her. Her heart ached with yearning to reach it.

Someone sobbed. Tears changed into an avalanche of blood, and she fell, her chance to reach the citadel gone.

Waking up, María rubbed her damp eyes. Beside her, Catalina sobbed into her pillow. Her golden city receding farther and farther into the mists and wisps of half-forgotten dreams, she touched Catalina's wet cheek with a sigh and wound her arms around her. Catalina's body trembled, her tears soaking through María's shift.

Catalina broke away from her and stared up at the ceiling. "Another nightmare."

María swung out of bed and relit the night candle. She returned to the bed. "Do you wish to speak of it?"

Catalina shook her head so hard the bed creaked in protest. "It was just a bad dream, that's all."

María rested her head close to Catalina. "I had one too." She shivered, remembering the earth changing into congealing blood in her dream.

Catalina clasped her hand. "It is no wonder – not after what happened today in the cathedral. But I have had this same dream for years. An eagle sits on my chest and dips its beak into my heart, over and over." Catalina looked aside at her. "When it flies away, I wake up, weeping. What can it mean?"

María shook her head, staring up at the ceiling too. Candle-light shimmered the gold of the intricate pattern-work. "Like you said, what happened today in the Cathedral disturbed us both."

Catalina sighed. "I spoke harshly to you before – before we went to sleep. Forgive me, my sister. Ever since we left the Cathedral, I have been wondering if the broken ropes of the Bota-fumeiro may be a warning about my marriage."

María turned to Catalina. "Why think that?"

Catalina visibly trembled. "Ever since we received news of the Earl of Warwick's death, I have believed myself cursed. I do not wish to speak against my parents. I know they demanded it because they wanted to make England safer for me. But his death was wrong."

"You cannot blame yourself, Catalina. You did not want him dead."

"I hear what you say, my sister, but it makes no difference. He stood in the way of my marriage, and died because of it. Latina taught me enough about England and its people for me to know Warwick had a cursed life. He was only a boy of ten when the English king imprisoned him in the Tower. Latina told me that he was deprived of books and education. Imagine, four-teen-years of deprivation and then to be executed at the end of it. His story breaks my heart. And you're wrong. I am the reason and cause for his death. The blame is mine."

María tightened her hold on her friend, her own fear growing. *Was Catalina right? Could what happened in the cathedral be truly a warning about her marriage?* Pushing away the thought as ludicrous, she wished for the dawn to come – and quickly. The night seemed full of ghosts, and forebodings.

2

Even in a world that's being shipwrecked, remain brave and strong.

~ *Hildegard of Bingen*

July, 1501

Doña, my dear Latina,

We have been at A Coruña for weeks, waiting for weather to favour our departure.

Maria hurried towards the waiting boats, aware of the darkening sky. Moments before, sunlight shimmered on their wind-plucked robes, but in an instant the dazzle was gone, deadened by the dim light. Even the peacock colours of the grandees' cloaks became peahen.

Don Diego de Cordova, Count of Cabra – a loyal servant of Catalina's parents and a man they had known all their lives – stood close to the Archbishop of Santiago. The two men journeyed with them to England to act in loco parentis for the princess at her wedding. The count was tall, but beginning to lose the litheness and leanness of a lifelong soldier, while the Archbishop was stocky and short, his dark skin made darker by his black robes. Long, mature face and round, aged face, the men wore close to the same serious expression. Sailors helped members of their party into the boats that would take them out to the ships. When they lifted the blackamoor servant into a boat, the girl looked like she was going to her execution.

María scrutinised the sky again. An enormous purple-black cloud scudded across the sun, edged what seemed like a thin ribbon of cloth of gold. Sea birds flew through retreating slants of sunlight escaping from tiny cloud crevices. Moment by moment, the crevices sealed up, decreasing the light. Beating their wings against wind, the land-bound birds became first Midas-touched and then blended with the mounting darkness. They cawed a never-ending warning.

The strengthening gale wrapping her gown tight around her body, she paused again, her hand on her anxious stomach, glancing the way they had come. Despite the warmth of her mantle, she trembled, cold of body, cold of spirit, cold of heart. She pushed herself another step towards the boats, and then another step, then another and another – determined not to falter.

Again, the wind intensified, her ears buzzing with its aeolian whirr. It pushed her back, blowing the fine gossamer silk veil tight around her neck. Struggling to fix her veil, sea spray stung her eyes. She crinkled her nose at the smell of nearby rotting fish and human refuse, a stench overpowering the fresh tang of the sea.

Her veil at last untangled, she took in again the grey, endless ocean. For years, she had anticipated this day. Now she needed to surmount the reality. She heard in her mind the voice of her mother, "Dear one, I am here. I am here. Always," the words her mother had said on their last day together. The words no longer comforted her, but spoke of everything she sacrificed. An ocean of grief choked her. *I do not want to go. I do not want to leave here. How can I leave and know I will never see Mother once more?*

She looked ahead to Catalina, and her heart ripped apart. *I love her. I cannot leave her. I can do this. I can make a life in England as long as I am with my Catalina. I must. I promised.*

A short space away, Doña Elvria trudged purposely alongside her husband, Don Pedro Manuel. Head lowered, scowling as usual, the older woman also fought with the strong wind. She dropped her skirts to hold onto her head covering and tripped over her dragging gown. Her husband grabbed her arm, preventing her from falling to the ground.

A loud, cut off laugh came from a stone's throw away. Clumped close together, watching the princess and her party's departure, twenty or so villagers stood not far from the row boats tied to the quay. Two older men pushed a white-faced youth behind them, protecting him from view. They need not have feared. Nearby, sailors assisted their party into boats. The day brought greater concerns than giving mind to a peasant who mocked his betters.

Some distance from the shore, three of the king's galleons –

turned into rocking toys by the strong gale – lay ready to catch the morning tide. As soon as they boarded, the ships would sail out to sea. She took a deep breath, and tried to calm her quailing heart, drumming in her ears. Grief swished and churned within her like the currents of the foaming sea.

María fought anew with her veil, caught again by the wind. Sunlight broke through the cloud. Bright light, silver-flecked, showered the squadron of galleons, the sea around them turned into a glittering, huge, swelling pond. The light seemed alive, rippling, pulsing, a continual interflow between sea and sky, as if angel wings quivering between Heaven and Earth. One moment, so fierce and frightening; the next moment, a vision of beauty.

Driven on by the wind, María came to stand beside Catalina, gazing with her at the sky and sea in silence. *Why speak when I know someone's heart as well as my own?*

The Count of Cabra approached and bowed. He lifted Catalina aboard the closest boat. Settling the princess in, Cabra draped a thick blanket over her lap and legs, and smiled in reassurance. He stood arrow-straight, the proud, tall commander beckoning to the rest of the party. "Hurry! The tide waits for no one! To the boats," he boomed, in a voice fit for the battlefield.

Helped by one of the sailors into the same boat as Catalina, María twisted around. Shadowed by Farum Brigantium, the ancient lighthouse, a white, stony beach formed a barrier between sea and harbour town. Sunrays lit up the narrow stretch of beach before the deluge of darkness from the heavy clouds swept over it.

Two days later, Catalina rolled in the narrow box bed and muttered, keeping María from sleep. "Traitors...Die...Die...," Catalina repeated, and repeated. She flung out her arms, forcing María to balance on the bed's edge, moving out of her way.

Should I wake her up? She wiggled back beside Catalina, sighing, trying to ignore the smell of vomit and unemptied night buckets permeating the cabin. *Let sleeping dogs lie*, she reminded herself. What happened in real life gave more cause for fear. Already, the other women in the cabin, woken up from the storm, prayed for their lives.

The sides of the galleon groaned, timbers cracked, as if timed to the thunder bursts from the storm. The vessel pitched one way, then another, like an unbroken horse bearing a rider's weight for the first time. A wind from hell bayed for blood outside, its wails echoing in their cabin. Flashes from the lightning bolts darted like sharp, silver tongues through timber cracks.

She peered through the hole closest to her. Ripping asunder the night, lightning illuminated the evening sky, each flash offering brief visions of other worlds. In a blink of an eye, these worlds turned from gold to blue then finally purple, before disappearing into darkness. *What if the storm is too much for our ship?* Her stomach roiling, she checked Catalina. The pulse of light from the storm revealed Catalina still sleeping, seemingly oblivious to the roll and pitch of the ship.

Another ear-splitting boom of thunder shook their cabin. Catalina gasped, and bounded up, her eyes wide with fear.

María clasped her hand, keeping her voice calm. "You're all right. Were you having another dream?"

Catalina lowered her head in shame. "Si – another nightmare."

Catalina leaned against the back of the bed, hugging her knees to her. She stared ahead as if into another world. "The executioner swung the young man's head like a toy. There was blood everywhere." Catalina raised her hand to her throat. "In the dream, I had blood on me too."

"My sister, it is only a bad dream," María comforted. But she remembered all the bad dreams plaguing Catalina since the start of their journey. When the Botafumeiro broke free of its ropes in the cathedral, it seemed yet another bad dream, but one too terrifyingly real. María chewed at her bottom lip. *Why does Catalina keep having these dreams? Am I a fool to think Warwick is warning Catalina from the grave?*

Catalina pushed aside her blankets and soft animal skins. "I must get up. I feel sick." Not waiting for María to aid her, she swung around, attempting to stand, only to nearly slip on the slimy, water-drenched timbers.

The ship pitched. Storm water seeped over the boards. They had been placed in the captain's great cabin, on the upper level of the ship, supposedly the safest place on board for Catalina. It no longer felt safe. Close to them, water pooled, a steady tide on the rise. Catalina dropped to her knees, crossing herself before grabbing hold of the frame of the bed. "God, forgive my sins," she said. Then she whispered, "Please, God, I do not want to die."

Beside María, the crack in the wood revealed lightning bolts ripping apart the sky. In the cabin, women called out in fear, Inés and Francisca, like Catalina, precariously balanced on their knees, praying loudly as the ship pitched and rolled in quick succession. Others held onto whatever they could. María's heart beat so fast, as if trying to burst free from her chest.

The wind buffeted the ship without mercy. Suddenly, the storm-gale shrieked, a scream of such power it left María clinging to Catalina and silenced all around them. The ship heeled savagely over, toppling María and Catalina to the wet floor. Water streamed through every crevice of the upper cabin.

Doña Elvira screeched, "Mother of God. Save us! We're going under!"

The ship violently rocked, and everything turned black. Hurting from her fall, María held on tight to the nearest post for dear life.

In the darkness, unseen terror hunted her.

Just after dawn's first light, María stood beside Catalina on the gallery of the ship's great cabin, feeling as bruised and battered as their damaged ship. The endless, horrifying night had given way to a pearled, translucent dawn, the gale dissipating down to brisk sea breezes. Ragged dark clouds scattered in the western sky, the only remnant of last night's storm.

Humiliated, the galleons hobbled their way back to gentler harbours, seeking safety. With all the ships in need of much repair, the men and women on board praised and gave thanks to God for their escape from premature death.

The cold air making her feel more fragile, María drew her red mantle firmer around her, as the wind tugged it, and flapped it against Catalina's. She clutched her mantle's intricate border, embroidered in black wool. Her heart lurched, seeing in her mind her mother sewing it. She closed her eyes for a moment, and made herself think of other things.

Above her, gulls cawed. María watched their flight, her eyes watering against the wind's strong sea salts. Three days ago, another flock of gulls fought their way through the wind to shore. *Are they the same birds? Perhaps they are. Si – no matter what, life goes on.*

Catalina folded her arms on the rails and glanced at the sky. "Such a terrible storm." She studied the beckoning, gentle sea. "A new day – a new beginning. I feel like the phoenix rising from the ashes."

Looking at the birds again, María clasped her friend's hand. "A phoenix about to fly. It is a new dawn for both of us."

Catalina sighed. "So far to England."

Waves splashed against the side of the rocking ship, their beat reminding her of the lines of a poem. She recited softly without thinking:

"My thoughts hurl my heart like a boat by a flying sail on
    a stormy day.
I am destined to wander, by the book of God, and to roam
    over every land.
For all who are fated to exile move about like Cain and
    flee as Jonah."

"Did you speak?" Catalina asked.

María stilled, glancing at her friend. "It is not important," she said, staring down at the ocean. But the words kept drumming in her mind.

She was continually so tossed and tumbled hither and thither with boisterous winds.

~ Robert Grafton, 1502

Doña, my dear Latina,

We await ashore at Laredo for the ships to be repaired and ready once more to take to the sea. For three slow weeks we have waited. I am reading one of the books you gave me on our parting, the writings of Saint Hildegard. 'Of Causes and Cures' is indeed a wise book. It opens up my mind, my teacher. Was that your intention in giving me this book? You will be pleased to know I keep in mind your example; I write notes and drawings in my journal to help my learning. But I daily miss your counsel and our lessons. Away from you, I feel more unsuited than ever to become this healer you wish of me. I do not want to fail you, or my princess. I will not forget my promise I gave to you; I will build on the knowledge you have given me. It would only show my lack of gratitude for your good teaching if I did otherwise...

Cabra's gruff voice sounded outside Catalina's window. Catalina still fast asleep, María rose from her writing desk and looked outside, worried the men would wake her. The count stood next to the English sea captain, Stephen Brett. Sent by the Tudor King, he had arrived early yesterday. The short, dark-haired man, with the bowed legs of a lifelong sailor, spoke to Cabra in rapid French. "If the princess does not leave soon, Count, my king will need to postpone the wedding of his son. That would make my king most unhappy. Everything is arranged and awaits the princess's arrival."

"We are not ready to go," the count replied. He waved his hand in the direction where the seamen and craftsmen worked on the ships. All day long, men hammered and sawed, overhauling the damaged ships for another sea voyage.

"You better be ready soon, my Lord," the Captain said. "If you think the weather is bad at present, I can promise one more week will give us a crossing none will ever forget. I want us gone as soon as the repairs are done, otherwise I fear my first mate will lose my own ship in the Bay of Biscay. I know its sea storms too well. My king sends me to guide you to a safe English harbor, and I promise you, I will. But we must leave before this week ends."

The men moved on. María stood at the window, unable to rid from her mind the captain's words. *A crossing none will ever forget? Dear God, we have already been in one sea storm, and I never want to face another.* Catalina still sleeping, María decided to deal with her fresh anxiety by leaving her letter unfinished for a time, and to search for food.

In the outer chamber, Bella, Francisca and Inés sat close together, adding more embroidery to the princess's trousseau. The three girls lifted their heads at María's approach and then glanced at each other. "So – you come to join us?" Inés asked.

Surprised at their cold looks, María sat down near them. "Forgive me, but I will do anything to avoid the needle or distaff," she replied with a smile.

"Not just the needle and distaff. You make it clear where you'd rather be," Francisca retorted.

María stared at Francisca. "I do not know what you mean."

Bella shifted on her stool in obvious distress. "We have been here weeks," she said. "All that time you and the princess stay alone in her chamber. I think Doña Elvira is right – you wish to keep the princess to yourself."

María glanced around, making certain Doña Elvira was nowhere in sight. Annoyed, she shook her head at the other girls. "You listen too much to that woman. I have been with the princess since we were small children. I cannot help it if she prefers to remain in her chambers to read and write letters to her family and not sit and while away her time in idle chatter."

"Do you have to stay with her all the time?" Francisca snapped, her eyes hard and accusing.

María held her tongue on her desire to reply to Francisca in harsher words. She remembered Francisca's smile in the Cathedral at Santiago de Compostela. *We can be friends. No – we must be friends. Soon, we will be in a strange country. We will only have each other then.* Resolving to ignore Francisca's remark, María shrugged. "She wants me there – and we are well used to each other's company. I have letters I want to write too, and books to study. It keeps my mind off the coming sea voyage, which I dread as much as you, and I hazard a guess this is also the reason why the princess busies herself with so many letters." Inés yanked at her long plait hanging over one shoulder before touching María's arm. "Can you not convince her to come and speak to us too? We are leaving our families and country too. Surely these weeks together would have been better spent by strengthening the bonds between us? We are all here to serve her – not to become jealous of one another because we think she has taken favourites." Inés frowned at her sewing. "And you are not alone in wishing to avoid the needle. If you could loan me one of your books to read, I would be in your debt."

María rubbed her aching head. *Have I become my companions' advocate?* It was not a role she welcomed.

When María returned to the bedchamber, Catalina was awake and at her writing desk. She lifted her head, put aside her quill and smiled at her. "You have been gone for a while."

"I have been talking to our companions."

"Mm..." Catalina picked up her quill again, her attention returned to the parchment in front of her.

"Catalina – could you please listen to me for a moment?"

Catalina twisted around. "What is it?"

"I think it would be wiser if we are not alone so much. The other women are your companions too. They are unhappy. I do not believe it is simply due to this long journey."

Catalina pursed her mouth. "Do you know what troubles them?"

"They are jealous." María sighed.

"Jealous?" A frown so alike her mother's knotted between Catalina's thinned eyebrows.

María sighed again. "Of me. They are jealous of me."

Catalina looked taken aback. "But you and I have always been together."

María shrugged. "I think it would be wise to remember the queen's advice not to have obvious favourites. Once we are in England, your companions will form your inner court within your court."

"But I think of you as my sister," Catalina said. "Even mother kept those she trusted close to her, your mother for one."

"Si, and like my mother for your mother, I vow to serve you to the day of our death. But the other girls begin to trouble me. They are scared too about the sea voyage and, like us, they are leaving behind everything they love for England. Pray, for my sake, let us eat with them and spend more time getting to know them. I think if you befriend them, really befriend them, they won't be so jealous and cause mischief. I do not like their black looks."

***

Once more, they boarded their ship for England. As the sailors readied the ship to weigh anchor, María joined Catalina and the other women on the deck. The vessel rocked gently in the wind, its pale sails set against the pellucid skies. But blue skies turned grey too quickly, just as the wind changed from a siren's invitation to a wild, hungry, angry beast hunting for prey.

María fought against her queasiness, her stomach rolling like the ship's own deck. She grabbed the rail, gazing first to land, then to her princess. Catalina broke away from the chattering women, looping her arm through hers. "Fool- hardiness or bravery, do you think?"

Before María could answer, wind whipped her veils against her face and into her open mouth. She burst out laughing. She laughed at the black clouds already gathering on the horizon and a churning, endless ocean. She laughed at how small their ship was when compared to the sea's vastness. She swallowed, her laughter skating close to weeping, and met Catalina's troubled eyes. "I pray to get to England safely; I pray for all of us," she said quietly, with all the control she could muster.

By late the next day, the skies had turned black, and it seemed time repeated itself. Lightning bolts pierced the heavens, ferocious winds howled and high seas pounded against the ship. Again, pressed to remain in their cabin and hearing the groans of timber, María tried to block her ears. Thunder boomed over their heads, and she feared their vessel was about to break apart. A demonic sea tossed their ship, as if Satan himself indulged in murderous play.

When she had seen the ships for the first time, she had thought they looked like toys out in the ocean. They proved fragile toys. The howl of wind quietened for a moment, bringing with it the cries of the sailors fighting hard for the ship's survival; for the survival of them all. The ship pitched in the midst of mountainous waves. Cold, terrified and wretchedly seasick in their dark, sea-drenched cabin, she felt locked into an awful eternity.

But this time the sea squalls did not return them to home. Rather, the winds of hell brought them close to England, but not to land. For days, the contrary winds and winter storms made it impossible to approach shore, and the safety of harbour. Holding Catalina's hand, María huddled with her and the other girls. "Do you think we will die?" asked Francisca, asking the same question quailing María's heart. María could not answer her. None of them could. Hearing the wind howl again and ship's timbers groan, María clasped Francisca's hand too.

At last, the hour came when calmer seas allowed them to anchor. Beside Catalina on the poop, María watched men rowing out to them from the nearby shore, through the rough waters. The men would take them to shore.

Catalina's hands came together as if in prayer. She turned frightened, anxious eyes to María. "They tell me we are at Plymouth. We were supposed to anchor in Southampton, not here. Death stalked us twice, María. Twice."

Mists thickened and swirled at the English shoreline. Grey skies, grey water, grey shore covered with grey rocks – a grey world with little welcome. Even the large castle seemed grey, and ugly. It loomed as if daring them to approach.

"What if my marriage does not please God?" she asked. "Shhh – do not say such things." María took Catalina's arm,

gazing down at the sea. The waves crested and chopped against the rocking ship. "Thank God we soon leave this ship for land." She shook herself into movement, glancing around to check they were alone. "Come, my sister, let us return to our cabin and make ready for England."

The day was coming to an end when their boats were dragged on to the rocky shore near a stone wharf leading to the castle. Waiting Englishmen plucked out the women from the boats. María caught her breath, her heart beating fast, when one of the tall, grinning men scooped her up in his arms and carried her to the safety of the wharf, as if she weighed nothing at all.

Set on firm ground, she wobbled and raised her hand to her spinning head. No longer anchored to her body, she seemed to look down on herself. All around her, the sea air seeped the rot of dead things. She seized the last bit of her will power and forced her legs to obey her, joining the rest of her companions. Clumped together protectively around Catalina, everyone looked exhausted. Some looked ill. Don Alcaraz, the princess's physician, was so pale he seemed close to crumpling onto the ground.

Male voices sang. A group of roughly garbed men on the rocky foreshore came closer and closer. María could not understand a single word, but there was no mistaking they sang in welcome. Well-dressed men headed towards them. Pointing them out to Catalina, the count broke away from the large group and strode out to meet with them. At last, the count returned to Catalina. "My princess," he said with a brief bow, "the men are here to escort you to Plymouth castle."

They followed after the Englishmen, the singers trailing after them as a ragged escort. All the way, the men sang, their tunes changing from fast to slow, to fast again. By the time they reached the castle, the men had been joined by other singers – men, women and children.

When the castle door closed behind them, María smiled to hear them still singing. Don Alcaraz grinned too. "The English welcome the princess as if she is the saviour of the world," he said, loud enough for the others to hear.

Her legs still not feeling her own, she surveyed the dark interior of the castle. In spite of the tapestries hanging on every wall, the place appeared established for soldiers, and hardly a place fit to welcome Catalina on her first day in England – or to accommodate her. Its uninviting ugliness left her longing for the beautiful buildings of home.

She stepped on the rushes laid on the flagstone floor, crackling underfoot, and followed Catalina to a long and spacious candle-lit room. The smell of herbs wafted around her, but it did not disguise the other smells of human and animal waste kept too close, and another smell that made her stomach turn – the smell of rancid fat. It weighed down the very air she breathed.

Entering the room, she saw first a stone hearth as tall and wide as the height of a man. The fire within devoured huge logs, and glowed bright and warm its welcome. A long table loaded with food and drink was set at the end of the room.

Catalina collapsed in the nearest high-backed chair by the huge hearth, and gestured to her companions. "Please sit, if you wish. We all need rest." Sitting on a bench with visible relief, Don Alcaraz leaned forward, pointing to the open doorway. "Princess, an English lord comes."

Catalina turned her head. Gazing the same way, María saw an aged man coming through the door. Richly robed, he tottered slowly, his limping gait aided by a walking stick. Close behind him trailed a pretty woman, her hair covered by a white headdress. She looked young enough to be his granddaughter. A number of men dressed in red livery followed them. Cabra stood behind Catalina's chair. He bent to speak near her ear. "I recognise the badge, Your Highness. It is Thomas Howard, Earl of Surrey."

Catalina sighed, tugging with annoyance at the thin silk veil covering her face. "It seems I must greet him."

The count moved before her chair and bowed. "I shall bring the earl to you."

Cabra strode over to the door and bowed to the elderly earl. He spoke quietly to him and the young woman, before bringing them and one of the liveried men over to Catalina. The old man bowed over Catalina's proffered hand and spoke his welcome in French before gesturing to the woman. "My wife, the Lady Alice." María almost gasped her surprise. *That young girl his wife? Dear God – he is an old man.*

The Lady Alice curtseyed. "I am delighted to meet you, your highness."

"I have sent word to the king," the earl said, "to tell of your safe arrival." He gestured to the liveried man, who approached carrying a ruby encrusted gold pomander, placed upon a red velvet cushion. "Pray, your highness, accept this small token of my esteem. I am honoured to be amongst the first to welcome you to England."

Catalina took the pomander and smiled. "Earl, I accept your gift with great pleasure." Her eyes huge and glassy in her wan face, she flopped back in her chair.

Recognising the signs of her friend's deepening fatigue, María stepped closer, signing to Don Alcaz in passing. He moved over to the count, bowed to him before whispering in his ear. The count moved swiftly across and bowed to the Earl. "Forgive me, my lord, but can I ask for someone to show the princess to her chamber and for food and drink to be sent to her? Our princess needs to rest. Our journey to England has been difficult to say the least."

Catalina laughed tiredly, but held out her hand to the Earl of Surrey. "My good Count of Cabra speaks the truth, my lord. I look forward to sleeping in a bed which does not threaten to overturn me to the floor. Tomorrow, I hope you will escort me to the nearest church so I and my people can give thanks for our safe arrival."

Surrey took her hand and bowed again. "With great pleasure, my highness. I will go to the priest and arrange it now." That night, they all rested in comfort at the castle. Early the next day, clean again and robed in rich robes, they walked with their English hosts the short, but steep distance to the church of Saint Andrew's. Joined by more and more English, their number grew until at least double in size by the time they arrived. Just before entering the stone church, some of which seemed newly built, María turned to look at the harbour. A dense black cloud spread like spilled oil across the sky, and the darkened sea seemed endless. As the wind whipped her gown and veil and the waves crashed on the rocks of the beach, she remembered the day she first left the shores of her home for the waiting ships. Her heart aching at all separating her from her old life, she turned and followed after Catalina.

From Plymouth, only two days later, a group of English noblemen escorted them to Exeter. There, more members of the English court greeted them, their arrival swelling their retinue into the hundreds. They gave Catalina a message from their king and prince, a message welcoming her to England. Mounted on horses, the party journeyed on, riding through deer and tree rich woodlands, passing farmlands where peasants worked the fields, stopping before nightfall at a place readied in advance for the royal party.

Encased by filtered light of yet another dense forest, María twisted towards Catalina beside her. "It is much greener than home," she said.

Catalina glanced at her before gazing ahead at the road. "Home, María? We must think *this* home if we want any chance of happiness in our new country."

The next day, the weather changed again. The grey sky opened up, and rain fell without pause. Its downpour lashed the road into a mud bath, slowing their progress. Forced by the vicious weather to remain with her closest women in a litter brought for her use, Catalina took out her sewing. Skeins of coloured thread around her neck, she spent the long, dragging hours of the wet day embroidering. María wished she could do the same, but knew her skills would not be able to surmount the constant rocking of the litter, or the dim light. She tried to read, but gave up, her stomach aching with its emptiness. Sleep offered the only escape for her.

The days passed with early risings and brief stops. Every night, they slept at a place prepared to accommodate Catalina and her party. It was weeks before they arrived at the village of Dogmersfield. Closer to London, Catalina and her party were promised a longer stay and rest at Dogmersfield House, an episcopal palace.

Stepping out from the litter after Catalina, María paused to study her surroundings. A short distance from the palace, large ponds glittered and eddied in the afternoon sun. A young lithe man stood with a net at the end of a long pole at the edge of one pond. With unexpected grace, he swooped the long pole into the water to haul it out heavy with fish. Slinging the pole over his shoulder, he headed to a pathway skirting the palace.

In the distance, the spire of a church rose over the trees. The afternoon sun spun a net of gold over the landscape stretched out before her. She turned to the palace. Strangers bowed and greeted Catalina, standing apart from the rest of her company. Hungry and thirsty, María hurried to her princess.

María sprang up in bed, shocked at hearing Doña Elvira's raised, distressed voice. Outside Catalina's chamber, the woman argued with a man. The argument becoming louder still, Catalina awoke from her nap and turned on her side. She yawned and placed a finger on her lips, gesturing to María to remain quiet. As if Doña Elvira guarded the door, María heard her say, "The princess is sleeping; she sees no one."

Another man's voice spoke fast and furious in a language not their own. Underlined with steel, a quiet voice interrupted with what sounded like a command. Another man answered in Latin with annoyance, and the accent of home. "Doña, the king is master here. He will see the princess, no matter what you say." Humming voices seesawed, overlaying and overtaking one another, until it became a cacophony of confusion, the words impossible to decipher. A loud knock on the door was followed next by the entrance of a very flustered and unhappy Doña Elvira. "Your Highness, quick, I beg you. The king and his son, the prince, want to see you; now."

Catalina swung out of bed. María followed after her and seized their mantles from the nearby chair. She hurriedly tossed hers over her shift and then helped Catalina into hers, gathering up the two hanging sides, covering her chemise as well as she could. She muttered a few under-breath curses, as she straightened the mantle's folds, pulling it over Catalina's bare-head like a hood.

Her eyes wide with panic, Catalina snatched at it so it covered her face from nose to chin. "Come. Let's meet my new father and my husband," she said, her voice muffled by her mantle.

María padded into the next chamber – a chamber crowded with men. One approached Catalina and bowed. Dressed in Castilian garb, he also spoke in their tongue. "Your highness, I am Doctor de Puebla, your ambassador." He gestured to a man and youth. "I am honoured to introduce you to King Henry and Prince Arthur."

The king and prince strode over, their kinship announced by height, slender bodies, long faces, thin, wide mouths, hooded eyes. Backlight lit the boy's blond, shoulder length hair into a sheen of silver, while age thinned and dulled the greying locks of the older man.

Catalina curtsied. María dropped even lower, and remained kneeling on the floor. She raised her eyes to the prince. Head and shoulders taller than Catalina, his wan complexion rivalled that of a young maid. Little flesh thickened his bones, dark hollows pressed under his high cheeks. His gentle blue eyes were that of a dreamer, a poet, a singer of songs: the eyes of a delicate boy who suffered illness. A boy so slender a strong wind could blow him away. Disturbed, María bit her bottom lip, reminded of Catalina's brother, Prince Juan. Whilst a man and not a youth like this prince, Juan, in the final months of his life, had looked pale and ailing like Prince Arthur.

"Raise up, girl." The king took Catalina's hand, helping her to her feet. "Why cover yourself? Let me see the bride I've got for my son."

He spoke in effortless French. María wondered why he didn't speak to Catalina in Latin, the language of diplomacy, and one Catalina knew well. But then she recalled the letters exchanged between the two royal families. Queen Isabel, no doubt, had informed the English king Catalina spoke little English, but three years ago his wife had asked for their son's betrothed to be taught French, the second tongue of many at the English court.

María glanced aside at Doña Elvira. Kneeling beside her, the woman stirred in unhidden distress. Her skin grey and dark eyes bulging, she appeared overwrought, and ready to cry. María fought down a nervous giggle. She had never expected to witness Doña Elvira like this.

"Your Grace, good sire, I beg of you, it is not Castilian custom for the princess to reveal her face to her husband until after their marriage," the older woman said.

The king narrowed his blue eyes until he looked out of slits. His eyes sparked. "I care nothing for Castilian custom – not when it affects me or mine." His voice was soft, and of one used to obedience. "The princess is in my dominion. Reveal her to me."

Doña Elvira blanched to a sick pallor, but began to move as if to answer his command. Catalina's upraised hand halted her. "Stay. I'll do as the king asks."

Catalina pushed off her hood, but kept careful hold of her mantle, hiding her shift from view. Dipping her head, she offered to the king a brief, low curtsey. "My Lord King, I hope you find me pleasing," she shyly glanced towards the prince, "and also my Lord Prince."

Her nerves frayed near to breaking point, María wiggled, shuffling on her knees. Catalina stood all alone to face the taller king, yet a tiny smile teased at her mouth.

Henry Tudor rubbed the side of his beardless chin, reddening the tiny wart below his lower lip. He returned to Catalina a slight, tight smile. But Arthur though – his smile lit up his whole face.

Winking at his son, the king turned to the man introduced to them as Queen Isabel's ambassador. "Her fair beauty pleases us, as does her agreeable nature, Doctor de Puebla. With her good royal blood, she'll give us fine grandchildren." All the time he spoke, not once did the king address Catalina directly, Rather, he looked her over, up and down.

Still on her knees, María inwardly shuddered. In her mind came the memory of her father. His eyes had the same look as the king when he selected the young mares to serve his prized stallion.

She remembered all the times Queen Isabel had told Catalina she would be Arthur's consort, his queen. From almost the cradle, she had been trained for that role. Her life was not meant merely to serve, bed with him, and bear his sons, but to help him rule his kingdom.

King Henry talked rapidly to Dr de Puebla, María understanding only a few of the English words. *Does the king not see Catalina? Can he not see a too pale girl, her long, golden red hair unbound, her feet naked, her hands clutching tight her mantle, as if to stop them trembling?* Her princess hooded her eyes and bowed her head. *Si, Catalina knows the king's attention has gone on to other matters.*

María turned to the prince. The youth smiled and nodded at Catalina in reassurance, but then he turned from his bride to his sire, as if waiting and wanting to know what to do next. His body shared the same tautness as Catalina. María swallowed. *Si. A girl and youth with no other choice but to do their duty.*

The main part of the evening banquet over, it was time to entertain the king and his son. Smiling, Catalina rose from the royal dais and came over to take María's hand, leading her to the floor.

Rat tat tat rat tat tat beat the drummers, pipers and lute players threading their notes through the beats. María controlled her nerves and clapped with Catalina, once, twice, three times. Her body swayed to the music of home.

Above them, and too close for comfort, King Henry unsmilingly watched on.

The music swelled. María forgot the king, forgot everything but the dance. She stepped around Catalina, keeping her eyes on her friend. Her body aligned to Catalina's, she moved in a half circle, one way and back the other. The drums rolled again. She spun around on her heel, stepping out the five points of a star. Faster and faster she moved, her sweat beading her brow and dampening her gown.

The dance set her spirit free. She closed her eyes for a heartbeat, for a breath, for what seemed an eternity and touched the gates of Heaven before plummeting to earth. The music slowed. She encircled Catalina, and then Catalina her. The instruments quietened, reaching their final sobbing note. She stamped her feet in unison with Catalina's and clapped four times. The dance at an end, she caught her breath, and smiled at her friend as the audience applauded.

Catalina took her hand again, and they faced the king. His long, narrow face was expressionless. Together, in unison, they sank to kneel before the king, and lowered their heads.

María raised her eyes to the royal dais. The king pushed away from the table, leaving the room.

Catalina whispered in a rush, "Was he not pleased? Did we – did I – do something not to his liking?"

Still on her knees, María shifted closer to her friend. She did not know what to say; despair winged and nested its heavy weight in her heart. Catalina seemed nothing to him, this winter king, other than a symbol, or possession. He did not see Catalina, a flesh and blood girl, exiled a long way from home. She trembled, not daring to ponder what this meant for Catalina, or herself.

4

There Adam slept, and God formed the body of woman from one of his ribs, signifying that she should stand at his side as a companion and never lie at his feet like a slave, and also that he should love her as his own flesh.

~ *The Book of the City of Ladies*

In the bedchamber of Queen Elizabeth, María wiggled on the low stool, shuffling her throbbing, icy feet from side to side. Wind hammered rain against the thick glass; air-fingers slithered their chill through crevices of the ill-fitting window frames. The cold thrust its way through her thick layers of clothes. Drafts lifted and billowed out the heavy tapestries. They swelled and swayed, in an illusion of life. For days, the wind had howled and groaned – its voice throbbing a continual complaint, loud, soft and loud again through the royal chambers. Freezing air blew its breath down the corridors and galleries; so bitterly cold, unbelievably so. The strong, thick stone walls did little to keep any warmth in the chamber. Frost even edged a thin decoration on the large, polished bronze on the nearby wall. She shivered, and tried not to think about winter, yet still weeks away.

The bronze reflected the queen's huge bed. With its thick, heavy bed-hangings and covered with furs, the bed looked warm and inviting. Miserable, María wanted to curl up, back in the bed she had left only a short time ago, well beneath her own fur covers, and escape from the cold in sleep. Fingertips numbed and clumsy, she turned another page of her book, glancing yearningly towards Catalina. She wished she sat closer to the enormous fire burning with abandon in the huge hearth. But then María studied Catalina with far more attention.

Perched on the edge of her stool, Catalina kept changing her position, twisting one way and then another from the heat, the silk of her gown gleaming with the fire's orange and red glow. *They have placed her chair too close to the fire.* Catalina had other causes for discomfort as well. On high backed chairs overlooking her, a queen and a king's mother kept their eyes on the girl come to marry the heir to England's throne. María gnawed her bottom lip. *I am far better off here – even if I am freezing. I'd hate to be looked at like that.*

It was not the first time the two older women had met with Catalina since her arrival in London. Two days ago, the Countess of Richmond had hosted a banquet in Catalina's honour. The queen and the king had spoken to Catalina for a long time in French that evening.

Sitting with Catalina's other women, well away from the

royal dais, María had watched them speak, more certain as time passed the queen spoke to Catalina for purpose other than simple friendliness. All the time she spoke to Catalina, the queen seemed to be assessing Catalina, until Catalina also showed signs of anxiety. Today, for the first time, the three women came together without being surrounded by the king's court.

The English queen smiled, a sudden ray of sunlight bursting through the clouds of this dark, storm-plagued day. So fair of face, the queen's beauty could have belonged to an angel in mortal form.

"Daughter Katherine, I hope you are happy in your new home," she spoke in French. She gestured to the older woman beside her. "The Lady Margaret Beaufort and I want to help you learn the ways of England as quickly as you can."

Margaret Beaufort pursed her lips. Her narrow face was a composite of sharp elements: sharp cheekbones above concaved cheeks, sharp nose tapering over sharp, thin mouth, down to a sharp chin. She glared at Catalina, so much so, Catalina winced. The countess's thin mouth, so like her son's, the king, twisted into a smile, wrinkling the dull, white skin around it.

María lowered her head, surreptitiously watching the woman. *Margaret Beaufort has the look of one who smiles little, and judges much.*

"Your marriage pleases the king, my son; he desired this alliance for many years," the countess said.

Catalina smiled her most winning smile. "Likewise, my family wanted this union. *Non Mahi, non tibia, seed nobbies.*"

The king's mother frowned and rubbed together her knobbly, long fingers, heavily burdened with copper rings. She stared unblinkingly at Catalina. "You are learned in Latin?"

"Si..." Catalina's bright smile flickered out. She looked across to the queen for assurance. Elizabeth of York smiled her approval. "Good," the queen said.

The king's mother twisted around crossly to her daughter-in-law. "Women are not meant to be Latin scholars, Elizabeth. It's against the word of God." Her face stiffened with icy disdain. The queen smiled at Catalina, then faced the woman beside her. "Good mother – by the grace of God, Catalina will one day be Queen of England. The king and I knew and approved of her learning Latin, although Dr de Puebla has informed us it is a more classical Latin than we speak here. Classical or not, I am glad my new daughter knows the language. I have often regretted my own lack of the tongue. Whilst I understand it spoken and can write a few simple phrases, I remain clumsy speaking it, simply, I believe, because I never learnt to speak or read it as a child. Good mother, you've told me you too regret you cannot speak Latin."

Lady Margaret stared at the queen, her mouth a straight line. Queen Elizabeth frowned and spoke in a rush to Catalina. "I believe my new daughter is also an excellent embroiderer? And knows well how to use a distaff?"

Catalina looked across at the queen with gratitude. "Si, my Lady Grace. My mother, the queen, taught her daughters to be good wives. I hope to weave and sew Prince Arthur many fine shirts."

The good humour twinkling in the queen's eyes reflected back in Catalina's, too. The queen turned to her mother-in-law. "You see. She has been well taught, as I told you."

"Well taught." Releasing a loud huff, the king's mother

straightened in her chair. The fire flickered in her dark eyes when she looked again at Catalina. "I will see."

The queen frowned, glancing first at the king's mother and then at Catalina as she reached for the reassurance of her crucifix.

"I am remiss in my good manners," Queen Elizabeth said. "Pray forgive me, but I haven't yet asked you if you find Lambeth Palace to your liking?"

María took in with relief Queen Elizabeth's concerned face. *By all the saints, pray let the queen be what she seems: a good woman who wants to help Catalina.*

"I like it well..." Catalina offered a weak smile. "It is a pleasant place."

"Daughter, it must seem to you we have moved you from one abode to the next. After a few days' rest here, we'll see your formal entry to our fair city of London and your wedding to my son. It is much for you to deal with, I know."

Catalina lifted her chin, and straightened. "You'll not find me lacking. I am the daughter of Isabel of Castile. I know my duty."

"I am sure of that. Your noble mother's letters have told me that already." The queen looked at the woman beside her, catching her eye. Some wordless understanding passing between them, the queen nodded.

María realised the queen was looking in her direction. Embarrassed, she lowered her head and pretended to read.

"María de Salinas. She's your kinswoman, I believe? Your bedcompanion?"

Cocking her head, María covertly looked across at Catalina. Catalina nodded, her face puzzled.

"You trust her? Really trust her?"

"Si, Your Grace, with my life –"

María lowered her head for a moment, her heart warm with pride. *Si, I will be loyal to Catalina, always.*

The queen turned to her mother-in-law. "It is only wise my new daughter has someone she trusts in and can confide in. We already know these two are close. Her mother told me they have been brought up together since they were barely more than infants."

The queen turned to Catalina, her face grave. "You must understand what is said in this chamber goes no further."

Catalina nodded again.

"Not one word, my child. If the king knew of this conversation, we'd have much to answer for. And my son – it would hurt him deeply, to know his mother and grandmother's concern causes us to speak of this matter to you." The queen looked down to her lap, and sighed. "My son came early into the world..." Gazing into the fire, the queen sighed again.

Wondering where this conversation was leading, María was not surprised to see Catalina frowning with bewilderment at the queen and the king's mother. "Madam? Your Grace?"

The queen rubbed the side of her wan face, her fingers curling to rest on her cheekbone. She frowned a little. "Forgive me; it is a difficult matter to discuss." The queen lowered her head. "After my son's untimely birth, we feared daily for his life. His early years were much the same; I dread the coming of every winter. All through his life, his people have hidden how often they nursed him through sickness. The king, his good father, turns a blind eye to the fact that the strength of his first- born is not as it should be, and Arthur pushes himself to be what his father wants. My boy has a cough even now."

Elizabeth of York reached for a goblet set beside her and raised it to her mouth. She sipped, her eyes staying on Catalina until she caused Catalina to stir uneasily. With another sigh, the queen replaced the goblet on the small table. She did not notice its contents swilling overtop, puddling a swirl of ruby- red wine around the rim of the goblet's foot. "My daughter, you have seen my son. Tell me the truth, what do you see?"

Catalina flushed. "Good madam – I... I don't know what you want me to say..."

"I want you to speak the truth, my daughter. Fear not – it is Arthur's mother and grandmother you speak to, two women who love him dearly. We talk here only in his best interests."

Catalina straightened herself on the stool. She reddened and swallowed, speaking just above a murmur. "Your Grace – the prince appears frail... a frail stripling."

The queen considered the woman beside her. "See, good mother, she already knows. After just a few, brief meetings. We're right to do this. I love all my children, but Arthur's our hope; he is England's hope. He'll build well upon the king's work. We must do all we can to keep Arthur safe. My new daughter will help us. I see it in her eyes."

Catalina looked from one woman to the other. "Madam, I do not understand –"

"You will. But first swear you'll never speak of this conversation to any other than those in this room. Not even to your confessor. My son knows I planned to talk to you. He knows I am anxious about him." Queen Elizabeth reached for Catalina's hand. "Swear your silence to me, daughter."

Catalina blinked fast, her eyes frightened. She clutched at her crucifix. "That I will swear on the almighty God, by my life and my eternal salvation in the world to come."

The queen relaxed visibly, giving Catalina a slight smile. "Good. I believe you. I learnt early in life to know when someone lies. Watching and listening to people tells you much, remember that. I will allow your kinswoman to stay, but when you leave my chamber and return to yours, you must make your kinswoman vow her silence too. She stays because I know you two are like the closest of sisters." Shifting on her stool, María pulsated with pride again, but pride tempered by trepidation.

Again, the queen looked aside at her mother-in-law. "Good mother, it would be best now if you go. What you don't hear you can deny knowing. It is time to speak the truth to my son's wife."

The older woman nodded. Standing up, she straightened her unadorned, black gown. "We know little of this girl, Bess. Be careful," she said.

The queen smiled a strange smile, a smile speaking of many shared secrets. "You must know I am always careful. There's too much at stake to be otherwise."

Margaret Beaufort frowned. "The girl is a stranger to us...."

"Good mother, you can trust me. I am your 'Humble and Reverent' daughter."

The countess pursed her mouth for a moment. "Indeed," she said, a slight smile twisting her lips. María raised her head as the tiny woman left the chamber. The pride she had felt moments before dissolved to apprehension. She was no longer certain if she wished to remain in the queen's chamber, even for Catalina's sake.

When the door closed behind her mother-in-law, the queen moved a little in her chair. "Still so pious, and full of plots." She let out a deep breath. "Pray, give my mother-in-law no mind. When I first married her son, I did not understand her. Once I hated her, believing her responsible for so many of my sorrows. But the passing of time has helped me understand the fault was not hers, but others. I also understand better the road she has walked. From the time she was born, until she was a grown woman with the skill and wit to shape her own destiny, men have used her for their own ambition and desire for power. She was but thirteen when she brought her only child, my husband, into the world. It damaged her in more ways than just her body. I see beyond her stern façade, and do love her. She protects her blood with her life."

Sudden tears rushed to María's eyes. *My mother is exactly the same. How I want to be like her – a good mother for my children.*

Catalina's eyes widened. "Your Grace, I do not understand." The queen enclosed Catalina's tiny hand in both of hers. The English Queen wore only her wedding ring on her long, fine-boned fingers. "I know you don't. But there is much you need to know, if only for your own survival in England. My daughter, my husband's mother believes death will come for her soon. She strives hard to make amends while there is still time to do so, caring first for her soul. She and I work together when it comes to my children, her grandchildren. For those close to her she would walk through Hell. Indeed, that is a road she knows well, too well. We both do."

The fire raged with fury. Towers of wood flamed and crumbled, as if visions of blood-permeated cities set ablaze. For a long moment, the queen's eyes reflected the fire's embers. The older woman swallowed before next she spoke, her voice soft, barely above a whisper. "It is easy to hate, but I have found hate only destroys what we don't want destroyed." She eyed Catalina. "And I too pray for God's forgiveness. Even today, after years of forfeiting so much for peace, blood still spots my hands. Catalina, evil is a strong, cruel and pitiless foe and often victorious. I know this too well. Another thing I know; the crown of England has proven a curse to those of my blood. This is why I must speak to you."

The queen rubbed her palm on her temple. "My good daughter – when you bed with my boy, I want you to promise not to be a full wife to him. Do you understand what I mean?" Her eyes bright in a bloodless face, the queen moved closer to Catalina. "Not yet. Not until his sixteenth birthday. Pray God, he'll come into his full man's strength by then."

Catalina blanched, snatching her hand away as if scorched. "But, Your Grace –"

The queen bowed over her hands held as if in prayer. When she next spoke, her voice trembled. "I pray for your forgiveness, and God's too. What I ask goes against all what the priests teach to us. But I have thought hard on this matter. If it is a sin for a mother to try to save her children from what may destroy them, then it is my sin, not yours. My son coughs. He hides it from me, but his grandmother and I are well used to the signs and know when he is not well. He is growing taller day by day, and there is something else... something also sapping his strength. His doctors are worried about him, and so am I." She lifted her head. "My daughter, a full marriage might be too much for him at this time. It could turn his cough into a deadly one. I beg you for my son's sake, nay, for my son's life, to do this. I have spoken to Arthur in private; I have told him there's no hurry, no need for him to take the man's part until he feels ready. If you ask him to wait, to leave you a maid, my sweet boy will not force you. Arthur already likes you well. A little more time to get to know one another will not hurt the marriage, only strengthen it." The queen touched Catalina's hand. "Do I have your promise? Not until he is sixteen?"

María almost dropped her book. *Dear God – what is the queen asking of Catalina? Both Queen Isabel and King Ferdinand would be furious if they knew. She came to make a full marriage, and not to feign one.*

Catalina turned her head to the fire for a time. "Juan, my beloved brother, died at nineteen." She looked back to the queen. "Many said it was because he cleaved too well to his wife. You fear this same fate for your son?"

The queen bent forward to clasp Catalina's hand. "Aye. I say again, aye, aye, and aye. Arthur is the best of my children, the best of my two living sons. He's wise beyond his years. It is not only my mother's love telling me this. His tutors, as well as his often harsh and hard-to-please grandmother own this to be true. England does not need another wrong king. I have seen too much blood flowing from the crowning of a wrong king."

"But Arthur will be king –"

Altering her position, the queen stretched out her right hand, palm up, as if in offering. "If he lives." She swallowed hard. "If my eldest son dies, Harry, his younger brother, is next in line. Harry would not make a good King. Already I see he has all my father's worst qualities, qualities that brought so much ruin to England. I have spoken of this at length with the king."

She rubbed her temple once more. "We plan to place Harry in a religious order."

Catalina looked with confusion at the queen. "Your Grace, a religious order? For a second son?"

"It is the best course open to us. A life devoted to God will encourage the flowering of all that's good in Harry, and stamp out those parts of his character causing me many sleepless nights. Please don't mistake me. My Harry has much good in him. We have perhaps spoilt him; he is easy to spoil. He has all the gifts of my family, but all the flaws as well. One day, I believe he will be Adonis come to life again, and I doubt a religious order will keep him chaste. My heart quails at the thought of him ever becoming king. The crown destroyed my father; it destroyed my family. It would destroy Harry. My heart tells me this." The queen reached for the goblet beside her. Raising it to her lips, she wet her mouth, her eyes staying on Catalina before returning the goblet to the table. The queen leaned forward.

"Daughter, the bloody history of my family is not something I am proud of, nor something I ever want to see repeated. I saw my uncle Richard, a good and honourable man, a man I loved, take my brother's crown because he believed it was the only choice he had – and the only way to safeguard the life of his own son. He could do little to stem the evil let loose by my own father. Indeed, evil caught him too, forcing his back against a hard wall so he struck out in fear for those he loved.

"His end redeemed him. At Bosworth, I believe he resolved to be the scapegoat for his brother's sins when he galloped his horse towards the men surrounding my husband. My uncle's death cleansed England to begin again." The queen brushed away tears. "His death broke my young heart. I swore then I wouldn't let the deaths of him and my poor two brothers be in vain. So many deaths – and it is always the innocent sacrificed for the misdeeds of others.

"Even my cousin, Edward, the Earl of Warwick, only two years ago, was another sacrifice. May God forgive me, I could do nothing, nothing, to prevent his death. My husband's a strong king. He is a good king. But the crown weighs heavy on him, forcing him to protect it. But to execute my poor cousin Edward, poor Edward who never had a chance to live, really live." She tightened her mouth. "Another innocent dead – yet more blood poured on this altar called a throne.

"But I have Arthur. He is my hope; England's hope. If he lives, I believe we will see a final end to this bloodbath of those I love. But my boy must stay alive."

The queen reached for Catalina's hand again. "Can I rely on you for this? Have I your promise?"

Catalina squared her shoulders. "My brother's death ripped a hole in my family that nothing can ever heal – and destroyed all my parents' hopes to leave behind Castile and Aragon as united kingdoms. You have my promise, Your Grace. I vow to do what I can."

5

How was she created? I'm not sure if you realize this, but it was in God's image. How can anybody dare to speak ill of something which bears such a noble imprint?

~ *Christine de Pizan, The Book of the City of Ladies.*

Waking heavy headed and little rested, María rolled to the edge of her princess's bed and eyed the still asleep Catalina with envy. She settled back on to her pillow, listening to the rain pelting the tile roof and windows like small stones, a noise which had infiltrated her dream. The dream fast fading away, she still trembled with its warning of threat.

Deciding to get up, she eased off the thick layers of fur covers, careful to not wake Catalina when she pulled aside the bed curtains. She stood on the uncovered wooden floor and gasped, her good intentions forgotten, "Holy Mother of God!"

The freezing air assaulted her, knifing her without mercy to her bones.

Catalina stirred, sighed, but slumbered on.

María grabbed her mantle from the end of the bed and hurriedly tossed it over her shoulders, clasping it to cover her thin night rail. The cold floor making her feet dance, she dashed to the bowl of water placed upon a table close to the fire for their morning wash. Every step of the way, her toes stung and throbbed painfully, as if threatening to drop off. Cursing herself for not putting on her slippers, she ignored her breath turning into vapour, let go of her mantle and dipped her hands in the bowl for her fingers to break through a thin layer of ice. She gritted her teeth, close to howling in despair. Shattering the ice with her fist, she gritted her teeth once more, and scooped out handfuls of water. Freezing water struck her cheeks, and ran down her neck, beneath the loose neck of her shift, and between her breasts. Shaking with cold, she snatched one of the towels on the nearby stool to dry her face and grimaced at her blotchy, goose-pimpled chest. *A clean face must be enough today. I cannot bear cold water again.* She padded over to the hearth.

Only a few red embers remained in the thick carpet of ash from the night fire. Threads of blue smoke wisped and spiralled out toward her as it came down the chimney. Rather than summon a servant, she stoked the sluggish fire before feeding the fire with sea coal placed nearby for this purpose. Before she awoke Catalina, she wanted the chamber warmer and more fit for her princess.

María sat back on her haunches and noticed the room's large window. Last night, Catalina had drawn the curtains to look out at the moon. *She must have forgotten to close them.* A distorted grey world wavered through the thick glass. She remembered the dawns of home, blue, cloudless days and sunlit palaces of home where private chambers opened to gardens inviting morning strolls even in winter. She poked the embers crossly until they burst into flames. *I must stop grieving; I have made my choice; I must live with it.*

She thought about the coming day. Soon, she would break her fast with Catalina. They had done this all their life together, but more and more she grew troubled. When she closed the door on the other women, leaving them to break their fast together, their envious and jealous eyes bore into her. She sighed. There was no easy solution. Not when Catalina still preferred her companionship above all others. All she could do was to nurture the small signs of friendship between her and the other girls, in hope of true friendship. She stood and hurried to gather their clothes for the day to warm them by the fire as Catalina slept.

———

María giggled at Catalina's sour expression as she sat for breakfast. On the table was a dish of grey mass lumped into a bowl. Catalina pushed aside the bowl, reaching for the fresh white bread and hard cheese. She nibbled at these, picked up a goblet and sipped the beer.

"They cannot expect me to drink this," Catalina said, pushing the goblet aside too.

María chuckled again. On one of their first days in England, Catalina had turned to her when first tasting this English brew, whispering for her ears alone: "This is the sponge of ice and vinegar given to our Lord."

Gulping back another bubble of laughter, she swilled down a mouthful from the rejected goblet. "I'm becoming accustomed to it. It is different from what we are used to at home, but I do not mind it."

Catalina pushed her bowl towards her in answer. "If you like English beer, taste this then."

María picked up the bowl, sniffed, and put it down again. "Even for the love of you, I will not eat this. It may be that English dish of sheep brains Doña Elvira told us about." She peered at the dish, identifying cooked oats, cabbage, leeks and other pale vegetables. "The English have a liking for grey things." She nudged the bowl with her finger. "Perhaps it reminds them of the colour of their days." *How uprooted we all are – even from the colours of home.* She glanced at the closed door. "It would be wisest for us to break our fast with the others," she said slowly, thinking again about the other girls' unhidden unhappiness.

Two brisk, hard knocks sounded before Doña Elvira entered and curtseyed. "Your Highness, a summons comes from Queen Elizabeth. The queen greets you, bidding you a good morrow. She asks for you to again come to her chambers as soon as you break your fast. The messenger told me you may bring one attendant with you." Doña Elvira glowered at María. "I humbly suggest I accompany you this time."

Catalina reached for another piece of bread. "Other than take me to the queen's apartments, Doña Elvira, your time is too valuable to stay with me. My women need your guidance and attention. There's also that letter the queen, my mother, commands from you. I am sure Doña María won't mind coming again."

Doña Elvira muttered something under her breath, turned on her heel and left the room, closing the door behind her. If she had slammed it, María would not have been surprised. She crumbled up a piece of bread on her plate but did not eat it. Still disturbed by Doña Elvira's behaviour, she clasped Catalina's hand. "My *prima hermana*, do you remember our conversation at Laredo?"

Catalina lifted her head, frowning. "What of it?"

"The women are still jealous."

"But I am spending more time with them."

"Si, but remember, England is a strange place for them too. We need one another. Believe me, I will not be hurt if you ask one of the others to accompany you today."

Catalina chewed and swallowed some of the cheese. She smiled slowly. "Mother told me to listen to your counsel. And, believe me, I do listen. But I understand the queen's message. She wants me to bring you."

María met Catalina's eyes. "Because you trust me?"

"*Si*, my *prima hermana*."

María trailed after Catalina, her heart drumming loud in her ears. Entering the queen's chamber, she wished Catalina had not wanted her to come. *You should be grateful for this honour.* But, rubbing her anxious stomach, she would have been more than happy to put aside the honour today. She glanced at Catalina's squared shoulders and hands fisted into balls. *I am not the only one anxious.*

Queen Elizabeth stood by the hearth, little changed from the previous morning. In a dark blue gown of velvet with tight fitting sleeves of purplish-red silk, she welcomed Catalina, holding out her arms in answer to Catalina's curtsey. When the queen embraced her friend, María blinked. The queen's sleeves appeared the colour of blood against Catalina's dark green gown. *Why do I think such things? Catalina's nightmares and forebodings about her marriage is making me see things not there.*

The queen kissed Catalina, insisting she sit in the chair used by the king's mother the day before. The room lacked the disquieting presence of Margaret of Beaufort, but another woman stood next to the queen's chair. Younger than the queen and tall like her, she stooped, as if uncomfortable with her height. With a pleasant rather than pretty face framed by a matron's gable, she possessed none of the queen's fair, pleasing beauty, yet the hooded deep blue eyes gave away their kinship. María remained kneeling just inside the door, waiting to know what to do. Queen Elizabeth gestured to a stool, set to one side of the door. "Go, kinswoman of my new daughter, and sit. Remember, trust is precious, and once lost is difficult to restore. All you hear in this room must remain in this room."

María rose to her feet. She nodded in answer to the queen's look of absolute steel, and curtseyed before heading to the stool. Nearing the unknown woman, she breathed in her rose scent, very like to the queen's, but with an undertone of a flower María could not identify. Long face with a thin mouth, an over-long nose and chin, the woman radiated a sombre air of real humility. Beauty of soul seemed to exude from her.

María slipped her thin book of herbal lore from her skirt pocket, sat on the stool, and pretended to read it as she listened and watched.

"Catalina, pray meet my sweet cousin, Margaret. Meg is wife to Sir Richard Pole. You will know good Sir Richard soon enough. He is half cousin to my husband, and my son's chamberlain, and has worked tirelessly in ensuring all the preparations for your wedding are in place."

The woman smiled a beautiful smile and curtseyed. "Princess, I give you welcome."

Catalina beamed, dipping her head in greeting. "Thank you, Lady Margaret."

To Maria's relief, all of them conversed in French, the language she understood easily, unlike English. With a laugh, the queen yanked at her cousin's hanging sleeve. "Sit down, Meg." She waved her hand toward the same stool Catalina sat upon yesterday. "My neck hurts looking up at you!"

The queen turned a smile to Catalina. "Perchance I should introduce you as Katherine – for that is what you will be called here."

Catalina returned the queen's smile. "Katherine was my great grandmother's name. She who was known as Katherine of Lancaster before becoming Catalina of Castile."

The queen rested her hand on top of Catalina's. "And now it comes full circle. You shall be Katherine of England, a worthy and noble consort for my dearly beloved son."

Catalina's face lost colour. *Holy Mother of God – she is showing her apprehension about her coming marriage.* Maria felt relieved when her friend lifted her chin.

"Your Grace, I am blessed to have two mothers, and both

share the same name of Elizabeth, for that is what Isabel means in Castile. Strange, I only thought of this last night."

The queen tightened her hold on Catalina's hand. "Not strange at all. It was only yesterday we discovered we could love one another. I thank the good God for that."

Catalina smiled, a smile blazing a bridge of light even to María in her dark corner. "Si, God is good."

Margaret placed her hands palm to palm, as if in prayer. "God is good," she echoed. Her mellifluous and deep voice possessed all the beauty lacking in her face.

Queen Elizabeth turned to Margaret. "Cousin, you and I have both walked hard and painful paths. It has taught us much." The lady Margaret looked at the queen with love and tenderness. For the first time, María noted the marks of suffering around her gentle eyes.

"Joy and sorrow are the two sides of the coin we call life," said Lady Margaret. "They're part of our pilgrimage to God. Joy and suffering teach us loving is all."

The queen kept hold of Catalina's hand, but reached for the hand of her kinswoman too. "My Meg, my most faithful and trusted cousin, and friend."

Elizabeth of York faced Catalina again. "I desire you to take my kinswoman into your service, daughter. She will be a good friend to you, a friend you can trust, just as you do María. She will not only teach you English but also act for me. She'll protect you from the wolves."

Colouring bright pink, the Lady Margaret lifted her head, straightening her bony shoulders. "Bess, I will not fail you. I am good at being inconspicuous while at watch." She considered Catalina. "My princess, I'll teach you the game the queen and I learnt to play early in our lives – a game of silence and observation serving us well." The woman swallowed hard. "It has kept us alive, and safe."

The queen touched her kinswoman's knee. "Render to Caesar what is Caesar's, but remember our souls always belong to God." *Render to Caesar what is Caesar's?* María thought about the queen's meaning. *We wear masks of obedience, but never at the cost of our souls. First, we must serve God.*

The queen, her kinswoman and Catalina stilled, as if they all prayed a prayer together.

Uneasy, María took her eyes from the tableau they made together. She turned the page of her book. *Si – masks are forced upon women. We are forced to wear them to simply survive.* Stroking her cheek, she wondered at hers. Her youth often protected her but also left her maskless, or bestowed on her a mask as fragile as if spun from butterfly wings. One touch, and it shattered, dissolving as if it never existed at all. She shivered from sudden fear. She did not want to harden that mask, or wear it like a second skin. Such a mask would mean nothing remained of her innocence.

María followed Catalina back to her chamber. Entering the room, she fought back her surprise to find Doña Elvira rising from a stool near the door. The woman curtseyed to Catalina. "My princess," she said, "Don de Ayala waits to see you."

Catalina frowned and gestured María to the stool beside the fireplace. "You may sit," she commanded before heading to the nearest high-backed chair.

Seated, Catalina rubbed the side of her face in thought. "Don de Ayala? I have heard the name before." María had too – but could not remember when, or where. "Who is he again, Doña?" Catalina tapped her fingers on the armrest.

"Don Pedro de Ayala is your parents' ambassador to Scotland."

"Scotland? This is not Scotland."

"He signed his message this morning as ambassador to Scotland, and England. I believe he stays in London, and has done so for years."

Leaning her elbow on the armrest of her chair, Catalina cradled the side her face. "How can that be? Is not Doctor de Puebla my parents' ambassador to England? You say he is waiting to see me? Pray, bring him to me."

Doña Elvira soon returned with a tall, lean, handsome man. Garbed in rich clothes, he took Catalina's proffered hand and bowed over it. "Princess," he said, speaking in pure Castilian. "We have long waited the day to welcome you to England."

He lifted his head, his long black hair sweeping against his shoulders. Like many of the English, he wore his hair in the French style.

María shifted uneasily on her stool. *Catalina has already let her guard down. She already forgets what her mother told her: be careful of where you give your trust.*

Catalina gestured to another stool. "Pray sit. You wanted to see me, Don de Ayala?"

The man sat, and leaned closer to Catalina. "I am your servant, Princess, and wished to make myself known to you. Doctor de Puebla didn't speak of me to you?"

"No. I did not realise there are two ambassadors serving the English court."

"The man would not tell you this; he denies me the right to this title, yet I have been at the court of King Henry for the last four years."

Confused, María listened intently. Did not Doña Elvira say this man is the ambassador to Scotland? She knew very little about Scotland, other than it was like Aragon to Castile, a lesser kingdom to one more powerful. *Perhaps that is why Don de Ayala remains at the English court, and is jealous of Puebla.* A jealousy confirmed by de Ayala's next words. "The king likes me well; we hunt together with great regularity. I must warn you about Doctor de Puebla. The man is a braggart, a flatterer. If he is not a spy acting for the English, he serves King Henry before the queen, your mother, and the king, your father."

Catalina blinked. "If what you say is true, why then would my parents place such trust in him? When I left home, the queen, my noble mother, spoke highly of the man. She said I could trust him to serve me well."

"Forgive me; I do not wish to contradict our most noble queen, but she does not know him as I do. If she did, she would soon relieve him of his position, of which he is unfit to serve. There are things I would hesitate to speak of to you, but let me just say the man does not deserve your respect. Believe me, princess, he is the vilest kind of Jew. I humbly implore you to be careful of the man, and do not trust him."

María liked Don de Ayala less with each passing moment. He spoke charmingly and seemed a man of true breeding, yet her instincts screamed out to her that Catalina needed to be careful of this man, and not the elderly, unattractive and unkempt Doctor de Puebla. The old man seemed ill, worn out, yet he had done everything possible to ease Catalina's first days at court.

Catalina continued to speak to de Ayala in their native tongue. She leaned forward and spoke to him as if she had known him for years. María shut her mouth on a sigh. All of them were homesick – but Catalina's homesickness deepened daily with the approach of her wedding. María knew Catalina craved the comfort of the familiar. *So much so, she forgets many of her mother's warnings. I think she wants to trust Don de Ayala because he reminds her of home. But she shouldn't trust him. Should I tell her this?* María sighed again. Once Catalina made up her mind about anything, it was near to impossible to convince her otherwise.

Lambeth Palace, the tenth day of November

Doña, my dear Latina,

    The day has come for the princess's ceremonial entry into London...

María heard something thud to the floor in the next room. With a sigh, she put aside her letter to go and supervise the three English maidservants who readied the room for Catalina to bathe. One girl lit the candles and high sconces. Another drew the chamber's heavy curtains, and the last girl replenished the fire.

María sat by the tub, threw handfuls of rose petals into the steaming water and poured in rose oil. She leaned over the tub. The water reflected her solemn, wavering face, dappled with red and dark pink petals. Circled by light from an overhead sconce, she moved forward. The cords of her over gown yet untied, her even looser chemise drooped down a naked shoulder. Her long, black hair cascaded over it and fell towards the water. Her reflection quivered, as if she metamorphosed into a water dryad from an ancient Greek tale. The water- logged rose petals losing their vibrant colour, she drifted in a dream of flower-adorned nymphs stepping into the sea, as the sun sunk over the horizon. *If I slip into the watery world of the nymphs, will I feel as strange as I feel now? Would their world be just as strange to me as this one?*

A memory opened. She was twelve and sitting by one of the courtyard pools of the Alhambra. Like this present moment, she had been staring down at her reflection, daydreaming, when Latina's face joined hers. "Avoid the mistake of Narcissus. Self-love destroys the soul," her teacher had said. Roused from her trance, María protested she wasn't admiring her reflection, rather just simply daydreaming. Latina paled, and her eyes widened in fear. When Latina told her of the superstition, that daydreaming over your reflection somehow tempted death, the bright day left her brave enough to laugh.

Death.

Death had brought her out to the garden that day. The fear of death. The fear of Prince Juan's death.

On the day they had waited for news of Juan, a lone dragonfly had darted over the pool – its nacreous wings glistening dew-like in its flight. It had winged close to her and Latina; its perfection made her cry. Latina had taken her into her arms, but had no words of comfort. That beautiful day had been the harbinger of so much sorrow.

Days later, Juan's death had become a reality. Her heart broken, she had raged at God, unable to understand the rhyme or reason for his loss – a loss ripping a hole into all their lives. She still did not understand.

"*What we hold and love one day*
On another day we lose," she sang softly.

She started, and returned to the present. She had written those words later, in that same garden.

A maid servant jumped from the stool she had stood on to light one of the sconces. María began straightening the line of bath oils set on the low table. Next to the oils, was a small wooden chest half full of rose petals. Until more arrived, these were the last of their petals from Castile. The smell of roses bought back another memory of La Latina, when she and Catalina watched her make rosewater in her chamber. Almost every day of her shared childhood with Catalina, Latina had been there, guiding her. Her homesickness became so strong, so sharp, it stabbed her and left her heart aching. She closed the chest and snapped the gold clasp shut.

She half turned from the tub to thank the maidservants for their labour in readying the bath for Catalina. Shaping the unfamiliar English words, her tongue tripped. She tried again, this time more slowly. The girls exchanged glances, clearly amused at her attempt at their tongue.

One girl grinned at her, revealing a missing front tooth. In quick succession, the girls curtseyed to her. "We are glad to serve the princess," one of them said in French before stepping over to the huge fire hearth. Stoking and replenishing the low fire, the girl pulled the big pot of warm water over the flame. Two maids carried the wooden frame with Catalina's under clothes for the day closer to the heat. One laughed and pointed to Catalina's drawers, whispering something close to the ear of the other girl. The two girls looked at it as if they had never seen anything like that in their lives. María winced, remembering being told English women wore no drawers. Their most private parts were only covered when they had their menses. The first girl fingered Catalina's costly Holland chemise, edged with delicate lace, giving a long, envious sigh.

María sighed, too, but not from envy. The girl's fingers were likely still grubby from bringing up the wooden bath. Grubby fingers meant hunting out another clean chemise from the clothes chests. Catalina did not lack for costly shifts; Queen Isabel had sent her daughter to her wedding with at least fifty. The majority of Catalina's undergarments were made from either Holland or fine cotton. Amongst them, the queen also included in her daughter's trousseau five silk chemises; the first would soon be worn at the occasion of her wedding. All of them were examples of beautiful and skilful needlework. Each shift differed from the next, whether by embroidery or lace, or even gold buttons.

The maidservants grabbed the empty buckets. Bobbing quick curtseys, they left the room, swinging the wooden buckets against their dresses. The rush of their footsteps becoming softer in distance, María heard the girls' voices raised in song. She understood only few of their words, yet within her echoed the resonance of joy and youth. Alone, she finished readying the bath for Catalina.

The last tie looped and knotted, María joined the other women to behold their princess.

A lovely girl stood before them, dressed in the gown chosen for her entry to England's capital. Catalina wore a cap reminiscent of that worn by a cardinal, secured under her chin with cords of delicate gold. Her thick, auburn hair, shining with gold and red lights, flowed free over her shoulders, streaming down her back. Face pale, mouth a little open, Catalina clasped her crucifix, and let out a deep breath. "Tell them I am ready."

María noticed Catalina's frightened eyes. Her friend did not look ready at all.

Render to Caesar what is Caesar's, Queen Elizabeth had said days ago. María swallowed. *My friend is what is rendered to Caesar – by her parents, by life. She had never been given another choice. Given another choice?* María squirmed, wiping her hands up and down her gown. *What choice? Catalina has always been owned by Caesar.*

6

The bright star Spain, Hesperus, on them shone whose goodly
beams hath pierced mightily thorough this castle to bring this
good lady whose prosperous coming shall write joyful be.
~ *The Receyt of the Ladie Kateryne*

Outside the palace, María hesitated behind Catalina. The
air assaulted her with its strangeness – and its
unpleasant earthy headiness. Everywhere, crowds of people –
noble to humble, rich and poor, men and women, young and
old – pressed against one another, in a flurry of changing colour.
The English greeted their new princess with joy, their voices
vying with the fanfares of trumpet, pipe and drum. She could
not help smiling. *All England has come to welcome Catalina.*

Arthur's young brother Henry approached Catalina. Newly
arrived from his home at Eltham Palace, María had seen him for

the first time the previous night with his parents, when the king and queen introduced him to Catalina. Garbed in scarlet hose and white and red robes, the youngest son of the king already towered over Catalina. While his face was that of a beardless boy, he was close to the same height as his older brother, the Prince of Wales. His hair, gleaming with red lights, fell to his already wide shoulders. Under its straight fringe, his eyes, blue like his mother's, shone with excitement. Despite his young years, he had been trained well in his role as escort for his new sister-in-law. He reached for her hand, leading her to their waiting mounts.

A nearby English woman beckoned to María to move. Already, Catalina and the prince were mounted on their horses, a little distance away. The young prince's high, loud voice was easy to hear as he talked to Catalina. María studied him again before turning to the English woman beside her. "How old is Prince Henry?" she said in Latin, before remembering the queen saying Catalina had learnt a more classical Latin than that spoken at the English court. Since she had learnt the same Latin, she breathed a sigh of relief when the woman beside her answered her.

"Our Prince Hal? He's ten. He's a tall stripling. Takes after his grandsire, King Edward, the queen's father."

Strewing roses, lilies and nosegays of violets before them on the road, jostling Londoners lined either side of the throughway taking Catalina and her party deeper into the city. Every available window, their shutters wide open, had people hanging out of from them. From their high windows, men and women threw down what looked like snowflakes on the procession. María, her face raised, felt the gentle caress of falling rose petals.

With gestures of joviality, liveried guards kept the road

before the procession clear and the crowd behind rough and ready barriers. Whenever María passed a guard she received a smile and a glad greeting. At times, she relinquished her dignity and smiled in return.

Bells pealed over and over. A cannon fired. María jolted in her saddle as her frightened horse gave a half rear. She placed a hand over her fast beating heart before tightening the reins in both hands. Leaning close to the horse's ear, she spoke quietly to her trembling mount. She trembled too, and took a few deep breaths to steady her nerves. The cannon fired again and again; several steeds broke away and needed coaxing to return to the procession. "It is all right," she said to her horse. "Let's keep going."

Realising she spoke her own tongue to an English horse, she gulped back a laugh close to tears when her mount moved forward again. *Perchance God gave animals the ability to understand all languages.* She noticed other riders struggling to get their horses to obey them. *Or perhaps I have been simply well taught since a small child.*

María appraised the sky. Yesterday, it rained from morning long into the night. Now, only a few white clouds drifted on the gentle wind. Everywhere she looked, there was a new wonder to behold. On either side of the road rich tapestries draped tall wooden buildings either joined to one another, or so close together they seemed joined. She passed wooden castles, battlements, fountains gushing wine and mechanical zodiacs. In the procession, five men with long poles held up a pretend Tudor red dragon, chasing away its pretend enemies with red ribbons of pretend flame.

She passed ships and two mock mountains – one green for

England and one golden brown like earth scorched by the sun for Spain; Spain and England linked together by a golden chain, all of it hailing the joining together of two royal houses, and three kingdoms. The Tudor King had spent much gold on making certain none could say the English did not know how to stage a celebration.

Always some way ahead of her, Catalina would stop for a time at each of the six stages of the procession. Beginning by representing the realm of humankind, the six stages proceeded to that of heaven itself. Watching the English honour her friend and princess, María became prouder and prouder. Swept up by the joyful cries of the crowds, she no longer minded the unfamiliar, unpleasant smells or the strangeness of England.

Just as the day's proceedings played homage to a glorious future – a future when Prince Arthur and his bride would reign as England's King and Queen, the people alongside the road called out their homage and happiness to Catalina. Finding herself riding beside the same English woman she had met at the start of the procession, María shared with her a smile. The woman grinned back. "Aye – we are all happy to see this day finally come. We love our prince. He will be another King Arthur; today but celebrates that – and our hope his reign will be a time of legends."

By the time they arrived at the final stage of the procession, María felt light-headed with weariness, but she almost laughed at the sight of a man dressed as God. The man's false white beard looked like a sheep fleece. Sitting on a golden throne placed a dais painted with white clouds, the man seemed pompous rather than godly. When Catalina approached him, he recited a well-rehearsed verse:

> *"Look ye, walk in my precepts and obey them well,*
> *And here I give you that same blessing that I*
> *Gave my well-loved children of Israel;*
> *Blessed be the fruit of your belly."*

Catalina seemed focused on every word, a girl serious and proud, her back as straight as possible. *No need to remind Catalina to tread a God-fearing path; she is her mother's daughter; she will be true to God till death. Si.* María swallowed. *That expected duty weighs as heavy on Catalina's spirit as if the hoped-for babe already quickened in her womb.*

At Saint Paul's Cathedral the next day, Prince Henry was there again. María could not help comparing the two princes. Prince Henry was glowing with good health and vitality, while his nervous older brother had a translucent beauty which worried her. Catalina was right to call him frail. She rubbed her eyes and closed her mouth on a yawn. *Frail? After yesterday, I too feel frail.*

The boy prince grinned, seized off his cap with an exaggerated flourish, and bowed to Catalina. The morning sun, breaking through the gathering rain clouds, crowned his hair to a fiery red-gold, and glittered the jewels and gold bordering the silk veil covering most of Catalina's face. A breeze teased at the veil as Prince Henry raised Catalina's hand to kiss. Walking alongside, he kept his hand joined with hers, waiting to lead her down the long aisle of the Cathedral to his brother.

María fisted her trembling hands close to her sides, keeping them still. She hurried up to Inés, Bella, Francisca, and the English women of rank chosen for this day, to help carry Catalina's long train. Taking the silk train in her hands, she glanced at Margaret Pole aligned with the English women, and then at Francisca, standing opposite to her on the other side of the train. Francisca gave her a slight smile, before looking ahead, clearly waiting for the signal for them to start moving. People in the crowd outside the cathedral pointed to Catalina's white gown. María stroked one side of her own full skirt. *Have they never seen gowns like this?* Ringed by thin hoops like Catalina's, her skirt swung around her hips like a bell. An echo of Catalina's more voluminous gown, its movement comforted her. With so much different in her life, today she wore the fashion of home.

Long notes from trumpets reverberated in the cathedral, and Catalina and the young prince began their slow way down the aisle. Trying to time her pace to exactly that of Francisca's, María could hear the loud drumming of her heart. *There are people everywhere!* Doctor de Puebla, their ambassador, had told them last night that the king commanded the building of platforms especially for this day, providing the opportunity for many of his subjects to witness the marriage of his son. Now men and women jostled for position. A strong smell of incense could not cover the whiff of sweating bodies. María steadied her breathing, her shaking hands. *Do not be a fool. There are no eyes on you – or if there are, they are not interested in you or judging you wanting. They only want to see Catalina.*

Behind the decorative wooden rail of the high gallery at the front of the cathedral and way above the rest of the congregation, King Henry, Queen Elizabeth, their two daughters and the king's mother looked down at the proceedings. This day, Henry

Tudor truly looked the king. He was garbed in a gown of white damask, embroidered with Tudor gold and crimson roses, edged with ermine on the collar, and overtop a long-sleeved crimson undergarment; on his head was a black bonnet with a ruby sparkling in the blaze of candlelight. María blinked in awe. *There must be thousands of candles in the cathedral. Their light rivals the thin winter sunlight of outdoors.*

Hearing loud weeping overhead, María raised her eyes again to the gallery, inwardly cursing when she missed a step. Beside the king, his mother cried. Her son shrugged, smiled at his wife and clasped his mother's hand, his sudden movement swinging his black, jewelled scabbard so his steel sword caught the light. Lady Margaret wiped her eyes and smiled at the king. She said something to him. When the king laughed in response María started, surprised. *So – the king can laugh.* He leaned closer to the railing of the gallery, narrowing his already narrow eyes to peer at his son, and the girl come to marry him. He smiled, his eyes narrowing even more, as if struggling to see. María stored away her suspicion of the king's weak vision, to speak of it later to Catalina.

The queen wore robes of similar hue to the king's. As tall as her husband, Queen Elizabeth wore round her slender neck a thin gold collar of Tudor roses as well as long strings of pearls. A simple coronet of gold encircled her white brow, and her long silver-blonde hair flowed free. *So, it is true. The queens of England do reveal their hair in events like this. Perfect face, perfect figure – can she really be as old as thirty-five years? From this distance, she looks as old as me.*

Beside the queen stood her nephew, Edward Stafford, the young duke of Buckingham. Edged with sable, he too wore rich and heavily embroidered robes, his decorated with his emblems of golden antelopes and swooping swans. At the ready to come at their masters' bidding, a group of attendants stood a little behind, some in the livery of the duke and a greater number showing the green and white colours of the king.

Their faces bloodless and grave, Catalina and her prince reached the altar. María, with the other women, lowered the silken train to the floor before gathering together at the side of the altar as the prince and Catalina knelt on the red carpet before the Archbishop. "Our Archbishop of Canterbury, Henry Deane," Lady Margaret whispered in her ear.

María nodded. Archbishop of Santiago stood a little distance from the other archbishop, waiting for his part in the proceedings. Her eyes returned to the kneeling couple. The prince and princess did not look at each other, but straight ahead, their gazes locked on the crucifix at the front of the cathedral. *Praise God I am not marrying six weeks before my sixteenth birthday like Catalina. Praise God, I am promised I can decide my own husband.*

The archbishop turned towards the assembly. His voice boomed, echoing into the huge cathedral, as if he called across mountaintops. "Into this holy union Arthur, Prince of Wales, and Katherine, Princess of Aragon, now come to be joined. If any of you can show just cause why they may not lawfully be married, speak now, or forever hold your peace."

He glanced around the assemblage, blinking a few times as if gathering together his next words. "Are you both willing to proceed with the ceremony?"

No longer kneeling, Catalina and Arthur glanced shyly at

one another. In unison, their voices loud enough to carry far, they answered, "I am willing."

The archbishop turned to the Archbishop of Santiago standing next to Catalina. "Who gives this woman to be married to this man?"

Archbishop of Santiago stepped forward. He placed Catalina's hand in Arthur's. "In the name of our noble sovereign lord, Ferdinand, King of Aragon, I do." He bowed low to the royal pair, and then strode to the congregation.

In response to the Archbishop of Canterbury's nod, Arthur faced Catalina again, speaking in Latin. "In the name of God, I, Arthur, Prince of Wales, take you Catherine to be my wedded wife, to have and to hold, from this day forth, for better for worse, for richer, for poorer, in sickness and in health, till death us do part, if holy church ordains, and thereto I plight thee my troth." Arthur withdrew his hand from Catalina's.

With no time or even appetite to eat anything this morning –María swayed, light-headed. Her empty stomach grumbled. Hoping no one heard or saw her embarrassment, she closed her eyes, and took a deep breath, re-planting her feet firmly on the ground. She reopened her eyes to Catalina looking straight at her. Stabbed by her friend's lack of joy, María clasped her hands tight together, her stomach churning with her sense of helplessness.

Catalina raised her chin, and clasped Arthur's hand again. "In the Name of God, I, Catherine, take you, Arthur, to be my wedded husband, to have and to hold, from this day forward, for better for worse, for richer, for poorer, in sickness and in health, to be bonnier and buxom, in bed and board, if holy church will it ordain, and thereto I plight thee my troth."

The archbishop blessed the ring, sprinkling it with holy water from the altar. He turned to the couple and offered the ring to Arthur. The prince clasped Catalina's right hand. "With this ring I thee wed and this gold and silver I thee give, and with my body I thee worship."

He rested the ring on her thumb. "In the name of the Father." Arthur took the ring to the next finger, "and of the Son," then to the third, "and of the Holy Ghost," before slipping the ring on her fourth finger, saying, "Amen." Arthur and Catalina knelt again in front of the archbishop, who sang out his benediction.

María turned away, rubbing her tender stomach. Her heart drummed even louder in her ears. It was done. It had taken over twelve years, but, for better or ill, Catalina was Arthur's bride.

A three-course banquet followed at the Bishop's Palace near Saint Paul's before the couple was bedded. María was relieved to find herself seated beside Lady Margaret Pole. With each new course, Lady Margaret explained to her the perplexing English dishes brought out to the tables. María felt her eyes widen when servitors placed elaborative, huge white depictions of ships and castles near her. "They are called subtleties," said Lady Margaret. "Made out of sugar and egg whites." Margaret Pole picked up a dish close to her. "Try this." María forked out a piece of meat and bit into it. "Very tender. Is it chicken? I like the taste of lemon."

Margaret nodded and handed her a slice cut from a pie. The

pastry and the pork filling melted in María's mouth. "Delicious," she murmured.

"We call it royal flampayne," Lady Margaret said with a smile. "It is a favourite dish of many."

Margaret Pole pointed out people from the court. One, Bishop Fisher, María looked at him with closer interest, remembering people speaking his name. He sat beside the king's mother, a man with a cavernous face combined with aura of severity bringing to her mind Queen Isabel's Hieronymite confessor, Hernando de Talavera. Recalling de Talavera's many kindnesses to her as a child, María pushed down her homesickness as she watched the old man speak to the Countess of Richmond, and she with him. *They seem old friends – I must tell this to Catalina. It may prove important in the future.*

Covered by white cloths, going lengthwise down either side of the hall, two tables were laden with fowl, beef, all kinds of meat, and pastries of every shape and size. Seated at these tables, English Lords and Ladies ate as if none of them had ever heard of the sin of gluttony. She cringed at the noises made by her table companions. They belched and even farted as if they knew no better, or simply did not care about the impression they made to those foreign to their court.

On the raised dais with the royal family, Catalina, her table separated but close to Arthur's, picked at her food, just like her new husband did. The girl and boy wore the same, unsmiling look. Soon, it would be time for the next part of the proceedings.

María chewed at her mouth, distressed for her friend. *What can I do? Catalina's marriage is why we have come to England.* She pushed her food around her silver platter too, her unsettled stomach making it impossible to eat. Her mouth was so dry. She reached for the wine, her hand trembling so much she spilled red wine on the cloth. In the candlelight, it looked like blood. María gulped the wine. *The blood of a virgin on her wedding night.*

The edge of her silver platter shone in the light of a nearby candle. Everybody at her table had silver platters for their food, and those on the royal dais had gold. Close by, tall sideboards displayed gold and silver goblets adorned with jewels, and engraved bowls and plates. Undoubtedly, English goldsmiths had been busy of late – for Henry Tudor to proclaim his wealth to all.

María gulped down another mouthful of wine, turning her head towards the royal dais. Catalina looked scared, her eyes huge as she looked around at the English celebrating her marriage. *What does this all mean for her?* Raising her hand to her heating face, María lowered her head, her heart quickening with anger. *Catalina is flesh and blood, but it seems her parents, Queen Isabel and King Ferdinand, forget that – or do not care. She is simply a girl sent far from home; a lamb thrown to the wolves.* A memory from her twelfth year stirred.

Barefoot, she danced with Catalina on the beach at Laredo. A moment of innocence destroyed when Isabel, Catalina's older sister, dashed by them. Uncaring for her skirts, Isabel stumbled towards the surf. "One marriage is all I want," she screamed. Her brother Juan raced after her – and stopped her going deeper into the water. Both of them kneeling on the wet sand, he held her in his arms as she wept bitterly. "You speak of our mother's sacrifice, Juan?" Isabel said, refusing her brother's comfort. "I love Alfonso. I still love Alfonso. I do not want a second marriage. Ever." She wrenched away from Juan. "Brother, it is I whom our mother sacrifices." Isabel looked desperately at her sisters

Catalina and the infanta María. "All her daughters are! We are the lambs our parents sacrifice upon the altar of power. Sometimes I wonder if the profession of our parents' love is but the Judas sheep leading us to our fate."

Unable to silence her memories, they drove daggers into her heart. *Queen Isabel and King Ferdinand but sacrifice Catalina for their own gain. They sacrifice her to gain England as an ally, and to strengthen Aragon and Castile against the French. They sacrifice her for conquest, they sacrifice her for war.*

María blinked. *Si, with royalty comes duty, but does that make it right to sacrifice your children? Queen Isabel seemed no longer certain of that by the time she farewelled Catalina, her youngest child, but Catalina's father? I dislike the king. I have always disliked him. He was the one to insist his eldest daughter remarry again. He also told the queen not to delay Catalina's journey to England.*

Shaking her head, trying to clear it, María tried to think rationally, only to fail. *Soon, I and Catalina's other chosen women will take our princess to her bedchamber. We will wash her naked body with reverence and help her into the bed. And, there, Catalina will wait for Arthur.*

I am part of the ritual too. I am one of her women who will ready Catalina's body for the altar. María swilled down her wine so fast she gagged. *Altar? Si – the wedding bed is an altar. An altar that will be soon stained with Catalina's blood. Arthur's mother asks for it to be otherwise, but Arthur is fifteen. Surely, like so many boys of that age, he will wish to prove himself a man?*

Her head aching, María longed to escape.

Merry with drink, most of Arthur's men danced with women of the court. They waited like her for the banquet to come to an end, so they could prepare their prince for the bedding. Coming close to her table, she heard a few of them bantering with one another about the prince's prowess. One said loudly in French the prince would soon know the heat of Spain, and the woman he danced with laughed. María checked the prince and princess. *If I can hear them, surely they can too?*

Another loud, but younger voice drew her attention to the door. During his recent dance with Princess Margaret, his older sister, Prince Harry shocked María when he had stripped off his outer garb until he danced only in his small clothes, making the king and queen laugh at their son. The boy was still in small clothes, but there was no sign of any amusement on the face of the man, dressed in the robes of a priest, standing close to the prince. The portly, youngish man bowed his head in servitude, speaking close to the furious boy; he seemed to plead with Prince Harry. Bishop Fisher stood by, watching, his hands hidden in his dark robes, little hiding his distaste.

The distance prevented her from hearing the conversation, but she guessed the prince did not want to leave the festivities. "He is a handful," Lady Margaret murmured in French beside her.

María studied the Lady Margaret. The sweet-faced woman now attended Catalina every day and ensured she knew as much about the English court as possible. *I need to know too. The more I know, the more I can be of service to Catalina.* She pointed to the duke of Buckingham. "Does the king not mind his lords dressing themselves like royalty?"

Lady Margaret laughed. "A duke is royalty in this land. I heard my good cousin spent 1,500 pounds on his robes, nearly as much as the robes worn by the king." Margaret laughed again.

"My cousin Edward is the third duke of his name," she said. She slowly sipped from her goblet. "He has a good heart for those he loves. He holds the queen in high regard, but there is no denying he can be a vain, conceited cockerel like his forebears. The queen tells me she thinks her nephew wished to annoy the king by rivalling him, or more, by the coin spent showing his wealth at the wedding. He does not realise it does not annoy King Henry, but amuses him to see Edward spend his inheritance on such trifles. As long as Edward wastes his wealth on princely clothes and the enrichment of his estates, the king can rest easy he is not thinking of treachery."

María heard a loud young voice say, "You cannot command me to go." She turned her head towards the door. The Bishop approached Prince Harry and said something close to his ear, gesturing to the king and queen. The boy gazed that way too. Whatever the prince saw there, it bowed his head into submission, but not before he glared with hate and ferocity at the man of God. Prince Harry raised his head, signalled to a servant, and left the room. Fisher shared a glance of sympathy with the other man before they followed after the prince.

"The young prince is different to Prince Arthur," María said slowly. Unable to stop herself, she remembered Prince Juan again. From boy to man, he had never forgot his dignity, or his good manners. Sorrow surged, the sorrow of loss which never left her, and she turned to Lady Margaret, seeking distraction, seeking to hide her grief. "Very different," she said, hoping Margaret would talk more about the royal family – or anything to stop her from thinking of the past, or home.

"He is. But he is obedient to his parents." Lady Margaret's thin mouth sketched a slight smile. "His father because he both loves and fears him, and his mother because he adores her." This time, her smile lit up her face. "I have often witnessed his love for his mother. Just months ago, I was with the queen when she visited her children at Eltham Palace." She sighed. "Young Prince Edmund was ailing. God rest his innocent soul, the boy died soon afterwards. I remember Prince Henry rushing into the chamber as if with winged feet, leaving his sister Margaret well behind him. The day was a perfect, golden day, its light streaming into the palace from the high windows. It showered a haze over my cousin. Holding Edmund in her arms, my cousin looked like a statue of the Virgin Mary come to life.

"Seeing Prince Harry approach, she handed Edmund to his nurse, and beckoned to her son. The young prince's face when he knelt for her blessing – it competed with the sunlight, and all for his mother." She sighed. "You forgive a boy much when he shows himself capable of such love."

María studied the young couple. "Is Prince Arthur capable of such love?" She brought her hand to her hot cheek, not meaning to speak her question out loud.

Lady Margaret did not seem to notice her embarrassment, or act as if the question was peculiar. "He lives apart from his royal siblings and I know less of him than I would like, but he reminds me often of my..." She turned distressed eyes to María. "A dead uncle, who I loved greatly. If the prince is indeed like him, once he gives his heart, he will give it forever." Lowering her eyes, she paused for a moment, her fingers doodling a depiction of what seemed a wild, white rose on the white tablecloth. "Loyalté me lie," she murmured quietly.

María shook her head a little. *Loyalté me lie? What does she mean by that?* But Lady Margaret turned to her without explanation.

"You have been with the princess long?" the woman asked. "We are close kin. I have been the princess's companion since before my fifth summer...." María drifted in memories. "My parents served the queen. We saw them whenever the court came close to our home. In their absence, my grandmother cared for me, and my sisters and brothers," she said, reliving a time long gone. "But one time, my mother and father came home without warning." She smiled. "I still remember the rain and wind, the drum of horses' hooves, and my grandmother standing at the door, laughing with relief. The wind was so strong it snatched the door from my grandmother's grasp." She paused in silence, remembering how the rain spotted her grandmother's face and clothes, her black widow's gown and veil flapping like raven wings taking senseless and panicked flight as a gale blew into the alcázar.

Lady Margaret touched her arm. "What happened then?"

"The queen and her court happened," she replied, grinning. "The weather drove the queen and her four daughters to seek shelter at our home. Their entourage filled every chamber, every hall, every space possible. They stayed three days with my family."

She fell silent again. In her mind, she saw the deluge of humanity brought to them by the day's deluge of rain that morning. By the afternoon, candlelight lit the dark day bright. Their guests no longer in travelling clothes, light gleamed off golden gowns, robes of rich colours, gold and jewellery. Lute and hand harp strummed a continual underlay to the murmur of song, the cadences of adult prattle, the measured movement of graceful strangers. Before the hour of supper, her mother had summoned her household to greet the queen and pay her homage. Hiding well behind her mother, María had taken in the queen and her family.

Lady Margaret laughed beside her, returning her to the present. "So, you met the princess then?"

"Si." María started, realising she spoke in her own tongue. The memories swept her back the years, back to home. Her first home. Queen Isabel's smallest child had stood across from her. Sleepy, her eyes two-thirds closed, she nestled under the arm of her older sister. A girl of fifteen, Isabel seemed already an adult. Isabel and Catalina wore rich robes made from the same brocade as their mother's, as did the queen's other two daughters. With an instinct unique to children, María knew the smallest infanta was her own age, or close to it. They took each other's measure, a slow smile dimpling Catalina's cheek. María had smiled in answer, nodding to something unsaid between them. Deep within her, her universe shifted. By the time the queen and her court prepared to leave, they had become inseparable. The queen had then asked for her to serve as her youngest daughter's companion, and her parents could not say no.

María gulped down her wine, yearning to numb her pain. Her longing for home threatened to overflow.

Lady Margaret briefly rested a hand on María's. "I too am close to my kinswoman, the queen. I would do anything for her." María returned her eyes to the dais. "I likewise with my princess," she murmured. *Si – even if it means I am exiled from home forever.*

Lady Margaret sighed. "It does not make for an easy life."

She studied María, her mouth thinning. "And yours will be harder still."

Perplexed, María met Margaret's kind eyes. "Why do you say that?"

"You're beautiful, my dear. I thank God I am not that. Most men never notice me – excepting for my husband, and my boys, who value me for other reasons. You, my dear, will need to be careful. Men will seek after you, and try to woo you away from loyalty to your princess."

Straightening her shoulders, María shook her head. "No man could ever do that."

Lady Margaret laughed a little, and raised her goblet. "There speaks one who has never been in love."

7

Nothing is sweeter than love, nothing higher, nothing stronger, nothing larger, nothing more joyful, nothing fuller, and nothing better in heaven or on earth.

~ *Thomas à Kempis*

At last, the evening drew to a close and María joined the women escorting Catalina to the bedchamber prepared for the prince and princess. The wine gone to her head, María did what was expected of her, but it all felt a dream. Or a nightmare. She could not decide which.

The moments passed and the women washed Catalina and helped her into the warmed bed, drawing the coverlet up to her chin. Her pale face was stripped of all expression, her eyes huge and shining in the candlelight.

Should I offer her a goblet of wine? I'd want wine if I was

bedded with a boy I only met and spoken to a few times in my life.
But the chamber door opened, closing the door to any chance of
speaking to Catalina. Prince Arthur, garbed in a nightshirt with
a dark red robe cast over his shoulders, entered the room, carried
on the shoulders of his men. The king and two of his priests
followed close behind.

Without further ado, the men put the prince down. One
of them took off Arthur's robe and the prince joined his bride,
laying a little distance from her. The priests stepped forward,
and one blessed the bed, intoning in Latin. In her head, to
calm her nerves, María focused on translating the words in
English: "Protect your servants as they rest in this bed from all
the imaginary and unreal apparitions of the demons. Protect
them so they can meditate on your precepts as they sleep. So
that here, and in all parts, they are made safe by your
protection."

One of Arthur's attendants did what she had wanted to do
for Catalina, and passed a goblet of wine to the prince. Prince
Arthur pushed aside his pillow, leaned against the bedhead, and
drank deep. A young man considered the prince, and turned to
the king. "Your Grace, may I have your permission to tell a
bawdy tale?"

María lowered her head, squirming when the king laughed.
"Why not?" He winked at his son. "Some levity on a wedding
night never goes astray." All the intoxicated men laughed, even
the priests. Catalina's women, though, gathered together in a
silent knot.

"Have you heard of The Blacksmith of Greil, Your Grace?"
asked the young man.

The king laughed again. "Many times – and from your own

sire and grand sire, Gruffydd." He waved a hand. "You tell the story, boy."

The young man grinned at the white-faced prince. He seemed to want to reassure him. "God had blessed him with a magnificent prick that served women as a treat. They said it was shaped so fair, with a shaft two palms in length and wide as a fist." Catching the unsmiling eyes of the prince, he paused, and also seemed to notice Catalina for the first time. Fear shone in her eyes. The young man sobered, straightening up. "Methinks I will end it there. It is a but a silly tale."

"I can do one better," another young man.

The king chuckled, but contemplated his silent son and daughter-in-law. "I am certain you can, Tom, but I think we have overstayed our welcome. Time for us to leave, and let my son enjoy the first night of his marriage."

The prince passed his goblet back to his attendant. He replaced his pillow before laying down beside Catalina again.

Relieved the king had not allowed the stories to continue, María began following Catalina's other women. She glanced over her shoulder at Catalina. Utterly still in the huge bed, her friend stared up at the ceiling and gripped the coverlet so tightly her knuckles were the same colour as the white sheets. Close beside her, her young husband did not look her way.

The last to leave the antechamber, María waited as the guard shut the heavy oak door. Everything around her seemed to spin – and not just from all the wine she had drank that night. Her world had shifted. Shifted in a way that left her struggling for a sense of solid ground. She seemed falling into darkness, with nothing to hold onto.

I came to England because I couldn't bear being separated

from Catalina, but I never thought about what this night would mean to me. What if marriage changes my sister? What if she no longer needs me – or no longer wants me in her life? I've lost my homeland, my mother, my beloved teacher. What if I lose Catalina too? I could not bear it. Not exiled in England, so far from all else I love.

Inés took her arm, gazing at her in sympathy. "Come away. You cannot help her now. None of us can."

Unable to speak, she met Inés's eyes, and allowed her to lead her down the hallway. María took one step, and then another towards the women's chamber, wondering how she would sleep this night. She wondered if Catalina would sleep at all.

Francisca had already dressed Catalina when María, early the next day, returned to Catalina's bedchamber. In the antechamber, her face tight with concern, Francisca looked around before she whispered, "Prince Arthur was not here when I arrived. Nothing happened last night. The princess's servant is remaking the bed."

Burdened with the secrecy of Catalina's promise to the queen, María met Francisca's troubled eyes. "I shall go and see if our princess needs anything."

She knocked once on the bedroom's door. "It is María," she said, knocking again. Catalina's muffled voice answered. María opened the door, then closed it behind her. Catalina sat on a chair facing the door, close to the fireplace and the crumpled bed. A picture of gloom, she glanced towards María before staring at the fire.

The Moor servant girl lifted her head at María's arrival, and then returned to straightening the bedsheets, the colour of her skin contrasting vividly against their whiteness. The sheets, too, told the same story as Francisca – the sheets had no evidence of virginal blood. María approached Catalina. When Catalina glanced in her direction, María hesitated before bobbing a curtseying. *I must always remember to curtsey to her. Even when we are alone like this. She is wife to a king's son. One day, she will be queen.*

Glancing first at the servant, Catalina turned to the fire, her fingers curling underneath the end of the wooden armrest of her chair. She laughed – a strained laugh with no hint of humour – before speaking hurriedly in Latin. "I kept my promise to the queen, María. It was not hard to do, not when my husband was happy to just hold my hand and speak to me." She inhaled and exhaled a deep breath, and looked aside at María. "The queen is right. Her son is ailing. All night, he was racked by coughing. I fear it will be a long time before he is strong enough to consummate our marriage."

Troubled for her friend, María stepped closer and rested a hand on her shoulder. "You are not even sixteen for another month; the prince will not be sixteen for another nine. Time will make this right."

Catalina sat straighter, lifting her chin. "Do you think so? Oh God, María, even his lowborn servants are stronger and healthier than him. His coughing kept us both awake for hours." She shrugged. "It gave us the opportunity to talk long of his mother's conniving, of what she proposed. He is worried that his father may learn of what his mother asked of me – and of him – and be angry. I told him we can keep this secret, and that there is no need to say to his men any other than we are indeed husband and wife, but..." She bit her bottom lip, gazing at María with wide eyes. "A falsehood is not a good way to begin a marriage. A falsehood I cannot confess to any priest because of my vow to the queen..."

Wedding celebrations continued for weeks. After their time at the Bishop's Palace, they stayed at Westminster, entertained by more pageants and tournaments, before the royal family and its court travelled down the Thames to Richmond Palace.

Prince Arthur had his own barge. Settling herself in it for the journey, María sat behind Catalina and her prince with their other close attendants. She trembled as the afternoon wind blew cold and sharp, reminding her winter had truly arrived. Pulling her mantle tighter around her, she rubbed and warmed her hands under its folds. She wished she could untighten the new English gable headdress she wore. She wished she could fling it into the depths of the Thames. She hated how heavy it felt and its shape. It was like a cage – a cage making it difficult for her to look anywhere but straight ahead.

The Thames rolled beside her like a huge tapestry of unending colour. The calm, smooth river reflected the colour of the azure sky and the scattering of clouds, as well as the barges of the English court. For a few moments, she could forget winter, and believe autumn still ruled their days. From the barge of the king and queen, a little distance ahead of them, she could hear musicians playing upon their instruments and voices raised in song.

María noticed the prince pointing to the large barge and whispering close to Catalina's ear. Catalina laughed and whispered something to him. Gladness warmed María's heart. This journey brought Catalina and the prince closer together for once. Since the wedding banquet and their first bedding, the days saw Catalina and her new husband spending little time together. At last night's banquet, they even sat at separate tables and rarely glanced each other's way. María's moment of happiness melted away, and she squirmed in discomfort. *Is that surprising? Catalina and Prince Arthur know all eyes watch their every move.*

Now, relaxed in the company of their most trusted attendants, Prince Arthur grinned, pointing ahead to his wife. "Richmond Palace, lady wife."

"Oh," Catalina said. "It is beautiful."

María craned her neck to better see. A white, three-storey castle loomed in the near distance, its round and octagonal towers facing the river. Surrounded by green lawn and gardens, the stone castle, framed against a blue sky, seemed like a subtlety the English delighted in creating for their feasts.

"It was finished a short while ago, built to replace the Royal manor of Sheen," Arthur said. "Sheen burnt down when I was eleven, while I was at Ludlow. My mother tells me the fire was like Hell itself. Mother, Father, my brother and sisters and even my grandmother only escaped through the Grace of God. When my father escaped, a wall collapsed and could have cost him his life. I came close to losing all my closest blood kin that night and becoming too early England's king." He toyed with the ring on his little finger, before speaking again. "My mother greatly sorrowed about the destruction of her childhood home."

Catalina brushed her hand against his. "A fire nearly claimed the lives of my family as well. I was eight then. My royal mother had taken us, all her children, to witness the taking of Granada. Somehow, a fire started in my mother's tent. She and my sister Juana had to run for their lives. I am glad you were safely away and did not witness the fire that destroyed the manor."

María shifted, remembering the night Catalina mentioned. She remembered being bundled by the soldiers out of the tent she shared with Catalina and the other infantas. She remembered the flames consuming Queen Isabel's tent. She remembered the terror – and how she held onto Catalina for dear life.

Arthur glanced at Catalina, and then at the river. "For as long as I can remember, I have lived separately from my family because I am my father's heir and must have my own household. Do you think it makes it easier to know you are kept safe when your family are threatened with death? I wish I had been with them."

Catalina studied him for a long moment, and then took his hand. She kept hold of it for the rest of the journey to Richmond.

8

If you would reflect well and wisely, you would realise that those events you regard as personal misfortunes have served a useful purpose even in this worldly life, and indeed have worked for your betterment.

~ *Christine de Pizan*

The prince's barge entered the water-gate at the side of the palace. Alighting from the barge, María trailed after the prince and Catalina as they crossed the bridge over the narrow moat. She turned her head, her ears catching the sound of twittering birds in the nearby terraced-garden – sweeter birdsongs than she had ever heard in her life. Gentle light deepened the green of the well-maintained lawns spread out from the palace to the riverbank. *A different kind of beauty from home – lush, and rich, the colours deep and vibrant.* She strode towards the palace.

The towers and walls reached to the almost cloudless sky. Seemingly without end, an orchard stretched out on the left. A two-storey gallery formed a wall for the palace, edging the garden, separating the palace from a small church.

Catalina and Arthur entered the palace to the welcome of the already arrived king and queen. Going together to the Great Hall, the king proudly showed his daughter-in-law around. Rich tapestries covered stone walls. Turkish carpets covered much of the stone floor. Gold and silver plate, and glass and precious metal goblets filled sideboards far taller than men.

Like many other places María had seen in England, the palace also had an open hammer beam ceiling, but it seemed to possess more windows than usual to let in the light. Welcoming fires burned bright not only in the huge brick hearth in the centre of the Great Hall, but also two other large fireplaces at either end of the chamber, warming the room against the growing chill of the afternoon.

Catalina and Arthur retired alone to their chambers, set close together in one part of the palace. Up since dawn, María decided to follow the young royal couple's lead and rest for a while before the evening festivities, reading one of her books in the chamber with the other women.

During another long and seemingly endless dinner that night, María sat between Bella and Francisca, with Inés next to Francisca. Catalina's fool entertained the king and queen and their court with acrobatic feats before the arrival of the second course. When he hung by his teeth on a rope secured from one side of the Great Hall to the other, María gasped in disbelief. Francisca laughed at her, and leaned closer to her ear.

"If you had not spent all your time with our princess at

Laredo, you would have seen the man practice his craft on the beach. He did not mind us watching him to pass the time."

The hours sped by and the king and queen began the dancing, before returning to their dais to look on as others of their court danced. Weary from her long day and yearning for bed, María remained seated, content to watch. Only a handful of English dances had been taught to them before they left Queen Isabel's court – all of them far more dignified than the dances she loved at home. Now she discovered the English too enjoyed dancing to a fast beat and the challenge of complicated steps.

After dancing once with her husband, Catalina danced with the duke of Buckingham. Arthur kept his eyes on his wife, a smile teasing his mouth. Candlelight left hollows in his wan face and lit up his deep blue eyes. The dance ended, and Catalina laughed at something the duke said. He bowed and she offered a brief curtsey before returning to her table.

The prince rubbed his eyes and covered a yawn. His paleness became translucent. María chewed her mouth. *The prince is over-taxed.* One of his men must have thought so too, because he came to the table and whispered in the prince's ear. Arthur glanced at him and nodded. He rose and came to Catalina's table to bid her good night.

Catalina watched him leave the evening festivities, worry unhidden on her face. The duke of Buckingham approached Catalina's table, bowed and spoke to her for a few minutes. Catalina nodded to the duke and gave him a strained smile.

"I wonder what the duke said to her?" Bella said softly beside her.

"You can always ask her later. I suspect he reassured her about the prince." María swallowed. "No words of reassurance can change what we all can see. His health is not improving." She bent her head, pushing away the image of the princess's brother, and her sorrow for his loss.

"What will happen if the prince's health fails completely? What will happen to our princess then? And to us?"

"I do not know."

"Surely we would go home then?" asked Francisca.

Arthur is not Juan. He is not Juan. "I do not know," María repeated, relieved when Catalina rose and signalled to her women to follow.

Doña, my dear Latina,

Forgive me for not writing to you in recent weeks. I am certain you have heard of my princess's marriage to Prince Arthur. The English still celebrate the wedding of the heir to their throne. The prince is very beloved, but he is not strong. My princess sleeps as she has done since childhood, and I remain her bedcompanion and reside with her in her rooms.

Seated near the roaring fire in Catalina's antechamber, María replaced her quill in its ink pot and stared out the window. Thick, distorted glass made the falling snow seem like a misty cloud. They had been at Richmond for a week – time enough for the weather to change, for the worse. The wind screamed, lifting white flurries to hit against trees in the garden, and breaking up the snow-cloud before her eyes. Gusts of freezing air came through the ill-fitting window, ruffling the papers on the near table, causing her to shiver once more. A candle flickered, illuminating a pile of unused parchments and the books Catalina had borrowed over the last week from the king's library to read.

María turned when the bedroom door opened with a loud creak. Catalina held their winter mantles. "Come. I refuse to stay here one more moment until someone remembers me; I want to explore this palace." She tossed María's mantle to her. Putting on her own, Catalina pulled the hood over her head, casting her face in shadow.

María gathered her mantle around her. Drawing the hood over her head too, she eyed the roaring fire with regret. "Is it wise for us to leave the chamber?"

Catalina turned. With a start, María realised her friend was paler than ever.

"My lady mother allowed us to wander as we willed, as long we remained within the confines of the royal apartments and gardens. I feel trapped, treated like a caged bird. Doña Elvira busies herself with another letter reporting all to my lady mother, so let us fly free and hunt out more books in the king's library. We can use the staircase near here, and return to my cage before the bells ring out the new hour."

María giggled, closed her eyes, reciting:

> *"When you are depressed,*
> *make strong your heart,*
> *Even while standing at death's door.*
> *There is light in the candle before 'tis put out*
> *And in the gored lion, a roar."*

"Let me hazard a guess –" Catalina grinned, "yet another poem of Samuel Ibn Nagrela?"

María shrugged. "If my mother is able to recite the poetry of our illustrious ancestor for every moment of the day, why should I be any different?"

Catalina's smile widened. "I don't want you any different. It reminds me of home. But I need exercise, not poems. Exercise of body and exercise of mind, as Latina often told us. I would settle better in my cage if I had new books to read. Let's go."

María laughed a little. "You smell books, si, like a hunting dog? But pray, I beg you, only for a short time. I do not wish for Doña Elvira to know we have flown from our coop and send people to seek us out. She'll find more cause to grumble at me because she fears to grumble at you."

She closed the door to their chamber as quietly as she could, trailing after Catalina down the spiral stone staircase, keeping her footfalls soft and light. Cold, strong draughts pulled at her heavy mantle, guttering the torchlights in the high sconces. She shivered, thinking longingly of the fire left behind, gorging itself on heavy logs of wood like one famished.

María stumbled on the final, uneven step, almost falling into a dark hallway. An awful smell hit her like a solid wall. She gagged, edged closer to her friend.

"Saint Michael's sword." Catalina held a pomander to her nose. "Have we walked into a privy?"

Wishing she had remembered to bring her own pomander, María raked her eyes over every bit of floor near them. The light was too dim to see properly. "Perchance there is one near here. What else explains it?"

The vile stench wafted over from the side of the stairwell. María paced a few cautious steps forward, thinking she might see a privy door, and stepped into a puddle. The stench hitting her like never before, she jumped back in disgust. "By all the Saints in good Heaven!" *The privy nearby? Jesu', I but stand in it.*

María lifted her skirts higher from the ground, treading more warily, and moved to stand by Catalina. Hurrying with her down the hallway, she asked Catalina, "Can you imagine what the queen, your mother, would say?"

Catalina screwed up her face in unmistakable abhorrence. "My mother does not expect her subjects to act worse than animals, fouling where they live. When I am queen, this will not happen. I cannot believe Queen Elizabeth brooks such behaviour."

María lifted an eyebrow. Catalina rarely spoke about her future. *My beloved kinswoman will be queen one day.* She shivered with both excitement and dread, until they became neither one nor the other: until she shivered with terror. *Why am I so frightened? Nothing has changed. My life has always been intertwined with Catalina; it shapes my own fate, and I accept it.* Moving far enough away from the stairwell for the smell to become bearable, and to where there was better light, María glanced over her shoulder. "Must we return this way?"

Catalina frowned and rubbed a knuckle up and down her cheek. "Do you remember the other way for us to return to my chambers? My head spins."

Catalina's question defeated her – and she held her palms upraised in answer while she thought. "I think we should make a return, even using that awful way," she said slowly. Neither you nor I want to ask for directions if we get lost."

"Catalina!" Prince Arthur hurried in their direction,

followed by two men, his friend Gruffydd and another companion.

María met Catalina's anxious eyes before shrugging. "Better Prince Arthur, your husband, than his father, the king," she murmured under-breath as she stepped behind her.

María curtseyed low at the prince's approach, Catalina doing likewise.

For the first time, he looked unyielding like his father. "My lady wife, what do you do here, alone?"

Catalina glanced over her shoulder at María. "I am not alone, Your Highness, my good husband. My companion Doña María is here."

"That is not what I mean." The prince spoke as if annoyed. "Two young women, walking here, unprotected. My God – Kate, I did not believe you could be so foolish. Thank God, we found you before any harm befell you."

Catalina offered an uncertain smile. "I thought it safe, my Lord. I did not realise I placed Doña María and myself in any danger."

The prince's thin, long face relaxed back to one belonging to a boy, and his look softened. He stepped towards her, took her hand and enfolded it in his. "Why are you here, my lady?"

Catalina lowered her head. "I wish to borrow new books from the king's library."

He exchanged a smile with his companions over his shoulder before speaking again to Catalina. "More books, my Kate? Soon all my father's library will reside in your chambers."

Catalina grinned in response to his obvious amusement. "Do you mind, my Lord husband?"

The young prince shook his head. "No, my lady. It gives us much in common." He held out his arm. "Shall we go together?"

Catalina's eyes blazed alight with her smile, her teeth glinting pearl like under the light of a torch set high in the wall. María stepped away to allow Catalina and the prince some privacy. She found herself walking alongside Arthur's unknown companion. A handsome man, he walked with the bearing of a soldier and the aura of a leader. A small jagged scar scored his cheek and a dimple cleft his square, strong chin. When his deep blue eyes glanced her way, María's heart did a strange flip.

He greeted her with a dip of his head. Her face warm, she lowered her eyes.

"Lady, may I beg the honour of your name?"

With another quick glance at him, she sketched a brief curtsey and inwardly cursed at its involuntary wobble. "Doña María de Salinas –" Her heart drummed loud in her ears. She inhaled another deep breath. For two years or more, schooled with Catalina, French had fallen off her tongue like pollen to a bee. Her mind blank, she struggled for Latin, or Castilian, but her tongue no longer obeyed her.

The stranger came closer. His smell – a newly washed body mixed with worn leather and the smell of horses – did peculiar things to her insides. Her heart beat faster, and unfamiliar emotions swirled like a rising deluge seeking to drown her. Well behind the rest of their party, she quickened her pace. His long-legged stride easily kept up with her. "Doña María de Salinas – I have heard the prince speak of you. You're the princess's favourite companion?"

She glanced aside at him. Dark eyelashes and eyebrows contrasted with his silver-blond hair. Surrounded all her life by fair men and women, she had never noticed blond hair could be so alike to gleaming threads of silver, or perhaps she never had reason to notice it. A light trail of stubble brushed his jaw line. She clutched her dress, denying her desire to touch it. Raising her hand to her hot face, she stared unseeingly at the ground. "Si, her companion from childhood, and her kinswoman." Her voice sounded odd and hoarse to her ears, and she found herself no longer walking, but standing alone with him. When he smiled, she found it impossible to look away. Reeling, one hand grasped at her rosary at her waist, and the other rose to her chest. *Why does my heart hurt?* Her legs quivering like jelly on top of feet of lead, she forced herself to move forward again.

His hand grazed against hers, and scorched her flesh, halting her again. He reached out and clasped her hand. As quick as he took it in his, he freed it, letting her loose. But not before a lightning bolt smote her heart. Her blood turned into honey, honey seeping down to her woman's parts. She floundered, breathless, helpless against the winds of fate.

"Forgive me. I have no right to touch you. By all the good Saints, no right. God's wounds, you are beautiful."

No man had ever said that to her before. Not even her loving father. Knees still weak, she raised her eyes to his. Time stood still in silence, a waiting moment before the tempest gathered its strength, taking all in its path.

At last, she rediscovered her tongue. "Good sir, pray tell me, what's your name?"

The young man dipped his head. "I am remiss. I crave your pardon, my lady. I am William Willoughby de Eresby, Baron. It is an old barony in this kingdom, held by my family for centuries. But pray give that no mind. I would regard it a great honour if you call me Will." He smiled, showing white, strong teeth. "May I speak to you again, my lady?" He paused for a moment. "Just speak to you."

Up ahead, Catalina and the prince slipped through the library's doorway. Sir Gruffydd followed, shutting the door behind him. *What would Catalina say? What would Doña Elvira? My mother?* Their voices chorused in her head: *María, have you learnt nothing? You should know better than speak alone to strange men. You but ask for trouble.* Yet her heart told her he was no stranger.

Confused, pulled one way and then another, María turned to Will. His gentle smile and eyes seemed to embrace her. Unknowingly, she had waited for this moment all her life. And hungered for it. Now, an emptiness within her yearned and cried out for fulfilment. Demanded it. *Si, he is no stranger.* She curtseyed again and smiled at him. "*Si*. You may speak to me. I would be also honoured if you call me by my given name."

He took her hand and kissed it with a lingering tenderness. She turned away, not wanting him to see how much he moved her.

"I best go and attend to my princess," she said in a rush. Retrieving her hand, she wanted to run away from him – terrified she would forget herself and fall into his arms. Frightened too at this new, unexpected world opening before her. She toppled between her life as a maid, a maid who loved no man, and a new life where she was no longer a girl, but a woman who, for good or ill, had given her heart.

Out of breath, María hurried to the library's door – glancing at him one last time before she entered the chamber. Leaning against the closed door, she shook her head, praying he would not follow. Not until she regained control of herself. *I am losing my wits. This cannot be happening. I promised. I promised I would not leave her alone. Not now. Not yet.*

9

For weal or woe I will not flee
 To love that heart that loveth me.
 That heart my heart hath in such grace
 That of two hearts one heart make we;
 That heart hath brought my heart in case
 To love that heart that loveth me.

~ Unknown author, C. 1500

Doña, my dear Latina,

 Prince Arthur and my princess no longer live separated lives. Each morning, the prince seeks out his new wife. They are a young man and woman learning to like one another.

While Catalina looked forward to her husband's daily visits, María hoped for another occasion to speak to Baron Willoughby. Will. She said his name over and over, as if a prayer, as if it would conjure his presence and salve her hurting heart. She did not understand this passion – a passion that had her in its grips. Day and night, her thoughts spun around this man, this beautiful man she had only spoken to once. This beautiful man who had turned her life upside down. She did not want to desire him, but she did – a desire sweeping her beyond her depth. Frightened by the strength of her feeling, she felt consumed by it; drowned by it. She feared meeting him alone again, but she longed for it too - with all of her heart.

When Will Willoughby accompanied the prince, she often sensed his seeking eyes upon her, his unvoiced question. But when she lifted her eyes to his, he broke his gaze to look at something else. That day of their first meeting, he begged to speak to her, but now he avoided her. Confused and hurt, she kept remembering his hand aflame upon hers. She decided to seek him out, determined to discover the reason why he no longer wanted to speak to her.

Fate decided to help. On the sixth day after their first meeting, she opened the door of the prince's private chamber and entered his antechamber, sent there by Catalina to retrieve her lute. Near an unlit fireplace, Will, wearing but his top small clothes over his dark hose, dozed on a high-back chair. With his hair dishevelled and his body relaxed, Will seemed no longer a grown man, but a youth. A vulnerable youth.

María looked over her shoulder at the open door of the prince's private chamber. Catalina sang accompanied by her husband's lute. Stumbling over a verse together, they laughed and started the song again. Occupied with one another, they would not notice her slow return. In truth, the two of them might be happier for her absence.

María shut the door with care and crossed to the fireplace, lavender rushes snapping underfoot as her gown's skirt brushed against them. The whisk-whisk-whisk of her skirt and her beating heart seemed the only sound in the world. Stopping close to the chair, she gulped down her heart, smoothed out the folds of her gown and stepping hard on the rushes, intentionally breaking twigs, smelling the pleasant perfume of the rushes. *I begin to understand why the English use rushes to cover their floors.*

When breaking twigs didn't rouse Will, she gathered the last remnants of her fast disappearing courage, cleared her throat, bending down close to him, murmuring, "My lord?"

Will's eyes opened, and he lost colour, jerked upright. He looked at her in undisguised dismay. Shattered, she raised her hands to her hot face and moved away to give him more space. "Lady! Forgive me. Does the prince call for me? God's teeth, to fall asleep in broad daylight. But I've slept little of late." María licked her dry lips. "Nor me." She looked at him, shuffling her feet on the rushes, wondering if he took her meaning. Telling herself the heady perfume of the rushes explained the gnawing in her stomach. Again, she took hold of her courage. "Pray forgive my forwardness. I lack experience, my lord..." She gulped down a deep breath. "The day we met, I thought –"

He came closer and placed his hand on her arm for a moment. A brief, brief touch, but the heat of it seeped through her sleeve to her bare skin. "I beg you, say no more." His jaw hardened. "I am married."

Her whole world cracked opened and threatened to swallow her up. Her mouth dry, feeling ill, she met his eyes. Moment by suffocating moment, a wall of silence built between them. She put out her hand, trying to push the wall down.

"Married. You're married? But when we met –?" Her words squeaked out so high it no longer sounded like her voice. The searing pain of her wounded heart threatened to tear her into pieces. Staring through her tears at the rushes, she wished the floor would open up and she could disappear.

"Forgive me. I was wrong to speak to you that day. I blame myself – but when I saw you – 'twas like I've always known you, and the fates meant for us to meet." His voice caught. "I forgot the fates are rarely kind."

María glanced up at him. His deep blue eyes glittered brightly with unshed tears. She wanted to be angry, but how could she be when he seemed so miserable? She turned her anger on herself, hating how she wanted to throw her arms around him, hold him and not let go. She wanted to kiss him, kiss him, kiss him, tell him it didn't matter. That nothing mattered but them. To tell him knowing he returned her feelings was enough. *Si, fate betrays us*. But her own shaking body betrayed her more. Sicker than ever, she wanted to hit him. She wanted to hold him tight. She wanted his lips on hers, his hands on her body. She wanted him. Only him. She had met him only a week ago, but her heart told her this man was meant for her, and her for him.

She raised her hands to her hot face, her shame at her unbridled feelings crashing down upon her like a trapdoor. Picking up her skirts, she spun on her heel, running from the room, and out into the hallway. He called out, "Come back. Do not leave like this. Let me explain..." Unable to block her ears, she ran faster, not knowing, or caring, where her path ended. Never in her life had she felt so alone, so hurt. Not even when her twelve-year-old heart had broken over Prince Juan.

Mama – oh, Mama. I need you. I need you more than ever. I want to go home. The newly laid down rushes in the hallway meant their smell swept after her as she scurried away from her humiliation, constricting her chest even more. From this day onwards, she knew she would hate the perfume of lavender.

Dark, miserable days followed – days without end. That is, for her. Her heart seemed to bleed, irreparably broken into tiny pieces. Her resolve to stay strong was an unwinnable battle. Watching Catalina and Arthur every day did not help. Though still not a full marriage, it was clear to all Catalina was well matched with her prince. Day by day, their relationship and happiness grew, whilst María struggled to ignore the presence of Will. It was impossible when he attended the prince every day.

She was grateful when a new bundle of medicine books from Latina gave her excuse to linger in Catalina's chamber whilst Catalina dallied with her husband and his friends.

One day, seated deep in the window-seat, she tried to read one of her new books. But, hearing the laughter of Catalina, her prince and his companions outside, she found it hard to focus on the words, reading the same passage, over and over.

She twisted around and looked out at Catalina and Arthur competing against one another in a game of archery. Catalina positioned her bow with skill. She pulled the string and the arrow flew and hit close to the bull's eye. Will, Arthur's best friend Sir Gruffydd and the young Duke of Buckingham clapped next to the prince, now waiting his turn, while Bella and Francisca watched on. "Best of three," the prince called to his wife. Catalina took another arrow from her quiver, and aimed again. This time, the arrow struck the edge of the board. The third arrow landed on the other side of the bull's eye. Will was smiling broadly, joining in with the laughter of the others.

She wanted to weep. *He is not heartbroken like me. He has forgotten me.*

Something dropped on her lap. She turned around. Doña Elvira stood over her, scowling. María took a deep breath, and gathered all her willpower not to snap. She glanced down at her lap and picked up a torn sleeve. She lifted her eyes to Doña Elvira.

"Why should all the other women mend the princess's gowns while you sit around and waste your time doing nothing but reading. Find a needle and thread, and fix that sleeve," the woman commanded. "Prove to me you have some use, other than to be the pampered pet of the princess."

Stunned into silence, María stared at Doña Elvira as she left the room. Their journey to England and the time since arriving had not changed Doña Elvira's long-held dislike of her, rather the opposite. María shook her head, pondering why it was so important to Doña Elvira to have full possession of the princess's ear.

María curtseyed low at the door. Coming deeper into Catalina's chamber, she curtseyed yet again, a little hurt when Catalina did not notice her. Seated on a high-backed chair near the fire, Catalina kept her eyes on her husband as she leaned towards him. Arthur sat at the feet of his wife, speaking softly to her:

Thy lips, O my spouse, drop as the honeycomb:
honey and milk are under thy tongue;
and the smell of thy garments
is like the smell of Lebanon.

Arthur reached up to Catalina and took her face between his hands. They looked long at one another before joining their lips in an inexpert kiss. They broke away and laughed at one another, and Arthur stroked his wife's face. "I am glad we take our time. It will be all the sweeter for the wait when September comes."

They remained in a world of their own, and still oblivious to María's presence. She slipped back, returning to Catalina's antechamber. She had seen enough lovelorn youths, especially when Juana and Isabel, Catalina's beautiful sisters, resided at their mother's court, to recognise the prince was also one such. He was completely changed from the reserved, uncertain boy who first greeted Catalina. María had suspected his apparent lack of interest in his bride was due to shyness. That was all changed. They grew more enamoured of each other as they spent more time in each other's company.

She stamped down her envy – an ugly, preposterous beast destroying her peace of mind. *Forget Will. He is not for you. It is a sin to love him. Stop being a fool. You just think you are in love. How can you love a man you have only spoken to twice?* But her heart told her otherwise. She looked for him, yearning to see him, while another part wished him absent. "*I am married,*" she heard in her mind. *"I am married."* Her heart sat in her chest, heavy and jagged like a sharp rock, tearing at her every waking moment.

The door left open between the two rooms, she heard Catalina read to her husband in French, the language Arthur and she both spoke with fluency.

"And then he dressed his shield and his spear, and cried aloud unto Sir Tristram and said: Knight, defend thee. So they came together and Sir Uwaine bruised his spear all to pieces upon Sir Tristram's shield, and Sir Tristram smote him harder and sorer, with such a might that he bare him clean out of his saddle to the earth."

María decided to re-enter the chamber. She curtseyed again and cleared her throat to get their attention. "My lady princess and lord prince, a message has arrived from the queen."

Handing the folded message to the prince, she stepped back and waited.

The prince scanned the letter, frowning a little in concentration. "We are to make ready to leave on Friday for Windsor."

"Windsor–?" Closing the book and placing it on her lap, Catalina turned questioningly to her husband. He grinned, taking her hand.

"Close by to here. It is one of my father's favourite residences. I also have news. My Lord father advised me this morning to ready myself for my return to Ludlow Castle – a place I love like none other. Sweet wife, at Ludlow Castle I govern my own court."

Catalina bent, peering down at his face. All at once, her animation vanished. "Must we part so soon, my lord?"

Arthur raised her hand to his lips. "That is not my wish.

And it gladdens my heart that you feel the same. Sweet Kate, I have asked my father if you could come too."

Catalina's smile returned. "I would like that. No, I want that."

Arthur took her other hand, kissing the inside of her wrist. On his face, thick down mingled with the beginning of true beard bristles.

María swallowed – unable to rid from her mind the image of Will on the day of their first meeting. The dark bristles on his jaw line. Fighting her desire to touch him. A desire igniting, burning stronger each new day until it became a raging fire. A fire she found impossible to contain. A fire she fought to contain. She had to contain it. She could not even speak to Catalina about her heartbreak. Will was married. To love him was a sin.

Arthur spoke again. "I thought... I hoped that would be your wish. Many here, both your people and mine, believe you too young and new to England to go with me to Ludlow." The prince laughed. "As if our ages matter at all. I am nine months younger than you. My father has written to your parents for their thoughts on the matter. Once he receives word from them, he'll make his decision." He sighed. "Marriage or not, we are still commanded by our parents."

Catalina smiled. "I am glad of it. I for one feel not ready to steer my own life without guidance."

Aware they had forgotten her, María crossed to the window seat where Catalina's sewing basket had been left. She began to sort through the cards of skein, returning them to order by their colour. *Oh, Catalina – you should be ready to steer your life. I know you are not yet sixteen, but you will be soon. And you are married. It may not be a full marriage – but it is still a marriage.* María replaced the card of costly purple thread with care. *And one day you will be queen. You've been trained to be a queen.*

Uneasy, María chewed at her mouth. In the security of her mother's court, Catalina had rarely doubted her abilities. But leaving her mother, leaving Castile, had changed her, and left her less confident. It made her more reliant on those older than her. In England, she seemed another person. Perchance we all are. María saw again in her mind flower-adorned nymphs returning to their home, the sea. *Si – like them, we are strange creatures, but we are unable to go back home. We go from one strange place to another.*

María realised she knew nothing about Ludlow Castle. If she knew nothing, that likely meant Catalina knew nothing too. *Margaret Pole. I will seek her out – and find out for both of us.* She glanced up from her task, relieved when Catalina lifted her chin with pride. She almost knocked the sewing box to the floor. *Do you not realise what that means for you? You well know Catalina's look of determination, of stubbornness.* Most of the time, María admired Catalina for these traits, but she dreaded them too. Once Catalina became fixed on her course, it was almost impossible to persuade her to take a different road. Now her look presaged another long journey, after only a short time at the English court. *I should think myself fortunate. I should wish for the distance between Will and I.* She had overheard the prince telling Catalina Will had left the court to return to his estates, and his wife, for the Christmas season. He had left before the weather worsened into true winter.

Her princess's next words confirmed she was right to feel

anxious about being uprooted again. "My parents will want me to stay with you," Catalina said.

Arthur beamed at her, and Catalina smiled back. A sudden, icy draught blasted through the open door. Candles blew out, dimming the chamber. María shivered, her heart struck cold. During their brief marriage, Prince Juan and his wife Princess Margot had also gazed at each other like Arthur and Catalina – as if their world was made anew, as if there were no one else in the world but them. For Juan and Margaret, their joy had ended too soon. She blinked, praying for the shadows to be gone, and the memories banished with them. But the shadows remained, and lengthened.

At last, wedding celebrations at an end, the court of the English King moved to Windsor. The days moved closer to the time for Prince Arthur's return to Ludlow Castle. María had learnt from Margaret Pole the castle was located in the Welsh Marshes, an area separating England from Wales. If Catalina accompanied him, it meant weeks of travel – again.

But before the day of the prince's departure came the departure of others. On a grey, dismal day, María stayed seated on a stool in the shadows of Catalina's antechamber. Their first greetings done, the Count of Cabra and the Archbishop of Santiago faced Catalina, standing close together. María covered her mouth, wishing again to laugh at their difference in height. Her desire to laugh became a sigh. Catalina feared losing the guidance of these two men – men her parents trusted.

Her pale face framed by a dark matron gable, Catalina

gripped the top of the high-backed chair so hard it left her knuckles bloodless before she moved from behind the chair and closer to the men. Bowing low, Cabra strode forward with a wide, measured step, kneeling at her feet. He kissed the hem of her dress and stood again, gazing at her with kind, dark brown eyes. "Our ship sails early on the morrow, madam. I ask for your blessing and prayers for a safe journey."

Catalina crossed herself. "I bless you with my whole heart, Count, and you have my prayers." Knotting her hands together, Catalina glanced at one man and then the other. "But need you go so soon? My wedding was only a few weeks ago – can I not beg you to stay with me, if but awhile longer?"

The bishop dipped his head low and his heavy cross swung, the gold catching the light of the torch guttering in the high sconce. The reflected light from the metal flashed, winked and twirled a fast dance of glittering specks of gold on the grey stone wall.

"Your Highness, the queen, your noble mother, commands we make our return to Castile as soon as possible. Your royal parents, our beloved King and Queen, have approved you accompanying the prince, your noble husband, to Ludlow Castle. They have also sent the English king the instalment of your dowry. My daughter, there's nothing left for us to do here. But what joy and comfort I can give to the queen when I tell her how well the English care for you."

"I have finished a letter to my mother. It tells her the same." She gestured to María.

Rising, María picked up the folded letter from the nearby table. She passed it to the archbishop before returning to her place.

"Give it to her when you return," Catalina said quietly.

"Of course, Your Highness. My last advice to you is this – learn well the language of your new country. Do this with great speed."

María closed her mouth on a groan. *Great speed? How can we learn it quickly when everyone speaks to us in either French or Latin? It is enough to learn the ways of the English, let alone their tongue.*

"I humbly also suggest to you make yourself known to Bishop Fisher," the archbishop continued. "He is a most Godly and saintly priest. You can trust his counsel."

Catalina nodded. "Si. I have spoken to him." Catalina knelt at the archbishop's feet. "Give me your blessing before you go, my Lord bishop."

He rested his hand on her bowed head, a compassionate smile softening the hard lines of his face. "*Veni sancte spiritus, reple tuorum corda fidelium: et tui amoris in eis ignem accende,*" the bishop's voice reverberated in the room.

Kneeling, her heart heavy for Catalina, María bowed her head. Seeking distraction, she translated in her mind the archbishop's words into English: *Come, Holy Spirit, fill the hearts of the faithful and kindle in the fire of Thy love.* She raised her eyes. Catalina, her form outlined by mellow candlelight and diaphanous winter sun, remained on her knees.

"Raise up, my daughter," the archbishop commanded.

Taking his beringed hand in both of hers, Catalina raised it to her lips and kissed it. She stood, and moved away from the light as if she wished to hide her face. María saw her brush tears away. "God speed, you go with my prayers and blessings. May the good Lord keep you safe from harm. Farewell."

The two men bowed low. Backing away from her, they bowed again at the door, and shut it as they left.

María picked up her skirts and dashed over to take her friend in her arms. Catalina rested her face on her shoulder. "With every new day, another cord cut. They cut me from my mother, father; my country." She whispered, "And I weep." She laughed with bitterness. "My father would be angry with me, si?"

María massaged Catalina's tight shoulders. "You're tired. Santa María, we all are. Since our arrival, the English have rarely left you alone, let alone give you time to rest. Thank God we are going away to Ludlow Castle. The prince will give you the time you need to restore your spirits."

Breaking away, Catalina laughed and laughed. "Oh María. Do you realise how long the journey is to Ludlow?"

"Si." She grinned. "But we are used to that. Once at Ludlow, you will go to bed and stay there until I tell you otherwise. I tell you, you need rest."

Catalina shook with more laughter. "You speak like Doña Elvira! Am I to have everyone around me telling me what to do? Soon I'll be obliged to remind people whose daughter I am, and that I will be queen of England one day." She hiccupped. "Oh María, I am full of foreboding. I wish my parents had not demanded Warwick's death. My heart tells me it was wrong – and my awful dreams tell me too." She turned wide, desperate eyes to María. "Please don't ever leave me!"

María wound her arms around Catalina again "My sister, I promised to stay with you long ago. My life is with you; you must know that."

Tightening her hold on Catalina, María shut her eyes, and prayed: *God give me strength. God help us both.*

Doña, my dear Latina,

I send this letter home to you with one who soon returns to our queen's court. Many have left for home. Most carry with them gifts from England's King. My heart breaks a little every time our number diminishes. My heart breaks more to see the light in my princess's eyes dim, and her spirits dragged down, day by day. I worry for her. The prince, her husband, is worried too...

Arthur had been with Catalina since morning Mass when someone knocked on Catalina's antechamber door. María opened the door to see a young page with a parchment in his hand. "From the king," he said, "to be given to the princess." He handed the parchment to her, hurrying away. María stood for a moment, turning the folded missive one way, and then another. *This is the first time King Henry has sent my princess a private message. I hope it is happy news.* She took the message to Catalina, who read it quickly.

"The king wishes us to come to his private library," Catalina said.

Arthur's eyes shone with humour as he held his hand out to his bride. "Come. When the king, my Lord father, commands, we must obey."

Catalina sighed, looking longingly at the closed door of her bedchamber. She put her hands in both of his and Arthur pulled her to her feet.

The prince kissed her hand. "Sweetheart, I promise, you will not regret obeying my father. Doña María can come too. I know you do not like being separated from her." He reached for her other hand and kissed one hand and then the other. The good prince glowed when Catalina smiled at him.

Here is a youth struck with Cupid's arrow. I must be happy for Catalina. María tried to smile, but the prince and the princess's deepening affection for each other just reminded her of her own heartache. *Is it wrong to wish for happiness too?*

It was a question that stayed with her every step of the way to the king's chamber. When they arrived at its closed door, the prince turned aside to Catalina and smiled with merriment. As if catching his mood, Catalina beamed at him. María forced another smile, curious about what waited for Catalina in the royal chamber.

A guard opened the heavy door for them. The door closing behind her, María stepped back, confused. The prince's companions remained out in the hallway. *The prince must have arranged that before coming.*

In the centre of the large chamber, Queen Elizabeth sat on a floor cushion. The queen's hair, parted in the middle, fell in two long, thick plaits, one swinging over her lap, and the other down her back. She seemed a young maid rather than a queen and a mother six times over. Nestled beside her was Mary, her blonde, five-year-old daughter, a small replica of the queen. A pup curled up on the queen's lap, watched over by an adult whippet sitting next to Queen Elizabeth.

At last, María remembered to drop a deep curtsey. The lavender rushes crackled loudly beneath her, their smell over-whelming her with another reminder of loss. She pushed away the image of Will, and waited for Catalina's command, waiting for someone to tell her what to do. No one spoke to her. She seemed invisible to them – even to Catalina. Uncomfortable on her knees, she turned her head right and left, seeking a place to retreat. She shuffled farther away from the royal family, closer to the fire-darkened wooden panels and the nearby shadows. Her heart drubbed fast.

Queen Elizabeth bent her head, checking over the pup, uncaring that it chewed and pulled at the drawstrings of her sleeve. The whippet came around the queen and sniffed the pup. White, delicate and long-legged, the bitch licked the queen's hand before licking the pup. Her black eyes shone with a true mother's pride. Her work done, the bitch lowered her haunches, twisted around and scratched her back quarters.

King Henry rested his finely boned hand on a huge, closed tome upon the tall bookstand in front of him. His slanted blue eyes peered at his wife and daughter. Laughter lines etched deeply around his eyes and a smile tugged the corners of his mouth. All his coldness gone, he looked at his wife with tender love. He raised a hand. His ink-stained fingertips caught a beam of light, and time stood still. María saw in her mind La Latina in the sunlit courtyard of the Alhambra, telling them a story, adding flavour and weight to her words with the movement of her hands. Like the king's this morning, her fingers always showed the evidence of hours with the quill. Rubbing her wet eyes, María returned to what unfolded before her. She shook her head, unable to believe her ears when the king said, "Madam, if that pup soils my carpets, you may discover yourself in danger of my anger."

The queen looked up at her husband and grinned. "You frighten me, my Lord." She held out her long-fingered hand to him; the loosely tied murrey sleeve fell down to her elbow, revealing a shapely arm the colour of white marble. Again, the queen wore no jewellery on her fingers other than a simple gold wedding band. Her exquisite hands needed no adornment. "See how I tremble, Harry."

His eyes warm and doting, King Henry guffawed, his laughter loud and uninhibited. More bewildered than ever, María watched King Henry cross the floor to his wife. He bent and took her hand in his and cupped it against his cheek before taking the palm to his mouth to kiss it.

María shook her head. *Am I dreaming? I must be dreaming. This cannot be the same king I feared only short weeks ago at our first meeting.*

Still holding the queen's hand, the king caressed his wife's thin shoulder whilst bending down to listen attentively to their daughter. He was a man transformed, and all for the good.

Prince Arthur beamed at his parents. Releasing Catalina's hand, he strode toward them and knelt, receiving his parents' blessings, a boisterous welcome from the dog and his small sister. Shoulder to shoulder, he stood next to his father, and beckoned to his wife. Catalina picked up her skirts, padding hesitantly in his direction.

Giggling at some remark of her father, the Princess Mary glanced at Catalina. Her bright blue eyes flashed with sudden decision. She jumped up from her mother's side, rushed over to Catalina, grabbing her hand. "Come, my sister, and see my new puppy. Mama says she is the pick of Dora's litter."

Dora, hearing her name, raised her ears, and stopped scratching. She dashed back and thrust her face into the queen's lap, her lolling pink tongue licking her pup again. The queen rubbed Dora's ears, bent down, crooning softly to the bitch. Like her husband and children, the dog looked at the queen with adoring eyes.

The princess pulled Catalina over to her mother. Catalina curtseyed low. She glanced up at the queen, collapsing from her curtsey to the fresh rushes. With a bemused shake of her head, Catalina laughed. "May I please have permission to stay here on the floor with you?"

The queen tossed her head, her shoulder plait swinging over to join the other. "Fiddlesticks, child, pay no mind to me – or the king, your new father. If you wish to sit, or stand, please do so. In this place we keep different rules and remember we are a family." She held out a hand to her daughter-in-law. "I'd like you to stay close by me." She grinned cheekily at Prince Arthur and the king. "Let our husbands be our lackeys for a time."

The king raised his scanty brows, scratching the crown of his thinning hair. He glanced aside at his son. "Perhaps it would be wiser not to follow my example as a husband, my boy. Your mother often thinks I am her lackey. Even when I remind her other men beat their wives she just chuckles."

The queen tossed her head back, and laughed. The sound rang out like bells. Barking with excitement, Dora jumped, scampering all around her mistress. The queen laughed again, grabbing her dog's jewelled collar. "Sit, Dora, sit girl. Did you not hear the king? Our good lord talks of beatings."

Dora turned her long-lashed, black eyes on the queen, and wagged her short tail. Settling her rump against the queen's thigh, she sniffed and licked her pup again. The queen tilted her head to one side, beaming at her husband before proffering a hand to her son.

"If Catalina loves Arthur as much as I love you, he'll never have cause to beat her. Husband, can you not see what a good wife we have here for our son?"

The king eyed Catalina without emotion.

Lowering her head at his stern look, Catalina stared at the floor. King Henry glanced again at the queen. "If you say so, Bess."

The queen's eyes journeyed from her husband to Catalina and then back again. She tightened her full mouth, shaking her head at him. "Dear Heart, must you put up your walls of suspicion for a girl not yet sixteen? Kate is married to our son; truly, there's no danger here. She's no enemy. She's our new daughter."

The king locked his gaze on the queen, his mouth thinning to an unsmiling slash. María swallowed, her heart cold. His face seemed as shuttered as the day when she had first saw him. The queen shook her head again and sighed. She patted Dora's head, now resting on her lap next to the puppy. "Doesn't my husband know yet my instinct is like yours, Dora? We know who we can trust. Our daughter Kate is our friend."

King Henry crossed to the bookstand and stood behind it. Shifting uneasily, he sucked in his top lip before dipping his head at Catalina. "Forgive me. I do not mean to make you fearful. I am proud to call you daughter, and shall do my best to be a good father to you."

Nodding her approval, the queen smiled. She turned eyes shining with love, love embracing her husband, her son and her small daughter. She smiled again, a smile directed to Catalina. "My husband has something for you."

Prince Arthur rested a hand on his wife's shoulder. "Kate,

my lord father is famed in England for his wisdom. I asked him to find something to make you less homesick."

Merry again, the king seemed at once younger and less careworn, a kinder man no longer behind the austere barrier forming his aegis against the world. He beckoned to Catalina. "Come – see what I have here."

Catalina hesitated, biting her lower lip. The queen stood, the sleeping puppy cradled in one arm, and took Catalina's hand.

"Don't be afraid. The king and I want you happy in your new home, and family. Already we see how content you have made our son. Come and see what my lord has for you."

Catalina stood beside the queen and king behind the bookstand, and looked down at the open large tome. Her eyes widened, and a slow smile spread across her face. The king and queen exchanged a long look; the queen grinned, looping her hand through her husband's arm.

Unaware of anything but the book, Catalina stepped closer to the stand. She raised her hand to touch it, but jerked back in a kind of panic. Flustered, she glanced aside at the king. "Your Grace, I –"

The king laughed. "Rest easy, my girl, it is here for you. Go on –"

Catalina gave him a shy smile and bobbed a brief curtsey. She returned to the book, beginning to turn its thick leaves.

María straightened and craned her neck, seeing music notes on one of the pages. Her grief swelled at another reminder of home, and the years of shared lessons with Catalina learning to read music, and make it.

"Your Grace!" Catalina raised eyes lit with joy. "I have never seen anything like this in all my life. Music, my Lord King, pages and pages of it."

A smile softened the harsh lines of the king's thin face; moving closer to Catalina, he seemed a gentler man.

"This book and two more have just come from Venice. The *Harmonice Musices Odhecation,* a hundred goodly songs in three volumes." He glanced at his wife. "Already the queen has made me glad of paying the heavy cost of gold for the book by singing a dozen or so to me. Sweetheart, what say you? Could you not play your lute for us?"

The queen blushed a little before turning to give the puppy to Mary. She glided over to the window seat and picked up a lute resting there. Sitting down, she began to strum a chord. The queen looked across at her husband. "My love, why not you and I sing together that song from last night?"

Mary squealed with delight and fairly danced over to her mother to sit at her feet. Her blue eyes beseeched her father. "Oh please, my lord father. You and mother rarely sing together." The king stroked his thinning crown of hair and looked askance at Prince Arthur. "Methinks your sister has a short memory or has forgotten the song we sang to her but yesterday. What say you, my son?"

The prince gave a half bow. "My lord father, I add my voice to Mary's. We never get enough of hearing you and mother sing together."

The queen strummed another chord and her laughing eyes met the king's. He nodded, and stepped forward to the book-stand to turn the pages to close to the middle of the book. "When you're ready, sweetheart."

Her head bent to the lute, the queen plucked out a melody

of notes. She gave a signal; together a sure tenor joined with a heavenly soprano, and they sang:

Fortuna desperate iniqua maledicta che
di tal dona electa la fama ay denegata.

María shuddered – thinking about the words of this popular song. *Is fate so malicious to blacken the name of women even when we do not deserve it?* She sighed. *It seems life is designed from the beginning to defeat us, and keep us in the dark.*

10

Kings ought to marry princesses from neighbouring countries, not from faraway lands.

~ *Saxo Grammaticus in his 'Gesta Danorum', written in the thirteenth century.*

María had just pushed aside her half-eaten bowl of pottage when Prince Arthur came upon his wife early the next day. His unexpected entrance caused a fluster of panic amongst the princess's women as they ate their breakfast. María and the others all stood to curtsey, vacating the benches set either side of the long trestle table in such a hurry the wooden benches screeched in complaint against the wooden floor.

Seated alone on a small table set upon a dais where she broke her fast, Catalina, rose up, startled. "My Lord husband."

Catalina touched her uncovered hair, blushing. "Forgive me, I did not expect you so early."

Taking off his feathered, velvet bonnet with a flourish, Arthur smiled, and dipped a deep bow. "Surely I can visit my wife if I wish?"

Catalina came away from the table, curtseying low before standing near Arthur. "Pray, my husband, did you not tell me last night you were going to Eltham this morning, to bid farewell to the prince, your brother, and to your sister, the princess Margaret?"

Replacing his bonnet on his tousled hair, the prince smiled. "For certes that was my plan last night, but the queen wishes to see us. Are you done here, Kate?"

Catalina glanced at her plate. Making a wry face at what remained of her English breakfast, she nodded. Bella hurried over, bringing Catalina's favoured headgear. She carefully placed it on Catalina's head, sweeping her loose hair under its long veil. The prince held out his hand to his wife. "Anon, sweetheart."

Flocking with the other women, María hurried after Catalina, wondering what was so important for the queen to wish to see Catalina and Arthur so early in the day. The prince's attendants waited for him in the corridor outside. In quick order, the women grouped two by two with the men, following the prince and princess to the queen's compartments. At the doors, the prince gave a meaningful look to Sir Richard Pole, his chamberlain, and one of the oldest of his many attendants. María saw Catalina gesturing to her. She trailed after Catalina and the prince as they entered the queen's chambers. Once again, the queen was with her small daughter, playing on the floor with Mary's puppy. A young woman, dressed in the dark robes of a religious order, sewed silently by the light of the window. María blinked. Last night, at supper, she had seen for the first time the queen's youngest sister, Bridget, and had overheard others speak about her. Closer, María saw the girl's exquisite beauty – a beauty at odds with her black habit.

Perchance that explains the foul rumours. People little believe a beautiful woman can be chaste. Stranger, a beautiful princess who is a Bride of Christ. King Ferdinand would never have permitted it of his daughters. María remembered Catalina's sister Isabel begging her parents to be allowed to take the veil after the death of her first husband. But as the eldest daughter of Queen Isabel, she was too close to the Castilian crown, and a far too important matrimonial prize, for her desire to be granted.

At the sight of her brother, Mary bounded up with a cry of 'Arthur' and ran over to embrace him. The queen rose too, the puppy squirming in her arms. She smiled at them in welcome, and gestured to the seats near the hearth.

"Come Arthur, come my Kate. Sit with me." The queen gave the puppy to Mary. "Child – time to take Patch to his mother. She will be missing him by now."

Mary's eyes welled with tears. "Why cannot I stay with you and my brother? And I don't want to take my puppy back. I want to keep Patch with me."

Her smile gone, Queen Elizabeth cocked her head and considered her small daughter. She touched Mary's wet, flushed cheek. "What is this behaviour, child? And to weep because I wish to speak to your brother alone? Or is it for your puppy you weep? Do you see your new sister Kate weeping for her mother and father? She loves them both. The separation is a great sorrow to her. But if she weeps about it, it is not in the view of all. Ones of our station weep not for trifles."

Shamed-face, Mary lowered her head. "Forgive me, Mama."

María also bent her head. *I too am separated from those I love – from Latina, from my mother. And I cannot cry – not when I must stay strong for Catalina.*

"Good girl," the queen kissed her daughter's cheek. "Of course you are forgiven." Queen Elizabeth turned to her watching sister. "Bridget, would you mind going too?" the queen asked. "I want this time alone with Arthur and Kate before they leave for Ludlow." She wound her arm around Mary in half an embrace.

"Mary will enjoy speaking to the kennel master." The queen laughed. "I know you will like that as well, sister. I promised you a puppy to take back to the convent – why not make your pick today?"

The queen turned a smile to María. "I already know I dare not separate you from your princess. There is a basket at the side of the window-seat. Bridget and I are sewing new altar cloths for the chapel. We would both be grateful for your help."

Sewing one of her most hated pastimes, María wished she had been dismissed. She noticed Catalina's look of amusement, pursed her lips and padded slowly to the basket. Taking out a cloth with its edges yet untouched, she located a threaded needle and sat amongst the cushions in the window-seat, starting to hem as best she could.

"News has come from Eltham,' the queen said. "I know you wanted to go to visit your brother and sister, Arthur, but I must ask you to change that plan. Indeed, I will be leaving on the morrow to see Harry and Meg." The queen sighed. "Your brother and sister have been fighting again. They are locked in their chambers until I speak to them."

"Locked in their chambers?" Arthur raised an eyebrow. "Not for the first time. They fight in public, but are worst behind closed doors. Not too long ago, servants, servants mind you, had to pull them away from one another when they acted like two snarling dogs. Harry and Meg egg each other on to the great distress of their tutors, and servants. I warned them last time that if they laid a hand on each other in violence again, it would result in them being locked in their chambers. From what I gather, Harry has a cut lip and Meg is nursing a sprained wrist. I am ashamed of both of them. Alas, it means I must bid you two farewell earlier than I hoped. I must go and stay with your brother and sister until I am certain they have seen the error of their ways. My wayward children must realise that their royal blood means duty and service too." The queen smiled at her eldest son. "I have never had to tell you this lesson. You knew it from the cradle."

Arthur leaned forward and held his mother's hand. "I want you to be proud of me."

The queen took his face between her hands, her eyes brimming with emotion. "Oh, my boy, I am proud of you; I have always been proud of you." She released him, and looked at Catalina. "And now my son is married. What a king and queen you two will make for England one day. You will write once you get to Ludlow? You, my son, and –" she clasped Catalina's hand, "you, my new daughter?"

"Of course," replied Arthur, Catalina smiling beside him.

María pricked her finger, and let out a soft cry of pain, and dismay. Her blood spotted the white silk of the altar cloth. The queen and her son and daughter-in-law remained oblivious to this minor mishap. The three of them talked and laughed together.

Abandoning the altar cloth, she sat watching them. Arthur held Catalina's hand all the time they spoke to his mother. The queen glanced at their linked hands before asking Catalina a question. She talked to them as if storing up memories forever. María hid a smile. *Catalina is truly loved – not only by her husband, but by the queen.* Her moment of happiness snuffed out, as if wet fingers grasped the wick of a lit candle. Will had been gone for weeks. Gone to his wife. No one seemed to know when he would return. She told herself it was for the best. But it did not help her aching heart.

December drew to a cold close. Preparing for their journey to the Welsh Marshes at Baynard Castle, María helped Francisca oversee the packing of Catalina's clothes. Making certain they had plenty of furs for their journey, she gazed out the window at the grey skies and sighed. "I do not like us travelling in winter." She realised she had switched from English to the comfort of her own tongue. *Does it matter? Everyone at court speaks to us in French or Latin. I begin to believe I do not need English at all.*

Francisca shrugged, speaking in Castilian too. "It is not snowing. I am certain we would not be going if the English thought it was dangerous."

"Perchance they take it for granted. Have you listened to them? They speak of the weather all the time."

Folding more clothes and placing them into the open

coffers, Francisca grinned at her. "Si, you are right. I have started to think the weather possesses the same importance to the English as the second coming of Christ."

Startled by Francisca's remark, she stared at her for a moment, and then burst out laughing. "I am not certain our confessor would approve of the allegory, amiga." She sighed. "The English expect the weather to grow still colder." She laughed again. "We become like them. All our talk has been of weather. But already, these dark days leave me famished for the sun of home."

The queen still away at Eltham with her other children, María gathered with Catalina's other women, watching the king and his mother bless Catalina and Arthur before they began their journey. Strongly guarded, accompanied by a great company of lords, ladies, and knights, as befitted the heir to the throne and his wife, they started their way to the Welsh Marshes. They stopped at inns along the way to eat, and for sleep when night fell.

Travelling either on horse or English litter gave María another chance to see the famous, great forests of their new country. Trees grew thick and close together, their bare branches blocking out the thin sun of winter, making the going dark and dismal. Along the way, she saw ruins reclaimed by nature and places where young trees began to shadow the remains of broken walls. Prince Arthur pointed these out to them and told them of recent battles fought and won. "In summer, I would like us to go on pilgrimage to Saint David's in Pembroke. It is close to where the king, my father, was born – and the place he came with his men, before going to England to fight the usurper. My lord father knew the Welsh would not betray one who was also Welsh and descended from Welsh princes. He could trust them with his life." Arthur grinned over his shoulder at Sir Gruffydd. "I share his view. The grandsire of my kinsman Gruffydd not only strengthened my lord father's cause, but was the one who brought down the usurper, that evil child-killer, with his poleaxe on the battlefield."

Thoughtful, María lowered her head. *All the time we have been in England, few named the previous English king. Do they fear if they call him Richard he will live again, even in just memory?*

The day arrived when María saw a grey stone castle dominating the winter blue skyline. Perched over the Welsh Marshes, she was reminded of their first English castle in Plymouth, months ago. Whilst a far smaller castle than that one, it too seemed to grow out of the landscape, grey and ugly. Arthur trotted his horse close alongside Catalina's mare.

"There it is, sweet madam, Ludlow Castle. How does your new home look to you?"

Turning to him, Catalina's eyes warmed the winter day. "My lord, it looks well secure," she laughed a little, "if perchance not overly inviting."

María took in the busy marketplace outside the castle walls. *Not overly inviting? Si, the English can create places of great beauty, but it seems beauty comes second to withstanding weather and war.*

"That will soon change," Arthur now said. "In recent times, it has been left empty bar for a few loyal men to ensure its upkeep – and it has been little more than a worthy watchdog for my Lord Father. It is but my second sojourn here and there's still much to do. But our people make it a fit home for my bride."

Doña, my dear Latina,

We celebrate Christmas at Ludlow Castle. We arrived just in time. The winter promised by the English is here. The days are too wet and miserable for us to go outside. I feel walled in by the castle's grey stones. At times, I think Ludlow is a place of desolation. I pine for the warm hills and plains of Castile.

All day and night, María listened to the wind as it whistled and whined like a death's screech. It blew under eaves and around the castle, icy drafts pushing their way through the cracks in the stone around the windows. In these dark days, María started wondering if she would ever see sunlight again. She had never known such cold existed. Her very bones ached, no matter how many furs she wore or tossed onto Catalina's bed. The cold made her thankful she was still Catalina's bedcompanion on most nights. But it made no difference she had Catalina's body warmth beside her; no difference the fire in the large hearth burned throughout the night, or thick drapes covered the many windows.

The bitterly cold nights caused her to sleep fretfully. Some nights, she had only just managed to fall asleep when servants woke them for Prime and she had to force herself out of bed to go to another freezing morning Mass. Dressing in the low grey slants of light of yet another dismal, stillborn day, María barely felt her own fingers, all of them numbed and made clumsy by the cold.

Mass was held in the Saint Magdalene chapel, a short distance from Catalina's apartments in the North Range. María thanked God that the wall of its nave joined the wall of the castle. Whenever she stepped out to the inner bailey and faced the elements, the icy, strong winds pushed her back and she had to fight her way forward. The chill seeped through her fire- warmed clothes, goose pimpled her skin and made her eyes smart with tears.

But the easy access to the chapel meant stepping into warmth. All day long, servants kept the braziers alight to heat the enclosed space, heady incense infiltrated the air in the beautiful rotunda. Carvings of scenes from the Bible ornamented the walls of the nave and the rotunda. There were also paintings of Christ in his passion, and his mother Mary. Simply by being there lifted her spirits.

One morning, as they made their way to morning Mass, Prince Arthur paused beside Catalina, waving a hand around the chapel's small interior. "See the workmanship – don't you agree little compares with it?"

Halted behind them, María saw Catalina grin at her husband. Amber candlelight made her friend look even younger than sixteen. "Sir Gruffydd tells me the chapel's design was inspired by the Holy Sepulchre in Jerusalem?" She gazed around the rotunda. "I like it well," she said.

Arthur took her hand. "Aye – it was built by crusaders – those who had returned from the first crusade." He lowered his head. "I wish I had been older so I could have joined your noble mother's holy crusade and proved myself her valiant knight."

Catalina smiled again, touching his face. "Arthur, none are more valiant than you. You've nothing to prove."

Still holding hands, the boy and girl walked together towards the altar. Holding the skirt of her new crimson gown away from her feet, María noticed Arthur glancing in her direction. He began speaking in Latin. She stilled, and averted her face. *Does he not know I am also fluent in the language? I must ask Catalina to tell him.* Wishing to give them more privacy, she stepped away from them, letting go of her skirt. Over long, it spilled out on the stone floor all round her.

"Sometimes –" the prince had said, stopping alongside Catalina. He had reached to take her other hand, continuing to speak in Latin. "Sometimes I wish my parents named me other than Arthur."

Catalina turned. "But why?"

Arthur's eyes seemed the only vivid colour in his face – a face paler than usual. "Arthur is a name for legends – a name for heroes – a name for the bards to make songs of. Who am I, Catalina? In truth, I am but an untried youth...my father's heir," he winced, "like it, or not. My father, and mother, expect much of me. What if I prove unworthy of them, unworthy of the name they gave me?"

Arthur averted his face and coughed; a coughing fit not the first that morning. Catalina studied him with unhidden fear. "Come," Catalina said, leading him to the pew near the altar. "Look around you, people love you, Arthur, from high to low. I do too. I love this Arthur. This Arthur is all I want."

María trembled, and then clasped her hands together. *Stop comparing Catalina's husband to Prince Juan. Si – Juan too was never strong. He too carried the heavy burden of being the heir to a throne. For Juan, it had been the double burden of two thrones.*

But Arthur is alive – and Juan is dead. Fear froze her heart. She remembered Latina speaking of life repeating itself.

She began listing in her mind all she had in her medicine coffer that might help the prince: rose petals, honey, essence of lemon oil, rosemary, borage, oregano and perchance a clove of garlic and balm for the prince's melancholy. If she had anything to do with it, Arthur would make old bones, and be Catalina's husband for a long, long time.

11

Think what a scandal it is to be happy
   When you are faced with sorrow from both sides:
   You cried when you came into world
   And another will weep when you leave it.
   ~ Samuel Ibn Nagrela

Early one morning, María wandered down the great hall. She had escaped the women's chamber in search of time alone. Time away from Doña Elvira's jealous remarks, and the noise of other women. Often, their close proximity to one another destroyed her peace of mind. She swirled around to the elaborately carved doorway opening to the Great Chamber, and the raised royal dais. An oaken under-croft stretched across the high ceiling of the chamber. Since they had arrived, the prince and Catalina had spent much of their day here, playing their part in all the ceremonial and public occasions. Several times a week, they all gathered together to break their fast in the Great Hall, and Arthur and Catalina supped on the dais. The dais was also where Arthur dealt out his judgements with a confidence which belied his age.

Reaching one of the tall windows recessed into the walls, she sat on the stone ledge of its embrasure. A haze of thin sunlight filtered through thick glass windows and netted her within its fragile, silver veil. There were windows everywhere in this building. Windows with a Y tracery and trefoil lights that looked out to the inner bailey, and narrower windows on the north wall of a simpler design. Despite the light streaming in the hall, the winter sun gave little warmth. The emptiness of the hall began to oppress her; she almost regretted her decision to leave the women's company.

The wind whined to a long scream, the ill-fitting window-frame letting in the smell of farm animals. She crinkled her nose. Ludlow castle looked after most of its own needs. Pigs, cows, horses and hens were kept sheltered in the grounds of the castle. *Home – I want the smells of home.* She closed her eyes, conjuring in her mind the image of well-kept walled gardens shadowed by orange, lemon and pomegranate trees heavy with fruit, where water flowed from the mouths of stone lions into the waiting deep stone basin, and the sweet fragrance of azahar blossom drifted in a spring breeze.

Cattle lowed outside, answered by other animals. Gathering her mantle around her, she swung around on the window-seat, hugging her knees. Again, she looked around the empty hall, wondering why Arthur loved this castle when she came close to hating it. She hated how she never felt warm. She hated its dark chambers, the night wind which kept her awake and the savage winter keeping them, like the animals, confined behind the walls, caged.

In the corner of the window ledge curled a piece of silk green ribbon: a remnant of their recent Christmas celebrations. She reached for it, and held it to the light, before winding it round her fingers. *I can still be happy. I was happy on Christmas Eve.*

It had been a bitter-sweet happiness. On Christmas eve, she had sat with Francisca and Inés, listening to a Latin ballad sang by a children's choir from St Lawrence's church. The last verse repeated in her mind:

Hail, Mother of our Lord,
who brought peace back
to angels and men
when you bore Christ!
Pray your son
that he may show favour to us
and blot out our sins,
giving us help
to enjoy a blessed life
after this exile.

...after this exile... the words had stabbed her then, and stabbed her now. She was not only exiled from the home she loved, but also exiled from the man her heart desired. She stared down at her hand, realising she had pulled the ribbon too tight around her fingers. So tight, it hurt. *I lie. I only pretended happiness.*

During the twelve days of Christmas, in this very hall, they had banqueted and danced night after night. She had sought oblivion by drinking too much, and dancing to exhaustion. Only Catalina's concerned and too watchful eyes prevented her from forgetting she was María de Salinas, the kinswoman of Princess Katherine, wife to the heir to England's throne. If not for Catalina, she would have encouraged the men who spoke sweetly to her; she may have allowed them to persuade her to come out of the hall with them, alone. She lowered her head in shame. *Just because my heart is broken is no excuse to cast aside my virtue.*

Later that morning, María accompanied Catalina and her husband to the battlements. Walking a little distance from them, she stilled, eyeing the journey of a snowflake. It fluttered near her, and she held out her hand from underneath her mantle. The snowflake landed on her skin-tight sleeve, and began to melt. Cold water seeped to her skin, and caused her to shiver and tug her mantle tighter around her. She peered up at the clouds, blinking against the bright snow light. The snow light seemed far brighter than that of home. *Delight in it. Revel in England's differences. This is your home.*

This is your home.

She tried to hold on to the words, but they did not help. Wrenched and wretched, she just yearned for Castile. Another burst of snowflakes drifted down. Determined to change her mood, she popped her tongue out to catch one, unintentionally moving closer to Catalina and the prince.

Catalina laughed. "Be careful. Arthur has warned me about frozen tongues. They are not unknown in these parts."

María rolled her eyes and poked out her tongue at her in answer.

Arthur's laugh joined his wife's. "Is that another Castilian custom?" he asked, standing closer to Catalina. A deeper pink flushed Catalina's cheeks, a pink not explained away by the cold. She smiled at him and headed over to the battlements, her long mantle trailing in the snow. Snowflakes criss-crossed a pattern on the mantle's black fur. She pointed east. "If I remember right, London's somewhere in that direction."

Arthur came to stand beside her. He leant his elbow on the grey stone of the battlement, cupping his cheek on his palm. María noticed again his fine, long fingers – they were as beautiful as his mother's, the fingers of a lute player, fingers of a young man who always touched Catalina with gentleness. María squashed her rush of envy.

"Aye." He reached for Catalina's hand. "London is England's heart. One day I shall rule from there, with you beside me as my queen. But not for many, many long years, God willing."

"Si. God willing," Catalina said.

María turned a little and looked out on the mist-shrouded hills in the distance. A white landscape stretched before her. The morning light dulled and turned lugubrious. Winding cloths of fog drifted toward the castle.

"Tell me, is it true your mother holds the greater kingdom?" the prince asked.

Catalina turned a puzzled face to Arthur. "What mean you, my prince?"

"Have you forgotten to call me Arthur?"

Catalina smiled at him. "Arthur. What do you wish to know, Arthur?"

"My father told me your mother rules the more powerful kingdom. Does King Ferdinand not care Queen Isabel holds the upper hand in their two kingdoms?"

Catalina gazed away from him, leaning on the battlement. "He does at times," she replied slowly, "but my mother never forgets she's my father's wife. Mother..." Her eyes shining, Catalina bit her bottom lip before speaking. "My mother taught all her daughters the art of ruling, but first and foremost, my mother trained us to be helpmates for our husbands. I shall do my utmost to be a good wife to you, and one day a worthy consort and aid you as king, in whatever ways you desire." Catalina flushed a little. "God willing, I pray to give you many fine sons."

Arthur reddened. Before he remembered her presence, María leaned on the battlements and attended to the winterscape, pretending to focus on that alone. The prince coughed. *Dear God – he sounds unhealthier than ever.* The wind blew down to her his soft words, and that of Catalina's.

"I am stronger. Is it not time for us to have a true marriage?" Catalina reached for his hand. "I want you first well, truly well, with that worrisome cough of yours gone." Catalina smiled at him. "I vowed to your mother we would wait until September. You will be even stronger then. We are young. God willing, we will have many years together." Arthur raised her hand to his lips. "Aye. God willing.

'I was alone till cruel Love arrived.

> *I couldn't dismiss him even if I wanted:*
> *I'd first have to separate myself from my limbs'."*

He smiled at Catalina before taking her in his arms, kissing her brow, her cheeks, her mouth. The kiss became long and deep: a man's kiss, and no longer a boy's. Catalina's mantle gusted out in the strengthening wind; the twin red dragons, embroidered from shoulder to hem, seemed alive as the mantle twisted around their intertwined bodies, before the prince broke his lips away, turning his head to cough and cough.

María touched her own lips – seeing Will in her mind. *What did it feel like to be kissed with such passion?* She raised her hands to her hot cheeks, fighting down the surge of emotions, at the sudden pull and ache between her thighs. *Stop being a fool.* Muttering under her breath a curse, one she had learnt from her mother, she stamped on Will's image as if it were a fire threatening to jump out of containment. She turned tear- blurred eyes to the road leading to London, and back again to the love-locked couple, counting on her fingers the months to the prince's sixteenth birthday in September. *Only Catalina's vow to the queen prevents her from becoming a full wife to the prince. Si, a vow Catalina no longer wishes to keep.*

That night, Catalina and Arthur shared a bed again. Answering Catalina's summons the next morning, María wondered if this day would be the day when all would be at last changed. Going through the antechamber where the other women busied themselves, she entered the open door to Catalina's bedchamber, and curtseyed. Arthur was already gone.

Catalina stood by the burning fire, a servant helping her finish dressing. Half-turning, she smiled, a smile saying so much – of resignation, of acceptance, of regret. María did not need to look around at the white, barely rumpled sheets to realise Catalina and her prince had once again kept a chaste night. The final cord of her gown tied, Catalina gestured to the servant. "Thank you. You can leave me. I wish to speak to Doña de Salinas alone."

The servant curtseyed and left the chamber. María crossed to Catalina. At last, Catalina shrugged, sitting on the elaborately carved chair close to her. She waved to the stool next to it. "Pray sit, my sister." She bent her head, sighing. "Arthur's cough will not leave him alone at night, not enough to consummate our marriage." She reddened. "Something else also causes him pain, and stops him as much as his cough whenever he tries to play the man's part. He refuses to confide in me – and tell me what the matter is. But his night cough... can you think of something we can try? His cough exhausts him."

María shook her head. "I have scoured my books in my desire to help the prince, but all I can suggest are the usual remedies. I know much less than the prince's own physicians." "I disagree. Latina taught you well these past eight years." Catalina sighed again. "No matter. Winter will be over soon. Once we have blue skies again and warmer days, my husband's health will improve."

"Where is the prince?"

"He wished to break his fast with his men and deal with correspondence from the king. He plans to return to my chamber later in the day with his harp, the gift he received at New Year from Sir Gruffydd. Arthur wants to teach me more English songs. Why not put aside your books and join us? The other women will be there. It would help us learn English, and you could sing to us. I've missed you singing these many weeks." María swallowed and turned to stare sightlessly out the window. *I have sung only sad songs these past weeks. If I share those songs, it would only disturb Catalina's own happiness.* She swallowed again, confused once more at the strength of her feelings; her inability to keep them in check. *Should I tell Catalina about Will? But what use would that be? There is nothing to tell. I must forget him; I must stop being such a fool. I cannot be in love; not with a married man.*

María hurried to attend Catalina and her prince after supper. Daylight of a warmer winter day still lingered when she entered the chamber, its golden gloaming light settling over the others already there. Lady Margaret Pole, Inés, Bella, Francisca, Sir Gruffydd, and few more of the prince's closest companions, gathered in chattering groups or close to the royal couple. She averted her face from the men. *Do not think of Will. Do not think about him home with his wife. You cannot love him. You cannot love him. Dear God, help me. I must douse my desire – and make my heart stop yearning for sight of him.*

Her head pounding, María passed Inés talking animatedly to Doctor Linacre. "I'd rather read Livy than Tacitus," Inés said to the respected scholar. "I prefer the telling of legends than to dwell on the ugliness and brutality of history. Although, I wish I could read it in Greek, like you do."

María continued on to Catalina and curtseyed to her friend and the prince. "Look at this gift from my husband," Catalina said after smiling in welcome, pointing to a closed thick book placed on the lectern by the window.

Prince Arthur laughed. "A late gift – I wanted to give it to you for New Year, but it only arrived today. I did not think it must come all the way from Venice," he shrugged. "They could not find a copy worthy enough for my wife in London."

"*De institutione musica*," María said, reading the title. She grinned at Catalina. "A treasure indeed, my princess."

Catalina smiled again. "The book has caused the prince and I to speak about the belief that the stars themselves make music. It is a beautiful thought, do you not agree, that music is everywhere? We may not be aware of hearing it, but it is still there."

"Si – a beautiful sentiment," she replied.

Catalina turned to her husband and seemed to forget her. María wanted to feel joy for her friend that she was happily matched with Arthur. But it just reminded her of Will – and that he had already been matched with a wife.

She slipped away from Catalina and her prince, glancing over her shoulder at the book. She seemed to smell summer roses – and the rosewater perfume of her teacher. She slipped into memory when sunlight shone bright on a tiled courtyard and water babbled its continual song as it poured from fountains into the pool. The lace-like stone of the palace was reflected in the long expanse of water.

It was two days before she farewelled the Alhambra forever, and Latina had come to sit beside her for their final lesson.

Latina held in her hands her own copy of *De institutione musica*. As if desiring to not waste one moment of time and ensure this morning was imprinted on both of them, Latina turned the pages and read: "...music is so naturally united with us that we cannot be free from it even if we so desired." Latina had clasped her hand. "The ancients believed music and medicine should be combined. I believe it, too. Music nourishes the soul just as surely as poetry. I have treated much illness in my life. I believe the first battle is won if the mind is healthy – and music is indeed medicine for the soul. Music is too much part of us for us to ever ignore it in the treatment of those in our care." Realising Latina had chosen the art of healing for her last lesson, María had looked up at her teacher in panic. Latina tightened her grip on her hand. "Fear makes us human, María. I would rather you be fearful, than arrogant. Leave arrogance for the princess's physicians. But if the physician advises a treatment for the princess you do not think right, then you are there to ensure the princess knows of it, and what else can help her."

"I do not deserve this trust," she had said.

Latina had smiled at her and wound her arm around her shoulders. "Child – all we can do, is to do our best – and be willing to learn. I believe in you, and know you will take as your creed *'do no harm.'* Your doubts will mean you surmount the storms with sails furled with caution – a far wiser course than not. Women, I believe, have better instincts than men when it comes to matters of the body. But I want you to go to England with what I have taught you these past eight years, but also questioning it too."

Missing her teacher, she closed her eyes, fighting against sorrow. Sorrow for many causes. Someone took her arm. She looked aside at Inés's concerned face. "You are troubled?" whispered Inés close to her ear.

María tried to smile. "It is of no matter."

Inés raised her eyebrows. "I do not believe it. You have been glum for weeks." She glanced towards Catalina and Prince Arthur. "If the princess was not so enamoured of her husband she would realise something is wrong. It is more than simply homesickness. You smile with the same brittleness of this English winter, and eat so little I fear you will soon fade away." She met Inés's troubled eyes, and shrugged. "Blame it on greensickness." She looked towards Catalina. Arthur held her hand palm up in his, and caressed it slowly as if wanting to memorise every bone from finger to wrist. "Watching the prince and princess has made me envious. I too would like to be loved like that."

Before Inés had the chance to reply, Sir Gruffydd sat on the stool at the neck of a huge harp. "With permission, my prince, may I play for the princess a Welsh song composed by the famed Dafydd ap Gwilym?"

The prince smiled at his friend. "I would like that well, Gruffydd. Could you play for us the lark song?" He enclosed Catalina's hand in his and sat next to her.

Gruffydd closed his eyes, plucked the strings of the harp, singing in a rich tenor:

"Sentinel of the morning
> *light! Reveller of the spring!*
> *How sweetly, nobly wild thy flight,*
> *Thy boundless journeying:*
> *Far from thy brethren of the woods, alone,*

A hermit chorister before God's throne!

> *"Oh! wilt thou climb yon heavens for me,*
> *Yon rampart's starry height,*
> *Thou interlude of melody*
> *'Twixt darkness and the light,*
> *And seek with heav'n's first dawn upon thy crest,*
> *My lady love, the moonbeam of the west?*

María's heart broke anew. *My lady love? No man had ever called me that – yet my heart has been pieced by Cupid's arrow.* She turned away from Inés's unhidden concern. *I must rid myself of these thoughts. I must think only of my princess, and how to serve her. That is my course – my only course.*

A week later, María paused walking down the nave of the chapel, and looked out the window. Spring had finally arrived, and the snow melted and turned the world green. The light from the window seemed to wrap around her. She quickened her pace, catching up with Catalina and Prince Arthur. Her eyes adjusting to the candlelit interior, she sniffed the heady smell of incense combined with sour wine coming from the nearby altar, and fought back a sneeze.

Shortly after dawn, she had come to the chapel for time alone, and to pray for God forgiveness for her sin of loving Will. She found it impossible to pray – or to be alone. Not when two monks washed the altar clean with sour wine, others swept the floor and set up the Judas Cup and the Paschal Candle, and a group of choristers practiced their songs for the day's Maundy Service. Now those same choristers sang out their hearts to the prince and his wife.

Seated on one side of the flower-decorated chapel, fifteen youths, their feet already resting on stools, waited for the prince to wash their feet. Overseen by the prince's chaplain, servants with bowls and towels washed the right foot of each boy.

Catalina knelt at the royal pews. María knelt behind her, beside Margaret Pole. Lady Margaret had explained to them last night this English Easter custom, when one of royal blood washed on Maundy Thursday the feet of the same number of poor people their own age.

Arthur crossed himself, smiled at his wife. He strode over to his chaplain and took from him a long towel and put it around his neck before the next part of the ritual. A cushion was placed on the floor in front of the first youth, and the prince sank to his knees and took the youth's foot in his left hand. A servant approached him with a bowl, and the prince washed and dried the foot and then signed it with a cross before kissing it. Fifteen times he did this before going to a table laid out with platters of bread and salted fish. Taking up one platter, he began distributing the food to the boys. Time after time, servants would bring to the prince a fresh platter until all the youths had been given food. The prince repeated this with wine, clothes and, finally, a leather purse of coins.

Arthur returned to the royal pew and knelt beside his wife. Lowering his head in prayer, he reached for and held her hand.

María could not take her eyes away from his face – a face as white as snow.

Doña, my dear Latina,
I include a message for you to send to my mother.

María glanced at Catalina. She tossed and turned in fever, but still slept. María twisted away from the writing table, and brushed away her tears. She wished there was a direct way to write to her mother. Her mother lived far away from court, on the family estates. Her best route of getting letters to her mother was to send them via Latina.

María blinked – caught up in the memory of her last visit home. She had kneeled before her mother for her blessing, aware of the apprehension in her mother's eyes, aware of her hard face. "You walk upon a road taking you far from my care, you do not understand how far," her mother said

"Mama, I love the infanta. Please, I beg you, don't ask me to leave her. I would die," she had answered. She refused to lower her eyes from her mother's, praying, 'Dear God, let her understand.'

Her mother's eyes at last softened. "You're young, my daughter," she said, helping María to her feet. "But love is a two-edged sword. Once we have that sword, none of us can put it down." Her mother averted her face and sighed. "If you really wish to do this, go with my blessing."

María rubbed her wet eyes. She wished her mother knew how to write, but she had never learnt the skill; she had only learnt the skill to read. The circumspect letter she sent to Latina to send on to her mother was not the letter she wished to send. It said little of what she ached to say. She did not desire her mother scribing to her priest a letter of pity. A letter which would come to her in the voice of the priest, and not her mother's.

Exhausted, María began writing again. This letter would be different. She could unburden her heart to Latina.

Why did you want me to be a healer? What use is learning if it means you can do nothing which really helps? Catalina and her husband have both fallen ill. I am so full of fear, Latina. Catalina is close to death, and we hear the same of her husband...

Catalina moaned and called out "Arthur" in her sleep. María put aside finishing her letter for another time, and returned to her friend.

Catalina clung onto life. María did not care if she risked her own life, and refused to leave her for more than a few minutes. The other girls begged to relieve her so she could rest, but María only trusted Bella with Catalina. During these weeks at Ludlow, María Rojas, who had kept the name of Bella ever since that long-ago day when the women had bathed together at Lavacolla, had become one trusted by Catalina. Little able to sleep, María watched over her friend, watched her chest rise and fall, listened to her every gasp for breath. Terrified, more exhausted with every passing day, she feared Catalina would stop breathing if she left her friend's sickroom. As it was, her friend seemed to be on the threshold of one world and the next.

María cooled Catalina's forehead and wet her friend's lips, and prayed.

On the fourth day, the second day of April, Catalina gulped down a deep breath and opened her eyes. "María," she said, moving her hand to feebly clasp María's hand.

María didn't need reassurance from Don Alcaraz, the princess's physician. *Her hand is cool, thank God. The danger is over. Catalina has returned to us.* Catalina shifted her head and smiled weakly at her. She licked her lips and tried to speak. She swallowed, and tried again, "Arthur?" she croaked.

María squeezed her hand. "Remember, you both became ill."

"He is well now?"

María glanced across the bed. Don Alcaraz shrugged – a gesture that indicated he did not know the answer. She helped Catalina sit up, and brought a goblet of watered-down wine to her lips. "Pray, drink. They will tell us about your husband when they know anything. Rest, amiga. In a little while, I will send down to the kitchen for broth."

It was noon when bread soaked in chicken broth was brought up. Catalina, now wide awake, fretted over Arthur. Trying to allay her fears, María helped Catalina sit up amongst her pillows, preparing to feed her when Lady Margaret entered the room with a low curtsey. She lifted her head. Her hooded eyes seemed gored into her fleshless face, a face no longer young and etched deeply by new lines of sorrow. The physician joined her at the door. Bowing to her, he spoke a soft question. Lady Margaret shook her head, and gazed despairingly over to the princess. Catalina stared at her, the silence lengthening like a night shadow. Outside, courting birds broke into song. "No, no, no," Catalina cried out, her sudden movement overturning the bowl of soup set beside the bed. Its contents spilled and spread out over the timbered floor.

"Madam," Lady Margaret said, stepping closer to the bed. "I am so sorry."

"Oh God, dear God. Arthur cannot be dead." Catalina attempted to sit, only to fall back onto the pillows.

"His soul left us less than one hour ago, my princess."

"He cannot die," Catalina repeated. "Arthur cannot die."

María reached for her, but Catalina pushed away her hand.

Catalina looked around the room, her wild eyes returning to Lady Margaret. "You – you brought me the news. Oh God. I cannot bear this. Go. Go – I command you to go."

Paling, Lady Margaret looked at Catalina and then at María. With surprising strength, Catalina sat upright, pointing at Lady Margaret. "Why are you still here? Why are you still here tormenting me? I said go, and do not return." She burst into tears and collapsed back onto the bed.

Casting a glance of sympathy to Lady Margaret as she left the room, María turned to Catalina. She tried to comfort her, but Catalina's sorrow broke her until she wept too.

Once again, María watched over Catalina day and night when her friend suffered a relapse. But it was a different kind of relapse to that caused by fever. Catalina's young body wanted to live, in spite of her broken heart. Curled up in a tight knot in her bed, she refused to speak, refused for days to face the reality of

Arthur's death. In the long hours of silence, María returned to writing her lengthy letter to her teacher...

I have failed. I have failed my princess, my Catalina. Her husband is dead. Si, the prince is dead. We had celebrated Easter, the resurrection of Christ, but now the spring flowers adorning the chapel are being torn down. Our days are dark, my teacher, spring is forgotten. And for good reason.

Spring brought death with it. I first knew illness came to us when Sir Richard Pole told the prince and princess about the sudden deaths of English soldiers. As you had told me to do, I spoke to Doctor Linacre, the prince's tutor and one of his physicians, to discover more. He was willing to indulge my interest and answer my questions. The men were all young and strong – yet they died just days after first falling ill. Soon others became ill, Catalina and her husband amongst them.

I tried to help the prince's physicians, but they turned me away. I am only a girl of sixteen. It means nothing to them that I have learnt from a woman celebrated in my own country for her medical knowledge. I spoke those words to Linacre who first told me of this terrible illness. He told me to trust them and not to concern myself with the prince's care. Thank God, Catalina's physician knows I was schooled by you. Don Alcaraz was pleased to allow me to assist him in caring for my princess. The prince's physicians wanted to bleed Catalina to rid her of her fever. They told us to do anything other would be a death sentence. They cursed Don Alcaraz and called him a fool when he refused to bleed the princess more than the once. Told him he had ensured Catalina's death.

I believe the prince's physicians bled him out; a boy whose grip on life was too fragile for such treatment. The strong wind I feared when I first beheld Prince Arthur has blown and stolen him away from Catalina.

His cold body, embalmed and wrapped in its winding cloth, lies in state in his presence chamber at Ludlow. He will be soon taken to the Abbey of St Wulfston for burial in his waiting tomb.

Catalina is slowly recovering her lost ground. Even if Royal English protocol permitted otherwise, Catalina's health gives her no other choice but to let him go on his final journey alone. She has had no strength or heart to leave her chamber.

All I think of is my failure. I should have made the English physicians listen to me. You have taught me much, and I know by heart all the treatments for fever which should be first tried before choosing to bleed someone already close to death.

I have failed Catalina. I hear you in my mind; you would tell me it was ill fortune; the fates, and not me. But you do not hear Catalina cry. I cannot comfort her. She loved Arthur. Loved him. Now she is a sad widow of sixteen and the alliance between her parents and England lies in tatters...

María began to breathe easier by the closing days of April. Colour returned to Catalina's cheeks, and she ate the food brought before her. But she still spent her days in her chamber – either abed, asleep, or in a wide awake, dry-eyed silence, curled up in the cushioned window-seat, her mantle wrapped around her. Day by day, night by night, María stayed with her. Reminded yet again of the long days of sorrow following the death of Prince Juan, María prayed her presence gave Catalina some comfort.

Not long after breaking her fast on the final day of April, Catalina returned to her bed to sleep again. María picked up her copy of Saint Hildegard's *Of Causes and Cures* and sat near the window. Since the day she knew Catalina was on the road to recovery and out of danger, she had scoured all the books of medicine her teacher had given her. *They would have listened to me if I had more knowledge. If I knew more, I could have done more to help the prince. I could have saved the prince.* The words repeated in her mind until her head pounded and ached.

A crow cawed somewhere near. She winced at the reminder of death, and twisted around, looking out the window at the cloudless sky. She peered down at the garden. Spring spread out its invitation of delight: lush green grass, a garden edging the castle's walls bursting into colour from its countless flowers. *Delight?* María winced, and wiped at her wet eyes. *In this dreadful time, in this dreadful place, how dare I even think of delight?*

A movement of dark blue in the castle grounds caught her eye. Shifting closer to the window, she recognised the woman who strode with long-legged determination in the kitchen garden, and glanced aside at her sleeping friend. She put down her book and, careful to not make a noise, padded to the door, forgetting her mantle in her hurry to reach the garden. Since the prince's death, she had not seen Lady Margaret to speak to her. She needed to speak to her. She needed to speak to her about the princess.

Lady Margaret was still there when she arrived. Kneeling on the ground, she pulled out weeds growing too close to the herbs.

María, first meeting the woman's eyes, dropped down beside her and started to do the same. She swirled for a moment, remembering all the times she had helped her teacher weed the herb gardens of home. So many, many herb gardens – it seemed they all merged into one – bathed, like today, in the light of spring. She sunk her fingers into the rich earth, feeling for the long roots of a stubborn weed.

The older woman considered her. "Our princess must be better for you to leave her side." Spoken in French, it was a statement, not a question.

María pulled out another weed before replying in the same language. "We have missed your company, lady."

Lady Margaret stared at her. "Missed my company? Princess Katherine told me she didn't want to see me. She commanded me to get out of the room, and not return."

María sighed again. She studied Margaret's pale, pleasant face. "She was sick – and just learnt about Prince Arthur."

"That little explains why she looked at me and spoke like she hated me."

"She does not hate you, Meg. May I call you Meg?"

Lady Margaret rubbed the side of her face, leaving smudges of dirt on her white face. She shrugged, staring down at her dirty hands. "You find me on my knees today, and more caring about the obedience I owe these herbs than to my rank." She raised her head, and laughed strangely. "And what rank is that? Royal blood or not, I am but a knight's wife. I would like to be your friend; if that is your wish too, pray call me Meg, and I will call you María."

María smiled in answer. "Meg – my princess cares for you. She only spoke the way she did because of her sickness." She swallowed, studying Meg for several heartbeats. "She believes herself cursed."

Meg lifted her head, her thin brows raised in her thin, pale face. "Cursed? What do you mean, cursed?"

María slipped her fingers under her tight gable hood; it always felt tight. She wished she did not need to wear it – ever again. *If only I could yank it off my head and throw it onto the pile of weeds.* She inhaled a deep breath. "She feels cursed because of your brother."

Meg's eyes widened. Her mouth opened and shut before she got out: "Edward? Cursed because of Edward?"

María tugged at another weed. Its deep, stubborn roots threatened to unbalance her. At last, she managed to pull the weed from the ground, and looked again at Meg. "You must know why."

Meg looked away, her mouth trembling. Her fingers rubbed at her cheeks for a moment, before she lowered her hand to clasp it with the other in her lap. "I do not blame her for Edward's death. Not her." She spoke so quietly María shuffled closer to hear.

Time stayed still. She swallowed again, gazing around. Close to her, new life pushed through the earth, reaching up to the light. She wanted spring to comfort her, but, as yet, it just deepened her grief. *Why did Arthur have to die? Why did God let Arthur die?* All his promise, all his goodness, all his youth – for what? Juan's death had made no sense to her at twelve. She was years older now, but Arthur's death left her even angrier at God. When she confessed this to their priest, he scolded her and told her to pray for God's forgiveness. The priest's lack of understanding left her more aware than ever of her separation from Latina. Latina always listened without condemnation, and knew the right words to salve sorrows.

María sighed, and looked again at Meg. "You may not blame her, but Catalina blames herself. She has had nightmares about it ever since the evil news of his death came to us. Then, on our journey to England, certain things happened... She did not believe God blessed her marriage. Arthur's death proves to her she was right."

"Arthur's death proves nothing. God rest his soul, my young kinsman had never been strong. None of it is her fault," Meg said. "The blood of my brother's death is not upon her, but others."

María shrugged. "You and I know that – but that will not stop her thinking otherwise. Be not deceived. You have seen Catalina calm and rarely unbridled, but in these cruel days you have met the Catalina I sometimes know. I have been her bedcompanion since childhood. I became her bedcompanion because of her nightmares. She comes from an uneasy family. Don't misunderstand me; she is her mother's daughter. But still waters run deep. Seeing you when she learned about Prince Arthur's death just reminded her of what was done to cement this alliance. She cannot forget or forgive herself for your brother's death."

Meg stopped weeding. "Would she listen to me if I told her not to blame herself?"

"Perhaps. But not yet – she is too raw; too overcome with sorrow. Her physician judges her well enough to return to London, if it be in slow stages. Once in London, I will tell her of our conversation today and ask her to speak to you."

María returned to Catalina's chamber to find her perched on the edge of the bed. She hurried over to her, resting a hand on her arm. "Do you want to sit by the window?" she asked.

Catalina lifted huge eyes. "I must see Arthur. Doña Elvira came and told me tomorrow they will take him from the castle to his tomb at Worcester."

María sat and clasped her hand. "Dear One, all you will see is a closed coffin."

"I don't care. Take me to him, I beg you."

María chewed at her bottom lip for a moment. "I am not certain it would be wise. It is not an easy way from this chamber to the chamber where they have the prince's body. The castle's staircases may be beyond your strength."

"Pray, María, take me. We can go slow. I may never have this chance again to grieve by my husband's body."

Catalina's expression brooked no more argument. María helped her rise and dress in a warm day gown, and next her hooded mantle. Shrugging on her own mantle, she supported Catalina as they made their slow way to the prince's presence chamber. They stepped through the open doorway. At each corner of a long table, a tall candle burned bright. Light flickered on the large gold cross on the top of the large table, and danced on the gold cloth draping it. The coffin with the embalmed body of the prince lay underneath the table.

The guards around the chamber stood straight and unmoving, with shadowed faces. At sight of them, Catalina lowered her head under the hood of the mantle. Breaking away from María, she came deeper into the room and knelt at the top of the table.

María crossed the room to kneel beside her. It seemed a long time before Catalina lifted her head. "Doña Elvira says Arthur requested his heart remain at Ludlow. Do you think it may be Arthur's last message to me?" she asked softly.

María clasped Catalina's hand. "You made him happy. He would want you to know that."

Sighing, Catalina touched his coffin, leaving her hand there. "He is not the only one who will leave their heart at Ludlow." She crumbled against María. "Oh, Arthur. Arise, my Arthur, my beautiful one. Without you, it will be always winter, and the rain of my tears will never stop. The time of our singing is over, and will never be heard in this world again." She leaned her forehead on his coffin. "Oh, Arthur – how do I face a future without you? So many hopes, for you and I, and now nothing. Nothing. God, help me. Help me. I wish I had died too."

María rubbed her wet eyes. *Dear God – pray be merciful. Let us go home. Let us go home where we belong.*

12

I have loved, because our Lord:

will hear the voice of my prayer.

Because he hath inclined his ear to me:

and in my days I will call upon him.

The sorrows of death have compassed me:

and the pains of hell have found me.

I have found tribulation, and sorrow:

and I called on the name of our Lord. O Lord, deliver my
soul, merciful Lord.

~ *Psalm 116:2*

Where am I? Confused and disoriented, María awoke to a world without light. She held out a hand, thinking she was still in the enclosed litter sent to bring Catalina back to the court of Henry Tudor. Black, inside and out: black velvet, black cloth, black ribbons, Catalina wearing the black of mourning; all of them wearing the black clothes of mourning. The long journey to London was one of silence. All the way back to the English court, Catalina's women feared to say the wrong word and set Catalina weeping again.

María shook her head. Hazy memories of arriving just before the fall of night returned. *I am in bed. Back at court. But where's Catalina?* She tried to roll. Her body, heavy and aching with exhaustion, reminded her of the many hours travelling on terrible roads.

Voices murmured nearby, and someone – *Catalina?* – sobbed. María parted the bed-hangings and peeked out. Catalina knelt beside the seated Elizabeth of York, her head on the older woman's lap. Catalina wept. She wept as if her tears refused to stop. Heartsick, María let go of the bed- hangings, and pulled back into the darkness of the bed. She could still see the queen and Catalina through an opening in the bed-hangings.

"Hush, child," the queen said, stroking Catalina's loose hair. Her red-gold tresses blazed a living fire against the queen's black robes.

María brushed away her own tears. Once, another queen did exactly the same to another young, heartbroken widow. She had been a child when Catalina's eldest sister Isabel returned to her mother's court a widow. Isabel had hair the same colour as Catalina, hair the envy of many women. But not that day. She had shorn off all her long hair with her dagger. María would never forget Isabel's grief – or the jagged scabs of half-healed wounds on her scalp.

Just like she would never forget Catalina's weeks of sorrow – or her sorrow at this very moment. Pulling back deeper into the bed, she drew up her knees, hugging them to her, unable to take her eyes from her friend and England's queen.

Catalina wiped her face with the back of her hand. "I kept my promise to you, but still Arthur died."

The queen sat straighter against the high-backed chair, her gaze going to a crucifix in the nearby private altar. Flinching, she closed her eyes for a time before she spoke. "I was wrong to ask that of you. It was in God's hands. I should have left it so. I crave your forgiveness, as I pray for God's. My boy is dead. Nothing will change that." She rubbed her face. "I blame myself. I must do what I can to heal the damage this promise has done."

Catalina visibly started, her eyes flashing with anger. "How can you or anyone heal this? Arthur's dead." She swallowed hard. "He is dead. Nothing heals this loss – not now; not ever." The queen blinked. Her grief raw and tangible, it marked and aged her to heartrending fragility. María hugged her knees tighter. The queen looked a woman in torment.

Catalina seemed to think the same. She sat back for a moment, biting her bottom lip, then leaned across, wrapping her arms around the queen. "I beg your forgiveness, madam. You bore Arthur into the world and loved him well. We're both losers here. I know that." Catalina broke away, her face wet with tears. "I just wish we had had more time."

The queen touched Catalina's face. "Look at me, child." Catalina raised her eyes. "Tell me true – would you rather not have known my boy?"

Catalina leant her face against the queen's hand. "No – never that. Arthur gifted me with a season of joy and..." she took a deep breath, "and so much tenderness and love in our few months together."

The queen took Catalina's face between her hands. A slight smile touched her lips. "You had your season and I close to sixteen years. Arthur well knew how to love – it was his gift."

The queen kissed Catalina's forehead before dropping her hands to her lap. She clasped them together. "He held all our hearts as tenderly as one would hold a helpless babe. There was no malice ever in him. I give thanks to God you came to us and gave my sweet Arthur your heart. And he gave you his. All saw this. Let that give you some comfort, as it does me." The queen gestured to the chair next to her. "Sit, my daughter."

Catalina sat. María followed her gaze to the nearby crucifix. The nearly naked ivory figure of Christ sagged in his moment of death; his face no longer suffered but looked like one asleep, at peace.

"At least I can be comforted knowing that nothing can hurt him again," Catalina said slowly.

The queen turned her eyes to the figure of Christ, too. "My sweet boy hurt too easily. Too much sickness in his young life made him sensitive to the pain of others; all he wanted was to take pain away." The queen blinked and rubbed her wet eyes. "I tell myself God knew best to call my boy before he need arm himself against all comers as king – as my husband has had to do over and over in his reign. It is not easy to be a strong king." Catalina flushed, her eyes afire with fury. "Arthur would have been a strong king. He would have been a great king, the greatest and best to ever sit on England's throne."

"Child, I believed that too. But we will never know if we were right. Perhaps the way of the world might have been too hard for Arthur to surmount and still stay the Arthur we loved." She sighed. "Arthur's reign might have seen him end like my uncle Richard. That bloody road I never want to see in my life again." Flushing, Catalina tilted her head. Shadows of thought flickered over her face. "Your Grace...I know of this King Richard. How can you compare him to Arthur? Didn't he...did he not murder your two brothers?"

The queen placed her hands, palm-to-palm, close before her mouth as if in prayer. A log in the fire broke apart with a loud *pop,* and shot forth sparks, some striking close to the two silent women. But they did not seem to notice. Their eyes only stayed on the other.

At last, Elizabeth of York sighed, her gaze drifting unseeingly around her chamber. She rubbed her forehead. "I will not speak against my husband, the man who is the father of my children... God help us, how black these times make my uncle's name, when he was only a good man who succumbed to the evil that lays in wait for every king. My uncle Richard did not murder Edward and Dickon."

Catalina blinked. "Who did then?"

The queen shook her head. "I cannot speak of it to you. I cannot, for it is only guessing on my part, but I believe a good guess. All I can tell you is that my uncle Richard, though he died blaming himself, did not order my brothers to be brought to an early death. That he never wanted; it destroyed him to know he failed my brothers as a king and kinsman."

Elizabeth sat deeper in her chair. "Alack, daughter. It is a hard pilgrimage God gives us in this life – especially those in positions of power. Days as dark as these give me cause to cry out to God he asks too much, that the sorrow life gives me will make me fall into the blackness of despair. And I'll be no more. Lost forever. But then I hear a lark or blackbird sing or see a rainbow bridge its way across the horizon. My heart knows God's comfort then."

Catalina kissed the queen's hand again. "Be assured, my queen, only two women I know in this world are already worthy of heaven – my mother and you – a woman I am also proud to name mother."

Elizabeth of York bowed her head and wiped her face on the sleeve of her chemise, puffing here and there through the cords of her gown. "God bless you, child. Catalina, we must talk of your future…"

Silent, Catalina sat straighter before twisting towards the fire. Elizabeth of York clasped her hands in her lap. "I understand, a future without Arthur. It is a cross we will bear while we draw breath. Still, we are here and, like it or not, the future must be faced. We must continue to live, Catalina. As for me…" The queen shifted uneasily. "I am with child, my daughter…after Christmastide, I shall ready myself to bring forth a new babe…"

Catalina turned a face drained to a sick white. "Madam, what mean you? A babe?"

Queen Elizabeth settled back, sputtering out a grim laugh. "Pray, no need to be so shocked. I am not an ancient crone and am still yet a wife. You'll learn, my child, men and women give each other what comfort they can; in these hard days, the king and I have needed much comfort."

She looked at the fire before returning her attention to Catalina. "The king loves me greatly and wished to spare me more childbed, but we have only one son now. Meg's letters told me enough to know you kept your promise to me. I must then do my duty as England's queen. I must remind you of your duty too, my daughter...When he is of age, I want you to marry my Harry."

Catalina shook her head a little, her mouth trembling. "Marry...your son? The boy you say should never be king? Madam, I do not understand."

Elizabeth took Catalina's hands in hers, and moved closer towards her. "Daughter, there is no choice now. Listen..." She took a deep breath. "Forgive me. I know you will find this painful, but a virgin wife is no true wife. You can marry Arthur's brother with an easy conscience."

Catalina snatched her hands away. Clutching her crucifix, she stared at the queen and spoke in a rush. "How can you say that? I was Arthur's wife. I gave my heart wholly to him, if not my body. And I only did not give him my body because I feared the same as you." She bounded up. Anger flushed her cheeks and glittered her eyes. "The six nights we lay in each other's arms –" Catalina touched her lips and closed her eyes. "I counted them – each one of them. I will never forget the feel of his mouth on mine, my body aflame by the touch of his gentle hands. We kissed over and over. It seemed to never come to an end. Nor did I wish it." She looked again at the queen. "No one will ever know what it cost me, not to beg him to go on, not to beg him to pull away the blanket we kept between our bodies. But always...always – I...I could see how weak he was; it took no time at all before he became breathless when he kissed me. I feared to make him worse, and he was always relieved when I told him we should stop. He had little energy to continue. God help me, I wish I hadn't. It sickens me to know you are with child." Catalina bent her head, speaking through her tears. "It should be me feeling a child stir within me, not you. My sweet

Arthur dead while I remain alive, and cursed. I killed my only chance for his son – our son…"

Paling, the queen swallowed. "God help me – and you. All I wanted was to safeguard Arthur's life. You're justified to be angry. Nothing I can say can make it right again. All I can do is try as I have before: plant the right seeds for the future." She rested her hand on her belly. "I pray to God this child will be one of those seeds –"

Catalina glanced at the queen's flat belly with a coldness María had never witnessed from her before. "You think you can replace Arthur?"

The queen winced. "I am not that foolish. You can never replace those death takes from you. But I must think of Harry; he is the son I must aid now. I pray I make wiser decisions for him than I did with my first born."

Catalina eyed the queen, and sniffed. "This child, if you bear a son, can never be king while an older brother lives."

"Of course, daughter. But I also know the more I surround Harry with good the more hope we have to allay our fears. From the time he was a little child, I have seen much evidence of good within him. I believe Harry wants to be good. It is only he often fails." Elizabeth sighed, rubbing the side of her face where her headgear framed too tight against her cheek and left a red weal. "When he fails, he not only hurts himself but others too.

"His sister Margaret weds soon the King of Scotland and is acknowledged by all at Court as Scotland's queen." The queen shook her head. "He knows full well that being prince gives him greater right than an ordinary child. But the day when he needed to give precedence to his sister, may the good Lord have mercy on us. The temper! I wish to speak no disrespect of the dead, but his temper is evil, just like my mother's, God give her peace. My son is only a boy but so tall and strong. If you gave him a quick glance, you'd be forgiven for thinking Harry a young man already. I fear he won't be much longer without knowledge of women."

Catalina looked at the queen with wide eyes. "Why me? Why do you want me for your son?"

The queen inhaled a deep breath, sucking in her lower lip. She lifted her chin; her blue eyes glowed like sapphires set in ermine. "My Kate, because you fear God. With God's help, and with yours, I hope to see all my fears about Harry come to nought."

Catalina rubbed her eyes. "Madam, I do not want to think of another marriage. It is too soon." She stared again at the queen. "My sister Isabel said this when she lost her first husband. You know she died in childbed when she married a second time?"

The queen rested her hand on her belly. Pursing her lips together, she tilted her head to one side, as if gathering together her words with great care. "My dear, we are women. That risk shadows our lives the moment we become wives. But to bring into the world another new life – believe me, it is a risk I do willingly, for the love I bear my husband. And for the love I bear for England."

Catalina breathed quickly, raising her hands to her face. "My sister did not want it. She did it because it was her duty."

The queen nodded. "A royal duty; a duty one day you will do too. The Spanish ambassador has been to see us, Catalina. Your parents agree to you marrying Harry when the time comes."

Catalina gulped down a deep breath. "My mother and father want this – they have said so?"

The queen nodded, clasping Catalina's hand. "My child, I would never lie to you. Your parents do not desire to cut the tie between our houses. They suggest your marriage to my son when Harry is fourteen and of legal age."

Catalina leaned closer to the queen. "But why cannot I go home, and return to my mother? Forgive me, this is what I want."

The queen turned to Catalina eyes full of pity. "You are a princess, daughter."

As if she no longer could bear to look at the queen, Catalina lowered her head. Her tears spattered her robes. "Si, I do my duty."

María swallowed the lump in her throat, a lump which felt like her heart.

I do my duty.

Catalina's words throbbed in her – tore at her like pent up sobs. *I hoped to go home. I cannot go if Catalina stays.* María sighed. *I too know my duty – and do it. Like Catalina, I keep my vows.* María saw Will in her mind. *Dear God – help me.*

María slipped away to the chapel. The first days of her return had disappeared in a haze of ill slept nights and sorrowing hours from morning to night. Depressed and desperate for better days, she wanted time alone, time to think. But solitude was denied to her. Margaret Pole was already in the chapel, praying. Kneeling near her, María bowed her head. *Dear God,* she prayed, *please help my friend. Help her find her way back from this dark night. Help me to be strong. Help me cast Will out of my heart so I can serve Catalina with a single mind.*

The long months of not seeing Will had not helped her forget him. Since Prince Arthur's death, she thought of Will more, not less. Will was alive, she was alive. *What if I never find another man who makes me feel like Will does? Oh – stop being a fool. You can count the times you spoke to him on one hand. Stop thinking you love him.* She emptied her mind, listening to the chapel's choristers practising their songs. The music salving her spirits, she rose straightening the folds of her gown.

As if she had been waiting for María to move, Meg stood and greeted her. They walked out of the chapel together talking of little things, but when María moved to make her return to Catalina's chambers, Meg took her arm and spoke. "Is this a good time for me to come with you and speak to the princess? I cannot forget what you told me at Ludlow. It weighs heavily on me."

María eyed her. Meg was at least a decade older than her and Catalina. She too had lived through terrible times of grief and loss. *If I do not have the words to comfort Catalina, maybe she does.* "Come then," she said, "I am certain my princess will speak to you."

Meg's long legs and swifter stride made it difficult for María to walk beside her. She found herself almost skipping or jumping with every third step to keep up with her. They entered the antechamber, where Catalina's other women either sewed or read. Ignoring Doña Elvira's glowering look, María knocked on the door of the bedchamber, to signal to Catalina she returned. Hearing Catalina's voice answering, she opened the door and stepped inside, Meg following behind her. Catalina was still seated before the fire, staring into the flames. Less than an hour ago, she had been in the same place, in exactly the same position. But at least she lifted her head at their arrival – and smiled at seeing them. María and Meg both curtseyed, and approached Catalina. She held out a hand to Meg. "I am glad to see you. I wish to ask for your forgiveness. I spoke harshly to you when...when my husband died. I would call back the words if I could."

Meg curtseyed again, and then took her hand. "There is nothing to forgive."

"That is not true. You did not deserve to be dismissed in such a way, not a woman who has only offered me friendship and loyalty since I first arrived in London." Catalina gestured to the nearby chairs. "Pray, sit down. Both of you." She smiled a little. "María tells me she now calls you Meg. May I also have that honour?"

"Of course, Your Highness."

Catalina leaned towards Meg and began speaking. "In the privacy of my chambers, could you not call me...." Looking first at María and then at Meg, she looked both downhearted and confused. She shook her head. "It must be Kate, I suppose. It still feels strange to me."

Meg sat on a stool, and smiled. "I would be even more honoured if you allowed me to call you Catalina. It is the name your mother gave to you – and the name you have been called most of your life."

"I would like that," said Catalina, smiling slightly. "Forgive me. I do not think I have ever asked you about your children, not even when I first discovered you were a mother at...at

Ludlow. It is no excuse, but since arriving in England, I have had so much to learn. It has quite made me forgetful of my manners." "Pray, do not concern yourself. In your shoes, I would be the same. I have four sons. Henry is nine, Arthur's seven, Reginald three and Geoffrey only one."

"Four sons? God has truly blessed your marriage – and a son already nine. You must have been my age when you first became a mother."

"Yes. Sixteen." Meg met Catalina's eyes. "I was married at the same age as you, my husband eleven years the older. It is a good marriage, a very good marriage, but if God ever blesses me with a daughter I would want to match her with someone closer to her age." She touched Catalina's hand. "That is because I saw the love flower between you and Prince Arthur. Whatever happens in your life, you will always remember the sweetness of young love."

"Si." Saying nothing more in reply, Catalina turned to the fire, held out her hands to its warmth before returning them to her lap. She looked across at María. "Pray, sister, fetch my shawl. I am cold."

María settled the shawl around Catalina's shoulders, tucking it in on her sides. Her hand brushed against Catalina's; she touched it again. Catalina didn't feel cold, but clammy, as if fevered. She inwardly sighed. She wished for many things, but mostly to see Catalina healthy again. No treatment she or the physician gave to her seemed to make any difference.

"Forgive me," Meg said, "if my words opened the wound again."

Catalina shrugged. "The wound has not closed. Sometimes I wonder if it ever will."

"You're right. The wounds scored deeply by sorrow never close up. Rather, we learn to live with them, and learn to hide from the world when the wounds re-open, and weep. I was three when my mother died in childbirth, five when my father died in the tower. My brother, as you know, was executed over two years ago. Edward was twenty-four. I never forget them, just as I never forget the babies I have borne into the world to bury too soon after. But my faith saves me from despair."

"Si. I hold onto my faith like a raft. Prayer gives me comfort....and...and I find some comfort in my memories." She looked across at Meg. "Suffering, don't you think, deepens our awareness of God?"

Meg turned her face away for a moment. "It can be for some. It has for me, and for you. But for others...I have seen many broken by suffering. I would never wish for it. I fear the day will come when I will be broken by it too."

Catalina stared again at the fire. "I cannot lie; Arthur's death has broken me." She twisted towards Meg. "His death reminds me of other deaths; my brother, my sister Isabel, who was like a second mother to me; her infant son. I also think of your brother, he who they executed for my marriage to Arthur. I think of his death every day..."

Meg leaned closer to Catalina and took her hand. "Look at me," she said.

Catalina turned, her eyes like that of a whipped dog. María held her breath for a heartbeat. *God, dear God – let Meg find the right words to help Catalina.*

Meg shook her head. "My dear, Edward's death is not at your door."

Catalina rubbed her temple, her lips trembling. "How can

you say that? My parents refused to send me to England until your brother was dead."

"I heard rumour of the demands of your royal parents. Believe me, the queen, my cousin, has more influence on her husband than most surmise. If Edward had not tried to escape, he would be alive today. Elizabeth told me this herself. She would not lie to me. As for your parents' demands...." Meg shrugged. "If I remember right, you were not even three when you were promised to our noble prince, God bless his soul. Time was on your parents' side to pressure King Henry for my brother's death. But at the end, they needed this alliance as much as he. You would have been sent to England, Catalina, even if Edward still lived." She let out a sigh. "King Henry was just waiting for good enough cause to kill him. When Edward attempted to escape, he signed his own death warrant. No, Catalina, you do not have my brother's blood on your hands. The king does. Henry Tudor knows this too."

13

What is better than wisdom? Woman.
And what is better than a good woman? Nothing.
~ *Geoffrey Chaucer*

The warmth of June beckoned María out into the garden the next day. The early morning light spread out its path before her, as if wishing to lead her somewhere. Where, she did not know, or even care; she was just content to follow the trail of light as it took her farther away from the palace. She looked around at the well-kept garden, happy for once. After speaking to Meg, Catalina seemed changed for the better. So much so, she had finally left the darkness and seclusion of her bedchamber to come and sit with the other women.

Richmond palace did not possess the heart-stopping beauty shared by many of the royal residences of Castile or Aragon.

Still, it had its own beauty – a fresh beauty too. Henry VII had spent much gold readying the palace to mark the triumph of his son's marriage. Like the prince himself, the triumph was simply dust. She pushed her thoughts away, refusing to let unhappiness stalk her present mood.

She rounded a corner, planning to go to the herb garden, but stopped. Will stood a little distance away, turned towards her. *So – this is where the light was leading me. Why am I not surprised?* She swallowed again, and made herself to move forward. Closer to him, she gave a brief curtsey. "My lord."

He stepped closer and smiled. "We permitted each other our first names when we last met."

How long ago that now seemed. She looked at him, her heart hurting, aware time apart had not altered her feelings, rather deepened them. Dizzy, she searched for somewhere to sit. A bench close by, she hurried over before her legs gave up on her. *Don't be a fool. He is married.*

Will approached her. His blond hair shone in the light, and he gazed at her in a way making her thankful she had found this seat. "May I sit beside you?" he asked.

She nodded, unable to say one word.

He sat too close for her comfort and heaved a sigh. "Life plays on us evil games," Will said. "I thought stories of love just that. I never believed in the arrows of Eros. Then you came into my life. I married at fifteen, to the girl chosen by my father, a girl I liked. I thought my liking close enough to love and was content. But now? Now when I close my eyes at night, all I see is you. All I want is you. I no longer desire my wife because she is not you. Aye – I was content; now no more."

She looked down into her lap. The silence grew between

them, moment by moment, linking them in mutual heartache. She sighed. "What do we do?"

Will took her hand, and dropped it as it burnt him. "I want to take you in my arms, but I dare not...I cannot trust myself"

She met his distressed eyes. "What do we do?"

He hunched his shoulders and lowered his head. "I do not know."

She did not know too. All she knew was a silence fell upon them again – an awful silence speaking of an unwinnable situation.

Will stirred at last. "If you were not highborn, I would beg you to be my mistress. But that lacks honour, and truth. I do not want to soil the love I bear you. I would marry you, if I could. But that cannot be. When I heard the Princess of Wales had returned, my heart leapt with joy. I wanted to see you again – to hear your voice, to speak to you. I thought at first it was best to avoid you, but I kept on thinking of Prince Arthur. Life is short, María. When I saw you walking towards me, I realised it would be a kind of death to never see you again. If we cannot be married or lovers, do you think we can console ourselves with friendship? It is little, I know, but better than nothing."

She risked holding his hand for a moment. She smiled at him, but turned from him her tears. "Friendship is more than nothing. In truth, that is all I give you too. I promised to stay with my princess while she needs me."

But she realised her promise to Catalina would crumble at his word, his touch. All she wanted at this moment was to feel his mouth on hers. To give into this torrent of desire sweeping her away from shore, filling every part of her with the ache of yearning. *Honour?* She trembled; she had no honour when it came to him.

Early the next morning, María met with Will in the garden, while Catalina met with her ambassador. The day before, Will had told her he would be returning home for a month by the end of the week, and they arranged to meet in the garden each day after Prime, making good use of their brief time together.

María found Will sitting on a bench with a lute beside him. She sat next to the lute and touched it. "Are you going to play it?" she asked with a smile.

"Before I returned to my estates last Christmas, I heard you sing in the princess's chambers. Since then, I have dreamt of playing my lute for you, and us singing together. Pray, grant me my desire for us to teach each other songs – songs from your homeland, and songs from mine." Taking hold of his lute, he stood and held out a hand to her. "Shall we find a more secluded place than this – somewhere we can be assured of greater privacy?

María laughed, and let him help her rise from the bench. "So, you sing too?"

"I sing too."

She considered him for a moment. "I beg you to sing the songs of your homeland in English. I need to learn English quickly."

Will grinned and squeezed her hand before releasing it. "I would never sing the songs of my country in any other language."

They walked for a while, away from the palace and deeper into the garden. At last, they sat together on the thick grass, under the shade of an ancient oak tree. Will played his lute as they sang songs they both knew. They laughed together, getting their voices in perfect harmony. Sometimes, her heart ready to burst with happiness, María remained silent and listened to his voice, pitched to hit every note with emotion and soul. Too soon, María heard the distant ringing of the church bell. Affright, she rose to her knees, twisting towards the palace. "I must go," she said.

"Wait awhile." Will rested a hand on her arm. "I want to tell you more about my life before we meet again…if you wish for us to meet again."

María sat back on her hunches and tried to smile at him. "I wish I did not wish it. Or desire it." She swallowed down her sense of panic. "Do you think we are strong enough to be just friends?"

Will met her eyes, and put down his lute. He clasped her hand briefly. "Aye – it will be hard for us, but this is what we must do – if we wish to meet again. For ourselves – and the others we love. María – I do love my wife. Not like you, beloved, but I have known Mary all my life. We're cousins – and neighbours. I always knew Mary would one day be my wife. We were married on my sixteenth birthday – four years ago. I thought I was content – but then I met you, and discover myself a selfish man. I want you in my life. I need you in my life. I do not want to give you up. But I do not want to hurt Mary too. My heart may be unfaithful, but not my body. Not if I can help it. Friendship between us two must be enough."

That night, María told Catalina about Will. Catalina stayed silent for a long time. At last, she sighed. "I should forbid you to see him again, but I cannot do it. Not when I see your heart shining in your eyes." She reached out and took her hand. "You must promise me one thing."

Ashamed, she could barely meet Catalina's eyes. "What's that?"

"No matter what, you must stay only friends with him. Doña Elvira will inform my mother if she ever suspects you have given yourself without marriage, and you will be sent home in disgrace. I could not bear that."

Squeezing Catalina's hand tighter, she leaned closer. "I will not disgrace you, or my family. In any case, I could not marry him even if he was free. You need me with you."

María lowered her head, again aware her long ago promise to Catalina was under threat. All that kept her falling into an abyss of unfettered desire was her terror of losing the good opinion of Will, Catalina, her family. She no longer knew herself, or what she was capable of.

Turning from Catalina's unhidden concern, she bit her bottom lip. *Catalina is my lodestar.* She closed her eyes for a moment. *She has always been my lodestar.* But it was Will she kept seeing in her mind.

Rain trickled down the chimney. Sparks crackled, bursting like tiny shooting stars. María scampered back from the fire, but not in time to prevent some of the sparks from scorching the skirt of her gown. Acrid smoke from the burning sea coal blew out from the hearth. Coughing, her hands already chilled again, she examined the cluster of tiny black spots on her gown. She shook her head with weariness. How the nearness of the fire mimicked the rhyme and metre of her days in England. One moment she was too hot, the next knifed by cold.

Catalina – cocooned in furs – reclined in the room's stone window seat, half twisting to peer out the thick, greenish glass of the window. The light cast a strange jaundice colour upon her face, but failed to lift the gauze of shadow from her slender form. Catalina planted her hand on a diamond pane, her short fingers spread out like a star. Her hand slid downwards, and she let out a sigh.

"Lo, fate buffers us like a gale force wind buffers a lone ship upon the sea." She seemed to speak only to herself, but then turned to María. "Today's the first of September – Arthur's sixteenth birthday. The day my vow ended...I would have been Arthur's true wife today..."

Placing her book on the nearby stool, María joined her at the window-seat, sitting at the other side. She contemplated the rain-drenched garden, distorted by the convex of the thick glass. The voice of the wind whined strong and furious, bending trees in its unceasing journey.

María shivered at the freezing draughts allowed in by the cracks between wooden window-frame and undressed stone. She flexed cold, stiff fingers, rubbing her hands. "You'd think it's the first day of winter rather than autumn."

A gentle smile touched Catalina's lips. Sorrow and days of sickness left hollows in her cheeks and purple shadows under her eyes. She seemed older than just sixteen. *Si, suffering made her so.* Yet, she still could laugh, like she did this moment. "María, you complain of the English weather overmuch." Disquiet puckered her brow, and clouded in her eyes. "You don't want to go home, do you?"

María reached for her curled-up hand, resting upon black furs. She held it, and shook her head. "My home is with you. Always."

Catalina's chapped mouth trembled, and her hand tightened its grip. "You need not walk this road with me. You can go home, if that's what you want."

María met Catalina's eyes; her friend spoke the truth. She glanced back at the garden. Driving rain showed no sign of relenting; it pierced the earth like myriad silver daggers, pounding the garden into drenched submission. She slowly spoke. "Prima hermana – long, long ago, by our own blood, we bound ourselves to one another."

Where were we then? I cannot remember. But she did remember the child Catalina holding up her right hand, a needle gripped between two fingers, her stance reminiscent of her noble mother. Called Princess of Wales from her earliest years and a royal daughter twice over, Catalina, from childhood, wore her mantle of royalty to every inch of her being. "Let's swear to be together even unto death," her princess had said.

"God willing, I swear this."

Without thinking, the child María had echoed the words she often heard her parents say. She never suspected where those words would lead her. That long-ago morning, she only felt curious why Catalina held up her needle – and then bewildered at Catalina's serious look. Her friend's eyes bore down on her until she could no longer concentrate on her sewing until her stitches no longer resembled a rose but became a mess of threads. She had tossed aside her embroidery hoop and met her friend's eyes. "What is it?"

"Let's make a vow," Catalina had said, "let's swear to be friends and sisters, truly sisters, forever. I know a way. We will prick fingers, the finger with the vein going straight to our hearts, and join them together."

The reflected candlelight flickered across the diamond pane window and broke into her memories. She grinned at her distorted reflection, and rubbed her finger. It throbbed as if pierced by the needle once more. She returned her gaze to Catalina. "How can I leave you? You are my sister; my other half. Separated from you, I am cast adrift and lost. I'll will never leave you, not while life lasts."

Catalina lowered her head.

María shook her friend's hand to get her attention. "I want to be here when you become England's queen."

But I will not be Arthur's queen." Catalina squared her chin and shrugged. "If the winds of fate ever blow me to that harbour."

María rubbed her temple. One thought came to mind. "Prince Arthur would want you to help his brother," she said quietly.

Catalina's eyes rested on her. "Yes – you are right. Arthur would wish this of me. He would want me to be England's queen – even if it means marrying his brother."

14

O! ye that put your trust and confidence
    In worldly joy and frail prosperity,
    That so live here as ye should never hence,
    Remember death and look here upon me;
    Ensample I think there may no better be.
    Yourself wot well that in this realm was I
    Your queen but late, and lo now here I lie.
    ~ Thomas More

Heavy of heart, María returned from the chapel to the royal apartments. Somewhere near, a child wept. She turned into the corridor leading to Catalina's chamber, and the sound of sorrow surmounted the crackle of rushes underfoot. Prince Henry wept outside his father's chamber, its guard doing his best not to look the prince's way. Face and hands against the wall, the boy hid his tears, but he could not hide the way his body shook, or silence his sobs.

Fighting her own tears, María trod wearily on to Catalina's chamber, pulling the mantle made by her mother tighter around her body, yearning that the mantle was her mother's arms. Longing for her mother, she kept walking, but every step seemed to take her deeper into unassailable despair. She turned another corner taking her to the long gallery, confronted by more grief. On a wooden bench, blind to all else, a man sat with his hands clasped in his lap. Eyes red-brimmed, his face was white, and despairing. Leaning his shoulder on the wall near him, a young, dark haired man rubbed his wet eyes, his face consumed with grief. María remembered meeting him once at Richmond– not long after Catalina wed Prince Arthur. *Si, Thomas More. That is his name.*

The news had spread like wildfire throughout the court: Queen Elizabeth dead. The good Queen dead. England's most virtuous and gracious Queen dead. Dead. Dead. Dead. She hated the word, more than hated it, and all it brought with it.

The queen died in the early hours of the morning, on the eleventh day of February, the very day marking her own birth thirty-seven years ago, nine days after being brought to bed of a girl-child on Candlemas day. They christened the king's new daughter Katherine. The queen had wished to honour her daughter-in-law and show her love of Catalina to the court.

María entered Catalina's chambers, passing the other women knotted in grief. Afraid of bursting into tears if she spoke to them, she dashed over to Catalina's bedchamber and knocked. "I'm back," she said. Hearing Catalina's reply to enter, she opened the door and stepped into the room, shutting the door behind her. She closed her eyes for a moment, her head pounding.

Her back towards her, Catalina sat at the table, with a half- written parchment on her portable, slanted writing desk. "Any news about my small namesake?" she asked, twisting around. Catalina's light blue eyes seemed huge in her white face.

Maria fought the smart of tears again and stepped deeper into the room. "I spoke to the queen's midwife. Alice is beside herself." She reached the table and gripped its edge, aware of the heat radiating from the fire burning in the hearth behind her. "The child is weak. The little princess seems likely to follow the mother."

Catalina winced and crossed herself. "Pray God that willnot happen. She wanted this baby so much." Tears rolled down her cheeks. "I have lost another whom I loved, and the only person with any true power to help me in England." She lowered her head and began to cry, her sobs competing with the savage storm lashing the chamber's windows.

Feeling too sad to offer Catalina any comfort, María rubbed her wet eyes and sank to the floor, bowing her head over her knees. Catalina collapsed beside her, and clasped her hand. The wind blew down the chimney and drove the smoke back into the chamber. Despite the lit candles and fire, the room seemed darker and colder. María leaned her head on Catalina's shoulder, and sat with her in silence.

The midwife was proved right. The little princess soon gave up her weak hold on life, going the way of her mother. In the cold and merciless winter, María gathered with Catalina and her other women to watch the pomp of the queen's funeral. On the bier in the abbey, they placed the baby in her mother's arms before they entombed them both.

Walking down the aisle to the abbey's doors, María pulled her mantle closer around her body. All around her, the court sorrowed for the loss of its queen. She closed her eyes for a moment, listening to the chanting of monks. Her heart a lump in her throat, she just wanted to weep and weep. Outside the abbey, crowds of people, crowds of people huddled together – their faces scored with grief. Ignoring the freezing day, she stilled. Sorrow swelled from hundreds of people like a tidal wave striking at rocks. Sorrow tore her heart into pieces. *Dear God – you ask too much of me. Catalina's grief asks too much of me. Dear God, I am but sixteen. I beg you, I need Will. Pray him defy winter and this terrible weather, and return to me. I need him. I need him now.*

May 1503, Richmond

Doña, my dear Latina,

Forgive my tardiness in replying to your recent letters. What can I say – other than the sad days continue.

King Henry's sorrow has changed him, and not for the better. His wife's death leaves behind a shell of a man; a man whose walls remain up more often than not. The only ones with any power to return him to that kinder man I once witnessed when we first arrived at court are his children and his mother. Since the queen died, we all inhabit a dark night at court with no promise of dawn.

I try to lift my princess's spirits by encouraging her to take an interest in the news shared by Doctor de Puebla about Princess

Margaret's coming marriage to the King of Scots. King Henry's eldest daughter left for Scotland at the end of June, taking with her many new gowns and robes, and jewellery befitting her new status. Her marriage preparations reminded me of when Queen Isabel did the same for her daughter. How long ago that now seems.

Our princess and her household remain at Richmond, but Puebla keeps us well informed of Margaret's journey. He tells us the young princess spent a week with her father and grandmother in Colyweston before they blessed her and placed her in the care of two English lords: the Earl of Surrey, and the Earl of Northumberland. They will escort her to Scotland, where the King of Scots waits to receive his young bride.

A sharp rap at the door was followed by it swinging open. Princess Mary slipped into Catalina's bedchamber leading two leashed whippets. Putting down her quill, María rose and curtseyed. Also at her writing desk, Catalina smiled in welcome to her sister-in-law.

Through the open doorway, a rattled Doña Elvira looked ready to scream. María closed the door as she pushed down a bubble of laughter. Doña Elvira did not know what to do with a child princess who had had taken to visiting her sister-in-law without warning, and without formality in her father's absence. The king had accompanied his daughter Margaret on part of her journey to Scotland. If it was not for the girl's rank, and the fact her father adored her, Doña Elvira would likely refuse her admittance.

"You promised you would come and walk with me and

Patch and Dora today. Did you forget? I waited and waited for you."

Rubbing the side of her face, Catalina glanced down at her half-written letter. "Forgive me, child – I forgot the time, that is all." She looked again at the letter. "I always do when I start writing."

Mary came over to Catalina. She untangled the leashes of the two dogs and got them to sit. "Is the letter important? Would you like to make another time to walk with me?"

"It is important," Catalina rose and stood away from the table. "But it can also wait for later."

"I do not wish to take you from important matters. Mother...mother always told me we had to attend to important matters before we dallied in more pleasurable activities."

Catalina's eyes briefly met Maria's. For months, any mention of her mother would have the girl in tears. Catalina had spent long hours comforting the princess. She was one of the few who could. "For the queen, your mother, duty, and the welfare of England, directed her life." Catalina bent down and patted both Patch and Dora. Sad eyed Dora had regained all the weight she had lost in her months of pining for the queen. For weeks after the queen's death, they thought the dog would die as well. "I remember her example always."

Mary swallowed. "I do too."

Returning to her writing desk, Catalina studied the letter again. "I will finish writing this after I return from our walk. Time outdoors will do me good – and help me work out what I must say in my letter." She grinned at Mary. "I write on behalf of one of my women. Did you know Bella has given her heart to the young heir of the Earl of Derby? I am delighted in the match, and so is the Earl. Rightly so. My kinswoman is the only living child of her parents, and will one day inherit great wealth. I write to her parents asking their permission for Bella to wed. Bella is very dear to me. If her parents grant this permission, then her marriage to an English lord means Bella will remain in England with me."

For the past year or so, Bella shared with María the position of the princess's bedcompanion. It was not something María begrudged, not while Catalina still called her *sister*. She was also grateful to have more of her nights alone since her involvement with Will. At times, Catalina caused her pain when she told her bluntly she should stay away from Will when he was at court. It did not help she knew this too – but he was the one person in her world who asked of her nothing more than she was content to give and gave her the support she craved.

The child Mary glanced around the room distractedly, holding out her hand for Dora to lick. "Did you hear my Lord Father will be returning soon?"

Catalina picked up her mantle and looked up in surprise. "No – I have not heard that. When will we make ready to welcome your father, the king, back to Richmond?"

"I hear in about three days."

Tossing her mantle over her shoulders, Catalina smiled at Mary. "For your sake, I am glad he is returning soon." She looked at the dogs. "Am I to take Patch's leash again?"

Mary handed over the leash for her dog. "Yes. Dora still refuses to go with anybody but me." Frowning, she glanced at Catalina. "Are you not looking forward to my father's return?" Taking Mary's hand, Catalina did not answer but began heading towards the door, Patch and Dora following close behind.

"Come Patch," Catalina called, tugging at the leash. "Time for us to go to the garden." She grinned at María. "Return to writing your letter, or your book, if you like."

Deciding her letter could wait for later too, María sat on the stool and opened her book. Mary's unanswered question hung in the air of the empty chamber. She stared unseeingly at the words on the page, remembering Catalina talking to her the day before. "He told me he would be a good father to me. Why does he treat me then with indifference? I do not know if he means for me to marry his son. And if he does not – then why must I stay in England?"

María swallowed. *And if Catalina returned home, I would go too. I would never see Will again. Could I bear that? Dear God, how could I bear that?*

June 28th, 1503

Doña, my dear Latina,

Today, I accompany the princess from Durham House to the London home of the Archbishop of Salisbury for my princess's betrothal to Prince Henry. The young prince also celebrates his twelfth birthday on this day.

A promised bride once more, Princess Catalina no longer wears the colour of mourning....

María entered Catalina's chambers, holding her vihuela, dreamily thinking of the garden she had just left. She touched her lips, still feeling Will's chaste kiss. *Chaste kiss? Not quite. No, not quite.* Every morning, when he was at court, she spent an hour with Will, making music with him. It was a time she treasured. Playing their instruments together and practicing new songs provided them with an intimacy otherwise missing in their thwarted love affair.

Deep in the antechamber, by the window, Bella and Francisca sat close together, sewing, and talking softly. She wondered if Bella was again talking about her marriage hopes. Thinking about Bella's good fortune, trying to push down her envy, distracted María for a moment.

The two women paid no mind to María until she stood near them. Startled, they both raised eyes glittering with what seemed guilt. Resting her vihuela against the wall, María cocked her head, considering them. "What are you two chattering about?"

Bella caught Francisca's eyes. She shrugged, gazing back at María. "The dispensation for Princess Catalina's betrothal to the young prince. Is it true it says the marriage between the princess and Prince Arthur was consummated, when we know differently?"

Taken aback, she stared at one girl, and then the other. She picked up her vihuela and sat beside them. "Where did you hear this?"

"A servant of Doctor de Puebla told me," Francisca answered. She sighed, thinking, once more, Francisca allowed her tongue too much freedom. Like all of them, she had long, empty days to fill with some kind of occupation. Francisca amused herself by talking to servants, anyone new coming to see Catalina, anyone happy to talk to her. "Princess Catalina told me the wording." She shrugged. "It protects the princess. Her royal parents wished to ensure there will be never any question about the legitimacy of Princess Catalina's new marriage, therefore, the legitimacy of her children. The wording of the document safeguards the future. The king and queen do not doubt our princess's virginity – not with Doña Elvira telling them what she did."

For months, the question of Princess Catalina's virginity had been a thorn in the side of Dr Puebla and his negotiations for a new royal marriage. A constant stream of probing letters from Catalina's parents had resulted in a major falling out in the household of the princess. Bishop Geraldini, Catalina's confessor and tutor, had written to one of his friends, hinting the relationship of Catalina and Arthur had been closer than others told. The letter had been intercepted by one of the spies – God knew who – of Queen Isabel and King Ferdinand. Catalina's parents had been furious with him. Likewise, Catalina too. She had wept with the knowledge of her confessor's betrayal. "I told him I loved Arthur," she had said to María. "I told him of my desire, and how, if Arthur had been stronger, I would have gladly given him my body. I asked him if I sinned by always remembering my brother's death, and keeping my promise to the queen. It seemed wisest to wait until Arthur was stronger. I hoped and prayed that by September he would no longer be ill. All I wanted was for Arthur to be well, and no longer in pain. I see my confessor believed I lied about my nights with Arthur. He must think my confessed love for Arthur means I am no longer a virgin."

Catalina was relieved when her parents dismissed her confessor from her household and summoned him back to Castile. She no longer trusted the man, and never wished to see him again.

Francisca giggled. "As Doña Elvira so aptly remarked, the princess is exactly as she was when she left her mother in Castile. None of us – not even the princess's servant and namesake, ever saw any sign of blood on the princess's sheets on those few nights she shared a bed with the prince. The boy was a weak boy, and already claimed by death."

María sighed and held her instrument closer, wishing it could have been otherwise. There was no doubt in her mind; Catalina could have been happy in her marriage with Prince Arthur. "We can be thankful those rumours about King Henry came to nothing," she murmured.

Bella visibly shivered. "Such evil rumours. Imagine the king wishing to marry his daughter-in-law. Our princess wept for hours when Francisca told her what she had heard from Dr Pueblo's servant."

"There must have been some truth to it," said Francisca. "It was not long afterwards Queen Isabel wrote to Princess Catalina to make ready to come home."

Bella let out a deep sigh. "She was so happy to receive that letter, but only a week later Queen Isabel sent her another to say she would stay in England to marry Prince Henry when he reached fourteen years."

María leaned back, remembering the day that letter arrived.

"It is my duty to obey my parents," Catalina had said, repeating the lesson she had learnt from early childhood.

Her friend's obvious sorrow, and disappointment caught her own heart. María had rushed over to her, embraced her, and murmured words of comfort. Besides listening, it was all she could do.

Catalina had propped against her, her body shaking. "My

marriage to Prince Henry is an important alliance and will strengthen my parents' hands against the French." She released a shuddering breath. "Oh, María. I want to go home."

María had held her friend for a long time, wondering if she betrayed Catalina by no longer wanting the same. If she returned home, she would never see Will again.

She pushed away her thoughts, taking up her vihuela. Plucking its strings, she found herself singing a song from home, a song of duty, and its cost.

Tresses, my tresses,
The king has sent for them,
Mother, what shall I do?
Daughter, give them to the king.
Ringlets, my ringlets,
The king has sent for them,
Mother, what shall I do?
Daughter, give them to the king.

The carved settle and other gifts arrived at the same time as the messenger from Castile. The bench, a gift sent from Catalina's parents on her betrothal to Prince Henry, had already been unpacked and left in her chambers for her inspection. Large scallop shells and figures depicting Catalina and her mother, a bearded guard on either side of them, decorated the top of the bench. Elaborately carved in the Moorish style, it was a reminder of another place; another time.

The messenger from King Ferdinand had followed a

different route to the one chosen for the gifts. White with exhaustion, and emotion, the messenger knelt before Catalina, holding out the letter to her, seemingly unable to speak. Catalina took the letter from him, read for a moment and let out a terrible cry. Dropping the letter to the floor, Catalina pulled out her meat dagger from the pocket of her gown and slashed at the settle.

María rushed over, and held Catalina tightly in her arms. "What is it?" she asked.

The dagger fell from Catalina's hand – and hit the floor with a loud thud. Catalina fell weeping to her knees, dragging María with her.

"Catalina? Tell me, please."

Catalina leaned against her as if she no longer had the strength to rise. "My mother is dead. She is dead."

15

Every heart sings a song, incomplete, until another heart whispers back. Those who wish to sing always find a song. At the touch of a lover, everyone becomes a poet.

~ *Plato*

December, 1504

Latina, my dear teacher,

I thank you for your recent letter. When I gave it to the princess, as you asked of me, she was comforted to know her mother had you by her side in the days leading up to her death.

Latina, I write to you for advice about my princess's fevers. She has been stricken with them since the death of the prince, her husband. She became worse when news came about the death of the queen. For nights I have listened to her teeth rattle as she tosses and turns. I hear you tell me that is only expected, and that her fevers are a consequence of these times of sorrow. But I write to you in hope you may advise me of something I can give to help her.

No doubt you know of the new treaty for Catalina's marriage to Prince Arthur's brother, Prince Henry. The new treaty does not favour my princess. Si – the Pope's dispensation protects her; the question of the consummation of her marriage to Arthur is of little consequence, but this treaty allows her no income.

King Henry treats my princess shamefully. Since her mother's death, little money has been given to maintain her household. As for new clothes – she has had to make do for months. Her very existence is at the king's mercy.

No wonder she becomes ill.

<hr>

Back at Richmond Palace after a stay at Durham House, María padded down the path to the herb garden. She shifted the weight of the empty wicker basket onto the crook of her arm, and headed straight to the tall, flowering stalks of Valerian. Placing the basket down on the ground beside her, she touched the delicate lace of the white petals. She knelt on the ground, pulling at the stalks close to the earth, yanking out the roots. With her dagger, she cut them away from the plant before placing them and some of the cut-up stalks in the basket. She searched the garden. *What else do I need?* Her supply of Valerian at an end, thanks to Catalina's struggles to sleep at night, she thought of all the other herbal remedies in need of replenishing.

Contentment stirred in her heart, the morning stretching out before her in promise of usefulness rather than the too often tedium and boredom marking her long days.

The garden was quiet, awash with the light of dawn. She laid the dagger on the grass and rested her hands on her lap, listening to the chirping of birds and the breath of wind. It was so quiet she could hear wind rustling the leaves in the nearby trees. A lark sang its spring song. From a distance, dogs barked and cattle lowed, calling to one another.

Light, quick footfalls sounded in the garden, coming closer. Annoyed to have this time of peace disturbed, she turned; Prince Harry walked down the same path she had followed only a short time ago. His determined stride and eyes directed towards her made it clear where he was heading. The boy grinned.

She bounded up and curtseyed. "Your Highness."

Not yet fourteen, he towered over her. His face was clean shaven, his skin pink and glowing, flushed a little with exertion. Despite his height and broad shoulders, his face seemed pretty rather than handsome. He glanced down at the basket between them, and looked at her again. "I've heard Princess Katherine call you María?" His voice was high, but pleasant on the ear, like that of a young singer.

"Yes, Your Highness. María de Salinas, her kinswoman." *By all the saints in Heaven, I have lived in England over three years and this is the first time he has ever acknowledged me.*

He reached down, picked up one of the Valerian stalks and brought it to his nose. His face screwed up in surprise. "What do you do with this? It is...unpleasant."

She smiled. "Only when you are too close to it. From a distance, I think the flowers of the Valerian plant smell sweet –

like cherries. But the flowers are of little use to me. It is the leaves, and the roots I am after today."

"But – what for?"

She looked at him, surprised. "Surely, my prince, you cannot be interested in herbal medicine?"

The young prince grinned. "Why not?" He studied her for a moment. "My cousin Lady Margaret told my mother you are learned in such things. Would you teach me?"

She blinked, more surprised than ever. "Teach you, my Lord Prince? I would not presume to teach one of your station."

The youth frowned, tossing the Valerian stalk back into the basket. "If I wish you to teach me, then so be it. Too many presume to know what is in my best interests. I can do what I want–" He looked uneasily around the garden before returning his eyes to María.

"How does the princess? I grieved for her at the news of her mother's death."

She sighed. "We've all grieved for her – and for ourselves. Queen Isabel was greatly loved." She gestured to the basket. "The Valerian is for my princess. She has not slept well since the news came." She risked speaking bluntly to the prince. "We wonder at your father's silence. All the princess has heard in recent days comes from our ambassador. He told our princess the king complains again about her unpaid dowry. The princess has such little money she cannot even pay her servants."

The prince jerked his head, his small bud of a mouth shutting tightly. He sniffed and narrowed his eyes. "You speak against my father, the king?"

She cursed herself. "Forgive me – I did not mean to offend you, Your Highness..."

The prince averted his face, lifting his chin. "I must be away." He looked at her again and offered a slight smile. "Will you be in the garden again tomorrow? I spoke true when I told you I want to learn the uses of herbs. It is of an interest to me."

"If this is truly your desire, Your Highness, I can come again tomorrow. What hour would you like me to be here?"

Once again, the prince looked uneasily around the garden. "Shortly after dawn is good. The king, my father, is busy by then. I think he will not notice if my return from chapel is overlong…"

She studied the youth. *How strange. He has no servant or attendant with him.* Not wanting to anger him again, she put aside her questions. "I will try to be here, my prince, but my first duty is to the Princess Katherine. She may have need of me."

She stepped back at the fury in the boy's eyes. "You are wrong," he said. "Your first duty is to my father, and then to me. If I command you to be here on the morrow, you will be here whether the princess needs you or not."

Silenced by his icy look, she raised her hand to her mouth. She hadn't thought he looked like his father, but he did now. She curtseyed and wished the boy gone. The peace of the garden had disappeared – and with it, all of her own peace. "As you say, Your Highness."

"Tomorrow then – at this hour. I expect to find you here."

"As you say, Your Highness," she repeated, glad and more than simply relieved to see Prince Harry turn on his heel and hurry down the garden path towards the direction of Richmond palace. Before she lost sight of him, the boy tossed the hood of his mantle over his head as if he wished to disguise himself.

Not long afterwards, as they broke fast together, she told

Catalina of her strange meeting. Crumbling up her bread on her plate, Catalina frowned. She pushed aside her barely eaten meal. "This boy will be soon my husband, yet I know little of him. I can count on one hand the times we have talked together. Would you mind me companioning you tomorrow?"

Without thinking, María huffed.

Catalina lifted her eyebrows. "What does that mean?"

She screwed up her mouth, one way, and then the other, thinking over what she should say. She decided on the truth. "Perchance it is good you have spoken to him only a few times. I like not this prince."

The prince did not hide his surprise to find Catalina with María the next morning. So surprised, she wondered if the youth was going to bid them both farewell and go on his way. Catalina must have noticed his unease too. She picked a sprig of rosemary and handed it to the towering prince. "For remembrance of those we have loved and lost, Your Highness." She smiled at him. "Pray forgive me speaking in French, but my English is poor. My lady tells me you wish to learn about herbs and their uses. I too like to learn of such things. I hope you don't mind me joining you this morning?

"Perhaps if María can school us about herbs, you could teach us both English?" She turned her eyes toward the nearby entrance to the garden. With grey clouds gathering in the sky, shadows deepened and spread out from the high walls of the enclosed garden. "It would be a great favour to me. Weeks go by without the chance to practise the tongue of my new country."

She blushed. "I would like to learn the language of the man I have been promised to."

The youth also blushed. "I will soon be a man."

"Yes, I know," Catalina replied quietly.

María winced at the look Catalina gave to him. It seemed to beseech, and demand to be seen – but all with an air of hopelessness. At nineteen, Catalina had learnt hard lessons. One of the hardest had been whatever power she possessed could disappear on the whims of two kings. Her mother's death had brought with it not only more heartbreak, but the knowledge the Tudor King regarded her as less of a prize. King Henry left her with little money, her father even less. She was simply a pawn in a power game between two kings; a too often cruel game. But the prince before her also had little power to change the current status quo.

Almost every day thereafter, the three of them met for one or two hours in the herbal garden and María identified countless herbs and explained their uses to Prince Henry. She told the prince some of the legends and folklore she had learnt from Beatriz Galindo.

"Your Highness, do you know the story of the Pied Piper of Hamelin?" she asked him one day.

The prince turned to her with curiosity. "Hamelin? Where's that?

"A town somewhere in the Holy Roman Empire, Your Highness," said Catalina, smiling at María. "Go on, María. You tell the story better than me."

María grinned and sat on the grass. "It was three hundred years ago when the town of Hamelin was overwhelmed by a plague of rats. The rats were everywhere; they even came into homes at night and ate babies in their cribs. The townsfolk tried everything to rid themselves of the pests, and were at their wits' end when a stranger arrived in their town. He was a piper. He told them, for a bag of gold, he could make the rats go away. And he did; playing his flute, he led the rats to the river and there they drowned." She smiled at the listening prince. "But it was not the music of his flute, but the valerian in his pockets, which seeped through his clothes, that helped rid Hamelin of its rats. Rats delight in the smell of valerian and will follow it everywhere."

"Is this story true?" asked the prince.

She shrugged. "I cannot say, but it is true that rats do like the smell of valerian."

"You forgot the end of the story," said Catalina.

Henry glanced at her and then back at María. "What was that?"

"The town people refused to pay the piper. The piper got his revenge. He played his flute so beautifully that all the town children followed after him. The people of the town never saw the piper again, or their children."

The prince laughed. "I think it a true story. The piper's punishment of the town folk was just, and right."

María swallowed. *Does he really think it right for a town to lose all their children, just because of a bag of gold?*

The youth was once more talking to Catalina. He seemed innocent, and charming. But he made María's skin crawl.

The meetings with the prince left María more bemused with

each passing day. Not only because her confusion about the prince. Catalina never revealed to the prince that she, thanks to sharing the same teacher, knew more about herbs than was expected of a princess. Rather, Catalina was content to let María demonstrate her knowledge and be the one to answer the prince's questions. Still, with every day, it was clear the prince enjoyed Catalina's company. Soon, his questions turned from learning about herbs to asking about Catalina's life at her mother's court. Or the prince would tell her of what he had done the previous day. Hiding her amusement, María watched as Catalina allowed him to dominate the conversation. When the betrothed couple started to talk of books and what the prince was studying with his tutors, or taught each other the tongues of their birth, she took it as permission to forget the prince's morning's lesson, and returned to adding herbs to her basket to replenish her supplies.

Looking around the garden for more to add, she paused, running the names of the herbs through her mind. It came to her that names possessed power. Named plants had a dominance over all the unnamed plants in the garden. A name gave more than simply dominance and power – it gave meaning, and the right to exist. The right to be loved. She smiled, seeing Will in her mind. She knew his name, and he hers. It linked them for all time.

A few days before the prince's fourteenth birthday, they gathered as usual. María was once again happy to see the prince spread his mantle on the grass for him and Catalina to sit together and talk of their books as she weeded the garden near them.

Twigs snapped. María looked up. The Countess of Richmond and the Duke of Buckingham hurried towards them, accompanied by a young servant dressed in the prince's livery. Moved from one place to another, Richmond Palace, Durham House, Westminster, Windsor, Fulham Palace, Catalina and her household saw the tiny Countess only rarely. Prince Henry clearly was not expecting to see her. He bounded up, helping Catalina to her feet. María stood up in her confusion, but then fell to her knees again. *What will the king's mother think of finding her grandson engaged in talk with Catalina?*

The king's mother and the duke less than a stone throw away from them, Catalina curtseyed and Prince Henry bowed. The prince's servant fell to his knees beside María, casting her a look of apprehension.

"Grandmother – I bid you good morning," said the prince. "And to you, my cousin Edward."

"Good morrow to you, too, Harry." She cocked her head, and raised her eyes to her tall grandson. Her mouth pursed, and she glanced towards the prince's servant. "Your man was in such a hurry he almost knocked me over." She glanced at the duke next to him. "Fortunately, Edward was with me, and he seized your servant. We got it out of him the reason for his rush and his little care for what stood in the way of getting to you." She shook her head. "You best be away, Harry. Your father has gone to the chapel in search of you."

The blood disappearing from his face, Prince Henry met his grandmother's eyes. He bowed to her, and then to Catalina, picked up his mantle from the ground. He clicked his fingers at his servant who rose from his knees. Both of them hurried down the garden path.

Lady Margaret looked after them for a time, and then

turned to Catalina. "I must say it was a pretty and peaceful sight to see you with my grandson, Kate. I think this is not the first time?"

Catalina blushed, and lowered her eyes. Then she stood straighter, and taller than the king's mother. María swallowed back a bubble of laughter. Catalina was so petite; it was hard to believe there was one more diminutive still.

"I do not think there is anything wrong to speak to the prince I am promised to in marriage."

Lady Margaret exchanged a look with the duke. He shrugged, and glanced at Catalina with sympathy. The countess sighed. "Believe me – I do not think there is any wrong in you and Harry speaking together. It is always a blessing when a friendship is formed between two who one day will be husband and wife." Lady Margaret considered Catalina. "According to the treaty, your marriage to my grandson will happen soon. But I do not like Harry deceiving his father. I have no choice but to tell him of these meetings."

Catalina plucked at her shabby gown. "I do not understand why I cannot see the prince. We do no wrong by talking together."

"I am certain you do not. I know you well enough to know you were indeed worthy of Arthur, and I am in favour of your marriage to Harry, who I also love. But in this, we must also remember the wishes of the king, my son. He knows better than us about what should be done for you and the prince. I will speak to him – see if I can convince him that these meetings should be encouraged, but no longer under such clandestine conditions as this." Lady Margaret bowed her head to Catalina. "Good morrow to you, princess." Without another word, she turned on her heel, and headed down the path to the royal palace.

Gazing at Catalina, the duke stood there for a moment as if wishing to speak. He turned his eyes in the direction of the countess before looking at Catalina again. "I must follow, but it has been a delight to see you after all these weeks. I will speak to the Lady Margaret and beg her to reconsider speaking to the king." He bowed low, and hurried after the king's mother.

That same evening, Catalina received word from the king. He commanded Catalina and her household to go, early the next day, to Fulham Palace, one of the homes of the Bishop of Ely.

On the way to the palace, María held Catalina's hand in the litter. "The king does not want me to see Harry," Catalina said yet again in bewilderment.

Bewildered, too, María grabbed at straws. "There might be another cause." Her words sounded hollow to her ears, she feared to say anything more.

"I suppose I should be grateful the king sends me to a residence where I am promised full control of my household. At least, I hope that will be the case."

The Bishop's small palace was very pleasant – and Catalina was royally welcomed on her arrival. But by the end of the week, Puebla arrived with unwelcomed news.

"The prince is now fourteen," he said to Catalina. "and of legal age to marry you, my highness. But the king will not speak to me of this. Rather, the prince has protested against marrying his brother's widow, and he has done this legally, in front of witnesses."

Catalina looked close to crying. "But he likes me," she sputtered.

Puebla shrugged. "That matters little, Your Highness. The king commanded him to do this, and the prince obeyed. It is as simple as that. With your permission, I will take your leave, Your Highness."

"Si – go," she murmured, her face averted from him.

María waited for the door to close before going to Catalina. "What will you do?" she asked, resting a hand on Catalina's arm.

"Do? I can do nothing. I am nothing."

María swallowed her sense of helplessness. "That is not true, Catalina. Do not give up. Better days will come."

"Better days? I wish I could believe that," Catalina said quietly.

"They will come," María said, but she lowered her head, not wanting Catalina to see her doubts.

16

The lady who has faith in virtue
      surely ought to put her faith
in a knight of heart and worth;
when she knows how worthy he is,
let her dare reveal she loves him;
a lady who reveals her love
hears virtuous, pleasant people say
only pleasing things about her.
~ *Medieval song*

A warm day again summoned María to the privacy of the enclosed herb garden at Fulham Palace, a day seducing her to forget the worries of the present. But when she knelt to garden, it was to the sound of her worn skirt tearing. Yet again. She slipped a finger into the reopened rent, the threadbare fabric ripping more. Irritated, she thought of all the time she had wasted repairing the skirt. She mended her gowns now. She had no other choice. For one proud of her royal blood, even if royal blood on the wrong side of the blanket, she lived a much simpler life than she had been used to in the past. *My clothes fast become rags – and they hang off me because I have lost so much weight.* She sighed. *None of us have had had new clothes for years. Not even Catalina, a legitimate princess of two ruling monarchs.* Her stomach grumbled. Yet again, she had eaten a sparse breakfast, little liking the food offered for them. *Our food is unsuitable for our princess, let alone the household.*

Over and over, María yanked out weeds. But it did not make her feel better. She yearned more than ever for another time; another place. *I wish Catalina and I were children again. I wish we were in the gardens of our homeland. I wish for sunlit mornings when I could feel the heat of the day to come. I wish for Catalina gardening beside me as our beloved teacher schooled us about herbs, the best ways to harvest them.* For months, Catalina spent most of her days in prayer, or writing more begging letters to her father, her deepening melancholy about their circumstances often causing her to withdraw emotionally and physically from those around her. María sat back on her hunches, and tossed weeds to the pile beside her. *I wish Catalina would speak to me like she used to. She shuts me out too.* Raised, angry voices from somewhere near broke into her thoughts. She lifted her head. *Is that Bella shouting?* Arguments between the women were not rare – not with them all closed in together for hours in Catalina's chambers. But Bella rarely argued with others, or shouted. Bemused, María shook her head. *Rarely? Bella never shouts.*

A gold crucifix swung at the end of rosary beads and flashed as it caught the sunlight. Bella held up her skirts from her feet, almost running down the garden path. María straightened and waved to her. Even though she headed towards her, Bella did not acknowledge her greeting. María called out, "Good day, amiga." Bella stopped, glanced over her shoulder, and then lumbered over to María like one walking in her sleep. Close up, Bella's eyes were red rimmed and shining with tears.

"What's wrong?" María asked. She feared Bella's answer. Every day seemed to bring them more bad news.

The young woman took from the deep pocket of her gown a letter and held it out. María wiped her grubby hands on her apron, took the letter and scanned its contents.

"Oh," she said. She swallowed, her heart filling with compassion. "I am sorry."

Bella dropped to her knees. Her hands on her lap, she glanced around the garden. "I do not understand. It is not as if the man I love is a penniless nobody. He is the oldest son of a great lord." She shook her head, and rubbed her wet eyes. "Now my father refuses to pay the dowry so I can marry him. I do not understand."

María re-read the letter. "Your father writes he wants you to marry a grandee of Castile. He says he and your mother want you home – to raise your family in your homeland."

"In other words, my parents dictate my life, and marry me to a man who I do not love." She spoke in a rush. "Doña Elvira caused all this, and she does not deny it. I showed her the letter just before, and she laughed. I hate the woman. Our English servants call her a bitch behind her back, but that does disservice to dogs. Pray, watch her, María. The princess trusts her. I do not believe the woman deserves it. She told me she is the one who wrote to my parents about my English lord and proposed I marry Antonio, her son, in his stead. Now look what has happened! My parents refuse both matches, and command my return home."

Inwardly sighing, María reached for Bella's hand.

I have come close to hating the woman for years, but never knew others felt the same. Is Bella right, and Doña Elvira does not deserve Catalina's trust? "Have you told our princess about the letter?" The other girl shook her head again. "I dread telling her. She was happy thinking I had found love with an English lord, and he with me, and that I would live here, in England, for the rest of my days. I wanted this, too. I never thought the marriage would be forbidden by my parents." She blinked away tears. "Somehow, I must find the strength to tell two people I love this awful news." She met María's eyes. "How do you tell the man you love, a man who also loves you, you cannot marry him? I wish I was dead. I'd rather be dead, than break his heart. I would be better off dead than to marry a man I do not know or love. And my princess. My news will bring her more sorrow."

María took Bella in her arms. The girl crumpled against her and wept. Helpless to give Bella any real comfort, she saw Will in her mind, then Catalina and Arthur locked into an embrace as snow drifted down on the battlements at Ludlow castle. *Why cannot one of us be lucky in love?* Fate seemed to conspire against them, and deny them happiness.

María lowered herself to a stool by the hearth, and stared at the sluggish flames. Despite the afternoon's chill, there was never enough money to keep Catalina's chamber warm all through the day. Her spirit as cold as her body, she listened to Bella tell Catalina of the letter from her parents.

Catalina crossed the room to sit on the nearest chair. She lifted her chin. "There is no recourse, you must obey your parents."

Bella fell to her knees, and took Catalina's hand. "I would never leave you if not for this letter." Bella leaned her head on it. "If I had courage, I would break the sixth commandment for you, and for John. I wish I was brave enough to do so."

Catalina stroked the top of Bella's fair head. "I would not ask that of you, amiga. I could not bear to see you disowned by your family on my behalf. Your father writes he has already arranged your marriage. You have no choice but to go home."

Bella remained silent at the feet of Catalina.

Despondent, María twisted towards the hearth. *Sí – fate conspires against us... Or is it people? People like Doña Elvira.* María started, then stilled. *Is the woman really untrustworthy? The woman is often in deep conversation with Don de Ayala, only for them to break off talking together on seeing me. Could they be sharing secrets? But what secrets?* She thought hard. *Doña Elvira is a proud Castilian, like me. She is from one of our noblest families – like me. Since Queen Isabel's death she has spoken glowingly of Queen Juana's husband, Philip the Fair. Sí – whenever Catalina voices her bewilderment and hurt about her father's lack of help, Doña Elvira advises her to write to King Philip, her brother-in-law.*

It makes little sense. Or does it? She assembled the facts in her mind. Doña Elvira never spoke highly of Philip of Flanders before Queen Isabel's death. But her devotion to Queen Isabel never included King Ferdinand, other than as the queen's husband. *There is little doubt that Doña Elvira favours the husband of the new Queen of Castile over King Ferdinand. Si – Philip is now known as King of Castile. I think Bella is right. Doña Elvira cannot be trusted.*

Days later, María opened a letter from home and read its contents. She dropped the paper as if it burnt her fingers and raised her hands to her face. *Oh – what do I do?*

"What is it?" Putting aside her sewing, Catalina hurried over to the table. "What does Latina say?"

María licked her lips. "The letter is not from Latina. It's from my mother, written by her priest." She lowered her head. "Bella is not the only one called home. My family has arranged a marriage for me too." Willing the words to be different, she read the letter again. More defeated than ever, she shoved it over to Catalina.

Taking it, Catalina read out loud:

Daughter, you are nearly twenty. Unless you wish to join a religious order, which I know you do not, you cannot remain in England a woman without a husband. The time for your marriage is long overdue.

I do not desire for my daughter an unnatural life. If you remain unwed in the world, I fear that fate for you.

Your brother's friend has agreed to marry you. He is Flem-

ing, but has Castilian blood through his noble grandmother who was, like us, close kin to the royal family. He inherited lands not far from ours, and yearly spends spring and summer overseeing his property, which is how your brother first befriended him. Alas – his family asks for a larger dowry than we can pay, but surely your long years of service to the princess will solve that shortfall...

Catalina rested a hand on her shoulder, placing the letter on the table. Silence grew heavy in the room, pregnant with so many unsaid things. Finally, her princess sighed. "First Bella, and now you. Do you desire this marriage, amiga?"

She inhaled a deep breath, her eyes travelling around Catalina's bedchamber. *I am sick of walls; sick of living this half- life. Every new day, my life is more constricted, more caged. More hopeless.* She swung her gaze back to her friend. *It is the same for her. Worse for her. They might as well just imprison her in the Tower.* She swallowed. "I do not know. I only know I do not want to abandon you."

"But you want a husband and children. You always have. I remember you saying at twelve you wanted many children."

Catalina's words doused her in cold water. It seemed Will stood in the room Without meaning to, she let out a cry, and clasped her hand over her mouth, staring at her friend in dismay. She sputtered out, "Forgive me. I never expected to receive this letter."

"There is no need to ask for forgiveness. If anyone should ask for forgiveness, it should be me. Your mother is right. This life is unnatural. I may be forced to live it, but that does mean you must live it as well." She sighed. "Wife or nun – the two choices for ones of our rank. I think of taking the veil…often. My María, a nun's life is not for you. I see how you look at Lord Willoughby. You cannot hide your passion for him, not from me."

María rubbed her wet eyes. She had last seen Will three weeks ago. He had asked for the king's permission to return to his property; because of her, he needed to cool his blood. María trembled, her heart beating faster as she remembered their last time together. They had come close, too close, to becoming full lovers. Will had been so angry at himself for his weakness, while María had wished he had been weaker still.

Now he was gone, gone back to his wife. He vowed he no longer touched her, and had stopped sharing a bed with her when he first fell in love with María. In truth, María would not blame him if he did bed his wife. *Unnatural life? Just because I live one, does not mean I should begrudge him his chance for some kind of fulfilment.* She glanced at the letter. Perhaps it was better to wed a man she did not love than to forever yearn for a man beyond her reach. *Will – oh, Will. Our love is hopeless. Our love has always been hopeless. If I continue like this, I will soon be sent home in disgrace. I cannot dishonour my family. I would die first before bearing a bastard child.*

She turned back to Catalina. "You are right. I want children." She looked around the room, desperate and despairing. "This may be my only chance to have them. But I do not wish to abandon you."

Catalina sat on the chair beside her and clasped her hand. "And I desire you to have the life you should have; the life you always wanted. You have a chance of that. Me? I no longer hope for anything." She rubbed the side of her face. "I shall write to my father and ask him for the dowry."

She closed her mouth against reminding Catalina of all the begging letters she had written to the king, her father, in the last two years. There was rarely a time when King Ferdinand came to her rescue. He made excuses, or ignored or treated her heartfelt requests as if beneath his notice. For all that, Catalina still loved him, believing he wanted to help her. He just couldn't. *Or wouldn't.*

María stood at the window in Catalina's chamber at Fulham Palace overlooking the small, circular courtyard. Beside her, Catalina waved at Bella. María swallowed her heavy heart, and raised her hand too. Already mounted on her horse, Bella waved back. Three of Catalina's household were accompanying her to the waiting ship. One of them, her princess's Moor maidservant, was returning with Bella to Castile. With the household struggling to find enough coin to feed the mouths it had, it was easy for Catalina to grant the homesick girl permission to go with Bella. Catalina clasped Maria's hand as they watched Bella and her party ride through the courtyard's gateway. When the entrance closed after them, Catalina half-twisted towards María. "Do you think it true," she asked, "Doña Elvira deliberately destroyed Bella's chance for happiness?"

María shrugged. "I am not the best person to ask. Doña Elvira has never liked me, or I her."

"I know. But my mother always trusted Doña Elvira. Surely,

she is not self-serving, as Bella believes. Surely Doña Elvira's loyalty to me cannot be doubted?"

María listened as Catalina tried convincing herself she could trust a woman who had been part of her life since childhood. *What can I say, other than I believe Bella speaks the truth.* Catalina's last arguments petered out, and her princess stared sightlessly at the window. "You would never betray me, would you?"

Taken aback, María spun around to her friend. "I, betray you? Never!"

Catalina reached for her hand. "Forgive me – I should know better than ask you such a question. But hard times like these are when we learn who deserves trust."

María tightened her grip on Catalina's hand before releasing it. "Come away from the window. Let us join the other women. They too sorrow about farewelling Bella. The day is warm – we all should go to walk in the gardens to lift our spirits."

Richmond Palace, 1505

Doña, my dear Latina,

I hope to ask of you a great service. Could you please go to my mother and beg her not to sorrow on my behalf? She had hoped the king would provide the shortfall required for my dowry. Alas, the king writes nothing about this request. In truth, I am

relieved. In my weakness, I believed I wanted to return home; I wanted the children a marriage would give me. But I cannot abandon my princess.

How can I leave her when she is neglected by the English king, and her own father too? Neither of them provides her with enough money. Their neglect leaves her vulnerable. People recognise she is not in favour. Once, my princess was invited by King Henry to join his hunts. She enjoyed these outings – and the opportunity to speak to the king, as well as to Don de Ayala and the duke of Buckingham, both men whose company she enjoys. She has not been invited to hunt with the king for months. He does not he inquire about her indifferent health, which often keeps her abed. She loses hope – hope about marrying the prince, or ever finding happiness again...

María chewed at her bottom lip, wondering if she had said too much, and thinking of all the things she could not say in her letter. Her mother's attempt to find her a husband had seemed a rope flung out to one drowning. Si – she wanted to go home. She would always want to go home. But how could she go if it meant deserting Catalina to what seemed an endless winter? It would but make of her a traitor.

Receiving her mother's letter had also seemed a way of escape from her own predicament. She feared succumbing to sin; she feared her desire for a married man, a desire which threatened to control her. She feared how much she loved him, body and soul, until it seemed no sin at all.

María stepped through the library door, eyeing the books laid out on the shelves stretching down the wall of the narrow room. When Inés spoke, she nearly dropped the book she was returning. Deep in the room, Inés was in deep conversation with William Blount, Baron Mountjoy. Inés blushed and gestured a greeting to María. She swung around to Mountjoy. "Have you met Dona María de Salinas?"

Mountjoy bowed. "I have seen you before, and know your name, but never had the pleasure to speak to you."

"Lord Mountjoy is loaning this book to me," Inés said to María, holding out a thick manuscript with a decorative cover.

María read out loud the title. "*Herodotus' Histories.*"

Inés hugged the book to her. "How I can thank you, my lord? I did not think it was possible for you to find it." She blushed again. "Are you certain you wish to loan it to me? This is a valuable book."

"Of course I wish it. As for finding it – anything is possible if you have wealth to pave the way."

María reached out and touched it. She removed her hand, and flexed her fingers. She remembered holding the book as a child, and the weight of it. Latina reading from it. "Si – valuable. I remember my teacher telling me so when I asked to borrow *Herodotus's Histories* from Queen Isabel's library," she said softly.

"When Inés told me of *Herodotus's Histories* in the royal library of Castile, I had to address my own library's lack of it. It needs to be included on the shelves of King Henry's library as well. I know I give this book into good hands. It will give me reason to return to speak to you, lady, if you wish. I have met few women in my life who make a study of philosophy."

Inés's smile lit up her face. "Not even your wife, my lord?"

"My wife does not read. She disapproved greatly when I insisted our daughter be schooled in both reading and writing."

"I did not know you have a daughter, my lord."

"Gertrude is only four. Alas, my son died not long after his second birthday."

"I am sorry to hear of your loss. It is painful enough to lose a child newly born, but at two..." Inés sighed, and touched Maria's arm. "Do you remember the princess's little nephew?"

"How can any forget a child we all loved."

"Si – and a beautiful child too. One day he was alive, so, so alive, a child who laughed and played, and the next, dead."

Mountjoy lowered his head for a moment. "It was the same with my small lad." He sighed. "My study of philosophy consoled me in my sorrow, and still does. My poor wife finds it harder. If I speak of philosophy to her, she just becomes angry. Even scripture helps her little."

María noticed Inés's troubled face and decided to speak. "She is a mother who has lost her child. I can think of no greater grief."

"Yet it is a grief shared by many." Mountjoy frowned. "Do you mind if we speak of other things?" He toyed with his food dagger sheathed at his waist. "When I first met Dona Inés, she astonished me with her knowledge of Plato."

Inés laughed softly. "You make it seem I've read all of Plato's philosophies. I have only skimmed the cream from the milk. María knows his writings just as well as I."

"Have you two ladies a favourite passage from his work?"

María shrugged. "I – I think all of us – like his thoughts about women..."

Mountjoy raised an eyebrow. "All of us?"

When Inés reddened and seemed too flustered to answer him, María spoke again, "The princess speaks with us about Plato, and other philosophers. She was well schooled about them in Castile. Our princess likes this from Plato: 'We can easily forgive a child who is afraid of the dark; the real tragedy of life is when men are afraid of the light'."

"Aye – I like that too. The princess reads philosophy then?"

"She loves the ancient philosophers" Inés flushed, speaking in a rush. "Just the other day, I heard her speak her desire to read more philosophy books. She has read all the books owned by the king."

"It would give me great pleasure to right that particular problem. Do you think she would do me the great honour to accept books as gifts from me?"

Inés gazed at María with wide eyes. *She looks like a doe ready to flee at any moment. Mother of God – she too is in love with a man she cannot have.*

"I can ask her," María answered Mountjoy. "She has no money to buy new books for herself, but I cannot see why she would refuse such a kindness from you."

Mountjoy bowed to them both. "Time for me to go." He bowed again to Inés. "Pray keep the book for as long as you wish. But I do hope to see you again and continue our past discussions."

The man gone, María considered Inés. "Past discussions?" Inés reddened again, but then straightened her shoulders.

"You cannot speak. I have stopped counting the times I see you stealing away to see your English Lord."

She sighed. "You are right. I cannot judge – but I would wish for my friend not to have the same pain as I have suffered since giving my heart to a married man. Because I cannot shame our princess, or my family, I cannot even be his mistress. All I have are short hours in his company. Hours of torture because I want him so much."

Inés clasped the book to her breast and sat on the bench beneath the high window. "It is the same for me. I have given my heart, too." She leaned back on the wall, drawing her face into the shadows. "Oh, María, what am I to do?"

She sat beside her and reached for her hand. She had nothing to say. There was no easy solution for either of them. She sighed. *It seems no sin at all.*

Doña, my dear Latina,

Do you know anyone King Ferdinand will listen to? I cannot tell you how desperate we all are. My princess struggles to pay her debts because no money comes from her father, or King Henry. As I write to you in my princess's bedchamber, I hear Doña Elvira and Don Pedro de Ayala in the princess's privy chamber. The ambassador insisted on this audience – and Doña Elvira insisted on my princess listening to him. Doña Elvira was not pleased when my princess permitted me to stay when she sent out the other women. They seek to persuade my princess to sell silver vessels, brocade and a collar of linked gold. My princess is unhappy to do so. These pieces are from the dowry meant for her second marriage.

Hearing Doña Elvira and Don de Ayala leave, María put aside her unfinished letter to join Catalina in the privy chamber. Her friend paced up and down, wringing her hands. "I do not know what to do," Catalina said to María. "I must write to my father again. Surely if he knew the true state of my affairs…"

María doubted it would make any difference to King Ferdinand. She offered the only advice she could think of, "Why not speak to Doctor de Puebla?"

"What help has he ever given me? The man is an incapable fool. He lets me down, time after time. Thanks to him, we reside at Richmond, rather than at Fulham Palace. I know I complained of living there, but at least I was away from the king. Everyone spies on me here."

María contemplated the closed door, turning over in her mind all she knew about de Puebla. *Si – the man has disappointed Catalina time after time, but at least he tries to help. I do not believe him a fool, rather a man often faced with an uphill battle to win over King Henry.*

But Catalina was not wrong about spies. Leave this room, and all eyes followed her. Most of the time, boredom explained it. They had nothing to do but to watch one another. But placed as she was, being spied upon was the natural order of the world. She sighed. How could any tell whether people meant well by their princess, or sought to do her a disservice? It was impossible. "How can you be so sure it is his fault? The king brought you here, not Doctor de Puebla," she murmured.

"Who else am I to blame? Doctor de Puebla tells me he has the ear of the king, yet he fails to use that ear in his duty to me. I am without money to pay my servants and my debts. Look how we suffer here. We are kept cold, and I have no money to support my household. We are poor. I can hardly bear it."

"We all in your household share your tribulations – and are honoured to do so."

"Tribulations... Si – you describe well our lives. We are afflicted, and more than you realise. Did you know Doña Elvira leaves soon for Flanders?" María started. "Why?"

"She does not wish to leave me, but it is her eyes. She has lost sight in one of them. Her brother, my father's ambassador to Flanders, knows of a Flemish physician who cured the infanta Isabel of the same complaint. With my permission, Doña Elvira wrote to him, begging him to come to England, but he refused. I cannot say to her nay and hinder her journey." Catalina shifted in her chair angrily. "As for Puebla. I asked him to beg help from King Henry on my behalf. All I wished was for the King to find an old English woman to take her part whilst Doña Elvira is in Flanders. Or, if he could not do that, then let me return to court while Doña Elvira is absent and be, God help me, under the king's eye. At least at court we have some chance to alleviate our boredom. But when I asked this of the doctor, I was told my English servants would be dismissed, and I will no longer be the mistress of my own home. I must write my father. Surely this news will disturb him; I am his daughter; my treatment is an insult to him. He must send to me someone he can trust to deal with the king; someone I can trust, too." Her face shimmering with the sheen of fever, Catalina spoke in a rush, and erratically. She coughed and coughed, collapsing on the nearest chair.

María approached Catalina. "May I make you something to soothe your cough?"

Catalina raised her face. Blue shadows etched deep beneath her eyes. "That would be a true kindness. I would rather your remedies than those given by my physician. Sometimes I wonder if he desires to poison me."

Laughing, she rested a hand on Catalina's shoulder. Under

her hand, there seemed no flesh, only bone. "I will go to the kitchen and see if they have fresh chicken, or chicken gizzards. I think the best thing I can prepare for you is a chicken broth. It will keep that cold of yours at bay."

María grabbed her shawl. Slinging it over her shoulders, she hurried through the antechamber and headed in the direction of the distant kitchen. Angry male voices speaking in Castilian drifted towards her. The voices came from within a chamber where the door had been left ajar. She padded softly over to it, shaking her head as she leaned against the whitewashed wall. *Dear Lord, I am but a spy too.*

"You dare to speak to me in such a manner, you lowborn scum? You, who should never have been given the trust of our noble Queen, God rest her soul, or her royal husband. Look at you. You do not even dress as one would expect of a royal ambassador. It is no wonder the princess listens to me, and not you."

"Can I help it if I have not the fortune you have, Don de Ayala? I am in debt because of my loyalty to our king. I do not possess the coin to dress as you do. I do not have coin to pay for servants. But perhaps that is all for the good. I would not like to have servants like yours, brawling and committing murder in the very streets of London. Even your priest cools his heels in Newgate prison with blood on his hands. You think me unworthy of respect? If the king was to know the truth about you, you would find your shoe on the wrong foot. I have been patient with you, but no more. I will no longer allow you to undo all I do for the king, and his daughter, the princess. I am no fool; you are in the pay of King Philip."

María blinked at Doctor de Puebla's contempt; it dripped like congealing blood with every word he spoke.

"I refuse to stay here in the same room with you for one more moment," snarled de Ayala.

Heeding the warning in those words, María lifted her skirts and ran to the nearby corner of the hallway. She prayed to reach there and be out of sight before the ambassadors chanced to see her.

A few days later, Catalina agreed to give Doctor de Puebla an audience. María rose from her stool and stepped closer to kneel by Catalina's side, wishing to give her friend the only support she could. *Did I do right by not telling her what Doctor de Puebla said about Don de Ayala? My princess is ill. I need to be certain before I trouble her without cause.*

Doctor de Puebla looked terrified when he entered the chamber, and spoke in a rush before Catalina had a chance to stand from her chair and greet him. "Princess – it is true you sent to King Henry that letter?"

Catalina looked at him, surprise plain on her face. "My letter? What of it? I only relayed my brother-in-law's desire to meet with King Henry at Calais."

The old man shook his head as if in dismay. "Princess, do you not realise what you have done?"

"Done? All I have done is open the door to two kings becoming better allies."

"Better allies...my princess, can you not think what this would mean to the king, your father? King Henry and King Philip better allies would mean your father's hand is weakened." Catalina paled and sat back on her chair. "I do not understand.

Doña Elvira told me Don Juan, her brother, believed it would be good for King Henry and my brother-in- law to meet."

"Good for them, princess – and especially for King Philip. King Philip wishes for your father to be removed as regent of Castile. As your sister's husband, he desires control of the regency. Don Juan may be your father's ambassador, but he and his sister are both Castilians. They would rather King Philip be the regent on behalf of his wife than your noble father, the King of Aragon." Puebla considered Catalina with compassion. "You must know, princess, I have learnt Doña Elvira has long been a spy on her brother's behalf. Her desire to go to Flanders is not simply because of her eyes, but because she knew she would be soon found out."

Catalina slumped back in her chair. Pursing her lips, Catalina looked at the ambassador. "What do I do – how do I make this right?"

Puebla gestured towards Catalina's writing desk. "You must write to King Henry. You must tell him to disregard your first letter. Tell him he must value the king, your father, higher than King Philip. And then you must send Doña Elvira and her husband from your household and never allow them to return."

María shifted on her knees deeper into the shadows. Forgotten by the door, she studied King Henry, Catalina kneeling before him. He had changed since his last visit to Catalina. Loss of flesh meant his clothes hanged as if from bones. His eyes shone unnaturally in a face jaundiced and hollowed with illness. María shuddered. His eyes also glittered with rage. Catalina's eyes shone too in her white face. Trembling again, María felt Catalina's fear as if it was her own. How could she not fear? The sending of Catalina's letter had brought the arrival of a furious king on the same day. "Madam– I command you, write to your father. If I am to place such value on your royal father, he must stay true to his promises," he said, coldly and slowly.

Catalina reddened and then paled. "I have written to him."

María stirred, her fingers clutching at her skirt. *Does the king have no pity? She has written her father countless letters. She exhausts herself with writing them."*

"Write again," said the king. "He must pay me your promised dowry."

"Sire, what of the jewels and plate I brought at my marriage to your son?"

"The jewels and plate you use? You think I should regard that as your dowry? I would but rob you of your possessions if I took that."

"But, Sire, with respect, it was you who told me to use these things. I was a stranger to your dominion. I did not know if I used the jewels and plate the ownership passed to my husband, and made them worthless to you, and no longer the dowry my father intended."

The king lifted a scanty eyebrow. "Are you claiming I deliberately set out to deceive you?"

"No, Sire. But –"

Henry VII raised a hand to halt Catalina's attempt at explanation. "I possess many jewels and plate. What need I of your used goods? I'd pay you a paltry sum for them, for they have little value to me. Your father promised me money, and money I shall have. So, Madam, you will write."

Catalina bowed her head. She coughed and cleared her throat. "Si, I shall write."

The king stormed passed María without even glancing in her direction. Rising, she rushed over to Catalina, and helped her up from her knees. "What will you do?" she asked.

"What I said – I will write, and beg my father to send the king my dowry."

Realising Catalina was shaking, María wrapped her arm around her. "But, Catalina, you have begged your father for years."

"What else can I do?"

María had no answer.

17

Ah, child and youth, if you knew the bliss which resides in the taste of knowledge, and the evil and ugliness that lies in ignorance, how well you are advised to not complain of the pain and labour of learning.

~ *Christine de Pizan*

January 1506, Fulham Palace

My dear Latina,

The years pass too quickly. You would find me very changed from the girl of fifteen you once knew. My princess is a woman of twenty summers – and I too will soon reach that age.

I wish I write of happier times. Perhaps my princess, and those like myself who remain with her out of love and loyalty, could have found some contentment if my princess had been allowed to rule her own household. At court, she is made to feel unwanted, forgotten, and of little worth. Although, at last, the English king has sent to her new clothes, as befitting her rank. But for a purpose. She has been told to make ready to welcome Queen Juana and her husband, King Philip. Their ship, on its way to Spain, was driven by sea squalls to shelter in English ports.

María replaced her quill in its inkstand, lost in memories. Nine years. Nine years since she danced barefoot with Catalina on a golden, seemingly endless stretch of beach. Nine years since they had bid farewell to Juana, hours before Catalina's older sister boarded the ship taking her from her homeland to a husband she had never met. María blinked – seeing in her mind's eye Juana weeping in her mother's arms. She had felt so helpless, her morning joy doused by witnessing her cousin's heartbreak.

Catalina's brother Juan and sisters Isabel and María had been there too – the last day the five siblings were ever together in this mortal life. She would never forget how Isabel had wept in her brother's arms, her sister's marriage reminding her that she too would soon go to another diplomatic marriage bed. Only two years later both Juan and Isabel were in their tombs. After Isabel's death in childbed, her sister María had wedded her sister's widower and became Queen of Portugal. She was now a mother many times over. And Juana? Juana was crowned Queen of Castile.

Nine years. Nine long years. At last, she and Catalina would see Juana again.

Catalina curtseyed and greeted her brother-in-law, Philip the Fair. Kneeling close by, María eyed the tall, slender, black haired man who stood beside King Henry. He was sallow skinned and sullen of expression, very different from his younger sister Margaret; Margot deserved the byname of fair, and not her brother. During her marriage to Catalina's brother, Margot had shone a bright light, inside and out.

"Where is my sister – where's the Queen of Castile?"

Catalina asked. María wondered at Juana's absence too, and leaned forward to hear the king's answer.

"My ships found safe harbour at Dorset. My wife remains there until I summon her," he said, nodding his dismissal, and then returned to talking to King Henry who gestured his leave to go too.

Ignored by both men, Catalina half-twisted away from them, her face flushed and despondent. Disappointed too at Juana's absence, María clenched her hands by her sides. Catalina had yearned and prayed to see someone from her family for years. *But not someone like Philip who treats my princess with disdain.*

María drew Catalina's attention towards the solitary Princess Mary. Now a girl of ten and already promising to surpass her mother's beauty, she stood some distance away, looking cast down too. Catalina curtseyed to the kings, the men so deep in conversation they paid her little mind, and made her way to the young princess. María rose to trail close behind, reaching Catalina at the same moment she greeted Mary.

"I'm glad to find you here, sister," she said with a smile.

Mary grinned too. "Father wants me to help entertain the King of Castile. Have you met your sister's husband before?"

Catalina looked towards the men. "Never," she murmured. "This was our first meeting."

María bent her head, fighting the urge to laugh. *I suspect she wishes it was the last.*

Mary clasped her hands before her and shuffled her feet. "I was hoping you might know what he likes. No matter – I will play my lute. At least that will please my lord father."

"It will be pleasing to us all." Catalina frowned and gazed around the chamber. "Is your brother not here?"

"He is ill." Mary shrugged. "But I did not believe he was so ill he had to be left behind. He spent the first week entertaining King Philip in showing his strength of arm in a jousting tournament our royal father held for our royal visitor. Harry impressed the king, but it came at a cost. Our lord father said Harry acted the fool by bearing arms meant for a grown man, and not one still a youth. On a hot day too. My father commanded my brother to remain at Richmond, resting. Harry was not happy at being left with only the company of his tutors. He liked King Philip, and King Philip him. Harry told me he should be here with the King of Castile. He also wants to meet the Queen of Castile." Mary glanced at her father. "Of course, he would not tell our father that." Mary laughed. "Aside from my grandmother, I am the only one in my family who dares to speak their mind to the king, my father. Everyone else dances around him like cowards. So, sister, what do you plan to do to entertain your brother-in-law?"

Catalina pointed to herself and then María. "You speak of dance... See how we are dressed?"

Mary frowned a little. "I remember," she said slowly, grinning. "You wore a gown like that when I first met you. It is not the fashion of your country?"

Catalina bent her head, and straightened her skirt with care. "I stored these gowns away after my wedding to...Arthur, your dear brother. When I left Castile, it was the fashion. I expect when I see my sister, she will tell me the fashion is something else entirely now. But back to your question. You are right, we wear the clothes of the country of our birth. María and I plan to dance together tonight."

Mary's eyes widened with her smile. "Will you dance with me too? It has been months since the last time we danced together."

"If you wish, my sister." Catalina's smile disappeared. "But I cannot promise any great skill. I spend little time dancing."

Without thinking, María shifted closer to Catalina, and then remembered they were not alone. Stepping back again, she wondered if it was wise for her friend to dance tonight. Catalina's times of illness left her with little energy. Today, when they practised, it had not taken long before she became breathless.

María caught sight of a man she remembered well from Queen Isabel's court. She edged closer to Catalina, bobbed a curtsey and whispered near her ear, "Look over by the door – it is your mother's painter."

Catalina, infused with delight, grabbed her hand. "Come with me." She glanced at the young princess. "Forgive me, but there is someone here I must speak to," she said.

Catalina weaved through groups of courtiers until she reached the thin, aged man leaning on the wall. His eyes shut, he started when Catalina's shadow fell upon him. Staring for a heartbeat, his face broke into a wide smile before he bowed to the princess. "My Lady Princess," he said in Castilian. "It has been too long."

Catalina grinned back at him. "It is an unexpected pleasure to see you again, Master Sittow," she said, replying in the same language. She gestured towards María. "Do you remember my companion, Doña María de Salinas?"

Master Sittow dipped his head to her. "Doña, you were once a beautiful child, and today a beautiful woman. Long ago, I sketched you on paper. Now I desire to capture your image in paint."

Aware of her heating cheeks, María bent her head and murmured her thanks. She glanced aside at Catalina, blushing again at the laughter lighting up her friend's face. "María thinks her beauty is something she needs to deny. She wishes to be given admiration only for her mind. But what of me, Master Sittow? Have you no praise for me?"

Sittow bowed low. "My Lady Princess, what praise I have for you cannot be expressed in words. Pray, let me paint you; let me make your beauty of youth immortal."

María gulped back a laugh. Catalina's blushing cheeks became exactly the same colour as the red-pink of a rose she had seen in the garden this morning.

"Master Sittow, I – I –" Catalina swallowed, staring at María in bewilderment.

Sittow stepped forward, and leaned closer, as if to speak confidingly to Catalina. "Madam, think how pleasing such a painting would be for your father."

Catalina gazed at María in question.

She shrugged. "Why not, my princess. We look to be here for

a long while yet; it would be good to send a portrait home to the king." She shut her mouth, afraid she would speak her thought out loud: *And remind him he has a daughter.* Catalina nodded. "For the king, my father then. Shall I send for you in the morning, Master Sittow?"

"The morning it is." He rubbed his hands and bowed. "I wait with impatience to start."

María danced with Catalina. *Forget the kings. Forget everyone in the room watching you. Just dance.* She clapped and stepped around Catalina, her spirit fused with her body, at last erasing from her mind the people in the room, her movements timed and measured to perfection with the beat of music. She closed her eyes for a moment, awash with nostalgia, recalling sunlight so bright it changed stone paving paths of courtyards to blinding white. Water glittered as if with diamonds as it poured into stone basins of fountains. The dance came to an end, and she stopped the sorrowful flow of her memories. In control again, she caught her breath, curtseying in unison with Catalina.

The young princess joined Catalina, María curtseyed again and broke away to stand with Francisca and Inés as the two princesses danced together a slow, sedate dance. María shared a look with Francisca and Inés, knowing they shared her relief that their unwell princess had managed two dances without mishap. With the show of their skill done, Catalina took the princess's hand, gazing around the room. Catalina led the princess across the wide chamber. Margaret Pole, garbed in her widow weeds, stood a little away from the other courtiers, but she smiled at the approach of the two princesses. She curtseyed before starting to talk to them.

"Our princess looks happy," Francisca said in Castilian.

"She will be happier when she sees her sister," María replied. Men and women of the court grouped together for the next dance.

"Still, she is happy this evening," said Inés.

"Si – and would wish you two some joy too. The dance is about to start – go and join in. I will attend to the princess."

María hurried over to where Catalina stood with Meg and the young princess. Catalina smiled at her approach, continuing to speak to Meg.

"My friend, let me say in person what I wrote to you two years ago. I grieved for you at the news of your husband's death. Sir Richard was a good man – one Prince Arthur trusted, and loved."

Meg lowered her head. "I miss him more than words can say. Although, I am blessed to have sons who remind me of him every day."

When Lady Margaret remained silent, María met Catalina's bemused eyes, and shrugged.

Catalina rested a hand on Meg's arm. "Is something wrong?" she asked. "I did not expect the pleasure of seeing you at court."

"I needed to speak with the king's mother. She is a close kinswoman to my husband." Meg sighed "Since my husband's death, I have been driven to live at Syon Abbey with my children. I took my third son to Sheen Priory this week. It is hard to explain to a child not even seven why I thought this wise. Reginald is the most gifted of my three older boys – and I want him to receive the education he deserves." Meg sighed again. "My boy believes I desired to rid myself of him. I am at my wit's end. If the king does not listen to his mother, I do not know what I will do."

Catalina glanced in the direction of the king. "The king is not the same man we knew when Arthur and Queen Elizabeth lived." She glanced with unhidden worry at the young princess beside her. "Forgive me – I should not speak of the king, your father, thus."

Princess Mary shrugged her thin shoulders. "You speak only the truth. Since my mother left us, it has been like my father lives in the night."

Catalina took Mary's hand. "He loves the children he has left – sister, you give him light."

Mary shrugged again. "But my lord father always returns to the dark. And every time he returns, it is harder to bring him back out again."

Meg also gazed towards to king. "The queen, your mother, knew how to do that. He loved her greatly; we all loved her." Meg swung around to Mary. "She would not have wanted you to take on the burden of helping your father in his black days. She would have wanted you to be carefree, while you could; you are so young. The court is already a sad place without our sweet princess losing her joy."

"I refuse to lose my joy; I promised mother that before she died."

Catalina wound her arm around her young sister-in-law. The ten-year-old girl was already taller than her. "Tell Meg your news, Mary."

Meg hunched over, lowering her head to the same level as

the princess. Mary was tall for her age, but Meg was as tall as most men at court. "What news is this, Your Highness?"

Mary blushed. "The king, my father, and King Philip speak of betrothing me to Prince Charles."

Catalina grinned. "My nephew."

Mary screwed up her face. "He is four years younger than me."

Releasing Mary from her half-embrace, Catalina shook her head. "And your brother is over five years younger than me. Believe me, for those placed in positions like ours, age means nothing. You are also your father's favourite child – he is not likely to send you away from England until the time comes for your true marriage. By the time you go to marry my nephew you will be a grown woman. I know you will be a worthy helpmeet for a youth who will one day rule a kingdom greater than any have seen for centuries."

Mary paled. "I did not realise he ruled a great kingdom..."

Catalina clasped her hand in reassurance. "Why should you? You are only ten. Time enough to think of these matters when you are older."

Catalina looked around before straightening her shoulders. "I must speak to my brother-in-law." She padded over to the two talking kings, María following a few paces behind. Catalina curtseyed, smiling brightly at Philip. "Brother, will you not dance with me?"

The king offered her a brief bow, "I am happy enough where I am." He offered what seemed to be a smile of apology to King Henry. "She is like her sister. My wife always forgets herself and interrupts when she is not wanted."

María flinched when Catalina lost her animation. She decided she disliked Prince Philip.

Catalina lifted her chin and stood her ground. "But it would be a great joy to me to dance with you. It has been so long since I have danced with a brother."

"It is a joy I must deny you. I am a mariner, not a dancer. As your sister has learnt, if I want to dance, I will do so, but only when I wish it." He waved his hand in dismissal. "Leave us. I wish to speak alone with King Henry."

Rebuffed, Catalina left them to sit next to Princess Mary. The cloth of estate of both their royal houses hung behind them, lifting and fluttering a little, now and then, whenever a draft escaped through an opening door. Wishing to give her friend support, María knelt by her princess's side. Catalina looked at her. "I could not even ask him about Margot, let alone my own sister," she said. She covered her face for a moment, hiding her distress.

María touched her hand in sympathy. *Margot was as different as day to night to her brother. No matter their station, she had reached out to people with intelligence and grace. Her brother blusters with arrogance and ill temper.* "He has probably forgotten his sister was ever your brother's wife." She studied Philip. He was laughing, his head close to King Henry. He raised his goblet to his mouth, the red wine dribbling down his chin and staining his white satin doublet with spots. More than ever, María wanted the evening to come an end, and for them to leave. Her eyes still on Philip, she wondered at Juana's continued absence. *Juana is Queen of Castile. Her husband is only king because he is wedded to her. She should be here. Philip the Fair said she waits for his summons. Summons? The Queen of Castile waits for her husband's summons? More and more, I begin to think Philip the Fair would be better named Philip the Foul.*

February 1506, Windsor Castle

Doña, my dear Latina,

We have been at Windsor for seven long days. Queen Juana's husband and King Henry spend their days either hunting, or with the English King's councillors. Every day, my princess is ignored by them.

Sitting in a pool of light, María wrote her letter on a table close to where Master Sittow painted his canvas. From his skilful sketch, the depiction of Catalina came to life, and regained the beauty robbed from her by illness. With immense care, the painter painted the gold edging of the headgear framing her young face. Set back on her head, it revealed her golden-red hair parted in the middle.

Sitting on a high-backed chair, Catalina moved restlessly, straightening the skirt of her brown gown, its neckline adorned with the scallop shells of Santiago de Compostela. A beam of sunlight shone on her necklace of linked Tudor roses. María sighed. Arthur had been buried with a similar chain. Queen Elizabeth had gifted this necklace to Catalina before they left for Ludlow.

Arthur; Queen Elizabeth – both of them long dead.

María wished Catalina had chosen a different necklace. She wished she had chosen a different gown – a less sombre one. Despite the slight smile depicted in the painting, she seemed what she was: a sorrowing widow. A widow with what seemed a halo spilling out behind her head.

But Master Sittow still captured the Catalina María knew so well. He had caught her wistful expression, her eyes lowered as if she desired to keep her thoughts private. She wondered what King Ferdinand would make of the portrait. Would it remind him he had a daughter in need of his aid? A daughter he forgot when it suited him. If only Queen Isabel had not died. She would not have allowed the English to treat her daughter as they did.

***

Will was once more at court. María joined him at morning Mass and then slipped away with him afterwards. They walked and talked in the gardens, speaking of books, of music, of matters concerning her princess.

"Tomorrow, shall we find somewhere to sing together?" Will asked. "You can practice your English, if you wish."

María inwardly sighed. *He keeps his distance from me. How I wish otherwise.*

Rain began to fall. First, a few drops – and then a short shower burst. "Hurry before it starts again," Will said. "The library is close by. Let's go there."

In the library, a man was taking a book from its shelf. Will's eyes brightened. He smiled and bowed in greeting, and then gestured to María.

"Do you know my friend Edmund Dudley? Edmund – this is Lady María de Salinas. She serves the Princess Katherine."

Bobbing a quick curtsey, María glanced up at the handsome,

dark-haired man and gave him a smile. "I have seen you going to the king's apartments many times. It is good to know your name."

Dudley gave a short laugh. "Good to know my name, lady? I am but a loyal servant to the crown and beneath your notice." He grinned at Will. "Rightly, I should be beneath Will's notice too, and not one he calls friend."

"God's oath, Ed, you are married to my close kinswoman. Your children are my blood kin – why should you not be my friend? And what do you do here, so early in this day?"

"King's business." Dudley scowled, and his unsmiling mouth closed tightly.

Will considered him, and then rested a hand on his arm. "The same business, my friend?"

"The same." He stared at the thick book he had picked up on their arrival. "I never thought I would regret my study of law. Good you call me friend, Will, but many do not." He sighed. "I must return to my employment. Why not come and share a meal with me and Elizabeth tonight?"

"I will be honoured."

Will watched Dudley stride away – and then turned back to María.

"He does not look happy," she said.

"No – King Henry employs him in work he would rather not do."

Will brushed against her. Unable to stop herself, María reached out, clasping his hand, before breaking away as if she touched fire. Since his return to court, he rarely now touched her, or she him. Burnt into both their memories was how close they had come to weakening and becoming full lovers. "I want us to remain friends," he had told her. "And that means not making it harder than it is already. I am a man, María, being near you is temptation enough. I sin enough in my thoughts, pray help me keep what honour I can."

María averted her face, not daring to look at him, aware her honour could and would crumble at his touch. Friendship was not what she wanted from him, but it was all that she had.

The messenger gone, María sat next to her friend. "I am so sorry you never saw Juana," she said.

Catalina lowered her head. "I do not understand. We have been here for over a week, more than enough time for my sister to come to Windsor. Now I am told to make ready to leave."

María clasped her hand. "I wished to see her too." She tightened her grip. "She is my cousin as well as my queen, but I know this strikes at you harder. Shall I let the others know, and call for servants to begin packing?"

A knock sounded at the door followed by Francisca's muted voice. "Madam, another message has come from King Henry." María opened the door and took the parchment to Catalina. Catalina bounded up. "She's here! She is with the king."

King Henry was embracing Juana in welcome when they arrived. Releasing her from his arms, the king gazed at Juana as if seeing a vision.

María knelt by the door. She also could not take her eyes away from Catalina's older sister. Now in in her twenty-fifth year, Juana was greatly changed from the sixteen-year-old girl she remembered. Thin and pale, she was more beautiful than she had been at sixteen, but it was a beauty of brittle fragility. King Henry took her hand again and kissed it tenderly. María winced when Juana removed her hand and glanced at her husband with terror.

King Philip grunted. "No need of that, brother Henry. You give my wife too warm a welcome."

Juana stepped away from the English King and lowered her head.

King Henry gestured towards Catalina. "There's one who is eager to see you."

Juana turned toward Catalina, looking on with bewilderment, but then back to her husband.

"You wish to spend time alone with your sister?" he asked. Her face stark and white, Juana nodded.

Why does she fear him? She is Queen of Castile, and the daughter of Queen Isabel – she should not fear anyone. Catalina, too, standing as if rooted to the floor, seemed stunned by what was happening in this room.

"Go," King Philip said. "But expect my summons soon."

Casting a backward look at her husband, Juana approached Catalina. Catalina smiled at her sister, curtseyed and then took her into a tight embrace. At last releasing her sister from her arms, Catalina kept hold of Juana's hand. "Come. Come with me to my chamber."

Once there, Juana looked around the room. Visibly relaxing, she smiled at her sister. Noticing María as if for the first time, her eyes widened. "Cousin, I see little has changed. You still shadow my sister."

Happy to see at last the Juana she remembered, María shut

the door and fell to her knees. "My Queen, it has been too many years."

"Too many years...yes, it has been that." She waved her hand. "Pray get up, María. You're my cousin. Besides, few give me such homage."

Catalina led her sister to the four chairs by the fire. "María, pray sit with us too."

Sitting on the chair closest to the fire, Juana held her hands out to its warmth. "This English weather – how do you stand it, sister?"

Catalina grinned aside at María. "It is our cousin's constant complaint too." She turned back to her sister, hooding her eyes. "In truth, I also like it little. I do not think I have had one winter when I have not sickened. But winter is over. Soon, the days will be pleasant again. Juana, I cannot tell you how much it means to me to see you. I thought I would never see any of my family again."

Juana sat back in the chair, contemplating Catalina. "I am glad to see you, Chiquitina."

Catalina started, and tears welled in her eyes. "The last person to call me that was our mother." She swallowed. "How I miss her."

Juana broke her gaze from her sister, and sighed. "I miss her too – in more ways than I can say. It is true we had many disagreements, but my life changed for the worse when she died."

Catalina reached to take her sister's hand. "Mine too. But, sister, you are Queen of Castile. Surely that gives you some say over your destiny?"

Juana hunched over, toying with the rings on her right hand.

The rubies in her rings caught the firelight and flashed a dance of red on her bent head. "I have no destiny other than that allowed by my husband." She pursed her lips for a moment. "He owns me, body and soul."

"Juana – I do not understand what you mean. No one can own your soul, not even your husband. Your soul belongs to God."

Juana looked aside at Catalina. "Is it true you are still a virgin?"

Catalina blushed. "My husband, my sweet Arthur, was unwell all of our marriage, and too unwell to consummate our marriage."

Juana lowered her head, playing again with her rings. "That explains your question. A virgin could not understand how a man can own you." She leaned back in her chair. "Many times, I've wished for the return of my virgin state."

"But then you wouldn't have children."

"Si – there is that. I have children. Four of them. What comfort that gives me, I do not know."

"Juana – what is wrong? You make no sense."

Juana stared at Catalina. "That's what my husband says. That he cannot make sense of what I say. He tells me to remain silent; that he hates the sound of my voice "

María swallowed her shock at the torrent of pain revealed by Juana's words. *By all the Saints, what has her husband done to her? Her spirit is broken.*

Catalina bounded up, kneeling at her sister's side. She enclosed Juana's restless hands in hers. "Oh sister, dear sister. What has happened to you?"

Leaning back in her chair, Juana stared sightlessly at the fire.

"I cannot tell you, Chiquitina. I do not want to speak of it – not to you, not to anyone." She turned back to Catalina. "But I do wish to warn you be careful of who you trust. Did you know your old dueña, Doña Elvira, was long in my husband's pay?" Catalina visibly swallowed. "Doña Elvira?" she said softly.

She glanced at María, clearly not wanting Juana to know she already knew this.

"Yes – her brother may be in name our father's ambassador, but he is Castilian to the core. He has no loyalty to our father, and Doña Elvira is the same. She only asked permission to leave your service and come to Flanders because too many people were beginning to suspect. Rightly, she feared the vengeance of our royal father. Fortunately for her, she has a clever brother – one who hinted to our father that certain documents would come to light if any foul play ever comes his sister's way."

"What documents are these?"

"Who knows? I only know Doña Elvira served our mother for years before coming to England. I suspect the woman knows many secrets involving our father." Juana cocked her head towards her sister. "That is past, and matters little to me. Do you know – can you tell me what my husband and the English King have been speaking of in these days since they first met?"

Catalina shook her head. "I do not know."

Twisting the ring on her hand again, Juana frowned. "Hmmm – Don de Ayala is loyal to me. I will speak to him."

María shifted uneasily in her chair drawing the eyes of both sisters to her. Catalina studied her. "You know something, María?"

She shrugged. "A trusted friend told me something yesterday." Thinking over her conversation with Will, she glanced first at Juana and then at Catalina. "The king has signed a treaty with King Philip."

The sisters stared at each other, and looked again at María. "Did your friend tell you the meaning of this treaty?" Catalina asked.

María stared at her hands for a moment. "Forgive me for remaining silent, but I wished to wait for a better time to speak of this. You were already distressed at not seeing Queen Juana."

"Worry me? María, you should know to tell me everything." María glanced at Juana, fearful of her reaction. "It is a secret treaty. King Henry has agreed to support Juana's husband against your father. My friend told me King Ferdinand has been making approaches to Castilian grandees. Forgive me, my Queen, but it seems King Ferdinand has been saying you and your husband are unfit to rule."

Rubbing the side of her face, Juana turned. "Our father... Our father seeks to betray me?"

Catalina shook her head. "We do not know if this is true. Perhaps...perhaps it is not you who our noble father doubts, but your husband."

Juana pursed her lips and considered Catalina. "You have not changed. Even as a child you defended our royal father." She jutted out her chin. "I, on the other hand, I stopped trusting him years ago. Chiquitina, listen to one who knows. One day he will break your heart, as he has done mine, over and over.

Break Catalina's heart... *By all the Saints in Heaven, why does Catalina, without fail, keep her faith in her father?* From childhood, they had both known of his betrayals, his many lies, but Catalina always made excuses for him. It was as if her whole world depended on believing in him.

María glanced aside at her friend, wondering if she realised yet this treaty also affected her. *If Philip the Fair and Henry VII unites together against King Ferdinand, that will lessen her father's power. And, as a princess of Aragon, lessen Catalina's value as a bride for Prince Henry.*

María kept back one piece of information for when she could speak to Catalina alone, knowing how much it would upset her. For Henry VII's support, Juana's husband was willing to pay in flesh. He was returning to the Tudor King a man in the protection of his father: Edmund de la Pole, the Earl of Suffolk. Will had told her that King Philip had only agreed to this when the king had promised this would not cost the earl his life. But the man would be placed in the Tower, likely for the rest of his days. Another 'White Rose' dealt with and taken off the chess board, and one less fear for Henry VII. María feared telling her would bring a return of Catalina's nightmares – the nightmares she had for years about the death of Warwick. As it was, her princess had nightmares enough.

18

In me the false-speaking gossips find no ally,
    for no one can be honoured who conspires with them;
    they're exactly like the fog that spreads and makes
    the sun lose brightness;
    for that I love no wicked people.
    ~ *Songs of the Women Troubadours*

At the evening banquet welcoming the Queen of Castile to the English court, María sat at the table just below the royal dais, counting the times King Henry turned to Queen Juana beside him. Often, he spoke at length to her, time and again breaking into the conversation she was having with Catalina. It did not take Catalina long before she lost her smile, and she wore her unreadable face. By then, she tapped the fingers of her right hand on the table in what María recognised as annoyance.

The king speaking again to the queen, María recalled the times she had seen him talking to his wife. His eyes had been dead since her death, but not so tonight. He leaned towards Queen Juana as if eager to hear every word she said. He spoke close to her ear, and Juana looked at him with widened eyes and laughed. María blinked. *Saint Michael – King Henry has found his heart again. He is in love – with Catalina's sister.*

King Philip spun around from talking to the man next to him. Splashing red wine from his goblet on her, he slipped his hand inside the neck of her gown. Juana started, twisted around, staring at him in silence. An expression of pain tightened her face to a white stillness. Philip laughed, withdrew his hand, and locked eyes with King Henry. Shocked, the English king glanced at Juana with sympathy before turning away.

Catalina, too, seemed shocked. She lowered her eyes, taking her hand closest to Juana off the table. Juana glanced at her, and then hooded her eyes too. Stunned also by King Philip's behaviour, María guessed Catalina clasped her sister's hand out of sight. King Philip either ignored his wife for the rest of the evening, or belittled her, or mocked her. He drank and drank until he was drunk, all the while the Queen of Castile ate little on her plate. *Poor Juana. She seems too frightened to speak – even to her sister.*

María gasped, waking up from a dreadful dream. Catalina stirred restlessly beside her. Her heart beating fast, drumming loud in her ears, María rolled onto her side, curling up. Fearing to sleep again, she took deep breaths. Wax dripped down the night candle near the bed as she remembered her dream. She shuddered at the images in her mind. *King Philip threw blood over Juana, and shoved Catalina away. She came to their aid, but the king grabbed her by the throat, and began to squeeze. She could not breathe....*

Still trembling, María closed her eyes. *Dear God, let me sleep without nightmares.*

María met Will after morning Mass. Thinking him unusually quiet as they walked side by side in the gardens, María rubbed her eyes, and yawned. "Did you sleep badly too?" she asked.

"Well enough," Will answered. "I heard something from my manservant this morning."

"Oh?" She yawned again, and tried to clear her mind. It felt as foggy as the morning mist before her eyes.

"It concerns your princess."

She rounded on Will, at last woken up. "You best tell me then."

"King Philip did violence to his wife last night."

"What – are you certain?"

"My servant is certain – and I believe him. He passed the queen's apartments in the night. He heard breaking furniture, the smack of blows, the queen pleading with her husband." Will reddened. "He believes the king took the queen like a beast. She was weeping, and begging him to stop."

"God's teeth – how am I to tell my princess this?

"Must you tell her?

"I have to – it is something she needs to know."

Leaving Will, María arrived back to her princess's chamber at the same time a message arrived from Juana. Catalina read it, then handed her the brief letter.

Chiquitina,

My lord husband commands I return to our ships without delay, and wait for him there.

Farewell.

"Why has she gone so soon?" Catalina asked. She dropped into her chair, her eyes bright with tears.

María chewed her mouth, and decided to give her friend a watered-down version of what Will had told her. "She had an argument with the king, her husband, last night."

Angrily, Catalina turned to her. "Phillip is unworthy of her. He gives my sister none of the respect owed to her as Queen of Castile. I know he is her husband, but to allow him to command her. I do not understand." She brushed her wet eyes. "I had only one hour in her company. It is cruel to her, and to me."

María clasped Catalina's hand. *King Philip is cruel. But do I tell her how cruel?* She took in Catalina's too pale, distressed face. *Not yet. Not yet. No – not yet.*

October 1506, Fulham Palace

Doña, my dear Latina,

News has come to us of the death of King Philip. Is it true what they say about the queen – that she refuses to give up his body for entombment?

With little desire to think or write of death, even the death of a vile man like King Philip, María put down her quill and peered out the window. Through the ripples of the thick glass, she could see a golden light washing over the garden as if bidding the day farewell. Autumn had arrived. Leaves fell from the trees and spread a thick carpet on the ground. She was glad they were here, and not at Richmond. She liked the peace, the gardens, and the privacy which Richmond Palace never had. She picked up her quill and penned another line.

Do you think it is true what they say about the king?

She stared at what she had written, chewing her bottom lip. *Can I write that? Even to Latina, can I write a question like that?* She reached for her knife, scraping away her words, all the while thinking of the power struggle between Catalina's father and Henry Tudor. Juana and Philip's departure saw the ill use of Catalina resume in full. King Henry's treaty with King Philip soon led to the English King publicly stating the betrothal between Catalina and his son was invalid. The relationship between Aragon and England was at an end until King Ferdinand paid what he owed of Catalina's dowry.

Both kings seemed not to care the bone they fought over was a young, increasingly despairing and ill woman. The English King gave King Ferdinand six months to pay Catalina's dowry. The six-month deadline passed, and King Henry extended it for a further three months. But when King Ferdinand refused to budge, Catalina became the butt of the king's anger.

King Henry has cut off the pittance he gives to maintain my princess's household. She has put herself into debt again to ensure there is food for us to eat. Thank God King Ferdinand sent her some money – but it is not nearly enough. My princess has pawned close to everything she has to pawn.

It feels to me my days are more difficult than my princess. Her faith has always been stronger than mine. These hard days have made her faith stronger still. Besides the consolation of prayer, my princess was also comforted when her father offered her proof of his care and respect of her by naming her his ambassador to the English court, which also gave her some income. Prince Harry also gave my princess comfort for a time. The youth escaped his father's eye to spend time with her. He played her his songs and my princess shared with him the books she read. The boy strutted like a cock at my princess's words of praise. It was clear the prince relished her approval, and he sought it out more and more.

But even that small comfort was taken from her. When King Henry discovered the reason behind his son's daily excursions, he speedily commanded her to leave the court and return to Fulham Palace. He covered his hand by saying it was out of concern for Catalina's health. The king's command only served to make my princess sicker.

Now Catalina is heartsick about her sister, Juana. She sent a strange letter to my princess...

María put aside her quill again, thinking of what happened that morning when Catalina read the letter.

"Juana believes our lord father had her husband poisoned." Catalina had leaned forward and given the letter to the fire. "It is true what we hear; my sister has lost her mind in her grief. Our father does not do murder."

Murder? King Ferdinand does not do murder? Latina called him a murderer. María, her head pounding, looked down at herself as a child, standing outside of Latina's bedchamber. Inside, Latina was praying, and weeping. That morning, Catalina's sister, Isabel, had died in childbirth. Latina had been with her for the birth. And she, a child, unable to comfort Catalina about the news of her sister's death, had gone to Latina in search of comfort from the adult she most loved at court. She had never expected to find Latina sobbing.

"Dear God," Latina rambled through her tears, "King Ferdinand is evil. Evil, I say. Isabel's blood is on his hands. He killed her as surely as he murdered her first husband. How could she live learning of her husband's murder? Forgive me, God, but I curse the King; I curse him for what he has done to me, and to others."

María had run away, not wanting to hear anything more. She had never told Catalina about what she heard. First, because of Catalina's grief about losing Isabel. Later, she had started to believe Latina had spoken wildly through her sorrow. The memory became like a confused nightmare. A nightmare belonging to a day of tragedy. It was easier to think it a nightmare and push it deep into the recesses of her mind.

And she had not told Catalina of her memory that morning. Despite everything he put her through, Catalina wanted to

believe in her royal father. She did not want to think ill of him –
even if this became more of a struggle with every new day. When
Juana departed England, Catalina blamed King Philip for her
new problems, not her father.

*If Catalina ever saw the king at last as others do, it could
break her as it did Juana, and also her sister Isabel. I love her too
much to ever risk her sanity.*

At last surmounting her helplessness, María returned to
writing her letter to Latina.

*The princess received news today that we return soon to Durham
House. The king treats my princess like a pawn – to be moved at
will. But at least Durham House is a place we all like...*

María lifted her eyes again to the autumn day. The gateway
of the herb garden was open. The footpath before it was awash
with light, as if inviting her to go out and enjoy the final hours
of day. *Si – I like Durham House, but not as much as here.
Fulham Palace is my favourite place of all.* She sighed again. *The
machinations of King Ferdinand and the English king turn us all
into pawns. We have little power to win this game. Not even my
princess.*

The angry spring wind bent young oak trees, breaking branches,
battering down flowers, scattering and swirling leaves and petals
in its wake. Its voice whooshed like a torrent of water over-
whelming its banks. María tightened her hold on her full basket
of herbs, as she fought the powerful wind to return inside.

Holding down the contents of her basket, she glanced at the afternoon's ominous dark clouds. A lightning- bolt forked the sky, then another. She quickened her step. A heavy raindrop struck her almost like a small stone and shattered to soak into her gown before the rain fell. The worsening weather seemed a portent for her day; or perhaps of the continuation of these terrible days of trial.

Going inside, she blinked and adjusted to the change of light in the long gallery. Darkening outside, inside was darker still. They had no money to waste on candlelight. The few candles they used were in the rooms of Catalina and her women.

Heading back to these rooms, María corrected herself. Not just the rooms of the women. There were a few men who were part of Catalina's household – and another man had joined them at Durham House three weeks ago: Fray Diego Fernández, a Franciscan priest, now Catalina's confessor.

María saw him walking straight towards her. She halted in her steps, and then continued on. A lightning flash illuminated the gallery – delineating his lean, hooded figure. Before María blinked again, his brown Franciscan robes seemed transmuted into cloth of gold. Closer, he still seemed not to notice her, but that did not surprise her. Since his arrival, Catalina was the only person he took care to cultivate, and to influence. In the short time he had been with them, he was already making his presence known, a watchful presence often imposed upon the women. *Whether we wanted it or not.*

They were side by side now. When he glanced her way, María lowered her eyes. He did not say a word of greeting, just continued on his way. For a man of God vowed to celibacy, he was handsome: fair hair, blue eyes, high cheekbones, closely shaven skin, a full, well-shaped mouth. *Si, too handsome for those of small minds and loose tongues.* Unlike so many Franciscan priests, there was no doubt he bathed and wore clean robes. Today, María sniffed the rose water as he passed her.

Do I do him a disservice in my lack of trust? Am I right to be worried about the priest? Coming from Castile, with Bella's recommendation, Catalina had welcomed him with little question about his character, just relieved to gain a confessor from an order she revered. With the passing of only three weeks, she also respected and revered him. *I wish Catalina was more cautious about where she gave her trust. Bella admitted she only had brief knowledge of him, but others thought well of him. Si – he is a man of God, but Catalina should not relax her guard so soon. He is a stranger to us.* She sighed. *If I speak of my concerns I may upset Catalina for no good purpose. I may simply misjudge the man.*

Content to be away from the other women, María took her basket to the room set up by the physician as his stillroom – one he was happy to share with her as long as she was willing to prepare some of his concoctions. Their day by day confinement in the chambers allowed to them sometimes reminded her of travelling in the andas back home. That, too, had imprisoned her in boredom. On the table near the room's only window, she cut up mint, putting it in a measure of vinegar before pouring it into a flask to ferment.

At least, she had this time alone. Her unacknowledged role in caring for Catalina's well-being and health gave her the excuse she needed to escape to the herb garden whenever the weather allowed, or to keep up her learning by reading. She could never be bored in the garden or the stillroom. Her time in both places allowed her to think, to read, to learn.

A girl's laughter cut through the whine of the wind and shook María from her musing. Leaving her knife beside the chopping board, she padded to the open door and looked down the corridor. Francisca was deep in conversation with the middle-aged Grimaldi. One of their princess's many creditors, he belonged to a banking house which held power over King Ferdinand due to his many debts. His banking house also had Catalina in its power.

Grimaldi put his hand under Francisca's chin, lifting her face. Surprised Francisca did not break away from him, María drew back little, hoping they did not see her. Grimaldi pulled Francisca into his arms, and kissed her. Once again, Francisca made no effort to resist his advances, rather, she kissed him back as if this was not the first time, but one of many encounters. Francisca laughed again when one of his hands began to untie her bodice and the other pulled at her skirt, but this time she broke away from him. She said something – and blew a kiss his way, before heading back to Catalina's chambers. María returned to the mint on the chopping board and picked up her knife. She swallowed, staring at the uncut herb, tempted to gulp down one of her concoctions to settle the unease churning in her stomach. *Should I tell Catalina?* She began chopping again. *Catalina is already worn out dealing with the troubles brought about by her father and the English King.*

She has far greater concerns than Francisca's ill-judged romance. Surely this is a little thing – too little to bother Catalina about?

Francisca was no longer a girl, but, at twenty-one, well into womanhood. She should know better. But, like all of them, she saw few men, and only irregularly. María put down her knife, looking at the jars on the shelf. All of them represented the many hours of her lonely life. *God knows, all of us are women denied husbands and children. Is it wrong she dallies with a man? Have I not done the same thing - and with a married man? I am no innocent to cast the first stone.* She picked up her knife again. *But with Grimaldi? A man not only decades older than her, but also one with no noble blood. A man who is a money lender. A man who already has a too great a hold over our princess. I will talk to Francisca, and warn her to be careful.*

Morning prayer in the chapel finished, María broke away from the women returning with Catalina to her chambers and took the path to the herbal garden. Arriving there, María noticed Francisca coming through the back gate some distance away, heading back to the princess's apartment. *Strange. She is all alone. And she was missing from chapel this morning.* She put Francisca out of her mind and weeded for the next hour, and then worked on in the stillroom. Her morning tasks completed, she went to change her clothes before re-joining the other women. She took in the antechamber and swallowed back a sigh. Catalina's chair was empty again. In the window- seat near it, Francisca bent her head, repairing a sleeve. Light streamed through the window, showering over her slim figure, delineating her in its haze.

She shut the door, picked up the book she had started reading the day before, and sat next to Francisca. "Where's everyone?"

Francisca made a face. "Where do you think?"

She sighed. "With Fray Diego? Perhaps we too should find the time to listen to him read from the Holy Bible."

"Holy Bible?" Francisca sniffed. "If it only was the Bible that Fray Diego concerned himself about."

María looked aside at Francisca. Her eyes focused on her task, Francisca sewed fast, and angrily, patching up a rip in the sleeve. *She too distrusts Fray Diego. But for what cause? Perhaps, for both of us, there is no cause other than jealousy since Catalina spends most of her free time with him. But I think Francisca is angry for another reason.*

"What's troubling you?" María asked, leaning closer.

Her hands stilling, Francisca lifted her eyes, frowning. "Who says I am troubled?"

"Amiga – you do. I can see it by your words, by everything you do today." She pursed her lips. "I saw you this morning, in the garden. You were coming through the gate." She met Francisca's eyes. "Where did you go?"

Francisca flushed, and lowered her head. "It's none of your concern, María, and I do not wish to speak of it."

María decided to take the bit between her teeth. "Was your morning excursion anything to do with Grimaldi?"

Dropping the sleeve to her lap, Francisca stared at her, and then burst into tears. As suddenly as she started crying, she stopped, rubbing her eyes. "What do you know, María?"

"Little enough. I saw you yesterday with him – and now today I saw you come in through the gate as if returning from somewhere. I know Grimaldi lives close by because our ambassador lodges with him." She released a long breath. "None of this seems wise."

"Wise? What would be wise would be the princess

dismissing her foolish priest. Before he came, Princess Catalina listened to Don Fuensalida – as she should to her ambassador. But she now only listens to the priest. Do you know he has arranged for more of the princess's goods to be sold?"

María sat back against the cushions, holding her book to her chest. "When did you learn this?"

"I heard Princess Catalina argue with Don de Cuero. Poor man. Bad enough he has had to live with the English humiliating him at every turn by calling him a lowly usher, when he is her treasurer, but now the princess tells him he is a traitor because he refuses to hand over a valuable plate to sell. In two weeks, Fray Diego has arranged the sale of enough of the princess's goods to realise two hundred ducats. Cuero told me most of it will be spent on books, and to pay the wages of the princess's confessor."

María rubbed the side of her face. She knew all this – but had thought it not the case for the rest of the household. *I should know better. We live too close together to hide matters like these.* "I do not think it matters," she said slowly. "The princess needs to get money from somewhere. I would rather see her sell the goods of her dowry, than to keep going to creditors. But you have changed the subject, Francisca. Grimaldi and you...I do not think that is wise at all."

Francisca reddened. "He wishes to marry me."

Stunned, María considered her. "He is what – fifty? And he is not noble."

"So? He is rich, and clever. And he adores me." Francisca turned to her. "I have not told him yes. Tell me true, do you not think it is time for the princess to see she will never marry the English prince? Henry Tudor wants a better prize for his son.

Can you not tell her to write to King Ferdinand and tell him it is time for us all to go home?"

María shook her head. "It is not my place to tell her such things."

"Why not? You have been with the princess since a child – and none are close to her as you are. Surely, you want to marry, to have children?"

"Si. I want to marry, and have children," she said quietly, all the time thinking of Will. Those few, fleeting and infrequent moments in his company gave her life its only joy. She turned to Francisca. "I made a promise to our princess long ago I would stay with her. It is for her to decide when to write to her father. It is for her to decide if I ever return to Castile. And I don't think you are right about her betrothal to the prince. She has told me it cannot be undone, not unless they wish to humiliate the royal house of Aragon. She would die before she saw that happen. Duty is our princess's lodestar. My princess is mine. What about you, Francisca? What is your lodestar?"

Francisca averted her face, staring out the window, saying nothing.

19

All my youth I have loved, often; long loved and keenly yearned, and it has cost me dearly!
~ *Anonymous medieval lament*

Alone in the gallery at Richmond Palace, María plucked at the strings of her vihuela, and hummed. Will had gone home for a month, and she sorely missed him. She tried not to think about his wife.

She shifted to the deeper shadows in the window seat, and once again tried to capture the music and words beating a pulse in her head. She played awhile in thought, trying to find the right notes. A slow, soulful song birthed, stretched and fluttered its wings in her mind; she needed to find a tune to marry with it. She wanted her song whole, released, no longer a ghost of possibility, but something real and alive. She wanted her song to fly.

She sang quietly, tasting the words one by one as they melded in with the notes:

Oh, my aching heart
Be still
And quiet
'Tis useless to wish for
What you cannot have.
She sighed. *Si – what I cannot have...*

Footsteps echoed, light, unhurried footsteps. María raised her eyes. Prince Henry approached her. She had chosen this place with care, and hoped its distance and seclusion from the royal apartments would give the privacy she craved, time to spend alone with her vihuela; for a chance to compose this song which demanded birth. *Now I must put aside my instrument to curtsey to this spoilt, arrogant youth. A youth I daily struggle to like.* She smiled her false smile, and prepared to playact yet again.

The prince waved a hand at her. "Sit; keep playing." He sat close by, and looked aside at her. "I heard you in the library. You have a good voice." He grinned. "I too sing well; Even the king, my father, says so." His blue eyes once more considered her. "What song was that? I do not think I have heard it before?"

María rubbed the side of her face, shifted a little away from him. "It is a song I was composing, Your Highness."

He appeared taken aback. "Words and music?"

"Yes, Your Highness."

The prince shook his head. "I have known few women who know how to write songs." He looked troubled. "My mother was one; my sister Mary is like her and also composes music.

Other than that..." He turned towards her. "Does the Princess Katherine write and play music?"

"The princess does not write music, but she knows how to play the harp and will sometimes practice a new song by use of her clavichord. But she prefers to show her love of music by listening, and dancing."

The youth grinned. "Good. Any wife of mine would need to love music – and know how to dance. I would not like it if she didn't." He reached over and took her vihuela, brushing his blunt fingers against the strings. He did it again, but this time – to María's surprise – strummed a confident chord. "This instrument is from Castile?" he asked.

"Yes, Your Highness." María shifted again, pushing down her annoyance and urge to snatch her vihuela off him. She rarely allowed others to touch it; a long-ago gift from Prince Juan, it was too precious to her to risk it to strangers – or those she had not learnt to trust. And it was her vihuela. The prince had taken it without even asking if he could.

Unaware of her impatience to see him gone, the prince strummed a short melody. When his fingers stumbled over the notes, he sniffed and passed the vihuela back to her. "I prefer the lute. It has a better sound."

"If you say so, Your Highness."

He frowned at her. "You do not agree?"

María shrugged. "All musicians have their own preferences; for me, I have played a vihuela since childhood." She smiled. Pulled by the strong current of memory, she saw a sunlit chamber and Prince Juan, blond, with gentle eyes, his smile lighting up his handsome face as he murmured words of encouragement. How patient he had been with her; even as a five-year-old, she knew the honour of receiving her first lessons on playing a vihuela from him. He had given her this vihuela for her twelfth birthday, not long before his death.

She glanced at the prince beside her. Prince Henry was so different; a bold, strutting cock, while Juan had been like a caged nightingale. Despite the cage, while he lived, Juan sang, to touch all hearts, a song of goodness and nobility of soul. She inwardly sighed. His death, and Arthur's, seemed so wrong, a jest of God's which still made no sense.

"Play me your song again," the prince commanded.

María shuttered away her memories of one prince, and attended to another. She lifted her chin. "Forgive me, but I have not finished it yet." She swallowed. "It is not ready for Your Highness's ears."

His small slit eyes narrowed. "It sounded good enough to me when I heard you in the library."

María shifted away from him. She wanted to say, *Foolish boy, do you not know that you cannot expect to receive everything you ask for? I have no wish to share this song with you. I write this song for the one I love. Sharing it with you would only serve to tarnish my gift, and I would no longer wish to give it.* She met his eyes, thinking fast. "I would prefer to hear a song of yours, Your Highness, than any of my unworthy attempts to be a songstress. It would honour me to hear you sing."

"Would it?" He brightened, his previous annoyance seemingly all forgotten. He bounded up from the seat. "I will go and fetch my lute then."

María watched him hurry down the corridor until she saw him no more. She sighed, strumming notes on her vihuela, and singing softly under her breath.

Oh, my aching heart
Be still
And quiet
'Tis useless to wish for What you cannot have...

She lifted her fingers from the strings, transfixed. It came to her that Prince Henry was one who would never be quiet, or still. As for knowing the uselessness of wishing for what he could never have? He was more likely to think everything he wanted was his for the taking – even if it meant destroying everything else that stood in his way. *Am I wrong to think this? He's only a boy. The years could teach him a greater wisdom – a knowledge of humility. He may yet learn what love means; you cannot take it, or own it.* But she doubted it. Despite his handsome looks, there was something rotten about him. He reminded her of a beautiful apple, red and appetising to look at, but rotten at its core. He still caused her skin to crawl. She hoped and prayed his long dead mother was right. Once married to Catalina, the good in Henry would have its chance to flourish over the bad. She sighed. Her doubt remained fixed, immovable. A loud crash and a cry close by woke her from her musing.

Setting aside her vihuela, she hurried towards the sound. She let out a cry. A wall of the gallery had collapsed. Beside the rubble, the prince sat on the ground, rubbing the top of his head. María rushed over to him and knelt by his side. "Are you all right, my prince?"

All the colour fled from his face, the youth had a red wheal on his forehead and a tiny wound dribbled blood near to one eye. "My God," he said, "That was close. One more step and I would have been under that wall. One of the beams knocked me down."

"Your Highness, you know I have some medical knowledge," María took out the folded, unused white handkerchief from the pocket of her gown and showed it to him. "With your permission, may I clean the wound and examine you?"

Prince Henry grinned. "Go ahead, my lady."

María wiped away the blood, and then checked his eyes. His pupils were normal: no sign of serious head injury. The wound was barely a scrape, a superficial scratch at most. Heavy, running footsteps sounded behind her. She turned to see two of the king's guards and John Skelton, the tutor of the prince, and Wolsey, one of the king's chaplains, now fast approaching them. Prince Henry smiled slowly and took between his fingers a long strand of her hair which had freed itself from her headgear. "Hair shimmering with the blue-lights of a crow's wing and black doe eyes to entrap a man with one glance. You are Helen born again; there is none to compare with you at my father's court." He laughed. "I was starting to think you didn't like me."

She smiled at him, both flattered and admiring his bravery. Perhaps she was wrong. Perhaps there was more about this prince to give them hope of a better tomorrow.

The other men reached them. Wolsey and Skelton helped the prince up and one of the guards assisted María from the ground. Supported on either side by Wolsey and Skelton, the prince started to walk with them, going back the way they had come. He stopped, and stared at her. "Tomorrow, come you to the place I found you today. Tomorrow you will play me your song." Without another word, he turned and headed to the apartments of his father. Watching him go, she stood there for a long time, gazing at the ruins of the gallery. It seemed to her the ruin of all hope.

The cold nights meant she was once more Catalina's bedcompanion. In the princess's bed that night, she remembered the prince's demand. She tossed and turned until her anger brewed and threatened to bubble over, at last waking Catalina up.

"What's wrong? Are you not well?" Catalina asked, sleepily, rolling onto her back.

"I'm not ill."

"What is it then?"

María sighed. "Forgive me for not telling you, but Prince Henry found me this morning when I was composing my song for Will. The prince wants me to play it for him tomorrow."

Catalina turned, facing her. "He does? Why?"

María sniffed. "The young prince wants to show he has the upper hand." She pumped her pillow, and laid back, staring at the ceiling. "He has no right to ask this of me. I do not write this song for him."

"And I have told you – you should not be writing songs for a married man. It is a sin, María."

"I know, and I confessed it to our household's priest. You know Will and I have vowed to friendship only."

"Still, you write him songs."

"I love him. I cannot help loving him. But it is not Will who is my concern tonight. I do not want to obey the prince's command and meet with him tomorrow."

Catalina remained silent for a long moment. "If he commands you, María, you must obey. What if I go with you – would that help at all?"

"But the ambassador is coming tomorrow. That is too important a meeting to cancel for a spoilt prince."

"I forgot. You are right; I must meet with the ambassador. And you must meet with the prince. I do not like it that you think so little of him. I do not think him spoilt, but only young. He loves music, and so do you. Perhaps if you spend more time sharing this love with him, you may yet find a common ground and grow to like him. I hate the thought that my sister thinks so little of the man who, God willing, will one day be my husband."

Husband? By all the Saints, the boy is an arrogant, overweening rogue.

Catalina shifted as if in discomfort. "María –"

"Si?"

"It worries me that you never think to take someone with you on these daily excursions of yours. You put yourself in unnecessary danger."

María shrugged. "I am twenty, and a grown woman. There are guards everywhere, at every entrance. We have a river on one side of us, and high stone walls on every other side. I never go out at night. I am as safe here as if I was imprisoned. Sometimes, I think we are, that the king means for us to be imprisoned." She moved a little away from Catalina. "Our teacher never had someone shadowing her every move, why should I?"

Half-listening to Catalina list all the reasons she should not be alone a memory came to her – one she had pushed into the far recesses of her mind.

Sent by the nuns to gather some herbs from the royal garden, she had found her teacher there, dishevelled, walking as if a sleepwalker. Green light pooled over her and darkened the red ugly marks on her neck.

Down the many years, María heard her child-self voice say: "Something is wrong, my teacher." She had not known what it was, only that Latina wanted to hide something.

Latina's behaviour and words had bewildered her, and for the first time in her life, her teacher spoke to her in anger: "Go from here, María. Go and enjoy these days too soon ended, when childhood gives you freedom denied to us who are no longer children."

She saw again Latina's face; it had been wet with tears.

Thinking back now, the pieces of her bewilderment came together and began to make sense. María shivered, recalling other times when Latina had stepped back into the shadows, her face paling in fear. Then she would shake herself, straighten her shoulders and move forward again, all the time averting her eyes from King Ferdinand, as if she refused to see him, and wished to erase him from her life. Latina's hatred for King Ferdinand had only deepened María's own innate distrust of the king.

"María – are you listening to me?"

"Si." She rolled on her side, pulled at the cover of the bed, curling up for warmth. She fought back tears. If what she suspected of the king was true, she had one more secret to keep from Catalina.

"Will you please take a companion with you in future?"

María smiled slightly. "You do not command it?"

Catalina sighed. "I do not want to command you. You are my sister, si?"

María reached for Catalina's hand. "Si, your sister. I promise you, I will take a companion if I believe there is risk of danger. But pray put your mind at rest. We are too well guarded here, and I know how to look after myself."

I know how to look after myself. The next day, at the same time and place, she put down her vihuela on the window-seat and began to pace, recalling Catalina's concern with growing annoyance of having no choice but to obey the prince.

Her footsteps the only sound in the gallery, she became aware of time passing and wondered if her fortune had changed for the better. Perhaps the prince was not coming. She returned to the window seat and picked up her vihuela. Perching on the edge of the seat, she prepared to fly at the next ringing of bells calling for prayer. She cradled her vihuela and plucked its strings in thought. She blinked at the sudden burst of the light from the window; it captured her in its warmth, and she turned towards it, reminded of a song. Settling herself deeper in the window-seat, she plucked the strings of her vihuela again, but this time sought to remember the tune. At last, she knew it. Shutting her eyes, she joined her voice to the notes of her vihuela:

> *Take to your place at the window*
> *Please come and catch my love!*
> *My eyes are very tired, I am weary of looking out for*
>   *him...*

Hands clapped and clapped. Startled, she opened her eyes.

The prince grinned at her. "No need to be weary; I am here."

She swallowed. *Arrogant boy. First, you command me to play you the song I wrote for my lover. Now you think this song I sing because I miss him is for you. You think too much of yourself.*

The habit of long years of service to royalty reined in her anger, reminding her she had forgotten to rise and curtsey. Doing this quickly, she now said, "I am here as commanded, Prince Henry."

"And I was tardy. The king, my father, needed to speak to me this morning about what happened yesterday. He has imprisoned the builders who built that gallery. The king is furious; their trumpery work almost killed me. I am pleased you waited for me." He sat on the window seat and gestured to the space beside him. "Pray sit, and play me that song from yesterday."

Perching yet again on the edge of the seat, she looked aside at him. "The song is still unfinished, Your Highness. Could I not play you something else?"

His eyes narrowed in what seemed annoyance. "I begin to think you do not want to play me your song."

She bent her head, hoping he would not see how true that was. "Your Highness, it is an unfinished song. It may never be finished. I do you no honour by playing a song that is not yet a true song." She considered him for a long moment. "I know of other better songs."

The prince scowled. "Sing me one then," he said.

Annoyed by yet another command, she shook her head, and tried to force herself to pick a song, but all the songs coming to mind were love songs. She had no desire to sing love songs to this youth. At last, she remembered a song that seemed safe. She played its opening chord, and sang:

Lovely Yolanz in a quiet room
unfolds silk fabric across her knees.
She sews with one golden thread, another of silk.
Her cruel mother chastises her:
"I reproach you for it, lovely Yolanz."
"Mother, why do you reproach me:
Is it because of the way I sew or cut
Or spin or embroider?
Or is it because I sleep too much?

The prince laughed, and reached out a hand to touch her cheek. She shifted away from him, placing her vihuela to the floor. When she straightened, the prince seized and pulled her towards him, and kissed her clumsily.

She broke away. Furious, she grabbed her vihuela as if a shield and stood. Wiping her mouth, wanting to spit at him, she stared at him. The anger brewing from last night frothed, and bubbled over. "You dare to kiss me?" It no longer mattered he was prince. He was a boy who had overreached himself.

Lounging back in the window-seat, he laughed. "I like you. I told you yesterday, you are the most beautiful woman at my father's court. You also have spirit." He reached for her, but she moved away from him. The prince flushed then, and stood, over towering her. "You should be honoured."

She thought fast. "Your Highness, you are a most handsome and gifted youth, and I pray you forgive me for my first shock and angry words. You do honour me by your attentions, but you must understand my close relationship to the Princess Katherine, your betrothed, does not allow me to even contemplate a dalliance with you. Not ever." She met his eyes. "Besides that, I too am of royal blood, and I will be no man's plaything. Your Highness, I am twenty to your fifteen. Ask me to play for you, write songs with you, teach you about herbs or medicine, but there can be nothing else between us. The princess is my kinswoman and my dearest friend. And you are betrothed to marry her."

He broke eye contact, his face flushed with shame. He straightened his shoulders, and met her eyes again. "As I said, I like your spirit. Perhaps I was wrong to kiss you; but it was suggested to me by my men that I should learn something of women before I wed the princess. I am fifteen, well time for me to act a man in all ways. You are beautiful, and I like you, and thought you liked me."

She stared at him, unable to believe her ears. *The boy chose me for his mistress?*

"I do like you," she lied. "But only as one who desires to offer friendship. I am a chaste woman of noble birth, Your Highness. I would die rather than bring dishonour to my family. I am loyal to, and am trusted by the Princess Katherine. You look in the wrong place, Your Highness."

The prince shrugged. "You are right. I forgot your relationship with the princess." He waved a hand. "Go then. I will find another woman who knows, as well as appreciates, the honour bestowed upon her by my interest."

María curtseyed. She looked at him. "Pray, you do understand why I must refuse you?"

He rose from the window-seat, screwed his mouth, looked her up and down. "Aye. I expect my people to be loyal, and I am glad my future bride has one such as you amongst her women. My father tells me loyalty should always be rewarded. No doubt you will show your loyalty in other ways." He pointed at her vihuela. "I would like us to make music together in future, and continue learning from you about medicine."

María curtseyed again and straightened. "That I am most happy to do, Your Highness. I bid you good day."

Walking down the long gallery, knowing she had not asked his permission to leave, she felt his eyes boring into her back. All her instincts crying out to hurry, she had to use all her control to keep her steps normal. She was thankful he could no longer see her face. Nauseous, aware of her fast beating heart, she did not need a mirror to know her face would be stark and white. She wanted to run from him. *He is a boy. A boy.* She tightened her hold on the vihuela, holding it to her. *A boy who will one day be king. How do I avoid him? I must avoid him. I never want his hands on me again.* She shivered with disgust. *Dear God, help me.*

That same afternoon, it seemed God had heard her prayer. Catalina received notice from the king that she would be moved from Richmond again. Two days later saw them returned to Fulham Palace.

20

If beyond earthly wont, the flame of love
  Illume me, so that I o'ercome thy power
  Of vision, marvel not: but learn the cause...
  ~ *Dante*

María sat on the stool near the fire. Kneading her aching stomach, she locked her eyes on Catalina. For yet another time, since dawn, in the closet of her private altar, her princess was on her knees, praying. Her hair unbound, Catalina tugged at the rough neckline of the brown robe she had taken to wearing in recent weeks, exposing her red and irritated skin. The scapular, the robe of the third order of the Franciscans, did little to disguise her growing thinness.

María recalled their final years in Castile. Sorrow had

followed sorrow. Catalina had learnt the consolation of prayer then. She sighed. *I wish I could say the same. All I learnt then was doubt, and to struggle for my faith. It seems a lifelong struggle – but one I think healthier than being obsessed with prayer like Catalina. She has been even more obsessed since Fray Diego became her confessor.*

Four, five, six, seven or more times a day, Catalina knelt before him, and prayed. It was his influence which had brought Catalina to the wearing of the religious robe. It was his influence which led to more days of fasting. María hurled a small log onto the fire, wishing she could do the same with the priest's influence. *Is there any wonder Catalina is fatigued and prone to illness?* She hurled another log on the fretful fire. *And I do not believe Catalina's physician makes matters any better.* The man insisted a monthly bloodletting would improve her health. But since beginning this harsh practice, Catalina's monthly bleeding had become fitful and scanty.

In bed that night, María stared at her friend's back when Catalina rolled over. Her thin chemise slipped down one arm to reveal her thin, naked shoulder. She could even make out Catalina's backbone. She pulled the blanket up to cover Catalina's shoulder, her fingers touching her friend's naked flesh. She yanked her fingers away. There were times, like now, when sleeping close to Catalina stirred up feelings which left María confused, and perturbed. She closed her eyes, wanting Will's lips and hands on her body. Wanting Will here in the bed beside her, and not her closest friend. She closed her eyes, pushing away her sinful thoughts. She opened her eyes, worrying again about how much weight Catalina had lost in recent weeks.

"Why fast every day? Surely to fast on Friday is enough for anyone," María grumbled.

Catalina rolled in the bed, facing María. "I am ill enough. It is easier to go without, than suffer the consequences of bad food. We are given fish even when I am too ill to eat it. Even if I was dying, they would send me fish. I'd rather not eat at all."

"You're right. They send to us food none of us want to eat, but if we don't eat it, we will starve. Even King Henry is concerned about how little you eat. Why else would he ask the pope to give Prince Henry the right to order you to not to fast so often? Could I not cook for you? I could make you a soup to settle your stomach."

Catalina clasped María's hand. "Do not worry about me. Let's go to sleep." Catalina turned away, rolling over to face to the other way.

María lay back in the bed and stared at its dark canopy. *Not worry? I cannot help but worry. Catalina's despair frightens me. Every day, she talks of death. I wish the priest did not have such a hold on her.* She tightened her lips. It was easy to see the reason why. All of them were caged – living unnatural lives. Catalina more than anyone else because of her rank. These long days, months, years of enforced loneliness would leave any young woman vulnerable to the words of a charming, too handsome man. She knew Catalina was innocent of any wrongdoing, but she was not too certain if the same could be said of the priest.

Si – this priest...he has far too much power over my princess, and desires it so. Unable to sleep, María shifted uneasily, thinking about what had happened only last week. King Henry, sending his daughter Mary with his message, had summoned Catalina to come to Richmond. Catalina had been unwell all through the night, but the unexpected summons had restored her spirits; at times, she thought the king forgot her. She had gone to Mass with Mary and was breaking her fast with the thirteen-year-old princess when Fray Diego had been announced. Sitting on the window-seat, María lifted her eyes from the book she was reading when he bowed to the two princesses.

"I believe you have met my confessor?" Catalina had asked her young sister-in-law.

Mary nodded, gazing with unhidden interest at the handsome man.

"Is it true you plan to go to Richmond, Your Highness?" Fray Diego asked bluntly in Latin.

"Si – once I finish breakfast, good Father. The king wishes to see me."

"You cannot go," the priest demanded.

Mary swung around to Catalina with wide eyes.

Catalina flushed. "I cannot go? What do you mean, Father?"

"I have been informed you were not well last night."

María had felt her own eyes widen then. *Who told him? I know I did not tell anyone about Catalina vomiting in the night. It must have been the servant who took away the bowl.*

The priest approached Catalina until he stood over her.

Startled, María almost dropped her book. *By all the Saints. Catalina may owe him her obedience as her confessor, but I still think the man oversteps himself.*

"You look ill even now – far too ill to go to Richmond," the priest said.

"But I am much better." She gestured over her empty plate. "I have even eaten today. Believe me, I am well."

"I say otherwise. As your confessor, I command you not to go."

Flushing again, Catalina glanced at Mary. "But Father…I do not want to stay here all alone."

"You will not be alone. I will be here, and your women. If you stay well today, you may go to Richmond tomorrow." He bowed again, and backed out of the room.

Mary blinked, and whispered close to Catalina's ear as the man disappeared. Catalina shook her head. "Believe me, sister, he is faithful, and his advice wise. He is the best priest a woman in my position ever had." She sighed. "I will stay here today. Tomorrow will be soon enough to go to Richmond."

Still wide awake, María rolled in bed, remembering how furious King Henry had been when his daughter returned without Catalina. He had accused her of having an evil relationship with her priest, and Don Fuensalida had taken the king's side. He hated Catalina's confessor and how he influenced her; he expressed no sympathy for the princess, "I acquit the king of the blame, and do not wonder at his anger," he had said to her.

January 1509, Richmond

Doña, my dear Latina,

Our lives are improved since King Ferdinand has appointed his daughter ambassador to the English court. The position means the princess has some money to pay her servants and maintain her household. It matters little if it came about simply because her father, the king, grew tired of the princess's many letters complaining of her ill use by the men who were supposed to be serving both King Ferdinand and herself.

At the beginning, she placed all the blame onto the shoulders of Doctor de Puebla – even, in her anger, ignoring his failing health. By the time the poor man died, my princess had reason for shame, and guilt.

More guilt. At least, he died knowing the princess thought far better of him because she sent him a letter asking for his forgiveness for all her past errors of judgement. In truth, Fuensalida's appointment some months ago opened the princess's eyes to Doctor de Puebla's true worth. Fuensalida's behaviour brought England and Aragon close to war. King Henry hates him so much he has commanded his guards to refuse him admittance to his chambers. My princess says at least Puebla understood the English and knew how to deal with them. He would never have embroiled her in affairs as Fuensalida has done.

But enough of kings and courts. At last, we look forward to the wedding of Inés. It seems the first joyful occasion in years.

Standing close to Francisca, María clutched at her mantle, wishing the wedding service was over. There was not even a brazier provided in the church to give them some warmth. *Remember your good fortune. Lowborn English marry on the church porch, no matter the weather, and not near the altar – as what happens today.*

"I, William, take you, Inés Vanegas, to be my wedded wife, to have and to hold, from this day forward, for better for worse, for richer, for poorer..."

She looked at William Blount, Lord Mountjoy. It seemed so long ago since she consoled Inés about loving a married man in the library. He was handsome, taller than most men, older than Inés by only six years – a good match for her friend. No one had wished for his wife to die in childbirth; was it wrong if years of sharing his interests with Inés had become something else? Was it wrong for Inés to marry the man she loved?

Was it wrong for her to think of Will on this wedding day – and wish for...she swallowed. *Dear God – what evil am I thinking? Forgive me, forgive me, forgive me...*

When Mountjoy placed the gold wedding ring on Inés's finger, she caught Catalina's smile. She hoped it meant Catalina had put aside her unhappiness about the dowry. It had been a sore point ever since Mountjoy had asked for permission to wed Inés. Catalina had only very little to give her. Mountjoy told her it did not matter. He was a wealthy man who was happy to wed for love. He had even paid for the wedding banquet.

Trying to warm them, María rubbed her hands underneath her mantle. Despite the winter chill, Catalina continued to smile brightly and seemed a different person all through the ceremony. The events of today, without doubt, lifted her spirits. *Praise God. Catalina badly needs some joy in her life.*

At the banquet, María was relieved to be seated beside Francisca, on a table just below the dais with the wedding party. As the guest of honour, Catalina sat next to Inés and Mountjoy, with the priest who had married them today beside her, and Fuensalida, another ambassador of her father's, next to him.

"So – one of us has found a husband – and a wealthy one too," Francisca said quietly, close to her ear.

"Wealthy or not – it is a love match, and we can only be happy for Inés."

Francisca shrugged, and reached for a chicken leg. "I am happy for her. I just desire the same state for myself. More with every day." She gnawed the flesh of the chicken. Wiping away the oil from the meat running over her lips, she murmured, "I hope it comes for me before it is too late." She glanced at María. "At least, thanks to the generosity of our friend's wealthy husband, we will be ensured of food suitable to our station today." Francisca spoke in a rush, as if she wished to forestall any questioning. She turned her head towards the dais. "Is our princess ignoring Fuensalida? It seems to me the man is trying to get her attention."

Taking some fish and bread for her plate, María decided to leave Francisca to her secrets. Her princess gave her enough to worry about. She lifted her gaze to the dais, watching for a few moments. Catalina spoke to Inés, her new husband, the priest, all the while Fuensalida kept his eyes on her, his displeasure becoming more apparent with every passing second. At last, the man swilled down the contents of his goblet and leaned closer to Catalina, forcing the priest to sit back to make room for him. "I have done what you asked, Your Highness," he said in Castilian. "I have written to the king. My letter is gone, as is the one you gave me to send to your royal father."

María let out a gasp. She lowered her warming face, hoping no one heard. *The man forgets himself.* She reached for her goblet and gulped down a mouthful of wine. "Could he not wait for another time to speak about this? This is a happy day," she said softy to Francisca, falling back on her own tongue too. "What letter is he speaking of?" Francisca asked, replying in the same.

"Just another letter to King Ferdinand," she said slowly before sipping her wine.

But it was more than just another letter. Catalina wrote to her father enough was enough. Her only desire was to close the door on these painful years. Like her sister Isabel had done when she lost her first husband, she had begged in her letter to be allowed to return home. She begged her father to be allowed to enter a convent and take the veil.

Will the letter make any difference to King Ferdinand? Will he at last care?

Catalina, her face stripped of all expression, turned to the ambassador. "How long do you think before the king, my father, sends his answer?" she asked, also speaking in the tongue of her birth.

The ambassador shrugged. "You must be patient, Your Highness."

Catalina raised her hand, her fingers tightly fisted. "I am patient. For years, I have been patient. That time is at an end. I have little money left – nothing of value to pawn. I must go home."

"Believe me, I have begged the king to send a ship to take you to Aragon."

Catalina lifted her chin. "We will speak more of this matter at another time, ambassador." She glanced at the priest beside her. "Forgive us, Father," she said in Latin. "My ambassador needed to ask of me a question. Now – what were you saying?"

"Our princess writes so many letters to the king, her father," Francisca said with a sigh.

"Si." María sighed too. *Most of them he ignored. Will this one be any different? But what if Catalina does go home?* María broke a piece from the small loaf of bread before her and began to eat it. *If I return to Castile, I leave my heart behind in England.*

She swung her attention to the newly married couple. They

only had eyes for one another. *Will – oh, Will. I do not want to leave you, but we have no future. What is there for us other than shame and despair? What chance is there for a day like this for us?* She shook her head. She loved and wanted only one man. If she could not have him, she believed she could find contentment by remaining in the service of the one she had loved since her childhood.

Even in a nunnery? She swilled down the last of the wine and stared down into the empty goblet. It did not give her any answer.

Two weeks later, a new letter came from Catalina's father. The king had disregarded his daughter's pleas to come home, and that of his ambassador. Yet again, Catalina ate little, and became sicker.

Catalina was not the only one in their group to suffer from ill health. María watched Francisca with increasing anxiety. Day by day, the girl became paler and paler. One morning, sitting with the women breaking their fast, she pushed away from the table and asked permission to return to the chambers shared by Catalina's attendants.

María spoke briefly to Catalina, and followed after Francisca. Francisca rushed down the corridor, heading towards the privy. Reaching the closed door, María waited for her to come out. Listening to Francisca gag and vomit, she leaned against the wall. *Dear God, do not let it be that. Not that.* But her growing suspicion of the last week or so – a suspicion she had refused to believe – solidified as the slow minutes passed and became impossible to push aside until she wanted to vomit too.

At last, the door opened and Francisca emerged, so white she could have been a ghost. Her eyes widened. "Why are you here?" she asked, her voice panicked and hoarse.

"I am concerned for you." She checked all around before taking Francisca's hand. "Come – come with me to the stillroom. Besides me, the only other person to use it is the physician – and I know he visits a friend today. I promise you, we can talk there without being disturbed."

Francisca met her eyes, then nodded. Side by side, they walked without hurry, as if by not rushing the coming, dreaded conversation could be avoided for all time. Her hands deep in her gown pockets, María discarded thought after thought, each one heavier than the last. By the time they reached the stillroom, she found herself walled in by increased helplessness.

Leading the way, she opened the door to the stillroom for Francisca, letting her go in first. The room was dark, so she kept the door open until she drew aside the thick drape over the room's small window. The sunlight pooled over the large table and stools while not touching the rest of the room. Closing the door, she contemplated Francisca. Seated on one of the table's four stools and with her elbows leaning on its surface, Francisca cradled her head in her hands. María sat on the stool beside her and touched her hand. "You are with child?" she murmured.

Francisca lifted her head, her eyes wide with panic. "I have only missed one menses; surely there could be another cause?"

Thinking, Maria sat straighter, realising she had scored the tabletop's soft wood with her nail. She considered Francisca. "Are your breasts tender?"

Francisca nodded and rubbed her eyes. "Yes, but I cannot be pregnant; how can it be when it was only the once."

"*Si, non caste tamen caute,*" Maria said without thinking.

Francisca frowned at her. "Are you saying I should have used precautions? What precautions are they? And do you know of any that really work, bar for abstinence? I am twenty- three. How long can any of us be expected to live this life of enforced chastity? The only fortunate one amongst us is Inés. She may have married a widower, but at least Baron Mountjoy is young, and she loves him. He is also wealthy, and noble born. Marriage to him will also ensure Inés a place at court with our princess. The princess may talk of entering a convent, but I for one would rather die than be a nun."

"Forgive me," María said, digging her nail deeper into the wood. "I spoke unwisely." *Si, if you can't be chaste, at least be careful.* She trembled, closed her eyes, remembering how close she had once come to surrendering her virginity. *Will's hands on me. My hands on his buttocks, his erect penis between my thighs, rubbing and rubbing against my protected woman's parts until he convulsed with release. No wonder Will dared not come near me for weeks.* She looked aside at Francisca. "It could be me sitting in your place." She smiled with bitterness. "I too do not desire to be a nun. I do not keep my virginity because I fear your fate, not really, but because the man I love has too much honour to see me disgraced." She shrugged. "I am not as brave as you."

Francisca lowered her head; its shape cast a grey shadow on the table. "I am not brave. I am terrified. Help me, María."

María licked her lips. *Francisca has only missed one mense. She may not be with child at all. And if she is pregnant? A child has no soul for at least forty days, or until it quickens.* She rose from the stool and looked at the shelf where she kept all her medicine books. Taking one down from the shelf, she searched until she found the right page. "Here," she said, pointing out the passage to Francisca.

Take root of the red willow with which large wine jars are tied and clean them well of the exterior bark, and, having pulverised them, mix them with wine or water and cook them, and in the morning give them in a potion when it has become lukewarm. Grind madder and marsh mallow, and mix them with barley flour and white of eggs, and then make from them little wafers. Also good for provoking the menses is a fumigation made from these same herbs.

"Hmmm – I do not think there is anything listed here likely to hurt you, but let me have a few days to hunt down a few others too. You must understand, they may not work; Nothing may work." She clasped Francisca's hand. "I can make no promises, other than I refuse to give you something that has any chance of causing you greater ill."

"Greater ill?" Francisca rounded on her. "For women like us, can you think of any greater ill than to bring a bastard child into the world? I would be dead to my family."

She tightened her grip on Francisca. "Before we try anything, can you not speak to your lover? Perhaps he would offer you marriage if he knew. It would be a way out for you."

Francisca sat for a moment, staring out ahead. "I will go to him this day." She sighed. "He says he loves me, and is devoted to me. Now is the time to find out if he speaks the truth."

Later that same afternoon, Francisca knelt on the grass before Catalina, her hands together as if in supplication.

"I forbid you to see him again," Catalina commanded. "I cannot believe your disloyalty. You – you who have been with me ever since we left Castile."

Standing less than a stone's throw away from the two women, María, her heart brimming with pity for Francisca, cursed again the ill timing that had brought Catalina out to the garden in search of her just as Francisca came back alone to the palace grounds.

Shocked at first that one of her women would throw caution to the wind and leave the grounds without a chaperone, Catalina had been even more shocked when Francisca told her she was returning from the home of their ambassador. When asked why, Francisca paled, looked desperately at María and then back at Catalina. "Madam," Francisca said, "I spoke to Don Fuensalida out of my great love for you. He needs to know Fray Diego encourages you to stay in England. He is wrong to do so. There is nothing for you here. I asked the ambassador to write to King Ferdinand and beg him to dismiss the priest."

Catalina stared at Francisca, and María swallowed. *The ambassador does not trust Francisca – or he would have told her their princess had ignored Fray Diego's advice and wrote to her father, begging him to let her come home. Francisca thinks to cover her shame by telling our princess of what she believes is a forgivable betrayal.*

"You told this to the ambassador?" Catalina asked.

"Your Highness, you must listen to me. Don Fuensalida is

right to call Fray Diego a pestiferous priest. Your confessor persuades you to declare everything to be a mortal sin, however innocent it might be, just to prove his power over you. His influence causes evil tongues to talk."

Catalina shifted angrily and lifted a hand. "Be silent. I'll hear not another word against a man who has discharged faithfully the duties of my confessor and chancellor. You could learn what it means to be faithful and loyal from him."

"Madam –"

"Say no more. I do not want to see your face, not now, not tomorrow, not the next day. Remain in your chamber until I summon you again."

Francisca wept, stood up, and stumbled and walked and stumbled again towards the women's chambers. María watched her go, and rushed over to Catalina. "She did wrong, but she spoke the truth when she says she loves you. I beg you to forgive her."

Catalina's eyes glittered with fury. María stepped back.

"Better to know she betrayed me? She asked my ambassador to use his influence to dismiss my confessor. I will never forgive her." Catalina waved a hand. "Stay here in the garden. Your herbs would be better company than me today. I will speak to you later." She turned on her heel, and hurried back in the direction of her apartments.

Waiting until Catalina disappeared inside, María hurried after Francisca to the women's sleeping chamber, finding Francisca at the room's writing desk. María closed the door and stood with her back against it.

Francisca stopped writing, and looked over her shoulder. Her clothes coffer was no longer at the end of her bed, but shut and locked by her side. She returned to her task, and wrote another line before signing her name with a flourish. Placing her quill beside the letter, she stared at the black ink staining her finger-tips. She wiped them with a cloth, sprinkled pounce on the parchment, shook off the excess and then picked it up.

"I will read it to you," she said, looking towards María. "Madam, I go to marry Grimaldi. It is what I could not bear to tell you in the garden. Pray, remember my loyalty to you for the last seven years, and know I will always love you. Francisca." She put the parchment down and lifted wet eyes. "Do you think I should write more?"

Resting a hand on her friend's shoulder, María licked her lips, guessing Francisca did not desire an answer. "I could speak to our princess and tell her the whole story..."

"What use would that be? You heard her today. I am already a traitor in her eyes." She shook her head a little. "I do not wish for her to think me a whore as well. Promise me, I beg you, do not tell her of my disgrace."

María tightened her grip on her friend's shoulder. "But..." she swallowed. "The truth might help her understand..."

Francisca broke away from her, moving to stand by the window. "I do not want her to know. It is hard enough you know the truth...today, today only brought everything to a head. Francesco promised to wed me the moment I told him I feared I was with child. He is organising a priest to do this today. Pray, promise me you will not tell her of my troubles. It will serve me little if my parents ever learn Francesco was my lover before he made me his wife. It will distress them to know I married beneath me, but they will forgive me in time."

María crossed to Francisca and took her hand. "If this is

what you truly wish, I promise you, I will say nothing." *I will say nothing? Say nothing to Catalina?* Sudden sorrow swept her down the long years, to the day when childhood had ended for her and Catalina.

> *Hand of its clouds, winter wrote a letter*
> *Upon the garden, in purple and blue.*

"We vowed to tell each other everything. Everything!" she had told Catalina. At eight, she had understood little of what she had witnessed that terrible day, a day which had begun so bright and happy. So innocent. The family of Jews in their broken-down cart; a young girl with a face of a virgin labouring with her first child. Prince Juan white-faced and disturbed, becoming angry at Catalina's questioning as to why they could not help them. Catalina had gone to her mother in search of answers. She had returned hours later not wanting to speak. Finally, Catalina told her the queen believed it right to drive out the Jews from Castile. That the Jews had crucified a baby and wanted the death of all Christians.

Si, childhood ended then.

Confused, she swallowed, aware her life broke apart from Catalina's in a way she had never expected.

Francisca gestured to her coffer. "Will you find me servants to take my things to the home of the ambassador?"

María nodded, and began heading back to the door.

"Wait," Francisca said. She turned. Francisca held out the folded parchment. "Can you make certain she gets this?"

Taking the parchment from her, Maria slipped it into her deep pocket. She looked again at Francisca, her spirit weighed down by yet another farewell. "You have my word; she will get your letter, but I will stay silent about everything else. As you say, it helps or changes nothing if she knows."

María swallowed again, her childish words echoing in her mind. *We vowed to tell each other everything! Everything!*

How many times she had broken that vow over the years.

Wanting to weep, she embraced Francisca, and kissed her cheeks. "I'll send for the servants. Farewell, my friend. I'll pray for you."

María released Francisca, knowing she farewelled her forever. *Francisca has made her choice. And Catalina is mine.*

María returned to Catalina's chambers. Entering the privy chamber, her gaze fell on the empty window-seat. For years, she had come to this room to find Bella, Francisca and Inés seated there, their heads close together, chatting. She would never find her three friends here again. She lifted her eyes to Catalina's bedchamber, wondering if she should disturb her. She guessed the privy chamber remained empty of people because Catalina had told them to go, but also suspected Catalina would want to see her by now. She knocked on the bedchamber's door. "Can I come in?" Hearing a soft yes, she opened the door, and entered.

Catalina was seated on her favourite chair by the window, overlooking the garden. Sunlight flooded over her for a moment and lit up her hair, but then the light dulled. Rain spattered the window, and the day turned dark. Catalina held out her hand. "Forgive me. I was angry at Francisca, not at you." Taking her hand, María knelt by her side. "I know." She inhaled and exhaled a deep breath, taking the letter from her pocket. "Francisca asked me to give you this."

Catalina took it, and scanned the contents. She dropped the letter to the ground. "Do you know what it says?"

"She loves you, my sister."

"Loves me? She not only betrayed me, but has married without my permission – and to my money-lender. She saw a way out of these dark days and took it. And she says she loves me. If she loved me, she would not have done any of this."

Unable to tell Catalina the real reason for Francisca's marriage, she lowered her head.

"You would not do this," Catalina said.

Startled, she glanced up. *Does Catalina voice a question, or a command? How can she ask this after all our years together?* Shifting a little on her knees, she murmured, "I stay true to you. Always." She placed a hand on Catalina's knee, leaning closer. "You look tired, my sister."

"You know I struggle to sleep at night." Catalina twisted in her chair towards her. "Do you think the dead stay with us? At night, when I lay awake, I sometimes hear Arthur's lute. It lulls me back to sleep, and I dream of him. We walk together in a sunlit land."

María peered down at the garden. *Si – she has not forgotten Arthur. But why should she? She loved him. We never forget the dead we love.* The rain and wind easing for a time, a slant of light burst through the dark clouds and lit a clearing between the trees. Somewhere, a bird sang, soon joined by the calls of other birds. Seizing on this as a promise of better times to come, her spirits lifted. "Si, I believe you have the rights of it. I also feel the comfort of the dead. But they are not dead – are they?" She raised her eyes to Catalina. "Just gone from us and our grey world – into their new, unending morning. Perchance their love for those they leave behind pulls them back to the threshold between the living and the dead; and there they hold the door ajar for us so we see the glimmer of dayspring waiting for us too."

Leaning closer, Catalina peered out the window. "Like a candle in the window to help us find our way home?"

María gripped tighter her friend's hand. "Si, like a candle."

PART 2

Daughter,

Do I still need to beg you for forgiveness?

You are so alike to me, and I know forgiveness is hard for

women. Women do not forget.

I cannot forget.

I do not want to forget.

I feel my queen's presence all around me. For her I tell this

story. And for me, but especially for you.

There is so much more I need to write.

I must keep writing my story to the end.

1

I am rejoiced to find you love each other so supremely and hope you may be happy to the end of your life; a good marriage being not only a blessing for the man and woman to take each other, but a blessing to the world outside.

~ King Ferdinand II of Aragon

Yawning after an almost sleepless night, María emerged from the chapel at Richmond Palace. Catalina had tossed and turned for hours before begging her for a sleeping draught. With Catalina at last asleep, she mixed another cup of the sleeping potion for her own use, and drank it. But her mind refused her rest until she feared waking Catalina with her own tossing and turning. She gave up any hope for sleep when she heard the birds greet the dawn, and dressed. Leaving Catalina in the care of her other women, María had made her way down to morning Mass.

Her stomach reminding of its emptiness, she stepped towards the palace, her eyes watering at the sudden assault of bright light from the rising sun. She lifted her hand, protecting her eyes, risking a glance at the sky. Blue and clear, nothing suggested anything other than a day when spring came early. The bright morning did not bespeak death – or the death of a king. But other things did; the increased activity in the royal apartments and the absence of the prince from his father's chambers. All yesterday, he had remained locked away with the king's councillors.

All yesterday, time seemed waiting, and they waited too.

Catalina had spent the day praying in her closet. She did not tell María what she prayed for, but María could guess. Walking on, María pondered the letter Catalina had sent to her father at the beginning of the year, after King Henry clawed back from his first close call with death. When she settled a shawl on her friend's shoulders, María could not help reading some of the letter. In her mind, María saw the words once more:

You ask what prevents my marriage to the prince?

King Henry prevents it. He would need to be first dead before I could wed his son.

María stopped on the path, her heart quickened. Soon after Catalina sent that letter King Henry became ill again. Everyone knew it was just a matter of time before he would be no longer ill, but dead.

She raised her hand to her face again, her heart still beating fast. Her head felt ready to burst. *Could King Ferdinand be responsible for the Tudor king's death? They said he poisoned King Philip from afar – why not the English King too? Is not one of his physicians Spanish?* The world around her began to spin.

Oh God – what if the king was responsible? She swallowed. *And if he was? If he hastened the death of King Henry, would it not mean he acted for the first time like a father who cared what happened to his daughter?* She swallowed again. *I know the herbs to use. If we lived close enough to the king, could I have done this for Catalina?*

María staggered, and then crossed herself. She heard the voice of Latina as if she stood right next to her, "Do no harm, my child, do no harm." *Jesu' – I think of murder. Forgive me. I would never have done it. Forgive me for desiring the king's death so much I pray for it. And hope for it. But I would never have murdered him.*

An unending void opened at her feet. *What kind of woman am I?* She gazed over her shoulder at the chapel. *How can I go to Mass if I think such things? Dear God, forgive me. Deliver me from evil.*

Her head pounding, María started walking again. The wind dropped, its voice exchanged for running water and the burr of male voices. She turned towards the nearby water fountain. Will stood on the other side, deep in conversation with his friend, Edmund Dudley. She lifted up her skirts and hurried over to them. Will noticed her first, his serious face breaking into delight. He bowed in greeting, and then gestured to the man beside him. "Do you remember my friend, María?"

She curtseyed. "It is good to see you again, sir."

Dudley bowed. "Lady, you and Will are the first today to

give me a friendly greeting." He gave a peculiarly strained laugh. "To see the rats run in the opposite direction at my approach reminds me what my loyalty to the king has cost me." Dudley cocked his head towards Will. "I must be away. My wife will worry if I do not return soon." He bowed again, and sped down the path heading to the river.

Staring after him, she turned to Will. "What was that all about? The man scurried away like a whipped dog."

"He is frightened, and well he should be." Will paused, visibly disturbed. "Love, Edmund told me what many of us already suspect. The king died a day ago."

María swayed, and held out her arm to keep her balance. Will took her hand in his and enclosed it with his other.

"Are you certain?" Not waiting for his answer, she spoke in a rush, "I must wake my princess and tell her." She let go of Will, whirling towards the royal chambers.

Will grabbed her arm. "Wait."

"What is it?" Bewildered, she rubbed the heel of her hand against her aching temple. She wondered if she was dreaming. "Why haven't they proclaimed the king's death?"

"The old king's councillors wish to ensure the change from one reign to the next goes smoothly. King Henry, the seventh of his name, did not think to die so soon. Edmund told me the old king neglected to school his son about kingship. We have a youth of not even eighteen taking his father's crown."

María saw in her mind that same youth forcing his mouth on hers. She shuddered and looked down the path that Dudley had taken moments before. There was no longer any sight of him. She turned to Will. "Why is your friend frightened?"

"Because he served the old king. Poor Edmund. For years,

the king made use of his knowledge of law to fill his coffers. He is hated by many at court. I judge no man, let alone a man whose only real crime is being loyal to his king. This morning he heard rumours he will be thrown to the wolves. He also heard… more than just a rumour concerning Princess Katherine."

She stepped closer to him. "Tell me."

"Our young king is determined to marry her."

She shook her head. For two years or more, his father had made it clear he was no longer interested in matching his son with Catalina, and his son seemed to desire more to follow his father's lead than to marry Catalina. "Why?" she asked, more of herself than of Will.

"I am not certain of the reason, but Edmund told me our new king told his councillors his father made him promise to wed Katherine. He plans to have her at his side as his wife and queen for his coronation."

Swallowing, María clutched his doublet like one drowning. "You are certain of this?"

"My love, if there is one man whose word I will never doubt, it is Edmund Dudley. Believe me, Princess Katherine will be soon Queen of England."

The weight of seven dark, hopeless years lifted from her heart and soul. María threw her arms around him, and burst into tears. Wiping her eyes, she lifted her face and kissed him, then broke away from him. "I must be away without any more delay. I must tell my princess. She needs this good news."

Will grinned at her. "It is good news." His face sobering, he took her hand. "It gives me hope for a day when there will be a good and happy outcome for us too."

She shook her head. "How can it be? You do not wish for

your wife's death." She bit her bottom lip, remembering her evil thoughts coming out of the chapel. "Nor do I wish for it." She reached for his hand, holding it for a heartbeat. "What we have must be enough."

The proclamation of King Henry's death came the next day, and with it the news of the arrest of Edmund Dudley. "How can our new king do this?" Will asked her. "Edmund has only done the bidding of his sovereign – and with great loyalty too. And it has been to his detriment. His service troubled his conscience and resulted in the curses of many, but what could he do other than obey the commands of the king? Now they accuse him of treason."

Walking beside him in the gardens, María took his arm. "Surely they will give him a fair trial? Surely the king cannot execute a man for serving well his father?"

Will halted beside her, bringing her to a stop too.

She reached to take his face between her hands. "What is it, love?"

Will looked at her with haunted eyes. "You do not know the Tudors well if you say that."

Dropping her hands onto his shoulders, María glanced all around, making certain they were still alone. "I know the Tudors well enough to know they deceive and like well their gold, as do many in positions of power; but surely they would not kill a loyal servant, especially a man who is no threat to them?"

Will inhaled and let out a deep breath. "Have you ever heard what happened after the battle of Bosworth Field?"

"Bosworth Field? The battle when Henry Tudor seized the crown from Richard, the third of his name? Or should I call him the usurper – as do many at the court? Of what import is that? Surely it has nothing to do with Edmund Dudley?"

"Aye. Nothing – excepting for this. After he seized his crown by killing the anointed king of England, Henry Tudor made all those who fought for Richard – a man once known as England's king – traitors. King Henry was more than willing to see many men die because of their loyalty. Now Edmund is accused of treason. My cousin Elizabeth, his poor wife, is at her wit's ends. She tells me she knows not the charges, only that Edmund has been taken to the Tower with Richard Empson, the other man he worked with – in the name of his king, a king who knew he did wrong. Why else would Henry Tudor, in the days he approached death, ask Edmund to go through his books so he could make restitution to those he wronged? My friend does not deserve this."

"Shhh." María wrapped her arms around Will, trying to comfort him. "This is a new king. We do not know yet what kind of king he will be." *What kind of king he will be?* María pushed down all her fears. "God willing, these arrests are all for show. Pray, let us not worry until we know more."

No one expected the young king to propose marriage to Catalina until after his father's funeral, and the passing of a respectable time of mourning. But where the weeks, months and years of waiting had once been dark with despair and the destruction of hope, this time was different. Conditions in her chambers improved. Her debts were paid. There was a sudden influx of new servants, servants who treated Catalina with respect and fidelity. In the lead up to his father's funeral, the soon-to-be crowned king spent hours with her, asking her advice in ensuring all the planning for the funeral was as it should be. Every morning, a message arrived from King Henry – asking after Catalina's health and happiness, or requesting another noble woman from the court join her household. One noble woman Catalina requested for herself. To María's great joy, Margaret Pole returned to court. Two of the women requested by the king were the two sisters of Edward Stafford, the Duke of Buckingham. Their acceptance soon brought a request from the duke for a private audience with Catalina. When he came to speak with her in her privy chamber, María remained with Catalina. Receiving permission to read, María sat near the window, recalling the duke at Catalina's wedding to Arthur. He had been young and slender then. Now he was a tall man in his early thirties, fast running to fat. She recalled his arrogance as a youth, knowing that had been deepened by the passing years. Yet with his pride there was also charm, and a generosity of spirit he showed to people he liked. *Si – and he likes Catalina.*

Sitting near one another on high backed chairs, Catalina and the duke soon fell into easy conversation with each other. They had met infrequently over the years at court, and then Catalina had been cautious about speaking to men near to her own age – in case it set off the wag of evil tongues. Now, it seemed, those brief meetings had been enough to sow the seeds of friendship.

The duke spoke of his devotion to his close family, and his desire to ensure his sisters had been placed in trusted positions in Catalina's household suitable to their rank. Half listening to Catalina's reassurance, María hid a grin when the duke relaxed and began talking of the improvements he was making to his country estates. *As a youth he liked showing off his wealth – and he does the same as a man.*

Whilst Catalina and the duke were deep in talk, a messenger came bearing a gift and letter from the king. María pursed her lips. *The third gift and letter today. The king too likes showing off his wealth.*

Taking both from the messenger, with her thanks to the king, Catalina placed the letter and gift next to her writing desk, and returned her attention to the duke. Blushing, she smiled at him. "I will send a message of thanks to the king shortly," she said.

Edward Stafford laughed a little. "Well, the king, my cousin's purpose is plain, and I am glad of it. He could not ask for a better or more royal wife than you." He leaned closer to her. "I tried to help, madam. Many times, I spoke to the countess and begged her to speak reason to her son. She was once my respected guardian, and I think highly of her. But she told me she could not intercede on your behalf. It was a matter of politics, she said. I can tell you true, most of the court were shamed about your treatment by the first Henry Tudor. I pray this new Tudor treats you always as you deserve."

Catalina leaned back, and frowned. "Deserve," she said slowly as if she weighed the word to find its measure. "My Lord Duke, if there is one thing the years have taught me, it is the knowledge that we gain nothing in life by expecting our deserts." She eyed the crumbling fire. "Or perhaps, in truth, I did deserve these past years."

Lowering her head, María brushed at the smart of tears. *How can she think that? No one deserves seven years of abandonment.*

Through tear-glazed eyes, she saw the duke peering at Catalina in puzzlement. "What mean you, Your Highness?"

Catalina shrugged. "For years, the death of Warwick has weighed heavily on me. Many have told me the blame was not mine, but so much has happened to make me doubt their reassurance. I wonder at times if my life is cursed because of Warwick's unjust death."

Sitting rod straight in his chair, the duke stared at her. "Madam, you cannot be serious."

Catalina met his eyes. "I have never been more serious." She laughed a laugh dead of any trace of joy. "If the king does indeed marry me, I pray it means the curse is at an end."

Her tears splattering the open pages of her book, María twisted towards the window. *She still believes she's cursed. Dear God – show her it is not true.*

The first days of June brought with them warm winds – warm winds stirring in María memories of another time and place. Memories that tumbled and crumbled like autumn leaves before the onset of winter. She raised her head. *Exile in England is not winter. Lift your heart. It is no longer winter, but summer. The summer of your life.*

With the first days of June also came Henry Tudor's request for a private audience with Catalina. María listened to her friend acquiesce as if she expected a conversation of trivial matters. *Si – Catalina's dealings with the old king have taught her well the skills of pretence, of hiding her true feelings in public. It is only for the good.*

Within the hour, like a gusty, whirling wind himself, the young king was announced and he asked to speak to her privately in her closet. They were alone for close to an hour before they emerged, hand in hand, flushed and happy. King Henry grinned at the waiting women. He glanced aside at Catalina. "You do not mind if I tell them?"

Catalina blushed, and smiled at him before lowering her head. María smiled too, joy lightening her heart. She could not remember the last time Catalina smiled like that. She had begun to fear she would never see Catalina happy, really happy, again.

"Your mistress will soon be my mistress too – and the mistress of this land. Aye, your mistress has agreed to be my wife." He raised her hand and kissed it. "When I am crowned King of England, you will be crowned my queen. I leave you now to begin your preparations."

The young king departed the room just like he had arrived – full of energy and youth. María shook her head. *Short months ago, Catalina had given up all hope of this day ever arriving. How quickly life changes from one moment to the next.* Deep in the chamber, seated by the window, Catalina looked out on the summer morn.

María approached her, and touched her shoulder. "All's well?" she asked.

Catalina looked aside at her. "We go to Greenwich early on the morrow; we will be wed at the Friary by the Archbishop of Canterbury. Because the prince..." Catalina shook her head. "I misspoke. Because the king is in mourning, the ceremony will only be witnessed by a few. You, of course, I want... need with me." Catalina's hands gripped the carved armrests. "I do not know if I believe this yet. After all these years, I will be wedded to Harry. Warham, the archbishop of Canterbury, expressed his concern about my prior marriage to Arthur, but he could not argue against the papal dispensation for this marriage." She sighed. "For the last year, I have not thought of marriage– other than becoming a bride of Christ. Now all I think of is Arthur… how young we were when we wed… a boy and a girl… the years since… so many years since… I am old, my sister."

María smiled at her. "Twenty-three is not old. Did I never tell you Latina believed women should not marry until twenty-five – when they had lived long enough to become wise wives, and mothers."

"Not many would agree with our wise teacher. But I have, we all have, lived through more than enough since Arthur's death – enough for me to feel aged."

Catalina speaks of Arthur. It has been so long since she last spoke of him. María sighed. It seemed this impending marriage to his brother had reopened the scar. She rested a hand on Catalina's arm. "Are you not happy? Don't you wish to marry the king?" she asked softly. She averted her face. She did not dare to remind Catalina that her marriage to Arthur had not been a full one. "You can wed him with a free conscience," she said, looking at Catalina again.

Catalina's eyes filled with tears. She covered her face with her hands and let out a sob – a sob changing to a laugh close to mania. Dropping her hands, she clasped them tightly in her lap. She lifted her eyes. "Happy – what is that? And you should know better than to ask me what I wish. Has it ever mattered? I cannot remember a time when England did not own my life."

The morning after Catalina's wedding, María walked alone in the garden. Catalina and the king were still abed. When she had entered Catalina's antechamber to begin her day of service, there were no mistaking the noises coming from the bedchamber. Catalina was a true wife, at last. Glad to hear also Catalina's laughter, she had slipped away – scolding herself for the sadness settling on her spirit. *I should praise God. Catalina has a chance of a whole life. I should be happy for her – even if I have little prospect of ever experiencing the same.*

Quick footsteps padded behind her. She glanced over her shoulder. Buckingham, dressed in his riding clothes, advanced towards her.

She curtseyed as he drew near. "My lord Duke," she murmured.

He gestured with a plump hand for her to rise, his double chin quivering.

"Is it true?" he barked out, his cheeks reddening in his fury.

She stepped back, stunned at his anger. "My lord Duke, I do not know what you speak of."

"Do not play around the bush with me, woman; is it true the king married Princess Katherine yesterday?"

She studied him, pulling at her bottom lip for a moment in thought. It was clear the news of the marriage was already known at court for the duke to want to question her. She shrugged. "It is true, my Lord."

"Why was I not invited to witness the wedding?" The duke seemed to swell up before her eyes. "My cousin knew I was staying at my London property."

She lowered her eyes, uncertain how to deal with the enraged duke. Once more, she shrugged. "My lord Duke, the king is still in mourning. He only asked for a few to witness the marriage. The Spanish ambassador was the only other man of noble blood to be there – and that was because of the princess... I mean, Queen Katherine."

She paused, breaking eye contact with the duke. This was the first time she had called Catalina Queen Katherine. In the quiet garden, it seemed the title echoed as if trumpeted. She returned her attention to the duke.

She swept him a deep curtsey. "Duke, it is not for me to say; I only obey. Forgive me, I must ask your permission to continue on my way."

The duke waved a hand at her. "Go then. I will speak my mind to young King Henry when I see him next."

Walking away from him, María wondered if it would be wiser for him to hold his tongue. The duke was a prideful man; but so was the king. Even more so.

2

Now the people, freed,

    run before their king with bright faces.

    Their joy is almost beyond their own comprehension.

    They rejoice, they exult, they leap for joy

    and celebrate for their having such a king.

    ~ Thomas More

Doña, my dear Latina,

*   Happy days have come for us. My princess is at last married to the young Henry Tudor, England's new king. I daily struggle to believe it – my princess is queen. There is such change in her. Even her confessor remarks on her happiness, and says she is the most beautiful creature in the world. Tomorrow, Catalina of Aragon will be crowned. She will wear the mantle her royal mother, Queen Isabel, readied her for from childhood.*

One of the four women selected for the task of carrying the silken trail of Catalina's coronation robes, María jigged a step behind Catalina as she studied the sky. The blue sky of the midsummer English day seemed to join her joyful mood, giving promise of a bright future.

María returned her gaze to Catalina. Her long hair flowed free, and resplendent, shining golden in sunlight. When María had helped Catalina robe this morning, Catalina seemed transformed. A short woman became a towering presence; a woman no longer the girl hiding her fears on her long ago first wedding day, but a woman ready to face her destiny. María almost skipped again. *Our darkest night is over, and today begins the new dawn. At last, Catalina is in her rightful place. Praise God.* Cold water seemed to wash over her, dousing her joy. She swayed a little, pushing down her urge to touch her mouth, remembering the lips of the youth Henry on hers. *Why think of that? Forget it. He was a boy then, and now he is a man. A man married to my friend. A man who is a king.*

Smiling at the Londoners milling close by, Catalina walked out from the palace, going to stand under a canopy held by the Barons of Cinque Ports, behind the canopy held over the uncrowned, bareheaded king. He wore his hair the same as from boyhood – in the French style, although cut longer to the shoulder and with a fringe straight across his forehead. He was not quite eighteen, his birthday still four days away. Today, Catalina looked just as young as him. Following the English sacred coronation rituals of hundreds of years, they trod barefoot on the striped cloth – stretching out before them as far as the eye could see. Under their separate canopy, the royal couple passed cheering crowds. Glancing over her shoulder, María saw people breaking through the barriers. They flung themselves down to cut a piece of cloth before rushing after the king and queen as they made their way to the Abbey. *Meg Pole said this may happen – people wishing to keep a sacred token of the day.* Entering Westminster, the uncrowned queen and king moved towards the archbishop and knelt at his feet.

María moved aside for a time, standing with the other women. A fanfare of trumpets signalled the beginning of the crowning ceremony. *How different to their wedding.* That day had been subdued, attended by few witnesses. Today's only similarity saw Catalina again in a white gown, but this time not because of the virginity she brought to her marriage bed, but white for that of England's uncrowned queen. Even her pretty face was white as she contemplated the altar. *She looks so solemn – she looks like a queen.*

Meg Pole nudged María. Together they returned to Catalina for their part in the coronation rituals. María met Catalina's eyes for a moment, and then helped Meg loosen the cords at the top of Catalina's gown, baring the top of her breasts before stepping away. The archbishop came from anointing the chest of the king to anoint Catalina with the same thick oil. Slowly sliding down Catalina's skin, María could smell it even standing at a body length distance away. Woody, but potent – it skirted close to an unpleasant pungency. The archbishop next crowned the new king, then he took the smaller crown from its cushion to crown Catalina. Overcome with pride, María shut her eyes against unsought for tears.

"Yea! Yea!" reverberated in the Abbey, and a roar answered from outside.

María opened her eyes. The archbishop stood by King

Henry's side, smiling as the people called their acceptance of the new king. Close to the altar, Lady Margaret, the king's grandmother, bent her head, and wept. María remembered her doing the same at Catalina's first wedding, so long ago, but this time, bereft of her beloved son, she wept and dried her eyes alone, before gazing again at her grandson with unconcealed pride. A handsome figure of surprising lithe grace, the young king towered over everyone. Despite his youth, he blazed with confidence. While that did not surprise María, his aura leadership did. *Perhaps it simply comes from the crown he wears.*

Standing apart in their royalty, hand in hand, the new king and queen accepted the homage of their people. The glitter of the jewels on their robes and their crowns conjured a sparkling aura around them, as if the king and his wife shone like stars in the firmament.

María watched the proud English lords kneel, one by one, before her friend. Placing their hands between Catalina's, they swore their loyalty to her as they had done the king. The last allegiance sworn, the queen stepped forward and spoke. "My good people – go now to Westminster Hall. A banquet awaits us to feast together on this auspicious day."

Once more, the king and queen walked under the canopies, but this time crowned.

The polished flagstone floor reflected back countless torches from the high walls. Long, wooden trestle tables covered with white tablecloths and decorated with herbal wreaths stretched down the hall. Side tables leaned against the walls, laden with food ready for serving the thousands of people attending the banquet. María, ushered to her place near the royal dais, sat next to Margaret Pole.

María forced herself to stop looking around the room for Will. "Keep your distance from him tonight," Catalina had said to her this morning. "If the king ever guessed you two are heart-sore for each other, he may think the worse and not allow you to keep your position in my household. He does not know you like I do – and you would not disgrace yourself." She had been thankful Catalina spoke to her while writing a letter. It had given her time to school her face. Again, she tried to forget Will and smile back at Meg's smile of welcome.

"Do you remember we sat together at Queen Katherine's first wedding?" Meg asked.

"Si, I remember." María eyed the dais. The heads of Catalina and her husband were close together as they talked, the symbols of their estates behind them trembling and stirring in the draft. Catalina and the king only had eyes for each other. More than once, the king held her face and kissed her in full view of all, a kiss Catalina returned. "Prince Arthur and my princess, as she was then, could barely look at one another."

"That soon changed," Meg replied, her eyes returning to the dais too. "Watching them grow to love each other is something I have never forgotten."

The king kissed Catalina again, and wound his arm around her shoulders.

"Has she forgotten Arthur, do you think?" Meg murmured.

"No, she will never forget Arthur. She carries his memory in her heart," María said slowly. "But she deserves joy after all the years of uncertainty, and despair. She is ready to be England's queen."

"She *is* England's queen. At last." Meg looked around the hall. "The whole kingdom seems here tonight."

María twisted around too and caught sight of Inés and her husband, Mountjoy, now serving as the queen's chamberlain, on the other side of the room, talking across their table with an old man and Thomas More. Wondering when it would be a good time to go to talk to Inés, she glanced at Meg. "The queen told me her husband wished to outdo his father's coronation banquet, and that of the usurper, Richard of York. They say his banquet fed three thousand or more."

Meg lowered her head. "I was there that night, and remember it well. My uncle Richard came down from the royal dais to speak to me, a child of ten. He kissed me with affection when it was time for me to return to my chambers." She sighed. "He believed he was right to take the crown. But it weighed heavily on him. At the end, it brought him only grief and death." A trumpeter blared out a fanfare, announcing the serving of the banquet food about to start. María's stomach grumbled in response, but then she forgot all about her hunger, covering her hand over her mouth. A rider trotted a horse through the open door, followed by another rider on a horse covered with cloth of gold.

She turned to Meg Pole, lifting her eyebrow in question. Meg whispered back, "The Duke of Buckingham."

Dressed gloriously as a prince of the realm, he was barely recognisable from the furious man Maria had spoken to more than a week ago, the morning after Catalina's wedding. Behind the duke and his companion followed a host of servants carrying more huge trays of food. The delicacies set before them depicted mottoes and strange devices, many of them decorated in gold leaf or coloured with the yellow of saffron. Seeing others eat them, she took one and studied it more closely. "What is it?" she asked.

Meg glanced at it. "Can you not see?"

She looked at it again, recognising the arched grated gateway common to many of the older castles she had seen in England. "Oh. I know what it is. But what a strange thing to make for us to eat."

"Not as strange as all that." Meg reached for one of the same delicacies and nibbled at it. "It is the Beaufort Portcullis, from the Château de Beaufort in France – once a stronghold of John of Gaunt, the third son of Edward III, and the queen's great grandfather. It is part of the heraldry of the countess, the king's grandmother."

María began eating, asking more questions of Meg in her efforts to puzzle out other delicacies set on the table. Servitors carried straight to the royal dais two of these dishes – cubes of lamb in a rich sauce and a whole grilled porpoise. *Porpoise?* She could not remember the last time Catalina had her most loved meal. María looked at King Henry. He and Catalina now crossed arms and drank from each other's goblets.

All through the years since their first meeting, he confused her. At times, she wondered why she disliked him but, as what happened today at the coronation, she would then remember how he forced his lips on hers when he was fifteen. It always came back to that – the final drop overflowing her cup of repugnance. María could not forgive his action which forced her to keep another secret from Catalina. Day after day, she fought to hide her feelings about the king from Catalina, but then he perplexed her again by doing something kind and thoughtful like this. It must have been him who had commanded the cooks to prepare Catalina's favourite dishes. *Perchance one day I will change my opinion of him, and put aside the past. Perchance.*

María gulped down her wine and turned her mind from thinking about the king. She saw again Inés and her husband on the other side of the hall. Making her excuses to Meg, María crossed over to them. Inés smiled brightly seeing her approach, and shifted on the bench-seat to make room for her at their table. When María sat beside Inés, Mountjoy broke his conversation with More and the old man and smiled in her direction. "Doña de Salinas, you honour us by your company." María grinned. "We both serve the queen and I see you every day, my lord, but it appears you have kept your wife away from court since your marriage."

Mountjoy laughed. "I believe my wife wishes to familiarise herself with all the books in my library before returning to the queen's service."

Inés giggled. She playfully grabbed María's arm and came closer as if wishing to confide to her. She chuckled again. "My beloved husband believes it is books which keep me away from court."

More smiled across the table. "I envy your husband. When I first married my wife, she protested she preferred not to read." The old man regarded him with amusement. "You told me you needed to speak to her father to make of her a docile wife."

More laughed. "I do not believe in the beating of wives – but to persuade them by other means. Jane was only sixteen when we wed – and raised in the country. I confess, she had much to get used to in the first year of our marriage – including a husband who loves books and learning – and wished the same said of his wife. Jane not only reads the books I give her, but has come to welcome my tutorage." More said it kindly, and with warm eyes and great charm. María could imagine a woman coming to enjoy his schooling – even one who happened to be also his wife.

María looked around the table of mostly men. The only young women sitting amongst them were her and Inés. "Is Mistress More not here?" she asked More.

"To Jane's great regret, she is not yet churched of our new child. We have a son to add to our three girls."

"I congratulate you," María murmured, returning her eyes to Inés. "And is your husband right – is it his books which deprive us of your company?"

Inés laughed. "Not just his books. My husband forgets he has a young daughter I must woo so she trusts and likes me, and a very large estate I need to become familiar with to ensure its smooth running. Once those two things are well in hand, I will make my return. The queen has already written to me asking it be soon."

María smiled back at the friend. "I am glad of it. I have missed you." She blinked, realising she had spoken in Castilian. "I have missed you, too." Inés replied in the same tongue, but then she grinned across at her husband, and spoke in English. "But, in truth, I miss my husband more. I am looking forward to coming back to court so we are not so often separated. But talking of company – do you know our Master Erasmus? He is a good friend of both Thomas and William, and my husband's guest in London, while he pens a new book. You would remember Master Erasmus's *Collectanea Adagiorum*. We all read it with enjoyment with the princess... forgive me, the queen, one winter at Durham House. Master Erasmus – you will enjoy speaking to Doña de Salinas. She is a scholar in her own right."

María laughed. "Scholar? I am no scholar compared to a man who writes such works."

Erasmus looked in her direction and smiled kindly. "If Lady Mountjoy describes you in such terms, you must deserve it."

"Doña María is a student of the healing arts. All the years we waited for happier days for our queen, María spent her days reading medicine books or keeping busy in the stillroom. Her medicines became sought after and far more preferred than the ones prepared by the household physician."

María laughed again. "Only because I was always able to get more honey from the kitchen for my potions. One of the servants took a liking to me."

Mountjoy raised his goblet to her. "I can guess it was a man – and a man likely mooning still about the beautiful woman who was beyond his reach like the moon itself."

Inés widened her eyes at the husband. "Should I be jealous of my friend?"

His amused eyes resting on his wife, Mountjoy raised his goblet again. "Why should I wish for the moon when I have the sun? I am the most fortunate of men."

Lowering her head, Inés blushed. She laughed a little, turning aside to María. "You must see why I am impatient to re-join the queen's household. Every day without my husband seems a day of winter."

María squeezed her friend's hand, and did her best to smile.

Be happy for Inés – and Catalina. Be happy even if you cannot share the same happiness as them.

The next morning, the king took part in a tourney celebrating his coronation. Tired from the long night before, María hid a yawn as she stood amongst the other attendants of the queen in the stands, surprised Catalina looked not tired at all. Ready to watch the king compete, Catalina smiled her welcome when her husband strode over to her, smiling even wider when he asked for her token. As yet unarmoured, the king was garbed in a velvet tunic, one side green, embroidered with gold edged pomegranates, the other side, white, decorated with gold edged Tudor roses. Catalina passed to him her scarf. As he threaded it through one of his shoulder straps, she leaned down and touched his clean-shaven cheek. María trembled, remembering touching Will's skin with her own fingertips – wishing she could do the same as Catalina, but without the sin, or the guilt.

The king flushed like a blushing maid, before placing his hand over Catalina's. He stood there as if rooted to the ground, eyeing his wife. The wind strengthened, the plume of golden damask on the helmet under his arm began to blow one way and then the other.

The ground began shaking with the approach of mounted horses. Eight fully armoured knights rode in formation. Underneath their armour, the knights' robes of green silk, decorated with gold bramble branches embroidered in gold thread, could be seen. Their mounts' trappings were the same. Horns sounded. Men dressed from cap to toe in Tudor green and white rushed out, carrying green and white fencing. With surprising speed, they set up an area on the grass like a forest – with a small herd of fallow deer, artificial trees, bushes and ferns.

Terrified, the deer huddled together in the temporary enclosure. The animals raised heads and cocked ears, their huge eyes looking left and right, seeking escape. Despite their fear, they moved with grace and beauty. A horn trumpeted a long note in signal. Men dashed over, opened the gates, the deer ran free. Greyhounds bayed their strange howl and surged as if one towards the deer, the kennel masters struggling to keep hold of their leashes. Another long note trumpeted out, and the freed greyhounds set upon the deer.

Sickened, María averted her face. The awful screams of the dying animals seemed to never end. The English, men and women, cheered and cheered. At last, the knights brought the bloodied carcasses over to the queen, placing them on the grass in front of the royal stands. Hearing her thank them, María shivered, seeing in her mind the bullfights of her childhood. She always hated them. Thinking of the beauty of those deer moments ago, deer now dead before her friend, she hated what happened today even more. Catalina's thanks to the knights also hid her hatred of such sports. María knew they both would dream dark, disturbed dreams tonight.

The strange, violent playacting continued. It became more of a nightmare when Will competed in a swordfight, one that cut deeply into her own heart. A clumsy sword stroke from his opponent brushed Will's neck, and caused blood to flow down his neck like a crimson tide. She collapsed on a seat and held on to it with her strength. *Do not run to him – do not cry out.* Dizzy and ill, she watched as the physician attended to his injury, and

Will returned to win his match. Will receiving the congratulations of the other competitors, she slipped away from public view and vomited. It took some time before she could stop shaking and return to the stands.

After the king gave out the trophies, Will stood on the trampled grass before the royal stalls to begin the next proceedings. He held before him his trophy, a golden lance. Catalina leant forward to greet him, her husband coming to re- join her.

María stared at the lance, reminded Will would soon compete again. She trembled with fear – a fear she had to keep to herself. She could not even speak of it to Will. He would make little of the danger to his person, despite the terrible injuries already happening elsewhere to others. Trumpets throbbed long notes again, followed by shorter ones. Will raised his arm, and bowed low to the queen and king before standing again.

"Noble King and Queen," he bowed once more, "I serve the goddess Diana with my good knights. We have hunted since dawn, but word has come to us that Athena's knights make ready to perform feats of arms. We wish to fight for the love of her whom we serve. If we lose, all we ask for are these dead deer and the greyhounds that slew them, but if we win, we desire the swords of our opponents.

The queen smiled at her husband. "My Lord husband, what reply should I make?"

The king grinned back, but then looked serious. "Sweet lady wife, there is a grudge between these two bands of knights. To grant this request may lead to more unpleasantness. Pray, do not consent to these terms. Rather, permit the knights to fight the tourney, but with a limited number of strokes."

"My king and husband, I shall do as you advise." She turned to Will. "Good sir, leave the field with your men, but prepare yourself to joust with these men who serve Athena. We shall reward you your deserts."

Smiling, Catalina glanced aside at her husband. "And you, my Lord? Will you joust today?"

The king raised her token to his lips and kissed it. "I will. Married to you, I can only be triumphant." He took her hand and bent closer to kiss her.

A messenger broke into this happy moment – giving the king a folded parchment. King Henry read it, and paled. He looked a boy when he gazed back at his wife. "I must be away – my grandmother has fallen ill. The letter says she is close to death."

He looked around. María also scanned the fields around her. For as far as her eye could see, hundreds revelled in festivity and costly tournament. "We will have to bring these celebrations to an end if my grandmother dies," he murmured, his moment of vulnerability replaced by annoyance. He kissed Catalina's hand. "Sweetheart – stay here and enjoy the day. I hope to come back soon." The king strode away with his closest men.

Two hours later word came that Margaret Beaufort had died.

"From joy to sorrow again," Catalina murmured later, watching from her window for the king's return.

"It means nothing," María replied. But she wondered about it too; the new king and his grandmother had argued daily in recent weeks. The countess made it clear she did not approve of many of his decisions – especially that of the arrest of Dudley and Empson. *These arguments? Had they hastened her demise?*

"You know how she grieved for the loss of her son. I believe she but waited to see her grandson crowned king before letting death take her. She was an old woman; it was her time to go."

Catalina turned and contemplated her in silence.

Written on the twentieth day of September, 1509

Doña, my dear Latina,

I pray you understand the long delay since my last letter. The coronation of my princess...forgive me – I must now write queen, was soon followed by another royal funeral – that of the Lady Margaret Beaufort. I then received your letter telling of my mother's death. I cannot find the words to tell you of my sorrow. My mother's last letter begged me to return. She said she did not care if I had no husband, only for me to be with my family again. She told me she feared for me.

August and early September ran together in a fog of grief. The queen tried to comfort me. My other friends too. Little helped. At least I could grieve alone in my chamber at Richmond. With the queen married, I, as a mark of her favour, have been given my own rooms.

She forced herself to write of other things:

The queen grows happier with her husband with each new day.

It is good they share a love of learning and books. The king seems all heart and kindness to the queen and wants to be with her every moment of the day and night. He gives her a constant stream of gifts – from trifles, to costly palfreys. Last week, he even gave her a gift of a monkey, after discovering how much she loved these animals as a child. Every morning, when the weather allows, the queen accompanies the king to hunt with him. He enjoys hunting with hawks and falcons as much as she does. Do you remember the time when King Ferdinand took over one hundred falconers out with him? Do you remember the day we all hunted with Prince Juan?

María put down her quill, seeing in her mind Prince Juan waiting for Catalina to mount her horse, his hooded falcon on his wrist. How he had smiled when he saw María trailing behind. "I ask my sister to ride with me and again she brings her shadow," he had teased.

The amber light of autumn streamed through the uncovered window. A bird twittered, and then another. She looked again at the letter. There was too much she dared not to pen. *No – I cannot write to Latina of how Catalina remains blind to her husband's shortcomings.*

For a long time, María had seen him as a boy and now a man who put his own desires above others. She remembered his temper as a ten-year-old, his arrogance as a youth. His arrogance when he assumed she would be honoured to become his mistress. *Kingship little changes him. He wants all to go his own way.* What troubled her more was witnessing his acts of merriment and goodwill alongside other darker acts. She had heard him speak cruelly to older members of the court, and then with pure vindictiveness to Bishop Fisher who was grieving at the loss of Margaret Beaufort. Fisher loved the countess – and wished to ensure all was done as his friend would have wished. But when he had spoken to the king, he had been told harshly it was none of his affair. There were also rumours the king had already been unfaithful to the queen.

María glanced at the timepiece in the chamber, threw her mantle over her shoulders, and headed to the gardens. This morning, Will had sent her a message telling of his long- awaited return to court from his estates and asking to meet with her in the herb garden.

She found him standing by the dense border of rosemary. Seeing her, he held out his arms for her to go into. "My love," he said, tightening his arms around her, "forgive me for not being here when news came of your mother's death."

Leaning her face against his chest, she sighed. She had wished to be in his arms for weeks. All her pent-up grief released, and her tears flowed.

She gulped down a long breath, rubbed her eyes, and looked up at him. "I did not know my mother was ill. I remember the last time I saw her. She was not old then. In my mind, she will never be old."

"Do you not think it a good way to remember her, Dear Heart?"

She broke away from his embrace to snap off a piece of rosemary. Looking at it, she twirled it between her fingers. "Thomas More spoke to the queen recently about how he allows his rosemary to grow wild in his garden. It is sacred to memory, he said. I look at it and think of my mother on her funeral brier, lying on a bed of rosemary, without me there to mourn her. I was not there when she died, and I was not there when they entombed her." She shook her head. "I wish..."

Will clasped her hand. "What do you wish?"

She raised her eyes to the cloudy sky. The weather turning

cold, she shivered. "For too many things I cannot have. I'll never have. And what is the point of wishing for them when I am rich enough? I have your love, and my queen's." She tried to smile. "And – in spite of sorrowing for my mother – I must be happy. Do you know the queen is with child?"

"I should have guessed it – she seemed, somehow, different."

"She is happy in her marriage – and even happier about this coming child. I have tried not to weep too much about my mother. I cannot burden her with my grief."

Will took her again in his arms. "Burden me then. If you need to weep, weep."

Without another word, she rested her face on his doublet, and wept again.

The queen's pregnancy was soon common knowledge. One evening, María hurried back to the royal chambers. As if in wait, Don Luis Caroz, the new Spanish ambassador, stepped out of a doorway. He hailed her. It was not the first time the annoying man had waylaid her at court.

Tempted to ignore him, she paused and looked back the way she had just come. But she waited too long, and he came closer. She bobbed a curtsey and greeted him in Castilian. *At least meeting him gives me a chance to speak in my own tongue.*

Don Caroz swung out his both arms one way and another, as if trying to keep afloat, or wishing to hit something. "I have waited for weeks and still I have not seen the queen. I am insulted," he spat out, without the courtesy of greeting her by name in return.

"I am sorry to learn this, Don Caroz." She lowered her eyes so he did not see she was not sorry at all. "I am certain my queen does not intend any insult to your respected position."

"Then why am I refused private audience with her? I have had only one conversation with Queen Katherine, and that was shortly after my arrival in England. Now, I am expected to communicate to her through you, and her other women. Let me not speak of her useless confessor. The man gives me nothing more than soft words and excuses."

María considered her reply with caution. The man was so arrogant he did not realise how much he had angered Catalina at their first meeting by insisting she take back Francisca de Cáceres as one of her women. "It is true she served me before she was married," Catalina had told him, "but she proved unworthy of any position at court. She is a perilous woman, and a danger to me." Caroz refused to listen, insisting again on the employment of Francisca. The third time he argued with her Catalina told him to go, and wait for her summons. He kept speaking to those high in the queen's household, hoping to convince someone to help him with his demand. The man was clearly frustrated by the stone wall of loyalty around the queen. He wanted someone close to the queen who he believed would be loyal to him. The man was blind to everything else.

María shuffled her feet uneasily. She had not seen Francisca since she left to marry the money-lender. She missed her. But she could never see her again – not when her first loyalty was to Catalina. *Francisca must be desperate to reclaim her place as one of Catalina's women – so desperate she must have agreed to be the ambassador's spy. If I suspect this, so would Catalina. And the man wonders why my sister refuses to see him.*

"Don Caroz, the queen is with child," she said softly. "The physicians counsel her to rest as much as possible. We have told you this for weeks. I do not understand why you see this is an insult. Surely the queen's health must be our first concern." "Of course, of course. But I am the ambassador of King Ferdinand. I refuse to sit idly by while the queen listens to bad advisors."

María knew the advisor the ambassador disliked the most. Friar Diego told the queen repeatedly, "Forget Spain and gain the love of England." But it was advice María agreed with, and also told to the queen. She hated the loyalty and devotion Catalina gave to her father. King Ferdinand had abandoned his daughter to the wolves for seven long years. *It is only good Catalina breaks away from her father in this way. For once and for all, my sister must recognise the pack she belongs to, and must hunt with.*

"Good Don, you but do the queen great disservice by not giving her any credit for her wisdom. My queen has lived through a hard schooling since coming to England. She is no longer a child to be told what to do, but a woman who acts with care and caution."

"How am I to know the truth of what you say when the queen insults me by refusing to see me?"

"And I say to you again there is no insult intended. You must know the many hours she spends with her husband at court, and also attending to her duties as queen. The brief hours she has alone must be for rest, for the sake of her health, and the child she carries." María curtseyed. "I bid you good afternoon." She spun around, shutting her ears to his demands for her to stay, aware she had ended their conversation in English.

No matter what – the side Catalina belongs to, is mine too.

3

When you know what a hero he now shows
    himself, how wisely he behaves, what a lover he is
    of justice and goodness, what affection he bears
    to the learned, I will venture that you will need
    no wings to make you fly to behold
    this new and auspicious star.

~ William Blount, 4th Baron Mountjoy to Desiderius Erasmus on the ascension of Henry VIII

Richmond, October 1509

Doña, my dear Latina,

My queen is happy and I struggle not to show my own unhappiness. I am surrounded by content women. The queen is not the only one looking forward to bringing forth her first babe.

Inés tells me she is with child, and so is Maud Parr. She is a girl of sixteen, newlywed and newly appointed to the queen's chamber. Already, her belly is swelling. I can barely look at the girl.

María re-read her letter, wincing at her words. She could not tell Latina she was in love with a man she could never have. A man she loved too much to accept anyone else in his place. She could not write and tell her of the daily battle to bear without bitterness her barren life. She took her knife and scraped away the basest of her words, and pushed herself away from the table. *The letter can wait until I am less melancholy.*

Will, too, was unhappy, but not just because of their hopeless situation. He spent his days at court going from one person to another in hope of finding a way to save his friend, Dudley, now in the Tower accused of treason. Dudley was said to have written to his friends and ordered them to assemble in arms if he sent them news of the old king's death.

"What an evil lie," Will told her one warm evening, as they strolled in the enclosed herb garden at Richmond. No one else in sight, María dared to hold his hand as they walked side by side. "There is only one reason for his imprisonment. He served his Tudor king too well, and now must suffer for it. God's teeth – the king robbed his subjects of their wealth, not my friend. It is not his fault he also became wealthy over the years of serving the king." His voice rose, loud with passion. "He only did the miserly bidding of our late king – a man who kept his subjects in check by putting them into debt."

María grabbed his arm, halting him in fear. "Be careful of what you say."

Will paled. His eyes travelled around the garden, and a slight smile touched his mouth. "We are alone."

"Thank the Good Lord for that. You do not want to end up imprisoned too."

Will seemed lost in thought, his gaze locked upon a nearby lavender bush. Again, she took hold of his arm. "What is it?"

Will still did not look her way. "I have joined with other friends of Edmund," he said slowly. "We plan to help him escape from The Tower."

María stared at him, her heart beating fast in fright, unable to believe her ears. "Escape? From the Tower? That is impossible."

At last Will looked her way. There was no mistaking his desperation. "I cannot let Edmund go to his death without trying to save him. He is my cousin's husband, and a good man." *By all the saints – Dudley may be good man – but to turn traitor for him? These weeks of worry and sleepless nights cause Will to lose his reason for him to listen to these friends.*

Her fear becoming pure terror, she wrapped her arms tight around him, hoping to talk sense to him. "I know, and I know you love him," she said. "But he would not be a true friend if he expected you to put at risk your own life."

"I would not be his true friend if I did nothing."

The breeze lifted strands of his thick blond hair, revealing his ear and the silvered scar running down his neck, the injury gained in the tournament celebrating the coronation of the king and queen. *How close I came to losing you that day.* Terrified once more, she tried to grab hold of her courage, only for it to dissipate like smoke. María leaned her face against his chest, listening to his heartbeat as she regained her self-control. Years ago, she had been drawn to Will for reasons she could not explain, or put words to. She believed it love then, but the passing years had taught her otherwise. At near sixteen, the strong gale of attraction had caught her unyieldingly in its grip, but the long years since had deepened desire to real love, and devotion. He was a good man too – a brave man – a man who held his honour as a shield of truth before him. *I do not want to live without Will. Ever.*

She held her tongue on everything she wanted to say, acknowledging the emptiness of so many of her arguments. If she said, "What of us?" she opened the floodgates to arguments sounding petty and selfish. If she begged him not to help his friend escape the Tower, was she not asking him to betray himself – to be a man other than who he was?

She reached up, touching his scar. Her fingers shifted across a little, resting on the blue vein where she could feel the pulse of his heart. Only good fortune that day had prevented the blade from striking deep, or on this spot; if it had, it would have cost him his life. She swallowed. And he put his life at risk at again. But was not this a better cause? *Will would do much for his friends. Is that not one of the reasons I love him so much?*

He placed his hand over hers, and bent to kiss her lips tenderly. "I must do this. I refuse to let fear prevent me from doing what is right," he said, bowing his head to rest it on hers. The shadows lengthened in the garden – reaching out to them. Reaching out to him. María shuddered, leaning her face on his doublet, listening to his heart again before reaching up to touch his neck once more. His scar would make it easy for the headman's axe to find its mark.

Days later, Will sent her a note.

My love,

Parliament does not confirm Edmund's attainder. There is hope we will see him pardoned and freed. Sweetheart, I beg you, speak to the queen. The king listens to her. He must be made to understand that Edmund's imprisonment makes for a mockery of justice.

Written by one who leaves his heart in your safekeeping.

María folded the note and slipped it deep in the side pocket of her gown. She glanced over to her sleeping friend. Now in her fifth month of pregnancy, Catalina no longer glowed with youth and health, but, weighed down by the coming child, became more swollen and ill looking day by day. Her many duties as queen kept her busy, and wore her out. In recent weeks, Catalina had written out rules to tighten up the running of the royal palaces, and given them to the king for his approval. Like Catalina, he too loved beauty, and wished not to have it concealed under filth. Catalina had found it easy to persuade her husband on the need to lay down rules for those at court. Especially when he was draining his treasury to refurnish his palaces. New carpets had replaced old, walls had been freshly whitewashed, and more tapestries and furniture were ordered from abroad. The glorification of the king's royal residences went hand in hand with the glorification of the king's person – every day, the king changed his costly clothes from morning to night.

At his nightly banquet, it seemed he was robed in yet another new garment adorned with more jewels. Catalina, too, had new gowns, but the additions to her wardrobe were necessary to her rank, and did not go to the same excesses as her husband.

The excesses carried over to the nightly revels, until María began wondering why Catalina remained silent about the king's extravagances. Catalina seemed happy just to sit beside her husband as he entertained his court. *Perhaps that is why she is silent. She is happy in her new role – and does not wish to risk her happiness by angering her husband.* Being big belly with child, Catalina no longer danced with him – it left her too breathless – but watched on as her young husband danced with the women of his court. He seemed oblivious to his wife's unhealthy pallor, but Catalina refused to leave her place on the dais until the king signalled an end to the night's festivities.

Listening to Catalina stirring and murmuring in her sleep, she thought with exasperation about Will's note and wondered what to do. *Sweetheart, I beg you, speak to the queen. The king listens to her.* Will had taken up Dudley's cause as if a crusade, as he elected himself Dudley's own knight errant. His involvement in a foolish scheme to rescue his friend proved he no longer thought rationally, or with reason. Now he wished for her to speak to the queen.

María rose from the table and stepped lightly to Catalina's bed. She pulled a blanket of woven wool over her friend's body. No – she could not ask this of Catalina, but perhaps she could speak to the king.

Since that time when he forced his lips upon hers at Richmond, she had made certain she was never alone with him. Nowadays, he rarely looked her way. *Three years is a lifetime for a fifteen-year-old youth. He is married to Catalina, and soon to become a father. He has no doubt forgotten that day.*

She gazed back at Catalina. Every day, the king would come to spend time in private with his wife. *If I wait at the door, I can ask the king for a private audience before leaving them alone together.*

As good fortune had it, Catalina had not woken up when the king arrived. María curtseyed to him at the door, the king scowling when she remained before him, rather than going into the next room. "Do you wish to speak to me?" he asked.

Forget fear. I do this for Will. She curtseyed again. "Sire, may I have time to talk to you alone? Not at this moment, of course, but at a time and place of your choosing. Believe me, it is important."

The young king glanced towards his sleeping wife. "Important, you say." He considered her for a moment, his eyes warming. "Meet with me early on the morrow – when I return from my morning hunt. I will seek you out in your herb garden – as I once did in the past."

María curtseyed her thanks, and left the room. *I do this for Will.*

The usual disapproval of the other women followed her when María broke away from them after Prime. Few of the English noblewomen knew her well as yet; none of them had experienced seven terrible, desperate years when all seemed dark and hopeless. Her mornings in the herb garden had been her main comfort during these years, and she continued her habit now

Catalina was queen. She needed her time with her herbs too much to ever concern herself about what the other women thought of her going to the herb gardens, alone.

Strolling to where the king asked to meet her, María breathed in the fresh, sweet smell of newly shorn grass. The morning rain some time ended, dazzling specks of light danced through windblown grass and leaves. Everything shimmered in the morning light. Birds chirped in the trees and the strengthening wind sang its song through the trembling branches of the trees, its breath tinged with salt from the river. María sat on the stone bench and waited. *What do I say to him? How do I convince the king to give mercy to Dudley? The king. Strange to think of this youth of eighteen as a king.* She closed her eyes, seeing him again as a boy of ten, gazing on Catalina in awe on her first wedding day. Had he, even as a boy, envied his brother his bride? Arthur was long dead and gone, but the boy Henry became a man who had claimed Catalina for himself.

Light footsteps crunched the earthen pathway. María opened her eyes to the king heading her way. He was alone, still dressed in his hunting clothes. The feather in his cap was limp and bent over from the recent shower. She once more admired him for his grace. For a tall man, he moved like one comfortable in his skin, and with the light step of the dancer he was. The king now three body lengths away, she rose and kneeled on the ground, waiting for him to reach her.

"You asked to speak to me in private." He sat on the bench, and stretched out his long legs before him. "God oath, I rode hard today." He screwed up his face, and laughed. "I angered Brandon today, something I find difficult to do. He told me I risked breaking my neck, and my mount. I disagreed. My neck is safe enough, and the horses sent by the King of Aragon are meant to be ridden hard. They are horses meant for battle." He waved a hand at her. "Get up, woman. I have known you long enough for ceremony to wait for more public times. What did you want to say to me? Is it about my queen? Do you wish to add your voice to that of her physicians, and tell me of your concern for her health, and how she is not finding the bearing of this child easy?"

María rose and shook the leaves off her gown. "True, Your Grace. The physicians are right to speak to you of the queen. She needs early nights and careful care, but that is not why I asked for this meeting." She decided to not beat around the bush. "Your Grace, I asked to speak to you to beg mercy for Edmund Dudley. He was loyal to your father, Sire, and he is loyal to you."

The king's small blue eyes narrowed. He stood, casting her in his shadow. "You asked me to meet with you to talk about Dudley?"

"Yes, Sire."

"What is he to you?"

"I know him only a little, Your Grace, but he is a good friend to a good friend of mine."

"Who is this friend?" He waved a hand and scowled. "No – you do not need to tell me. I see you often in conversation with Lord Willoughby. Willoughby is becoming a nuisance. I am tempted to throw him into the Tower to see if that will bring the fool to his senses." He pulled at his earlobe. "Perhaps I should if he is getting women to speak for his cause. Dudley's fate does not concern him, or you."

He rested his eyes on her again, and then he looked thoughtfully around the garden. "If he was fool enough to ask you to do this, perhaps it is true, perhaps he was fool enough to do the other thing..." He cocked his head, and considered her. "I was told yesterday of a conspiracy that came to nothing. A number of the guards at the tower were offered gold if they would help Dudley escape. Lord Willoughby has the wealth to bribe an army of guards, if he wanted to. Tell me, do you know anything about this?"

His question left her shocked, struggling for words. Her heart beating fast, María spoke in a rush. "Why should I know?" "And why do you look like you have seen a ghost?" he said slowly. "You do know what I speak of."

Her heart seemed choking her. María swallowed. She had never expected him to know of or bring up Will's foolish escape plan. "Believe me, Lord Willoughby is loyal to you, Sire."

"You avoid the answer. Perchance I'd be wise to place Lord Willoughby under arrest and have others ask him these questions."

Dizzy, María closed her eyes for a moment, inhaling and exhaling a deep breath. "If you do that, Sire, you could not avoid arresting me too. As I say, Lord Willoughby is my friend, and we often speak together for all to see. If you arrest him, you would need to arrest me too. I would hate to think what that may do to the queen."

The king seemed an uncertain boy for a moment before rounding on her in fury. "You dare threaten me – and with my wife?"

María raised her hands to her hot face. Every moment, this conversation was taking her deeper and deeper into a cesspool. She shook her head. "I do not threaten you with the queen. I only speak the truth." Her legs wobbling, she fell to her knees before she collapsed. Gazing up at the king, she held her hands out to him in supplication. "Pray, Sire – do not arrest the baron. He has been a good friend to me since I first met him, when he served your brother, Prince Arthur, God rest his soul. I will do anything you say, but do not arrest him."

He looked long at her, and then reached down to stroke her face. "Anything?"

Her blood running cold, she met his eyes. For a moment, she could not speak, too shocked at his unhidden lust. "You cannot mean...?" she spluttered.

He took a loose strand of her hair between his fingers and studied it. "Why not? Ever since I was a boy of fourteen, I dreamt about you, dreamt of you naked in my bed. You are fair, María. You were fair to me as a boy, and even fairer now. I am king; you should be honoured that I offer you this pleasant way to keep your friend safe."

María fought down her terror, thinking out her words with care. "I am honoured you think me fair, but you cannot ask me to bed with you. I am high born, your wife's kinswoman, and," she bent her head, "I am also a virgin, and must remain so until my marriage." She looked up at him in desperation. "What you ask is a betrayal of your wife. Think you what would happen if we bedded together and a child resulted from it. There is much the queen, your wife, can forgive, but not that."

The king pursed his lips, his small yet full mouth like a pink rosebud. A mouth which had seemed so innocent. A mouth disgusting her. "She is my queen, and will shut her eyes." He lowered his head, appearing uncertain. "I have no wish to hurt my beloved wife. She means more to me than I can say." He shrugged. "While she is with child, I am forbidden her bed. I need a woman, a woman who knows how to keep her mouth shut and her rightful place. I thought perhaps you were an answer, but I need no virgin in my bed. My father, the king, always told me high-born virgins are for wives, not mistresses." He turned his gaze upon her. "Still – we have a bargain to make. You do not want me to arrest Lord Willoughby; and I, one day, wish to indulge my desire to bed the most beautiful woman at my court. So – this is what you will promise. Once you are married, you will answer my summons and come to me. If you promise this, I promise I will overlook Willoughby's moon-struck behaviour in these last weeks. And you would be wise to speak sense to him. Dudley's fate is not for him to decide. It is mine."

Her head swirling, María shook and shook. *Will – oh, Will. What a sordid mess you have placed me in.* "You ask me to promise to bed with you when I marry?" She wanted to vomit. "That is what I ask. And I am not a greedy man; I also recognise your long, close relationship with my beloved wife, and do not wish to distress her – not without need. I ask only for one night and your debt to me will be paid. One night with you I can easily hide from my wife."

"You vow you will not arrest Lord Willoughby?"

The king grinned like a wicked boy. "He's lost his wits, and I should arrest him, but I find I like this game better. Every time I see you now I will imagine you in my bed. The years leading to my marriage taught me the truth of Aristotle's words: Patience is bitter, but its fruit is sweet. I am willing to wait to have you in my bed. One night with you will indeed be sweet." "Sire, while the queen needs me, I have no plan for marriage."

"Yes – my wife, the queen, has told me you desire of all

things to remain with her. You serve her well, not only as her chief confidant, but with your knowledge of healing arts, which she heeds much more than the advice of the royal physicians. But you will marry. A woman of your noble blood and beauty will be claimed one day. I am willing to wait for a better served time, when my dear wife is less likely to find out, and the fruit will indeed be sweet. So, I have your promise?"

Her sight blurring, María bowed her head in submission. *If I stay silent, pray he will think he has my promise.* She lifted her head to feel whipped by the king's grin.

"Today was a good meeting – and a happy outcome. We shall speak no more of this until you are safely wed. Until then, we shall please my wife by being friends. I bid you good day, María."

María bowed her head again. *Friends? Is he fool enough to think we can ever be friends after this day? If I cannot marry Will, I will never marry. Age will soon rid me of this cursed face the king thinks so fair. Will is safe. That is all I care about. Will is safe.* She raised her head, and froze in fright. *But what if the king ever suspected I love Will, and he me? That I am not as inno-cent as I led him to think. Could he use Will to call in his debt then? I know him, he will watch us, and closely.* Her heart beat faster. *Oh God – what if the king had anything else to hold over me? What would be the consequences, to Will, to me? I must end it with Will. I must end it.*

4

~ Medieval Portuguese verse

Another dawn broke, and its light fell over her as María paced up and down in the garden. Not the same garden as the day before, this secluded garden held a special place in her heart. She spent many mornings in this garden with Will, whiling away the hours playing their instruments and melding their voices together in song.

She shook her head, her heartbeat drumming loud in her ears. *Will may not come.* But the servant she sent to Will last night had returned and told her he would be here. She could not think of one time when he failed to come to her.

The morning birdsongs did not comfort her today. Her meeting with the king yesterday pushed her back into a dark world, stripped of any illusion of possessing any power over her life. She dropped to her knees beside a garden bed of basil and began wildly tugging at the weeds, tossing them in a pile next to her. When Will rested his hand on her shoulder, she almost jumped out of her skin.

"What is wrong, María?"

She wiped her wet eyes with her sleeve, and sat back on the grass. Will crouched down next to her, gazing at her in bemusement. "Love?"

She closed her eyes. *Dear God, help me. Please help me.* Averting her face from him, she locked her eyes onto the purplish-pink foxgloves growing in a clump in the corner of the garden. Dappled by light, the bell-like flowers bobbed back and forth in the breeze. They did not look deadly – but pretty, enticing, inviting the touch of hand. If they did not treat dropsy, she would have pulled them all out and add them to her weed pile. *Si, beauty often hides ugliness too.* She stole a look at Will. *Like my love for him. It makes of me a sinner, consuming me with desire until I hate my virginity and wish to sin.* "I cannot do this anymore," she said.

Will frowned. "You cannot do what?"

"Us. I cannot be simply your friend. It's destroying me."

He stared at her, the bones of his face becoming distinct. "You want to end what we have together?"

María entwined her fingers into the grass at either side of her, and held on. "What do we have, Will? We cannot marry, and I cannot be your mistress. We decided this years ago. I am who I am, and you are a man who wishes to remain a man of honour. The queen has never been happy we continue to meet.

And for what – for us to keep alight a fire burning which rightly should have been put out years ago?"

He shifted closer, resting his hand on hers. "You cannot mean this. You have my heart, and only you. As for the fire – it did not give us any choice. Who can choose where they love?" Removing her hand from underneath his, María clasped hands on her lap, and shut her eyes, unable to look at his white, agonised face for one more moment. *I must stay strong. There is too much at stake for the king to know I love Will, heart and soul. He will only use the knowledge to destroy the man I love – and destroy me by doing so.* Opening her eyes, she stared at her hands. Dirt from the garden was ingrained under her short finger nails and into the lines of her skin. She held her hands until they hurt, and her knuckles became bone white. *Make an end, fool – do not draw it out.* She gathered her courage and raised her eyes to his. "You also love your wife."

"Yes, I have never lied to you about that. But it is not like the love I bear for you."

"No matter, Will. The love you give to me is rightfully hers. It is wrong you avoid her bed because you wish to be faithful to me. We must face how things truly stand between us. You need an heir; an heir I cannot give to you. I can no longer bear to think I have robbed you of children – or from a woman who deserved better from us."

"I do not understand. Only days ago, you did not speak of this. All then was as it ever was." His eyes widened. "Is it because of Edmund? Are you angry at me because I sent you that note? I only asked you to speak to the queen because we are hopeful for Edmund and Empson's release. Who better to intercede to the king for the lives of two innocent men than his wife?"

His probing came too close to the truth. She gripped her hands again, lowered her head, and spoke quietly. "This has nothing to do with Dudley, but only us. I just never spoke of it before. I kept silent because I could not let you go. You are my first true love. You will always be my first true love." She swallowed, and braved to look his way. "But I must speak to you the truth. This wall we keep between us... oh God, Will, it is too hard. Either it must crumble, and all Hell lets loose, or we must end it. I am no longer a sixteen-year-old girl, but a grown woman. I have long been a grown woman. Every time we are together, I grow weaker. Even now. I look at you, and want your lips on mine, your hands on my body. I want you in my bed, but not for careful, cautious love games, which years ago we once risked. How many years have we not dared to really kiss or lay in a bed together, for yet another time of unfulfilled desires? I cannot go on like this. If you love me, and truly wish for me not to be shamed at court, you will let me go. Pray, I beg you, Will, let me go."

Will touched her cheek, and she swayed towards him. She stiffened, jerked her face away from him. *No. It must end.*

"You truly want this – forever?"

María could not look at him. "We can speak together in public, where others can hear. But we can no longer be alone. And you must go home and make a true marriage with your wife."

"I cannot believe you're saying this. You break my heart."

María rose from the ground, unable to stop her tears. It was the hardest thing not to look at him again. "My heart breaks too, but for seven years we lied to ourselves, thinking what we did was right. We were wrong. What we did was always for us – and without care for those we hurt. The time has come for us to open our eyes and make amends – you to your wife, and I in service to my queen. If you love me, you must let me go." Picking up her skirts, she turned on her heel and ran from him, trying to block her ears as Will called after her. His voice broke apart into a terrible cry. It sounded like a death knell.

5

Everyone can see the king is vexed with the Queen Katherine and she is vexed with him. No one knows how it will end. The storm is at the height.

~ *Don Luis Caroz to Miguel Perez de Almanza, 1510*

"The time has come for us to open our eyes and make amends – you to your wife, and I in service to my queen." María's words seemed to follow her everywhere. It proved easier to say them than to live them, live them when her heart was breaking, and her whole life seemed over. She lost her taste for food and struggled through each day in a mist of depression. For a week, she sent away Will's messages – and then wept anew when she heard he had returned to his estates.

Catalina soon noticed the change in her, but was relieved

when told the reason. "It is for the best. Find someone else to love, someone who is not already married."

She could not tell her she never wanted to marry. Even Will. Marriage would mean the king's summons to his bed. She had nightmares about that, nightmares leaving her too terrified to sleep. Even the rosemary sachet she placed under her pillow helped little. She told herself it was good Will left for his home, and his wife, and it was good he had not returned. She did not want her strength or resolve tested through seeing him every day.

Autumn drew to a close, and winter fell upon them with all the savagery of a starving wolf. The dark, bitterly cold days echoed her low spirits, every new day a new struggle to accept Will's absence in her life. Despite the lit fires and the sea coal braziers in all the chambers at Richmond Palace, she could never feel warm. All she wanted to do was to curl up in bed and stay there – forever. She could not stop thinking of Will, and thinking of him broke her heart anew. Thinking how he had called after her, his heart breaking in his voice, destroyed her.

But Catalina needed her. She was not carrying her first child well – and she was still months away from her confinement. Refusing to let her ill-health interfere with her duties as queen, day after day, Catalina sought more improvements at court, and ways to support men of learning and piety. She was now the patron of scholars, of poets and musicians. She kept herself informed of all the important decisions put in force by this new reign, including that of Edmund Dudley and Empson. One night, not long after María's meeting with Will, Catalina spoke to the king at supper. "Would it be wrong to be merciful? I have been told they only served your father as he wished."

Close by, María pulled back into the shadows. *If I had only waited, I could have avoided speaking to the king, and I would not needed to forsake Will.*

For the first time in their marriage, the king raised his voice, speaking angrily to her: "This is none of your affair. It is my decision, and mine alone." He stormed from her chambers and did not return for a full day. By then, María had persuaded Catalina she must think of the coming child and not bring up Dudley and Empson again.

Henry and Catalina celebrated their first Christmas together, enjoying the entertainment of three plays and a concert with the court. On New Year's Day, the king delighted his wife by giving her a missal which had belonged to his mother, and even more by the message he wrote in it:

I am yours, Henry R., forever.

Taking the small book from him to place on her desk, Catalina smiled. "And I am yours, Harry," she said. "Until my last breath, I vow to be your faithful and loving wife. Si, until my last breath."

Seeing the king go to embrace Catalina, María pushed down her misery. For years, she had received a gift from Will at Christmas. *Perhaps his continued absence at court is my gift. I am not ready to see him again.* She shook her head, tearing her thoughts from Will to return to the present. She wondered about Catalina's words. *Did she wish to remind him of his unfaithfulness?* If that was her intention, the king appeared oblivious to it.

María lingered for a while in the chapel after Vespers to pray alone before returning to Catalina's chambers. She prayed for God's help – she prayed for forgiveness. She could not stop thinking of Will – or loving him. She could not stop her despair darkening her days. Daylight diminishing with every breath, servants lit the torches in the high sconces along the gallery leading to queen's apartments. At last, she arrived at Catalina's door, but the young guard, white with alarm, refused her admittance. "The king is with the queen," he said, refusing to look her way.

The king's loud voice reverberated through the thick wood. "Hold your tongue," he shouted.

Another voice, so like the king's, yelled back, "I say it again. My sisters are not for the likes of the Comptons, or the Tudors."

A door slammed in the inner chamber, and the door of the entrance flung open. The Duke of Buckingham emerged, his face red with fury. He glanced blankly at María. Without one word of greeting, he stomped his way down the corridor, heading in the direction of the stables. When the guard broke his stance and turned his head to watch the duke's departure, she seized the opportunity to slip into Catalina's antechamber, shutting the door behind her.

The door of Catalina's bedroom was closed. Fearing for her friend, she tiptoed to the window-seat near the door, and slipped behind its drawn curtains, all the while listening to the king roar: "I will not have your people spying on me, madam, or a meddling wife who minds not her business."

"Not my business? You take Anne Hastings to your bed and tell me it is not my business?"

The king and Catalina spoke in Castilian. She had never

before heard them speak like this to one another – terse and furious.

"What of it?"

"What of it, my husband? We've not been yet wed a full year. I bear your child; am I also to bear your unfaithfulness?"

"Be reasonable, Kate. You are with child and your bed is forbidden to me. Anne is married and no threat to you."

"No threat to me... you take a mistress, and you say it is no threat to me? Husband – a mistress is always a threat to a wife."

"Jesu'– you would never have known except for Buckingham's loose tongued sister. She should have stayed silent. Now Anne Hastings is gone, I know not where, thanks to Buckingham ordering her husband to send Nan away from court. And you are angry at me for no good purpose."

"No good purpose, Harry?"

"Nan was only a dalliance. I have no mistress, wife."

"A dalliance? My heart breaks over this so-called dalliance. And why should not Elizabeth tell me, and the duke, her brother, of this so-called dalliance? She is devoted to me, and devoted to her sister. Can you not understand why? Anne's good name is no more."

"You make too much of it. And my cousin, Buckingham, too. God's oath – did you hear his parting shot? His sisters are too good for the Tudors? He forgets his place. I tell you true, I am tempted to have my cousin cool his heels in the Tower."

Silence ruled for several heartbeats until it was broken by Catalina's strained voice: "You must not do that."

"'Must not?' You are my wife, and I love you, but 'must not' are words you must never use with me."

"Husband, if Buckingham was placed in the Tower over this

matter, then all the court would know," Catalina spoke slowly, as if drawing out each word caused her deeper pain, "if they did not know already, you have bedded Anne, and used William Compton to hide your dalliance. I believe you would prefer to keep it that way – if only for appearances sake." Once more, silence reigned, giving María time to think. In recent weeks, the king was often in Compton's chambers. He had told the queen they were playing cards. It appeared the king made use of Compton to play at other games. But to play with Buckingham's sister Anne? *The king is a fool if he did not expect Elizabeth, Buckingham's other sister, to tell her brother.* "You break my heart, Harry. I did not expect your unfaithfulness so soon after our marriage."

"I say again, you upset yourself for no good cause. It is thosewho told you and meddled in what was best left alone who are at fault in this. I command you send from the court Elizabeth Radcliffe, and your meddlesome priest. They should have held their tongues. This matter only concerned me, and none other." "Husband, it will always concern me when you bed another woman. They were right to come to me and tell me."

María winced, remembering the rumours she had kept silent about. *Did I do wrong? But what if I had worried her for no cause? She should not be vexed when she is carrying a child.*

"I disagree," said the king. "I want them gone from my court. I want them gone for a long time."

"You cannot be serious about me sending them away?"

"I am serious. And merciful. You do not know how close I came to ordering their arrests. But, as you reminded me, I want this matter to be forgotten. I will not forget it if I see these spies of yours creeping around at court."

"They are not spies."

"Wife, do I need to see to their removal, or will you?"

Another silence. "I will see to it, my king."

A longer silence fell before the king spoke again. "You do not look well."

Catalina's laughter had a bitter ring to it. "Are you surprised, my lord husband? Have I not cause to be unwell?"

"Your noble mother overlooked your father's dalliances, and you, wife, will overlook mine. Go you to bed. In the morning, you will see this in a better light. I'll kiss you now and bid you goodnight."

The door protested as it opened, and the floor creaked and shook a little as the king strode with a quick, angry step to the other door. Hearing it open and close, María waited several moments to ensure the king did not return and then rushed into Catalina's bedchamber.

Catalina lay on her bed, staring up at nothing. Climbing onto the bed beside her, María held her hand. "Catalina –"

Catalina turned a face blotchy and ill. "You'd never lie to me?" Unable to speak, María shook her head in denial, refusing to think of all the little lies she had told Catalina over the years. All the little lies spoken, and all the lies of omission. All because she loved her – and did not want her burdened with truths either unnecessary or too heavy. *Do I do right to keep so much from her? Over and over, I have broken my vow to never keep anything from her. My head hurts thinking about it.*

Catalina wiped at her wet eyes. "Did you know my husband has been unfaithful?"

María took a deep breath. *Dear God – what do I say?* She rubbed Catalina's hand, wincing at how clammy it was. This came at the worst of times. Meeting her friend's eyes, the suffering she saw there made her flinch. "It means nothing."

María flinched again knowing there was no consolation in her words.

Catalina closed her eyes, rolling her head one way and another on the pillow. "I do not know how to live with this. If I can live with this."

"You will. Women always endure such things. Especially wives of kings. Your father too had his women, and he esteemed, no, loved your mother. You bear the king's child. Sister, think with your head, not your heart. The king only appeases his lust, out of consideration for you."

Catalina seemed paler than ever. "We vowed on our wedding day to cleave only to one another." Fresh tears streamed down her face.

She swallowed, and tightened her grip on Catalina. *Did she truly expect a man like the king to be faithful to her? Does she know him at all?* She swallowed again, her head aching. *Catalina needs my comfort, and to not hear what I believe the truth about the king.* "Hush," she said instinctively. "The king still loves you – he cleaves to you in that. This woman means nothing to him, and she should mean nothing to you too."

"Nothing? She means nothing? You argue that word overmuch, María." Catalina rolled over, sobbing into her pillow. Miserable for her friend, María reached out to lay her hand on Catalina's shoulder. "Hush, my sister. Think of your babe. Please."

Catalina turned. Tears fell from her eyes. She no longer looked young. "I cannot, not when my heart breaks. Every time I think of my Harry with another. He told me he loved me. I believed he loved me. How can he love me when he tears me apart with his unfaithfulness? I am bleeding inside, María, bleeding." She held out her wet fingers. "See my tears? They are blood. Blood from my heart."

Wanting to cry too, María wound her arms around Catalina. Her heart reminded her of her own loss. She imagined Will in the arms of his wife. *I cannot think of him of being unfaithful to me. For seven years, we were the ones tottering on the sin of adultery. How do I know if his wife did not weep, like Catalina does now? The pain I must bear is my penance for all those years of sin.* The babe stirred uneasily between them. Catalina began weeping again.

She whispered, "Hush, my sister." Rocking Catalina gently in her arms, she sang to her, softly and slowly, in the language of home:

> *Let us all sing together:*
> *Hail Mary*
> *When the Virgin was alone,*
> *An angel appeared*
> *He is called Gabriel*
> *And is sent from Heaven.*
> *Radiant he said*
> *(Listen my dear ones):*
> *You will conceive, Mary.*
> *You will bear a son...*

6

Your daughter, our dearest consort, has conceived in her womb
a living child, and is right heavy therewith, which we signify to
Your Majesty for the great joy thereof that we take, and the
exultation of our whole realm.

~ Henry VIII to Ferdinand II of Aragon

Catalina looked more aged and ill when she returned to
her place by the king's side. She hid her pain, her anger,
but she could not hide her feelings about Anne Hastings. "I
never want to see the woman again," she told María before
telling the king the same. The king seemed bemused at seeing his
wife so stubborn, and unbending. He had never seen that side to
her, but, for the child she bore him, one he was now willing to
indulge. Anne Hastings was told to stay away from a court, for a
time.

Catalina's heartache over the king's unfaithfulness deepened María's own shame about the years she had wished Will would do likewise. But while she grappled with the shame, the grief of their parting only increased until the day came when she put aside all thoughts of her own sorrow to pen a letter.

Doña, my dear Latina,

A little princess was born last night, on the last day of January, but before her time.

The room was so cold she could feel the tracks of her tears freezing onto her skin. Rising from her seat, she sat on a stool closer to the fire holding her painful hands out to its warmth. Once again, the English winter had caused her fingers to swell and her skin to redden and crack. It had taken years before she saw it as an inconvenience, an excruciating inconvenience, of the cold days in England. Her medicine books reassured her it would not cause any permanent damage to her fingers. Bathing them in a warm mixture of beaten eggs, wine and fennel lessened her physical pain, but not the pain of life. Her sore fingers were a reminder her sufferings measured little against those of others. She returned to her writing desk, and re-inked her quill.

She was too tiny for any chance of life. She did not even take one breath.

It is custom here to not allow unwed women in the birthing chamber. My poor queen overrode the disapproval of her women, and the midwife, insisting I stay with her.

All through her labour, she held onto my hand and spoke to me in Castilian, blaming herself for the premature birth. That she should have listened to me and rested more in these last weeks, rather than concern herself with the Christmas entertainments for the court. But she was heartsore. Keeping busy left her little time to weep. I am certain you have heard rumours about the king of what I dare not pen.

With the birth not expected for months, the queen's chambers had not been readied for her confinement. When the pangs of childbirth came upon the queen, we all knew, at six months, no babe is born with any chance of life.

I write this letter to you in great confusion. Have you ever heard of a woman giving birth to one twin and with the remaining twin still alive in her womb?

The royal physician has convinced the queen she is still with child. I do not know what to believe. My queen is so swollen, unchanged from when she began her labour, it could be so. Alice, the queen's midwife, tells me it can happen as the physician says. But she can hear no heartbeat. She believes the physician wrong to tell the queen there is another child. She thinks the queen suffered from an illness caused by pregnancy, and this is what caused the child to be born early. She thinks the early birth saved her life...

For weeks, María stayed with Catalina in her chamber, comforting her, attending to her needs. The winter wind howled through the days and nights, pounding the palace with an unyielding fury. One night, when Catalina wished to sleep alone and Maria slept in the next chamber, the screech of its voice assaulted her dreams – forcing its way in. She dreamt the king seized her and refused to let her go; she dreamt he and Will fought to the death, the king's two-handed sword, the one he used in jousting competitions, soon overpowering Will's lesser sword, she dreamt he threatened everyone she loved. She woke, screaming, ready to fray at any moment, thankful she did not have to explain her tears to Catalina.

By the time the weeks became a month, María had let go of any hope that Catalina could still be pregnant. But Catalina was not ready to let go of her hope. She hoped and prayed for the physician to be right, and she still carried a child after birthing her dead daughter. Not so the king. By the end of four weeks, the king made it clear he believed Alice Massy – a midwife who had seen his mother through seven childbirths. He returned to his wife's bed. His needs, both as a king and a man, came first and outweighed the disapproval of those who still believed Catalina carried a child.

By the final days of April, Catalina faced the truth at last. There had been no unborn twin, and now she showed all the signs of early pregnancy.

"I am a fool." Catalina sat at the table, staring aside at the silver font sent by Margaret of Austria. "I allowed myself to believe for weeks I was still with child when there was no child. A child for which all is readied to greet its birth. What do I with all the gifts we have received? Shall I just send the font back with my thanks? What of the yards of Holland cloth? Do I send that back too?"

"Be happy you are once again with child," María realised she spoke in Castilian. She switched to English, "You cannot remain in this dark chamber forever."

Alice Massy approached and curtseyed. "My queen – you cannot be blamed for believing the king's physician. It was an easy mistake to make – when we wish to believe the evidence told by our eyes, but fail to consider other causes. The physician made a mistake, that is all. Send back the gifts, and begin again. You are in your twenties, in your prime. There is no reason for you not to hope all will go well this time."

So, Catalina returned to court to sit beside her husband, smiled and laughed again. That evening, María watched on as Catalina wrote to her father to tell him her news. With each line penned on the parchment, Catalina looked more defeated, and miserable.

Crossing the room to her friend, María rested a hand on her shoulder and glanced down at the letter. Phrases jumped out at her: *Please do not be upset with me. I prayed to God. It was God's doing.* But she did not tell her father how long it had taken her to face the fact her pregnancy was no pregnancy, rather she wrote in such a way to give the impression she had recently miscarried. Gently, María squeezed Catalina's shoulder. *What of it?* But the letter left María troubled. *Catalina hates falsehoods – and now she writes a letter with this falsehood to her father. Does she want to believe she has indeed just miscarried?*

Once more, María held her tongue. *What of it? Lie to her father, lie to herself, all that truly matters is she no longer secludes herself in her chamber and refuses to leave it.*

But, the days following, María became more disquieted by Catalina's behaviour. Much of her waking life was spent in prayer, but she also seemed a woman sleepwalking in her life. She returned to speaking of carrying the guilt of Warwick's death, when her eyes seemed dead. One day, after her women readied her for another of the king's nightly banquets, Catalina stared at the mirror. She stirred to the sparkle of jewels. Her robes of cloth of gold seemed to glitter in the candlelight. María set the queen's coronet on Catalina's unlined brow, and brushed her hair one more time until it shimmered. "I am not meant to be happy," Catalina murmured.

María glanced at the other women, relieved none of them were close enough to hear. She wished they were alone so she could speak to her. *But what can I say? Is lasting happiness a reality for any of us?* Walking behind Catalina to the banquet room, María thought of her own situation. Will had returned to court. Day after day, seeing him in the king's company tortured her; tormented her.

After Catalina returned to her bed that evening, María sat with Meg Pole, also newly come again at court to attend the queen. Without meaning to, she blurted out to Meg, "Why must happiness be elusive?"

Meg considered her inquisitively. "You speak strangely," she said.

"Forgive me – you are older than me, and have already lived through so much. Now you have regained your rightful inheritance. Does that make you happy?"

Meg broke her eyes away and screwed up a wry face. "Do you wish for the truth?"

"We are friends. You can tell me the truth."

Meg yanked at the neckline of her shift, straightening it so the blackwork of pansies could be seen. "My inheritance has been due to me overlong. I am pleased I can better assist my children to take their rightful positions at court, but as for happiness... that is a different thing. We must treasure happiness when we have it; it is the golden thread which lights up the too often dark tapestry of our lives. I have lived too long without wealth to ever think of it as a means to happiness. My change of position has given me power over my life – but power does not mean happiness. But I will be happy to see my change of position lighten the queen's undeserved and too heavy guilt over the death of my brother."

"She has also spoken about this to you?" María asked with a sigh.

"Aye. But she has taken the loss of her first child hard. It is her sorrow which has stirred all this up again. Once she holds her living child, she will put all this behind her." Meg looked at her. "I gather you are not happy too?"

María bent her head, staring at her clasped hands. She sighed. "I remember when we first talked together, you rightly told me I had never been in love. That has been long changed." Meg peered at her. "And you are still unwed." She leaned back, her eyes widening. "I hazard a guess you cannot marry this man. Who is it, my friend?"

"William Willoughby." She lifted her eyes to Meg's. "Will Willoughby," she said again. It seemed forever since she had spoken his name out loud.

"Ah – the very handsome, very married Baron. Does the queen know?"

"Yes – but I can no longer speak to her about it. She was pleased when I ended the attachment. Will is back at court and seeing him every day reopens the wound, a wound oozing at the slightest touch."

"You have my sympathy. But you made the right decision not to continue your association with the baron. You are too close to the queen to ever forget your honour."

"Honour, Meg?" María bit her lower lip, meeting Meg's eyes. "When I see him, I care little for my honour."

Meg shook her head. "You would sing a different tune if you found yourself with a bastard child. It is good you are free of him," Meg said. "Find someone worthy of you – someone you like and who is free to marry you."

She winced at what seemed the echo of Catalina's words. How simple it sounded. *As if I can ever be free of Will. No other man will ever measure up to him. I want him, only him. Find someone else? Impossible.* She trembled. *And the king makes it impossible too. As long as I remain virgin, I remain safe from him.*

Only the years of discipline, long, difficult years of learning to hide her feelings, helped María through those first unhappy days of seeing Will at court, and rarely speaking to him. But the nights when the king bedded with Catalina, her pregnancy yet unannounced to the court, and María slept with the other noble women who attended the queen, she could not help but fight back her tears. Her self-forced loneliness was like an expanse of ocean – stretching out without mercy, without end. For her, there was no sight of any shore. There could be no shore, not while life, and a king's desire, separated her from Will.

Catalina's new marmoset screamed and tore out of María's arms when the king rushed into the queen's chambers one morning with fifteen of his closest men – all of them dressed in green, short tunics, hose and hoods, carrying bows, arrows and swords. Behind them followed musicians. While the musicians piled in and filled an empty space in the chamber, María coaxed the frightened animal back into her arms, and knelt with the other women. Catalina first looked shocked, but recovered to laugh as her husband took her in his arms for his kiss.

Catalina gave the command for her women to stand, and María rushed to the deepest part of the chamber, cradling the marmoset. The heart of the poor little animal seemed ready to burst out of its skin.

"Let the music begin," the king commanded with a shout. He kept hold of Catalina's hand and led her to a clear space in the middle of the room to begin a dance. Servants came in bearing platters of food – and before the first dance was over, the room had changed from that of mostly silent, sewing women, to one of merriment, revelry, and youth.

The marmoset at last settled, María considered the royal couple. *Did the king do this because he noticed Catalina's low spirits?* Now Catalina glowed with happiness when her husband embraced and kissed her again in front of all the company. He glowed too, and caressed her flat belly. "The queen is with child. This time a son," he announced to the room.

The light dimmed once more in Catalina's eyes before she smiled brightly at the king. He kissed her again and bowed deeply to her. "Time to be away, my love. Wolsey wishes to see me this afternoon on some matter. Stay here, Kate. My musicians can stay here too – and play to you while you rest. I will speak more to you at the banquet tonight."

Dudley and Empson finally met their deaths on Tower Hill in the middle of August. María almost broke seeing Will haggard with grief. She wanted to comfort him. But she could not; she had to stay away from him, for both their sakes. One day, María caught him gazing at her, not hiding his hurt, his despair, his confusion that she avoided him, even in a crowded room at court.

His face haunted María that night – and kept her from sleep. As light of dawn broke into her chamber, the floodgates opened, and she wept and wept. *Oh, Will – if I weaken, the wall would tumble. I would beg you to take me for your mistress. But it is no longer as simple as that; it has never been simple. And I fear the king. If he knows I am your mistress, he will demand the same privilege. Everything I know of the king tells me this. And what would you do, my love? I know you well too. You would likely rage against the king, like Buckingham once did for his sister. But you are not Buckingham. The king hesitates to kill his cousin, but he would not hesitate to kill you. I protect us both by keeping the king's respect – his respect for my high birth, and his respect for my virginity.*

Richmond Palace, December 1510

Doña, my dear Latina,

Yet another winter has arrived. The queen has taken to her chambers, in wait for another childbirth. Unlike the first time when her too early labour caught all unprepared, all is readied and waiting for the birth of a prince.

Many candles lit up the birthing chamber – a room as warm

as any could make it this winter night. A well-stocked fire blazed in the huge fireplace and coal braziers burned merrily throughout the night, their fuel replenished by maidservants whenever necessary.

Catalina's labour had started that morning – on the last day of 1510. Her hair unbound, she laboured on a richly dressed pallet bed dwarfing her tiny form.

Once again, María held Catalina's hand, speaking softly to her in the tongue of their birth when her travail was at its worst. Then, she sang and encouraged Catalina to sing too, to ride out the pain. In the lulls between the pangs of labour, María distracted her by talking about the stories depicted in the tapestries hanging on the walls in the chamber. Most of them were of Biblical stories, but there were a few which told other tales. María drew back, staring at one of them, the tapestry strung up behind her friend. Candlelight shimmered the threads of the tapestry and its bold colours of summer. Hearing Catalina's strained laughter, she broke her eyes away.

"I have stopped counting the times you have looked at that," murmured Catalina.

María shrugged, tightening her hold on Catalina's hand, "I confess, it disturbs me." She looked again at the picture of the young man and woman sitting close beside one another in a sunlit garden, not touching with their bodies, but locked together in eternal, joyful longing with their eyes. "I know the story well. It makes a promise of a happy outcome. But the picture is a lie."

"You grow too cynical, my sister. Tristan and Iseult's love was not a lie. I do not believe love is ever a lie." Catalina writhed, throwing her head back. "Dear God, dear God," she moaned.

Alice came to the bed and placed The Girdle of Our Lady in Maria's waiting hands. The girdle sent from Westminster Abbey for the queen's labour, María wound it carefully around Catalina's swollen belly. "My queen," the midwife said, "this will give you ease. I do not think you will be waiting much longer before you hold your babe."

Alice was proved right. The last day of December ended and the first hour of January brought with it the cry of a living child. "We have our prince," said Alice in triumph. The boy's lusty cry rang out in the room, making some of the women laugh with relief. One woman sped from the room to take the good news to those waiting outside the chamber. Catalina fell back onto her pillows, her hands held out for her child. The midwife placed the precious boy beside her while she attended to the final matters of childbirth. The baby squirmed, his little red face grimacing, his thin arms flailing above the blanket. María touched his cheek, his skin feeling like silk beneath her finger. The child was perfect.

Tears falling down her face, Catalina stretched a finger out to her child, and the boy enclosed it in his tiny fist. She laughed. "My son is strong, thank God." She raised her eyes. "Does the king know yet?"

As if in answer, the door swung open, and the king rushed in, kneeling beside his wife and child. He looked at his son as if in awe, and touched the child's face. A light touch, as if fearful to hurt the child. The king grinned. "Look at the sheen of his hair, sweetheart, my love. He has our colouring, but mayhap his hair is a deeper red."

The midwife let out a guffaw. "Your Grace – your son, the prince, is newly born. Once we bathe and swaddle him, and dry the prince's hair, I think you will see your first instinct was right, he shares the same hair colouring as you, Your Grace, and the good queen."

Catalina clasped her husband's hand. "I have given you your prince, a healthy son."

The king grinned. He looked a youth granted his spurs. "That you have. I loved you before this day, but now my love has no bounds." He leant across and kissed her lips. "I will leave you and the boy to rest. I wish to go to the chapel and give my thanks to God for your safe deliverance, and that of our son."

The door closing behind the king, María relaxed her clenched hands. She hated being too close to the king. *No – it is the king I hate.* She raised her eyes to the only window left uncovered in the chamber. Outside, there was a flare of lit torches, one after another. Church bells rang out, joined by more church bells. Soon, it seemed a sea of voices cried out for joy. She turned back to Catalina. Catalina's eyes remained on her son. *Forget the king. Smile for Catalina. Smile for the boy.*

Named for his father, tiny Henry was christened five days later, his great-aunt, Lady Anne Howard, stood proxy for the child's godmother, Margaret of Austria and Richard Foxe, Bishop of Winchester stood in proxy for the child's other royal godparent, Louis XII of France. The King of France sent as a christening gift a gold salt holder and a gold cup. For days and days, from Land's End to John o' Groats, bonfires blazed out the news of the birth of the prince.

Catalina stayed at Richmond with her baby until she was churched. For forty days, María watched her friend's love for her little son grow as the child flourished, going from newborn babe to one who smiled seeing his mother. By then, the king had pilgrimaged to the shrine of Walsingham to give thanks and ask for the Virgin's protection for his son. Then he returned to Westminster and began planning his great celebration for Prince Henry's birth. Catalina, now churched and recovered from the birth, cradled her baby one last time before handing her son over to Bessie, his nurse.

Catalina had spent hours with her son each day – glorying in him, amazed at the miracle which had birthed from her body. All the long river journey back to Westminster, María wondered how Catalina managed to hold back her tears. She shook the thought away. *Catalina is right. The child is well, and in good hands. Like her own mother, Catalina will always be queen first, mother second.*

The king summoned her back at Westminster. It was time for her to show herself to the people and take her rightful place beside her husband, and return to his bed.

Ten days later, María stood in Westminster Hall with five other women, smoothing down her green and gold satin gown. It had been brought over from the royal wardrobe at Baynard Castle after being used for other royal events. One of the court seamstresses had spent the afternoon ensuring the gown fitted perfectly.

María was glad the gown was only borrowed; she never felt comfortable wearing the Tudor colours. She only wore it to please Catalina, who had asked her to take part in the celebrations tonight.

Five men on the other side of the hall, also in green and gold, milled around the towering king. Clothed in purple, on the upper part of his doublet was embroidered in gold "Sir Loyal Heart." *Sir Loyal Heart?* She wanted to laugh at the absurdity of it. The king was not loyal. He was unfaithful to his wife, and thought little of coercing her best friend to betray her. *Si – I have many reasons to doubt he has a heart – let alone a loyal heart.*

The hall had been recast as an arbour – greenery everywhere. The tapestry dividing the hall swung open, and Catalina glided in with more of her women. Her loose hair cascaded down her back, the light of torches gleaming it to a rich gold. Her hair seemed brighter and more glorious than the jewelled coronet she wore around her brow.

The king greeted her, kissing her on her lips with gusto. Since Catalina's arrival back at court, the king had come to her bed each night. They had returned to the young lovers of the early days of their marriage.

María inwardly sighed. She was still not resigned to her grief about losing Will. *You are a fool. He was never yours to lose.* But María could not make herself believe that. She could not stop missing what they once shared together. She avoided playing her vihuela for it reminded her of all the times they had made music together. When she played it, she wanted to weep because of her loneliness. Will was her love – her only love; his absence in her life blighted her days. But she had to keep away from Will to keep him safe.

The king led Catalina by the hand to her seat on the dais, and sat in the throne beside her. A trumpet blared out a long note.

"Stand aside, stand aside," the king's chamberlain called.

Two enormous horses, bigger than María had ever seen in her life, pulled into the hall an enormous pageant car, as high as eight feet at least and just as wide. Both horses were attired in elaborate costumes; one horse was disguised as a lion and the other an antelope. It was a good thing they were strong beasts; not only did each horse carry a woman of noble birth as its rider, but she counted seven men on the car. And not only men. A green velvet forest rose around a miniature gold castle, on which a man sat making rose garlands in a garden blooming with all the colour of spring. Three foresters, garbed in the same green as the forest and holding spears, walked alongside the car.

The court called out and clapped loud its approval as the pageant car made its slow way to Catalina, coming to a stop in front of her. The foresters blew their horns, and the car opened up. Out stepped four men from inside of the car, shouting their challenge for the next day's joust.

Ten days of celebrations continued. Ten days of celebrations and pageants when María remembered she was still young, only twenty-five, and could find some joy in life. But then the news came from Richmond.

Less than an hour later, the king and Catalina travelled down in their barge to the palace. Their little son lay in his cradle, wrapped in his swaddling cloths. The beautiful boy looked asleep. Bessie, his nurse, knelt by his cradle. "Your highnesses," the woman said through her tears, "I found him like that. He was well and lusty last night, but he did not wake this morning. He did not wake…"

Catalina fell to her knees on the other side of the cradle. She leaned on her son's cradle, and wept. The king knelt beside her, pulling her into his arms, weeping too. "It is God's will," he said.

María brushed away her own tears. *God's will? I cannot think of a child's death as God's will. There is no comfort in that – only a cruel God. I do not want to believe in a cruel God. I need to believe there is some plan – even if a plan beyond my understanding. A plan belonging to a loving God. Si – His plan where there is no more death, no more broken hearts, and love soars to the Heavens, for all eternity. I have to believe that – or else go mad.*

After the boy's funeral, María sat beside Catalina in a window-seat at Greenwich, gazing down at the Thames. The same Thames which had brought back the boy's small coffin over a week ago. The river reflected the grey day, and the grey mood of all at court. "Do you remember the last time we saw my son?" asked Catalina quietly.

María squeezed Catalina's hand.

Catalina did not look her way. Peering out the window, she appeared lost in her own world of memory. At last, Catalina lifted her head, her mouth trembling. "When I took him in my arms to kiss him farewell, he smiled at me. More. My little Henry laughed."

"I remember." María wound her arm around Catalina's shoulders.

"He was perfect; a perfect, beautiful child."

"Yes."

"And healthy. He was healthy... My son was healthy...."

"Catalina, please don't torment yourself."

"I cannot understand. A dead girl, and now my little Henry.

You are a healer. Can you not help me understand why both my babies are dead?"

María twisted around to the window. The sky and river both grey, she shivered, her stomach churning like the river below her. "All I know is what our teacher told me, and you too," she said slowly. "There is so much we don't know. While we live, we do the best we can, and go on."

Catalina seemed not listening. "Perhaps I made the wrong choices for the people to look after my son."

"You made the right choices, my sister, but there is no point in blaming yourself – or others. Remember Isabel's child, your little nephew. For almost three years, he was cared for and loved. So loved. And he lacked for nothing – and we could do nothing – nothing – when the fever came and took him. Your Henry was younger still. Latina told me the younger the child, the more chance of the illness taking hold in such a way that there is no hope of saving them. Pray take comfort that every day of his short life, your little boy knew love and the devotion of many."

Catalina glanced at her. "I tell myself that; I tell myself to possess memory of my laughing little son, is better than to have no son to remember. I tell myself he is with God – and one day I will hold him once more. None of it comforts me."

"My sister, your child has died." María tightened her hold on Catalina. "You are grieving. The only thing that will help is time. The passing of time will help you live with your grief."

"You speak of time...." Catalina swung around, staring at her. "I believed time would rid me of this burden of knowing an innocent man died because of my marriage to Arthur. My night-mares have returned." She fell onto her knees, dragging María down beside her. "Let us pray. I must pray for God's forgiveness. I must pray for Warwick to forgive me."

Taking Catalina in her arms again, María just wanted to cry. "Oh, he has. You *must* stop blaming yourself. None of it is your fault. Warwick is at rest, and at peace. You must believe that."

Catalina rocked and rocked, tears running down her face.

María trembled. *God help me – I do not know what to say, what to do, how I can help her? There is nothing I can I do.*

"I do not believe Warwick is at peace. How can I believe I am not cursed when my babies die?" She grabbed at María like a mad woman. "Pray with me. Please pray with me. Please pray for me."

María swallowed, and took Catalina's hand. "Whatever you want, I will do."

She tried to pray, and not to curse God.

Richmond Palace, the fifth day of April, 1511

Doña, my dear Latina,

I have nothing to write to you but of sorrow, not only for my poor queen, but for others at the court. The funeral of the little prince was soon followed by the funeral of the baby of one of the queen's English noblewomen. Maud Parr is a young woman of no more than seventeen and is heartbroken at losing her first child. The only good thing, if you call such things good, is it forced my queen to put aside her own grief to console her. Then a sorrow came even closer to home. Inés, bearing her first child, became ill. For days, she fevered, and was stricken with the lung disease. I did what I could, but nothing helped. She miscarried her child, and died the next day. Her husband, mad with grief, has returned to his country holdings to bury yet another wife.

María put aside her half-done letter, and rubbed at the smart of tears. She shifted on her stool by the fire and gazed at Catalina. Her friend was sewing by the light of the window, as pale and taut as the cream thread she now pulled through the king's shirt. For days, she had wept about Inés.

They both had.

They both had wept in each other's arms at night until they fell to sleep in exhaustion.

Beside Catalina, her confessor continued to speak of God's will. "It is time for you to put aside your sorrow," he said. There was no comfort in his words. Catalina pierced her fabric with her needle without reply. The priest leaned closer. "You must trust in God, my queen."

María trembled. Cold, she held her hands out to the warmth of the fire. *Trust in God? He speaks as if it is easy. But is keeping faith ever easy?*

Catalina met his eyes, and sighed. "I do. But I am a weak woman. You cannot tell me I do not have reason to question God's purpose."

"You know his purpose."

Catalina groaned, and put her sewing down on the small table next to her. "For the perfection of my soul? Good Father, if all the trials in my life do indeed serve for that purpose, then I find myself understanding why so many turn away from God." She settled back in her chair, averting her face from him. "I am only a woman – a weak woman. How much grief am I supposed to bear?"

The friar smiled a little and glanced towards María. "My queen, I speak to you as your confessor when I say you echo the doubts of Doña María."

María liked and respected him well enough now to shrug back. She even managed a wry grin.

"You must remember sorrows are part of a mortal life," the priest said.

"Good Father, I do not believe God would blame me for harbouring the same doubts – especially in times of grief. I would like some happiness in my life. I would like my friends to find happiness too. I would like my friends to not die. I cannot help thinking my life is cursed."

"Dear queen, I have told you before my thoughts about this so-called curse of yours. As your confessor, I commanded you to put it out of your mind – for once, and for all."

María stirred uneasily, clasping her hands upon her lap. *Once more, he speaks as if it is easy. I wish a command would put Catalina's mind at rest. But it is not as easy as that. Especially when Catalina believes she is responsible for a death of an inno-cent.* "You're not cursed. God does not curse his people. Death is the other side of life. None of us can escape it. It is what we do while we live which is what matters, and learning to turn from ourselves to God. Look beyond yourself, my queen, look beyond your grief. See it as a gift or the perfection of your soul. Believe me when I say I believe God loves you greatly to give you such trials."

"If I did not indeed know and trust in God's love, I would question you more about why God gives those he loves so many hard trials." Catalina sighed. "I know I must think of the world to come – and to see my trials as readying me to meet God. But, today, this does not comfort me at the loss of my friend, or make losing her any easier."

"Doña Inés would not wish for you to sorrow overmuch – especially when she is now with God."

Catalina did not reply, but picked up her sewing again.

The priest knitted his brow and leaned closer to her again. "Perchance if you thought of something you could do in her memory – something which could be her legacy. Something to help you find peace."

Catalina contemplated him. "I would have preferred her to have lived and had a family as her legacy." She sat in silence for a moment and then twisted around to Maria. "What legacy do you think our friend would have wanted?"

Maria let out a long sigh. "Like you, I think Inés would have wished the legacy of a family. The only other thing I can think of is that our friend was a lover of learning and books."

"Learning and books." Catalina frowned, and toyed with her rings for a moment. "I know what I will do. I will do what I can to help the universities of England become greater still. I will do this for Inés. If Inés could not leave behind children, I will make for her another kind of legacy to live on forever in this world."

Maria met her friend's eyes, and nodded. She tried to smile. Nothing would ever replace Inés, but neither would Catalina let her be forgotten.

Summer arrived – a summer when sorrow laid heavily on many at court. Walking in the long gallery one morning with Meg

Pole, María passed Thomas More, garbed in mourning. María lifted an eyebrow to Meg in question.

"He lost his wife in childbirth three weeks ago," Meg said. "She was only twenty-three – and the babe died with her."

María took a few more steps and halted, and Meg stopped beside her.

"What is it?" Meg asked.

"I hate this year. Every time I feel the dark cloud lift a little from my spirits, I hear of another death."

Meg sighed and glanced back at More. "He weds soon a new wife."

María stared at her. "His wife died three weeks ago, and you say he is to be wed. Already?"

Meg lifted her eyebrows, clearly baffled at María's outburst. "My dear, he has four young children. We English are practical about these matters. I do not blame him for marrying so soon, and finding a woman to care for his home, and his children. I would not be surprised if Mountjoy soon begins to look for a new wife. He needs someone he can trust to look after his young daughter and his country estate."

"I do not believe Mountjoy will marry for a while yet. Since he returned to court, he busies himself as the queen's chamberlain to deal with his grief. He has spoken to me about not ever marrying again."

She looked back over her shoulder. More spoke to Wolsey, Canon of Windsor and one of the king's ministers, near one of the tall, wide windows lighting up the gallery. Smiling, his face animated and alight with charm, Wolsey lifted a stubby- fingered hand, the gems on his rings catching the light from the window.

A dance of red, green and blue coruscated on the window near him. Beside the grand, stout Wolsey, More's appearance was plain, dreary. Sunlight struck the man's face, and she remembered seeing More on the day Queen Elizabeth had died. Then, like this moment, grief devoured his eyes. Always a slender man, his leanness today stood out against the plumper man next to him. He was gaunt; painfully so. His face was hollowed, the bones under his skin clearly visible. More seemed ill – or eaten away by sorrow. Pity filled her heart. It no longer mattered he married so soon after his wife's death. *All of us do what is necessary to live.*

"Are you certain you know where to find the queen?" Meg asked, stepping out of the entrance of the high gallery into the sunlight of the garden.

"The queen will be where I left her." María glanced down at the folded shawl she held in her hands. She had returned to Catalina's chambers to fetch it. "She was talking to the Flemish gardeners about the new fruit trees they have planted in the orchard."

"I would like to talk to them too. My head gardener tells me the last time we had a cherry or plum tree bearing fruit was not long after I was born. The orchard was burnt to the ground when my father rebelled against his brother, King Edward." Going deeper in the garden towards the large orchard, María strolled alongside Meg in companionable silence. At last, she saw Catalina in the distance talking to three men, two young and one elderly. The two young men broke away, picked up shovels and saplings from the ground, the sapling roots protected in matting. They had disappeared into the orchard by the time she reached Catalina. Catalina turned to them and raised her hand in greeting. "Good morrow, my friends." She gestured to the old man. "Do you remember Doctor Linacre? He was at Ludlow with us."

María glanced at Meg. "I remember."

"I too," said Meg. "You were one of Prince Arthur's tutors. The good prince once told me none could read the Aeneid like you."

"You were also one of the prince's physicians." María swallowed. She had tried to speak to him at Ludlow when the prince was dying.

The man bowed to her. "Forgive me, Lady de Salinas. I was terse with you when we last met, speaking harshly to you out of my own fear and grief. We knew we had little chance to save the prince – not when the youth had been already ailing for months." He glanced at the queen. "Queen Katherine tells me she thinks higher of you than most of the royal physicians. As I am honoured to be one of the king's physicians, it is praise I envy."

María raised a hand to her warming face, glancing at Catalina who smiled back at her. "The queen praises me overmuch. I do not deserve it. Have I seen you before at court?"

"Doctor Linacre serves as a rector in Kent," the queen said. "He but comes to London when the king summons him. You would have seen him before today, María. He has been one of the king's doctors since the coronation. He is not only one of the king's physicians, but Wolsey's and Archbishop Warham's too. He asked to see me today because he wishes to form a college of physicians. He believes, by doing so, we will ensure a better and higher standard of physicians throughout the land."

Turning, María studied him more closely. The man was at

least fifty, if not older. But his eyes were not of an aged man – they were determined, far-seeing, visionary.

"It is not a little thing you wish to do," she murmured.

"No, not a little thing." He bowed to the queen, and glanced around the orchard. "But the queen encourages me to plant this seed. I do not expect to see it grow this year or the next year. There is much I need to do first – and many I need to speak to. But the queen promises to speak to the king when I see the first shoots burst forth from the ground. Like the saplings here, I hope to see it flourish to a tree which will bear much fruit for England's future."

He bowed again. "I must ask your permission to depart, Your Grace, before the tide keeps me another day in Richmond."

"Of course, Master Linacre. As they say, time and tide wait for no man. I bid you good day."

Watching the old man walk towards the Thames, María thought of all the other men Catalina encouraged to achieve their hopes and dreams. She had never been prouder of Catalina. Roused from her grief at losing her son to comfort Maud Parr in her own loss, Catalina had become committed to service to her subjects – and not just those who resided at court. Many rich men were making themselves richer by forcing their tenants to make way for sheep. Deprived of their only homes, a flood of people poured through villages close to the royal palaces, most of them heading to London in hope of finding work and somewhere to live. Catalina taught some of these impoverished women lacemaking skills so they had a chance to support themselves. She walked to the villages to give alms to those in need.

Mountjoy also looked beyond his own grief, helping her in his role as her chamberlain – adding from his own fortune to the queen's income to help the poor and desolate. María looked at Catalina, now in deep conversation with Meg Pole and the gardeners. *Si – the English love their queen – and rightly so.*

7

Just as women's bodies are softer than men's, so their understanding is sharper.

~ *Christine de Pizan*

September 1513, Richmond

Doña, my dear Latina,

You no doubt heard of the recent English victory over the Scots...

María pondered the nearby fire, thankful for its warmth, thinking, shaping and testing in her mind the words she wanted to write. *Needed to write.* Next to her, with her own writing desk, Catalina also wrote.

Glancing back at her barely started missive, María gulped back a cry of frustration. Ink from her quill had pooled and blotched on the parchment as if marking it with a large thumb print. Putting aside her quill, she sprinkled on pounce and shook the parchment until it was dry, and then scraped away at the surface until the blotch was no longer visible. She tugged her furs tighter around her chilled body, flexed her swollen, cramping fingers, glancing at Catalina's letter, reading a line:

...you shall see at length the great victory that our Lord hath sent your subjects in your absence....

Catalina dipped the quill in ink and kept writing, all the while shifting in discomfort. Big belly with a new baby, these last weeks had worn Catalina down to a state of exhaustion.

Unable to take her eyes away from Catalina, María rested an elbow on the table, cupping her cheek in the palm of her hand. It took all her willpower to keep her tongue still. *Catalina should be resting, not writing to the king.*

As the nearby golden table clock whirred away the minutes, Catalina's quill glided down the parchment. The ink running dry, the nib began to scratch on the surface. Catalina re-inked her pen; started writing again.

Infuriated by so many things out of her control, María shifted on her seat. *The king should not have gone and left her to face these weeks alone.* But he had. In June, King Henry had departed England to fight the French, appointing Catalina his regent.

"Your royal husband just wishes to play the King Knight and outdo Henry V," María had told Catalina in private, the evening before the king's departure. "If he can. But why concern himself about that, when it means leaving you with the heavy burden of governing the kingdom? You are unwell."

She remembered Catalina's annoyed reply to her. "The queen, my mother, ruled a great kingdom from the early days of her marriage. She bore me, her fifth living child, during the Holy War. Only good fortune prevented me from being born on a battlefield. Should my Lord husband expect any less of the daughter of Queen Isabel of Castile? In any case, England is at peace, not at war."

María had struggled then to remain silent. It would be cruel to remind her of two dead babies. Catalina already knew the importance of her pregnancy. She would not agree with her that the king's desire for vainglory outweighed the need for a wife untroubled during these months of bearing their child. *Untroubled? He had not even considered her feelings when he decided to execute Edmund de la Pole.* Edmund de la Pole had been imprisoned in the Tower for seven years. When de la Pole's brother joined the French, it gave the king the reason he needed for de la Pole's execution. He told Catalina it was necessary for the safety of the kingdom. He could not understand why she wept, and spent more time in prayer. *Safety of his kingdom? Is he too blind not to realise la Pole's death reminded his wife of Warwick's death? Catalina carries the guilt of it every day of her life.*

Thus, the king had departed for France, to meet with frustration after frustration in Europe. Meanwhile, as soon as Henry VIII left England, the Scottish king had gathered his fighting men and crossed the English border. Catalina, by both horse and litter, had travelled from London to Buckingham, bringing the banners she and her women had started at Richmond Palace. They had worked for hours readying them, Catalina refusing to rest until the work was done. She even refused to find time in these days to entertain the captive Duke of Longueille, sent to England by the king from one of his own small battle conquests. Lodged in the royal apartments of the Tower, the duke was far more the king's guest than prisoner. The banners finished, she joined Lord Howard and the English armies at Buckingham before sending them to face the Scottish King.

The long distances Catalina travelled dismayed all her women. Alice, the royal midwife, was not only dismayed, but stripped of her normal placidity. Before they left Richmond, she fumed at María, "Surely if you spoke to her she would see sense, and not go to the Lord Howard? She should not risk her babe as she does."

But María knew Catalina too well. She had been left as England's regent, and she would not fail in that task. To fail, would be to fail her mother, her husband, and the country she took to her heart. England needed her as its Queen – and not as an ill, pregnant woman. All María could do was to coax her to rest more, to avoid fasting and unnecessary bloodletting. Almost daily, she prepared strengthening potions known to ward off illness and ensured Catalina drank them.

María held her hands out to the warmth of the fire. *The Scots King deserved his death and more for endangering Catalina's health at such a time.* He had also put at risk his own pregnant wife. Margaret Tudor had begged him on her knees not to go and invade England, but he ignored her impassioned pleas. He too desired the same vainglory sought by his uncle, King Henry.

Catalina stopped writing, put down her quill, and sprinkled powder on the wet ink before picking up the parchment to read. For a time, the room was silent excepting the crackle of the burning fire, the whirring of the clock and the whine of a wind belonging more to winter than to autumn. *Pray, this cold does mean not another winter I will curse. So many freezing English winters. Too many.*

Catalina spoke at last. "I will tell my lord husband I had thought to send him the body of the King of Scotland, but the hearts of our men would not suffer it. Instead I will send to him the coat of the king, as I promised him in my last letter."

Not knowing what to say, María wondered if Catalina's seeming cold desire to send the body of the Scottish king to her husband spoke of her own true feelings about being forced to protect England when her belly swelled with a new baby. Catalina was fragile and weak in body after weeks of anxiety and travelling for days. *Si, Catalina is proud of her victory over the Scots, but she will be prouder still to hold her prince.*

María stopped behind Catalina when she paused at one of the tall gallery windows, looking out on the sunlit day. "The morning is too good for us to return to my chambers. Let us all walk to the Abbey."

María stepped nearer and curtseyed. "Are you well enough, my queen? The walk is close to one hour."

Catalina turned her head, her eyes amused. "One hour? Do you wish for us to walk a snail's pace? A brisk walk along the river will be good for me. You must know one of my most favourite walks is that to Syon Abbey. I will send the barge ahead to take us across to the Abbey."

It was one of María's much-loved walks too. Even on grey, chilly morns, the dance of light on the river, the sight of fallow deer grazing, so used to men and women none raised their heads at their passing, and wild birds flitting over the river before diving into the water to bring out a fish glittering in sunlight would always lift her spirits.

By the time they reached the queen's barge, the hour was well and truly passed. They did walk briskly when they could, but Catalina also stopped to speak to men and women she met along the way. After years of walking this pathway, or visiting them in their village, Catalina knew many of the villagers by name. She had taken gifts to them on news of weddings, the birth of children – or gone to console them over the loss of loved ones.

Halting one more time as Catalina spoke to villagers, María rubbed the chill from her hands, and moved from foot to foot. No matter where they were, the common people loved Catalina – and not only because she always returned from these walks with an empty purse. They loved her because she spoke to them with love, with compassion, concerned to know if all was well with them. Some of the women were forward enough to ask the same of Catalina. "I pray for you, madam," one of them said, carrying her own young child at her hip. "I pray for your good health, and that, in good time, you will one day walk along this path with our prince – or a bonny princess. Boy or girl, we do not care. Our good queen will be its mother. We will love your child as we love you."

A bird broke into song – and Maria smiled, and brushed at the smart of tears. The bird song seemed to echo the burst of joy warming her heart. *Twelve years of exile, four of them as queen – si, only four years to gain England's love. How glad I am to witness it. It salves the sorrow of my own exile, and my exile from the man I love.*

Written on the tenth day of October, 1513, Richmond

Doña, my dear Latina,

The days grow colder and darker; soon, winter will fall upon us. And with the return of these cold days comes the return of the king. Winter and warfare marry not, so a treaty has been made. The queen tells me the king plans to return to his battles in France next year. The court now makes ready to welcome the king back to England...

The day drawing to an end, María twisted on her stool in the queen's bedchamber, hearing trumpets in the distance. She bounded up. Ribbons of jubilant notes – long and short – came muted through the door, louder with every moment. Catalina rose from her chair and stood in front of a window. Blocking out the light, she straightened her gown. Her face was too hard to see in the haze of light, but the backlight transmuted her loose hair to a fiery red. She tossed her head a little and laughed, caressing her swelling belly. "My son welcomes his father's return." Catalina stepped away from the window. "Let us go into the antechamber and join my women. I will wait for the king, my husband, there."

María opened the door for Catalina and waited until she was well into the next room before following after her. The other women rushed around the room, packing up their sewing, their books, their musical instruments. Despite the buzz of excited women, she heard the stamp of many feet coming closer before a voice called out, "Make way for the king, make way for my lord grace!"

The king's young voice shouted, "Kate. Where's my Kate?" Doors crashed opened. The king entered, dressed still in his riding gear, with all his gentlemen behind him. All the queen's women fell to their knees. The king looked a youth with his tousled hair, and his face newly shaved. He held in his right-hand large keys, his eyes searching the room. "There she is. My queen! My love! My Kate!"

Henry rushed over to Catalina and knelt at her feet, offering up the keys. She took them from him as he put his hands on her belly. He looked up at her, his eyes bright with emotion, and grinned. "I give you the keys of my victories, the keys of the cities I won in France, and you, my love, will give me my son."

Catalina rested her hand on his head and smiled. "Welcome home, my lord husband."

María shifted on her knees. She focused on the rushes on the floor, trying to restrain her fury. *It sounds like he demands from her a son. How dare he demand anything after these past months. Catalina saved his kingdom for him.*

On the trestle bed, Catalina screamed out one more time and collapsed back into María's arms. Cushioning her friend's body with her own, María looked across at Alice and Meg Pole. Alice bent between Catalina's legs and pulled out a tiny boy, raising eyes of sorrow. Blood and more blood gushed from his mother's body.

"Our queen has fainted, my lady," the midwife said. "Can

you please massage her belly to help bring forth the afterbirth? That will close the womb and bring the bleeding to an end."

Gently placing Catalina on her pillows with Meg's help, María began to knead Catalina's slack belly. To her relief, afterbirth soon came away, but the blood did not stop. Praying, she kneaded harder, trying to control her panic, her desperation when she could not feel her friend's womb tighten. "Catalina, oh, my sister," she whispered in Castilian, tears falling down her cheeks. "Do not give up."

It had been another long and hard childbirth – made harder by the knowledge the child came months too early. Catalina had laboured through the hours knowing she birthed the promise of death, not life.

Tenderly cradling the baby, Alice gazed around at Meg Pole and the other women in the birthing chamber. "He is alive, but will not live." She looked down at the boy. "This babe is so tiny, too tiny for any hope. I will baptise him, and we will keep him warm, but that is all we can do. The poor mite has not even tried to cry." She sprinkled the child with holy water, and baptised him quickly before giving the wrapped baby to one of the women. "Take him." Her apprehensive eyes returned to Catalina. "I do not want him here when she comes to. And pray none tell her she birthed a living child. What good would that be? The boy will soon leave us. She can learn of her son later when she is stronger."

Freed of the baby, Alice came back to the bed, resting a hand on María's shoulder. "Let me do that, my lady," she said. "You look exhausted after the long day and night we've all had."

Alice took over, kneading Catalina's belly with grim determination. María had seen her look that way before – Alice would not let Catalina die if she had anything to do with it. Meg returned to the bed with fresh towels. Together, they changed the bloodied towels, uncaring for their own clothes. In silence, they took the bloodied towels to the large basket by the door and returned to the bed.

Fighting her lack of sleep, María swayed, Alice's form blurring for a moment before she saw the midwife move away from Catalina with a smile of victory. "The bleeding is easing, thank God," the woman said. But then she looked at them with disquiet. "The queen has lost a lot of blood. She is not out of danger yet. We must pray for her."

Helpless, holding onto her arms, María stared at Catalina. *So pale. She could already be dead.* Again, she wondered why she studied the healing arts. In matters of life and death, she seemed in as much darkness as everyone else, without any power save Catalina's life. The only thing she could do was what Alice said – pray.

Too tired to protest, María let Meg take her arm, and lead her to the nearby chairs by the fire burning furiously in the hearth.

"Sit," Meg commanded, "before you faint as well."

Sitting on the edge of the seat, María leant forward, holding her head between her hands, drowning in fatigue. She felt Meg rest a gentle hand on her head. Her head still spinning, María looked across at Meg seated on the other chair. She caught the tired eyes of her friend. "I blame the king," María said softly, her resentment oozing out with each word. "The strain of the past months caused her to lose the child – the strain of keeping England safe, and the strain since he returned. How many banquets did he need to have to celebrate his little victories? And why blame her for her father's treacheries in France. How could he do that?"

At a loud snap, María twisted towards the fire. In the hearth, a smaller log split and crumbled into the red flames. In her mind, she heard the king shouting at Catalina, uncaring that the room was full of his wife's women, "Madam, your father has betrayed me." As if she had been the one to cause it, King Henry had then listed all her father's betrayals. He did not notice how pale his wife became, how sick looking – or how she sought for a seat to sit on as if blind.

Meg sighed loudly beside her. "Be reasonable, my friend. The king was right to feel betrayed by the queen's father. Unfortunately, wives, no matter their ranks, are always the butt for their husband's anger. In truth, our queen should have listened to Alice. His Grace, the king, would have forgiven her if she passed on her apologies and rested in her chambers, rather than partake in the nightly revels – especially if it had resulted in a strong prince likely to live. Our poor queen is a good woman, none better, but she is stubborn at times, and it leads to her downfall."

María recalled Queen Juana's words from years ago: "Even as a child you defended our royal father. I, on the other hand, I stopped trusting him years ago. Chiquitina, listen to one who knows. One day he will break your heart." How right those words proved. Catalina's labour had started hours after her husband had lashed her with his tongue about the treachery of her father.

Tasting her bitterness, María gripped the armrests of her chair. *I hate two kings. Si, Catalina is stubborn, but it is the men she loves who lead to her downfall.* She glanced at Meg. "This time, her stubbornness was rooted in fear." She heaved a sigh. "You know the king took another mistress in France?"

"Yes – I heard. What of it?"

"Catalina heard of it too. She fears if she leaves her husband to his own entertainments, he will but find another woman."

Stilling, Meg hooded her eyes for a moment. "Wearing herself out at the nightly revels would not change that. My royal cousin will always desire his playthings." She shrugged. "He is a king and does what so many kings do. I only wish I had come sooner. I would have talked to her and tried to convince her to think first of the baby. Once she gives him a son, the king's women will little matter."

"They matter to her. She loves him, and she wants him to love her. Every time she learns about another woman, it breaks her heart anew."

Meg looked towards the bed. Catalina stirred, and Alice moved closer to take her hand. Turning to María, Meg wiped her wet eyes with her sleeve. "And when she learns about this babe will not her heart be broken again?"

María locked her eyes on the bed. She felt transfigured into stone by both fear and exhaustion – and the weight of her lack of power. *I would pull out my own heart if it would help Catalina.* She rubbed her tired eyes. *Sometimes it feels like I have – but it has not helped at all....*

***

For two days, Catalina lay in bed, fighting for her life, her hold so fragile, any moment the thread could snap. For two days, Alice and María worked together to save her – trying every strengthening remedy they knew – chicken broth, gruel, or the mulled wine Alice prepared, which she called caudle. María also scoured her books for anything else to try, but, in the end, she faced what she gathered from books compared little to Dame Alice's skills as an experienced midwife. As for Catalina's son – no one thought of the boy Catalina had borne into the world as a living child, but only waited for him to die. The king did not even give his son a name.

The only dark blessing was Catalina was too weak and ill to know her child had lived. She was so weak there was no need to bind her breasts to stop them swelling with milk.

Her heart heavy, María remembered the two other times she had bound her friend's breasts. Catalina, as queen, never nursed her own babies after childbirth. The only chance she ever had to feed one of her babies was for the little boy who had lived for two months. *Would it have eased Catalina's sorrow at losing him to remember feeding him, holding him, his little body close to her skin, and heart?* María sighed. *Would I be strong enough to nurse my own child, if I am ever blessed to bear a child, knowing how many babes come into the world only to die?* She rubbed her wet eyes, close to completely breaking down.

She stared at her sleeping friend. It came to her how love is an act of courage. Living is an act of courage. "Do not leave me," she whispered close to Catalina's ear, "do not leave me alone. My life is with you – it has always been with you." She had lost Will; the thought of losing Catalina, too, threatened to shatter her like a ship upon rocks. She remembered all those already taken from her by life: Prince Juan, her father, her mother. She shook her head, hearing Latina's voice in her mind: *To really live is to love. Love even when with loving comes the sorrow of loss.* Latina was grieving when she spoke those words. She had lost her husband in the same battle which had taken María's father. She shook her head a little. *But I would never wish to not to love. Loving someone makes them a part of you – for all life, for all time.*

On the afternoon of the second day, Catalina opened her eyes, and weakly reached for María's hand. "Another dead babe," she whispered. "Three dead babes."

Tightening her grip on Catalina, she looked away. The boy, living longer than Alice predicted, had died only a short time ago. She could not tell Catalina that yet. She dreaded the coming day when she would have no other choice but to tell her.

***

Spring arrived at last. For days, winter had refused to release its tight grip. Not only was it freezing, but it rained and rained, keeping them indoors at Richmond Palace. When the skies finally cleared on a new day, María broke her fast, grabbed her mantle and hurried outside before anyone had a chance to lay a claim on her, or her time alone. For days, she had been surrounded by squabbling women close-confined in their chambers.

María yearned for the peace of the garden, to be able to think without the constant interruptions of court life. Service to the queen entailed a hefty sacrifice of her hours, day and night. Most of the time, she was grateful for her busy days. It helped surmount those times she saw Will, but could not speak to him alone. But today she begrudged it – all the demands on her time weighed her down.

Walking in the privy garden, María lifted her head and

realised she had taken the path leading to the Friary Church. She stopped and stared at the small church a short distance away. *I do not want to go there. I have prayed enough for this morning.* She decided to follow the path going to the orchards. Approaching the well-maintained orchard, she halted, hearing the sound of soft footfalls, and laughter.

Princess Mary, the king's sister, ran, weaving around the trees, holding her skirts free of her feet, her hair unbound and flying behind her like a golden cloud. The smiling girl kept gazing over her shoulder. Not far behind her, Charles Brandon, the new Duke of Suffolk and close friend to the king, ran too, his eyes on his prize. His long, unhindered legs soon caught up with her. He seized her in his arms, pulling her behind a spreading apricot tree. Mary's laughter chimed like bells, and all became silent.

Aware of the quickening beat of her heart, María remained still and thought hard. Princess Mary had not long celebrated her eighteenth birthday. Her childhood promise of beauty was now a reality. England's Rose, they called the princess at court. *Mary should not be alone with Brandon in the garden. And Brandon?* He was twelve or more years her senior. *What is the rogue thinking? Or is he thinking at all?* He liked women, and women liked him. Time after time, he entangled himself in another flirtation. Sometimes more than a flirtation. María had heard the rife rumour he had married one woman and then married another while still wed to the first. *But a dalliance with an unwed princess? A princess who had been put forward as a royal bride for emperors and kings since her earliest years? The new duke cannot be thinking.* Even now, King Henry negotiated Mary's betrothal with the King of France.

Gazing around the garden, María shuddered. Years ago, the king had headed in her direction in this same garden. That day had ended her small moments of true joy. *Si, a woman's beauty can be a curse. It makes many men fools.* She returned her attention to the tree, worried about the continued silence. Brandon, as one of the king's closest friends, should know better. *Mary is young; not so him. I will sing, let them know they are not alone. And then I will speak to Catalina about her young sister-in-law.* She cleared her throat, grabbed the first song to come to mind, and sang:

I must sing of what I'd rather not,
I'm so angry about him whose friend I am,
for I love him more than anything.

María faltered on the last word, seeing Will's face in her mind. She swallowed. *I love him more than anything. I will love Will until I die.* Close to tears, María sought for another song to sing. The only other song to come to mind was one she had heard Will Skelton, in service as the king's sage fool, sing the day before:

With lullay, lullay, like a child,
Thou sleepest too long, thou art beguiled!
"My darling dear, my daisy flower,
Let me," quoth he, "lie in your lap."
"Lie still," quoth she, "my paramour,
Lie still hardily, and take a nap."
His head was heavy, such was his hap,
All drowsy, dreaming, drowned in sleep,

That of his love he took no keep,
With hey, lullay, like a child.

María reached the edge of the orchard, stepping off the path, deliberately treading on dry leaves to create more noise announcing her approach, stopping when she skirted the edge of the shadow of the apricot tree. Silk whispered, then rustled. Mary emerged from behind the tree, smoothing down her gown. Brandon was nowhere to be seen.

"Good morrow, Princess," María called. "Have you come out like me to enjoy the fine morning?"

Mary blushed and lowered her head. Coming beside her, the princess glared at her and whispered in a rush, "You saw, didn't you?"

María met the princess's guilty, angry eyes. The girl's lips were red and a little swollen, and her bodice clumsily retied. Hoping to reassure her, she rested a hand on Mary's shoulder. "Let's speak about this inside."

María walked in silence behind the girl. *So – it will be me who will talk to Mary.* She touched the wisps of fine hair coming free of one of the snoods she wore most mornings. *I am ten years her senior. She likely sees me as an old woman. Perhaps I am in truth.* In her mind flashed Mary's guilty face. She touched her mouth. *Four years – four years or more since Will last kissed me.* At times, she regretted her inability to give her heart or body to any other man. Her love for Will froze her in the frustration of her virginity.

Taking the secret way known only to the royal family and their closest attendants, Mary walked on to her chambers. There were outdoor and indoor guards aplenty at Richmond, which meant her door could be left unguarded. She opened it and turned to María. "You better come in. We will be alone. I told my servants I wished to be alone, and undisturbed, this morning." Anger gone from her wan face, the girl's apparent guilt remained.

María closed the door behind them as Mary strode over to the windows and pulled open the heavy curtains. The morning light poured in, lighting up Mary's slim form and hair. Mary spun around, her long gold-red hair twirling around her face as if living fire. The girl lifted her skirts from her slippered feet, and dashed over to the nearest chair. She waved a hand at the other chair facing it.

"Come and sit. And let us talk truthfully."

Sitting, María straightened her gown, clasping her hands in her lap. She considered Mary, thankful she had known the girl long enough to speak freely. "You ask for the truth, Princess? I think if it had been anyone other than me to see you in the garden today then we would have had a scandal impossible to keep silent. Princess, do you not know you risk your good name? Even today, the king, your brother, is entertaining the French ambassadors. The king hopes to see you Queen of France."

Mary's face tightened until it looked birdlike. "I do not want it." The girl swallowed visibly, reaching for María's hand. "I love Charles." Releasing María, she stood, tears falling down her face. "I have always loved Charles."

María sighed. "Pray, sit, my princess, or I will need to stand too."

Perched on the edge of her chair, the girl seemed ready to bolt at any moment. "I do not wish to marry the French King. He is old. My skin crawls at the thought of him, let alone him touching me. Can you blame me for arranging to meet Charles in the mornings? I have gone walking in the orchards at Richmond since a child. I believed we would be safe there. I have never seen anyone there at dawn break; no one until this morning."

María touched Mary's knee, shaking her head. "Princess, you cannot and should not assume that. If you have not been seen already, be thankful for your good fortune. If there is one thing I have learnt in my years of service to the queen, it is the near impossibility of keeping anything secret at court. There is one other thing: if you really love Brandon, have you thought what would happen to him if he was found kissing you? Princess, he may be your brother's best friend, but if the king ever knew Brandon played love games with you, he would be a dead man."

Mary stared at her, her eyes shining with unshed tears. "Truly?"

María leaned across and clasped her hand. "Truly."

The girl bit at her bottom lip and bent her head for a moment before gazing at María. "I have been a fool, haven't I?" María let go of Mary's hand. For a moment, Will seemed to stand before her – and all the pain and grief came back. She lifted her chin, but no longer saw Mary clearly. Her tears made that impossible. "Love makes fools of us all," she said.

8

The man or the woman in whom resides
    greater virtue is the higher;
    neither the loftiness
    nor the lowliness of a person lies
    in the body according to the sex, but in the
    perfection of conduct and virtues.
    ~ Christine de Pizan

Months later, María sat in the window-seat of Catalina's chamber, gathering her furs tighter around her. The air grew colder with each new day as winter approached. Not only was her body cold, but her heart too. Once more, life repeated itself and another young woman wept to be consoled by one older. Near where María sat, Princess Mary knelt by

Catalina's side, her head in her lap. Her shoulders heaved, her fingers snatching and releasing Catalina's gown, over and over.

"Come," Catalina said. "This will not do. You are a princess of England. Your marriage is for the good of our country."

Mary raised a face red and blotchy. She wiped her running nose on her long sleeve. "You never wanted me married to France. You wanted me married to your nephew. At least Prince Charles is young, and not the old man my brother has sold me to."

Catalina sighed. "If only my nephew had been sixteen, and not fourteen, perhaps then you would already be his wife. Alas, the marriage treaty has been declared null and void, and Wolsey has got his way. Believe me, if it was not to achieve peace between France and England, I would have spoken louder to your brother against this marriage." "Like I said, I have been sold."

María winced, remembering Catalina's first wedding. *I believed then Queen Isabel and King Ferdinand sacrificed Catalina on a bridal altar. I still believe it. Thank God I possess some choice over my life.*

Catalina touched Mary's face. "Sweet sister, you are a royal daughter. I left my parents at fifteen. At least, your brother did not seek to see you leave England until you were a grown woman."

Mary leaned her head on Catalina's knee. "I do not feel a grown woman."

Catalina stroked her hair. "I know; and I know you go to a man who is not your first choice." Catalina raised her head, staying silent for a long time.

María sat back and blinked. It seemed she saw the shade of

Prince Arthur, lithe and tall, a wisp blown away by time. Blinking again, she saw only her friend. Arthur was long gone, but the memory of love and tenderness still lingered.

"Perhaps we did wrong by you by allowing you to remain with us until you reached the age of eighteen," Catalina said softly. "If you had left us at fifteen, you would not have bound yourself to Brandon."

Mary half rose, staring at Catalina. She spun around and glared accusingly at María. "Did María tell you?" It seemed Henry VII spoke again, but the cold yet angry words came from his daughter's mouth.

Catalina glanced at María, and lifted an eyebrow. "You knew too, amiga?"

María shrugged. "I knew, but the princess promised me she would no longer see Brandon in private. I believed the matter was dealt with, and did not see the need to worry you – not when you have been so ill." She glanced at Catalina's swelling belly.

"Another saw the need to worry me" María cursed that someone when Catalina tightened her mouth and shifted as if in discomfort. She would not have worried Catalina for the world, but far too many at court took pleasure in their loose tongues.

"The princess did not keep her promise." Catalina turned to her sister-in-law. "Did you, Mary?"

Mary reddened. "I only saw Charles to tell him of my marriage contract. I met him to bid him farewell."

"I believe you did more than bid him farewell. I believe there was weeping and embraces fit to make Cupid hide his face in shame for your lack of decorum. Thank God, the person who saw this farewell is someone we can trust to keep silent. Oh, my sister, once you are in France, we will not be able to protect you. At all times, you must behave with great caution and be circumspect. France has a long, painful history of removing queens it no longer wants."

"Would it matter? My life is over in any case."

Catalina shook Mary's hand. "No, it is not. Look at me, Mary." The girl raised her tear-filled eyes. "You marry a sick, old man. I do not believe you need to wait long before you are a widow."

Mary pursed her mouth for a moment. "A widow? You speak the truth?"

Catalina leaned back in her chair, and smiled slightly. "Have I ever lied to you, Mary? Believe me, I am in communication with people who know these things. I heard from one of them the French king's physicians advised him against this marriage. I am told the king is dying."

Mary sat back on her heels, gazing out in space before speaking slowly, and softly. "So – if I do my brother's bidding, I may yet achieve my heart's desire."

Catalina frowned. "You mean Brandon? The king is not likely to agree to matching his sister to one who is but a subject of the crown. Brandon may be my husband's best friend, but he is not a match for your royal blood. I advise you to put that idea out of your head, Mary."

"But, sister, I could still wed Charles. I will marry the King of France, but before I go to France I will go to my brother and weep and weep until he promises me I can choose my next husband."

Catalina settled back again. "My husband does not like his women weeping. And he loves you; if you weep, you will get his promise." She stroked the side of her face in thought. "But you must realise getting him to keep his promise is a different matter entirely."

Keep his promise? María chewed her bottom lip. *What of the promises – or even half promises made to him? Dear God, why do I remember that? Put it out of mind. It is long ago. From what I hear, he likes his women young. As young as Mary. I am no longer that.*

That same afternoon María wrote to Latina while Catalina sat glumly reading a communication written in cypher from Margaret of Austria.

"Listen," Catalina said, "Mary is not the only one not happy about her coming marriage. Margot writes our nephew Charles is distressed and angry too." She lifted her eyes from the parchment. "No wonder. My nephew has thought of Mary as his bride since he was a boy of nine, and called her his *wife*, just as we called Mary *Princess of Castile*. Charles blames the broken betrothal on his advisors. Year after year, it was his council who prevented Mary from coming to his court." Reading the letter once more, she laughed with bitterness. "Margaret writes Charles paid gold for an untrained hawk to be brought to his council meeting. He sat there, plucking it in front of his councillors. When they asked what he was doing, he said, 'Because the bird is young he is held in small account, and because he is young he squeaks not when I pluck him. Thus you have done by me. I am young, you have plucked me at your pleasure and I know how I must complain. Bear in mind for the future, I shall pluck you'."

The light of day withdrew from the chamber. Catalina rubbed her head and put the letter down on the table. "Margaret also writes of her unhappiness. She says the penance of breaking the betrothal is too great for their offence of delaying the marriage again. I am unhappy too. But what can we do? In the end, the decision must come from the king."

***

Another week passed. A week of rain, when it seemed the Heaven itself wept about Mary's marriage to the French King. The court at Greenwich for the ceremony, María lingered at the top of the spiral staircase, catching her breath from her climb up to the huge Presence chamber. *Truly, I am becoming an old woman.* She dropped her gown and shook out its skirts, watching the king, queen and Princess Mary go through the open doors. Men milled in the room, all of them richly robed; gold twinkled and glittered, and silks shimmered every time a man changed position.

Entering the chamber, she looked around. Close by, the Duke of Buckingham spoke unsmiling to the French duke. Edward Stafford detested the French, and rarely bothered to hide it, but, despite his cold eyes, he seemed civil enough today. His cloth of gold robes competed with the gold robes and ash-colour satin top of the king and seemed to merge with the cloth of gold arras covering the walls behind him. His elaborate gold chain, hanging low around his neck, was clearly weightier than those worn by the other nobles. But the king's gold collar was heavier still – and his robes, like the queen's, embroidered with many jewels. Standing with the French ambassadors, the Duke of Longueille also wore a gold collar, a recent gift from the king. The gold links stood out against the purple, chequered satin encasing his upper torso; the rest of his robes were cloth of gold. *Perhaps I should have taken more care about my choice of gown.* She had ensured everything was done perfectly for the queen's robes, but forgot about her own. She stroked her red silken skirts. *No matter – this gown is one of my best.*

Catalina glanced at the French duke, her unhappy, hard face almost ugly. The French duke had acted as the go-between for this marriage, negotiating the peace between France and England. The peace was not of her desire, for it severed the tie between England and Castile. Today, nothing made that clearer than the absence of the Spanish ambassador.

Princess Mary reached the side of the Duke of Longueille, who acted as proxy for Louis of France. The girl concealed well her true feelings about the match. Garbed in a gown of purple satin, with an underdress of the same ash satin as that of the robes of her brother and sister-in-law and wearing a cap of cloth of gold like the queen, Mary shone in beauty and youth, and brought all eyes to her. The Archbishop of Canterbury spoke a sermon in Latin, telling all that they had come this day to witness the marriage of Princess Mary to the French King. One of the French ambassadors next spoke in the name of his king, agreeing to this marriage. The Duke of Longueille then took the hand of the princess and placed a ring upon her finger. María swallowed. She saw in her mind Mary running from Brandon. She saw the joy lighting the girl's face when Brandon took her in his arms. How carefree her laughter had sounded coming from behind the tree. Just weeks ago, Mary wept on Catalina's knee. *I am sold,* she said. *So – it is done. Mary will be crowned Queen of France.*

Hours later, replete with too much food, María leaned back from her table and sipped her watered-down wine, watching men and women dance close by. The king and queen on the royal dais also watched the dancers. Mary, though, Mary who loved to dance, sat with her eyes lowered, picking at her food.

María returned her eyes to the dancers, her foot tapping to the beat of the music. She rarely danced since ending her relationship with Will. She had not seen him at court for months. She heard he stayed at his estates because of his wife. *Perhaps, at last, she is with child.* She so hoped for Will's sake. She wanted him to have a child, even if not their child.

The music no longer stirring her feet, she sipped from her goblet, content to be left alone, content to observe the others in their enjoyment while she waited to accompany the queen back to her chambers. She almost choked on her drink seeing Charles Brandon, the Duke of Suffolk, approach her.

He reached the table, smiled at her winningly, and held out hand. "Lady Mary, come, dance with me."

María met the duke's dark blue eyes. She looked around the room, and back at him, struck dumb, confused at his notice.

He smiled again. "I refuse to let you say nay. A beautiful woman, one of the most beautiful to grace the king's court, should dance at least once on a night like this."

Narrowing her eyes at him, wondering the reason for his attention, María shrugged, rose from the table and walked over to him. Taking his hand, she walked with him to the dance floor, and joined the dancers.

When they linked hands together in dance, and swirled slowly around one another, María asked, "My Lord Duke, am I right in thinking you dance with me for a purpose?"

Charles Brandon glanced at the royal dais, and back at her. He shifted closer and whispered close to her ear. "That morning in the garden you saw us, but you kept silent. Can I ask you why?"

The music changed its beat, and they moved away from one another. She took hold of the duke's proffered hand, and they paced out a half circle and back again. Once again, they stepped closer to one another. She turned towards him, and spoke. "I saw no reason for not remaining silent. I love the princess. She realised I only spoke the truth when I told her to continue to meet with you would endanger your life and destroy her good name."

Keeping her hand linked with his, she stepped away from him as they paced out another half circle to the beat of the music before coming closer together again. Stepping out of the tighter circle to the dance, he bent his head, his shoulder-length coal-black hair sweeping against her face. His thirtieth birthday had just passed. Already, flecks of grey dusted his thick, black beard, but the signs of age were at odds with his clear, good skin and bright eyes. They belonged to a young man in his prime. But he had always been one of the most handsome men at court; the touches of grey increased his attractiveness.

"Believe me, I told Mary this too. She refused to listen to me. I never meant for the princess to fall in love with me, or I fall in love with her, but she wore me down. Three years it has taken, and my heart belongs to the most beautiful creature who has ever graced this court, indeed, I think the world. Now my sweet lady is married to another."

The music tempo swelled to its conclusion. She curtseyed to Suffolk and the duke bowed to her. He took her hand and escorted her back to her table. Returning to her seat, she touched his arm when he turned back in the direction of his own table. He looked at her in question.

"Did you expect any different, my Lord Duke?" she asked quietly.

He shrugged. "Of course not." He studied the royal dais. As if she sensed his eyes upon her, Mary looked his way. Her face white and still, she picked up her goblet and drank. When the Duke of Longueille, seated beside her, spoke to her, she lifted her head, smiled brightly and gave him her full attention.

María knew that smile; she had known that smile since first getting to know Mary when the girl was a child of five. The Duke of Longueille would not recognise it as a false smile. Charles Brandon's agonised eyes told her he knew, like her, Mary's smile denoted nothing today. The girl was a player in a mummer's play, acting her part.

Slumping his shoulders, Suffolk shifted closer to María. "If it would help at all, pray tell Mary my heart is hers, forever." He bowed to her, and strode back to his table.

She looked again at Mary Tudor. Her brittle gaiety seemed unrecognised by the Duke of Longueille. The man was clearly charmed. Mary's heart might be breaking, but no one would suspect it other than those who knew her closely. She held her head high like Catalina close to her. Mary faced her future with courage, a high heart.

María swung her eyes to Catalina's white face, and scrutinised her more closely. Her stiff posture and the way she gripped her hands suggested she was troubled. Beside her, the king's place was empty. María searched the room. At the end of the chamber, where the candlelight began to weaken, the king spoke to Bessie Blount. She was a beautiful girl of sixteen, and new to court. The king took Bess's arm and took her into the darkened corridor. Very soon, they were lost to view.

The girl is seven years younger than the king – twelve years younger than Catalina. Tonight, Catalina looks old enough to be Bess's mother. A sudden movement at the other end of the hall drew María's attention. In the shadows, Friar Diego spoke earnestly to a young, pretty woman. The woman looked distressed. When she tugged at his sleeve and jutted her face close to him, he glanced worriedly at the queen. He said something to the woman, and together they left the hall. Several heartbeats afterwards, the Spanish ambassador followed them.

María swilled her wine, unable to still her disquiet. *The queen is well used to the king's unfaithfulness, but if Friar Diego has a mistress too?* She swallowed another mouthful of wine, dreading what this could mean for her friend.

9

When someone finds himself quite unjustly attacked and hated on all sides, there is no need for such a person to feel dismayed by misfortune. See how Fortune, who has harmed many a one, is so inconstant, for God, who opposes all wrong deeds, raises up those in whom hope dwells.

~ *Christine de Pizan*

Written on the first day of February, 1515, Richmond

Doña, my dear Latina,

No doubt you heard the scandal about Mary Tudor. It was only five months ago she was crowned queen of France. They say King Louis doted on her, and refused her nothing in the short months of their marriage. They say Mary danced him into his grave.

King Henry wished to make for his sister another royal marriage once her time of mourning was at an end. But, after Suffolk promised he would remember he first served England, the king sent Suffolk to bring her home. Suffolk may have meant his promise. But the king forgot his sister. It did not take her long to persuade Suffolk to marry her.

They returned home to an angry king. A king already angry for other causes. A king angry at life – and too ready to take it out on his wife.

Sitting as close as possible to the sluggish fire, María put aside her quill. *Should I tell Latina about how the king dealt with Friar Diego? The priest is already on his way back to Castile. She will hear the news before she receives my letter.* The words on the parchment no longer registering, she shifted her chair closer to the sluggish fire, flinching when a loud snap from the fire broke the silence. To calm her nerves, she lit the candles in the room, taking comfort from the smell of beeswax. It reminded her of childhood, and days with far less cares.

María rubbed her stomach. Every passing moment increased the ache which seemed to burn a hole in her. She breathed slowly in and out and settled back, locking her eyes on the doorway to the closet. So quiet in the bedchamber. Too quiet. At the beginning, she had heard sounds coming from Catalina's closet – words of prayer, her agitated movements, weeping – but now she was aware of silence. Catalina had told her she did not want to be disturbed. But that was over two hours ago. Since the light of afternoon started to diminish, it had taken all her restraint not to disobey her sister's command. The silence fright-ened her. She remembered Catalina's sisters, Juana and Isabel, and Catalina's grandmother – all of them broken by life until driven mad.

As if she willed Catalina to emerge, Catalina at last came out, aged, frail, defeated. Her stomach already swelling with child. Yet another child. Catalina lost a third son not long after Mary's wedding to the French King. Unlike the last boy born too early, this babe – who should have lived – came into the world without taking a breath. Another winter babe born dead. They had shrouded him and took him away before his poor mother could see. Few at court believed Catalina able to bear a living child. But the king had still returned to her bed as soon as she had been churched. It had taken little time before she hoped to give the king the son he so wanted.

Catalina made her slow way back to sit in her chair. *Say something. Smile at her – let her know she is not alone. Comfort her.* But María floundered to find the right words.

Catalina leaned forward, cupping her forehead in her hand. "Tell me, do you think it true?"

María shrugged, almost grateful for the question which unfroze her tongue. "What of it? He would not be the first priest who betrayed his vows." She took Catalina's free hand. "You take this too much to heart, my sister."

Catalina stared at her. "Take this to heart? He has been my confessor for seven years. I never thought he would betray his God, let alone me."

Uneasy that Catalina was taking Diego's wrongdoing personally, María tightened her hold on her hand. "The man deserved mercy; he may have taken a mistress, but that does not mean he is any less loyal to you. My sister, I have had time to think while sitting here in wait for you. Once, I mistrusted your confessor, but no more. For seven years, Friar Diego has given you his loyalty. When it comes to you, he would sacrifice much, I think. Now the king orders him back home. Something does not smell right."

Catalina lifted her head. "Speak your meaning clearly."

María brought her fingertips together, tapping them lightly. "It is only a suspicion," she said slowly, "but I cannot help to wonder if Friar Diego's undoing may be due to others putting the right temptation in his way. It seems strange to me that a man who managed to stay true to his vows in a household of mostly women for two years, some of them young women often greensick due to their unmarried state, would now change his colours without there being more to the story. I believe your father's ambassador is behind this."

"My father's ambassador?"

María nodded. "The man hates Friar Diego. He has long resented all the times he could only see you by first speaking to him. The ambassador has had years to spy on your confessor. I believe he finally worked out what could make Friar Diego break his vows." She sighed and clasped her hands in her lap. "None of us are infallible, Catalina. We sin because we are human." Lowering her head, she thought of all the times she had broken faith with Catalina. Not because she wanted to break faith, but because life forced it upon her.

Catalina rubbed her cheek. "You may be right about my father's arrogant ambassador. So, I will pray for God's help to forgive Diego for the sorrow he has caused me by this scandal, and also for forgiveness of a man I detest." She breathed in and out deeply. "I am no saint. Forgiving betrayal is my lifelong struggle."

"Who wishes you to be a saint? Not I! But if my assumption is right, then the ambassador has betrayed you, my queen. That is a betrayal I am not prepared to forgive."

Catalina smiled tiredly. "I have said this before many times, but let me say it again: I am glad you have remained with me through the years." She released a sigh. For a long moment, she sat there in silence before another weak smile. "Although, it would also make me happier to see you wed."

Oh, why does she speak of this? María turned to the fire. Through the blur of her tears, the flames and the crumbling red embers seemed to turn into pictures of Will. So many nights he entered her dreams, dreams where they loved with all the passion they had fought hard to resist all through the years. Nights she woke alone, her body afire, frustrated by unfulfilled desire, hating her long, hopeless virginity. Twisting and turning in her empty bed, unable to sleep, for hours she thought about all the missed, and now regretted, opportunities. Times her heart had told her she could break through his determination to remain a man of honour who did not want to degrade the woman he loved by making her his mistress. As if he could ever degrade her in such fashion. Since breaking from him, the lonely years had only made her wish she had forced him to put aside honour. María shook her head. *I always feared I would lose his respect. Worse – he may have started hating me because I was the cause he could no longer respect himself.*

These days, at twenty-nine, her fear seemed foolish. To bed with Will would have been such a little sin. Or – did she see it differently now? She had lived a half-life as a girl, and continued to live a similar life as a grown woman. But the years brought with a continual struggle to combat bitterness and envy. They weighed on her until they seemed the greater sin.

"Before we left Castile, you promised me I would have choice about my husband." María stared down at her clasped hands. She wanted children, but the great stumbling block to gaining them was she wanted Will's children. The thought of marrying another man left her cold. She shrugged and eyed Catalina. "There is no man I desire to marry."

Catalina shook her head. "That is not true, my sister. There is one man. You still love the baron."

María bent her head. "I cannot help I still love Will." She tried to smile. "Since Mary returned from France as Charles Brandon's wife, I have thought long about marriages arranged without any thought of whether a man or woman are suited to one another. Mary is one of the few women I know whomarried a man she had already given her heart to. Mary does not care she and Brandon will be long in debt to the king because they dared to wed without his permission. She is just happy. If I cannot have that kind of happiness, then I rather not wed at all."

Catalina looked away. "Happiness can come after the wedding vows," she said slowly.

Reaching for her friend's hand, María knew Catalina was not talking about her marriage to King Henry. Since his first unfaithfulness, the king had been unfaithful with other women, most of them lowborn. He was discreet, always that. But court rumour claimed the king's frequent visits to Jericho Priory were for other reasons than the sake of his soul. There was always someone amongst the queen's women who would tell Catalina of his latest conquest. Even so, the king was good at play-acting, and so was Catalina. Their marriage was seen as a good marriage.

Most of the time it was; but the husband who had made Catalina truly happy was not Henry VIII.

She tightened her grip on Catalina's hand. "If I cannot marry the man I love, I am content to remain with you, my sister, who I also love."

"In May day, when the lark began to rise..." the king sang.

The king is good at play-acting. A stone throw from the king but hidden from view, María lounged on her mantle, in a secluded bower in the parkland near Greenwich palace. *He play-acts the good husband. Surely that means he cares about Catalina?* In her self-imposed solitude, she sipped her wine and chewed at her chicken leg.

"Trolly lolly lolly lo, Sing trolly lolly lo! My love is to the greenwood gone," the king sang now.

Catalina had sorrowed over the loss of her confessor and his return to Castile for weeks. *Is it any wonder the king organises a day of merriment for his wife and court?* Catalina had no notion that their departure from Greenwich palace would be interrupted by the arrival of Robin Hood, Maid Marian and Friar Tuck – or that a banquet would be prepared for their pleasure in this parkland – in a huge bower laid down with carpets and scattered cushions to sit upon. She had no choice but to put on a happy face for her husband – especially when the day was witnessed by foreign ambassadors. *Si – the king is good at play-acting, but so is Catalina.*

After the banquet when her head started to pound, María had taken possession of one of the smaller bowers, provided for those who wished privacy. After a little while by herself, María was not surprised to see Catalina approaching. She rose and curtseyed. Catalina gestured to her. "Pray sit down. I've told the others I am joining you for a time."

María sat again, wondering what caused Catalina to speak to her in their shared tongue.

"A pleasant outing, don't you think?" Catalina asked, sitting beside her.

"Si, very pleasant." Hearing the king's voice, María drew apart some of the bushes to peer out. His back towards them, the king stood with the Venetian ambassador, both them apparently admiring one of the bowers filled with singing birds of all descriptions. The organisation of this event must have taken days to prepare. Even the trees had been made more beautiful by the hanging of innumerable embroidered hawthorn leaves.

Thomas More broke away from the other courtiers, and began walking in their direction. María pulled back and released the bush. But he still noticed them. He ambled over and bowed to the queen.

Catalina laughed. "You have hunted out my hiding place, Tom." She glanced at María. "I should say 'our'. My good friend found it first. Would you like to join us?"

More bowed again. "I could not think of a greater pleasure." Watching him throw down his cloak and sit, María hoped no one else would seek them out. She sighed. *Catalina's time with me will likely be cut short as soon as the king realises her absence.*

"Are you writing anything new, Tom?" Catalina asked More. He laughed. "I am always scribbling something new."

"You do not want to speak of it?"

"I refuse to weary my queen on a day as agreeable as today

with talk of my unfinished works. If I did, I would risk my wife's scolding."

Catalina grinned. "Your wife scolds you?"

"Aye – she thinks I am but a foolish man at times." He laughed again. "If she thinks it, she speaks it. But she also ensures a good, and peaceful home too – and I thank her for that. It is what I most need for the health of my soul."

"I have spoken to Dame Alice over the years since your marriage. I delight in how she speaks her mind, and how much but she loves you, Tom."

Catalina turned to draw aside some of the bush. She sighed. "I wish I could stay longer, but I too love my husband. It is time to make my return to him. I bid you good day, Thomas – please send my greeting to Dame Alice, and tell her I hope to see her soon. María, if you have enough of seclusion for the day, perchance you could come back soon? I am lonely for you."

"I will return anon, my queen."

María watched Catalina go, aware of More's silence. At last, he spoke, "You do not wish to return?"

María met his curious eyes. "I will always wish to return to my queen. She knows me well – and understands my need to be away from people at times. Today was one such time. All the chatter hurt my head."

More nodded. He looked out towards the milling courtiers. Music, laughter, talking men and women strangled any chance for a moment of silence. "Yes – the court is not a place for peace, or for the health of one's soul."

An accented voice called out her name and that of Thomas More. Master Erasmus shambled over to them. More helped María up from the ground and they greeted the old man outside of the bower. Leaning on his walking stick, Erasmus bowed over her hand before kissing her with relish. María had to restrain herself from wiping her mouth of his taste of mint leaves and garlic. But she liked Erasmus, and was always happy to speak to him.

"Such a delightful habit of the English! I never tire of it!" The elderly man spoke fast in French, his eyes creased up in laughter-lines.

She laughed, replying in the same tongue. "I remember you in the first year of the king's reign. You sought out all the unwed girls."

"The kiss of greeting is a good custom of England. But then the English have a lot to make up to us for their weather – and other bad habits."

"Do we, my old friend?" More said with a laugh.

María glanced at More and back at Erasmus. "What do you speak of, Master?"

"Surely you know?" Erasmus shifted as if in pain. "I speak not of the home of our friend here. The home of Thomas More is a delight to visit. But there are English who dump upon their clay floors foul things. Their rushes conceal old bones, spittle, shit of dogs and cats, and everything under God's good Heaven to make a stomach turn." His face screwed up in disgust.

María smiled and gave a short laugh. "Once, those habits were shared by others. I remember my first days at the court of the king's father. I was shocked time after time by the behaviour of the English nobility. But the queen has long stopped that kind of conduct at court."

"Aye – conditions at court are greatly improved from the time of the old king. But, to my dismay, I find many other places are exactly the same as when I first came to England, when this King Henry was but a boy and still a prince at Eltham Palace."

"You met him then?"

"I hoped to gain patronage of the old king, as is still a common pattern to my life. I wished to make myself known to Queen Elizabeth. Thomas, you must remember the day?"

"Aye – we walked together from my home to Eltham. Prince Henry, as he was then, was with his mother. What a beautiful woman she was."

"Very beautiful – and a good woman too." Maria sighed. "Our lives changed for the worse after her death."

"Do you recall how she towered over most men – and stood eye to eye with her own husband?" asked Erasmus.

"Yes, she was tall, but it suited her," said María. "Tell me, what of the king as a boy? I met him a few times when he was boy, but I am curious to hear what you thought of him, Master Erasmus?"

"From the outside, all his mother's son. I remember he sailed his toy boat in the pond near the palace. In my mind's eye, I can see the day still. The water shimmered like a bright mirror in the sun. A touch of breeze swelled its surface and ruffled the feathers of the swans." He laughed. "Strange, is it not, the older you become, how rain spoils so few of our memories."

María looked all around. The parkland seemed washed with gold by the lowering sun. Sunshine or rain, an increasing shroud of sorrow wound tighter around each new day. For years, she had no longer wished to look forward. She turned back to the comfort of Erasmus' voice; it kept her safe in a past not her own.

"I did not know the boy crouching at the pond's edge was a

prince. Although, thinking back, there was a guard close to him. I thought him then a goodly made young lad."

"Yes – I thought that too when I met him for the first time not long afterwards. He escorted the queen to her marriage with his brother."

"The queen has been a good patron to me. She is a worthy daughter of the great Isabel of Castile." Erasmus seemed to no longer want to speak of the past, but the present. María repressed a laugh. *If I stay here for much longer, Erasmus will likely begin talking of a new book he wishes more coin from the queen to write.*

"The queen is indeed her mother's daughter."

Daylight beginning to ebb, the wind turned even colder. María curtseyed to Erasmus and More with great respect. "I must be away and return to the queen. I bid you both good day – and hope to speak to you more very soon."

She walked away, but cast a glance over her shoulder at the two men. Both of them were talking, and did not seem to care about the lengthening shadows – or that everyone around them began to ready to continue their interrupted journey. They were happy in their own world.

Later that same week, María made her way back to her chambers from the herb garden to get her mantle for Vespers. The servant appointed to serve the queen's women nowhere to be found, she lit the tall night candles around the room. The final candle lit, she stepped away from it and noticed a sealed letter placed on the table. Written boldly on the folded parchment was her name, written in the English style, in hand writing she did not recognise.

Shrugging on her mantle, María perched on the edge of the chair, broke the seal and opened the thick parchment. She read the first lines and rose, her heart in her throat. She stood again, taking the letter to the greater light of the tall candle by the window:

1515, Manor of Eresby To Lady Mary,

I write to you, a woman I have never met, a woman I should hate, to tell you this: my physician tells me I must make ready to meet my Maker.

So, this letter comes to you.

I have known about you from the beginning. Did Will ever speak to you about how we grew up on neighbouring estates and always knew we would one day marry? At fifteen, we spoke in jest to one another of Cupid's arrows striking us. We did not believe in Cupid's arrows. At fifteen, we believed ourselves too old to place credit in such things.

Life makes a jest of us all. Those arrows struck at all our lives.

From what Will has told me of you, I believe you did not choose to fall in love with my husband. You were young when it happened; we all were young. So young. I am glad womanhood opened your eyes to the rights and wrongs of loving a man vowed to another. At such times, I believe women are stronger than men. Or, perchance I speak of Will, who I know so well. He would never have broken up with you, after giving you his heart; only you had that power. I know it must have been hard for you

– and a dear friend at court tells me you have never married, but remain in service to the queen.

So, I am dying and will leave behind a grieving man. You and I both know Will; he is a good, kind man. He told me that you were never his true mistress. Despite the pull of both your hearts, he stayed faithful to his wedding vows. But his heart was long divided between you and me. Soon, there will be no cause for that. My death frees him to love you again.

I write to you to give you my blessing. I beg you comfort my husband, and love him.

Pray, give him this letter to read when you think the time is right. I want him to know he has my blessing too.

Written by the hand of Mary Willoughby de Eresby.

Aye – yet another jest played on us by life; we not only share the love of the same man, but the same name.

María folded the letter and held it to her beating heart. Vespers forgotten, she stood by the window, her tears falling down her cheeks as night took over day. Candlelight shone on the glass and the darkness beyond.

The garden still slept a winter's sleep – but while the air breathed a freezing breath on María's face, the morning's promise of rain remained just that – a promise yet unfulfilled. *Strange – the weather makes me think of promises and fulfilment on a day I hope for both.* María looked around. Will's note had told her to meet him in the garden they once knew so well – but she had come earlier than the time he had written in his brief letter, and he had not yet arrived. She sat on the nearby stone bench. Even through her layers of clothes she could feel it's chill. Six weeks ago, Will's long absence from court had been followed by the news of the death of his wife. María had written to him a letter of comfort. She wrote she did not expect a reply – but hoped to speak to him when he returned to court. She had not expected to learn of his return yesterday and to find his note in her chamber this morning. A footstep crunched. María turned her head to the sound. Will coming her way, she stood and waited, her heart pounding in her chest. Will halted an arm's length away – looking at her. María had not been this close to him in years. He was handsomer than she remembered. Her legs refusing to hold her up, she sat on the bench again. "Oh Will," she said. She could not think of what else to say.

He sat beside her. "My wife made me promise I would seek you out as soon as I returned to court. On her deathbed, she made me promise."

They sat in silence for a time – a silence heavy with the years, years of heartbreak, and words left unspoken. María drew her cold hands under her mantle – and stole another look at him. He was marked by grief, so much so she could not help but clasp his hand. "I wish I could have known Mary. I believe we could have been friends. She was always the better woman than me."

Will met her eyes. "She told me she wrote to you," he said

"She told me she was dying. She gave us her blessing to be together."

"Mary would do that. I came to be grateful you sent me home to her." He averted his face, but his hand remained in hers. "It did not mean I forgot you. But the years turned the memories into what seemed a dream. It seemed I had woken to live another life."

"I am glad." María sighed. "But it was never a dream to me. My heart ached every day I was apart from you."

Turning his head, Will studied her. "Yet it was you who broke off our attachment – and sent my letters back unopened."

"I told you why. I could no longer go on the way it was between us. I was so close to begging you to let me be your mistress. At that time, I found it hard to forgive myself for my weakness – and I hated the thought I could soon find myself risking your respect, and that of my queen's. I thought, too, that you had a chance of happiness if you made a true marriage with your wife."

Will tightened his grip on her hand. "You sacrificed your happiness for me?"

María looked at him. He spoke more of the truth than he could ever realise. She had sacrificed her happiness for him – but she would never tell him the real reason why. Six years left the reason well and truly in the past. "I would do anything for you," she whispered.

His eyes glittering with tears, Will touched her face. "I did not deserve Mary, and I do not deserve you."

María placed her hand over his. "I do not deserve you, my love." She sighed. "Life rarely gives us our deserts, but when it does, should we not take them?"

Will's hands cradled her face, his blue eyes locked on hers. "Will you be my wife, María?"

"Si mi amado. Pero vivo una vida media sin ti." María laughed, realising she had spoken in her own tongue. "Yes, I will marry you. If I did not, I would be only denying my heart."

Will bent his head and joined his lips to hers – and awoke the pent-up passion which she had kept at bay for years until it blazed into a raging fire.

***

María wiped her wet eyes as Catalina held out her arms to Alice for the crying baby. "Give her to me," she said, her voice a command. Not a command from a queen, but from a mother wanting her child.

Tears lighting up her eyes, the midwife grinned. Carefully, she gave the child to Catalina. Above the blanket, the top of the tiny girl's head could be seen, and the silver fluff of hair. The child squirmed, her little hand opening and shutting like a twinkling star above the blanket embroidered with a border of Tudor Roses. Catalina had embroidered it in the last weeks of her pregnancy, every stitch a prayer of hope, yearning and faith. She stitched it talking to María of her dead babies, and in the midst of the fresh sorrow caused by her father's death in January. This moment her grief seemed forgotten; her eyes brimmed with joy as she gazed down on her daughter.

King Henry stood still by the bed and considered his newborn daughter. His very posture, taut like a pulled arrow string, screamed out his disappointment. His mouth moved silently for a moment. He cleared his throat and spoke, as if to himself. "We are young enough. Sons will follow." Catalina didn't seem to hear – all her focus stayed on the babe.

Looking from Catalina back to the king, María wanted to vomit out her spleen. *Damn you. Damn to you to Hell. Where is your heart? I wish you could suffer the same agony as Catalina. I would have enjoyed hearing you scream. And you would have screamed. You think you are brave. If only you could bear a child in blood and agony, we would know then how brave you really are.* María took her eyes away from him. *Stop these foolish thoughts. He too suffered the loss of his children. I do not like him, I will never like him, but Catalina loves him. He has no idea what it costs Catalina to ignore his unfaithfulness. But he is young. A young king. He will not be twenty-five until June. To be fair, most of the time, he does make Catalina happy.* Or thought he did.

In recent weeks, she had experienced another side to the king, the side Catalina loved best. The king kept giving Will and her unsought after gifts. Will was rich enough, but, in the lead up to the wedding, the king made him richer still by increasing his land holdings.

The king also convinced Will to delay their wedding until June so it became a true court affair. Not only was their wedding to be witnessed by all the court, but a huge banquet was planned to follow it. If Catalina and Will had not been both thrilled about the king's decision, she would have found it difficult to excuse the weeks she now needed to wait before her marriage to Will. But she had waited years for this day. *Perchance the delay is best after all. It gives Will more time to mourn his first wife before taking a second.* María wanted nothing to spoil her wedding day – especially Will's sorrow for another woman. Even one who deserved the sorrow. That her joy came about thanks to the death of a good woman often left her cold. María looked back at Catalina. Her eyes, still lit with joy, remained on the sleeping child in her arms. The king, too, gazed at the perfect baby. This time, he reached out a finger, touching her hand. When the baby clasped his finger, he smiled in delight. *Perchance it is time to forgive the king for his behaviour as a boy, and his behaviour as a new king. It is all likely forgotten by a man who has been king for close to seven years.*

She closed her eyes. *Thank you, God. Thank you for this healthy child. This little girl seizes life, just as she seizes her father's finger. Thank God, this baby does not sleep the sleep of death.*

As was customary, the child was christened soon after birth, taken from her parents by her godparents to the chapel at Greenwich, the same chapel that had seen her parents wed seven years before. They named her Mary.

Catalina recovered slowly from another hard and difficult childbirth, but, as soon as she was churched, King Henry returned to her bed.

June arrived, and before María knew it, she walked hand in hand with Will, at last his wife. They made their way from the chapel at Greenwich to the chamber readied for the wedding banquet. She and Will sat on the dais in place of honour with the king and queen. The feast seemed to go for hours, and then the music began for the dancing.

Joining her hand with Will's, María paced with him the measure of the dance, her eyes unable to leave his, unable to believe they were at last wed. Unable to believe she danced with Will as her husband. It seemed a dream, a dream she never wanted to wake up from.

Their dance ended. Her hand still in Will's, she swung around to go back to the table, only to find the king before her. Will bowed, and she curtseyed, and the king held out a hand to her. He winked at Will. "Time for Mary to dance with me. That is, if her husband allows."

Will bowed again. "Of course, Sire." Will dipped his head to her. "I will await your return, wife, at our table."

Once again, María placed her hand in a man, but this time her partner was the king, and the dance one chosen by him. They came closer together, stepping around each other, but close enough to speak. "So, you are married now," the king said. Her heart full of joy, María looked at Will. He and Catalina were in deep conversation with one another. "Yes, truly wed, Your Majesty."

They stepped close together again, and the king grinned at her. "So, soon I will redeem your long-made promise."

María faltered for a moment in the dance. The king grinned and tightened his grip on her linked hand. María broke away from him, and then stepped closer. Her heart beating fast, it took all her control to not run from the dancing floor. Only practice and skill kept her feet moving to the steps of the dance. Shoulder to shoulder, they circled around each other.

"I – I – it was no promise. I have long forgotten it," she spluttered.

He shook his head. "You may have forgotten, but I have not. You denied my desire when I was a youth, but you cannot deny your king. Expect my summons when I send your husband to look over his new lands. I am in no hurry. I have waited long enough to be patient yet, and allow you to enjoy your marriage for a time."

All her joy gone, María realised how much she hated him. He had not changed since he was a boy. What he wanted, he thought he had the right to take, no matter who he hurt, or what stood in his way. Near him again, María decided to speak bluntly, "You can summon me, Sire, but I refuse to come."

The king narrowed his small eyes. "No one refuses me. No one," he said quietly. They stepped around each other, and he lowered his head towards her, continuing to speak softly. "Years ago, I ignored your husband's foolish efforts to save Edmund Dudley. But I asked Wolsey to keep safe the evidence of his involvement. If you refuse my summons, María, that evidence will come to light." He smiled at her. "Come – why look so downcast on this happiest of days? I will keep my vow to you it will be for one night only – one night for me to have you in my bed. So, the decision is yours. Be a wife, or soon a widow."

The dance at an end, the king bowed to her and María mindlessly curtseyed back. He returned to Catalina's side, and she to Will's. She grabbed her goblet of wine and gulped it down. Will clasped her hand and squeezed it. *Thank God he still speaks to Catalina.* It gave her the time she needed to pretend the conversation with the king had never happened. She did not want to think about it. Not on her wedding day.

10

As for those who state that it is thanks to a woman, the lady Eve, that man was expelled from paradise, my answer to them would be that man has gained far more through Mary than he ever lost through Eve.

~ *Christine de Pizan*

Later that evening, with Will in the bridal bedchamber, she had drunk enough wine to numb her fear about the king and his threats. *I will not let anything – especially the king – spoil my first night with Will.*

Will sat in the high back chair near the hearth and held out his arms. "Come here, wife."

Going over to him, María lowered herself onto his lap, putting her arm around his neck. Resting her face against his bristly cheek, she sighed.

"We do not need to consummate our marriage tonight if you are too tired, Dear Heart," he said.

María pulled a little away from him – gazing at him. In the light of nearby candles, his silver-blond hair seemed a nimbus, framing his face. As a girl not yet sixteen, she had thought him the most handsome man she'd ever seen in her life. Time had strengthened his face and deepened his lines of humour, and made him more beautiful in her eyes. María leaned her upper body on him, reaching up to cradle his face between her hands. "Will – I have desired you for over a dozen years. I have dreamt of us together for a dozen years. I want to wake up tomorrow and know I am your full wife at last."

She moved closer to him, and joined her lips to his. His mouth tasted of honey mead. He kissed her back, first gently, and then with a hunger which ignited her own hunger. She kissed him like one famished – like one starved for too many years. Through her wedding dress, she could feel his erect penis. She rose from his lap, and held out a hand to him. "Husband, come. Come, bed with me."

Laughing, Will stood and took her hand. He raised it to his mouth, kissing her palm, before winding his arm around her waist. "Wife – you do not have to ask me a second time."

Much later, María leaned back in the bath tub, the rosewater steaming and gently lapping around her. Opposite her in the wide tub, Will rested his head back, spreading his arms over the rim. Twisting, he grabbed a wet cloth hanging over the side and reached for the soap.

"Let me," she said. She wiggled closer to Will, her love, her sweet love, and leant her naked body against his. "I'll wash you," she said as he tilted forward.

Her nipples tingled as they brushed against his back. She lathered up the musk-scented soap in a cloth before massaging it into his skin. His body relaxed under her hands. "So good, my sweet María, my wife." He grinned aside at her, and turned around in her arms. "You're my baroness now, Dear Heart. The king may name you Mary, if he chooses, but you will always be my María, the woman who has my heart. Who always has had my heart."

His hand slid between her thighs, his slow fingers stroking, gently touching, working their way up as if he had all the time in the world. She closed her eyes, savouring the unbearable sweetness coursing in her veins. María smiled at him, closed her thighs, entrapping his hand. "Not yet. I haven't finished," she murmured, beginning to massage him again. Her fingers touched a scar running jagged down his shoulder blade. She followed its long journey down his back. Candlelight turned it into a thick vein of silver. "How did you get this?" María pressed her fingers lightly into his skin, the muscle underneath rippling in movement.

"How do men usually get mementoes like that? War. Or our king's idea of war, one of his battles in France. It could have left me with worse than a simply scar; the sword cut deep. I bled like a pig."

María swallowed. "I did not know – no one told me."

"I did not want it known. I also made little of it to the king – and he had other things on his mind and did not think to ask about my injury."

María swallowed another time, her fingers again exploring his skin. He turned his head, and she saw the jagged line on his neck from the coronation tournament so long ago. She shivered, an ache smiting her womb, at the core of her life essence. "No more tournaments, or wars, I beg you."

He shifted in the tub and held her face between his hands. "Tournaments I will try my best to avoid, but I cannot promise you no more wars. I must go where the king commands. Even without war, life is full of danger. We cannot hide from that."

She rested her forehead on his arm. "I know. But I have yearned to call myself your wife for what has seemed an eternity. I do not want it taken from me in a blink of an eye." She nestled into him like a frightened child.

Will wound his arms around her. "Be happy, like I am, that we have each other, and let's not worry about what the future will bring. Dear Heart, nothing can take from us the love we share. Not even death. Heart and soul, I believe that."

He kissed her, his hands cupping her breasts. She melted into him, all her fears slipping away. He feasted at her breasts, his penis hard against her. She opened her legs to him, moaning as he sheathed deep inside of her, and began moving. She moved to his rhythm, forgetting to breathe. The pleasure crested and crested until it seemed stars spun out of control and comets blazed across the heavens. She cried out, and Will groaned, tightening his hold on her. Desire dissolved into bliss. "Do not move. Don't dare move," she said, wrapping her arms tight around him. "I want you inside me. I want you inside me for all time."

Three months passed before King Henry sent Will to check on his new holdings, and María received her feared summons from the king. That night, María let her cloak's hood envelop her into its dark depths, as she made her way to what felt her place of execution. *I praise the Virgin Mother and her son Jesus. Vehemently I mourn my sins, constantly hoping in Jesus*, she prayed silently, trying to stop trembling.

Every step forward brought María closer to the Duke of Suffolk's chamber. *How like the king to ask one of his friends to make it easier for him to commit adultery.* María longed to turn and run back the other way, run back to her chamber. *Dear God, don't let anyone see me. What if Catalina ever finds out? And what about Will? What if he returns from his estates earlier than I expect? Mother of God – I mourn my sins, those of the past, and those yet to befall me. Jesus, forgive me. Forgive me. Forgive me. What else can I do? I've no escape. No true power. If I wish to keep my husband alive, I have no choice but to obey. Render Caesar what is Caesar's... I am only a woman... a woman caged.*

Reaching the duke's door, María crumbled against the wall. Resting her cheek on the cold stone, her head pounded, and her heart drubbed fast and hard against her chest. *Dear God – pity me, and strike me down dead. Give me some means of escape. I do not want this; I cannot bear this. I do not want to take another step.*

No thunderbolt came down from heaven. Painfully alive, fighting waves of nausea, María failed again to think of any way to escape. She forced herself to knock at the door, the beating of her heart sounding louder in her ears. She inhaled a ragged breath, and knocked harder, hurting her knuckles this time. She raised her sore hand to her mouth like a child.

The heavy door creaked opened. Standing there was the same page who had brought the summons. María almost gagged at his look of sympathy, his pity. He was only a boy, yet he pitied her. But she pitied herself. *Whore. Adulterer. Betrayer.* The words beat around her head until she swallowed the vomit rising to her mouth.

The page took her cloak and stood by the open door to the next chamber. As if going to her execution, María stepped towards the chamber, gazing around the room in confusion, in fear.

The king rose from his seat near the fire. He was in a red velvet dressing gown. It didn't hide his naked lower limbs and feet; the V opening at the top showed the golden-red hair curling on his chest. Falling to her knees, María lowered her head, and shut her eyes. *I praise the Virgin Mother and her son Jesus. Vehemently I mourn my sins, constantly hoping in Jesus.* Gripping her hands tightly together, she steeled herself for what lay ahead.

"You can go."

Praise God! María lifted her eyes in hope – only for it to dissolve into despair. He spoke to the boy, not to her. She stared at the floor, struggling to keep calm, preparing for a kind of death. The door softly shut.

"Come."

María looked up at him, and then at his outstretched hand. She almost gagged. "My lord king, I beg you, do not make me do this."

He padded across the room. With feet apart, he halted but a short distance from her. "I have been patient. More than patient. It is time for you to keep your promise."

María swallowed, keeping her eyes on his face. "My lord

king, think of the queen... it would break her heart. My husband's too..." A sob escaped her, and María raised her hand to cover her mouth. *Do not dare show him you are weak.* María lowered her eyes again, seeing his bare feet move closer.

"My wife knows when to turn her face, especially when she is with child. You know I am told to avoid her bed at such times. Would she not rather I bed with someone keeping her best interests at heart, than one of the sluts around my court opening their legs at my slightest touch?" The palm of his hand slipped under her chin to make her look up at him. "As for your husband – surely he would be honoured to know his wife beds with his king? I have rewarded you much, yet you have never paid the piper. You told me it would be different once you were wed – and why the fuss? Your virginity is no more."

María found it difficult to breathe. Eight years of kingship had taken him from youth to virile manhood. He stood tall before her – one of the most handsome men she had ever known. Magnetic blue eyes, skin unblemished and rosy with health and youth, perfect teeth; the lips of his small red mouth looked as if they had been rubbed with the juice of cherries. He was five years younger than her. A devil chanted in her ear. *Just the once. The king vowed it will be just the once.*

María remembered Catalina's broken heart at discovering his first unfaithfulness. She remembered Will brushing away his tears of joy on their wedding day. She remembered the scar on his neck – and how this man in front of her held both their lives in the palm of his hand. Her fear helped the devil lure her into hell. *The Devil? Dear God – does not love keep my heart safe, and my honour too? It is not my desire to be here.* She raised her eyes to meet the king's. She owed no love to this man. She owed nothing to this man. *Surely Catalina's belief in him cannot be so wrong. I know he has a heart. I have seen it when he grieved over his mother, his lost children. Perchance I can still save myself from Hell.* María gathered her courage. "I never promised, my Lord King. You misunderstood me," she said.

His hands moved with the suddenness of a snake. His fingers gripped her neck, his thumbs pressing for a moment into her throat. María cried out in pain, and terror, her brief moment of confusion dousing lust forever more. "My Grace –" she got out. "You hurt me."

He released her, and looked at her with cold eyes. "You play games with me. Think carefully – do you want a king for your enemy? Your husband would not thank you for it, not if he is in the tower waiting for the axe. Remember – I have everything I need to sign his death warrant."

Struggling to keep her breathing in check, María closed her eyes and licked her lips. She tasted the salt of her tears. She looked at him again, fighting her repulsion. *Please God, let him hear me. Catalina loves him – somewhere, there must be some good in him I can reach.*

"My lord King, I am your wife's best friend, her kinswoman. My husband's your loyal subject. If I bed with you, you but make me your whore."

He padded over to the chair near the fireplace. With a dancer's grace, he shrugged off his dressing gown, dropping it on the chair. The blazing fire cast a reddish light upon his athletic body – it turned the hair on his head to a fiery gold. The hair around his erect manhood was a dark red, like blood. María wasn't surprised. It was as if she had always known.

"I want you, my whore. Come here to me."

Vanquished, María rose from her knees. *Just the once. Only the once – the king's whore. Dear Jesus, I mourn my sins.* She walked to the king. *If he ever tries to coerce me to his bed again, I will not go. I'd slit my throat first.*

Later, curled up in the window-seat of her chamber, María could not stop hearing the king's voice speak in her mind – the memory of her terrible, nightmarish evening kept her imprisoned until she was ready to scream.

"Stop weeping. She'll never know unless you tell her. Don't fear. I will not speak of this to my wife. Always – always now – she looks at me with reproach. What happens here remains between just you and I.

If you keep crying, I will become angry again. You shouldn't have pulled your mouth away. I have had enough of you! A king favours you, and you weep. Go! Go I say! Why bed with a dry log when I can snap my fingers for a dozen women with more warmth than you? I pity your husband. At least my wife knows the meaning of passion. Go, and keep out of my sight."

María yanked her bed-gown tighter around her body. *I hate him. I hate him. I hate him.* Hugging her knees, she turned in the window-seat, and gazed out at dayspring. Birds chirped, trilled and courted – a lark on a branch near the window bursting into joyous welcome for the morning sun. Joy – her joy so hard won over the long years – was all gone. She wondered if she would ever regain it.

Her mind refused to let her alone, hearing again the king's words: "I want you no different from a whore." The memory of what happened in the duke's bed scored as deeply as the pain between her loins.

Dear God – please God – keep Will away. What if he returns to court today? How will I explain the bruises on my breasts, my thighs, the red marks of my neck? I already think myself enough the whore without seeing it in his eyes. What if I tell him the truth? Will he forgive me then, or hate me because I once bargained with the devil for his life? And Catalina. My sister, how do I face you? You know me too well, but this I must hide from you. Si, I must always hide what happened tonight from you.

María swallowed down bile and swung gingerly off the seat, returning to the washing bowl. She washed again, dousing more cold water between her legs. *I am dirty, as unclean as a leper.* Since her return to the chamber, her fear intensified about the king's seed. What if it planted and grew inside her? All night she wondered how she would know. On their wedding night, Will had repeated the story Latina had told her close to twenty years ago: a man needed to pleasure his woman to her highest peak to make a child. María had laughed at him as he pleasured her, not wanting to tell him he was wrong. *Dear God – take this cup from me. It's too much for me to bear. Will! O Will! My love, my love... would it have been better for me to die than go to the king's summons? What else could I have done? The king can destroy us both with a word.* María shook her head. *He has already destroyed me. I do not know how to come back from this.*

The lark sang again, and she returned to the window-seat. The sun showered its warm light through the window, all over her trembling body. María shivered and shivered, her heart cold, thinking what last night could mean for her. And for Will.

If Will ever finds out, God help me, I vow I'll kill myself. I couldn't bear seeing the hurt in his eyes. And if he finds out the king forced me into his bed with his threats?

It terrified her to think what he might do. Confront the king might be the least of it. Will refused to let fear dictate his life. He believed – for women as well as men – they possessed choice, power to make their own lives. *He also loves the king, and thinks him a man worth his loyalty... God help him and me. Why are men, even the best of them, so blind? Si, Will loves the king, but not as much as he loves me.*

María dashed over to the wash bowl and washed again. She could not stop trembling, or stop her teeth from chattering. Three months of wedded bliss and now this. Last night, the king had stripped her hard-won mask from her. She seemed naked, as naked as when the king unrobed her. So naked, she wanted to run and hide from the new day.

Dry retching, María hunched over. Her back ached and all her woman parts. *If men treated whores as the king did me last night, God pity them.* Last night was so different to the love she knew with her husband. The man she loved, body and soul.

Last night with the king did not change that. He had possessed her body, but not her heart. Last night had turned her barely bitten-back distaste for him into a beast of hate. Like an injured boar, her hate wanted to tear him apart. María wanted to hurt him as he had hurt her.

How am I to hide that hate? Not only from those around the court, but from the two people in the world who know me best. Will, my love, I didn't know what else to do... I could see no way to free myself from the king's power...

María sluiced more cold water between her thighs. Hot tears ran down her cheeks, dripping down her neck to her breasts. She lowered her head, trying to regain control. She hated her tears. She hated the king who caused these tears she could not stop. She hated this new day she had woken to – a day of living nightmare. Over and over, she prayed for Will's child, and never the king's.

María returned to the window-seat. Three days ago, Will had taken her to the moon and gifted her with stars. Knowing he returned the next day to his estates for several weeks, they had loved over and over, hardly sleeping till dawn. The first light of morning infused their chamber with silver light when they made love once more. Long hours of loving made them hungrier for each other. They had made love yet again; tender, gentle, their wave of passion crested towards the shore for seemingly eternity.

That morning, their coming together echoed in her the same pain of their first week as man and wife – the pain soon turning into a pleasure. A pleasure demanding appeasement. María had dug her fingers into Will's back and cried out to him to go faster, deeper, harder. They reached the mountaintop together, its snow-cap melting into a river of ecstasy. Will had laughed, collapsing on top of her. "Perchance it is good I go to see my new properties." He kissed and nuzzled the soft part between her shoulder and neck. "I need time away from you to regain my strength." His mouth nuzzled the top of her ear. María giggled, stroking his broad shoulders, feeling his muscles rise and fall under his skin.

"I am not as young as I was," he said, kissing gently her closed eyelids. "Our marriage does not sate my passion for you – it has enslaved me." His mouth journeyed from the side of her mouth to cover her lips. "I can't get enough of you."

Stroking his cheek, María kissed him back; his manhood

hardened again inside her body. Catching her breath, she rested her cheek against his, her eyes blind with tears. "I want your son, my love – I want your child. When you return, I pray to God I tell you our child comes."

He kissed her again, his tears intermixing with hers. One more time, one more gentle time, they made love until, in his arms, exhausted and spent, she fell asleep.

María had awoken to a chamber no longer filled with the silver light of morning spring. She rolled over into the still warm dip left by Will's body. She snuggled closer to his pillow, breathing in his smell. Something lay on its centre. She had reached over and took between her fingers an interwoven short lock of gold and black hair tied up with a piece of red cord. She had smiled, remembering the red cords of the doublet worn by Will at their wedding. It was the same cord.

Will. My sweet love. My husband. My heart is yours, and only yours. My body bears your children, your daughters and sons, and no one else's. María sluiced between her legs again, rubbing so hard until her skin felt flayed. She wept anew, hating again her tears, tears proving her a weak woman after all. She wanted no king's child. She wanted only Will's. He would give her strong babes, not ones born only to die and be swaddled for burial.

11

If you seek in every way to minimise my firm beliefs by your anti-feminist attacks, please recall that a small dagger or knife point can pierce a great, bulging sack and that a small fly can attack a great lion and speedily put him to flight.

~ *Christine de Pizan*

The hours dragged by. Getting out of bed, María yanked the thick, green curtains across the windows, blocking out the morning light, desiring entombment in a dark place. She never wanted to leave her chamber. Ever. Sick of heart, she sent her troubled maid with her excuses to Catalina, telling her to say to the queen she sickened and for the queen's sake, and for the sake of the child the queen carried, she remained in her chamber. More lies to Catalina; more lies forced upon her by life. María hated herself more with every passing moment.

By afternoon, María found her lie true – the pain below her navel, afflicting her so often weeks before her menses, was worse than ever. Bent over in agony, she warmed a brick in the fire. Pulling it out with tongs, she carefully wrapped it in a blanket, curled back in the bed with the brick close to her. Its heat did little to soothe the fire burning a hole deep in her belly. By the morning of the next day, her pain had eased, but not her despondency. She wanted to curl up in her bed forever. When her maid brought her food and expressed her worry, she answered by waving the tray away. She told her servant to leave, and turned on her side. Her maid returned in minutes, ushering in the queen's physician.

María bounded up in fright, cowering in the shadows of her bedhead. "I want to see no one! No one, I say!" Without thinking, she spoke in her own language. She pulled the bed coverings up to her chin, trembling, praying the darkness of the room concealed her from Vitoria's keen, prying eyes. Tall and lanky, he stood frowning and smiling by the bed, lighting a candle. The ruby embedded in his black velvet bonnet flashed in answer to the light. He held the taper closer and a wisp of smoke swan-necked before her eyes. María shivered with fear. "Doña María – I am here because the queen is worried. You do not want to cause her concern, do you?"

María shook her head, biting her bottom lip.

"Let me see if I can help." He placed the taper down and took her hand away from the blanket and placed his finger on her pulse.

"Your symptoms? What are they?" His face had that faraway look she often saw when he examined the queen.

María pulled her hand away. "I am sick," she said.

His dark eyes flashed and he grinned – his teeth lit amber by the lone candle. "Si. That is why I am here. I have also told you the queen is worried. Now, what is your problem, good lady?"

"My head hurts."

He rested his fingers lightly on her forehead. "No fever. But you are pale." He pulled down her bottom eyelid, and peered closer at her, his eyes glazing over in thought. His breath smelt of sweet wine. "How long have you been wed?" Not waiting for her answer, he counted the three months out on his fingers and smiled. "Do you think you could be with child? This would be happy news for the queen. When did you last bleed?"

María cowered deeper into the bed. "Over two weeks ago."

He pursed his mouth, his eyes narrowing. "Too soon, I would think. But sometimes two weeks is enough time for a woman to show signs she is with child, especially with a first baby. Are you using your bladder more often, Doña María?"

Raising her hands to her warming cheeks, María nodded. She had lost count of her times to the privy since her return from the king.

Vitoria smiled. "Not an uncommon sign in childbearing women. Drink as much as you can and that will soon pass. You are thirty, si?"

María wriggled with discomfort. "What of it?"

"Thirty is old to bear a first baby. Well past the ripe time for childbearing. It is possible you conceived just after the end of your courses. I suspect you feel the signs sooner because of your age."

María half rose, leaning her back against the pillows. Her heart grabbed hold of his words. "My belly hurts." She gestured to the spot. "Yesterday, the pain tore at me. Could that also be a sign I am with child?"

His dark eyes hooded and his mouth pursed again. "Are you bleeding?"

María shook her head.

"Good. Send word to me if that changes. Bed is the best place for you until we know one way or the other. I shall tell the queen."

Grabbing his hand, María moved closer to him. "You think I may have conceived weeks ago?"

"If your belly hurts as you say and you're voiding more often, I am confident a pregnancy could well be the cause of it. Stay in bed and rest for as long as you need. With good fortune, the pain will go and we will have happy news for both your husband and the queen. But if you begin to bleed in the next couple of days, send your maid to me and I'll ask Mistress Alice to see you. I will send her to you tomorrow, to see how you are." Settling back on her pillows, María listened to his footsteps petering away as he left her chambers, thanking God Vitoria gave her good reason to stay abed until the king's marks on her upper body could be hidden. *Pray God, Vitoria has the rights of it. Please God, let it be that already Will's child is making its presence felt and I need not fear about bearing the king's bastard.*

Two weeks later, María leaned on the cold stone enclosure of the window-seat. She drew up her knees, and hugged them to her, as she tugged around her the mantle made by her mother so many years ago. She kept it wrapped up in her clothes chest, regularly refreshing the cinnamon and cloves to keep away any pests in search of a dark place, or a feast of good wool. Good care had increased the softness of the wool, but it was no longer the vibrant red dyed by her mother. She did not often seek its comfort, but today she did. She twisted towards the window. Dark and still, the day waited, hushed by the promise of a new dawn. She watched the tide of night pull back. Moment by moment, darkness faded and the sky became washed by more light.

A bird sang, eager, full of joyful longing; it knew the moment had come, the promise fulfilled. Always there was a new day, a new dawning, a new beginning. She shifted on the hard, cold stone. Bird songs comforted her not at all. *And what new beginning is promised to me?* The days alone had built around her more stones of fear. She told herself she bore Will's baby, and not the king's – but how could she really know?

Two weeks had been long enough for other signs to add to the others. When she spoke of her tender breasts, Alice had laughed at her.

"My lady – if that is all in store for you, count your blessings. Believe me, it is safe for you to remove yourself from this room and tell the queen you both are with child. How delighted the queen will be when you share with her this news."

"I am truly with child?"

Alice came back to the bed and held her hand. "Although it is early days for you, I have been too long the midwife to not to feel it in my bones." Alice released her, and placed her palms on her generous hips. "Let me see – " Like Vitoria, she began counting out on her fingers, drumming them on her dress, but this time for longer than the physician. "Methinks, the middle of

June. Of course, you never can tell with first babies. They never come when you expect or want them. Now – how about I call your maid and we'll see about drawing a bath for you. A good soak and wash will do you good, and then you can get dressed. In sooth, my lady, I'm surprised you stayed in your chamber for as long as this. I did tell the physician that one week was more than enough time to tell whether we needed to worry about you." Alice shrugged. "Serving the queen makes the man overly cautious. But you are a healthy woman, my lady, and it is way past time to show that to the queen. Only your daily cry that your ailment could be something other than pregnancy has caused the physicians to forbid her to visit your chambers. The queen must think first of the child she bears."

The next morning, María resumed her duties with the queen. She curtseyed at the door and raised her head. Only her years of training prevented her from breaking down when she saw the joy shining on Catalina's face as she held out her hands in welcome.

Catalina showed her what she worked on during their time of separation – a christening robe for María's baby. One look at the delicate lace and painstaking embroidery, and María had to fight back her tears. She began babbling in Castilian. "Catalina – my sister."

She turned her face away, frightened her control would snap. *I hate the king. Hate him. Hate him. How am to live with this shame? The king forced me to betray the two people I love with all my heart. Dear God, let me die.*

Catalina approached her and clasped her hand. "What is wrong, María? You act strangely"

María forced herself to smile. "I feel strange. I did not expect to feel so ill, and weary."

Catalina smiled. María almost winced seeing her face. Her soul seemed in her eyes, eyes haunted by sorrow. "Not many women escape the illness of these early weeks. You will feel better." She smiled wider. "Even if it means you will be forced to drink the remedies you have forced upon me over the years. You will feel better once your child quickens inside you. And you will forget every day of illness when you hold your living child. I pray for that for both of us."

For weeks, María battled her depression, trying to disguise it from Catalina, from everyone. Will's frequent messages made her even more depressed. He soon sounded baffled, wondering why she wrote little back to him.

Her pregnancy gave María the excuse she needed to slip away whenever the king visited his wife in her chambers. Unlike the early years, this was no longer a daily event. The king still enjoyed his wife's company, but he spent most of his free time with his mistress, Bessie Blount, rather than the queen.

At last, Will returned to court, tired and saddle weary. By then, there was no more doubt; she carried a child, but she knew not whose child.

Will's joy broke her. It was like a torturer had tightened a rope around her skull. María leaned against him, and wept.

Will gathered her tighter in his arms. "Are you not happy? You told me you wanted children." He looked at her in confusion.

"Yes. I yearn to hold your son or daughter in my arms."

"Why do you weep then?" He searched her face. "My María only weeps for a cause."

She gulped down her tears, tightening her hold on his body, as the rope tightened. She rested the side of her face on his doublet, not wanting him to see her face until she had schooled it. "Women do cry when they are happy," she said, praying he would accept that, and not force upon her a downright lie. "Bearing a child also makes women cry more easily."

Will laughed, and kissed the top of her head. "So, my wife weeps because of joy?"

Clutching his doublet, she nodded, her head about to split open. "Why else would I be weeping?" She broke away from him. "I must go to bed and rest." When he seemed ready to say something, she placed a finger on his mouth. "Shhh – no more questions." She leaned forward and kissed him. "I know this must seem a strange homecoming, but I am old for a first babe, the physician tells me. Already, the babe is making its presence known, and making me ill. Give me an hour or two to myself, and we will speak more later."

Before he could say one more word, she slipped into the bedroom and closed the door.

12

Dare to declare who you are. It is not far from the shores of silence to the boundaries of speech. The path is not long, but the way is deep. You must not only walk there, you must be prepared to leap.

~ *Hildegard of Bingen*

May 1517, Richmond

Doña, my dear Latina,

Queen Katherine still has only one living child, a baby daughter, Mary. My queen hoped this year would bring her another child, but, alas, it proved not to be.

But how proud you must be hearing of your former student. Of course, I speak of the queen, rather than myself. My queen becomes more like Queen Isabel, her noble mother, every day. The English love her even if she has not given them a prince.

So many have reason to thank God for her good influence on the king. The king's sister, Margaret, Queen of Scotland, for one. A rebellion in Scotland forced her, big with child, to seek refuge with her brother, the king. Queen Katherine convinced him he could not abandon his sister. As if any man should need convincing of helping a sick, pregnant woman in such a time – a woman who is also his sister.

Queen Margaret was delivered of a daughter, and resides at court for the time. Strange – since Mary Tudor is also here – to think we have three women at court with the right to be addressed as queen.

There has been civil unrest in London. Hundreds of young men, many of them just beardless boys, rampaged against foreigners making their livelihood in London. A priest ignited these riots after preaching foreigners take the bread from poor fatherless children. The king's nobles soon restored peace, but London's dungeons overflow, for it is treason in England if the king's subjects attack foreigners ruled by those who have a truce with the king. Because they rebelled, the young men – some as young as thirteen, were put to death with great violence and cruelty. I hear their bodies are left hanging in the streets...

Uncomfortable, María put down her quill, pushed away from the table and stood. The baby kicked and tried to tumble what seemed head over heels. The child was heavy inside her, but not as heavy as the burden of terror she had carried for months. *Do not think of that – think of other things. The child is Will's. It has to be.*

Swallowing down bile, María blinked away tears and stared at the crumbling fire. *Think of something else before you make yourself ill.* She glanced back at her letter. *I should finish that.*

A knock on the door was answered by another of Catalina's women. "The cardinal desires to speak to you, madam," the woman said.

A skein of white silk around her neck, Catalina carefully folded the king's shirt, putting it aside. "Tell him he may enter." The stout man came through the open door as María and the other women rose from their various tasks to give him reverence. For a moment, there was a lull as the cardinal's red robes swept on the rushes. Wolsey bowed to the queen. Firelight caught the rings on his hand, and sparkled rubies and sapphires. As a canon of the church, he had well liked to show off his finery, his costly jewels. Now the king's Lord Chancellor, and two years a cardinal, Wolsey had taken his 'prince of the church' status to heart. The number of jewels he had on his person competed with the king himself. He even built his own palace close to Richmond palace. Since acquiring more wealth, his entertainments had become legendary – and the man grew stouter in consequence. Catalina did not much like the man; not with his French leanings, his unhidden mistress and bastard children. *But he serves the king and England too well for her not to respect him. He respects Catalina too. I wonder what has brought him here today?*

Wolsey wasted no time in arriving to the point. "Madam, I like not the mood of London. You must speak to the king; if these executions continue, I fear showing my face to the common people. In truth, the king should fear too."

Speaking without a trace of his usual charm, Wolsey had explained the situation in bleak terms, leaving her chambers only when the queen promised to use her influence with the king. After the door closed after him, María counted the slow seconds as Catalina stood staring sightlessly ahead. *I wonder what she is thinking?*

As if in answer, she turned to María. "When we were children, the queen, my mother, told us the story of how she rescued my older sister when she was held hostage as a child. My mother did not hang the common people in retaliation for their rebellion – rather, she soothed them, and made efforts to discover what had brought them to such acts. It distresses me Harry thinks first to bring these young men to death without discovering the reason for their rebellion. My husband should be merciful with his own people, if he can." Sitting in her chair, she clasped her hands and lowered her eyes, her face taut with thought. A few minutes passed before she clapped softly. "I have a plan. Ask my chamberlain to invite my royal sisters to my chambers to share a glass of hippocras with me."

One hour later, the three queens had finished talking, and plotting, before leaving it to Catalina to put the plan in motion. María almost rubbed her hands in anticipation of seeing Catalina manoeuvre the king like a pawn to her desires.

That evening, the king came for a private supper in the queen's privy chamber, as he usually did when he and queen stayed under the same roof.

María offered the king her reverence and asked permission to go to the chamber's window-seat – and wait there for the queen's command. It was as far away from him as she could get. Ill at ease, the child restless within her, María shifted and shifted deeper and deeper into the seat. *I should ask Catalina's permission to leave. I should ask if another woman could attend on her when she dines in private with the king.* María sighed. *But Catalina would ask me why.* Privacy for kings and queens was almost as rare as sightings of white unicorns. Even now, there were servants waiting on them – and Catalina always had one of her women at hand, to call upon. In the last few weeks, knowing María would soon leave the court to have her child, her royal friend had wanted her close. María reminded herself the king paid her little attention these days. There had been only one time when she caught him glancing at her belly.

For a time, the king's behaviour towards her had bewildered both Will and Catalina. María had spoken to them both with annoyance, using the same explanation: "Why should the king want to look at me? I am a woman bearing a child when his own wife is not."

It had first upset Catalina to think of it that way, but Will and Catalina soon both accepted the excuse. María lived in terror all the weeks of her pregnancy that either Will or Catalina would grow suspicious. As it was, Will found it difficult to understand why she wept so often. She was just thankful her time at court was, for a while, coming to an end. Very soon, María would leave and go to stay at Will's London property by the Thames, and wait for the birth of the child. Will was coming too. He swung from terror about the pending birth to joy that he was at last to be a father.

Her own plate barely touched, Catalina turned to the king, watching him eat while she sipped from her gold goblet. She began to speak of commonplace things – or not so commonplace things. They spoke of trees bearing their first fruit in the garden. They spoke of the pope, Leo X, and the recent Council of Lateran and its implications. They spoke fearfully of the recent sweating sickness striking Oxford. They spoke of the death of Catalina's older sister María, but the king quickly put that aside. María, like Catalina in her second marriage, had spent her married life going from one pregnancy to the next. But most of her babies lived, unlike Catalina's. She had died in childbed, but left behind a living child. María trembled, feeling ill. *I think the king would be happy to see a prince born even at the cost of his wife.*

Catalina led the conversation to the unrest in London and the hundreds of young men now waiting to hear their fate. "Do they need to die, Harry?"

The king pushed his empty plate away. A waiting servant offered the king a gold metal bowl and white cloth for him to wash and dry his hands. "You ask a woman's question," he said, wiping his hands. His grin left María cold. For years, he had respected Catalina – but time had seen this respect erode away by his sense of royalty, and increased disdain.

Catalina shifted a little closer to him. "My Harry – most of them are no more than sixteen summers. Your Londoners would love you more than they do already if you show mercy to their sons."

King Henry sniffed. He raised his goblet to his lips and gulped down a mouthful. "Mercy? That but shows I am a weak king."

"Mercy does not show you weak, not if you do it in the right way... my Harry, pray, can I tell you what I have in mind?"

He looked at her, gulping down another mouthful. He grinned. "You have aroused my curiosity. What are you thinking?"

Catalina settled back in her chair and smiled. "Methinks you will like it well..." So she told him, and the king laughed. "I do like it, and if I like it, Wolsey will too. He has been in my ear daily about this affair. When do you suggest we do it?"

"The sooner, the better. Three days will be enough time to arrange it. Trust me, my love, we will do it so well that all will revere you as a king who is not only strong, but merciful."

The king guffawed again and gulped down more wine. Putting down his goblet, he glanced towards the closed door of Catalina's bedchamber. He loosened the strings of his under-shirt. On his hand, firelight caught and sparkled the rubies of his rings. When he toyed with a jewel in the neck of his doublet, crimson spattered his fingers.

Watching from the window-seat, María trembled. *Blood on his hands?* She chewed her nail, wondering why fear chilled her so. Catalina had nothing to fear from the king. *Or did she?*

King Henry's eyes darted around the room, lingering once more on the bedroom door. "I like this room," he said. "There are many happy memories here. Kate, I always find peace, sitting with you."

Catalina smiled. "A wife should bring her husband peace."

María realised the king looked towards her and the other servants, his face expressionless. "Leave us," he commanded.

Glancing at Catalina, María slowly rose from the window-seat, walking to the door leading to the long gallery. As one of the bowing servants opened the door for her, María turned and curtseyed.

"Tell my page I stay here the night with the queen. I will return to my chambers in the morning and make ready for the day's hunt."

María caught Catalina's eyes. Her friend blushed a little and lowered her head. Queen or not, she was first a wife – and must submit in obedience to her husband's commands.

Three days later, María looked out at yet another grey sky. Spring had arrived weeks ago in England; a fretful, sullen spring echoing the mood of London. The burden of her belly slowing her down, she lagged well behind Catalina, the king's two sisters and their women by the time she entered Westminster Hall. Despite the hundreds of candles all around the interior of this enormous, ancient hall, the light was dull and dismal. She inwardly sighed. *I exchange a dark day for this darkness.*

She blinked, her eyes adjusting to the light, and looked ahead, meeting Will's concerned eyes amongst the courtiers. Hoping to reassure him, she smiled. He lost sleep over her and the child she bore, and could not wait for them to leave the court.

Wanting to join the queen's women, María quickened her pace and hurried over to the royal dais. Lining the long wall on either side of the hall, people crowded in tightly, their number impossible to count. All the way to the queen's women, gathered below the dais, she felt many eyes upon her.

Standing near Meg Pole, María watched King Henry welcome his wife and sisters to the royal dais. The three queens, robed in costly gowns and their long hair netted in jewelled snoods, sat down, close together like a knot. A stone's throw away from the queen's women, Cardinal Wolsey and the king's nobles and courtiers stood as if waiting, all looking towards the hall's open doors.

The hall rumbled with what sounded like thunder. Startled, María placed her hand on her belly when the babe moved restlessly. Guards herded hundreds of prisoners towards the royal dais, all of them roped together with halters around their necks. When she noted women amongst their number, she gulped back a gasp. *And many, many boys. Too many boys. Some of them look younger than twelve.*

Thomas More stepped forward, his dark eyes looking at the prisoners. There was no trace of his charm and humour. As a London magistrate, he had been involved in the arrests and recent hangings. He watched the proceedings with a piercing, pitiless gaze.

María could smell the terror of the prisoners – stink of urine and shit permeated the hall. The week of imprisonment had left its mark upon them: dirty and torn clothes, dirty bodies; evidence of brawling, or having violence done to them. So many eyes wide with fear. Close to the dais, as if as one, hundreds fell to their knees, the sound thudding its echo in the hall.

"Mercy," they cried. "Mercy." Some wept, but most of the prisoners continued their piteous cries – until the guards moved in and pulled on the halters to quieten them.

Wolsey, as if judging the moment right, moved forward. "You should repent, for you have committed treason by taking up arms against peaceful foreigners, who should be welcomed to our land." Dramatically flourishing his ringed hands, he turned to the king and kneeled. "Despite their sins, I beg you, good Sire, to be merciful. These prisoners were led astray by ringleaders who have now been visited by the king's justice and executed. I beg you, noble king, grant these prisoners their lives so they can go forth to lead good lives, and comply with your royal will."

King Henry sat unmoving on his throne, staring out at the prisoners. Voices of the nobility rose, pleading for the king's mercy. Then the three queens stood, freeing their long hair from their snoods. All three women had golden-red hair, hair gleaming in candlelight as it flowed over their shoulders and down their backs. The three queens fell to their knees before King Henry. Tearing at their rich clothes, they raised their hands to the king. "Mercy," they begged, again and again.

Hiding herself behind Meg, María gulped back a laugh. For the last few days, the three women had carefully rehearsed this piece of playacting in Catalina's private chamber. She studied the king's face. She knew him well enough to feel certain he was enjoying every moment. *How long will he keep his wife and sisters on their knees? How long will he make them beg before he becomes the merciful king?*

At last, he stood, and helped his wife and his sisters to their feet, kissing their cheeks. Catalina shared a smile with her two sisters-in-law, taking their hands. Looking on, María sensed Catalina's relief as she seated herself back on the royal dais. The king could barely hide his amusement as he regarded the royal women, but then he schooled his face and turned to his subjects.

"Know this, I am a loving king to my subjects, and I heed the calls for mercy of the queen, my wife, and my royal sisters. I hereby grant a general pardon. You are no longer prisoners, but free to go to live good and loyal lives in service to the crown."

A young voice called in the hall, "God Save the King! God Save King Henry!" – a voice soon joined by others. The voices became louder and louder until the noise seemed to shake the walls of the hall. Wolsey signalled to the guards, and they released the prisoners. Freed, the prisoners threw into the air their halters and ropes. María placed her hand on her belly. *If only I could be free too. Free of this shame – free of all the lies.* The baby kicked and stirred. *Little one, it is not your fault. I do not wish to be free of you.*

A week later, the king was not quite as amused when he heard a new London song sung outside from the queen's apartments. The king came away from the window. "They are grateful to you, not I," he said.

Catalina rose and took his hand. "I am your queen. Their gratitude goes to you too."

Unnoticed, María slipped away. She wanted to weep again at all the lies forced upon women. Striding towards her chamber, she straightened her shoulders. Under her breath, she sang the final verse of the song Londoners sang for her friend:

For which, kind Queen, with joyful heart,
She heard their mothers' thanks and praise;
And so from them did gently part,
And lived beloved all her days....

The first day of June brought with it a warm, clear night, as if, for once, summer wished to make known its arrival. Grabbing her shawl, María glanced at their locked chests, ready for their morning departure.

Will put his arm around her. "I cannot wait to get you to my London home. My time at court or at my country estates caused me to neglect it. I forgot the manor house overlooked the river and how pleasant it is. The servants have readied it for our occupation – the walls are newly whitewashed, fresh rushes have been laid down and I have prepared you a stillroom fit for Galen. But it can wait while you rest, and read your books. These last weeks at court have taxed your strength." He looked at her, his concern on his face. "Are you certain you are well enough for this invitation of the queen's?"

María leaned on him, the babe stirring between them. "I will be leaving my queen for some time." She looked up at him. "If you get your way, months. I spent all day overseeing the packing for our journey, and saw the queen only briefly in the morning. You know the queen and I regard each other as sisters. I would much rather us stargaze and have supper with her tonight than stay indoors in our hot and stuffy chamber."

She did not tell him about the thoughts twirling around her mind while she packed their clothes, and the baby garments she had made over the last months. All that long, restless, too warm day, she struggled to find ease in a body no longer only. hers. Memories of dead babies, and dead women haunted her too: Catalina's sisters Isabel and María, Queen Elizabeth, Inés, the list of the dead seemed endless. Too many women, all them taken from life too soon. By the time she had finished packing, she needed to go to the stillroom and boil up some willow bark for a drink to combat her headache. *Staying in London means Alice will see me through my travail.* But even that knowledge little buffered her fears.

Will took her arm and grinned. "If you really wish to do this, we best start the climb to the roof."

The demanding climb of the well-lit spiral staircase seemed unceasing, the baby heavier with each turn. Will refused to leave her side for one moment, but halfway up he stopped her on the stairwell and tried to convince her to make a return to their chambers. María shook her head. "As long as we do not need to hurry, I can do this."

"Are you certain?" he asked.

Still catching her breath, she looked at him. The next day she would be leaving Catalina, and it could be forever.

She touched his face, and smiled. "I tell you true, I am well. Well enough to enjoy a last evening with the queen before we leave. We will go slowly up the stairs." It seemed more sensible to keep going than to return to her chamber and pretend to Will she was not fearful about giving birth.

He pulled her up the final step, and she emerged to a roof spread out with cushions and straw matting. A narrow length of costly Turkish carpet led from the roof's entrance to several chairs set near a long table covered with a white tablecloth. There was a feast of food on the table; so many dishes they concealed most of the white tablecloth beneath them. A tall torch had been placed on each of the four corners of the roof. While the torches lit up the edges of the turret roof, their light, flickering in a slight breeze, tapered off to a core of darkness in the centre of the turret, where everyone could gaze at the stars. Music of a harpist and flute player drifted from the other side of the roof. The men seemed to play to the night, to the stars; the soulful notes of the harp and flute reached out to María, piercing her heart.

Waiting for her to catch her breath again, Will wound his arm around her, and together they stepped away from the door. Catalina broke away from speaking to the king, Meg Pole and Thomas More, and hurried over to her. María curtseyed at

Catalina's approach. Or tried to. Her big belly made everything difficult.

"I did not expect you to come," said Catalina, kissing her cheek. She waved a hand at bowing Will. "No, put aside formalities, I beg you. You have given me such great pleasure by coming tonight." She smiled at Will. "María tells me you leave the court too for your child's birth?"

Will grinned broadly, holding onto her arm. "My place is by the side of my wife, Your Majesty."

Catalina reached out to clasp their right hands. "My lord, your words make my heart happy." She tightened her grip on María. "These last months I have seen why you refused to consider any other man. He is your perfect match."

María smiled at Will for a moment. "He is that, my queen." Dropping Will's hand, Catalina kept firm hold of hers. "Would you mind if I keep María by my side for a time? These coming weeks will be strange without her."

Will dipped his head. "Of course, Your Majesty. I will go now and give my reverence to the king." He bowed his head again. "I leave my wife in your good care, Your Grace."

As he crossed the roof, Catalina led her to the trestle table. "Would you like some food? The cook has prepared a number of Castilian dishes for our enjoyment."

"There is a bowl of ripe apricots too." María picked one up and took a bite, wiping the juice from her lips with one of the napkins placed near her. "It is good to see the trees from our homeland grow so well in English orchards."

"Our palace gardeners are good. I remember the care they gave to the saplings sent to us by my father in the first years of my marriage to the king. They lit torches around them in their first winter to keep the frost from them and did everything to ensure they survived to spring. All their effort was well spent. Sometimes, I think the fruit from our orchards in England is sweeter than the fruit I remember eating as a girl in our homeland."

María laughed a little. "That's a rare observation, my sister. Usually when we look back, we remember only the sweetness of the past – even when it was not sweet at all."

Catalina shrugged. "I do not often allow myself to look back. It is the present I concern myself with, and the future. And is this moment not sweet, my sister? The warm night allows us to gather together to stargaze on a clear, night sky. You are married to the man you always wanted, and bear his child." Ill and dizzy, María turned her face away, her heart beating loudly in her ears. She reached out to steady herself on the table. Catalina took hold of her arm, and took her to the nearest chair. "Sit, sit before you faint." Catalina dragged a chair to sit next to her. "What is it?"

Unable to look at Catalina, María shook her head. "Nothing. Nothing is the matter."

Catalina reached out to take both her hands in hers and began speaking softly in their shared language. "You avoid speaking the truth, amiga. Pray, tell me what is troubling you." María closed her eyes, her head pounding again. *I can never speak of what's troubling me, especially to you.* Desperate, she grabbed at the thoughts which had passed through her mind all through the long, warm day. María lifted her head and met Catalina's worried eyes. "I fear my coming childbed."

Catalina released her hands, and considered her with compassion. "We would indeed be foolish women if we did not fear giving birth. The only thing I can advise is to try give the fear to God. Let Him carry it for you."

María raised her eyes to the black velvet sky. Countless stars pricked through their light. She turned to Catalina, and shook her head again. "Your faith has always been greater than mine. Your times of trials increased your love and belief in God, but not so with me. With me, it served to do the opposite. All I can think of is all that can be taken from me in a blink of an eye." She looked across to where Will stood speaking to the king. Torchlight beamed down on the small table beside them, glittering the gold of the large armillary sphere, the assortment of astrolabes, the quadrants and all the other instruments set out for them to use to study the stars. "Sometimes, I even fear my happiness. If I lost it, would I ever find my way back from the dark like you have, time after time?"

"Sister – we all have our own journeys to walk. While it saddens me you struggle to find the peace I have found in my faith, it is not unusual for a woman heavy with child to be also heavy with what feels like the weight of the world." Catalina leaned closer and kissed her cheek. "As for myself, my dark times have taught me this: we do not come to Heaven without troubles. Troubles forge us and make us ready to meet God."

A dimming of the light from one of the torches caused her to glance over her shoulder. His body blocking out the light, Thomas More crossed the roof, heading in a straight line to Catalina. Nearing the queen, he bowed, and moved forward again.

Catalina shook her head. "Thomas, I told you before, I wish for informality tonight. This evening is for the king and I to enjoy the company of a few friends and for us to study the stars together." She smiled at him. "You do know the king and I both regard you as a good friend."

His body still blocking out the light from the nearby torch, More's face was hard to see, but his eyes suggested grimness. He moved to where light pooled from several torches. Looking at his animated, good humoured face, María wondered whether she had been mistaken before.

"I am honoured to be so regarded, Your Majesty," More said. "You must know the great respect I bear for you, my queen." He smiled. "Have I ever told you I saw you as a girl when you first entered London? I have never forgotten how lovely you were then."

Catalina chuckled. "Were then... My good Tom, it may be wiser for a man held in high esteem for his wisdom, to not risk the truth with your queen, who is still indeed a woman."

More's gentle smile gave his face an extra magnetism. "You are indeed a woman, my queen, and if you wish the truth, I say you have a beauty in these days that was denied to a girl who had not yet celebrated her sixteenth summer. Beauty of soul shines forth from your countenance more with each passing year."

Catalina laughed outright. "Methinks, you well know the skills of a courtier in spite of yourself, Thomas. I cannot tell you the pleasure it gave me when the king told me you have joined the privy council. You may have never wished for it, but of all the men I know, you are truly worthy of this position."

María saw him tighten his mouth. *Poor man. He tells the truth that he has little desire for this position.* More dipped his head to Catalina. "Your Grace, I hope I will never give you any cause to think any differently. With you I can speak plainly. You may say I have the skills of a courtier, yet I am but a simple man who enjoys life's simple pleasures. The king assures me my family will not suffer from me taking up this post, but I am not certain of this. If I had not come to believe God asks of me to take up this service, I would beg the king to allow me to continue as I have done these past years. Serving London as a Sherriff is also service to the crown."

"Tom, I will speak plainly too. You will serve England more through service on the privy council than by giving service to the city of London. My husband needs men such as you close to his side." Catalina smiled. "Vives has written to me. His letter spoke of reading a book you have penned. Vives is most impressed by it. I am astonished you have not told me of it, Tom – or given me the opportunity to read it too."

Thomas More's mouth shaped a slight smile. "I have only just finished writing it, Your Majesty. I sent a copy to Vives to read to get his thoughts. I am glad he liked it."

"He tells me you wrote of an imaginary country ruled by reason?"

"Utopia, your Grace. I use Utopia to explore my own thinking – and also reflect upon war and the need for princes to be aided by virtuous counsellors. In truth, I must confess recent events at home had much to do with the writing of this work."

Catalina pursed her lips. "I suspect you speak of the Pope's efforts to sow peace between Christian princes so they are able to combat the Turks, and Wolsey being made a Cardinal and Papal Legate so he could put into effect the perpetual peace promised by the Treaty of London?"

"You suspect right, my queen." He cocked his head, considering her. "If you wish to honour me by reading it, it would be my great pleasure to send a copy to you."

"The pleasure will be mine, Tom, I have no doubt on that score." Catalina smiled at him. "I forgot to tell you of another pleasure I had recently. Last time I walked to your home in Chelsea, I came upon your daughter, Margaret, in the garden. Every time I see her, she amazes me anew with her maturity and intelligence. You would not think her a girl of twelve – not with the depth and breadth of her conversation."

"She did not tell me she spoke to you, Your Grace."

Catalina laughed a little. "She was concerned you might not be pleased to learn we spoke together for such a length of time. Forgive me, I told her not to tell you, unless you asked why she had been overlong in the garden – and if I ever spoke of it to you I would tell you the time I spent with your young daughter in your garden lifted my heart and brought me to your door a far merrier woman than the one who arrived at your home. Your daughter is a delight, Tom, not only intelligent, but with a good heart. I would like the Princess Mary to be schooled in the same fashion." Catalina turned her smile to María. "I want my daughter to have the good fortune we had as girls. My royal mother chose well our teachers who gave us a love of learning and taught us its value."

María made a wry face and laughed. "You learnt that lesson earlier than me. I was eight before I stopped resenting the time I was forced to study books."

Catalina grinned. "By then, you not only read and wrote well, but our good teacher had begun teaching you the healing arts. It was of more interest to you than the study of the ancient philosophers."

"It is still of more interest to me than most things," María replied, laughing outright. The baby stirred and kicked. She cradled her hands on her belly. This child was daily making its presence more and more known. Thoughtful, she looked back at the girl she once was, wondering if Latina's decision to teach her medicine had come from recognising one of her students would never enjoy learning Latin without a purpose to learn it. She had never been a natural learner like Catalina, but her study of the healing arts had changed the course of her life. Once she started to learn about medicine, she had wanted to keep learning. With effort, she turned her mind back to attending to listening to the conversation between More and Catalina.

"Can you recommend a good teacher for my daughter, Tom, one who would teach her like your daughters?"

Thomas More laughed. "Already, my queen? The princess has not long celebrated her first birthday."

"She is the king's child. If we do not have a son, she will one day be Queen of England. My daughter may be small, but she already shows her intelligence. I, as her mother, oversee her learning in these early days, but I would like to place her future teacher in my household now, so my child knows and likes her teacher by the time she starts her lessons in earnest. It would also give me the time I want to judge the worthiness of this person. I intend to surround my daughter with people I trust and respect."

"If you wish for a teacher you can trust and respect, I have no hesitation in recommending Richard Featherstone to you. He is first a priest, indeed, he is a Doctor of Divinity, and second a scholar of Latin. He was awarded his Master's at Oxford. There are few who equal to him."

"Richard Featherstone? I know him, and like him. He is not only loyal to England, but loyal to God. I will send for him tomorrow and speak to him about teaching my daughter in the future. In the meantime, he can join my household as chaplain." Catalina turned, looking aside at María with concern. "Are you well again, amiga? Would you like something to eat, or do you feel up to returning to your husband and taking up an instrument to measure the stars? They predict our next full moon will be a Luna eclipse."

María took a chicken leg from the table. "Thank you, my queen, but I am content to stay here and eat."

The torchlight shone on More's teeth as he smiled. "Can I say what a pleasure it is to serve a queen who enjoys celestial phenomena through the eyes of reason. Too many men read but superstition in any movement of the stars."

"You praise me too high, Tom. As a girl, I would not have used reason. As a girl, I believed the movement of the stars made music we did not even know we heard." She lifted her head, looking up at the stars.

The harpist strummed a chord and began playing a song María first heard years ago at Ludlow. The present moment dissolved, and she heard in her mind a sure Welsh voice singing:

No woodland caroller art thou;
Far from the archer's eye,
Thy course is o'er the mountain's brow,
Thy music in the sky:
Then fearless float thy path of cloud along,
Thou earthly denizen of angel song.

María saw Catalina's eyes glimmering in the torchlight. *She is not looking at the stars. She is gazing back at a time when life contained love's promise and the sweet essence of youth.*

Confirming her suspicion, Catalina sighed, and said, "I am no longer sixteen and believe the stars make music. Astronomical phenomena are like the seasons; they are only the design of God, and to be accepted and welcomed as such."

Catalina laughed a little, and held María's hand. "I remember you thinking as a child the world was flat."

María shrugged. "And I remember you telling me otherwise." The night sky glittered with stars. "And what do you have to tell me about the stars we see tonight revolving around this Earth of ours?"

Once again, Catalina lifted her eyes to the heavens. "What can I say about the stars, other than their light links us to God, and eternity."

13

The sorrowful born child.
~ *Le Morte D'Arthur*

Will gathered the tiny child in his arms, his eyes locked on the sleeping baby. "We will name him Henry."

María's heart seemed to stop, and then jumped in her chest. Weakened from a difficult childbirth, energy ebbed and flowed through her body. Painfully, she rolled on the bed, closer to Will and the crib. She clasped her aching head.

Will raised his eyes, gazing at her with worry. He cradled the child nearer to him. "My love, should I call back the midwife?"

"I do not want to call him Henry," María said softly. She swallowed, wondering if Will had heard. "I do not want to call him Henry," she said again, but this time more loudly.

"Sweetheart, the king will expect it."

"Expect it?" María wanted to vomit. *My son is not the king's. He is not the king's.* She repeated it over and over in her head, but it did not help. Her head and heart pounded as if both were ready to shatter.

"Aye, love. Think you of the many wedding gifts he has given us and the favour he has showed to us both over the years."

Favour? María heard the king's voice in her mind: *A king favours you, and you weep.* Her aching head became a searing agony; the bright light streaming from the window hurt her eyes. "Will – draw the curtains, I beg you."

Gazing at her in obvious fear, he placed the babe carefully in the crib and did as she bid him.

"I never asked for or wanted his favour," María said weakly when Will returned to sit on the edge of their bed, clasping her hand.

"I know that," Will said quietly. "I also know the king never forgets the favours he gives his subjects. He always expects payment for them."

María swirled, all at once nauseous. "I am going to be sick," she got out.

Will fetched the bowl. His gentle hand rested on the back of her head, staying there until she finished vomiting. He straightened up, began walking towards the door with the bowl. "I will go and attend to this, and tell the midwife to return to you."

Left alone, María rolled on her back and stared at the ceiling. The baby whimpered. *Is he Will's son or the king's? How am I ever to know? Oh God – how right Will was when he spoke about the king never forgetting. I should be happy; I have a son. But I want Will to be my boy's father, not a man I hate. It was hard enough to hide my hate before this. I do not know how I will ever hide it now.* Her thoughts coalesced into a beast determined to destroy her; her head hurt more and more.

Alice returned with Will and took one look at María before coming back to the bed with a goblet. "You need to drink this poppy. You need sleep, my lady. Sleep will put all to rights."

The pain tightened its band around her head like a torturer twisting a rope. *Sleep put this to rights? Nothing will put this to rights but death.* Obediently, María gulped down the poppy. Her eyelids became heavy as Will sang a lullaby to the crying child.

With lullay, lullay, like a child,
Thou sleepest too long, thou art beguiled!
"My darling dear, my daisy flower...

Nothing will put this to rights but death.

Two weeks later, the words drummed and drummed in her mind, and heart. Will was prone beside her, his head resting on the bed. Again and again, María stroked his hair, then rested her hand on his shoulder, lifting and dropping with his sobs.

Nothing will put this to rights but death.

Her boy was dead. The child she had wanted, had dreamed about, for what seemed all her life. Like the queen's small son years ago, her baby had been found lifeless in his cradle that morning by his wet-nurse.

Nothing will put this to rights but death.

María closed her eyes tight. *Did I unwittingly curse my child, cause for him to die?*

His wet-nurse had voiced her worry about the boy two days

after his birth. "Ma'am, he does not suck like my strong boy," the young woman had said. "Often, your babe brings back most of his milk."

Rousing from her depression and still weeks away from being churched, María had asked for her child. She laid him beside her in the bed, stripped off his swaddling cloths. The silver-blond baby had seemed perfect to her; she told herself she had been a fool to think the child the king's son. He was Will's, and hers. Just because the king's daughter was born with a similar hair colour as her son did not mean anything. María had gathered him in her arms, lifting him to her nose. His baby smell pulled at her insides, and made her breasts ache. For the first time, she regretted her decision to not feed him herself.

And now her child was dead. The swaddling cloths she had so carefully removed from his tiny body less than two weeks ago would be his winding cloths. Will had not stopped crying since they had held their dead child that morning; María could not cry. She wished she could.

From her earliest years, she had kept in check her tears, or tried to. These last months of her pregnancy, to Will's bewilderment, she cried at the slightest cause, as if the tears she had stopped herself from crying since before her fifteenth year now demanded release. But now she could not cry. If she started, she would weep an ocean of tears. An ocean of tears drowning her.

Nothing will put this to rights but death.

Nothing will put this to rights but death. Nothing will put this to rights but death.

María wiped tears from her eyes. *My boy would have been a man now. If he had lived, his sister would not have been an heiress, and of little interest to men such as Brandon.* She rose stiffly from her chair to throw another log into the fire. Warming her hands, she glanced at the pages of parchment on the table beside her writing desk. She had written for hours – and still she had not reached the end. The light from the room's candelabrums could not chase away the shadows. In her tiredness, they seemed to take shape of the many ghosts from her past. Silent ghosts, but her heart knew they wanted her to speak for them. She straightened her shoulders, and returned to her chair. *I not only write for Kate, but for them. It is their story too.* She picked up her quill again.

Have I shocked you, my daughter, in writing about the death of my first born, your brother? My small son who died too soon for me to ever know for certain whether he was the king's, or your father's. When he died, I cared little about his parentage. I just wanted my baby alive.

But we can never determine our fates. I wish we could. I have had joy in my life, but sorrow too – as all of us do. But even this great sorrow paled into insignificance when compared to the sorrows faced by Catalina in her life.

We are young enough, there will be sons to follow, so said the king on the birth of Princess Mary. The king was young enough, but Catalina no longer so. After Mary's birth, she miscarried early in a pregnancy and then two long years passed before she became heavy with another child. When we visited Merton College that year, Catalina pilgrimaged to St Frideswide to pray for a living child. Her prayers proved in vain. She birthed a weak daughter who died within days. Life followed by death repeated again in Catalina's marriage to the Tudor king.

My daughter, I carried you in my womb when I told my friend of her dead baby. I was so aware of you, my darling. You stirred and quickened between us when I held her in my arms as she wept. Catalina clung to me like one drowning, digging her fingers into her arms, hiding her face in my breast. I found myself thanking God for my own dead child, for the sorrow we shared – and would always be a part of us.

No more babies followed, and I thanked God for it. Catalina's heart had been ripped out with each dead babe and drove her to take solace in God; her faith kept her going, her love for her daughter, Mary, her love for the king – and her love for England. But I doubted her sanity would have withstood losing one more child.

Little Mary grew and flourished. To Catalina, the child was the answer to her prayers. She devoted her days to overseeing the wellbeing of her only child.

Mary brought Catalina the joy she needed in her life.

I did not have the heart to tell her what your father told me in the privacy of our chambers. The king seethed with dissatisfaction. He wanted sons, not daughters, with all the inherent problems royal female heirs had brought to England in the past. He did not see it as Catalina did – her own mother was a strong and capable queen – why not their daughter?

Speaking to your father, I struggled to understand why the king was so determined to gain his prince, ignoring all the capable women he knew and had known throughout his life. He forgot his mother, his grandmother, his sisters, and his wife. He forgot how Catalina had proven herself when he had gone to

France and left her as England's regent. Perchance he wanted to forget. Her victory over Scotland was still celebrated by the English, and deemed far greater than his little victories in France. He forgot the victory had cost her another child, the son they both wanted.

But they had Mary, a girl child who was the granddaughter of Queen Isabel of Castile. A princess who was close kin to the most powerful royal house in Europe. In her mother's eyes, Mary was given to them by God to succeed as England's next monarch.

But the king did not see this.

14

We cannot live in a world that is not our own, in a world that is interpreted for us by others. An interpreted world is not a home. Part of the terror is to take back our listening, to use our own voice, to see our own light.

~ *Hildegard of Bingen*

1520, Syon Abbey

Doña, my dear Latina,

We will be at the Abbey for a week – leaving behind a court readying for the visit of Emperor Charles and the approaching journey to Calais. Yes, I am glad of this week's sanctuary, even if the reason for it takes me from my infant child and causes me much disquiet...

María rubbed her strained, watering eyes, and looked out the large window of Catalina's chamber. Her sight still blurring, she secured her needle into the tiny gown she was making for her infant daughter, and placed her sewing back in the basket at her feet. The passing years had not dulled her dislike of the needle, but she found a perverse pleasure sewing for her child. She would do anything for her daughter – make any sacrifice – even spend hours straining her eyes and pricking her fingers as she made yet another tiny gown.

María arose from her chair and stepped in front of the window. Silken gauzes of pink cloud streaked a lowering sky. None of the silk threads in her sewing box came close to capturing the colours of the ebbing day. Tomorrow, she would join the nuns in their herbal garden and garden to her heart's content. She flexed her aching fingers. *Si – tomorrow I will delight in using my hands.* She looked towards Catalina and the tiny princess.

Catalina brushed her daughter's silver-blonde hair. María remembered the king snatching off Mary's hair-net when the child was two, revealing her silver-blonde hair to the French ambassadors. She sighed. Catalina had not enjoyed the sight, or the reason her daughter was on show. Catalina hated the fact her small daughter had been betrothed to the French infant prince. At a banquet given in honour of the French, the king also showed off his infant son to the French ambassadors – a bastard son, born to his mistress, Bessie Blount. A bastard the king recognised. The boy was named for his father: Henry, Henry Fitzroy.

Princess Mary was almost two years older than her half-brother. The boy was said to be a bright child, but there was no question Mary was brighter. Even at two she had impressed those around her with her intelligence when she amused the court calling out 'Priest' to Friar Dionysius Memo, a Venetian musician employed by the king, and had commanded the man play music to her. For the last two years, Friar Dionysius had been the little girl's music teacher. He taught her well. The child could already read music and play the virginals.

One reason they had come to Syon for a time was because of the increasing tensions between Catalina and the king. He insisted on treating his bastard son like a true prince. King Henry doted on his daughter and called her his pearl, but he also spoke to his wife in private about making his infant son a duke. When he suggested a possible marriage between the boy and his daughter Mary in the future, Catalina had lost her control and stormed at him. She refused to speak about his son – now, or all the future. Humiliated and hurt, Catalina had sought the peace of the abbey so she could calm herself and take stock of the situation before the arrival of her nephew.

María padded over to Meg Pole sitting near the fire. Meg was so engrossed in her book she did not even raise her head when María sat in the chair across from hers. Settling back, María caught Catalina threading her fingers through her daughter's hair. Time stilled, María seeing in her mind Queen Isabel doing the same to the child Catalina. An act of love then, it was an act of love now. María swallowed what seemed her heart in her throat. *Thank God the gift of love remains with us until our last breath. No – love remains with us forever.*

Catalina held out one strand to catch the last rays of daylight. "Such a pretty colour. It is so like your father's mother, your dear grandmother, God rest her soul."

The child preened and beamed. "Your hair is pretty too, Mama."

Catalina started brushing again. "They once said my hair was beautiful. Its colour has dulled with time, my child. So be it. While we live, nothing remains the same."

Bewildered, Mary looked aside at her mother. "Why are you sad?"

Catalina put down the brush and wrapped her arms around her daughter. "Sweetheart, I am not sad, but foolish. The king, your father, has sent me a letter setting out his plans for you in the future. When you are nine, you will go to Ludlow. It is right for you to learn to govern your own court when you are older. You will one day be queen, God willing. Not for many, many long years yet, but you do need to learn how to rule." Catalina sighed. "I cannot lie. I do not want you away from me, not at nine, not ever. But it is years away. I am a fool to think of it, when I have you with me for years yet."

Mary chewed her lower lip, tears beading her short lashes. "I do not want to leave you, Mama."

Catalina considered her daughter for a long moment. "Child, you will not be leaving me for a long, long time. But you are a princess, Mary, and your noble father's heir. It is your duty to do for your country what the king, your father, commands." She took her small daughter in her arms again. "Forgive your mother for unwisely speaking of it. You stay with me until you are old enough to go. And – when the time comes – I will not send you alone. Your godmother Lady Margaret will go with you."

Meg raised her eyes from her book, and smiled. "It will be

my great honour to serve and go with the princess to Ludlow. She and I already love one another."

Catalina nodded. "You will be my daughter's mother in my stead."

Mary wound her arms around her mother's neck, kissing her cheek. "I love my Lady Margaret, but I love you with all my heart. I have only one Mama."

Written on the twenty-eighth day of May, 1520, Canterbury

Doña, my dear Latina,

I write to you Whitsunweek. The court makes its slow way to Dover, where the ships wait to take us to Calais. I know I wrote to tell you of the English court's preparations these last months for the King of England to parley with the French King. We stay at the palace of the Archbishop of Canterbury, a short distance from Dover and the ships waiting to take us to Calais. But we presently delay our journey to welcome to England the queen's nephew, the Emperor Charles.

In the chamber prepared for the queen's use, María padded over to the queen's jewellery coffer, passing Maud Parr, who carried the queen's silver lamé underdress. Catalina held up her arms as Maud pulled the underdress over her head. Another of the queen's women, Joan Guildford, waited close by, holding the gold gown lined with violet velvet, trimmed with winter ermine. The light from the nearby fire, burning bright in the enormous fireplace, caught the gold Tudor roses embroidered on its trim.

For a breath, the roses glittered like stars. One of the many new gowns made for Catalina during the six months' wait for their expected journey to Calais, and their meeting with the French king, the gown glistened like fluid gold.

At last, María located the ropes of pearls and heavy diamond cross Catalina wished to wear. Picking them up, she stood looking at the lustre and iridescence of the pearls – they seemed alive in her hands. She brought them to Catalina, carefully pulling the strings over her queen's head, making certain the pearls hung perfectly, before attaching the cross to one of the strings of pearls. She next placed on Catalina's head her black velvet hood, adorned with dazzling jewels and glistening pearls. Stepping back to check everything, María noticed Catalina's hands trembling as she smoothed down the skirt of her gown. *I would be nervous, too. She not only meets for the first time her nephew Charles, but an emperor too.*

"Do you think my nephew will be proud of me? Catalina asked.

Laughing with the other women, María bobbed a curtsey. "Madam, I tell you true, you have no need to ask such questions. Ever. You are our queen, and we are proud to own you as such."

Catalina clasped her hands in front of her as if wishing to still them. "This is a special day for me. I have long desired to see my nephew, the emperor. If I was not Queen of this land, he would be my sovereign." She stroked the top of her bodice with both hands and firmed her shoulders. "Time for us to go."

Gathering behind Catalina with the other women, María followed the queen to the grand hall. Last night, Will had told her stories of many royal weddings and banquets held here in the past. Now, servants rushed about, preparing for another banquet – one held in honour of Catalina's nephew.

Catalina headed deeper into the chamber, towards her waiting husband. His sister Mary and her husband, long returned to the king's favour, stood near him, and a young, tall man with shoulder length dark hair. He had the strangest face María had ever seen in her life. Juana, his mother, and even Catalina, possessed a jaw which jutted out, but only a little; his jutted out so much María needed to look away to hide her first shock of seeing him.

But Catalina did not seem to notice her nephew's peculiar face. Approaching him, she started to curtsey to him, but he forestalled her by removing his bonnet and dropping to his knees before her. "I ask for your blessing, Aunt."

Visibly moved, Catalina straightened and rested her hand on his bare head. "With all my heart, I bless you, my lord and beloved nephew. Rise up, and let me embrace you."

Bounding up, Charles embraced Catalina. She held on to him tightly for a moment before breaking away to wipe her face. "Pray, forgive me, but I am so happy. I never thought this day would come."

Charles smiled at Catalina again, and then at a woman who stood a few steps behind him. Robed as if one of highest rank, the beautiful, dark-haired woman, close to María and Catalina's own age, curtseyed in answer to Charles's beckoning gesture and came forward to stand next to him.

"You will be pleased to greet this lady too. This is your step-mother, Germaine de Foix."

Catalina acted as if she did not know the woman was also her nephew's mistress. She greeted her father's widow in French with delight and charm. María joined the queen's women, standing some distance away as the English royals engaged in pleasantries with the emperor and his mistress. Time came for Catalina to bid her nephew a brief farewell. She returned to her chambers to rest before the evening festivities. The great hall looked very different when they returned. Long tables, set out with white tablecloths, stretched along the walls, with the royal tables being at either end of the chamber. Happy to be seated beside Will, María had just started eating the dishes of the first course when the trumpeter blew out long notes and the floor shook under her feet. The Duke of Buckingham rode in on a white horse, reining it in at the emperor's table. He bounded off to kneel to the royal visitor

"He wants England to strengthen its ties to the emperor, not to the French King," Will said quietly close to her ear. "I hear he is furious Wolsey was sent by the king to Dover to welcome the emperor and escort him to Canterbury. All know the duke believes the cardinal has too much power over the king."

María sighed. She remembered Catalina telling her Buckingham desired – no, demanded – the king's ear. He hated the man he called the son of a butcher, and claimed the cardinal preened his wealth like King Henry himself. "The king was furious at the duke for speaking as he did," she murmured. Will frowned. "The duke is not the only one to hate the cardinal. Did you see our archbishop of Canterbury's black- storm face when he welcomed the cardinal to his palace today? No love lost there either. The look Archbishop Warham gave the cardinal was not one I would expect for a man of God."

There was another grim moment during the emperor's visit. At the end of the first course, Buckingham, as the king's chief sewer, held the bowl for the king to wash his hands. Wolsey took the opportunity to wash his hands too. The duke's eyes blazed with fury and he over tipped the bowl. María heard a few cut-off titters of laughter as the water poured onto the cardinal's jewelled shoes. The cardinal glared at the duke as if he could murder him while the king looked on.

María clasped her hands to keep them from shaking. *The king appears amused – but his eyes...they are like a bird of prey – preparing for the kill.* She leaned closer to Will and whispered, "Buckingham should know the king tires of his arrogance. If his game continues with the cardinal, he is likely to come out the loser."

15

Dare to declare who you are. It is not far from the shores of silence to the boundaries of speech. The path is not long, but the way is deep. You must not only walk there, you must be prepared to leap.

~ Hildegard of Bingen

The twenty-eighth day of May, 1520

Doña, my dear Latina,

I wait at Dover to board our ship for the court's crossing to Calais. The queen is still overjoyed about the recent visit of her nephew. She looks forward to meeting him again at Gravelines after the summit with the French King...

María looked out to the white cliffs of Dover, the deck of *Katherine Pleasaunce* rocking with the waves under her feet. Many years ago, the storms bringing them to England had kept them imprisoned inside a dark ship cabin, forbidden from seeing their first sight of their new country. She was not even certain if that long-ago terrible journey would have given her view of these majestic white cliffs, more impregnable than any royal fortress. She only knew the cliffs left her in awe, and took her mind away for a time from fearing the coming journey.

The smell of rosewater wafted towards her and combatted the sea air. Mary, the Duchess of Suffolk, approached, making her way through the multitude of men and women on deck, bowing or curtseying as she passed. When Mary came to stand beside her, María curtseyed too.

"What a swarm of people," Mary said, "and this is but one of our vessels taking my brother's court to meet with the king of France. My brother boasts six thousand men and women are going across to Calais." She leaned her arms on the railing and looked out at the cliffs. "The last time I had this same view, I cursed my royal blood – and dreaded arriving in France. I was ill all the way – and not simply because of the rough sea voyage." Deciding to take liberty on their friendship, María leaned on her arms on the railing, too. "But look what happened. Four months later, you married the man you loved."

Mary turned her eyes to sea. She shook her head, and visibly swallowed. "My short marriage to the French King seemed an eternity," she said softly. "And I had to pretend to be happy, and welcome my old husband to my bed." She shrugged, and laughed a little. "He was gentle with me – and surprisingly a good lover. But... he wanted my show of passion to be real, when

I had to steel myself to smile and welcome his hands and lips on me. The only thing to get me through the nights was to close my eyes and pretend it was Charles, and not Louis." She visibly shivered. "In the end, I felt like a whore."

María shifted, her stomach roiling. *I want you, my whore. Come here to me*, the king's voice said in her mind. As a close attendant to the queen, it often seemed her close to daily contact with the king was her punishment for that night. That and her dead son. The king, on the other hand, treated her with friendliness. Will had become more loyal to his king after his many kindnesses after the loss of their first born. Once more, the king engaged her in conversation about herbal remedies and treatments for various ailments. It was like he forgot that night. She would never forget. At times, she tottered on the edge of madness, wondering if his new-found friendliness was due to relief about the death of her boy. He likely thought he had been freed from Catalina ever finding out about what happened between them. Like Mary with her first husband, María steeled herself to smile and act as if she welcomed his friendship – while all the time she hated him.

"Perhaps we are all whores, men and women alike," she said slowly. "We do what we have to survive."

"You sound world-weary, my friend."

She glanced at Mary. *Si – I can speak freely to her. I have always spoken freely to her.* "Tell me true, why do you keep the trappings and style of the queen of France if you hated your time in the king's bed?"

Mary's eyes widened. Flushing, she lowered her head. "You want the truth? I earned it," she said softly. She inhaled and let out a deep breath. "I was indeed a whore." Mary looked in the direction of where her husband stood talking and laughing to the king. "Men make us such when they give us no choice in the matter."

Mary's words piercing her heart, María blinked away the sudden smart of tears. "I think it would be best to talk about the weather," she said in a rush. "These blue skies promise a short and easy crossing, do you not think?"

Mary lifted an eyebrow. "Do you have a secret, María, one you do not want to share with me."

Aware of her heating face, María looked back out to sea. She swallowed down her panic. "We all have secrets," she said slowly. "As for sharing mine with you... some secrets must never be shared. They are our penance and must go with us to our graves.

Mary frowned, her eyes on her husband and brother. "Yes. You indeed speak the truth."

María bobbed a brief curtsey. "I must go and check on the queen. She is unwell, and our Countess of Salisbury is keeping her company. And I must check on my husband too. My strong man dreads the sea crossing and has already taken to his bed." Cold at heart, María weaved wearily through the courtiers, making her return to the queen's cabin. All the way there, she seemed to carry not only the burden of her own secrets, but Mary's too. *It is none of your business. She can keep hers, and I will keep mine.*

<hr>

María could not take her eyes away from Guisnes Castle as she rode beside Meg Pole, and behind the queen and the duchess. In front of the old castle, another palace rose to a height of about thirty feet. Canvas and timber walls gave the mock palace the illusion of brick, and the painted canvas roof with its tall chimneys looked like slate. Diamond pane glass stretched across half the building. Struck by sunlight, the palace sparkled like a jewel on a green hill.

Close to one of the drinking fountains set before the building, near its elaborate staircase, María gave her horse over to one of the waiting stableboys, then followed Meg. The king and his men had arrived some time before the queen and her party. She suspected Will was already in the palace, somewhere, likely occupied with the king.

Soon falling behind Meg's longer leg stride, María made her way through the gatehouse of the palace to inside the huge banquet hall, bigger than most of the king's other banquet halls in his palaces in England. Tudor roses decorated the gold ceiling and a set off at dawn to ensure all was ready for her, directed the queen and her party to her chambers, leading them through the pretend palace to a short bridge taking them to the castle, the duchess and her attendants going with her chamberlain in the opposite direction. All around, tapestries hung on the walls. Glitter of gold thread and the abundance of densely embroidered cushions were scattered everywhere.

With Mountjoy leading, they made their way through the state bedchamber towards the secret way taking them to the short bridge connecting the mock castle to the real one, where rooms had been prepared for Catalina. Close to the state bed, María paused beside the open door of Catalina's closet to peer in.

Catalina came back with Meg Pole. "Go inside and satisfy your curiosity," Catalina said.

María stepped into the closet. Its interior was decorated with pearls and jewels, and a cornice of gold. A window in the closet looked down to the chapel where there were twelve gold statues, as tall as a child, each representing an apostle.

"They say the chapel is as big as the banquet room," Catalina remarked beside her. "I asked Westminster Abbey to send over silver, jewels, relics and the rich vestments of the king's father. All is ready to impress the French." Catalina looped her arm through hers. "My sister, let's go to my bedchamber in the castle. I am tired."

They crossed over to the castle and arrived at her rooms. Less impressive than the rooms in the mock palace, built purely with the intention to impress the French, the castle's chambers were also smaller and more comfortable: one of the queen's own beds had been sent over for their stay. Catalina sat on the bed with obvious relief. "You may go," she said to her other women, "Find out where you are lodged for our stay. You too, my good Countess of Salisbury. The Baroness will keep me company while I rest and wait the arrival of the French King and his queen."

As the door closed on the last of the women, María crossed the room to Catalina and sat beside her. She looked at her friend, and away, trying to control her anxiety. Catalina's skin was as pale as milk, and she looked much older than her thirty-four years. María clasped her hand. "You're not well."

Catalina shrugged. "I will be better once I have a chance to rest." She laughed a little. "The girl I was at fifteen faced a more perilous sea crossing than the one we just experienced. I was resilient then, not so now."

"You are not well." María examined Catalina's hand. Her

friend's fingers were so puffy her rings dug into her flesh. "We must do something about this swelling. I shall prepare you a dandelion tea. That will help."

Catalina made a face. "If you must. All the dandelion teas you have made for me over the years, and I still hate the taste."

"It works, and honey makes it more to your liking."

Catalina glanced longingly over her shoulder at her bed. "I think one hour of sleep will put me to rights." She turned to María. "Pray, help me take off my gown, and I will lay down for a time. Then you can find that husband of yours and see where you have been placed, while I rest."

"You do not need me to stay?"

"I will always need you, but I need sleep more than your company at this moment. I must make ready to face these next two weeks."

The sun lowered in the sky, and three cannon shots shattered the peace, signalling the appointed hour for King Henry to ride out to meet King François on Corpus Christi day. Trumpets sounded long, throbbing notes, answered on the other side of the valley by the trumpets of the French.

María lifted a hand to protect her eyes from the rays of a sinking sun, glad the day's scorching heat had cooled, and became more bearable. Standing on the battlements of Guisnes Castle with the queen and the duchess of Suffolk, and a few of their favourite women, María watched the king ride his horse to the valley between Guisnes and Arde to meet King François alone She raked her eyes over the hundreds of horsemen who accompanied the king, trying to locate Will and his men. Her heart swelling with pride, she smiled when she identified his colours and banners.

A large gold marquee had been pitched beside the mock castle for the banquet taking place once the kings finished these first formalities. Gold seemed to be everywhere – not only in a field where golden grass grew, and the gold tents spreading out as far as the eye could see, but also in the golden chains of office worn by the nobles and courtiers of the English court. Erasmus had once told her the English courtiers liked to show off the massive chains on their shoulders because it not only showed how strong they were, but also how wealthy. Recalling his words, María came close to laughing out loud, but then a more serious memory stirred. She remembered the battlefields of her childhood – when Queen Isabel had taken her children to witness the final fall of Granada. The fall of Granada had come with a promise of peace, but the fighting between Christian and Moor continued on for years. One battle took the life of her father.

Today, on both sides of the valley, gathered thousands. *They said this summit too would bring peace – peace for all time between England and France. Both kings bring here an army, an army disguised in rich clothes, displaying the wealth of the nobility of both countries. But the English and French have always warred with one another. All I see is the reminder of the fragility of peace.* The steady movement of the courts of two kings caused dust to rise in the air. Most were foot soldiers, but standing out from the multitude of men were also hundreds of King Henry's archers. Selected for their height and skill, they looked distinctive in their red coats with a band of gold decoration.

"I wish we could hear what is going on," said Mary.

"We cannot hear, but we can see." Catalina pointed. "Look – there are the heralds of the kings. The king, my husband, told me they will tell everyone to stand still, and keep to their own side, while he meets with King François. The kings' retinues move on the pain of death."

Mary folded her arms on the battlements. "King François and my royal brother move towards each other," she said. "They are raising their black velvet bonnets to one another. They move their horses closer and embrace each other. See the Marquess of Dorset holding the king's sword? He has with him the greyhounds brought as gifts for King François. Oh – a French noble also holds the sword of his king." She pointed. "I recognise his livery. That's Louis, the Duc de Bourbon, the king's cousin. He is like Buckingham to our king."

"Does not my husband look handsome," said Catalina.

María recognised it as a comment, not a question, and hid a smile when several of the attending women chimed in with their agreement.

The two kings dismounted from their horses and embraced again. There was no mistaking King Henry. Dressed in all the trappings of his estate, he was tall, lean and – at twenty-nine – young. His garb of silver cloth ribbed with gold and studded with jewels shone in the sun. The wind caught the black feathers on his bonnet as the king placed it back on his head.

María cringed to see Catalina's look of love and devotion. All her life, she was blind to the men close to her. She believed they deserved her love; it was like she had to believe it for her own chance at happiness.

Her heart heavy for her friend, María turned her head and

studied the nearby tiltyard, said to be twice the size of the one used at Whitehall. One tall and broad artificial tree, with green damask leaves, was set at the top of the yard. A pretty sight, but one with a serious purpose. Tomorrow, the tree would be used to hang the shields of the competitors. Empty of people, the field seemed so innocent. María shuddered, her heart heavy for another cause. Despite her determined efforts to persuade him otherwise, Will had entered the lists. He told her he would be considered a coward if he did not. She told him she preferred a coward husband to a dead one. It had led to one of their rare arguments. She decided to hold her tongue, and prayed she would not regret it.

"He has skinny legs," Catalina said beside her.

Brought back from her musing, María looked again at the valley with its huge gathering of men. "Who has?" she asked, bewildered.

Mary laughed, looking aside at Catalina. "Methinks my good sister means the French king. He lacks the calve muscles of our three good husbands. His legs were but sticks when I knew him in France, and they are the same now."

"The king, my husband, and the French king go now to the marquee to talk. Wolsey goes with them." Catalina stood back from the battlements, taking the arm of her sister-in-law. "The king told me this meeting will likely be a long undertaking." She jutted out her chin, and pursed her mouth. "They ratify the treaty betrothing my daughter to the dauphin."

María lowered her eyes for a moment, suspecting the harsh words Catalina really wanted to say.

Catalina looked around at the other women. "Let's return to my chambers and eat together. All of us. Tomorrow will involve us more, and it would be good for us to talk about how we expect the day to proceed."

***

That night, King Henry and Catalina hosted the French king and his court at an elaborate banquet. María sat with Will on one side, and George Cavendish, the cardinal's gentleman- usher and secretary, on the other. She missed Meg's company – but Meg's higher rank and kinship to the king saw her placed on a table closer to the royal dais.

"The French say they never saw the like, nor me too," George said to them, before biting into one of the subtleties.

It was true – the cooks had out-done themselves. On the tables, the servants set out what looked like London itself: dishes shaped like castles, a huge replica of St Paul's church, even figures of people – some fighting with weapons, some jousting, men and women dancing. The room was ablaze with the light of countless candles, light glittering the gold on the table into a golden haze.

All through the long hours of the banquet, María kept glancing at Catalina. Finally, Will clasped her hand. "Dear Heart, you cannot always help her. Come, wife, come and dance with me."

Stepping out in a second dance with Will, María noticed Thomas More and Bishop Fisher leaving together, deep in talk. She wished they could do the same. But the Duchess of Suffolk, who led the dancing, had asked her to stay at the banquet until the dancing came to an end, and help make up the English party demonstrating their skill. Her eyes drawn again to Catalina, she thanked God the Duchess of Suffolk had agreed to lead the dancing and freed her far too wan queen and friend to converse with the French king and his nobles.

Does Catalina look so pale because she somehow learnt of what Will told me before the banquet? He had overheard the king speaking to Wolsey about his disquiet about his marriage. "God punishes me for marrying my brother's widow by giving me dead sons," King Henry had said to the cardinal. Then he had asked the cardinal for ways he could annul his marriage.

Two days later, early in the morning, one of Catalina's maidservants brought a message from the Countess of Salisbury. Meg asked her to come to the queen's chambers in the old castle, without delay. Going through the queen's privy room, the maid opened the door to Catalina's bedchamber. Meg stood white-faced outside of the stool room. Hearing a long moan come from the room, María hurried over. "Catalina...?" Answered by another moan – but much louder this time, María saw the fear she felt reflected in Meg's eyes. Without another thought, María pushed open the door. Catalina was down on her knees, her head bowed. Blood seeped through her shift, and spread out all around her. Gagging at the smell of blood in the enclosed space, María rushed to crouch down beside her. "Oh, my sister, my poor sister," she whispered.

Catalina held out a shaking hand. "Please help me up."

Gingerly threading her arm under Catalina's, María wound her arm around her back. It took all her strength to assist Catalina to stand and out of the stool room. "Are you miscarrying? Why didn't you tell me –?" Helped by Meg, María walked Catalina to her bed, thankful it was not the state bed placed in the artificial palace, a place for show and not for true habitation. "I'll go and find a midwife."

Leaning her head on her shoulder, Catalina shook her head. "Please, María. Not the midwife. I want you and Meg, and no one else."

Meeting Catalina's pleading eyes, María sat her friend on the bed, looking around for towels. She spied some on a small table beside a clothes chest. "Stay here with Catalina," she said to Meg. "Do not let her move." She raced across to grab the towels. Meg was trying to untie the laces of Catalina's shift when she came back to the bed. Catalina's eyes were sunk into a face the colour of milk curds. She looked moments from fainting.

María tossed out one of the large towels onto the bed, putting the other beside it. "Lie down. I will place a towel between your legs."

Helped again by Meg, María placed a pillow under Catalina's head and under her knees before cupping her hand on the side of her face, "Are you certain you do not want me to find a midwife? I am told there are several in the camp."

Catalina reached for her hand and kept hold of it. "I am not with child. Harry no longer beds with me."

María could not take her eyes away from Catalina. "But – this blood... it cannot be from your monthly courses....'

"Monthly courses. I wish I had monthly courses. Since the beginning of the year, I have bled every day. How can my husband bed with me if I am always bleeding? Alice has given me herbs to help me on these days. I did not ask her to come with us to France. If Alice was here, people would think I was with child. You must know of these herbs too?"

María swallowed, horrified. After the birth of her daughter, she lived part of the week at court and part of the week with Will and her child at their London home. When in London, and if weather allowed, she always tried her best to return to her child by nightfall. Meg lived rarely at court, so Catalina would have found it easy to hide it from her too. She shook her head, scolding herself at her blindness. "Yes, I have what we need," she said slowly, the guilt eating away at her. "I'll go for my medicine chest, and prepare you something to ease the bleeding."

Catalina tightened her hold on her hand and reached out to clasp Meg's too. "Please do not tell anyone about this. I do not want my husband to know I am ill."

María could barely look at Catalina. *I have been so caught up with my daughter, I failed my sister. Failed her. Si – failed her again.* "You can trust me to stay silent. I will go now. When I return, I want you to tell us why you never told me about your troubles."

***

The next day, María remained in the stands with the other women attending Catalina. Her stomach hurt – the gnaw of her insides increasing with every moment, as her apprehension for her friend competed with her apprehension for Will. Relieved her potion of herbs had managed to control Catalina's bleeding, she could do little to return her to good health. The loss of blood had aged Catalina beyond her years. She looked what she was – an ill woman.

María prayed Catalina would last out another long day without a collapse, thanking God Catalina did not need to walk to the tilt yard. Her open litter – clad in crimson satin embroidered in gold relief –waited to bear her there. Mary, too, would be taken in her cloth of gold litter, with its porcupine emblems of her dead royal husband, Louis XII of France. Their women followed – either in wagons festooned with gold or crimson cloth, or, as María and Meg Pole chose to do, on horseback. She wanted to laugh when she compared her rich red velvet gown to the horse's saddle – not too certain if her costly garb outdid the horse's rich trappings.

Young Wyatt approached the wagon with the other women. Not long at court, and the son of Sir Henry Wyatt, a loyal servant of the king, the seventeen-year-old youth was handsome, deep thinking and gifted. Catalina liked him well. Recognising his talents as a poet and lute player, she often invited him to her chamber to play to her and her women, entertaining them as they sewed or read. Wyatt helped the last woman into the wagon and turned, blinking against the sunlight. "Verily, good dames, we are ready to go," he said with a laugh.

María looked over her shoulder at the men on horseback. They wheeled their mounts, creating a dust storm, before reining them to a halt. The palfreys pranced as if ready to bolt at the slightest fright. Meg rode her horse beside hers and glanced at her. "You wear a strange smile, my friend."

María shrugged. "I am thinking men play silly games."

"Silly games?" Meg laughed grimly. "Deadly games more like."

A trumpet blared out a long and bold note, announcing the

arrival of Catalina. Trailing on the ground, her purple cloak opened to reveal glittering jewels in her gown.

María's heart seemed to stop in her chest. *Catalina looks like her mother, Queen Isabel, God rest her soul.*

Despite looking unwell, Catalina stood upright, every inch a queen, and greeted Queen Claude and Louise of Savoy, her mother-in-law, with charm and grace. Claude, a pleasant looking rather than pretty young woman, wore a silver gown over the top of a gold undergarment. Precious stones glittered in the necklace she wore around her neck. She did not hide her advanced pregnancy. Catalina tried to engage her and the king's mother in conversation, but both women seemed disinclined to speak. Claude narrowed her eyes at Mary as if she saw a snake.

Catalina took her seat in the gallery beside her sister-in-law and the French Queen sat with the king's mother, ready to watch the men compete against each other on the tilt field and to cheer on their husbands, or son.

María took her own seat amongst the forty or so women who attended the queens and King François's mother. She listened for a time to all the other sounds mingling with that of men and women of the two courts. Horses neighed. The pounding of horses' hooves shook the ground. The lowing of cattle and the baaing of sheep broke in often too – animals brought for the slaughter for nightly banquets. Hearing the crack of a whip and a horse scream, she winced. *Likely someone punishes the animal for its disinterest in today's competition.* María bent her head and prayed again. *Dear God – keep Will safe. Do not let him be hurt.*

The heat making her thirsty, María accepted a large flask of wine from Maud Parr, gulped down several mouthfuls before passing it back. When it became time for Will to join the competitions, she took the flask back from Maud, hoping the wine would dull her fear. When Will left the competition early after two quick defeats – first in the joust, and then fighting out his swordfight, she wanted to cheer, her joy at seeing him leave the field lightening her heart. But her joy did not stay with her for long. Soon after Will's defeat, a young French noble, jousting against his own brother, was killed before her eyes. Sickened, thinking how easily it could have been Will, María remembered from her childhood the roar of a crowd competing with a death scream. She saw in her mind the young matador fighting the bull like a dancer – each movement graceful and skilful, so certain of victory. One moment, he celebrated with the crowd, the next, the enraged, injured bull gored him to death. She had wanted to run from the stands then too – but, like this present moment, when a brother wept over his dead brother, she knew she must keep her seat. It did not stop her feeling ill, or help her contain her terror at the thought Will might decide to fight again. It took all her effort to school her face and keep her emotions under control.

Their faces still and expressionless, Catalina and Mary hid any trace of fear while watching their husbands battle it out with their competitors. María knew they feared for their men too, but they were also familiar with their husbands' skills. Today, King Henry and the duke, more often than not, claimed the victory.

That did not prevent King Henry from spraining his hand when he engaged in combat with King François. A terrifying fight to watch, the two men struck each other with such speed and force it caused sparks to shoot out from their armour. King François ended the day with a black eye, and also a dead horse.

María had enough of the day by then, and relieved when Catalina – who appeared more than simply unwell – decided Queen Claude's departure signalled her own departure. Fearing her friend had started bleeding again, María followed with the other women and made her way back to the queen's apartments. She was determined to make Catalina lie down again.

Leaving Catalina in a poppy-induced sleep, María slipped out of her friend's bedchamber and headed to the chapel. She wanted to pray, not only for Catalina, but also to give thanks her husband emerged unscathed from the lists. She entered the chapel, and once more took in the gold and silk interior, perfect for an altar covered with cloth of gold interwoven with an abundance of large, white pearls.

"How dare you?" Mary, the Duchess of Suffolk said in anger.

Realising how close Mary must be, María hid behind the silver organ in fright.

A man's voice spoke softly in French, his reply too soft to be clear. Deep and distinct, he spoke again. María covered her mouth, almost gasping out loud. It was the French King.

"I've missed you, my dear," he said. "I thought you might be bored by now with your English husband – and ready to resume where we left off. My dear, you are even more beautiful than I remember."

A smack resounded in the chapel. "Do not touch me. I was a fool to ever agree to this meeting. Let me go. Let me go before you live to regret it."

"Years ago, you sang a different tune. You could have been my queen, my dear."

"How could that be – you are married to Claude, and would never want to be married to you. I said, let go of me. I will scream. That would put an end to any chance of peace between you and my brother."

"And here I was thinking you would still be grateful for the service I did for you years ago."

"You made me pay for it."

"You should not complain. You gained the husband you wanted, and stole a fortune belonging to France. I should break your pretty neck, my dear."

"I am warning you, if you do not release me, I will scream for help. I do not care if you are the King of France. I am no servant girl for you to treat me like this."

"See how I obey you, Mary. How sadly changed you are, my dear. So – you do not care if your husband learns the truth about us?"

Terrified to move or make a sound, María became aware of silence before a swish of silk ripped it apart. "I thought I did. I only came today because your letter made me think you planned to tell him. But I know my husband – he will forgive me. I am willing to tell him if it means it finally frees me from needing to speak to you again. He will be hurt, and I wished to save him that, but I will see to it his hurt lasts only a short time. Farewell, and I vow this time it will be for good."

Air rushed past María as the duchess dashed for the chapel's entrance. Light, slow footsteps followed and the door of the chapel closed.

The chapel silent at last, María stepped out from her hiding place. *Poor Mary, I know your secret.* She sighed. *Perchance all women have such secrets.*

"Claude, Queen of France," Lord Mountjoy announced, falling back from the door of Catalina's private chamber.

María fell to her knees between Countess of Salisbury and Maude Parr, the three of them asked by Catalina to remain with her whilst she spoke to her royal counterpart, who entered the room, followed by several attendants. Catalina rose from her seat and crossed the room to meet her halfway. Both women curtseyed to the other. Claude's big belly made her curtsey clumsy and not as low as Catalina's.

Catalina took the younger woman's hand, and began speaking in French. "I am so pleased you accepted my invitation to come today. I wish to thank you again for my litter and mules."

"And I for my new palfreys. I look forward to the time when I can ride them."

"Let's talk privately while our husbands compete again on the tiltyard." Catalina gestured to the nearby high-back chairs. "Come and sit with me. Our women can sit together at the end of the chamber."

Seated across from Claude, Catalina smiled her most winning smile. "Are you hungry, Your Grace? I can send for food from the kitchen."

Claude placed her hand on her belly. "Wine would suffice, Queen Katherine. I have not long eaten, but this child of mine makes me suffer if I eat overmuch."

Waving for a servant to bring over a tray with wine and goblets, Catalina turned back to Claude. "I am the same when I'm with child."

Taking a goblet, Claude sipped for a moment before lifting a face of sympathy. "It grieved me to hear of your last misfortune. I pray for you that you will one day have your prince."

As she too took a goblet, Catalina averted her face. "I pray for that too, but for a prince who lives. I have had three sons God has called out of this world." She raised her goblet and drank deep, before lowering her head. "I know you too have lost children, but I am glad for you. You are blessed with two living sons, and I thank God for my daughter. If I have no son, she will rule England as its queen."

"I wish it was the same in France. As you know, I am Duchess of Brittany in my own stead, but both my mother and myself married France to protect Brittany. But I am happy to leave politics to my Lord husband." Claude clasped the crucifix hanging on her rosary. "My concerns are not of this world. I serve God."

Looking at Claude with greater interest, Catalina drank again. "I serve God, too, although I confess I do concern myself with worldly affairs. I have always believed queenship means serving God by doing right by my country, and my husband."

Claude's eyes narrowed. "We have spoken with honesty to one another, my good Queen of England. I did wonder to my husband how the king, your husband, managed to convince you of the rightness of the betrothal of our infant children – and spending of a kingly fortune for these two weeks of tournaments and banquets. I may not wish to concern myself with this world, but I cannot avoid it – especially when it concerns my sons. Katherine of England has never been a friend of France."

"Katherine of England is wife to Henry of England. If my lord husband commands me to be a friend of France, I will obey." Catalina smiled at the younger woman. "Queen of France, I do not like war. If these two weeks ensure peace between our two countries, I am more than willing to put aside my personal feelings about the French. I want what is best for England."

"You speak as one who loves a country not of their birth."

Catalina laughed a little, pointing at María. "You see there my lady? Lady María is my kinswoman and we grew up together at the court of my mother, the great Isabel of famed memory. Nearly twenty years of living in England has not made my kinswoman love the land. She says she hates the winters and the rain, but she is like me – we not only love our English husbands, but the people of the land – from high to low. And if she was truthful, she would admit there are many days in our adoptive country which make one think Heaven must indeed be heavenly if it compares more with the skies and green hills of England."

María could not help herself from grinning. She bowed her head to the French Queen. "The queen is right. There are indeed days in England which make me forget the winters, and forgive it for the rain. I forgive it even more now I am married to an Englishman."

Queen Claude smiled. "When I was a child, one of my nursemaids told me the English have tails."

María caught Catalina's eyes and they both burst out chortling. The French Queen laughed too, but then looked inquisitively from María to Catalina. "Can I ask you to share the reason for your great amusement?"

Catalina leaned her elbow on her armrest, and cradled the side of her face in a hand. She gave a short laugh. "When we were girls, we heard the same story – except the tails belonged to the French."

Claude cocked her head, her eyes full of mischief again. She spoke softly in Latin this time. "I am not French, but a woman of Brittany. Let's say no more."

By the time Queen Claude left Catalina's chambers, the two queens had bonded in a friendship displayed to both courts the next day. At Mass, when it came time to kiss the offered golden Pax, Catalina gestured for Claude to go first, then Queen Claude, and back and forth it continued until both women started laughing, waved aside the Pax and kissed each other instead.

The next day, the wind became even stronger. It howled and whined, cutting though the forest. Leaves and dust lifted from the ground, swirling upwards and gathering into a grey cloud of litter.

A whirl of leaves hit María, and dust blew into her eyes. Blinded for a few seconds, she rubbed her eyes, gazing up. Lightning bolts lit the dark sky. All around, the wind strengthened and screamed, bowing tops of trees in its path. Thunder boomed like cannon shots. When lightning struck a nearby tree, she nearly lost control of her bladder. Fighting dizziness from the fright of it and the smell of sulphur, she lifted her skirts from the ground and ran back to the pavilions as the rain pelted down.

"María," Will shouted. Her husband hurried to her. He grabbed her hand, and pulled her along faster.

"Wait!" María laughed. Halting, letting go of Will's hand, she shook the rain from her gable. Pulling her skirts through the girdle of her gown to free her feet, she clasped his hand again. Running together, they raced to the tent given for their use. With cold, clumsy fingers, she untied the cords of the opening to slip inside. She looked around, thanking God the opening had been securely closed. Everything was as when they had left it to attend to their duties, untouched by rain or wind.

"Yet another storm," Will murmured, helping her take off her cloak. "You're drenched through!"

In the dull light, María looked at his blond hair. Rain drops dripped from its ends. She laughed, caressing his wet cheek. Noting his smooth skin, she smiled. She had protested about his bristles this morning. Somehow, he had found time to shave. "You are too. I'll get us some dry clothes."

Since their handful of servants had been granted leave to go to the nearby fair, she hurried over to their clothes coffers and sorted out what they needed. She turned to find her husband barelegged, wearing just his shirt with the drawstrings pulled wide open. Nearing forty, he stood loose limbed and tall, his fair hair duller and shorter than when they had first met decades ago, but still thick enough for her to relish running her fingers through it. She delighted in him; her beloved husband, this man in his prime. A man always comfortable in his own skin, and his surroundings.

María put their garments on the spare pallet next to the

main one, took off her gable and began unlacing her gown. Will came over, tugged and loosened the cords. Her heavy skirt dropped to the ground, followed by the arms of her dress and her bodice. He slipped his arms around her waist, and nibbled at her neck. He slipped her loosened shift off her shoulders, letting it fall between them, cupping her naked breasts in his hands. She leaned back, closed her eyes, rubbing her bottom gently against him. She turned to meet his eyes. Yearning and desire weakened her knees, and drew up like a tide within her. She glanced at the entrance to the tent. It flapped like a mad thing in the wind.

"Wait," she said again, laughing. She broke away, secured the cords and returned to Will. She stroked his cheek again, this time, trailing her fingers slowly down his face. "Do you think we have time? There'll likely be a page here any moment summoning you to the king or me to the queen."

"In this storm?" Will turned her around. His hot mouth began sucking and kissing her neck slowly from ear to shoulder. "If it is anything like the last one, it will last for hours." His fingers caressed her nipples until they became hard. Her head began to spin while her insides ached and demanded release. "Listen to the wind, my María, my wife. Do you not hear its passion? It reminds me I haven't bedded with you since we came to France."

Twisting in his arms, she took his face between her hands and kissed him; there seemed nectar on his lips. She laughed a little. *Si, I am but the bee in search of it.* She shut her eyes, her head spinning more. Moaning, she sank to the ground, bringing him with her.

Something snapped outside and crashed to the earth. The wind blew in and out the sides of the tent canvas. She tightened her hold on her husband. "Will! The tent is going to fall on top of us!"

He kissed her, pushing her down on the bedclothes of their pallet. "So, if it does? It will not kill us. And if it does, can you think of a better way to die?"

María laughed up at him, wrapped her arms around him and kissed and kissed him until all the world and its cares disappeared.

King Henry met again with the French King. Whiling away the day with the other women, María listened to the wind blowing in fury outside. She lifted her eyes from completing the tiny bodice she sewed for her daughter. *I cannot wait to return home and hold my baby again.* Nearby, a young servant girl stood on tiptoes to light candles in the sconces with a long taper. The servant was quiet in her movements, but everyone in Catalina's chamber was quiet. Even when María pushed her needle through the thick scarlet damask, the sound of needle piercing fabric seemed magnified. For more than one hour, all Catalina's women remained as silent as possible while Catalina played chess with a noble English girl they had met for the first time at The Field of Gold. A noble girl who had lived in France for years in the household of Queen Claude.

The only real noise in the chamber came from the queen's two monkeys. Cradled by two of the women, the animals – recent gifts to Henry VIII from the Ottoman Sultan – chattered, gave an occasional shriek as they groomed themselves, pulling off the gold leaf from their fur. The animals stayed in

Catalina's chambers whenever King Henry did not want their entertainment. King François liked the trained monkeys so much he asked for them to be included at every banquet.

María started sewing again, pricking her finger when one of the monkeys screamed again. Threading the needle for safe-keeping in the bodice for her infant daughter, she sucked her finger, tasting the salt of her own blood, and returned her eyes to the chess game and its unfolding battle.

Catalina moved her chess piece, smiling a little at the dark haired, dark eyed girl who played against her. Light turned the grey-blue of Catalina's eyes to the colour of the shimmering sea.

Nan Bullen frowned, and frowned deeper when one of the monkeys broke out in a long chatter, all the while focusing on the chess board.

Still sucking her sore finger, María shifted on her stool, uneasy with how the game had gone from simple enjoyment to something more serious. The girl played the game to win, and so did the queen. Setting back in her chair, Catalina lifted her hand and rubbed her temple. It was a gesture taking María back many years, to another queen. Catalina's mother had done exactly the same in moments of stress.

The diamond panes of the near window criss-crossed both girl and queen with their shadows. The lowering sun shone harsh on Catalina. She screwed up her eyes as if struggling to see. But not one word of grievance passed from her lips. She just continued to concentrate on achieving victory.

Chess pieces clicked together on the board. Beaming with victory, Nan Bullen held out her palm to the queen with her black king piece on it.

Catalina sat back again. "You play an excellent game,

Mistress Bullen. When you return to England, I hope you will join my women. Few dare win against me; it is good to put my wits against a worthy opponent."

The girl bowed her head before offering a smile which competed with the sun pouring in through the window. "Your Majesty, I will join your women with joy." The girl, showing her years in France, spoke with an enchanting French accent. "I am not only trained well to play chess and cards, but can play a number of instruments with skill." She smiled again. "I also love to dance."

"Yes – I saw that myself when the French King pointed you to me. You and young Wyatt danced well together. At your age, I used to love to dance, too. Alas, I have not danced for some time."

The girl looked across at Catalina with what seemed compassion. "Madam, I brought my lute with me. Could I not play for you? The wind blows so dreadfully it disturbs all our spirits. My lute will make us forget it." Glancing at the monkeys, she pursed her lips with unhidden distaste. "It may even serve to quieten the animals."

Looking tired, Catalina rose from the table and waved a hand. "Pray do, Mistress. Music soothes and restores the soul." *Music soothes and restores the soul.* María folded her daughter's bodice, recalling the night before. She had wished to sing to Catalina then to soothe her – but they were not alone. They had been surrounded by too many women – and Catalina's mood did not encourage her to sing. Helping dress Catalina for yet another meeting with the French King, she had arranged Catalina's thick braid of hair so it fell over her shoulder and down the front of her gown. There was not one strand of grey. But dark rings under her eyes bespoke of ill health, and another sleepless night.

When she saw the other women gathering up the remains of the queen's toilette, she had shifted closer to Catalina and spoke only for her ears. "You think it wise to dress in the Spanish fashion? It might serve to anger the French King, and your husband, too."

"I want the French King to remember who I am," Catalina had said. "I'm Queen of England, but I never forget my blood. Last night, I was given silver plate for my meal when he and my husband ate off gold. If my behaviour today angers my husband, so be it. It might remind him he has a wife, and a wife of royal blood." She had stilled before scrutinising her women. "While I am willing to risk my husband's anger, I warn you all to be careful around the king. He is still in pain, and short tempered from his wrestling match with King François. He did not expect the French king to prove himself the better wrestler – and he believes he was cheated out of the victory. My husband is likely to take his present ill-mood out on someone." María inwardly shrugged. *I stay away from him in any case.* She sat straighter. *But I pray he does not take it out on Catalina.*

The Bullen girl returned with her lute. She curtseyed to Catalina, now seated on the high back chair near the window, cradling one of the monkeys in her arms. María started with surprise when the girl sat without permission. "I play one of the songs composed to celebrate these lists," she said. The girl plucked the notes of her lute and sang:

My sovereign Lord for my poor sake
Six courses at the ring did make....

María closed her eyes, listening to Nan Bullen sing. *The girl has a voice of an angel. She will make some man happy one day.*

No cost had been spared for the candles lighting up the chapel built overnight on the tilting field. The light inside was brighter than the light outside. Seated beside Will and waiting for the Mass to begin, María stared at Cardinal Wolsey's feet. Every movement he made at the altar sparkled the rubies and sapphires in his jewelled sandals. She had never seen such sandals – and never expected to see them on a man of God. Wolsey's liking of displaying his wealth grew apace with the years.

After two weeks of competition, both kings looked worse for wear. While he no longer wore a patch to cover his black eye, King François's overlong nose was bent over to one side after it had been broken in a tilt against the Earl of Devonshire. Scratches and scabs healed all over King Henry's face. Some of the visible injuries were caused by King François when he engaged his brother king in a wrestling match. From what Will told her, the French King could have broken King Henry's back, or neck with his French trick, in a match that had only lasted a matter of minutes.

Half listening to Wolsey's opening prayers, María changed her position again on one of the uncomfortable boards in the gallery now turned into chapel pews for the royal company and their retinues. Everywhere shone with gold or silver. Not only were there silver statues of the apostles, holy relics, two tall golden candle sticks, but also an enormous jewelled crucifix.

The Dukes of Suffolk and Buckingham, along with the Earl

of Northumberland, strode up to the altar to assist the Cardinal. Suffolk held the towel, Buckingham the bowl and Northumberland the assay. She shivered at the look given to the cardinal by three nobles. *Grant us peace? Dear God, how can there be peace when even the English hate each other?*

At the close of the service, María walked with Will out of the chapel. A sudden loud explosion was followed by people crying out, and pointing heavenwards. Will clasped her hand. "I think it is meant to be a dragon."

"Why set off fireworks in the morning?" she murmured, distracted from looking at the sky by the yells coming from a group of men nearby rushing around as if in confusion and distress.

"Look at those men. Someone must be hurt – or made an expensive mistake."

María winced and looked back at the chapel, and all around. The sun glittered the gold on the tents and shone bright on the glass windows of the mock castle. *Was all of this an expensive mistake?* She sighed. *England and France achieve peace for all time? I will believe it when the Earth swallows up the sky.*

She tightened her grip on Will's hand. All she wanted was for all this to come to an end, and be back home with Will and their little daughter.

16

Glance at the sun. See the moon and the stars.
Gaze at the beauty of earth's greenings.
Now, think.
What delight God gives to humankind
with all these things.
All nature is at the disposal of humankind.
We are to work with it.
For without we cannot survive.
~Hildegard of Bingen
The thirtieth day of July, 1520

Doña, my dear Latina,

Has news come to you about what many call The Field of the Cloth of Gold? A week ago, I heard the French Ambassador say to another French man, "Many English carried their mills, their forests, and their meadows on their backs." I could not help thinking how right the man was. My husband is one of the richest men in England – and he depleted his coffers in these last weeks. I would hate to know how much King Henry spent to finance his meeting with King François. To be truthful, if peace is indeed achieved, it will not be because of this meeting of the English and French, but because both countries can no longer afford war.

We returned to the castle at Calais to celebrate the king's birthday, and to prepare for a journey to Gravelines to meet with the queen's nephew. The queen surprised the king when she expressed her desire to go with him. I was not surprised. Already waiting at Gravelines to meet with King Henry and Queen Katherine are people the queen had looked forward to meeting for months. Especially one.

Alone together in the queen's litter for the first part of the journey while Mary, the duchess of Suffolk and Margaret Pole opted to ride for a time, María and Catalina spoke together in the language of their birth, remembering happy days of their childhood, before the long years of exile and grief.

"Life was simple and promised much then," Catalina said.

María shook her head. "Our lives were never simple. And there is no such thing as promises in life."

Catalina sighed. "Si – you speak the truth. At least I no longer believe my life is cursed. It is what it is – and I count my blessings, like your long friendship."

When they arrived at Gravelines, the sun was still high in the sky. María alighted the litter, helping Catalina out. At little distance away, the king and his men were already dismounted and gathered together with Catalina's nephew, Charles. The emperor, dressed in his favoured dark, plain clothes, stood out amongst the bright, bold colours of the English court.

Standing behind Catalina, María searched around for the golden hair of a woman they both loved, and yearned to see. A woman of middle age approached them. The woman looked like a nun; her white veil covered most of her forehead and below her chin. The woman came closer; a woman with a pert nose, a woman with shining eyes who smiled widely at them. Margaret of Austria.

Margot, Catalina's sister-in-law, had been a grieving widow of twenty when they had farewelled her at the Alhambra. She had returned to the Netherlands, and married the duke of Savoy not long afterwards. Once more, she gave a man her loving heart. Once more, she had a short time of true happiness, before Fortune's wheel turned and made her a young widow again. She vowed not to wed again. It was a vow she kept even when Maximilian I, her beloved father, tried to sway her to do otherwise. For sixteen years, she had ruled the Netherlands, acting as regent for her and Catalina's nephew, Charles, until he was old enough to rule himself. He was now twenty-two, and the Holy Roman Emperor and the ruler of kingdoms stretching from Spain to the New World.

Catalina let out a gasp and moved towards Margot. An arm's length from one another, they stopped, looking at each other. Margot curtseyed and rose, holding out her arms. Catalina rushed into her waiting embrace.

María drew near them. When the women broke away from each other and looked her way, she curtseyed low and remained on her knees.

The duchess of Savoy held out her hands. "Rise up, friend. Oh, María, it is so good to see you again. Come – I wish to kiss you, too."

Hugged by Margot, María kissed the older woman. Margot kept hold of her hand when she broke away from the embrace. She reached out to clasp Catalina's hand too. "I never allowed myself to hope for this day," Margot said, her voice quivering with emotion. "I cannot wait for us to speak together." She beamed the same gay smile she had had as a young woman.

Catalina smiled just as brightly. "We have so much to tell one another." She glanced towards the waiting men. "Tomorrow, we return with you to Calais to deal with the business of this new treaty. The treaty can wait until then. Once today's formalities are over, the king, my husband, has kindly granted me permission to entertain you in my chambers tonight. I hope you will dine with María, Mary, the king's sister, and my other good friend, Margaret Pole." Catalina laughed. "Two Marys, two Margarets, and one Katherine." She shook her head. "No, tonight it will not be Katherine, but Catalina."

Margaret raised her hand to touch Catalina's face, and spoke in pure Castilian. "Catalina, my sister. How my heart has longed for you and my eyes have wished to see you again." She clasped María's hand. "And you too. I have never forgotten the Alhambra – and the time we shared together."

María smiled. "Si – I have never forgotten too," she said in her own tongue. "The English name me Mary, but I will always be María. A proud daughter of Castile."

The first greetings done, María settled into the chambers readied for their brief stay, resting for several hours before supper. Refreshed, the grime of travel washed from her body, and changed into her court clothes, María left Will to attend the king while she hurried down to the chambers given to the queen at Gravelines.

A servant let her in, and she realised, with annoyance, she was the last to arrive. The other women stood at the open window, chatting quietly together, looking out at the sun setting over the channel which headed out to sea. The view opened up to a flat landscape, with none of the greenness or hills of England.

Catalina smiled in welcome at María's arrival and gestured to a table laden with food and wine; a woman servant waited to serve them. "Pray, let us sit and partake of our first course." Catalina grinned. "I hope you do not mind if we have one servant remaining with us in the chamber tonight. Bridget will summon other servants to bring in the next courses, but once they have brought in the food they will go. We are a small group of good friends. I want us to speak freely, and in no fear of being overheard or spied upon. Bridget has been with me for years. We can trust her."

Knowing this to be true, María nodded at Bridget in greeting before joining the other women at the table, Catalina beside Margaret of Savoy, with María, Mary, the duchess of Suffolk, and the other Margaret on the other side. Bridget poured wine into their goblets, and stepped back deeper into the room, waiting to be summoned again.

Catalina raised her goblet. "Let's drink to good health and friendship."

"Good health and friendship," the women said in unison.

María wiped her mouth and looked around the table. Tonight, in this chamber, the only woman who could still be called young was Mary, Catalina's beautiful sister-in-law. Now twenty-four, frequent pregnancies left her increasingly fragile, her skin bloodless. She had still not recovered from her last hard childbed of the previous year. But, the lust between her and Suffolk still burning strong, Suffolk had returned to her bed. María swilled back another mouthful of wine. *Was lust the real reason Suffolk now shared his ill wife's bed again? Or had he returned to her bed in hope of begetting more children of royal blood? For a man who professed to love his wife, he placed little store in giving her the time she needed to regain her health.* She inwardly smiled. *How blessed I am to have Will. He is patient –*

and willing to wait until I wish to bed with him again. So many men refuse to wait. Especially men in positions of power.

Their voices drifting down the table, Catalina and Margaret of Savoy spoke together as if not aware of the others. "I have treasured your letters," Catalina said.

"And I yours," replied the duchess. She leaned closer and covered Catalina's hand with hers. "My letters could never tell you how much I missed you, or how I grieved for your losses." Catalina averted her face. "I have consolations given to me by life. My daughter is one, and my faith another. God has carried me through every loss, and my faith has only grown stronger. As long as I have my God, I can bear anything. And I always remember, we never come into the kingdom of Heaven but by troubles."

"You are unusually quiet this evening," Margaret Pole murmured beside her.

María took her eyes from Catalina. "I find myself pulled back to the past – and remembering once more the first time we sat and ate together."

Meg glanced towards Catalina and Margaret. "Much has changed since then."

María looked across the room, to the end of the chamber, where candlelight failed to reach. The ebbing of daylight brought with it shadows, memories, and ghosts. She remembered a girl and boy who sat beside each other, their faces white and expressionless as they watched the dancers of a celebrating court. They did not look at each other, as if they feared by doing so their masks would break.

"True. Time has robbed us of people we loved, our youth, our good health." She smiled at Meg. "But time has given me other things – a husband I love with my whole heart, and a child." María took a chicken leg off a nearby plate, and smiled before beginning to eat it. "I can think of one thing which has not changed. And will never change."

"What is that?"

"I serve Catalina with my life, and will until I die."

EPILOGUE

And that I did, my daughter. I serve Catalina, even now, when her earthly body has been food for worms these last three years. Her soul, though, is with God. She is at peace, whilst I struggle on, alone.

There are so many memories. The memories I have written about here, and other memories. Your father's death I cannot bear to think of. We had ten years of happy marriage – and we had you, our one child God granted to live, and for us to love.

All the rest of it, King Henry's determination to rid himself of Catalina for the Bullen, the years my friend fought for her marriage. The day Catalina made my heart sing with pride. You know of it too. It is a tale that will be told down the centuries, the day when Catalina rose from her chair, pushed her way through the crush of people, fell to her knees before the king. Her emotion that day broke into the English tongue she had spoken well for close to twenty years.

"I beseech you for all the love that hath been between us, and

for the love of God, let me have justice and right. Take of me some pity and compassion, for I am a poor woman and a stranger born out of your dominion," my queen said, raising her hands beseechingly towards her husband.

King Henry just sat there, refusing to look at her. "Alack, my lord husband, what have I done to offend you?" my queen asked. On her knees, she had shuffled closer to him. "What occasion displeased you so for you to put me from you? I take God and all the world to witness that I have been to you a true and humble and obedient wife, ever looking to your will and pleasure. I never said or did anything against your wishes. I loved all those whom you loved, for your sake, whether I had cause or not, and whether they were my friends or enemies. For over twenty years I've been your true wife and by me you have had divers children. Although it hath pleased God to call them out of this world, this is not my fault!" She had lifted her chin, her eyes ablaze. "And when you had me at first, I take God to be my judge, I was a true maid without touch of man. And whether it be true or not, I put it to your conscience."

Her long speech availed her nothing with the king, but not so the English. Time after time, I hear men and women speak of Catalina's words and pride themselves they had such a queen.

But Catalina's last years of trial are not important to this story – not really.

I write this for you to understand the lives women must endure – and the life I have lived. I am not perfect; I have sinned – sinned against God, and those who I love. I ask for forgiveness – but it does not take away these truths: I have always loved you, your father, and my Catalina.

There is one last memory I wish to share before I come to my end. One last memory of love, of so much love…

María rode through the savage wind. Thomas, her servant, spurring his horse ahead of her. Heavy rain drenched her to her skin, turning the earth before her into rivulets of mud. Her horse slid, struggling to move any farther up the steep hill where the torchlights of Kimbolton Castle could be seen. "Muchacha, do not give up. We are almost there," she said. Only for the animal to stumble and slip. Nearly going down on its side, the horse tumbled her to the muddy ground.

Every part of her body crying out in pain, María sat on the rain-soaked earth, her cowl fallen from her head. She wiped the mud from her face, kneeled on the ground, and reached for her horse's reins. The well-trained mare stood still, its head lowered as if defeated. She straightened her lopsided matron's gable and stroked the mare's nose. The trembling horse snorted, pawing and limping a little way towards her, but then stopped and neighed, shaking its head.

Rain and wind bowing him low in the saddle, Thomas reined up his horse close to her side. "My lady – are you hurt?"

She peered up at him, pulling her cowl overhead, trying to laugh.

"My pride is hurt, that is all. I haven't fallen from a horse since I was a girl. I fear poor Muchacha is lame –"

When Thomas shifted in his saddle, as if ready to jump off, she raised a hand. "No, Thomas, remain on your horse. We'll just take our time, my poor horse and I." She rubbed rain away from her eyes. "Pray journey on, Thomas, and tell them at the castle I am on my way to them."

"My lady – I cannot leave you alone."

María placed her hand on her sore hip and laughed with grimness. "You know I'm used to being alone. Go, I beg you. If I tarry overlong, the castle can send down help to me."

Thomas cast a quick look towards the castle, and wheeled his mount to face the uphill trail, the animal fighting to regain solid ground. The horse gathered momentum, and began heading to the castle a short distance away.

María stroked her horse's nose. "Come, my Muchacha. You want your oats and I want my supper. Let's follow."

Her body stiff, María stood carefully, biting back against the pain of her back and injured leg, and limped beside her limping horse, leading it on the firmed down trail of mud left by the other horse. Under-breath, she sang in her own tongue.

Resplendent star on the mountain.
Like a sunbeam miraculously glowing,
All joyous people
Come together
Rich and poor
Young and old
Climb the mountain
To see with their own eyes
And return from it
Filled with grace.

The horse nickered, and rubbed its nose on her arm. María laughed. "You are of good Castilian stock, too. From a foal, you have liked me singing songs from home. Someone else I know loves that song too. Tonight, I shall sit at her feet and sing. Come on, Muchacha, the sooner we get someone to look at your leg, the better."

She yanked her horse's reins, focusing again on the unmade road before them, fast becoming a treacherous mud bath. She fought against driving rain and mud, her dragging skirts becoming sodden and heavy. Gaining ground, María neared the castle. The sound of sizzling rain came down to her as the wind blew it under the ledges protecting the torches. Nearby but unseen, dogs barked out warning. Dizzy with pain, she caught her breath. "Come on, Muchacha. Only a little more."

She fixed her eyes on the flame of the guttering torches, slogging step by step through the mud. Black shadows loomed, grew and took substance. Thomas rode to her side.

"My lady! They say they won't bring down the drawbridge."
"By all the Saints, do they indeed? Hold my horse, Thomas!" Handing over her reins to Thomas, María cursed in Castilian and picked up her skirts and limped up to the castle. She stopped at the edge of the moat, her eyes raking back and forth over the battlements. Over the stone-wall, a wan, bearded face peered. Torchlight turned his eyes luminous and spectre-like.

"You there," María shouted, caring not one iota for her dignity. She had left that behind days ago when she had left London. "Open up. I am Baroness Willoughby.

The man leaned across, holding his hands on either side of his mouth to amplify his voice. "Baroness, I beg you, go elsewhere! We cannot lower the drawbridge without the king's permission."

María could not believe her ears. "What do you mean you cannot? Will you have me die at your gates? Have you forgotten all the laws of hospitality? I have fallen off my horse, and I am bruised and need my injuries seen to. Besides that, my horse is lame. You have no choice but to open to me, unless you wish for my son-in-law, the Duke of Suffolk, to deal with you later."

"Baroness, the king's orders –"

"The king's orders." María shook her head, thinking fast. "There's no longer need to concern yourself over that issue. My Lord Cromwell promised me the king's permission will be forthcoming, perchance by the morrow." She straightened her stance, and made her voice into a weapon of steel. "The night is foul, good sir, and my son in marriage is a prince of this land. Lower the drawbridge before you live to regret it."

"Baroness, I beg you –"

"Santa María." She shook her dirty fist up at the quaking man. "You waste time, time that could be used for better purpose! I am here, good sir, and there's nothing you can say to make me go away. Unless you wish for me to die at your gates, let me in. Let me in, for I will not leave. Lower the drawbridge. Lower the drawbridge now."

With difficulty María held her tongue as Catalina dictated the letter to the king.

My Lord and Dear Husband,

I commend me unto you. The hour of my death draweth fast on, and my case being such, the tender love I owe you forceth me, with a few words, to put you in remembrance of the health and safeguard of your soul, which you ought to prefer before all worldly matters, and before the care and tendering of your own body, for the which you have cast me into many miseries and yourself into many cares.

For my part I do pardon you all, yea, I do wish and devoutly pray God that He will also pardon you. For the rest I commend unto you Mary, our daughter, beseeching you to be a good father unto her, as I heretofore desired. Lastly, do I vow, mine eyes desire you above all things.

Katherine, Queen of England

María had been in Catalina's chambers for two days. She had given those in the castle no choice about the matter. As soon as they had opened the doors to her, she had gone in search of Catalina with her saddle bag filled with a lifetime of medical knowledge. By the end of the first day, she had realised she could do little for Catalina. All she could do was to help Catalina's physician ease the final hours of her friend's life. With each breath, Catalina struggled to surmount terrible pain. She slept only with the aid of poppy.

After a horrible night of fretful sleep, Catalina had asked to write a letter to her husband and check her will one last time. The letter done, Francisco Felipez, her secretary, read her will to her. Debts had been paid, servants rewarded, her personal jewellery and valuable furs bestowed to her daughter.

Listening, María gulped down a bitter laugh. English custom prevented a woman from writing a will while her husband lived. *Trust Catalina to use the king's denial of their marriage as a way to ask him to do right by their daughter and her servants. How I hate Henry Tudor. She should not spend these last hours worrying for others. But Catalina is as stubborn as ever. More so in these final days. She insists on doing what she thinks is right even if it increases her pain.*

Wiping away her tears, María twisted towards the fire. The

blue sea coal flared and crumbled, begging for replenishment. She gritted her teeth, angry once more, and shovelled a few precious pieces of coal onto the burning embers. There was very little fuel left to warm this freezing room.

"The letter to my husband and my will are finished." Catalina outstretched a shaking hand. "Francisco, with my whole heart, I thank you."

Francisco raised his head, his face strained and tired. He stood from his chair and came to Catalina's side, sheltering her hand in both of his. "Noble queen, serving you…" His Adam's apple moved up and down. He released her hand and rubbed at his face with ink stained fingers. "It has been the greatest honour of my life." He bowed low to her.

Catalina smiled gently at him, settling against the pillows of her daybed.

Francisco stood, gazing down at Catalina. "Madam – I…" He looked desperately over to María, his dark eyes alight with unshed tears.

Catalina kneaded the sides of her temples. Recognising her friend's distress, María signalled him to go, fearing his naked grief would at last break apart Catalina's determination to remain stoic, and calm.

He cleared his throat. He squared his shoulders, tidied up his inkpots before lifting his head. "I'll never forget you, my queen."

Catalina smiled a little, and licked her bloodless, cracked lips. "God speed, Francisco," she said. María rose to fetch her some water, wincing when she heard Catalina say, "Pray… for me."

Francisco bowed low again. "I will, my queen. Farewell, may

the good God keep you in his care, Your Majesty." He turned on his heel, rushing to the door.

María shut the door and returned to Catalina with a goblet of watered-down wine and waited for Catalina to finish drinking. She took the goblet and replaced it on the table by the pitcher of water. She turned back at the same time Catalina reached for her comb on the small table beside her. Her eyelids fluttering, Catalina panted; even such a small exertion caused her to struggle to breathe. Her skin waxen, her whole being possessed the translucence of the dying.

Rushing back to her side, María picked up the comb. "Let me. Please." She started to comb Catalina's grey, thin hair and remembered the thick golden-red hair of Catalina's youth. Her throat constricted. Despite her gentleness, with each stroke of the comb, more of Catalina's hair came away. Catalina shut her eyes and groaned, the lines of age carved deep into her face.

María froze the comb in mid-air. "Did I hurt you?"

Catalina moved her head. "No, not you, my sister."

"Are you feeling worse?"

"No... no... Thank the good Lord... I am... a little better today, thanks to your care. But the pain's a wolf, waiting outside... outside the door. When the door opens, it tears me with its teeth." She breathed out a ragged breath.

María rested her hand on Catalina's shoulder. Her friend had lost so much flesh, her body seemed no more than loose skin on bird-like bone. "Try not to talk. It tires you too much. Do you want me to make you another mixture of poppy?

Catalina shook her head again. "It only makes me sleep.... I don't want to sleep... not yet... Time enough for that soon...

Pray, don't argue with me. The end is coming. Let me talk, while I can..."

María bowed her head. "I don't want to think of you gone from me." She swallowed, tottering so close to losing control.

Catalina reached for her hand. She held it weakly for a moment, then dropped it. "Sister, only gone... from this world... Be happy I go to God. All my troubles over. At peace, María, at peace..."

María tidied what she could of Catalina's dishevelled locks, tucking strands behind her ears. Time stopped still. She sighed, laying her fingers on either side of Catalina's clammy forehead.

"Do you remember the queen, your mother, combing your hair before we left Castile?"

Catalina smiled, and held María's hand for a moment. "Do you ever forget love?"

María met Catalina's eyes, and began to lose grip. She stared down at the floor, anger burning a hole in her heart. She railed against life. Angry at her helplessness, angry at God. More than simply angry at the king.

She took a deep breath, unclenching her fisted hands. "*Si* – I remember love. Every day of our friendship, all through the long years, I remember love." She shook her head. She refused to cry. *Not yet. My tears can wait for a time when they will not upset her.* "I cannot bear to think of us separated – with no hope of seeing you more in this life."

Catalina took her hand again. "My mother once told me we never lose those we love. I know it true. My mother's love warms me now as it did then, more so with every passing day. I think back to us on the balcony, before we left Granada. I said to you then, one day I would be with her again. My sister, she is with me now." Merriment dancing in her eyes, Catalina patted beside her on the bed. "Come, sit by me."

María sat, amazed at Catalina's apparent delight.

"I saw her... my mother, last night. Here... right by my bed. Her joy... shone like... the midday sun of home. It was like... she kept from me... a secret."

María clasped her hand, and tried to smile. "You saw the queen?"

"I swear it. And my mother is not the only one. These last days, I drift between this world and the next...."

María returned the comb to the table. With great care, she stretched alongside Catalina, pulling up the blanket to cover them both. She clasped Catalina's cold, yet clammy hand. Catalina shut her eyes, the pain deepening the lines on her face. María, unable to do anything else, stroked her brow with gentle fingers. She settled her head beside Catalina's. "How many times in our lives did we share a bed? I am glad I am here. I am glad I share your bed now."

Catalina turned, and smiled. "Our lives have always been part of one another's."

María nestled closer to Catalina, and breathed in her aroma. Catalina smelled of death. Unable to stop them, she let her tears begin to fall.

Catalina touched her face. "No tears, my sister – death will not... separate us."

María rubbed her eyes, and sniffed. She lifted her chin. "Si – death will not separate us."

Catalina breathed with difficulty. So laboured. Each ragged breath spoke of the pain tearing apart her guts. "Did you know

Chapuys asked of me... a deathbed confession. That I came... virgin to Harry?"

Angry, María stiffened. "Chapuys? He should remember his place as your nephew's ambassador and not plague you about such things."

Catalina shook her head. "He is right. It is for Mary... I...do this. A deathbed confession from her mother will protect her rights. The king knows the truth. I came to him a virgin, and am his true wife. I pray to God... one day the man I love owns to it."

María eyed Catalina, her rage about the king brimming over. "How can you still love him when he would not allow your own daughter to be at your side? Not even now?"

"My sister – you've known love... true love between... a woman and man. A woman and man who bedded together, and had children together. Buried children together. Understand... please... I can do no other... but love him. I pray for God's forgiveness... for my Harry. He is lost... only God... can help him find his way home."

María sniffed again and bit back the reply she yearned to say. Too many memories pulled at her, but one unfurled in her mind. "He's not coming back, is he?" Catalina had said, twisting in her favourite chair to the window as for answer. María had risen from her stool and rested a hand on her shoulder. Catalina knew the truth without her saying it for her. Catalina had turned to her eyes alight with tears. "He never came to say good-bye." She gave a short laugh. "My husband always sought to avoid awkward moments."

"I'll bring you some wine," María had said, not knowing what else to do. Catalina had been abandoned; pushed aside like so many other women. Pouring the wine, María had returned to her. Catalina took the goblet, and stared into its blood-like depths before lifting her eyes. "You added no water?"

"No, my sister. A time like this calls for strong wine."

Catalina let out a laugh strangled by tears, looking sightlessly to the ceiling. "My Almoner tells me they have gone to Greenwich."

María had shrugged. "The Bullen likes it there."

"So do I – so does Harry. Pray, bring me my writing desk."

Curious, she had grabbed the small desk on the table close to the fire. On it, Catalina's initials were interlocked with the king's. She came back to Catalina and handed it to her. Catalina opened the desk, taking out from its bottom drawer an untouched piece of parchment. Holding a quill, she placed the parchment on the slanted desktop.

"I shall tell him of my grief he never came to say farewell. If I could see him but one more time, surely, I could make him reconsider this decision. He is my husband. I love him. I can't let him go like this. He can run away from me, he can run from himself, he can run from God, but that will not make our marriage a lie."

María had watched Catalina write her letter knowing she wasted her time. But her tongue remained too craven to tell her so. In truth, what else could Catalina do? A woman always fought an uphill battle in a world ruled by men – women's powers and weapons often eroded and destroyed by time and circumstances beyond their control. Unable to watch her dearest friend torture herself for one more moment, María had gone to the window and looked out at the trees. Their branches danced in a strong wind, and then stilled. Birds sang. The world shimmered in a diaphanous light.

She had glanced at Catalina as her pen stroked and scratched its way down the parchment. *Life is cruel and a crucible for all fates. Especially if we are born women.*

And to become crueller still. Catalina had received an answer to her letter the very next morning. Her face had turned an unhealthy grey when she dropped the king's letter to the floor. She had put her hands over her face, and rocked in her chair. "Mother of God, please help me," Catalina had said, gasping for air as if in pain.

That awful morning, María had fallen to her knees beside her friend, as she had done so many times in the past, and taken her hand. "What is it?" she had asked.

Catalina had lifted her head, blinking like an owl. "My husband writes it is a lie I came to him a virgin. He commands I no longer call myself his wife." She lowered her head, and wept. "Oh, Harry! What have I ever done to deserve this?" she had asked, broken, old – bereft of all hope.

María had swallowed hard, knowing there was nothing she could do to help. Hatred for the king had squirmed like worms eating through her belly.

Now Catalina, her friend closer than any sister, struggled to breathe on her death bed. *I hate the king. He not only denies Catalina was ever his wife, but refuses her request to let their daughter come to her. I hate him, hate him, hate him.*

As if guessing her thoughts, Catalina touched her arm. "Forgive him... please... for my sake... and your own."

Catalina wants me to forgive him? I do not know how. Not after everything he did to me. Feeling small, and unworthy of her friend, María desperately searched the room as if for answer. Dark shadows encircled the bed, candlelight cloaked them in a boat of amber-gold; *we are alone in a harbour of safety while all around us darkness waits for us to fall. Dear God – let me remember love, and only love.* María returned her eyes to Catalina. *Si. Only love keeps us safe from the dark.*

Catalina gripped her hand. "Promise..."

María took a deep breath. "I refuse to lie to you. Not at this time. All I can promise is I'll try...."

Catalina's hand relaxed; she rested her head on María's shoulder. "That's enough. I will pray for you. With God's help... you'll forgive... as I have. It is not for him, but for you. For you." She closed her eyes. "I am tired. So tired. Let's try to sleep."

María dreamt. She dreamt she walked in a great, endless hallway, bewildered and lost. Light changed from one moment to the next: bright sunlight trying to win out over dark storm. Flashes of lightning illuminated a huge, dark tapestry billowing against the wall.

Nearing the tapestry, María saw a thousand images and more from her life. They came away from the tapestry and started slapping, like playing cards, on to a black shrouded table. She saw the brown vega, mountains and valleys of her home-land. An old woman heavy with sorrow. A virgin-faced girl heavy with child, heavy with death, the blood flowing like rivulets from beneath her clothes.

"Are you Jews?" asked Prince Juan in her dream, becoming a corpse in winding cloths.

A ship buckled in a monstrous sea of blood, sweeping her onto a beach. She was awash in the blood from executions.

Never ending executions. Feature-less, swaddled babes, carried away after birth, not to live life but for burial. A pomegranate crushed underneath a man's foot, its skin rent apart, its seeds burst forth like gushing blood. The innocent crying out in their death throes.

She looked at the tapestry, and saw the threads of gold. Her mother glanced up from her sewing, her brown eyes sparkling with love and wisdom. Heading toward his waiting horse, her father strode towards the king. Loose limbed, fearless, his hand already on his sword, her father turned and smiled at her. Two small girls danced upon a golden beach. Latina laughed and told stories of friendship and love, faith and the snow of almond blossom. A boy and girl kissed long and deep, their mantles blowing in a snow chilled wind, twin dragons slithering, twisting around their intertwined bodies. Will held her face between his strong, soldier hands, his eyes welling with tears when he kissed her on their wedding day. She nursed her baby girl, and promised she would protect her from every hurt.

Awaking in tears, María discovered Catalina writhing in agony beside her. Catalina groaned and turned on her side, gagged and then vomited. The smell of fresh blood drowned the stale air of her sickroom.

Halfway between dream and a nightmare reality mimicking it, María jumped out of bed. She sluiced a cloth in a nearby basin of water, washing Catalina's face and mouth. Her frightened, pain-filled eyes shining in candlelight, Catalina struggled for breath. "The wolf devours me. Hurry, fetch my confessor."

María ran, her feet winged.

María halted writing, gritting her teeth against the wail of grief rising within her. If she released it, the wail of winter wind buffeting against the walls of her home would be as if nothing. Regaining her control, she dipped her pen in the inkwell.

Daughter, I have lost many I loved in this life; your father, my queen; even Latina, my old teacher, who I thought would live forever, has been three years in the grave. Now I fear Meg Pole, my beloved friend cursed with her too royal blood, will not be long with the living. The king, her cousin, refuses her the comfort of friends and keeps her locked away in the Tower of London. He wants Meg forgotten, dead. I can no longer lift my heart in these sad days. All I want is for these dark days to come to an end. I write here only the truth. All I want, my daughter, is to be with your father, Catalina, my mother, Latina, all those I loved and still love, in an eternity where there will be no more hurt or pain. I have no hope left, daughter. The only thing truly left to me is my deep and abiding love for you, but I am lonely. So, so lonely it hurts like a dagger plunged and twisted deep into my heart...

Fingers cramping, María put the quill in the ink pot, rereading what she had written, waiting with impatience and annoyance for the pain of her rheumatism to subside. For her clawed fingers to obey her once again. *Dear God, let this letter help my Catalina understand. I do not want to die without my daughter understanding the difficult decisions forced upon my life... or hating me. I cannot die with my Catalina hating me.*

I began this letter because I did not want to die without your forgiveness. My sweet girl, you who I love with all my heart. I will ask for forgiveness, if you wish, but let me say this first. I could do nothing to change how it was for me, and for you.

Child, I never before sought to sway you from the hard opinion you hold of me. When you were a child, you always asked why you could not live with me. I did not know what to say; especially when I hoped you would find happiness in Mary Tudor's home; in another mother's arms.

I had known Mary since she was a child and I a girl of fifteen. By the time she married to Suffolk, I was honoured to call her my friend. I knew her worthy of your love. When she became your guardian, I had no wish to see you pulled in two directions by reminding you also of my love.

When your father died, I was a woman left with little power over the fate of her only surviving child; like my kinswoman, Queen Katherine, I too was not born in these dominions, but in a country far, far away, with a wide, terrible, treacherous ocean journey between England and my home. Before the birth of my children, the only blood-kin I ever had in England was my queen. At your father's death, her power over King Henry was no more. The only way I had to stop your father's brother from taking all that belonged to you was to beg Suffolk to take you under his protection. Believe me, child, whatever I could do for you, I did do. And I did it out of love. All of it I did out of love. By the cross of God and my hope of a life to come, I swear I write the truth to you.

Her sight blurring, María closed her eyes to rest them for a time. In her head, she heard again her daughter's young voice from three years ago. *"You are my mother, and you do nothing to stop my marriage to this old man. You sold me to him as a child, and see where it has led. I believed from childhood I'd marry Harry, not his lord father. Harry's heart is broken, and I hate you for causing it. And you did cause it; you sold me to the highest bidder."*

María picked up her pen once more.

I was sick at heart seeing you weep the day before your wedding, sick at heart seeing you married to the man you had called Lord Father from your earliest years. But Suffolk had your wardship, Catalina. I had no recourse other than to smile and pretend joy when my heart was breaking for you. If I did not, do you think I would have been allowed to attend you at your wedding? To do what little I could do as your mother – even if a mother you cursed. I believed, too, that Suffolk would be a kind husband to you. He was kind to your foster mother; indeed, he is a man kind to most women. I have never seen him raise a hand to a woman in anger – whether highborn, or a servant. And you were right to call your husband 'old'; he is as old as me.

Let me speak with honesty. I begged him to give you more time before he made you a mother. I believed he listened to me, but I should have known better. He had a dying son, and knew death looked over his own shoulder. He ignored your tender years and bedded you as soon as he wedded you. He proved himself a man who first thinks of himself before he considers the wellbeing of those he should protect, and nurture. Praise the good Lord, death will come for him soon. In the near future you will be a wealthy, young widow free to choose whether or who to marry as dictated by your heart.

Now I write to you, begging you as the mother who bore you into the world and who has loved you with great devotion every day since. When I die, and God grant that be soon, I beg of you to bury my heart with the person who I loved from childhood.

You know who I speak of; how could you not when you bear her name?

Replacing her quill, María reached for the goblet of watered wine on the table beside her writing desk and gulped down a mouthful. She was almost finished this letter. Then she too would be finished – and ready to meet death. She took hold of her pen.

A church bell tolls nearby. I have written all through the long night, burning down night candles to their wicks. Sunrays finger-creep towards me, reaching closer and closer, beckoning new morn. Even the snow has stopped falling. For a time.

For hours, I have written, slouched here at the table, weighed down with unendurable sorrow, thinking of all those I loved who are dead, and buried. Thinking of my dear friend Meg, who is shadowed by the axe.

My beloved daughter, this is the first time I have allowed myself to remember Catalina's death. Estimado Dios –while Catalina lived I never felt alone. Alone... my daughter, I cannot think of a more hateful word.

I believed I lived through the worst life could give me when I lost your father. But when my Catalina, the sister of my heart, died? When I think of her dead, it strangles me of all breath.

You know she died in my arms? These arms... dear God, my undeserving arms... arms holding her many, many times. I held her in illness, and also whilst in travail with child. Tighter still I held her when my queen grieved, sobbing, her heart broken, when she saw yet another shrouded babe hurried away from the dark-ened birthing chamber. She struggled like one drowning not to let her dark despair and heartbreak drag her into a deep pit. She always carried a greater burden than I. Si. Her burdens were always greater and heavier than most women.

The grief of losing Catalina turned my already broken heart into jagged lumps of stone. Each breath I took became as if a tide of agony.

But strange – writing my letter to you has lifted the heavy weight from my breast.

I wrote this letter to you because I wanted you to forgive me, but I see I also need to forgive. I have carried hate in my heart for too long, my daughter. My Catalina asked me to forgive her husband. I can do that now. He is who he is, and I am who I am. In the end, I am but a woman who lived the best life she could.

Writing this letter has turned my hatred into pity. There is much to pity of a man who had the seeds of goodness and kind-ness, but – for reasons he alone knows – allowed evil seeds to flourish. Perhaps it was not all his own fault. His mother once said kingship for her son would be a curse. She was right. And Catalina was right to ask me to forgive him. I believe she knew forgiveness would free me from the past.

Si – it was never for him, but for me.

Sweet daughter, I reach this last page remembering love. Only love. So much love. Its light surrounds me. It is true; at the end, we know love is eternal. It is the light I leave you – the light you will never lose.

Pray forgive your mother, the mother who loves you, and be at peace, my child.

Written by my own hand, María de Salinas Willoughby, Baroness.

INTERNET RESOURCES

Not long after I started on my own timeline, I chanced upon this excellent, online resource:

http://www.historyonthenet.com/Chronology/timelinecatherine.htm

I'd like here to express my sincere thanks to its author for all their work in compiling this excellent timeline.

Medieval wedding service
https://itsmypulp.wordpress.com/2007/05/20/medieval- wedding-ceremony/

The English sweat
http://www.foxearth.org.uk/blog/2005/05/english-sweat.html

I will publish on my website (*www.wendyjdunn.com*) my author's note about the writing of this work. Please subscribe to my website to find out more or my newsletter – *https://bit.ly/3hznQiV*

BIBLIOGRAPHY & SOURCES

Ackroyd, P 2012, *The Life of Thomas More*. Anchor.

Ackroyd, P 2001, *London: the biography*, Random House.
Anderson, RM 1979, *Hispanic costume*, 1480-1530.

Boruchoff, DA ed., 2003, *Isabel la católica, queen of Castile: Critical Essays*, Macmillan, Vancover.

Bruckner, M.T., Shepard, L. and White, S. eds. 2004, *Songs of the Women Troubadours*. Routledge, Vancouver.

Chapman, H 1969, *The Thistle and the Rose: The Sisters of Henry VIII*, Coward, McCann & Geoghegan, Incorporated, Vancouver.

Cunningham, S 2016, *Prince Arthur: The Tudor King Who Never Was*, Amberley Publishing Limited.

Dowling, M 1999, *Fisher of men: a life of John Fisher, 1469–1535*. Springer.

Dubin, NE 2013, *The Fabliaux: A New Verse Translation*, Liveright Publishing.

Fraser, A *The six wives of Henry VIII*, Arrow Books, 1998
Gitlitz, DM and Davidson, LK 2000, *The pilgrimage road to Santiago: The complete cultural handbook*, St. Martin's Griffin.

Harris, BJ 1986, *Edward Stafford, third duke of Buckingham, 1478-1521*. Stanford University Press.
Huizinga, J 2014, *Erasmus and the Age of Reformation*, Princeton University Press.

Jones, MK and Underwood, MG 1992, *The king's mother: Lady Margaret Beaufort, countess of Richmond and Derby*, Cambridge University Press.

Kipling, G 1990, *The receyt of the Ladie Kateryne*, Oxford University Press, USA.

Klinck, AL and Rasmussen, A.M. eds. 2015, *Medieval woman's song: Cross-cultural approaches*, University of Pennsylvania Press.

Luke, MM 1967, *Catherine, the Queen*, Coward-McCann.
Mattingly, G 1942, *Catherine of Aragon*, New York.

Mattingly, G 1940, *The Reputation of Doctor De Puebla*. The English Historical Review, 55 (CCLXVII), pp.27-46.

Melczer, W 1993, *The pilgrim's guide to Santiago de Compostela*, New York: Italica Press.

Paul, JE 1966, *Catherine of Aragon and her Friends*, Fordham University Press.

Plowden, A 2011, *The House of Tudor*. The History Press.
Read, E 1963, *My Lady Suffolk: A Portrait of Catherine Willoughby, Duchess of Suffolk*. Knopf.

Richardson, G 2013, *The Field of Cloth of Gold*, Yale University Press.

Russell, J 1969, *The Field of the Cloth of Gold*, London.
Sharp, J 1999, *The midwives book: Or the whole art of midwifry discovered*, Oxford University Press.

Strong, R 2004, *Feast: A History of Grand Eating*.
Tremlett, G 2010, *Catherine of Aragon: Henry's Spanish Queen*, Faber & Faber.

Wilson, D 2005, *The Black Legend of the Dudleys*, History Today, 55(1), p.30.

Wilson, D. 2013, *The Uncrowned Kings of England: The Black Legend of the Dudleys*, Hachette UK.

ACKNOWLEDGEMENTS

Like the writing of all my novels, this novel has involved me in a true journey – both intellectually, emotionally and physically. I look back at that journey with so much gratitude. Once again, I have been supported and encouraged every step of the way. Once again, I have so many people to thank – so many, I am anxious I may forget someone. If I do, please accept my apology up front.

My first thanks must go to my family. They are the core of my existence – and I would not achieve anything in my life without their belief and love.

I am so grateful for all the friends who have been part of the journey in the writing of work through support, encouragement or critical friendship. Sometimes all three! I especially thank David Dunn, Ingrid Ahmer, Adrienne Dillard, Catherine Brooks, Lauren Chater, Glenice Whitting, Ana Tinc, Kathryn Lamont, Cindy Vallar, Claire and Tim Ridgeway, Rachel Nightingale, Kathryn Gauci, Barbara Gaskell Denvil, Nerina Jones, Rebecca Larson, Gareth Russell, Angela Wauchop, Dr Carol Major, Natalie Grueninger, Dr Carolyn Beasley, Lyn Zelenkovic, Karina Machado, Carol Dixon, Kathryn Holeman, Kate Murdoch, Deb Hunter, Tina Tsironis, Kristie Dean, Valerie Clukaj, Dr Owen Emmerson, Christine Bell, Nik Shone,

Keren Heenan, James Peacock, Sarah Giles, Helen and Brian Brown, Michele Le Bas, Shane and Vikki Nash, Luke Rowlatt, Jason Minos, Ian and Margaret Pym, Paricia Edgoose, Sue Sizer, Jane Downing, Anne Casey, Oscar O'Neill-Pugh, Denise O'Hagan, Stewart Faichney, Eloise Faichney, Laura-Jane Maher, Alexandrina Stark, Val Strantzen, Alexandrina Stark, Michelle Duke, Sally Odgers, Anne Connor, Jimmy D, Bubblita, David Major, Lesley Harrison, Lydia Fucsko, and Carolyn Mumford.

LEAVE A REVIEW

If you enjoyed *The Duty of Daughters Duology*, please consider leaving a review at Goodreads or the place where you purchased the book. I read every review left online and really appreciate the time you have taken to read the book and comment on it.

ALSO FROM WENDY J. DUNN

Dear Heart, How Like You This?

The Light in the Labyrinth

The Duty of Daughters
(Falling Pomegranate Seeds, Book 1)

All Manner of Things
(Falling Pomegranate Seeds, Book 2)

Mi hermana, mi reina

Shades of Yellow

Henry VIII's True Daughter:
Catherine Carey, A Tudor Life